ELEANOR'S VICTORY

M.E. BRADDON

ELEANOR'S VICTORY

ALAN SUTTON PUBLISHING LIMITED

First published in 1863

First published in the United Kingdom in 1996
Alan Sutton Publishing Ltd · Phoenix Mill · Far Thrupp · Stroud
Gloucestershire

Copyright © in this edition
Alan Sutton Publishing Limited, 1996

British Library Cataloguing in Publication Data

Braddon, M. E.
  Eleanor's Victory. – New ed. – (Pocket
  Classics)
  I. Title II. Series
  823.8 [F]

ISBN 0-7509-1118-2

Cover picture: detail from Stolen glances *by Edward Killingworth Johnson (1825–1923), 1865
(photograph: Fine Art Photographs Limited, London)*

Typeset in 10/11 Bembo.
Typesetting and origination by
Alan Sutton Publishing Limited.
Printed in Great Britain by
The Guernsey Press Company Limited,
Guernsey, Channel Islands.

CONTENTS

BIOGRAPHICAL NOTE

MARY E. BRADDON by the time of her death in 1915 had achieved notoriety, literary fame and wealth. She was known as the queen of the circulating libraries; she counted among her admirers Charles Dickens, Thomas Hardy, Henry James, Charles Reade and Bulmer Lytton; she had survived and prospered despite a scandalous marriage and a disreputable past. Indeed her own life echoes elements of the Sensation novels for which she was renowned and which established her reputation.

Born in London in 1837, M.E. Braddon was the third child of educated middle-class parents. Her father, Henry, was a solicitor whose successes within the law were squandered by philandering and good living. Her mother, Fanny, was a resourceful Irish woman whose patience with her husband's excesses ran out when her youngest daughter was four. The couple separated permanently, divorce at this time being virtually impossible.

Fanny assumed custody and financial responsibility for her children and moved them to Sussex. They returned to London in 1843 and settled in Kensington, where M.E. Braddon received a sound education at a respectable private school. Like hundreds of other similarly well-brought-up, well-educated young ladies, she looked set to follow an established path of marriage, children and a life of prosperous suburban domesticity. However, something happened that irretrievably altered such plans. Fanny Braddon's money had run out and she was faced with the harsh reality of having to survive financially in a society in which middle-class women were neither expected nor trained to earn a living. It was her daughter who stepped into the breach.

M.E. Braddon left home in 1857 to work as an actress under the name of Miss Seyton − her mother's maiden name. This she continued to do for three years, appearing in a variety of popular plays across the country. No doubt her theatrical training contributed to the pronounced sense of the dramatic that features in her novels, for she had already begun writing. As a teenager she had written for 'amusement' but with the advent of her mother's financial difficulties writing for profit became more important. She could not expect to work on the stage indefinitely, particularly if she wished to be socially respectable. Acting was associated with commonness and lewdness; nice girls did not make public exhibitions of themselves. It was this episode in M.E. Braddon's life that was to earn her a reputation for having a disreputable past and it comes as little surprise to note that it remained largely unconfirmed until after her death.

As is the nature of rumour, speculation surrounds her amorous experiences as an actress and the reason why she abruptly gave up the theatre in 1860 to concentrate on her writing. According to Charles Reade, with whom M.E. Braddon regularly communicated, the young actress received the patronage of 'a simple, noble-minded Yorkshire Squire' called Gilby, who was a 'father, lover, and friend' to the aspiring author. Whatever their relationship it did not last, but he performed her an invaluable service: he enabled her to publish her first serialized fiction, *The Trail of the Serpent*. An unremarkable piece of work, it nevertheless established her writing career and also reveals her penchant for the lurid, ghastly and macabre. Less than two years later she published *Lady Audley's Secret* and became a leading popular novelist.

Lady Audley's Secret was initially published in serial form in 1862 by a publisher called John Maxwell. Thus began a lifelong personal and business partnership between M.E. Braddon and 'Max' which ended only with his death in 1895. However, it was not an easy relationship. When they met, Max was already married; his wife, having been pronounced insane, had been committed to a lunatic asylum in Dublin, leaving him to rear their five children. Quietly and unobtrusively Max and M.E. Braddon began living together as man and wife, she bearing not only his children but also the financial burden of supporting the entire household when Max was struggling in business. They eventually married in 1874 after the death of his wife.

Rumour and gossip surrounded their early relationship, particularly when it became public knowledge that they were living together unmarried. It is no coincidence that the first of their five children was born amid the creation of what M.E. Braddon called her pair of 'bigamy novels' – *Lady Audley's Secret* and *Aurora Floyd*. As with so many of her heroines, M.E. Braddon understood what it was like to struggle for money and reputation in a deeply censorious society. Like Dickens she wrote compulsively and prolifically, conscious always of consolidating her financial security. After its publication in volume form, *Lady Audley's Secret* was never out of print during her lifetime.

M.E. Braddon's literary output was phenomenal. She completed at least seventy-four novels between 1862 and 1915, including *Eleanor's Victory* in 1863; she edited a popular magazine, *The Belgravia*, which featured articles and serialized fiction, while also frequently submitting anonymous stories for the extremely popular 'penny dreadfuls' of the time. These tales she described as 'piratical stuff', full of 'crime, tragedy, murder, slow poisoning and general infamy'. They were written solely for profit and had no pretension to literary merit. While some of her novels can be similarly dismissed, and her writing was generally condemned and criticized by many contemporary reviewers for being immoral, outrageous and of harmful influence, it is not sufficient to limit her to such an assessment. She was a writer of extraordinary appeal and popularity as well as ability. Henry James, for example, described her writing as 'brilliant, lively, ingenious and destitute of a ray of sentiment'.

M.E. Braddon can in many ways be regarded as the founder of the Sensation novel as written by women for women. The principal subscribers to the circulating libraries that distributed her novels were middle-class women, confined by upbringing, society and expectation to limited lives of domesticity and dependence upon others. They were required to be passive, submissive, undemanding and selfless. Fulfilment was to be found through others: husbands, children and families. M.E. Braddon's novels feature much more resourceful, active women who exert themselves in order to achieve social respectability and financial security. Unlike the unattractive, masculine women of similar qualities depicted by a male Sensation novelist such as Wilkie Collins, M.E. Braddon is the 'inventor of the fair-haired demon of modern fiction' (Margaret Oliphant, 1867). Her women are respectable, 'the daintiest, prettiest of blonde creatures'; they are intelligent and retaliate against injustice, poverty, unfavourable circumstances as well as men, to whom they are often openly hostile. It could be argued that they articulate the suppressed grievances and frustrations of the ordinary women who read about them, hence part of their extraordinary popularity. They provided escapism, fantasy and release from the mundane, the oppressive and the unescapable.

Unfortunately M.E. Braddon was to some extent a victim of her own early success. Having achieved such popularity with her first novel she found herself compelled to write to a similar popular formula. What is interesting is how she manipulates this to produce changes and developments in the established Sensation novel form.

FIONN O'TOOLE

CHAPTER I

GOING HOME

The craggy cliffs upon the Norman coast looked something like the terraced walls and turreted roofs of a ruined city in the hot afternoon sunshine, as the *Empress* steamer sped swiftly onward toward Dieppe. At least they looked thus in the eyes of a very young lady, who stood alone on the deck of the steam-packet, with yearning eyes fixed upon that foreign shore.

It was four o'clock upon a burning August afternoon in the year 1853. The steamer was fast approaching the harbour. Several moustachioed gentlemen, of various ages, costumes, and manners, were busy getting together carpet-bags, railway-rugs, camp-stools, newspapers, and umbrellas; preparatory to that eager rush towards the shore by which marine voyagers are apt to testify their contempt for Neptune, when they have no longer need of his service or fear of his vengeance. Two or three English families were collected in groups, holding guard over small mounds or barrows of luggage, having made all preparation for landing at first sight of the Norman shore, dim in the distance; and of course about two hours too soon.

Several blooming young English damsels, gathered under maternal wings, were looking forward to sea-bathing in a foreign water-place. The Établissement des Bains had not yet been built, and Dieppe was not so popular, perhaps, among English pleasure-seekers as it now is. There were several comfortable-looking British families on board the steamer, but of all the friendly matrons and pretty daughters assembled on the deck, there seemed no one in any way connected with that lonely young lady who leant against the bulwark with a cloak across her arm and a rather shabby carpet-bag at her feet.

She was very young – indeed of that age which in the other sex is generally called the period of hobbledehoyhood. There was more ankle to be seen below the hem of her neat muslin frock than is quite consistent with elegance of attire in a young lady of fifteen; but as the ankle so revealed was rounded and slender, it would have been hypercritical to have objected to the shortness of the skirt, which had evidently been outgrown by its wearer.

Then, again, this lonely traveller was not only young but pretty. In spite of the shortness of her frock and the shabbiness of her straw bonnet, it was impossible for the most spiteful of the British misses to affirm the contrary. She was very pretty; so pretty that it was a pleasure to look at her, in her unconscious innocence, and to think how beautiful she would be by-and-by, when that bright, budding girlish loveliness bloomed out in its womanly splendour.

Her skin was fair, but pale – not a sentimental or sickly pallor, but a beautiful alabaster clearness of tint. Her eyes were grey, large and dark, or rendered dark by the shadow of long black lashes. I would rather not catalogue her other features too minutely; for though they were regular, and even beautiful, there is something low and material in all the other features as compared to the eyes. Her hair was of soft golden brown, bright and rippling like a sunlit river. The brightness of that luxuriant hair, the light in her grey eyes, and the vivacity of a very beautiful smile, made her face seem almost luminous as she looked at you. It was difficult to imagine that she could ever look unhappy. She seemed an animated, radiant, and exuberant creature, who made an atmosphere of brightness and happiness about her. Other girls of her age would have crept to a corner of the deck, perhaps to hide their loneliness, or would have clung to the outer fringe of one of the family groups, making believe not to be alone; but this young lady had taken her stand boldly against the bulwark, choosing the position from which she might soonest hope to see Dieppe harbour, and apparently quite indifferent to observation, though many a furtive glance was cast towards the tall but girlish figure and the handsome profile so sharply defined against a blue background of summer sky.

But there was nothing unfeminine in all this; nothing bold or defiant; it was only the innocent unconsciousness of a lighthearted girl, ignorant of any perils which could assail her loneliness, and fearless in her ignorance. Throughout the brief sea-voyage she had displayed no symptoms of shyness or perplexity. She had suffered none of the tortures common to many travellers in their marine experiences. She had not been sea-sick; and indeed she did not look like a person who could be subject to any of the common ills this weak flesh inherits. You could almost as easily have pictured to yourself the Goddess Hygeia suffering from bilious headache, or Hebe laid up with the influenza, as this auburn-haired, grey-eyed young lady under any phase of mortal suffering. Eyes dim in the paroxysms of sea-sickness had looked almost spitefully towards this happy, radiant creature, as she flitted hither and thither about the deck, courting the balmy ocean breezes that made themselves merry with her rippling hair. Lips, blue with suffering, had writhed as their owners beheld the sandwiches which this young school-girl devoured, the stale buns, the oval raspberry tarts, the hideous, bilious, revolting three-cornered puffs which she produced at different stages of the voyage from her shabby carpet-bag.

She had an odd volume of a novel, and a long, dreary desert of crochet-work, whose white-cotton monotony was only broken by occasional dingy oases bearing witness of the worker's dirty hands; they were such pretty hands, too, that it was a shame they should ever be dirty; and she had a bunch of flabby, faded flowers, sheltered by a great fan-like shield of newspaper; and she had a smelling-bottle, which she sniffed at perpetually, though she had no need of any such restorative, being as fresh and bright from first to last as the sea breezes themselves, and as little subject to any marine malady as the Lurleis whose waving locks could scarcely have been yellower than her own.

I think, if the feminine voyagers on board the *Empress* were cruel to this solitary young traveller in not making themselves friendly with her in her loneliness, the unkindness must be put down very much to that unchristian frame of mind in which people who are sea-sick are apt to regard those who are not. This bouncing, bright-faced girl seemed to have little need of kindness from the miserable sufferers around her. So she was left to wander about the deck; now reading three pages of her novel; now doing half-a-dozen stitches of her work; now talking to the man at the wheel, in spite of all injunctions to the contrary; now making herself acquainted with stray pet dogs; always contented, always happy; and no one troubled himself about her.

It was only now, when they were nearing Dieppe, that one of the passengers, an elderly, grey-headed Englishman, spoke to her.

'You are very anxious to arrive,' he said, smiling at her eager face.

'Oh, yes, very anxious, sir. We are nearly there, are we not?'

'Yes, we shall enter the harbour presently. You will have some one to meet you there, I suppose?'

'Oh, no,' the young lady answered, lifting her arched brown eyebrows, 'not at Dieppe. Papa will meet me at Paris; but he could never come all the way to Dieppe, just to take me back to Paris. He could never afford such an expense as that.'

'No, to be sure; and you know no one at Dieppe?'

'Oh, no; I don't know any one in all France, except papa.'

Her face, bright as it was even in repose, was lit up with a new brightness as she spoke of her father.

'You are very fond of your papa, I think,' the Englishman said.

'Oh, yes, I love him very, very much. I have not seen him for more than a year. The journey costs so much between England and France, and I have been at school near London, at Brixton; I dare say you know Brixton; but I am going to France now, for good.'

'Indeed! You seem very young to leave school.'

'But I'm not going to leave school,' the young lady answered, eagerly.
'I am going to a very expensive school in Paris, to finish my education;
and then——'

She paused here, hesitating and blushing a little.

'And then what?'

'I am going to be a governess. Papa is not rich. He has no fortune now.'

'He has had a fortune, then?'

'He has had three.'

The young lady's grey eyes were lit up with a certain look of triumph
as she said this.

'He has been very extravagant, poor dear,' she continued,
apologetically; 'and he has spent three fortunes, altogether. But he has
always been so courted and admired, you know, that it is not to be
wondered at. He knew the Prince Regent, and Mr Sheridan, and Mr
Brummel, and the Duke of York, and – oh, all sorts of people, ever so
intimately; and he was a member of the Beefsteak Club, and wore a silver
gridiron in his buttonhole, and he is the most delightful man in society,
even now, though he is very old.'

'Very old! And you are so young.'

The Englishman looked almost incredulously at his animated
companion.

'Yes, I am papa's youngest child. He has been married twice. I have no
real brothers and sisters. I have only half-brothers and sisters, who don't
really and truly care for me, you know. How should they? They were
grown up when I was born, and I have scarcely ever seen them. I have
only papa in all the world.'

'You have no mother, then?'

'No; mamma died when I was three years old.'

The *Empress* packet was entering the harbour by this time. The grey-
headed Englishman went away to look after his portmanteaus and hat-
boxes, but he returned presently to the fairhaired school-girl.

'Will you let me help you with your luggage?' he said. 'I will go and
look after it, if you will tell me for what to inquire.'

'You are very kind. I have only one box. It is directed to Miss Vane,
Paris.'

'Very well, Miss Vane, I will go and find your box. Stay,' he said, taking
out his card-case, 'this is my name, and if you will permit me, I will see
you safely to Paris.'

'Thank you, sir. You are very kind.'

The young lady accepted her new friend's service as frankly as it was
offered. He had grey hair, and in that one particular at least resembled her
father. That was almost enough to make her like him.

There was the usual confusion and delay at the Custom-house – a little squabbling and a good deal of bribery; but everything was managed, upon the whole, pretty comfortably. Most of the passengers dropped in at the Hôtel de l'Europe, or some of the other hotels upon the stony quay; a few hurried off to the market-place, to stare at the cathedral church of Saint Jacques, or the great statue of Abraham Duquesne, the rugged sea-king, with broad-brimmed hat and waving plumes, high boots and flowing hair, and to buy peaches and apricots of the noisy market-women. Others wandered in the slimy and slippery fishmarket, fearfully and wonderingly contemplative of those hideous conger-eels, dog-fish, and other piscatorial monstrosities which seem peculiar to Dieppe. Miss Vane and her companion strolled into the dusky church of Saint Jacques by a little wooden door in a shady nook of the edifice. A few solitary women were kneeling here and there, half-hidden behind their high-backed rush chairs. A fisherman was praying upon the steps of a little chapel, in the solemn obscurity.

'I have never been here before,' Miss Vane whispered. 'I came by Dover and Calais, the last time; but this way is so much cheaper, and I almost think it nicer, for the journey's so short from London to Newhaven, and I don't mind the long sea voyage a bit. Thank you for bringing me to see this cathedral.'

Half-an-hour after this the two travellers were seated in a first-class carriage, with other railway passengers, French and English, hurrying through the fair Norman landscape.

Miss Vane looked out at the bright hills and woods, the fruitful orchards, and white-roofed cottages, so villa-like, fantastical, and beautiful; and her face brightened with the brightening of the landscape under the hot radiance of the sun. The grey-headed gentleman felt a quiet pleasure in watching that earnest, hopeful, candid face; the grey eyes, illumined with gladness; the parted lips, almost tremulous with delight, as the sunny panorama glided by the open window.

The quiet old bachelor's heart had been won by his companion's frank acceptance of his simple service.

'Another girl of her age would have been as frightened of a masculine stranger as of a wild beast,' he thought, 'and would have given herself all manner of missish airs; but this young damsel smiles in my face, and trusts me with almost infantile simplicity. I hope her father is a good man. I don't much like that talk of Sheridan and Beau Brummel and the Beefsteak Club. No very good school for fathers that, I should fancy. I wish her mother had been alive, poor child. I hope she is going to a happy home, and a happy future.'

The train stopped at Rouen, and Miss Vane accepted a cup of coffee and some *brioches* from her companion. The red August sunset was melting into grey mistiness by this time, and the first shimmer of the moonlight was silvery on the water as they crossed the Seine and left the lighted city behind them. The grey-headed Englishman fell asleep soon after this, and before long there was a low chorus of snoring, masculine and feminine, audible in the comfortable carriage; only broken now and then, when the train stopped with a jerk at some fantastic village that looked like a collection of Swiss toy cottages in the dim summer night.

But, let these matter-of-fact people snore and slumber as they might, there was no such thing as sleep for Eleanor Vane. It would have been utter sacrilege to have slept in the face of all that moonlighted beauty, to have been carried sleeping through that fairy landscape. The eager school-girl's watchful eyes drank in the loveliness of every hill and valley; the low scattered woodland; the watering streams; and that perplexing Seine, which the rumbling carriage crossed so often with a dismal hollow sound in the stillness of the night.

No; Miss Vane's bright grey eyes were not closed once in that evening journey; and at last, when the train entered the great Parisian station, when all the trouble and confusion of arrival began – that wearisome encounter of difficulty which makes cowardly travellers wish the longest journey longer than it is – the young lady's head was thrust out of the window, and her eager eyes wandered hither and thither amongst the faces of the crowd.

Yes, he was there – her father. That white-haired old man, with the gold-headed cane, and the aristocratic appearance. She pointed him out eagerly to her fellow-passenger.

'That is papa – you see, – the handsome man. He is coming this way, but he doesn't see us. Oh, let me out, please; let me go to him!'

She trembled in her eagerness, and her fair face flushed crimson with excitement. She forgot her carpet-bag, her novel, her crochet, her smelling-bottle, her cloak, her parasol – all her paraphernalia: and left her companion to collect them as best he might. She was out of the carriage and in her father's arms she scarcely knew how. The platform seemed deserted all in a moment, for the passengers had rushed away to a great dreary *salle d'attente*, there to await the inspection of their luggage. Miss Vane, her fellow-traveller, and her father, were almost alone, and she was looking up at the old man's face in the lamplight.

'Papa, dear papa, darling, how well you are looking; as well as ever; better than ever, I think!'

Her father drew himself up proudly. He was past seventy years of age, but he was a very handsome man. His beauty was of that patrician type which loses little by age. He was tall and broad-chested, erect as a Grenadier, but not fat. The Prince Regent might become corpulent, and lay himself open to the insolent sneers of his sometime boon companion and friend; but Mr George Mowbray Vandeleur Vane held himself on his guard against that insidious foe which steals away the graces of so many elderly gentlemen. Mr Vane's aristocratic bearing imparted such a stamp to his clothes, that it was not easy to see the shabbiness of his garments; but those garments were shabby. Carefully as they had been brushed, they bore the traces of that slow decay which is not to be entirely concealed, whatever the art of the wearer.

Miss Vane's travelling companion saw all this. He had been so much interested by the young lady's frank and fearless manner, that he would fain have lingered in the hope of learning something of her father's character; but he felt that he had no excuse for delaying his departure.

'I will wish you good night, now, Miss Vane,' he said, kindly, 'since you are safely restored to your papa.'

Mr Vane lifted his grey eyebrows, looked at his daughter interrogatively; rather suspiciously, the traveller thought.

'Oh, papa, dear,' the young lady answered, in reply to that questioning look, 'this gentleman was on board the boat with me, and he has been so very kind.'

She searched in her pocket for the card which her acquaintance had given her, and produced that document, rather limp and crumpled. Her father looked at it, murmured the name inscribed upon it twice or thrice, as if trying to attach some aristocratic association thereto, but evidently failed in doing so.

'I have not the honour of – a – haw – knowing this name, sir,' he said, lifting his hat stiffly about half a yard from his silvered head; 'but for your courtesy and kindness to my child, I hope you will accept my best thanks. I was prevented by important business of – a – haw – not altogether undiplomatic character – from crossing the Channel to fetch my daughter; and – aw – also – prevented from sending my servant – by – aw – I thank you for your politeness, sir. You are a stranger, by the way. Can I do anything for you in Paris? Lord Cowley is my very old friend; any service that I can render you in that quarter – I——'

The traveller bowed and smiled.

'Thank you very much,' he said, 'I am no stranger in Paris. I will wish you good night; good night, Miss Vane.'

But Mr Vane was not going to let his daughter's friend off so easily. He produced his card-case, murmured more pompous assurances of his gratitude, and tendered further offers of patronage to the quiet traveller, who found something rather oppressive in Mr Vane's civility. But it was all over at last, and the old man led his daughter off to look for the trunk which contained all her worldly possessions.

The stranger looked wistfully after the father and child.

'I hope she may have a happy future,' he thought, rather despondingly; 'the old man is poor and pompous. He tells lies which bring hot blushes into his daughter's beautiful face. I am very sorry for her.'

CHAPTER II

THE ENTRESOL IN THE RUE DE L'ARCHEVÊQUE

Mr Vane took his daughter away from the station in one of those secondary and cheaper vehicles which are distinguished by the discriminating Parisian by some mysterious difference of badge. The close, stifling carriage rattled over the uneven stones of long streets which were unfamiliar to Eleanor Vane, until it emerged into the full glory of the lighted Boulevard. The light-hearted school-girl could not suppress a cry of rapture as she looked once more at the broad thoroughfare, the dazzling lamps, the crowd, the theatres, the cafés, the beauty and splendour, although she had spent her summer holiday in Paris only a year before.

'It seems so beautiful again, papa,' she said, 'just as if I'd never seen it before; and I'm to stop here now, and never, never to leave you again, to go away for such a cruel distance. You don't know how unhappy I've been, sometimes, papa dear. I wouldn't tell you then, for fear of making you uneasy; but I can tell you now, now that it's all over.'

'Unhappy!' gasped the old man, clenching his fist; 'they've not been unkind to you – they've not dared——'

'Oh, no, dearest father. They've been very, very good. I was quite a favourite, papa. Yes, though there were so many rich girls in the school, and I was only a half-boarder, I was quite a favourite with Miss Bennett and Miss Sophia; though I know I was careless and lazy sometimes – not on purpose, you know, papa, for I tried hard to get on with my education, for your sake, darling. No, everybody was very kind to me, papa: but I used to think sometimes how far I was from you; what miles and miles and miles of sea and land there were between us, and that if you should be ill – I——'

Eleanor Vane broke down, and her father clasped her in his arms, and cried over her silently. The tears came with very little provocation to the old man's handsome blue eyes. He was of that sanguine temperament which to the last preserves the fondest delusions of youth. At seventy-five years of age he hoped and dreamed and deluded himself as foolishly as he had done at seventeen. His sanguine temperament had been for ever leading him astray for more than sixty years. Severe judges called George

Vane a liar; but perhaps his shallow romances, his pitiful boasts, were more often highly-coloured and poetical versions of the truth, than actual falsehood.

It was past twelve o'clock when the carriage drove away from the lights and splendour into the darkness of a labyrinth of quiet streets behind the Madeleine. The Rue de l'Archevêque was one of these dingy and quiet streets, very narrow, very close and stifling in the hot August midnight. The vehicle stopped abruptly at a corner, before a little shop, the shutters of which were closed of course at this hour.

'It is a butcher's shop, I am sorry to say, my love,' Mr Vane said, apologetically, as he handed his daughter on to the pavement; 'but I find myself very comfortable here, and it is conveniently adjacent to the Boulevards.'

The old man paid the driver, who had deposited mademoiselle's box upon the threshold of the little door beside the butcher's shop. The *pourboire* was not a very large one, but Mr Vane bestowed it with the air of a prince. He pushed open the low door, and took his daughter into a narrow passage. There was no porter or portress, for the butcher's shop and the apartments belonging to it were abnormal altogether; but there was a candle and box of matches on a shelf in a corner of the steep corkscrew staircase. The driver carried Eleanor's box as far as the entresol in consideration of his *pourboire*, but departed while Mr Vane was opening the door of an apartment facing the staircase.

The entresol consisted of three little rooms, opening one out of another, and so small and low that Miss Vane almost fancied herself in a doll's house. Every article of furniture in the stifling little apartment bore the impress of its nationality. Tawdry curtains of figured damask, resplendent with dirty tulips and monster roses, tarnished ormolu mouldings, a gilded clock with a cracked dial and a broken shade, a pair of rickety bronze candlesticks, a couple of uncompromising chairs covered with dusty green velvet and relieved by brass-headed nails, and a square table with a long trailing cover of the same material as the curtains, completed the adornments of the sitting-room. The bed-chambers were smaller, closer, and hotter. Voluminous worsted curtains falling before the narrow windows, and smothering the little beds, made the stifling atmosphere yet more stifling. The low ceilings seemed to rest on the top of poor Eleanor's head. She had been accustomed to large airy rooms, and broad uncurtained open windows.

'How hot it is here, papa,' she said, drawing a long breath.

'It always is hot in Paris at this time of year, my dear,' Mr Vane answered; 'the rooms are small, you see, but convenient. That is to be your bedroom, my love,' he added, indicating one of the little chambers.

He was evidently habituated to Parisian lodging-houses, and saw no discomfort in the tawdry grandeur, the shabby splendour, the pitiful attempt to substitute scraps of gilding and patches of velvet for the common necessaries and decencies of life.

'And now let me look at you, my dear; let me look at you, Eleanor.'

George Mowbray Vane set the candlestick upon the rusty velvet cover of the low mantel-piece, and drew his daughter towards him. She had thrown off her bonnet and loose grey cloak, and stood before her father in her scanty muslin frock, with all her auburn hair hanging about her face and shoulders, and glittering in the dim light of that one scrap of wax candle.

'My pet, how beautiful you have grown, how beautiful!' the old man said, with an accent of fond tenderness. 'We'll teach Mrs Bannister a lesson some of these days, Eleanor. Yes, *our* turn will come, my love; I know that I shall die a rich man.'

Miss Vane was accustomed to hear this remark from her father. She inherited something of his sanguine nature, and she loved him very dearly, so she may be forgiven if she believed in his vague visions of future grandeur. She had never seen anything in her life but chaotic wrecks of departed splendour, confusion, debt, and difficulty. She had not been called upon to face poverty in the fair hand-to-hand struggle which enobles and elevates the sturdy wrestler in the battle of life. No, she had rather been compelled to play at hide-and seek with the grim enemy. She had never gone out into the open, and looked her foe full in the eyes, hardy, resolute, patient, and steadfast. She was familiar with all those debasing tricks and pitiful subterfuges whereby the weak and faint-hearted seek to circumvent the enemy; but she had never been taught the use of those measures by which he may be honestly beaten.

The Mrs Bannister of whom George Vane had spoken, was one of his elder daughters, who had been very, very ungrateful to him, he declared; and who now in his old age doled him out the meagre allowance which enabled him to occupy an entresol over a butcher's shop, and dine daily at one of the cheap restaurants in the Palais Royal.

Mr Vane was wont to lament his daughter's cruel lack of affection in very bitter language, freely interspersed with quotations from 'King Lear;' indeed I believe he considered his case entirely parallel with that of the injured British monarch and father; ignoring the one rather important fact that, whereas Lear's folly had been the too generous division of his own fortune between his recreant daughters, *his* weakness had been the reckless waste and expenditure of the portions which his children had inherited from their mother.

Mrs Bannister, instigated thereto by her husband, had protested some years before against the several acts of folly and extravagance by which the fortune which ought to have been hers had been fooled away. She declined to allow her father more than the pittance alluded to above; although, as she was now a rich widow, and of course entirely her own mistress, she might have done much more.

'Yes, my darling,' Mr Vane said, as he proudly contemplated his youngest child's beauty, 'we will turn the tables upon Mrs Bannister and the rest of them, yet, please God. My Benjamin; my youngest, brightest darling; we'll teach them a lesson. They may poke their old father away in a foreign lodging, and stint him of money for any little innocent pleasure; but the day will come, my love, the day will come!'

The old man nodded his head two or three times with solemn significance. The sanguine, impulsive nature, dwarfed and fettered by the cruel bonds of poverty, was too elastic to be entirely repressed even by those galling chains; and having hoped all his life, and having enjoyed such successes and good fortune as fall to the lot of very few men, he went on hoping in his old age, blindly confident that some sudden revolution in the wheel of life would lift him out of his obscurity and set him again on the pinnacle he had once occupied so proudly.

He had had a host of friends and many children, and he had squandered more than one fortune, not being any more careful of other people's money than of his own; and now, in his poverty and desolation, the child of his old age was the only one who clung to him, and loved him, and believed in him; the only one whom he loved, perhaps, truly and unreservedly, though he wept frequently over the ingratitude of the others. It may be that Eleanor was the only one whom he could love with any comfort to himself, because the only one he had never injured.

'But, papa, dear,' this youngest and best loved of the old man's children pleaded gently, 'Mrs Bannister, Hortensia, has been very good – has she not? – in sending the money for my education at Madame Marly's, where she was finished herself. That was very generous of her, wasn't it, papa?'

Mr Vane shook his head, and lifted his grey eyebrows with a deprecating expression.

'Hortensia Bannister cannot perform a generous act in a generous manner, my dear. You recognize the viper by the reptile's sting: you may recognize Hortensia in pretty much the same manner. She gives, but she insults the recipients of her – ahem – bounty. Shall I read you her letter, Eleanor?'

'If you please, dear papa.'

The young lady had seated herself, in a somewhat hoydenish manner, upon the elbow of her father's chair, and had wound her soft round arm about his neck. She loved him and believed in him. The world which had courted and admired him while he had money and could boast such acquaintance as the Prince and Sheridan, Sir Francis Burdett, Lord Castlereagh, Mr Pitt, and the Duke of York, had fallen away from him of late; and the few old associates who yet remained of that dead-and-gone cycle were apt to avoid him, influenced perhaps by the recollection of small loans of an occasional five-pound note, and a 'little silver,' which had not been repaid. Yes, the world had fallen away from George Mowbray Vandeleur Vane, once of Vandeleur Park, Cheshire, and Mowbray Castle, near York. The tradesmen who had helped him to squander his money had let him get very deep in their books before they closed those cruel ledgers, and stopped all supplies. He had existed for a long time – he had lived as a gentleman, he said himself – upon the traditions of the past, the airy memories of the fortunes he had wasted. But this was all over now, and he had emigrated to the city in which he had played the Grand Seigneur in those glorious early days of the Restoration, and where he was compelled to lead a low and vulgar life, disgracing himself by pettifogging ready-money dealings, utterly degrading to a gentleman.

He could not bring himself to own that he was better and happier in this new life, and that it was pleasant to be able to walk erect and defiant upon the Boulevards, rather than to be compelled to plunge down dark alleys, and dive into sinuous byways, for the avoidance of importunate creditors, as he had been in free England.

He took his wealthy daughter's letter from the breast-pocket of his coat; a fashionable coat, though shabby now, for it had been made for him by a sentimental German tailor, who had wept over his late patron's altered fortunes, and given him credit for a suit of clothes. That compassionate German tailor never expected to be paid, and the clothes were a benefaction, a gift as purely and generously given as any Christian dole offered in the holy name of charity; but Mr Vane was pleased with the fiction of an expected payment, and would have revolted against the idea of receiving a present from the good-natured tradesman.

The letter from Hortenisa Bannister was not a long one. It was written in sharp and decisive paragraphs, and in a neat firm hand. Rather a cruel-looking hand, Eleanor Vane thought.

The old man put a double gold eyeglass over his nose, and began to read.

Hyde Park Gardens, August, 1853.

My dear Father,

In compliance with your repeated solicitations I have determined upon taking measures by which I hope the future welfare of your youngest daughter may be secured.

'I must, however, remind you that Eleanor Vane and I are the children of different mothers; that she has, therefore, less claim upon me than a sister usually has; and I freely confess I never heard of one sister being called upon to provide for another.

'You must also remember that I never entertained any degree of friendship or affection for Eleanor's mother, who was much below you in station, and whom you married in direct opposition to myself and my sisters——'

Eleanor started; she was too impetuous to listen quite passively to this letter. Her father felt the sudden movement of the arm about his neck.

'Your mother was an angel, my dear,' he said; 'and this woman is – never mind what. My daughters chose to give themselves airs to your poor mother because she had been their governess, and because her father had failed as a sugar-broker.'

He went back to the letter, groping nervously for the place at which he had left off, with the point of his well-shaped finger –

'But you tell me that you have no power to make any provision whatsoever for your daughter; and that, unless I assist you, this unhappy girl may, in the event of your death, be flung penniless upon the world, imperfectly educated, and totally incompetent to get her living.'

'She speaks of my death very freely,' the old man murmured, 'but she's right enough. I shan't trouble anybody long, my dear; I shan't trouble anybody long.'

The tender arms wound themselves more closely about George Vane's neck.

'Papa, darling,' the soft voice whispered, 'you have never troubled *me*. Don't go on with that horrid letter, papa. We won't accept any favours from such a woman.'

'Yes, yes, my love, for your sake; if I stoop, it is for your sake, Eleanor.'

The old man went on reading.

'Under these circumstances,' the writer continued, 'I have come to the following determination. I will give you a hundred pounds, to be paid to Madame Marly, who knows you, and has received a great deal of money from you for my education and that of my sisters, and who will, therefore, be inclined to receive Eleanor upon advantageous terms. For this sum of money Madame Marly will, I feel assured, consent to prepare my half-sister for the situation of governess in a gentleman's family; that is, of course, premising that Eleanor has availed herself conscientiously of the advantages afforded her by her residence with the Misses Bennett.

'I shall write to Madame Marly by this post, using my best influence with her for Eleanor's benefit; and should I receive a favourable reply to this letter, I will immediately send you an order for a hundred pounds, to be paid by you to Madame Marly.

'I do this in order that you may not appear to my old instructress –
who remembers you as a rich man – in the position of a pauper; but in
thus attempting to spare your feelings, and perhaps my own, I fear that I
run some risk.

'Let me therefore warn you that this money is the last I will ever pay
for my half-sister's benefit. Squander or misuse it if you please. You have
robbed me often, and would not perhaps hesitate to do so again. But bear
in mind, that this time it is Eleanor you will rob and not me.

'The only chance she will have of completing her education is the
chance I now give her. Rob her of this and you rob her of an honourable
future. Deprive her of this and you make yourself answerable for any
misfortunes which may befall her when you are dead and gone.

'Forgive me if I have spoken harshly, or even undutifully; my excuse
lies in your past follies. I have spoken strongly because I wished to make a
strong impression, and I believe that I have acted for the best.

'Once for all, remember that I will attend to no future solicitations on
Eleanor's behalf. If she makes good use of the help I now afford her, I
may perhaps be tempted to render her further services – unsolicited – in
the future. If she or you make a bad use of this one chance, I wash my
hands of all concern in your future miseries.

'The money will be made payable at Messrs Blount's, Rue de la Paix.

'I trust you attend the Protestant Church in the Rue Rivoli.

'With best wishes for your welfare, temporal and eternal, I remain, my
dear father,

'Your affectionate daughter,
'HORTENSIA BANNISTER.'

George Vane burst into tears as he finished the letter. How cruelly she
had stabbed him, this honourable, conscientious daughter, whom he had
robbed certainly, but in a generous, magnanimous, reckless fashion, that
made robbery rather a princely virtue than a sordid vice. How cruelly the
old heart was lacerated by that bitter letter!

'As if I would touch the money,' cried Mr Vane, elevating his trembling
hands to the low ceiling with a passionate and tragic gesture. 'Have I
been such a wretch to you, Eleanor, that this woman should accuse me of
wishing to snatch the bread from your innocent lips?'

'Papa, papa!'

'Have I been such an unnatural father, such a traitor, liar, swindler, and
cheat, that my own daughter should say these things to me?'

His voice rose higher with each sentence, and the tears streamed down
his wrinkled cheeks.

Eleanor tried to kiss away those tears; but he pushed her from him
with passionate vehemence.

'Go away from me, my child, I am a wretch, a robber, a scoundrel, a——'

'No, no, no, papa,' cried Eleanor; 'you are all that is good, you have always been good to me, dear, dear papa.'

'By what right, then, does this woman insult me with such a letter as that?' asked the old man, drying his eyes, and pointing to the crumpled letter which he had flung upon the ground.

'She has no right, papa,' answered Eleanor. 'She is a wicked, cruel woman. But we'll send back her money. I'd rather go out into the world at once, papa, and work for you: I'd rather be a dressmaker. I could learn soon if I tried very hard. I do know a little about dressmaking. I made this dress, and it fits very well, only I cut out both the backs for one side, and both sleeves for one arm, and that wasted the stuff, you know and made the skirt a little scanty. I'd rather do anything, papa, than accept this money, – I would indeed. I don't want to go to this grand Parisian school, except to be near you, papa, darling. That was the only thing I ever cared for. The Miss Bennetts would take me as a pupil teacher, and give me fifteen pounds a-year, and I'd send every shilling of it to you, papa, and then you needn't live over a wretched shop where the meat smells nasty in the warm weather. We won't take the money, will we, papa?'

The old man shook his head, and made a motion with his lips and throat, as if he had been gulping down some bitter draught.

'Yes, my dear,' he said, in a tone of ineffable resignation, 'for your sake I would suffer many humiliations; for your sake I will endure this. We will take no notice of this woman's letter; though I could write her a reply that – but no matter. We will let her insolence pass, and she shall never know how keenly it has stung me here!'

He tapped his breast as he spoke, and the tears rose again to his eyes.

'We will accept this money, Eleanor,' he continued, 'we will accept her bounty; and the day may come when you will have ample power to retaliate – ample power, my dear. She has called me a thief, Eleanor,' exclaimed the old man, suddenly returning to his own wrongs, 'a thief! My own daughter has called me a thief, and accused me of the baseness of robbing you.'

'Papa, papa, darling.'

'As if your father could rob you of this money, Eleanor; as if I could touch a penny of it. No, so help me, Heaven! not a penny of it to save me from starving.'

His head sank forward upon his breast, and he sat for some minutes muttering to himself in broken sentences, as if almost unconscious of his daughter's presence. In that time he looked older than he had looked at any moment since his daughter had met him at the station. Watching him now, wistfully and sorrowfully, Eleanor Vane saw that her father was indeed an old man, vacillating and weak of purpose, and with ample need of all the compassionate tenderness, the fond affection, which overflowed her girlish heart as she looked at him. She knelt down on the slippery oaken floor at his feet, and took his tremulous hand in both of hers.

He started as she touched him, and looked at her.

'My darling,' he cried, 'you've had nothing to eat; you've been nearly an hour in the house, and you've had nothing to eat. But I've not forgotten you, Nell; you'll find I've not forgotten you.'

He rose from his chair, and went over to a little cupboard in the wall, from which he took a couple of plates and tumblers, some knives and forks, and two or three parcels wrapped in white paper, and neatly tied with narrow red tape. He put these on the table, and going a second time to the cupboard produced a pint bottle of Burgundy, in a basket; very dusty and cobwebby; and therefore, no doubt, very choice.

The white paper parcels contained very recherché comestibles. A slender wedge of truffled turkey, some semi-transparent slices of German sausage, and an open plum tart, with a great deal of rich ruby-coloured syrup, and an utterly uneatable crust.

Miss Vane partook very freely of this little collation, praising her father for his goodness and indulgence as she ate the simple feast he had prepared for her. But she did not like the Burgundy in the dusty basket, and preferred to drink some water out of one of the toilette-bottles.

Her father, however, enjoyed the pint of good wine, and recovered his equanimity under its generous influence. He had never been a drunkard; he had indeed one of those excitable natures which cannot endure the influence of strong drinks, and a very little wine had considerable effect upon him.

He talked a good deal, therefore, to his daughter, told her some of his delusive hopes in the future, tried to explain some of the plans which he had formed for his and her advancement, and was altogether very happy and social. The look of age, which had been so strong upon him half an hour before, faded out like a grey morning shadow under the broadening sunlight. He was a young man again; proud, hopeful, reckless, handsome; ready to run through three more fortunes, if they should fall to his lot.

It was past two o'clock when Eleanor Vane lay down, thoroughly exhausted, but not weary – she had one of those natures which seem never to grow weary – to fall asleep for the first time in four-and-twenty hours.

Her father did not quite so quickly fall into a peaceful slumber. He lay awake for upwards of an hour, tumbling and tossing to and fro upon the narrow spring mattress, and muttering to himself.

And even in his sleep, though the early summer dawn was grey in the room when he fell into a fitful and broken slumber, the trouble of his eldest daughter's letter was heavy upon him, for every now and then he muttered, disjointly, –

'Thief – swindler! As if – as if – I would – rob – my own daughter.'

CHAPTER III

THE STORY OF THE PAST

The history of George Mowbray Vandeleur Vane was the history of many men whose lot it was to shine in that brilliant orbit of which George, Prince Regent, was the ruling star. Around that dazzling royal planet how many smaller lights revolved, twinkling in humble emulation of their prince's glory. What were fortune, friends, children, wives, or creditors, when weighed in the balance, if the royal favour, the princely smile, hung on the other side of the scale? If George the Fourth was pleased to bring ruin upon himself and his creditors, how should his friends and associates do less? Looking backward at the spurious glitter, the mock splendour, the hollow delight of that wonderful age which is so near us in point of time, so far away from us by reason of the wide differences which divide to-day from that foolish yesterday, we can of course afford to be very wise, and can clearly see what a very witches' sabbath was that long revelry in which the Fourth George of England led the dance. But who shall doubt that the dancers themselves saw the fantastic caperings of their leader in a very different light, and looked upon their model as worthy of all mortal praise and imitation.

The men of that frivolous era seem to have abandoned themselves to unmanly weakness, and followed the fashions set them by the fat and pale-faced Royal Adonis, as blindly as the women of to-day emulate the Imperial caprices of the Tuileries, sacrificing themselves as burnt offerings to the Moloch of Fashion, in obedience to the laws made by a lady who lives in a palace; and who, when she wears her silken robe three yards in length and six in circumference, can scarcely be expected to foresee the nervous tortures by-and-by to be endured by Mr John Smith, of Peckham Rye, whose wife will insist on having a hoop and train à l'Oojénee, and sweeping her superabundant skirts into the fender and across the back of the grate every time she steers her difficult way about the worthy Smith's fourteen feet by twelve front parlour.

Yes, if Cleopatra melts pearls in her wine, and sails in a galley of gold, we must have sham jewels to dissolve in our inferior vintages, and sham gold to adorn our galleys. If Pericles, or Charles, or George, affects

splendour and ruin, the prince's devoted subjects must ruin themselves
also, never letting their master see anything but smiling faces amid the
general wreck, and utterly heedless of such minor considerations as wives
and children, creditors and friends.

George Mowbray Vandeleur Vane ruined himself with a grace that was
only second to that of his royal model. He began life with a fair estate left
him by his father, and having contrived to squander the best part of his
patrimony within a few years of his coming of age, was so lucky as to
marry the only daughter and heiress of a rich banker, thereby acquiring a
second fortune just at that critical moment when the first was on the
verge of exhaustion. He was not a bad husband to the simple girl who
loved and worshipped him with a foolishly confiding worship. It was not
in his nature to be wilfully bad to anybody; for he was of a genial,
generous spirit, with warm affections for those who pleased him and
ministered to his happiness. He introduced his young wife to very
brilliant people, and led her into sacred and inner circles, whither her
father the banker could never have taken her; but he squandered her
money foolishly and recklessly. He broke down the bulwarks of
parchment with which the lawyers had hoped to protect her fortune. He
made light of the settlements which were to provide for the future of his
children. They were only blooming and beautiful young creatures in
cambric frocks and blue sashes; and surely, Mr Vane urged, they had
nothing to complain of, for hadn't they splendid apartments and costly
dresses, nurses, governesses, masters, carriages, ponies, and indulgences of
every kind? What did they want, then, or in what manner did he fail in
his duty towards those innocent darlings? Had not his Royal Highness the
Duke of Kent himself come to Vandeleur to stand sponsor for Edward
George? Had not Hortensia Georgina received her second name after the
beautiful Duchess of Devonshire, in whose lovely arms she had been
dandled when only a fortnight old?

Were there any earthly honours or splendours, within the limit of
reasonable desire, which George Vane had failed to procure for his wife
and children?

The gentle lady was fain to answer this question in the negative, and to
accept it for what it was not; namely, an answer to the questions *she* had
ventured to ask touching the future of those unconscious children. Mr
Vane could always persuade his simple wife to sign away any of those
parchment defences the lawyers had devised for her protection; and
when, after an elegant little *tête-à-tête* dinner, in the arrangement of
which the *chef* had displayed his most consummate skill, the affectionate
husband produced a diamond bracelet or an emerald heart from its
morocco casket, and clasped the jewel upon his wife's slender arm, or
hung it round her delicate throat, with the tears glistening in his

handsome blue eyes, gentle Margaret Vane forgot the sacrifices of the morning, and all those shadowy doubts which were wont to torment her when she contemplated the future.

Then, again, Mr Vane had an unfailing excuse for present imprudence in the expectation of a third fortune, which was to come to him from his bachelor uncle and godfather, Sir Milwood Mowbray, of Mowbray Castle, York; so that there were no vulgar retrenchments either at Vandeleur Park or in Berkeley Square, and when Sir Milwood's fortune did come, in the due course of life and death, to his nephew's hands, it only came just in time to stave off the ruin that threatened George Vane's household.

If Mr Vane had then taken his wife's advice, all might have been well; but the Mowbray fortune seemed like the two other fortunes, quite inexhaustible; the sanguine gentleman forgetting that he was in debt to full half its amount. The French *chef* still prepared dinners which might have made Oude himself tremble for his laurels; the German governess and the Parisian lady's-maids still attended upon Mr Vane's daughters; the old career of extravagance went on. George Vane carried his family to the Continent, and plunged them into new gaieties at the court of the restored Louis. He sent his daughters to the most expensive finishing-school in Paris, that very Madame Marly's of whom mention has been made in the last chapter. He took them to Italy and Switzerland. He hired a villa by the Lake of Como; a chateau on the borders of Lucerne. He followed the footsteps of Byron and D'Orsay, Madame de Staël and Lady Blessington; he affected art, literature, and music. He indulged his children's every caprice, he gratified their wildest fancies. It was only when the sons saw themselves penniless and professionless, with the great battle of life all before them, and with no weapons wherewith to fight; and the daughters found themselves left portionless, to win the best husbands they might in the matrimonial lottery; it was only at this crisis that these ungrateful children turned round upon poor, indulgent Lear, and reproached him for the extravagances they had helped him to perpetrate.

This was a cruelty which George Vane could never bring himself to comprehend. Had he denied them anything, these heartless children, that they should turn upon him now in his old age – it would have been rather a dangerous thing for any one else to have alluded to his age, though he spoke freely enough of his grey hairs when bewailing his wrongs – and be angry with him because he could not give them fortunes? This thanklessness was worse than a serpent's tooth. It was now that Mr Vane began to quote 'King Lear,' piteously likening himself to that too confiding monarch.

But he was sixty years old now, and had lived his life. His gentle and trusting wife had died ten years before his money was gone, and of all his

four children there was not one who would say a word in his defence.
The most affectionate and dutiful of them were only silent, and thought
they did much in witholding their reproaches. So he let them go their
ways, the two sons to fight the battle of life how they might – the two
daughters to marry. They were both handsome and accomplished, and
they married well. And being left quite alone in the world, with nothing
but the traditions of a brilliant past, Mr Vane united his misfortunes to
those of a very beautiful girl, who had been his daughters' governess, and
who had fallen in love with his splendid graces in the very simplicity of
her heart, thinking his grey hairs more beautiful than the raven locks of
meaner men.

Yes: George Vane possessed this gift of fascination in a dangerous
degree, and his second wife loved and believed in him in the day of his
decline, as entirely as his first wife had done in the brighter hours of his
prosperity. She loved and trusted him. She bore with a life of perpetual
debt and daily difficulty. She sacrificed herself to the mean shifts and
petty stratagems of a dishonest existence. She, whose nature was truth
itself, humiliated herself for her husband's sake, and helped to play that
pitiful, skulking game of hide-and-seek in which George Vane hoped to
escape the honest struggles of poverty.

But she died young, worn out, perhaps, by these incessant miseries,
and not able to draw consolation from the sham splendour and tinselly
grandeur with which George Vane tried to invest his fallen state. She
died within five years of her marriage, leaving a distracted and despairing
old man as the sole guardian and protector of her only child.

This calamity was the bitterest blow that George Vane had ever been
called upon to endure. He had loved his second wife, the wife of his
poverty and humiliation, far more dearly than he had loved the obedient
partner of his splendour and prosperity. She had been more to him a
thousand times, this gentle girl who had so uncomplainingly accepted the
hardships of her lot, because there had been no idle vanities, no hollow
glories, no Princes and Beefsteak Clubs, to stand between him and his
love of her.

She was lost, and he remembered how little he had done to prove his
affection for her. *She* had never reproached him; no word of upbraiding
had ever crossed those tender lips. But how did he know that he had not
wronged her as cruelly as he had wronged those noisy children who had
betrayed and deserted him?

He remembered how often he had slighted her advice, her loving
counsel, so pure and true, so modestly offered, so gently spoken. He
remembered how many humiliations he had forced upon her, how many
falsehoods he had compelled her to tell; how often he had imposed upon
her affection, suffering her to slave for him in his blind selfishness.

He could remember all these things now that she was gone, and that it was too late; too late to fall at her feet and tell her that he was all unworthy of her love and goodness; too late to offer her even such poor atonement for the past as penitence and tears. A hundred tokens of her in his poor lodgings recalled her a hundred times a day, bringing the tears into his poor broken-down mourner's eyes.

He did not need the presence of his little daughter, whose dark grey eyes looked at him like hers, whose auburn hair had the same golden glory that he had so often seen glistening in the sunshine as he sat lazily watching the low evening light upon his wife's drooping head. It seemed only yesterday that she had stood in the window working for him – for him.

His affliction left him for a long time a broken old man. He did not care in this dull interval of despair to keep up those outward shams of prosperity which he had so persistently preserved. His fashionable coats and boots, treasured so carefully of late, were no longer objects of tender care and delight to him. He ceased to go out into that ignorant and careless world in which he could still play the fine gentleman. He shut himself up and abandoned himself to his grief, and it was a long time before his frivolous nature recovered the shock he had suffered. It is not to be wondered at that, in the agony of his bereavement, his youngest child became unspeakably dear to him. He had severed all the links which had bound him to the past, and to his elder children. His second marriage had made a new era in his life. If he thought of these elder children at all, it was only to remember that some of them were living in luxury, and that they ought to support him in his penniless old age. If he wrote to them, he wrote begging-letters, appealing to them in exactly the same spirit as he might have appealed to the Duke of Wellington or Miss Burdett Coutts.

Yes; his youngest daughter usurped the place of an only child in the old man's heart. He indulged her as he had indulged the ungrateful elder children. He could not give her carriages and horses, liveried servants and splendid houses, but he could now and then prevail upon some weak-minded creditor to trust him, and would come home triumphant to his shabby lodging, bearing spoils for his beloved Eleanor. He would hire a brougham from a confiding livery-stable keeper, and would take his little girl for a drive in the country. He would get her fine dresses from the silk-mercers who had supplied his elder daughters, and he would compensate her for the shabby miseries of her every-day existence by chance flashes of radiance and glory.

Then, again, he would very often obtain small sums of money, loans from private friends, it may be, or fleeting treasures from a mysterious source, of which his innocent little daughter had no knowledge. So, for the first ten or eleven years of her life, Miss Vane's existence was chequered by sudden glimpses of abnormal wealth – wonderful feast days of luxury and extravagance – which contrasted sharply with the dreary poverty of her ordinary experiences.

Thus it was no uncommon thing for this young lady to dine to-day in a tawdry and rather dirty parlour at Chelsea upon tea and red-herrings, and to-morrow to sit opposite her father in one of the sunny windows at the Crown and Sceptre, eating white-bait with the calm enjoyment of a connoisseur, and looking placidly on while Mr Vane gave himself ducal airs to the waiters, and found fault with the icing of his sparkling hock. There was scarcely any extravagance which this little girl had not seen her father perpetrate. She had received from him a birthday present of a two-guinea wax doll, at the very time at which her schooling account, at a certain humble little seminary near Cheyne Walk, remained unpaid, and her education was brought to a dead-lock by reason of this default. She had sighed for that golden-haired waxen plaything, and her father gave it to her because he loved her as he had always loved, weakly and foolishly.

She loved him in return: repaying him a hundredfold for his affection by her innocent love and trust. To her he was all that was perfect, all that was noble and generous. The big talk, the glowing and sentimental discourse by which he was wont to impose upon himself, imposed upon her. She believed in that fancy portrait which he painted of himself, and which he himself believed in as a most faithful and unflattered likeness. She believed in that highly-coloured picture, and thought that George Mowbray Vandeleur Vane was indeed what he represented himself, and thought himself to be, – an injured old man, a sainted martyr to the forgetfulness of the world, and the ingratitude of his children.

Poor Eleanor was never weary of listening to her father's stories about the Prince Regent, and all the lesser planets of the darkened sky in which Mr Vane's light had once shone. She used to walk in the park with the old man in the sunny summer evenings, proud to see him bow to great people, who returned his recognition with friendly courtesy. She liked to fancy him in the days that were gone, riding side by side with those mighty ones of the earth, whom he was now content to watch wistfully across the iron railings. She was pleased to stroll about the West End in the dusky gloaming of the soft May night, and to look up at the lights in that princely mansion in Berkeley Square which George Vane had once occupied. He showed her the windows which had belonged to this and that apartment; the drawing-room; the first Mrs Vane's boudoir; the little girls' nursery and morning-room. She fancied all those fairy chambers radiant with light and splendour; and then remembering the shabby rooms at Chelsea, clung closer to her father's arm, in her tender sorrow for his fallen state.

But she had inherited much of George Vane's sanguine temperament, and almost as firm as her belief in the past, which had been a reality, was her confidence in the splendid future which her father hoped in. Nothing could have been more shadowy than the foundations upon which Mr Vane had built for himself an airy castle. In his youth and middle age his most intimate friend and companion had been a certain Maurice de Crespigny, the owner of a noble estate in Berkshire, and *not* a friend of the Prince Regent's. So, while George Vane's two estates had melted away, and his three fortunes had been expended, Mr de Crespigny, who was an invalid and a bachelor, had contrived to keep his land and his money.

There was only the difference of two or three years between the ages of the two friends. I believe that Maurice de Crespigny was the younger of the two. And it was during their early college life that the young men had entered into a romantic alliance, very chivalrous and honourable in its nature, but scarcely likely to stand the wear and tear of worldly experience.

They were to be friends through life and until death. They were to have no secrets from each other. If by any chance they should happen to fall in love with the same person – and I really think these sentimental collegians rather wished that such a contingency might arise – one of them, the most noble, the most heroic, was quietly to fall back and suffer in silence, while the weaker won the prize. If either died a bachelor, he was to leave his fortune to the other, whatever less romantic and more commonplace claimants, in the way of heirs presumptive, might press upon him.

These vows had been made at least five-and-forty years ago, but out of this folly of the past George Vane built his hope in the future. Maurice de Crespigny was now a soured and hypochondriacal old bachelor, shut in and defended on every side by greedy and sycophantic relations, and utterly unapproachable to his shabby old bosom friend; who could as easily have made his way out of one of the lowest dungeons of the Bastille as he could force an entrance into that closely-guarded citadel within which his college companion sat, lonely and dismal, a desolate old man, watched over by sharp eyes, greedily noteful of every token of his decay, ministered to by hands that would have worked eagerly at his winding-sheet, if by so doing they could have hastened the hour of his death.

If George Vane – remembering his old friend, perhaps, with some latent feeling of tenderness intermingled with his mercenary hopes – made an effort to penetrate the cruel barriers about him, he was repulsed with ignominy by the two maiden nieces who kept watch and ward at Woodlands. If he wrote to Mr de Crespigny, his missive was returned

unopened, with a satirical intimation that the dear invalid's health was not
in a state to endure the annoyance of begging letters. He had made a
hundred attempts to cross the lines of the enemy, and had been mortified
by a hundred failures; but his sanguine nature was not to be subdued by
any humiliation, and he still believed, firmly and entirely, that whenever
Maurice de Crespigny's will came to be opened, his name, and his alone,
would appear as sole heir to his old friend's wealth. He forgot that
Maurice de Crespigny was his junior by some two or three years; for he
had always heard of him of late as a feeble invalid, tottering upon the
verge of the grave; while he himself was erect and stalwart, broad-chested
and soldierly-looking; so very soldierly in appearance that the sentinels
on guard in the park were wont to salute him as he passed them,
mistaking him for some military magnate.

Yes, he believed the day would come when poor De Crespigny – he
always spoke of his friend with a certain pitiful tenderness – would drop
quietly into his grave, and when *he* would reign at Woodlands with his
darling Eleanor, avenging himself upon his ungrateful elder children,
reopening accounts with his old creditors – in all his visions of grandeur
and patronage he never thought of paying his debts – and arising from
the dull ashes of his poverty, a splendid phœnix, golden-plumed and
exultant.

He taught his daughter this belief as religiously as he taught her the
simple prayers which she said nightly at his knee. With all his faults he
was no unbeliever, though the time which he devoted to religious
observances made a very small portion of his existence. He taught
Eleanor to believe in the day that was to come, and the little girl saw the
light of future splendour gleaming athwart the dreary swamp of difficulty
through which she waded patiently by her father's side.

But the day came when George Vane and his child were to be
separated, for a time at least. Eleanor's twelfth birthday was very near at
hand, and she had as yet received no better education than the rather
limited course of instruction which was to be obtained for a guinea and a
half a quarter at the day-school near Cheyne Walk. For nearly six years,
inclusive of many intervals of non-attendance consequent upon non-
payment, Miss Vane had frequented this humble seminary, in company
with the daughters of the butchers and bakers and the other plebeian
inhabitants of the district. But by the time she was twelve years old the
various sources from which her father's very desultory income had been
drawn had one by one run dry and failed him. The weakest and most
long-suffering of his creditors had crossed his name out of their ledgers,
his friends had ceased to believe in the fiction of delayed remittances,
urgent temporary need, and early repayment; and he could no longer
count upon an occasional five-pound note when the Chelsea landlady

became clamorous, and the Chelsea general dealer refused to send home another ounce of tea, except on payment of ready money.

A desperate crisis had come, and in his despair the old man forgot his pride. For Eleanor's sake, if not for his own, he must endure humiliation. He must appeal to his eldest daughter, the hard-hearted but wealthy Hortensia Bannister, who had lost her stockbroker husband a twelvemonth before, and was now a rich and childless widow. Yes – he wiped the tears of humiliation away from his faded cheeks as he arrived at this resolution – he would try and forget the past, and would take Eleanor with him to Hyde Park Gardens, and appeal to her cruel sister in her behalf. His determination was speedily carried out, for he went to work with something of that desperate courage which a condemned criminal may feel when he goes to execution; and one sunny morning early in the June of 1850, he and his daughter sat in Mrs Bannister's handsome drawing-room, fearfully awaiting the advent of that lady. She came to them after a very brief delay, for she was business-like and uncompromising in her habits, and she had been prepared for this visit by a long, pitiful, explanatory letter from her father, in reply to which she had written very coldly and concisely, appointing an early interview.

She was a severe-looking woman of about five-and-thirty, with a hard face, and heavy black eyebrows, which met over her handsome aquiline nose when she frowned, which she did a great deal too often, poor Eleanor thought. Her features were like those of her father, but her grim and stony expression was entirely her own, and was perhaps the result of that early and bitter disappointment of finding herself a portionless girl, deserted by the man she loved, who fell away from her when he discovered the state of her father's fortunes, and compelled to marry for money, or to accept the wretched alternative of a life of poverty and drudgery.

This harsh disappointed woman affected no pretence of tender feeling for her half-sister. Perhaps the sight of Eleanor's childish beauty was scarcely pleasant to her. She herself had drawn a dreary blank in the great lottery of life, in spite of her wealth; and she may have envied this child her unknown future, which could not well be so dismal as the childless widow's empty existence.

But Mrs Bannister was a religious woman, and tried to do her duty in a hard, uncompromising way, in which good works were not beautified by any such flimsy adornments as love and tenderness. So when she heard that her father lived from day to day a wretched hand-to-mouth existence, haunted by the grim phantom of starvation, she was seized with a sudden sense that she had been very wicked to this weak old man, and she agreed to allow him a decent pittance, which would enable him to live about as comfortably as a half-pay officer or a small annuitant. She

made this concession sternly enough, and lectured her father so severely
that he may be perhaps forgiven if he was not very grateful for his
daughter's bounty, so far as he himself went; but he did make a feeble
protestation of his thankfulness when Mrs Bannister further declared her
willingness to pay a certain premium, in consideration of which Eleanor
Vane might be received in a respectable boarding-school as an apprentice
or pupil-teacher.

It was thus that the little girl became acquainted with the Misses
Bennett, of Wilmington House, Brixton; and it was in the household of
these ladies that three years of her life had been passed. Three quiet and
monotonous years of boarding-school drudgery, which had only been
broken by two brief visits to her father, who had taken up his abode in
Paris; where he lived secure from the persecution of a few of his latter-
day creditors – not the west-end tradesmen who had known him in his
prime, *they* were resigned and patient enough under their losses – but a
few small dealers who had trusted him in his decline, and who were not
rendered lenient by the memory of former profits.

In Paris, Mr Vane had very little chance of obtaining any information
about his friend Maurice de Crespigny, but he still looked forward
confidently to that visionary future in which he was to be master of the
Woodlands estate. He had taken care to write a letter, soon after Eleanor's
birth, which had been artfully conveyed to his friend, announcing the
advent of this youngest child, and dwelling much on his love for her. He
cherished some vague notion that, in the event of his death occurring
before that of Maurice de Crespigny, the old man might leave his wealth
to Eleanor. The contumely with which he had been treated by the
maiden harpies who kept watch over his old friend had been pleasant to
him rather than otherwise, for in the anger of these elderly damsels he
saw an evidence of their fear.

'If they knew that poor Crespigny's money was left to them, they
wouldn't be so savage,' he thought. 'It's evident they're by no means too
confident about the future.'

But there were other relatives of the old man's, less fortunate than the
maiden sisters, who had found their way into the citadel, and planted
themselves *en permanence* at Woodlands. There was a married niece, who
had once been a beauty. This lady had been so foolish as to marry against
her rich uncle's wishes, and was now a widow, living in the
neighbourhood of Woodlands upon an income of two hundred a year.
This lady's only son, Launcelot Darrell, had in his boyhood been a
favourite with the old man, and was known to cherish expectations
about Maurice de Crespigny's fortune. But the maiden sisters were
patient and indefatigable women. No sacred fire was ever watched more
carefully by classic vestal than was the ireful flame which burned in

Maurice de Crespigny's heart when he remembered his married niece's ingratitude and disobedience. The unwearying old maids kept his indignation alive by every feminine subtlety, by every diplomatic device. Heaven knows what they wanted with their uncle's money, for they were prim damsels, who wore stuff shoes and scanty dresses made in the fashion of their youth. They had outlived the very faculty of enjoyment, and their wants were almost as simple as those of the robins that perched upon their window-sills; but for all this they were as eager to become possessors of the old man's wealth as the most heartless and spendthrift heir, tormented by Israelitish creditors, and subsisting entirely upon post obits.

CHAPTER IV

UPON THE THRESHOLD OF A GREAT SORROW

It was nearly noon when Eleanor Vane awoke upon the morning after her journey; for this young lady was a good sleeper, and was taking her revenge for four-and-twenty hours of wakefulness. I doubt, indeed, if she would have opened her eyes when she did, had not her father tapped at the door of her tiny chamber and told her the hour.

She woke smiling, like a beautiful infant who has always seen loving eyes watching above its cradle.

'Papa, darling,' she cried, 'is it you? I've just been dreaming that I was at Brixton. How delightful to wake and hear your voice! I won't be long, papa dear. But you haven't waited breakfast all this time, have you?'

'No, my dear. I have a cup of coffee and a roll brought me every morning at nine from a *traiteur's* over the way. I've ordered some breakfast for you, but I wouldn't wake you till twelve. Dress quickly, Nell. It's a lovely morning, and I'll take you for a walk.'

It was indeed a lovely morning. Eleanor Vane flung back the tawdry damask curtains, and let the full glory of the August noontide sun into her little room. Her window had been open all the night through, and the entresol was so close to the street that she could hear the conversation of the people upon the pavement below. The foreign jargon sounded pleasant to her in its novelty. It was altogether different to the French language as she had been accustomed to hear it at Brixton; where a young lady forfeited a halfpenny every time she forgot herself so far as to give utterance to her thoughts or desires in the commonplace medium of her mother tongue. The merry voices, the barking of dogs, the rattling of wheels, and ringing of bells in the distance, mingled in a cheerful clamour.

As Eleanor Vane let in that glorious noontide sunlight, it seemed to her that she had let in the morning of a new life; a new and happier existence, brighter and pleasanter than the dull boarding-school monotony she had had so much of.

Her pure young soul rejoiced in the sunshine, the strange city, the change, the shadowy hopes that beckoned to her in the future, the atmosphere of love which her father's presence always made in the shabbiest home. She had not been unhappy at Brixton, because it was her nature to be happy under difficulties, because she was a bright, spontaneous creature, to whom it was almost impossible to be sorrowful: but she had looked forward yearningly to this day, in which she was to join her father in Paris, never perhaps to go far away from him again. And it had come at last, this long-hoped-for day, the sunny opening of a new existence. It had come; and even the heavens had sympathy with her gladness, and wore their fairest aspect in honour of this natal day of her new life.

She did not linger long over her toilet, though she lost a good deal of time in unpacking her box – which had not been very neatly packed, by the way – and had considerable trouble in finding hair-brushes and combs, cuffs, collars, and ribbons, and all the rest of the small paraphernalia with which she wished to decorate herself.

But when she emerged at last, radiant and smiling, with her long golden hair falling in loose curls over her shoulders, and her pale muslin dress adorned with fluttering blue ribbons, her father was fain to cry out aloud at the sight of his darling's beauty. She kissed him a dozen times, but took very little notice of his admiration – she seemed, in fact, scarcely conscious that he did admire her – and then ran into the adjoining room to caress a dog, an eccentric French poodle, which had been George Vane's faithful companion during the three years he had spent in Paris.

'Oh, papa!' Eleanor cried joyously, returning to the sitting-room with the dingy white animal in her arms, 'I am so pleased to find Fido. You didn't speak of him in your letters, and I was afraid you had lost him, perhaps, or that he was dead. But here he is, just as great a darling, and just as dirty as ever.'

The poodle, who was divided in half, upon that unpleasant principle common to his species, and who was white and curly in front, and smooth and pinky behind, reciprocated Miss Vane's caresses very liberally. He leaped about her knees when she set him down upon the slippery floor, and yelped wild outcries of delight. He was not permitted to pass the night in Mr Vane's apartments, but slept in a dismal outhouse behind the butcher's shop, and it was thus that Eleanor had not seen him upon her arrival in the Rue de l'Archevêque.

The young lady was so anxious to go out with her father, so eager to be away on the broad boulevards with the happy idle people of that wonderful city in which nobody ever seems to be either busy or sorrowful, that she made very short work of her roll and coffee, and then ran back to her little bed-chamber to array herself for a promenade. She came out five minutes afterwards dressed in a black silk mantle and a white transparent bonnet, which looked fleecy and cloud-like against her bright auburn hair. That glorious hair was suffered to fall from under the bonnet and stream about her shoulders like golden rain, for she had never yet attained the maturer dignity of wearing her luxuriant tresses plaited and twisted in a hard knot at the back of her head.

'Now papa, please, where are we to go?'

'Wherever you like, my darling,' the old man answered; 'I mean to give you a treat to-day. You shall spend the morning how you like, and we'll dine on the Boulevard Poissonnier. I've received a letter from Mrs Bannister. It came before you were up. I am to call in the Rue de la Paix for a hundred and six pounds. A hundred to be paid to Madame Marly, and six for me; my monthly allowance, my dear, at the rate of thirty shillings a week.'

Mr Vane sighed as he named the sum. It would have been better for this broken-down old spendthrift if he could have received his pittance weekly, or even daily; for it was his habit to dine at the Trois Frères, and wear pale straw-coloured gloves, and a flower in his button-hole, at the beginning of the month, and to subsist on rolls and coffee towards its close.

He unfolded the narrow slip of paper upon which his eldest daughter had written the banker's address and the amount which Mr Vane was to demand, and looked at the magical document fondly, almost proudly. Any one unfamiliar with his frivolous and sanguine nature, might have wondered at the change which had taken place in his manner since the previous night, when he had tearfully bewailed his daughter's cruelty.

He had been an old man then, degraded, humiliated, broken down by sorrow and shame: to-day he was young, handsome, gay, defiant, pompous, prepared to go out into the world and hold his place amongst the butterflies once more. He rejoiced in the delicious sensation of having money to spend. Every fresh five-pound note was a new lease of youth and happiness to George Vane.

The father and daughter went out together, and the butcher neglected his business in order to stare after Miss Vane; and the butcher's youngest child, a tiny damsel in a cambric mob-cap, cried out, 'Oh, la belle demoiselle!' as Eleanor turned the corner of the narrow street into the sunny thoroughfare beyond. Fido came frisking after his master's daughter, and Mr Vane had some difficulty in driving the animal back.

Eleanor would have liked the dog to go with them in their noontide
ramble through the Parisian streets, but her father pointed out the utter
absurdity of such a proceeding.

Mr Vane conducted his daughter through a maze of streets behind the
Madeleine. There was no Boulevard Malesherbes in those days, to throw
this part of the city open to the sweep of a park of artillery. Eleanor's eyes
lit up with gladness as they emerged from the narrower streets behind the
church into the wide boulevard, not as handsome then as it is to-day, but
very broad and airy, gay and lightsome withal.

An involuntary cry of delight broke from Eleanor's lips.

'Oh, papa,' she said, 'it is so different from Brixton. But where are we
going first, papa, dear?'

'Over the way, my dear, to Blount and Co.'s, in the Rue de la Paix.
We'll get this money at once, Nelly, and we'll carry it straight to Madame
Marly. They had no occasion to insult us, my dear. We have not sunk so
low, yet. No, no, not quite so low as to rob our own children.'

'Papa, darling, don't think of that cruel letter. I don't like to take the
money when I remember that. Don't think of it, papa.'

Mr Vane shook his head.

'I *will* think of it, my dear,' he answered, in a tone of sorrowful
indignation – the indignation of an honourable man, who rebels against a
cruel stigma of dishonour. 'I will think of it, Eleanor. I have been called a
thief – a thief, Eleanor. I am not very likely to forget *that*, I think.'

They were in the Rue de la Paix by this time. George Vane was very
familiar with the banker's office, for he had been in the habit of receiving
his monthly pension through an order on Messrs Blount and Co. He left
Eleanor at the foot of the stairs, while he ascended to the office on the
first floor; and he returned five minutes afterwards, carrying a bundle of
notes in one hand, and a delicious little roll of napoleons in the other.
The notes fluttered pleasantly in the summer air, as he showed them to
his daughter.

'We will go at once to Madame Marly, my darling,' he said, gaily, 'and
give her these, without a moment's unnecessary delay. They shall have no
justification in calling me a thief, Eleanor. You will write to your sister by
this afternoon's post, perhaps, my dear, and tell her that I did not try to
rob you. I think you owe so much as that to your poor old father.'

George Vane's daughter clung lovingly to his arm, looking up tenderly
and entreatingly in his face.

'Papa, darling, how can you say such things?' she cried. 'I will write
and tell Mrs Bannister that she has been very cruel, and that her insulting
letter has made me hate to take her paltry money. But, papa, dearest, how
can you talk of robbing *me*? If this money is really mine, take it; take
every penny of it, if – if – you owe it to anybody who worries you; or if

you want it for anything in the world. I can go back to Brixton and earn my living to-morrow, papa. Miss Bennett and Miss Sophia told me so before I came away. You don't know how useful they began to find me, with the little ones. Take the money, papa, dear, if you want it.'

Mr Vane turned upon his daughter with almost tragic indignation.

'Eleanor,' he said, 'do you know me so little that you dare to insult me by such a proposition as this? No; if I were starving I would not take this money. Am I so lost and degraded that even the child I love turns upon me in my old age?'

The hand which held the bank notes trembled with passionate emotion as the old man spoke.

'Papa, darling,' Eleanor pleaded, 'indeed, indeed, I did not mean to wound you.'

'Let me hear no more of this, then, Eleanor; let me hear no more of it,' answered Mr Vane, drawing himself up with a dignity that would have become a classic toga, rather than the old man's fashionable over-coat. 'I am not angry with you, my darling; I was only hurt, I was only hurt. My children have never known me, Eleanor; they have never known me. Come, my dear.'

Mr Vane put aside his tragic air, and plunged into the Rue St Honoré, where he called for a packet of gloves that had been cleaned for him. He put the gloves in his pocket, and then strolled back into the Rue Castiglione, looking at the vehicles in the roadway as he went. He was waiting to select the most elegantly appointed of the hackney equipages crawling slowly past.

'It's a pity the government insist on putting a painted badge upon them,' he said, thoughtfully. 'When I last called on Madame Marly, Charles the Tenth was at the Tuileries, and I had my travelling chariot and pair at Meurice's, besides a britska for Mrs Vane.'

He had pitched upon a very new and shining vehicle, with a smart coachman, by this time, and he made that half hissing, half whistling noise peculiar to Parisians when they call a hackney carriage.

Eleanor sprang lightly into the vehicle, and spread her flowing muslin skirts upon the cushions as she seated herself. The passers-by looked admiringly at the smiling young Anglaise with her white bonnet and nimbus of glittering hair.

'Au Bois, cocher,' Mr Vane cried, as he took his place by his daughter.

He had bought a tiny bouquet for his button-hole near the Madeleine, and he selected a pair of white doeskin gloves, and drew them carefully on his well-shaped hands. He was as much a dandy to-day as he had been in those early days when the Prince and Brummel were his exalted models.

The drive across the Place de la Concorde, and along the Champs Elysées, was an exquisite pleasure to Eleanor Vane; but it was even yet more exquisite when the light carriage rolled away along one of the avenues in the Bois de Boulogne, where the shadows of the green leaves trembled on the grass, and all nature rejoiced beneath the cloudless August sky. The day was a shade too hot, perhaps, and had been certainly growing hotter since noon, but Eleanor was too happy to remember that.

'How nice it is to be with you, papa darling,' she said, 'and how I wish I wasn't going to this school. I should be so happy in that dear little lodging over the butcher's, and I could go out as morning governess to some French children, couldn't I? I shouldn't cost you much, I know, papa.'

Mr Vane shook his head.

'No, no, my love. Your education must be completed. Why should you be less accomplished than your sisters? You shall occupy as brilliant a position as ever they occupied, my love, or a better one, perhaps. You have seen me under a cloud, Eleanor; but you shall see the sunshine yet. You'll scarcely know your old father, my poor girl, when you see him in the position he has been used to occupy; yes, used to occupy, my dear. This lady we are going to see, Madame Marly, *she* remembers, my love. She could tell you what sort of a man George Vane was five-and-twenty years ago.'

The house in which the fashionable schoolmistress who had 'finished' the elder daughters of George Vane still received her pupils, was a white-walled villa, half-hidden in one of the avenues of the Bois de Boulogne.

The little hired carriage drew up before a door in the garden wall, and a portress came out to reply to the coachman's summons.

Unhappily, the portress said, Madame was not at home. Madame's assistants were at home, and would be happy to receive Monsieur and Mademoiselle. That might be perhaps altogether the same thing, the portress suggested.

No, Monsieur replied, he must see Madame herself. Ah, but then nothing could be so unfortunate. Madame, who so seldom quitted the Pension, had to-day driven into Paris to arrange her affairs, and would not return until sunset.

Mr Vane left his card with a few words written upon it in pencil, to the effect that he would call at two o'clock the next day, in the charge of the portress: and the carriage drove back towards Paris.

'Bear witness, Eleanor,' said the old man, 'bear witness that I tried to pay this money away immediately after receiving it. You will be good enough to mention that fact in your letter to my eldest daughter.'

He had carried the notes in his hand all this time, as if eager to deliver them over to the schoolmistress, but he now put them into his breast-pocket. I think upon the whole he was rather pleased at the idea of retaining custody of the money for the next twenty-four hours. It was not his own, but the mere possession of it gave him a pleasant sense of importance; and, again, he might very probably have an opportunity of displaying the bank notes, incidentally, to some of his associates. Unhappily for this lonely old man, his few Parisian acquaintances were of a rather shabby and not too reputable a calibre, and were therefore likely to be somewhat impressed by the sight of a hundred and twenty-five napoleons, in crisp, new notes upon the Bank of France.

It was past three when Mr Vane and his daughter alighted in front of the Palais Royal, and the coachman claimed payment for two hours and a half. The old man had changed the first of his six napoleons at the glove-cleaner's, and he had a handful of loose silver in his waistcoat pocket, so the driver was quickly paid and dismissed, and Eleanor entered the Palais Royal, that paradise of cheap jewellery and dinners, hanging on her father's arm.

Mr Vane bore patiently with his daughter's enthusiastic admiration of the diamonds and the paste, the glittering realities and almost as glittering shams in the jewellers' windows. Eleanor wanted to look at everything, the trinkets, and opera-glasses, and portmanteaus, and china, – everything was new and beautiful. The fountain was playing; noisy children were running about, amongst equally noisy nurses and idle loungers. A band was playing close to the fountain. The chinking of tea-spoons, and cups and saucers, sounded in the Café de la Rotonde: people had not begun to dine yet, but the windows and glazed nooks in the doorways of the restaurants were splendid with their displays of gigantic melons, and dewy purple grapes, cucumbers, pears, tomatoes, and peaches. George Vane allowed his daughter to linger a long time before all the shops. He was rather ashamed of her exuberant delight, and unrestrained enthusiasm; for so much pleasure in these simple things was scarcely consistent with that *haut ton* which the old man still affected, even in his downfall. But he had not the heart to interfere with his daughter's happiness – was it not strange happiness to *him* to have this beautiful creature with him, clinging to his arm, and looking up at him with a face that was glorified by her innocent joy?

They left the Palais Royal at last, before half its delights were exhausted, as Eleanor thought, and went through the Rue Richelieu to the Place de la Bourse, where Mr Vane's eager companion looked wistfully at the doors of the theatre opposite the great Temple of Commerce.

'Oh, papa,' she said, 'how I should like to go to a theatre to-night!'

Miss Vane had seen a good deal of the English drama during her Chelsea life, for the old man knew some of the London managers, men who remembered him in his prosperity, and were glad to give him admission to their boxes now and then, out of pure benevolence. But the

Parisian theatres seemed mysteriously delightful to Eleanor, inasmuch as
they were strange.

'Can you get tickets for the theatres here, papa,' she asked, 'as you used
in London?'

Mr Van shrugged his shoulders.

'No, my love,' he said, 'it's not quite such an easy matter. I know a man
who writes farces now and then for the Funambules – a very clever fellow
– but he doesn't get many orders to give away, and that's not exactly the
theatre I should like to take you to. I'll tell you what, though, Eleanor, I'll
take you to the Porte St Martin to-night – why should I deny my child an
innocent pleasure? I'll take you to the Porte St Martin, unless——'

George Vane paused, and a gloomy shadow crept over his face – a
shade that made him look an old man. His youthfulness of appearance
entirely depended upon the buoyancy of a nature which contended with
age. The moment his spirits sank he looked what he was – an old man.

'Unless what, papa, dearest?' Eleanor asked.

'I – I had an appointment to-night, my love, with – with a couple of
gentlemen who—— But I won't keep it, Eleanor, – no, no, I'll not keep
it. I'll take you to the theatre. I can afford you that pleasure.'

'Dear, dear papa, you never refuse me any pleasure; but it would be so
selfish of me to ask you to break your appointment with these two
gentlemen. You had better keep it.'

'No, no, my dear – I'd – it would be better – perhaps. Yes, I'll take you
to the Porte St Martin.'

Mr Vane spoke hesitatingly. The shadow had not yet left his face. Had
his daughter been less occupied by the delights of the Parisian shops, the
novelty and gaiety of the crowd, she must surely have observed the
change in that idolized father.

But she observed nothing, she could remember nothing but her
happiness. This glorious day of reunion and delight seemed, indeed, the
beginning of a new life. She looked back wonderingly at the dull routine
of her boarding-school existence. Could it be possible that it was only a
day or two since she was in the Brixton school-room hearing the little
ones – the obstinate, incorrigible little ones – their hateful lessons: their
odious monotonous repetition of dry facts about William the Conqueror
and Buenos Ayres, the manufacture of tallow candles, and the nine parts
of speech?

They strolled on the boulevard till six o'clock, and then ascended the
shining staircase of a restaurant on the Boulevard Poissonnier, where
Eleanor saw herself reflected in so many mirrors that she was almost
bewildered by the repetition of her own auburn hair and white bonnet.

The long saloons were filled with eager diners, who looked up from
their knives and forks as the English girl went by.

'We dine à la carte here,' her father whispered: 'this is a fête day, and I mean to give you a first-class dinner.'

Mr Vane found a vacant table in an open window. The house was at a corner of the boulevard, and this window looked down the crowded thoroughfare towards the Madeleine. Eleanor exclaimed once more as the prospect burst upon her, and she saw all the boulevard with its gay splendour, spread out, as it were, at her feet; but her father was too busy with the waiter and the *carte* to observe her manifestation of delight.

Mr Vane was an epicure, and prided himself upon his talent for ordering a dinner. There was a good deal of *finesse* displayed by him now-a-days in the arrangement of a repast; for poverty had taught him all kinds of little diplomatic contrivances whereby he might, as it were, mingle economy and extravagance. He ordered such and such dishes for 'one,' intending to divide them with his child. A few Ostend oysters, some soup – *purée crécy* – a little dish of beef and olives, a *sole normande*, a quarter of roast chicken, and a *Charlotte Plombières*.

It was a long time since Eleanor had eaten one of her father's epicurean feasts, and she did ample justice to the dinner, even in spite of the ever recurrent distractions upon the boulevard below.

The dishes followed each other slowly, for the unresting waiters had many claimants on their attention, and the sun was low in the cloudless western sky when Mr Vane and his daughter left the restaurant. It was nearly night; the lights began to shine out through a hot white mist, for the heat had grown more and more oppressive as the day had declined. The Parisians sitting at little marble tables on the pavement outside the cafés fanned themselves with their newspapers, and drank effervescing drinks pertinaciously. It was a night upon which one should have had nothing more laborious to do than to sit outside Tortoni's and eat ices.

The noise and clamour, the oppressive heat, the bustle and confusion of the people rushing to the theatres, made Eleanor's head ache. One cannot go on being unutterably happy for ever, and perhaps the day's excitement had been almost too much for this young school-girl. She had walked long distances already upon the burning asphalte of the wonderful city, and she was beginning to be tired. Mr Vane never thought of this: he had been accustomed to walk about day after day, and sometimes all day – for what should a lonely Englishman do in Paris but walk about? – and he forgot that the fatigue might be too much for his daughter. He walked on, therefore, with Eleanor still clinging to his arm; past the Ambigu, beyond the Barrière St Antoine; and still the long lamplit boulevard stretched before them, away into immeasurable distance, as it appeared to Miss Vane.

The hot, white mist seemed to grow denser as the evening advanced; the red sun blazed and flashed on every available scrap of crystal; the gas-

lamps, newly illumined, strove against that setting sun. It was all light, and
heat, and noise, and confusion, Eleanor thought, upon the boulevard.
Very splendid, of course, but rather bewildering. She would have been
glad to sit down to rest upon one of the benches on the edge of the
pavement; but, as her father did not seem tired, she still walked on,
patiently and uncomplainingly.

'We'll go into one of the theatres presently, Nelly,' Mr Vane said.

He had recovered his spirits under the invigorating influence of a bottle
of Cliquot's champagne, and the gloomy shadow had quite passed away
from his face.

It was nearly nine o'clock, and quite dark, when they turned towards
the Madeleine again, on the way back to the Porte St Martin. They had
not gone far when Mr Vane stopped, suddenly confronted by two young
men who were walking arm-in-arm.

'Hulloa!' one of them cried, in French, 'you have served us a
handsome trick, my friend.'

George Vane stammered out an apology. His daughter had returned
from school, he said, and he wished to show her Paris.

'Yes, yes,' the Frenchman answered; 'but we were aware of
Mademoiselle's intended return, and it was arranged in spite of that that
we should meet this evening: was it not so, my friend?'

He asked this question of his companion, who nodded rather sulkily,
and turned away with a half weary, half dissatisfied air.

Eleanor looked at the two young men, wondering what new friends
her father had made in Paris. The Frenchman was short and stout, and
had a fair florid complexion. Eleanor was able to see this, for his face was
turned to the lamp-light, as he talked to her father. He was rather
showily dressed, in fashionably cut clothes, that looked glossy and new,
and he twirled a short silver-headed cane in his gloved hands.

The other man was tall and slender, shabbily and untidily dressed in
garments of a rakish cut, that hung loosely about him. His hands were
thrust deep in the pockets of his loose overcoat, and his hat was slouched
over his forehead.

Eleanor Vane only caught one passing glimpse of this man's face as he
turned sulkily away; but she could see the glimmer of a pair of bright,
restless, black eyes under the shadow of his hat, and the fierce curve of a
very thick black moustache, which completely concealed his mouth. He
had turned, not towards the lighted shop windows, but to the roadway;
and he was amusing himself by kicking a wisp of straw to and fro upon
the sharp edge of the curb-stone, with the toe of his shabby patent
leather boot.

The Frenchman drew George Vane aside, and talked to him for a few
minutes in an undertone, gesticulating after the manner of his nation, and

evidently persuading the old man to do something or other which he shrank from doing. But Mr Vane's resistance seemed of a very feeble nature, and the Frenchman conquered, for his last shrug was one of triumph. Eleanor, standing by herself, midway between the sulky young man upon the curb-stone and her father and the Frenchman, perceived this. She looked up anxiously as Mr Vane returned to her.

'My love,' the old man said hesitatingly, nervously trifling with his glove as he spoke, 'do you think you could find your way back to the Rue de l'Archevêque?'

'Find my way back? Why, papa?'

'I – I mean, could you find your way back a – alone?'

'Alone!'

She echoed the word with a look of mingled disappointment and alarm.

'Alone, papa?'

But here the Frenchman interposed eagerly.

Nothing was more simple, he said: Mademoiselle had only to walk straight on to the Rue Neuve des Petits Champs; she would then, and then——

He ran off into a string of rapid directions, not one of which Eleanor heard. She was looking at her father, Heaven knows how earnestly, for she saw in his face, in his nervous hesitating manner, something that told her there was some sinister influence to be dreaded from this garrulous, eager Frenchman and his silent companion.

'Papa, dear,' she said, in a low, almost imploring voice, 'do you really wish me to go back alone?'

'Why – why, you see, my dear, I – I don't exactly wish – but there are appointments which, as Monsieur remarks, not – not unreasonably, should not be broken, and——'

'You will stay out late, papa, perhaps, with these gentlemen——'

'No, no, my love, no, no; for an hour or so; not longer.'

Eleanor looked up sorrowfully in the face she loved so dearly. Vague memories of grief and trouble in the past, mingled with as vague a presentiment of trouble in the future, filled her mind: she clasped her hands imploringly upon her father's arm.

'Come home with me to-night, papa,' she said. 'It is my first night at home. Come back, and we'll play écarté as we used at Chelsea. You remember teaching me.'

Mr Vane started, as if the tender grasp upon his arm had stung into his flesh.

'I – I can't come home to-night, Eleanor. At least, not for an hour. There – there are social laws, my dear, which must be observed; and when – when a gentleman is asked to give another his revenge, he – can't refuse. I'll put you into a carriage, my darling, if you think you can't find your way.'

'Oh, no, papa, dear, it's not that. I can find my way.'

The Frenchman here interposed for the second time with some complimentary speech, addressed to Eleanor, who very imperfectly understood its purport. He had slipped his arm through that of George Vane, taking possession of him in a manner by that friendly gesture. In all this time the other man had never stirred from his sulky attitude upon the edge of the pavement.

Mr Vane took his daughter's hand.

'I am sorry I can't take you to the theatre, my love,' he said, in the same hesitating manner. 'I – I regret that you should be disappointed, but – good night, my dear, good night. I shall be home by eleven; but don't sit up for me; don't on any account sit up.'

He pressed her hand, held it for a few moments, as if scarcely knowing what to do with it, and then suddenly dropped it with something of a guilty manner.

The Frenchman, with his arm still linked in the old man's, wheeled sharply round, and walked away towards the Barrière St Antoine, leaving Eleanor standing alone amongst the passers-by, looking wistfully after her father. The other man looked up as the Frenchman led Mr Vane away, and slowly followed them, with his head bent and his hands in his pockets. Eleanor stood quite still, watching her father's erect figure, the short Frenchman, and the tall, sulky stranger following the other two, until all three were out of sight. Then turning homewards with a half-repressed sigh, she looked sadly down the long lamp-lit vista. It was very beautiful, very gay, brilliant and splendid; but all that splendour and gaiety made her feel only the more lonely, now that her father had left her. The first day, the natal day of her new life, seemed to end very drearily, after all.

CHAPTER V

WAITING

Miss Vane walked very slowly homeward through the hot, breathless summer night. She was too sorrowful, too much depressed by the sudden disappointment which had fallen like a dark shadow upon the close of the day that had begun so brightly, to be embarrassed by any uncomfortable sense of her loneliness in the crowded thoroughfare.

No one molested or assailed her – she walked serene in her youth and innocence; though the full radiance of the lamplight rarely fell upon her

face without some passing glance of admiration resting there also. She
never once thought that her father had done wrong in leaving her to
walk alone through that crowded Parisian street. In the unselfishness of
her loving nature she scarcely remembered her disappointment about the
theatre: not even when she passed the brilliantly lighted edifice, and
looked, a little wistfully perhaps, at the crowd upon the threshold.

She was uneasy and unhappy about her father, because in all her
Chelsea experiences she remembered evil to have resulted from his going
out late at night; vague and mysterious trouble, the nature of which he
had never revealed to her, but whose effects had haunted him and
depressed him for many dreary days. He had been sometimes – indeed,
very often – poorer after a late absence from his shabby Chelsea lodging;
he had been now and then richer; but he had always been alike
remorseful and miserable after those occasional nights of dissipation.

His daughter was sorrowful therefore at parting with him. She knew
that, in spite of his declaration that he would be home at eleven, it would
be between one and two in the morning when he returned; not tipsy –
no, thank Heaven, he was no drunkard – but with a nervous, wretched,
half-demented manner, which was perhaps more sad to see than any
ordinary intoxication.

'I was in hopes papa would always stay at home with me now that I am
grown up,' the young lady thought, very sadly. 'When I was little, of
course it was different; I couldn't amuse him. Though we were very
happy sometimes then; and I could play écarté, or cribbage, or whist with
two dummies. If I can get on very well with my education at Madame
Marly's, and then get a situation as morning governess for a large salary –
morning governesses do get high salaries sometimes – how happy papa
and I might be!'

Her spirits revived under the influence of cheering thoughts such as
these. I have said before that it was scarcely possible for her to be long
unhappy. Her step grew lighter and faster as she walked homeward. The
glory of the gaslights brightened with the brightening of her hopes. She
began to linger now and then before some of the most attractive of the
shops, with almost the same intense rapture and delight that she had felt
in the morning.

She was standing before a book-stall, or rather an open shop, reading
the titles of the paper-covered romances, with the full glare of the
shadeless gaslights on her face, when she was startled by a loud, hearty
English voice, which exclaimed without one murmur of warning or
preparation, –

'Don't tell me that this tall young woman with the golden curls is Miss
Eleanor Vandeleur Vane, of Regent's Gardens, King's Road, Chelsea,
London, Middlesex. Please don't tell me anything of the kind, for I can't

possibly believe anybody but Jack-and-the-beanstalk could have grown at such a rate.'

Eleanor Vane turned round to greet this noisy gentleman.

'Oh, Dick,' she cried, putting both her hands into the broad palm held out before her, 'is it really you? Who would have thought of seeing you in Paris?'

'Or you, Miss Vane? We heard you were at school at Brixton.'

'Yes, Dick,' the young lady answered, 'but I have come home now. Papa lives here, you know, and I am going to a finishing school in the Bois de Boulogne, and then I am going to be a morning governess, and live with papa always.'

'You are a great deal too pretty for a governess,' said the young man, looking admiringly at the bright face lifted up to him: 'your mistress would snub you. Miss Vane, you'd better——'

'What, Dick?'

'Try our shop.'

'What, be a scene-painter, Dick?' cried Eleanor, laughing. 'It would be funny for a woman to be a scene-painter.'

'Of course, Miss Vane. But nobody talked of scene-painting. You don't suppose I'd ask you to stand on the top of a ladder to put in skies and backgrounds, do you? There are other occupations at the Royal Waterloo Phoenix besides scene-painting. But I don't want to talk to you about that: I know how savage your poor old dad used to be when we talked of the Phoenix. What do you think I am over here for?'

'What, Richard?'

'Why, they're doing a great drama in eight acts and thirty-two tableaux at the Porte St Martin; Raoul l'Empoisonneur it's called, Ralph the Poisoner; and I'm over here to pick up the music, sketch the scenery and effects, and translate the play. Something like versatility there, I think, for five-and-thirty shillings a week.'

'Dear Richard, you were always so clever.'

'To be sure; it runs in the family.'

'And the Signora, she is well, I hope?'

'Pretty well; the teaching goes on *tant bon que mauvais*, as our friends over here say. The Clementi is a little thinner in tone than when you heard it last, and a little farther off concert pitch; but as most of my aunt's pupils sing flat, that's rather an advantage than otherwise. But where are you going, Miss Vane? because wherever it is, I'd better see you there. If we stand before this book-stall any longer, the proprietor may think we're going to buy something, and as the Parisians don't seem a buying people, the delusion might be too much for his nerves. Where shall I take you, Miss Vane?'

'To the Rue de l'Archevêque, if you please, behind the Madeleine. Do you know it?'

'Better than I know myself, Miss V. The Signora lived in that direction when I was a boy. But how is it that you are all alone in the streets at this time of night?'

'Papa had an appointment with two gentlemen, and he——'

'And he left you to walk home alone. Then he still——'

'Still what, Richard?'

The young man had stopped hesitatingly, and looked furtively at Eleanor.

'He still stays out late at night sometimes: a bad habit, Miss Vane. I was in hopes he would have been cured of it by this time; especially as there are no dens in the Palais Royal now-a-days; to the honour and glory of Napoleon the Third be it spoken.'

'No dens in the Palais Royal,' cried Eleanor. 'What do you mean?'

'Nothing, my dear Miss Nelly, except that Paris used to be a very wild and wicked place.'

'But it isn't now?'

'Oh dear, no. Our modern Lutetia is a very paradise of innocent delights, whose citizens enjoy themselves virtuously under the sheltering dictatorialism of a paternal government. You don't understand me – well, never mind, you are still the bright-faced child you were in the King's Road, Chelsea, only taller and prettier – that's all.'

Miss Vane had taken her companion's arm, and they were walking away towards the Madeleine by this time; the young lady clinging to her new friend almost as confidingly as she had done to her father.

I don't think the confidence was misplaced. This young man, with the loud voice and the somewhat reckless manner, was only assistant scene-painter and second violin-player at a transpontine theatre. He was bound by no tie of relationship to the beautiful girl hanging upon his arm. Indeed, his acquaintance with Mr Vane and his daughter had been of that accidental and desultory kind out of which the friendships of poor people generally arise.

The young man had lodged with his aunt in the same house that for nearly six years had sheltered the proud old spendthrift and his motherless child, and some of Eleanor's earliest memories were of Signora Picirillo and her nephew Richard Thornton. She had received her first lessons upon the pianoforte from the kind Signora, whose Neapolitan husband had died years and years before, leaving her nothing but an Italian name, which looked very imposing at the top of the circulars which the music-mistress was wont to distribute amongst her pupils.

Richard Thornton, at eight-and-twenty, seemed a very elderly person in the eyes of the school-girl of fifteen. She could remember him years, and years, and years ago, as it seemed to her, sitting in his shirt sleeves through the long summer afternoons, under the shadow of the scarlet-

runners in the little garden at Chelsea, smoking dirty clay pipes and
practising popular melodies upon his fiddle. Her father had thought him
a nuisance, and had been lofty and reserved in his patronage of the young
man; but to Eleanor, Dick had been the most delightful of play-fellows,
the wisest of counsellors, the most learned of instructors. Whatever
Richard did, Miss Vane insisted upon also doing, humbly following the
genius she admired, with little toddling steps, along the brilliant pathway
his talents adorned.

I am afraid she had learned to play 'God save the Queen,' and 'Rory
O'More,' upon Richard's violin before she had mastered Haydn's
'Surprise,' or 'Ah, vous dirai-je, Maman?' upon the Signora's shabby old
grand piano. She smeared her pinafores with poor Dick's water-colours,
and insisted upon producing replicas of the young scene-painter's
sketches, with all the houses lop-sided, and the trunks of all the trees
gouty. If Dick kept rabbits or silkworms, there was no greater happiness
for Miss Vane than to accompany him to Covent Garden Market in quest
of cabbage or mulberry leaves. I do not mean that she ever deserted her
father for the society of her friend; but there were times when Mr Vane
absented himself from his little girl; long days, in which the old man
strolled about the streets of the West-End, on the look-out for the men
he had known in his prosperity, with the hope of borrowing a pound or
two, or a handful of loose silver, for the love of Auld Lang Syne; and
longer nights, in which he disappeared from the Chelsea lodging for
many dreary hours.

Then it was that Eleanor Vane was thrown into the companionship of
the Signora and her nephew. Then it was that she read Richard's books
and periodicals, that she revelled in 'Jack Sheppard,' and gloated over
'Wagner, the Wehr Wolf.' Then it was that she played upon the young
man's violin, and copied his pictures, and destroyed his water-colours,
and gorged his rabbits and silkworms, and loved, and tormented, and
admired him, after the manner of some beautiful younger sister, who had
dropped from the clouds to be his companion.

This is how these two stood towards each other. They had not met for
three years until to-night; and in the interim Miss Eleanor Vane had
grown from a hoyden of twelve into a tall, slender damsel of fifteen.

'You are so altered, Miss Vane,' Richard said, as they walked along the
boulevard, 'that I can't help wondering how it was I knew you.'

'And you're not altered a bit, Dick,' answered the young lady; 'but
don't call me Miss Vane – it sounds as if you were laughing at me. Call
me Nell, as you used to do, at Chelsea. Do you know, Dick, I contrived
to go to Chelsea once last summer. It was against papa's wish, you know,
that I should let them find out where I came from at Brixton; because,
you see, Chelsea, or at least the King's Road, sounds vulgar, papa

thought. Indeed, I believe he said he lived in Cadogan Place, when the Miss Bennetts asked him the question. He explained it to me afterwards, you know, poor dear; and it wasn't exactly a story, for he had lodged there for a fortnight once, just after his marriage with mamma, and when he was beginning to get poor. So I was obliged to manage so cleverly to get to Regent's Gardens, Dick; and when I did get there you were gone, and the Signora's rooms were to let, and there was a nasty cross old woman in our lodgings, and the scarlet-runners in the garden were *so* neglected, and I saw your rabbit-hutches, all broken and forgotten in the corner by the dust-hole, but the rabbits were gone. The dear old place seemed so changed, Dick, though Mr and Mrs Migson were very kind, and very pleased to see me, but they couldn't tell me where you and the Signora were living.'

'No, we moved two or three times after leaving Regent's Gardens. You see we're obliged to study the pupils, Nell, rather than our own convenience. Chelsea was a long way from the Waterloo Phoenix, in spite of short cuts; but wherever the Signora's pupils are thickest, we're obliged to pitch our tents. They're thickest about Tottenham-court Road and Euston Square way now; so we're living in the Pilasters, Dudley Street.'

'The Pilasters! That sounds quite grand, Dick.'

'Yes, doesn't it? *Magnifique et pas cher.* We've a chimney-sweep next door but one, and no end of mangles. The Pilasters would be very nice, if we'd two sides of the way, but unfortunately we haven't; the other side's stables. It isn't my prejudices make me object to that; but the grooms make such an abominable noise cleaning down their horses, and I wake every morning out of a dream in which it's Boxing-night, and my transformation scene is getting the goose.'

The young man laughed cheerily, and guided his companion across the road to the other side of the boulevard. It was past ten o'clock when they reached the corner of the Rue de l'Archevêque, and the butcher's shop was closed.

Eleanor knew that she had only to push open the little side door, and that she would find the key of her father's rooms in the custody of the butcher's wife. She was very tired, almost ready to drop, poor girl, for she had walked a long way since alighting at the Palais Royal with her father; but she was almost sorry that she had reached her destination. The sense of her loneliness returned, now that she was to part with her old friend.

'Thank you very much for seeing me home, Dick,' she said, shaking hands with the young scene-painter. 'It was very selfish of me to bring you so far out of your way.'

'Selfish of you! Why, you don't suppose I'd let you prowl about the streets by yourself, Nell?'

Eleanor's face flushed as her friend said this: there was a reproach to her father implied in the speech.

'It was my own fault that I was so late,' she said. 'It was only just nine when papa left me; but I loitered a little, looking at the shops. I shall see you again, Dick, I hope. But of course I shall, for you'll come and see papa, won't you? How long do you stay in Paris?'

'About a week, I suppose. I've a week's leave of absence, and double salary, besides my expenses. They know the value of a clever man at the Phoenix, Miss Vane.'

'And where are you staying, Dick?'

'At the Hôtel des Deux Mondes, near the markets. I've an apartment in convenient proximity to the sky, if I want to study atmospheric effects. And so you live here, Nell?'

'Yes, those are our windows.'

Eleanor pointed to the open sashes of the entresol: the fluffy worsted curtains were drawn, but the windows were wide open.

'And you expect your papa home——'

'At eleven o'clock at the latest,' she said.

Richard Thornton sighed. He remembered Mr Vane's habits, and he remembered that the little girl in pinafores had been wont to keep abnormal hours in her long watches for her father's coming. He had often found her, on his return from the transpontine theatre at one or two o'clock, with the door of the little sitting-room ajar, waiting patiently for the old man's coming.

'You won't sit up for your papa, Nell,' he said, as he shook hands with her.

'Oh, no, papa told me not to sit up.'

'Good night, then. You look tired, Nell. I'll call to-morrow, and I'll take you to the theatre, if your papa will let you go, and you shall see "Raoul l'Empoisonneur." Such a scene, Nell, in the seventh act. The stage divided into eight compartments, with eight different actions going on simultaneously, and five murders before the fall of the curtain. It's a great piece, and ought to make Spavin and Cromshaw's fortune.'

'And yours, Dick.'

'Oh, yes. Cromshaw will shake me by the hand in that delightful, gentlemanly manner of his: and Spavin – why Spavin will give me a five-pound note for my adaptation of "Raoul," and tell every member of the company, in confidence, that all the great scenes have been written in by him, and that the piece was utter rubbish till he reconstructed it.'

'Poor Richard!'

'Yes, Nell, poorer than the gentleman who wrote the almanack, I dare say. But never mind, Nell. I don't think the game of life pays for much expenditure in the way of illumination. I think the wisest people are those who take existence easily. Spavin's wealth can't give him anything better than diamond studs and a phaeton. The virtuous peasant, Nell, who can slap his chest, and defy his enemies to pick a hole in his green-baize jerkin, gets the best of it in the long run, I dare say.'

'But I wish you were rich, Dick, for the Signora's sake,' Eleanor said, gently.

'So do I, Nelly. I wish I was the lessee of the Phoenix, and I'd bring you out as Juliet, with new palace arches for the ball-room, and a lime-light in the balcony scene. But, good night, my dear; I mustn't keep you standing here like this, though parting is such sweet sorrow, that I really shouldn't have the heart to go away to-night if I didn't mean to call to-morrow. That line's rather longer than the original, Nell, isn't it?'

Eleanor Vane laughed heartily at her old friend's random talk, as she wished him good night. All the light-heartedness of her careless childhood seemed to return to her in Richard Thornton's society. Her childhood had not been an unhappy one, remember; for in all her father's troubles he had contrived to keep his head above water, somehow or other, and the influence of his over-sanguine spirit had kept Eleanor bright and hopeful under every temporary cloud in the domestic sky.

But she felt very desolate and lonely as she pushed open the door and entered the dark passage at the side of the shop. The butcher's wife came out at the sound of her footstep, and gave her the key, with some kindly word of greeting, which Eleanor scarcely understood.

She could only say, 'Bon soir, madame,' in her school-girl French, as she dragged herself slowly up the little winding stair, thoroughly worn out, physically and mentally, by this time.

The little entresol seemed very close and stifling. She drew back the curtains, and looked out through the open window; but even the street itself seemed oppressively hot in the moonless, airless August night.

Eleanor found half a wax-candle in a flat china candlestick, and a box of matches set ready for her. She lighted this candle, and then flung off her bonnet and mantle, before she sat down near the window.

'I shall have a very short time to wait, if papa comes home at eleven o'clock,' she thought.

Alas! she remembered in her old childish experiences, that he had *never* come home at the promised hour. How often, ah, how often, she had waited, counting the weary hours upon the church clocks, – there was one which chimed the quarters; and trembling sometimes at those strange sounds which break the night silence of every house. How often she had 'hoped against hope,' that he might, for this once, return at the time he had promised.

She took the candle in her hand and looked about for a book. She wanted to while away the dreary interval which she knew must elapse before her father's return. She found a novel of Paul Féval's in a dirty and tattered cover, on the little marble-topped writing-table. The leaves were crumpled, and smeared with stains and splotches of grease, for it was Mr Vane's habit to amuse himself with a work of fiction while he took his matutinal roll and coffee. He had taken to novel reading in his frivolous old age, and was as fond of a sentimental story as any school-girl, – as his daughter herself.

Miss Vane drew the lumbering little table to the open window, and sat down before it, with her candle close to her elbow, and the tattered book spread out before her. No breath of air flickered the flame of her candle, or ruffled the golden hair swept back from her brow.

The passers-by upon the opposite side of the street – they were few and far between by this time – looked up at the lighted window, and saw a pretty picture by the dim glimmer of that solitary candle. The picture of a girl, serene in her youth and innocence, bending over her book: her pale muslin dress and auburn hair faintly visible in the subdued light.

The rattle of wheels and the cries of coachmen sounded far off upon the boulevard, and in the Rue de Rivoli, and only made the silence more palpable in the Rue de l'Archevêque. Now and then a carriage came into that quiet corner, and Eleanor Vane looked up from her book, breathless, eager, expectant, fondly hoping that her father might have come back to her in some hired vehicle: but the solitary carriage always rolled away, until the sound of its wheels mixed with the rattle of the distant wheels upon the boulevards.

There were clocks in the distance that struck the quarters. How long those quarters seemed! Paul Féval was very interesting, no doubt. There was an awful mystery in those greasy tattered pages: a ghastly mystery about two drowned young women, treacherously made away with, as it seemed, upon the shore of a dreary river overshadowed by willows. There were villains and rascals paramount throughout this delightful romance; and there was mystery and murder enough for half a dozen novels. But Eleanor's thoughts wandered away from the page. The dreary river bank and the ghostly pollard-willows, the drowned young women, and the ubiquitous villains, all mingled themselves with her anxious thoughts about her father; and the trouble in the book seemed to become a part of the trouble in her own mind, adding its dismal weight to her anxieties.

There were splotchy engravings scattered here and there through the pages of Monsieur Féval's romance, and Eleanor fancied by-and-by that the villain in these pictures was like the sulky stranger who had followed her father and the Frenchman away towards the Barrière Saint Antoine.

She fancied this, although she had scarcely seen that silent stranger's face. He had kept it, as it seemed, purposely averted, and she had only caught one glimpse of the restless black eyes under the shadow of his hat, and the thick moustache that shrouded his mouth. There is always something mysterious and unpleasant in the idea of anything that has been hidden from us, however trivial and insignificant that thing may be. Eleanor Vane, growing more and more nervous as the slow hours crept away, began to worry herself with the vivid recollection of that one brief glimpse in which she had seen the silent stranger's face.

'He cannot have a good countenance,' she thought, 'or the recollection of it would not make me so uncomfortable. How rude he was too! I did not much like the Frenchman, but at least he was polite. The other man was very disagreeable. I hope he is not a friend of papa's.' And then she returned to the drowned young women, and the water-side, and the willows; trying in vain to bury herself in the romance, and not to listen so eagerly for the striking of the quarters. Sometimes she thought, 'Before I turn over to the next page, papa will be home,' or, 'Before I can finish this chapter I shall hear his step upon the stairs.'

Breathless though the night was, there were many sounds that disturbed and mocked this anxious watcher. Sometimes the door below shook – as if by some mysterious agency, there being no wind – and Eleanor fancied that her father's hand was on the latch. Sometimes the stairs creaked, and she started from her chair, eager to run and receive him, and firmly believing that he was stealing stealthily up to his apartments, anxious not to disturb the sleeping inmates of the house. She had known his cautious footfall sound exactly thus in her old midnight watches.

But all these sounds were only miserable delusions. Quarter after quarter, each quarter longer than the last, hour after hour struck from the clocks distant and near. The rattling of the wheels upon the boulevards had died gradually away, and at last had ceased altogether.

It was long past four, and Eleanor had pushed aside her book. It was daylight, – grey, cold, morning, chill and dismal after the oppressive August night, and she stood now in the window watching the empty street.

But still the quarters chimed from the distant clocks: those distant chimes had become terribly distant now in the early morning stillness. But the silence was not of long duration. The rumble of waggon wheels sounded far away in the Rue St Honoré. The rush and clatter of a detachment of cavalry clashed upon the asphalte of the Place de la Concorde. The early sound of a horn called out some wretched recruits to perform their morning exercise in the court-yards of the Louvre. The cheerful voices of workpeople echoed in the streets; dogs were barking, birds singing, the yellow sun mounting in a cloudless heaven.

But there were no signs of the coming of George Vane with the morning sunlight; and as the day grew older and brighter, the anxious face of the pale watcher at the open window only grew paler and more anxious.

CHAPTER VI

THE BLACK BUILDING BY THE RIVER

Richard Thornton was by no means an early riser. He was generally one of the last of those gentlemen who shuffled into the orchestra at the ten o'clock rehearsal of a new melodrama, in which all the effect of a murder or an abduction depended upon the pizzicato twittering of violins, and the introduction of explosive chords at particular crises in the action of the piece. Mr Thornton was a sluggard, who complained most bitterly of the heartlessness of stage managers and prompter's minions, who seemed to take a malicious delight in nailing cruel slips of paper to the door-post of the Phoenix; terrible mandates, wherein the Full Band was called at ten; 'no ten minutes;' the meaning of this last mysterious clause being that the ten minutes' grace which is usually accorded to the tardy performer shall on this occasion be cut off and done away with.

But Richard was out for a holiday now. The eyes of Messrs Spavin and Cromshaw would fain have followed him in his Parisian wanderings, to see that he did double work for his double wage; but the proprietors of the Royal Waterloo Phoenix not being blessed with the gift of clairvoyance, Mr Thornton defied and snapped his fingers at them, secure in the consciousness of his own value.

'If J.T. Jumballs, the author of all the original dramas they have done at the Phoenix for the last ten years, understood French, he'd do "Raoul" for two pound ten,' thought Richard, as he stood before his looking-glass in the blazing August sunshine, rubbing his chin contemplatively, and wondering whether the bristles would be too strong if he let them stop till another morning.

If the honest truth is to be recorded, it must be acknowledged that Mr Thornton was by no means too scrupulous in the performance of his toilet. He had a habit of forgetting to shave until his chin was covered by an appearance of red stubble, dappled here and there by patches of blue and brown, for his beard was wont to crop up in unexpected hues, which surprised even himself. He sympathized with the great lexicographer in not having any overstrained partiality for clean linen, and, indeed, usually wore a coloured shirt, the bosom of which was arabesqued with stray splashes of whitewash and distemper, to say nothing of occasional meandering evidences of the numerous pints of porter imbibed by the young artist during his day's labour. When Mr Thornton bought a new suit of clothes he put them on, and wore them continuously; and ate and drank and painted in them until they were so worn and frayed, and enfeebled by ill treatment, that they began to drop away from him in rusty fragments like the withered leaves which fall from a sturdy young oak. There were people who declared that Mr Thornton slept in his ordinary costume; but of course this was a cruel slander.

To walk eight or nine miles a day to and fro between the place of your abode and the scene of your occupation; to paint the best part of the scenery for a large theatre in which new pieces are brought out pretty frequently; to play second fiddle, and attend early rehearsals upon cold mornings; to jot down the music cues in a melodrama, or accompany Mr Grigsby in his new comic song, or Madame Rosalbini in her latest cachuca; and to adapt a French drama, now and then, by way of adding a few extra pounds to your income, is not exactly to lead an idle life; so perhaps poor Richard Thornton may be forgiven if his friends had occasion to laugh at his indifference upon the subject of soap and water. They even went so far as to call him 'Dirty Dick,' in their more facetious moments; but I don't think the obnoxious *sobriquet* wounded Richard's feelings. Everybody liked him and respected him as a generous-hearted genial-tempered, honourable-minded fellow, who would scarcely have told a lie to save his life, and who scorned to drink a pint of beer that he couldn't pay for, or to accept a favour which he didn't mean to return.

People at the Phoenix knew that Richard Thornton's father had been a gentleman, and that the young man had a certain pride of his own. He was the only man in the theatre who neither abused nor flattered his employers. The carpenters and gasmen touched their caps when they talked to him, though he was shabbier than any of those *employés*; the little ballet girls were fond of him, and came to tell him their troubles when the cruel stage-manager had put their names down for shilling fines in a horrible book which was to be seen on the treasury table every Saturday morning. The old cleaners of the theatre told Mr Thornton about their rheumatic knee-joints, and came to him for sympathy after dreary hours of scouring. He had patience with and compassion for every one. People knew that he was kind and tender-hearted; for his pencil initials always appeared in some obscure corner of every subscription list, against a sum which was bulky when taken in relation to the amount of his salary. People knew that he was brave, for he had once threatened to fling Mr Spavin into the pit when that gentleman had made some insinuation impeaching Richard's honour as to the unfair use of gold-leaf in the Enchanted Caves of Azure Deep. They knew that he was dutiful, and kind, and true to the old music-mistress with whom he lived, and whom he helped to support. They knew that when other men made light of sacred things, and were witty and philosophical upon very solemn subjects, Richard Thornton would leave the assembly gravely and quietly, how eloquent or lively soever he might have been before. People knew all this, and were respectful to the young scene-painter, in spite of the rainbow smears of paint upon his shabby coat, and the occasional fringe of mud upon the frayed edges of his trousers.

Upon this August morning Mr Thornton made very short work of his toilet.

'I won't go out to breakfast,' he thought, 'though I can get two courses and a dessert in the Palais Royal, to say nothing of half a bottle of sour claret, for fifteen pence. I'll get some coffee and rolls, and go to work at some of the scenes for "Raoul."'

He rang a bell near his bed, pushed a table to the window, which looked out into the quadrangle of the hotel, and sat down with a battered tin box of water-colours and a few squares of Bristol board before him. He had to ring several times before one of the waiters condescended to answer his summons, but he worked away cheerily, smoking as he worked, at a careful water-coloured copy of a rough pencil sketch which he had made a couple of nights before in the pit of the theatre.

He didn't leave off to eat his breakfast when it came, by-and-by; but ate his rolls and drank his coffee in the pauses of his work, only laying down his brush for a minute or so at a time. The scene was a street in old Paris, the houses very dark and brown, with over-hanging latticed windows, exterior staircases, practicable bridges, and all sorts of devices which called for the employment of a great deal of glue and pasteboard in Richard's model. This scene was only one out of eight, and the young scene-painter wanted to take perfect models of all the eight scenes back to the Phoenix. He had M. Michel Lévy's sixty centimes edition of the new play spread open before him, and referred to it now and again as he painted.

'Humph! Enter *Raoul* down staircase in flat. *Raoul's* a doctor, and the house with the staircase is his. The house at the corner belongs to *Gobemouche*, the comic barber, and the practicable lattice is *Madeline's*. She'll come to her window by-and-by to talk to the doctor, whom she thinks a very excellent man; though he's been giving her mild doses of *aqua tofana* for the last three weeks. *Catherine de Medicis* comes over the practicable bridge, presently, disguised as a nun. I wonder how many melodramas poor *Catherine* has appeared in since she left this mortal stage? Did she ever do anything except poison people, I wonder, while she was alive? She never does anything else at the Porte Saint Martin, or on the Surrey side of the Thames. I must sketch the costumes, by-and-by.

Raoul in black velvet and scarlet hose, a pointed beard, straight eyebrows, short black hair, – austere and dignified. Cromshaw will do *Raoul*, of course; and Spavin will play the light-comedy soldier who gets drunk, and tears off *Catherine's* velvet mask in the last scene. Yes, that'll be a great scene on our side of the water. *Charles the Ninth* – he's a muff, so anybody can play him – has just finished reading the arsenicated edition of a treatise on hawking, closes the last page of the book, feels the first spasm. *Catherine*, disguised as a nun, has been followed by Spavin – by the comedy-soldier, I mean – to the Louvre, after a conversation having been overheard between her and *Raoul*. The *King*, in the agonies of spasmodic affection, asks who has murdered him. 'That woman – that sorceress – that fiend in human form!' cries the soldier, snatching the mask from *Catherine's* face. – 'Merciful Heaven, it is my mother!' shrieks the *King*, falling dead with a final spasm. That "It is my mother!" ought to be good for three rounds of applause at least. I dare say Spavin will have the speech transferred from the *King's* part to his own. "Merciful Heaven, it is *his* mother!" would do just as well.'

Poor Richard Thornton, not having risen very early, worked on till past five o'clock in the afternoon before his model was finished. He got up with a sigh of relief when the pasteboard presentment of the old Parisian street stood out upon the little table, square and perfect.

He filled his pipe and walked up and down before the table, smoking and admiring his work in an innocent rapture.

'Poor Nelly,' he thought presently. 'I promised I would call in the Rue de l'Archevêque to-day, to pay my respects to the old chap. Not that he'd particularly care to see me, I dare say, but Nell is such a darling. If she asked me to stand on my head, and do poor old Goffie's gnome-fly business, I think I should try and do it. However, it is too late to call upon Mr Vandeleur Vane to-day, so I must put that off till to-morrow. I must drop in again at half-price at the Porte Saint Martin, to have another look at the scene in eight compartments. That'll be rather a poser for the machinist at the Phoenix, I flatter myself. Yes, I must have one more look at it, and – Ah! by the bye, there's the Morgue!'

Mr Thornton finished his pipe and rubbed his chin with a reflective air.

'Yes, I must have a look at the Morgue before I go,' he thought; 'I promised that old nuisance, J.T. Jumballs, that I'd refresh my memory about the Morgue. He's doing a great drama in which one-half of the *dramatis personæ* recognize the other half dead on the marble slabs. He's never been across the Channel, and I think his notions of the Morgue are somewhat foggy. He fancies it's about as big as Westminster Abbey, I know, and he wants the governors to give him the whole depth of the stage for his great scene, and set it obliquely, like the Assyrian hall in "Sardanapalus," so as to give the idea of illimitable extent. I'm to paint the scene for him. *"The interior of the Morgue by lamplight. The meeting of the living and the dead."* That'll be rather a strong line for the bill, at any rate. I'll go and have some dinner in the Palais Royal, and then go down and have a look at the gloomy place. An exterior wouldn't be bad, with Notre Dame in the distance, but an *interior* – Bah! J.T.J. is a clever fellow, but I wish his genius didn't lie so much in the charnel-house.'

He put on his hat, left his room, locked the door, and ran down the polished staircase, whistling merrily as he went. He was glad to be released from his work, pleased at the prospect of a few hours' idleness in the foreign city. Many people, inhabitants and visitors, thought Paris dull, dreary, and deserted in this hot August weather, but it was a delightful change from the Pilasters and the primæval solitudes of Northumberland Square, that quaint, grim quadrangle of big houses, whose prim middle-class inhabitants looked coldly over their smart wire window-blinds at poor Richard's shabby coat.

Mr Thornton got an excellent dinner at a great bustling restaurateur's in the Palais Royal, where for two francs one might dine upon all the delicacies of the season, in a splendid saloon, enlivened by the martial braying of a brass band in the garden below.

The *carte de jour* almost bewildered Richard by its extent and grandeur, and he chose haphazard from the catalogue of soups which the obliging waiter gabbled over for his instruction. He read all the pleasing by-laws touching the non-division of dinners, and the admissibility of exchanges in the way of a dish for a dessert, or a dessert for a dish, by payment of a few extra centimes. He saw that almost all the diners hid themselves behind great wedges of orange-coloured melon at an early stage of the banquet, and generally wound up with a small white washing-basin of lobster salad, the preparation of which was a matter of slow and solemn care and thought. He ordered his dinner in humble imitation of these accomplished *habitués*, and got very good value for his two francs. Then he paid his money; bowed to the graceful lady who sat in splendid attire in a very bower of salads and desserts, and went down a broad staircase that led into a street behind the Palais Royal, and thence to the Rue Richelieu.

He treated himself to a cup of coffee and a cigar at a café in the Place de la Bourse, and then strolled slowly away towards the Seine, smoking, and dawdling to look at this and that as he walked along. It was nearly eight o'clock, therefore, when he emerged, from some narrow street, upon the quay, and made his way towards that bridge beneath whose shadow the Morgue hides, like some foul and unhallowed thing. He did not much like the task which Mr Jumballs had imposed upon him, but he was too good-natured to refuse compliance with the transpontine dramatist's desire, and far too conscientious to break a promise once made, however disagreeable the performance of that promise might prove.

He walked on resolutely, therefore, towards the black shed-like building.

'I hope there are no bodies there to-night.' he thought. 'One glance round the place will show me all I want to see. I hope there are no poor dead creatures there to-night.'

He stopped before going in, and looked at a couple of women who were standing near, chattering together with no little gesticulation.

He asked one of these women the question, Were there any bodies in the Morgue?

Yes, – the women both answered with one voice. There had not long been brought the body of a gentleman, an officer it was thought, poisoned in a gaming-house. A murder, perhaps, or a suicide; no one knew which.

Richard Thornton shrugged his shoulders as he turned away from the idle gossips.

'Some people would call me a coward if they knew how I dislike going into this place,' he thought.

He threw away his cigar, took off his hat, and slowly crossed the dark threshold of the Parisian dead-house.

When he came out again, which was not until the lapse of at least a quarter of an hour, his face was almost as white as the face of the corpse he had left within. He went upon the bridge, scarcely knowing where he went, and walking like a man who walks in his sleep.

Not more than half a dozen yards from the Morgue he came suddenly upon the lonely figure of a girl, whose arm rested on the parapet of the bridge, and whose pale face was turned towards the towers of Notre Dame.

She looked up as he approached, and called him by his name.

'*You* here, Eleanor?' he cried. 'Come away, child; come away, for pity's sake!'

CHAPTER VII

SUSPENSE

Eleanor Vane and the scene-painter stood upon the bridge looking at each other for a few moments after Richard's cry of mingled terror and astonishment.

Had not Eleanor's mind been entirely absorbed by one cruel anxiety, she would have wondered at her old friend's strange greeting. As it was she took no heed of his manner. The shadows of the summer night were gathering over the city and upon the quiet river; the towers of Notre Dame loomed dimly through the twilight.

'Oh, Richard!' Eleanor cried, 'I have been so unhappy. Papa didn't come home all last night, nor yet to-day. I waited for him hour after hour until late in the afternoon; and then the house seemed unbearable; I *couldn't* stay in any longer, and I came out to look for him. I have been far up on the Boulevard where I parted with him last night, and all the way along the crowded streets about there: and then through other streets, till I found myself down here by the water, and I'm so tired! Oh, Dick, Dick, how unkind of papa not to come home! How unkind of my darling father to give me this misery.'

She clasped her hands convulsively upon her companion's arm, and bending her head, burst into tears. Those tears were the first which she had shed in all her trouble; the first relief after long hours of agonizing suspense, of weary watching.

'Oh, how can papa treat me so?' she cried, amid her sobbing. 'How can he treat me so?'

Then, suddenly raising her head, she looked at Richard Thornton, her clear grey eyes dilated with a wild terror, which gave her face a strange and awful beauty.

'Richard!' she cried, 'Richard! you don't think that there – that there is – anything wrong – that anything has happened to my father?'

She did not wait for him to answer, but cried out directly, as if shrinking in terror from the awful suggestion in her own words:

'What should happen to him? he is so well and strong, poor darling. If he is old, he is not *like* an old man, you know. The people of the house in the Rue de l'Archevêque have been very kind to me; they say I'm quite foolish to be frightened, and they told me that papa stopped out all night once last summer. He went to Versailles to see some friends, and stayed away all night without giving any notice that he was going to do so. I know it is very silly of me to be so frightened, Richard. But I always was frightened at Chelsea if he stayed out. I used to fancy all sorts of things. I thought of all kinds of dreadful things last night, Dick, and to-day; until my fancies almost drove me mad.'

During all this time the scene-painter had not spoken. He seemed unable to offer any word of comfort to the poor girl who clung to him in her distress, looking to him for consolation and hope.

She looked wonderingly into his face, puzzled by his silence, which seemed unfeeling; and it was not like Richard to be unfeeling.

'Richard!' she cried, almost impatiently. 'Richard, speak to me! You see how much misery I have suffered, and you don't say a word! You'll help me to find papa, won't you?'

The young man looked down at her. Heaven knows she would have seen no lack of tenderness or compassion in his face, if it had not been hidden by the gathering gloom of the August evening. He drew her hand through his arm, and led her away towards the other side of the water, leaving the black roof of the dead-house behind him.

'There is nothing I would not do to help you, Eleanor,' he said, gently. 'God knows my heart, my dear; and He knows how faithfully I will try to help you.'

'And you will look for papa, Richard, if he should not come home to-night, – he may be at home now, you know, and he may be angry with me for coming out alone, instead of waiting quietly till he returned; but if he should not come to-night, you'll look for him, won't you, Richard? You'll search all Paris till you find him?'

'I'll do everything that I could do for you if I were your brother, Eleanor,' the young man answered, gravely; 'there are times in our lives when nobody but God can help us, my dear, and when we must turn to Him. It's in the day of trouble that we want His help, Nelly.'

'Yes, yes, I know. I prayed, last night, again, and again, and again, that papa might come back soon. I have been saying the same prayer all to-day, Richard; even just now, when you found me standing by the parapet of the bridge, I was praying for my dear father. I saw the church towers looking so grand and solemn in the twilight, and the sight of them made me remember how powerful God is, and that He can always grant our prayers.'

'If it seems best and wisest in His sight, Nell.'

'Yes, of course; sometimes we pray for foolish things, but there could be nothing foolish in wishing my darling father to come back to me. Where are you taking me, Dick?'

Eleanor stopped suddenly, and looked at her companion. She had need to ask the question, for Richard Thornton was leading her into a labyrinth of streets in the direction of the Luxembourg, and he seemed to have very little notion whither he was going.

'This is not the way home, Richard,' Eleanor said; 'I don't know where we are, but we seem to be going farther and farther away from home. Will you take me back to the Rue de l'Archevêque, Dick? We must cross the river again, you know, to get there. I want to go home at once. Papa may have come home, and he'll be angry, perhaps, if he finds me absent. Take me home, Dick.'

'I will, my dear. We'll cross the water farther on, by the Louvre; and now tell me, Eleanor – I – I can't very well make inquiries about your father, unless I fully understand the circumstances under which you parted from him last night. How was it, my dear? What happened when Mr Vane left you upon the Boulevard?'

They were walking in a broad, quiet street in which there were very few passers-by. The houses stood back behind ponderous gates, and were hidden by sheltering walls. The stately mansions between court and garden had rather a decayed aspect, which gave a certain dreariness to their grandeur. The fashionable world seemed to have deserted this quiet quarter for the leafy avenues leading away from the Champs Elysées.

Richard and Eleanor walked slowly along the broad footway. The stillness of the soft summer night had some effect upon the school-girl's fever of impatience. The grave, compassionate tones of her friend's voice soothed her. The burst of passionate weeping which had almost convulsed her slight frame half an hour before, had been an unspeakable relief to her. She clung to her companion's arm confidingly, and walked patiently by his side; without questioning him as to where he was leading her, though she had a vague idea that he was not taking her homewards.

'I will not be foolish about papa,' she said; 'I will do as you tell me, Richard; I will trust in God. I am sure my dear father will return to me. We are so fond of each other; you know, Richard, we are all the world to each other; and my poor darling looks so hopefully forward to the day in which he will have Mr de Crespigny's fortune. I don't hope for that quite so much as papa does, Dick; for Mr de Crespigny may live to be a very, very old man, and it seems so wicked to wish for any one's death. The day I look forward to is the day when I shall have finished my education, and be able to work for papa. That must be almost better than being rich, I should think, Dick. I can't imagine any happier fate than to work for those we love.'

Her face brightened as she talked, and she turned to her companion, looking to him for sympathy; but Richard's head was averted, and he seemed to be staring absently at the houses upon the opposite side of the way.

He was silent for some moments after Eleanor had left off speaking; and then he said, rather abruptly:

'Tell me, my dear, how did you part with your father last night?'

'Why, we had been dining on the Boulevard; and after dinner papa took me for a long walk, ever so far, past all the theatres, and he had promised to take me to the Ambigue or the Porte Saint Martin; but as we were coming back we met two gentlemen, friends of papa's, who stopped him, and said they had an appointment with him, and persuaded him to go back with them.'

'Back with them! Back where?'

'I mean back towards a big stone gateway we had passed a little time before. I only know they turned that way, but I don't know where they went. I stood and watched them till they were out of sight.'

'And the two men, what were they like?'

'One of them was a little Frenchman, stout and rosy-faced, with a light moustache and beard like the Emperor's. He was smartly dressed, and had a cane, which he kept twirling when he talked to papa.'

'Did you hear what he said?'

'No, he spoke in a low voice, and he talked French.'

'But you speak French, Eleanor?'

'Yes, but not as they speak it here. The people seem to talk so fast here, it's quite difficult to understand them.'

'But the other man, Nell; what was he like?'

'Oh, he was a disagreeable-looking man, and seemed to have a sulky manner, as if he was offended with papa for breaking his appointment, and didn't care how the matter ended. I scarcely saw his face — at least only for a moment — just long enough to see that he had black eyes, and a thick black moustache. He was tall, and shabbily dressed, and I fancied he was an Englishman, though he never once spoke.'

'He never spoke! It was the Frenchman, then, who persuaded your father to go away with him?'

'Yes.'

'And he seemed very anxious?'

'Oh, yes, very anxious.'

Richard Thornton muttered something between his set teeth, something which sounded like a curse.

'Tell me one thing, Eleanor,' he said. 'Your poor father never was too well off, I know. He could not be likely to have much money about him last night. Do you know if he had any?'

'Yes, he had a great deal of money.'

'What do you mean by a great deal? A few pounds, I suppose?'

'Oh, much more than that,' Eleanor answered. 'He had a hundred pounds — a hundred pounds in new bank notes — French notes. It was the money my half-sister, Mrs Bannister, had sent him, to pay for my education at Madame Marly's.'

'Mrs Bannister,' said Richard, catching at the name. 'Ah, to be sure, I remember now. Mrs Bannister is your sister. She is very well off, is she not, and has been kind to you? If you were in any trouble, you would go to her, I suppose, Eleanor?'

'Go to her if I were in trouble! Oh, no, no, Dick, not for the world!'

'But why not? She has been kind to you, hasn't she, Nell?'

'Oh, yes, very kind in paying money for my education, and all that; but you know, Richard, there are some people who seem to do kind things in an unkind manner. If you knew the cruel letter that Mrs Bannister wrote to papa — the cruel, humiliating things she said only a few days ago, you couldn't wonder that I don't like her.'

'But she is your sister, Nell; your nearest relation.'

'Except papa.'

'And she ought to love you, and be kind to you. She lives at Bayswater, I think I've heard you say?'

'Yes, in Hyde Park Gardens.'

'To be sure. Mrs Bannister, Hyde Park Gardens, Bayswater.'

He repeated the name and address, as if he wished to impress them upon his memory.

'I will take you home now, Nell,' he said. 'My poor child, you must be tired to death.'

'How can I think about being tired, Richard,' exclaimed Eleanor, 'when I am so anxious about papa? Oh, if I only find him at home, what happiness it will be!'

But she hung heavily upon her friend's arm, and Richard knew that she was very tired. She had been wandering about Paris for several hours, poor child, hither and thither, in the long, unfamiliar streets, following all sorts of unlikely people who looked in the distance something like her father; hoping again and again, only again and again to be disappointed.

They turned into a wider thoroughfare presently, and the scene-painter called the first hackney vehicle which passed him, and lifted Eleanor into it. She was almost fainting with fatigue and exhaustion.

'What have you had to eat to-day, Nell?' he asked.

She hesitated a little, as if she had forgotten what she had eaten, or indeed whether she had eaten at all.

'There was some coffee and a couple of rolls sent for papa this morning. He has his breakfast sent him from a *traiteur's*, you know. I had one of the rolls.'

'And you've had nothing since?'

'No. How could I eat when I was so wretched about papa?'

Richard shook his head reproachfully.

'My darling Nell!' he said, 'you promised me just now that you'd be a good girl, and trust in Providence. I shall take you somewhere and give you some supper, and then you must promise me to go home and get a good night's rest.'

'I will do whatever you tell me, Richard,' Eleanor answered, submissively, 'but let me go home first, please, and see if papa has come back.'

The scene-painter did not for a few moments reply to this request, but he answered presently in an abstracted tone:

'You shall do what you like, Nell.'

He told the coachman to drive to the Rue de l'Archevêque, but he would not let Eleanor alight from the vehicle when they reached the corner of the street and the little butcher's shop, eager as she was to spring out and run into the house.

'Stay where you are, Nell,' he said authoritatively. 'I will make all inquiries.'

Eleanor obeyed him. She was exhausted by a weary night of watching, a long day of agitation and anxiety, and she was too weak to oppose her old friend. She looked hopelessly up at the open windows on the entresol. They were exactly as she had left them four or five hours ago. No glimmer of light gave friendly token that the rooms were occupied.

Richard Thornton talked to the butcher's wife for a long time, as it seemed to Eleanor; but he had very little to tell her when he came back to the carriage. Mr Vane had not returned: that was all he said.

He took his companion to a café near the Madeleine, where he insisted upon her taking a large cup of coffee and a roll. It was all he could persuade her to take, and she begged to be allowed to sit at one of the tables outside the café.

'She might see her father go by,' she said, 'on his way to the Rue de l'Archevêque.'

The two friends sat at a little iron table rather apart from the groups of animated loungers sitting at other tables drinking coffee and lemonade. But George Mowbray Vandeleur Vane did not pass that way throughout the half hour during which Eleanor lingered over her cup of coffee.

It was past ten o'clock when Richard Thornton bade her good night at the threshold of the little door beside the butcher's shop.

'You must promise me not to sit up to-night, Nelly,' he said, as he shook hands with her.

'Yes, Richard.'

'And mind you keep your promise this time. I will come and see you early to-morrow. God bless you, my dear, and good night!'

He pressed her hand tenderly. When she had closed the door behind her, he crossed the narrow street, and waited upon the other side of the way until he saw a light in one of the entresol windows. He watched while Eleanor came to this window and drew a dark curtain across it, and then he walked slowly away.

'God bless her, poor child,' he murmured, in a low, compassionate voice, 'poor lonely child!'

The grave thoughtfulness of his expression never changed as he walked homewards to the Hôtel des Deux Mondes. Late as it was when he reached his chamber on the fifth story, he seated himself at the table, and pushing aside his clay pipe and tobacco-pouch, his water-colours and brushes, his broken palettes and scraps of Bristol board, and all the litter of his day's work, he took a few sheets of foreign letter paper and a bottle of ink from a shabby leather desk, and began to write.

He wrote two letters, both rather long, and folded, sealed, and directed them.

One was addressed to Mrs Bannister, Hyde Park Gardens, Bayswater; the other to Signora Picirillo, the Pilasters, Dudley Street, Northumberland Square.

Richard Thornton put both these letters in his pocket and went out to post them.

'I think I have acted for the best,' he muttered, as he went back to the hotel near the market-place; 'I can do nothing more until to-morrow.'

CHAPTER VIII

GOOD SAMARITANS

George Vane did not come home. Eleanor kept the promise made to her faithful friend, and tried to sleep. She flung herself, dressed as she was, upon the little bed near the curtained alcove. She would thus be ready to run to her father, whenever he came in, she thought, to welcome and minister to him. She was thoroughly worn out, and she slept; a wretched slumber, broken by nightmares and horrible dreams, in which she saw her father assailed by all kinds of dangers, a prey to every manner of misfortune and vicissitude. Once she saw him standing on a horrible rock, menaced by a swiftly advancing tide, while she was in a boat only a few paces from him, as it seemed, doing battle with the black waves, and striving with all her might to reach and rescue him, but never able to do so.

In another dream he was wandering upon the crumbling verge of a precipice – he seemed a white-haired, feeble, tottering old man in this vision – and again she was near him, but unable to give him warning of his danger, though a word would have done so. The agony of her endeavour to utter the one cry which would have called that idolized father from his death, awoke her.

But she had other dreams, dreams of quite a different character, in which her father was restored to her, rich and prosperous, and he and she were laughing merrily at all the foolish tortures she had inflicted upon herself; and other dreams again which seemed so real that she fancied she must be awake: dreams in which she heard the welcome footsteps upon the stair, the opening of the door, and her father's voice in the next room calling to her.

These dreams were the worst of all. It was terrible to awake after many such delusions and find she had been again deluded. It was cruel to awake to the full sense of her loneliness, while the sound of the voice she had heard in her dream still lingered in her ears.

The dark hours of the short summer night seemed interminable to her in this wretched, bewildered, half-sleeping, half-waking state; even longer than they had appeared when she sat up watching for her father's return. Every fresh dream was a slow agony of terror and perplexity.

At last the grey daylight stole in through the half-closed shutters, the vague outlines of the furniture grew out of the darkness; duskily impalpable and ghastly at first, then sharp and distinct in the cold morning light. She could not rest any longer; she got up and went to the window; she pushed the sash open, and sank down on her knees with her forehead resting on the window sill.

'I will wait for him here,' she thought; 'I shall hear his step in the street. Poor dear, poor dear, I can guess why he stays away. He has spent that odious money, and does not like to return and tell me so. My darling father, do you know me so little as to think that I would grudge you the last farthing I had in the world, if you wanted it?'

Her thoughts rambled on in strange confusion until they grew bewildering; her brain became dizzy with perpetual repetitions of the same idea; when she lifted her head – her poor, weary, burning, heavy head, which seemed a leaden weight that it was almost impossible to raise – and looked from the window, the street below reeled beneath her eyes, the floor upon which she knelt seemed sinking with her into some deep gulf of blackness and horror. A thousand conflicting sounds – not the morning noises of the waking city – hissed and buzzed, and roared and thundered in her ears, growing louder and louder and louder, until they all melted away in the fast-gathering darkness.

The sun was shining brightly into the room when the compassionate mistress of the house found Mr Vane's daughter half kneeling, half lying on the ground, with her hand upon the cold sill of the open window, and her auburn hair streaming in draggled curls about her shoulders. Her thin muslin frock was wet with the early dew. She had fainted away, and had lain thus, helpless and insensible, for several hours.

The butcher's wife undressed her and put her to bed. Richard Thornton came to the Rue de l'Archevêque half an hour afterwards, and went away again directly to look for an English doctor. He found one, an elderly man with grave and gentle manners, who declared that Miss Vane was suffering from fever brought on by intense mental excitement; she was of a highly nervous temperament, he said, and that she required little to be done for her; she only wanted repose and quiet. Her constitution was superb, and would triumph over a far more serious attack than this.

Richard Thornton took the doctor into the adjoining room, the little sitting-room which bore the traces of Mr Vane's occupation, and talked to him in a low voice for some minutes. The medical man shook his head gravely.

'It is very sad,' he said; 'it will be better to tell her the truth, if possible, as soon as she recovers from the delirium. The anxiety and suspense have overtaken her brain. Anything would be better than that this overstrained state of the mind should continue. Her constitution will rally after a shock; but with her highly nervous and imaginative nature, everything is to be dreaded from prolonged mental irritation. She is related to you, I suppose?'

'No, poor child, I wish she were.'

'But she is not without near relatives, I hope?'

'No, she has sisters — or at least half sisters — and brothers.'

'They should be written to, then, immediately,' the doctor said, as he took up his hat.

'I have written to one of her sisters, and I have written to another lady, a friend, who will be of more use, I fancy, in this crisis.'

The doctor went away, promising to send some saline draughts to keep the fever under, and to call again in the evening.

Richard Thornton went into the little bed-chamber, where the butcher's wife sat beside the curtained alcove, making up some accounts in a leather-covered book. She was a hearty, pleasant-mannered young woman, and had taken up her post by the invalid's bed very willingly, although her presence was always much needed in the shop below.

'*Chut,*' she whispered, with her finger on her lip, 'she sleeps, *pauvrette!*'

Richard sat down quietly by the open window. He took out Michel Lévy's edition of 'Raoul', a stump of lead pencil, and the back of an old letter, and set to work resolutely at his adaptation. He could not afford to lose time, even though his adopted sister lay ill under the shadow of the worsted curtains that shrouded the alcove on the other side of the little room.

He sat long and patiently, turning the Poison drama into English with wonderful ease and rapidity; and meekly bearing a deprivation that was no small one to him, in the loss of his clay pipe, which he was in the habit of smoking at all hours of the day.

Eleanor awoke at last, and began talking in a rambling, incoherent way about her father, and the money sent by Mrs Bannister, and the parting upon the Boulevard.

The butcher's wife drew back the curtains, and Richard Thornton went to the bedside and looked down tenderly at his childish friend.

Her golden-tinted hair was scattered on the pillow, tangled and roughened by the constant movement of her restless head. Her grey eyes were feverishly bright, and burning spots blazed upon the cheeks which had been so deadly pale on the previous night. She knew Richard, and spoke to him; but the delirium was not over, for she mixed the events of the present with the Chelsea experiences of long ago, and talked to her old friend of the Signora, the violin, and the rabbits. She fell off into a heavy sleep again, after taking the effervescent medicine sent her by the English surgeon, and slept until nearly twilight. In these long slumbers her fresh and powerful constitution asserted itself, and took compensation for the strain that had been made upon it in the past day or two.

Richard went away in the afternoon, and did not return till late at night, when the butcher's wife told him that her charge had been very restless, and had asked repeatedly for her father.

'What are we to do?' the good woman said, shrugging her shoulders with a despairing gesture. 'Are we to tell her?'

'Not yet,' Richard answered. 'Keep her quiet; keep her quiet as you can. And if it is positively necessary to tell her anything, say that her father has been taken ill, away from home, and cannot be brought back yet. Poor child! it seems so cruel to keep her in suspense, and still more cruel to deceive her.'

The butcher's wife promised to do all in her power to keep her patient quiet. The doctor had sent an opiate. Miss Vane could not sleep too much, he said.

So another night passed, this time very peacefully for Eleanor, who lay in a heavy slumber broken by no cruel dreams. She was very, very weak the next day, for she had scarcely eaten anything since the roll and coffee which Richard had made her take; and though she was not exactly delirious, her mind seemed almost incapable of receiving any very vivid impression. She listened quietly when they told her that her father could not come home because he was ill.

Richard Thornton came to the Rue de l'Archevêque several times during this second day of Eleanor's illness, but he only stayed a few minutes upon each occasion. He had a great deal to do, he told the butcher's wife, who still kept faithfully to her post in the sick room, only stealing away now and then, while Eleanor was asleep, to attend to her business.

It was past eleven o'clock that night when the scene-painter came for the last time. Eleanor had grown worse as the evening advanced, and was by this time terribly feverish and restless. She wanted to get up and dress herself, and go to her father. If he was ill, how could they keep her from him, how could they be so cruel as to keep her from his side?

Then, starting up suddenly from her pillow, she would cry out wildly that they were deceiving her, and that her father was dead.

But help and comfort were near at hand. When Richard came, he did not come alone. He brought a lady with him; an elderly grey-headed woman, dressed in shabby black.

When this lady appeared upon the threshold of the dimly-lighted little bedchamber, Eleanor Vane suddenly sprang up in her bed, and threw out her arms with a wild cry of surprise and delight.

'The Signora!' she exclaimed, 'the dear, kind Signora!'

The lady took off her bonnet, and then went close up to the bed, and seating herself on the edge of the mattress, drew Eleanor's fair head upon her bosom, smoothing the tangled hair with unspeakable tenderness.

'My poor child!' she murmured again and again. 'My poor, poor child!'

'But, dear Signora,' Eleanor cried, wonderingly, 'how is it that you are here? Why didn't Richard tell me that you were in Paris?'

'Because I have only just arrived, my darling.'

'Only just arrived! Only just arrived in Paris! But why did you come?'

'I came to see you, Eleanor,' the Signora answered, very gently. 'I heard that you were in trouble, my dear, and I have come to you; to help and comfort you if I can.'

The butcher's wife had withdrawn into the little sitting-room where Richard sat in the darkness. Eleanor Vane and the Signora were therefore quite alone.

Hitherto the invalid's head had rested very quietly upon her friend's bosom, but now she lifted it suddenly and looked full in the Signora's face.

'You came to me because I was in trouble,' she said. 'How should I be in trouble so long as my father lives? What sorrow can come to me while he is safe? He is ill, they say, but he will get better; he will get better, won't he? He will be better soon, dear Signora; he will better soon?'

She waited for an answer to her breathless questioning, looking intently in the pale quiet face of her friend; then suddenly, with a low, wailing cry, she flung up her hands and clasped them wildly above her head.

'You have all deceived me,' she cried, 'you have all deceived me; my father is dead!'

The Signora drew her arm caressingly round Eleanor Vane, and tried to shelter the poor burning head once more upon her shoulder; but Eleanor shrank from her with an impatient gesture, and, with her hands still clasped above her head, stared blankly at the dead wall before her.

'My dear, my dear,' the Signora said, trying to unclasp the rigid hands which were so convulsively clasped together. 'Eleanor, my dear, listen to me: for pity's sake try and listen to me, my own dear love. You must know, you must have long known, my dear, that heavy sorrows come to us all, sooner or later. It is the common lot, my love, and we must all bow before the Divine hand that afflicts us. If there were no sorrow in this world, Eleanor, we should grow too much in love with our own happiness; we should be frightened at the approach of grey hairs and old age; we should tremble at the thought of death. If there were no better and higher life than this, Eleanor, sorrow and death would indeed be terrible. You know how very much affliction has fallen to my share, dear. You have heard me speak of the children I loved; all taken from me, Nelly, all taken away. If it were not for my dear nephew, Richard, I should stand quite alone in the world, a desolate old woman, with no hope on this side of the grave. But when my sons were taken from me, God raised me up another son in him. Do you think that God ever abandons us, Eleanor, even when He afflicts us most heavily? I have lived a long life, my dear, and I tell you NO!'

The Signora waited in vain for some change in the rigid attitude, the stony face. Eleanor Vane still stared blankly at the dead wall before her.

'You have all deceived me,' she repeated; 'my father is dead!'

It was useless talking to her; the tenderest words were dull and meaningless jargon to her ears. That night the fever grew worse, and the delirium was at its height. The butcher's wife was relieved by a very patient and accustomed watcher, for the Signora had sat by many sick-beds, hoping against hope, until despair crept into her heart, as the grey shadows of approaching death came over a beloved face, never again to pass away.

The fever lasted for several days and nights, but throughout every change the English doctor declared that Eleanor Vane's constitution would carry her through a worse attack than this.

'I am glad you told her,' he said one morning to the Signora; 'there will be less to tell her by-and-by, when she begins to get strong again.'

There was, therefore, something more to be told.

Little by little the fever passed away; the crimson spots faded out of the invalid's hollow cheeks; the unnatural lustre of the grey eyes grew less and less vivid; little by little the mind grew clearer, the delirious wanderings less frequent.

But with the return of perfect consciousness there came terrible bursts of grief – grief that was loud and passionate in proportion to the impulsive vehemence of Eleanor Vane's character. This was her first sorrow, and she could not bear it quietly. Floods of tears drowned her pillow night after night; she refused to be comforted; she repulsed the patient Signora; she would not listen to poor Richard, who came sometimes to sit by her side, and tried his best to beguile her from her grief. She rebelled against their attempted consolation.

'What was my father to you?' she cried, passionately. 'You can afford to forget him. He was all the world to me!'

But it was not in Eleanor's nature to be long ungrateful for the tenderness and compassion of those who were so patient with her in this dark hour of her young life.

'How good you are to me,' she cried sometimes, 'and what a wretch I am to think so little of your goodness. But you don't know how I loved my father. You don't know – you don't know. I was to have worked for him; I was to have worked for him by-and-by, and we were to have led such a happy life together.'

She was growing strong again, in spite of her grief. Her elastic temperament asserted itself in spite of her sorrow, which she never ceased to think of night and day, and she arose after her illness like a beautiful flower which had been beaten and crushed by the storm.

Richard Thornton's leave of absence had expired for some days, but the Royal Phoenix Theatre closed its doors in the hot summer months, and he was therefore comparatively free. He stayed in Paris with his aunt, for they were both bent upon one purpose, to be accomplished at any sacrifice to themselves. Thank Heaven! there are always good Samaritans in the world, who do not mind turning backward upon their life's journey when there is a desolate wounded traveller in need of their help and tenderness.

The Parisian atmosphere was cooling down in the early days of September – faint but refreshing breezes were beginning to blow away the white mists of summer heat upon the Boulevards, when Eleanor Vane was well enough to sit in the little saloon above the butcher's shop, and drink tea in the English fashion with her two friends.

She was well enough to do this, and Richard and the Signora were beginning to think of turning homewards; but before they could well leave Paris there was something that ought to be told to Eleanor – something that she *must* know sooner or later – something that it would be perhaps better for her to know at once.

But they had waited from time to time, thinking that she might ask some questions which would lead to the revelation that must ultimately be made to her.

Upon this September afternoon she sat near the open window, looking very beautiful and virginal in a loose white muslin dressing-gown, and with her long auburn curls falling upon her shoulders. She had been silent for a long time: her two companions watching her furtively, observant of every change in her countenance. Her cup of tea stood untasted on a little table at her side, and she was sitting with her hands loosely locked together in her lap.

She spoke at last, and asked that very question which must inevitably lead to the revelation her friends had to make to her.

'You have never told me how papa died,' she said; 'his death must have been sudden, I know.'

Eleanor Vane spoke very quietly. She had never before mentioned her dead father with so little outward evidence of emotion. The hands loosely locked together upon her lap stirred with a slightly tremulous motion; the face, turned towards the Signora and Richard Thornton, had a look of fixed intensity; and that was all.

'Papa died suddenly, did he not?' she repeated.

'Yes, my dear, very suddenly.'

'I thought so. But why was he not brought home? Why couldn't I see——'

She stopped abruptly, and turned her face away towards the open window. She was trembling violently now from head to foot.

Her two companions were silent. That terrible something which was as yet unrevealed must be told sooner or later; but who was to tell it to this girl, with her excitable nature, her highly-wrought nervous temperament?

The Signora shrugged her shoulders despondingly as she looked at her nephew. Mr Thornton had been painting all the afternoon in the little sitting-room. He had tried to interest Eleanor Vane in the great set scenes he was preparing for *Raoul*. He had explained to her the nature of a vampire trap in the wainscot of the poisoner's chamber, and had made his pasteboard model limp in his repeated exhibition of its machinery. The vampire trap was a subtle contrivance which might have beguiled any one from their grief, Dick thought; but the wan smile with which Eleanor watched his work only made the scene-painter's heart ache. Richard sighed as he returned his aunt's look. It seemed quite a hopeless case as yet. This poor lonely child of fifteen might go melancholy mad, perhaps, in her grief for a spendthrift father.

Eleanor Vane turned upon them suddenly while they sat silent and embarrassed, wondering what they should say to her next.

'My father committed suicide!' she said, in a strangely quiet voice.

The Signora started and rose suddenly, as if she would have gone to Eleanor. Richard grew very pale, but sat looking down at the litter upon the table, with one hand trifling nervously amongst the scraps of cardboard and wet paint-brushes.

'Yes,' cried Eleanor Vane, 'you have deceived me from first to last. You told me first that he was not dead; but when you could no longer keep my misery a secret from me, you only told me half the truth – you only told me half the cruel truth. And even now, when I have suffered so much that it seems as if no further suffering could touch me, you still deceive me, you still try to keep the truth from me. My father parted from me in health and spirits. Don't trifle with me, Signora; I am not a child any longer; I am not a foolish school-girl, whom you can deceive as you like. I am a woman, and will know the worst. My father killed himself!'

She had risen in her excitement, but clung with one hand to the back of her chair, as if too weak to stand without that support.

The Signora went to her, and wound her arms about the slight trembling figure; but Eleanor seemed almost unconscious of that motherly caress.

'Tell me the truth,' she cried, vehemently; 'did my father kill himself?'

'It is feared that he did, Eleanor.'

The pale face grew a shade whiter, and the trembling frame became suddenly rigid.

'It is feared that he did!' Eleanor Vane repeated. 'It is not certain, then?'

The Signora was silent.

'Why don't you tell me the truth?' cried the girl, passionately. 'Do you think you can make my misery less to me by dropping out your words one by one? Tell me the worst. What can there be worse than my father's death; his unhappy death; killed by his own hand, his poor desperate hand? Tell me the truth. If you don't wish me to go mad, tell me the truth at once.'

'I will, Eleanor, I will,' the Signora answered, gently. 'I wish to tell you all. I wish that you should know the truth, sad as it may be to hear. This is the great sorrow of your life, my dear, and it has fallen upon you very early. I hope you will try and bear it like a Christian.'

Eleanor Vane shook her head with an impatient gesture.

'Don't talk to me of my sorrow,' she cried; 'what does it matter what I suffer? My father, my poor father, what must he have suffered before he did this dreadful act? Don't talk about me; tell me of him, and tell me the worst.'

'I will, my darling, I will; but sit down, sit down, and try to compose yourself.'

'No, I'll stand here till you have told me the truth. I'll not stir from this spot till I know all.'

She disengaged herself from the Signora's supporting arm, and with her hand still resting on the chair, stood resolute before the old music-mistress and her nephew. I think the Signora and the scene-painter were both afraid of her, she looked so grand in her beauty and despair.

She seemed indeed, as she had said, no longer a child or a school-girl; but a woman, desperate and almost terrible in the intensity of her despair.

'Let me tell Eleanor the truth of this sad story,' Richard said; 'it may be told very briefly. When your father parted with you, Nelly, on the night of the 11th of August, he and the two men who were with him went at once to an obscure café in one of the streets near the Barrière Saint Antoine. They were in the habit of going there, it seems, sometimes playing billiards in the large open room on the ground floor, sometimes playing cards in a *cabinet particulier* on the entresol. Upon this night they went straight to the private room. It was about half-past nine when they went in. The waiter who attended upon them took them three bottles of Chambertin and a good deal of seltzer-water. Your father seemed in high spirits at first. He and the dark Englishman were playing *écarté*, their usual game; and the Frenchman was looking over your father's hand, now and then advising his play, now and then applauding and encouraging him. All this came out upon inquiry. The Frenchman quitted the café at a little before twelve; your father and the young Englishman stayed till long after midnight, and towards one o'clock they were heard at high words, and almost immediately afterwards the Englishman went away, leaving your father, who sent the waiter for some brandy and writing materials. He wanted to write a letter before he left, he said.'

The scene-painter paused, looking anxiously at the face of his listener. The rigid intensity of that pale young face had undergone no change; the grey eyes, fixed and dilated, were turned steadily towards him.

'When the waiter took your father the things he had asked for, he found him sitting at the table with his face hidden in his hands. The man placed the brandy and writing materials upon the table, and then went away, but not before he had noticed a strange faint smell – the smell of some drug, he thought; but he had no idea then what drug. The waiter went down stairs; all the ordinary frequenters of the place were gone, and the lights were out. The man waited up to let your father out, expecting him to come down-stairs every moment. Three o'clock struck, and the waiter went up-stairs upon the pretence of asking if anything was wanted. He found your father sitting very much as he had left him, except that this time his head was resting upon the table, which was scattered with torn scraps of paper. He was dead, Eleanor. The man gave the alarm directly, and a doctor came to give assistance, if any could have been given; but the drug which the waiter had smelt was opium, and your father had taken a quantity which would have killed the strongest man in Paris.'

'Why did he do this?'

'I can scarcely tell you, my dear; but your poor father left, among the scraps of paper upon the table, one fragment much larger and more intelligible than the rest. It is evidently part of a letter addressed to you; but it is very wildly and incoherently worded; and you must remember that it was written under circumstances of great mental excitement.'

'Give it me!'

Eleanor stretched out her hand with an authoritative gesture. Richard hesitated.

'I wish you to fully understand the nature of this letter before you read it, Eleanor; I wish——'

'You kept the story of my father's death from me out of mistaken kindness,' the girl said, in an unfaltering voice; 'I will try and remember

how good you have been to me, so that I may forgive you that; but you
cannot keep from me the letter my father wrote to me before he died.
That is mine; and I claim it.'

'Let her see it, poor child,' said the Signora.

Richard Thornton took a leather memorandum-book from one of the
pockets of his loose coat. There were several papers in this book. He
selected one, and handed it silently to Eleanor Vane. It was a sheet of letter-
paper, written upon in her father's hand, but a part of it had been torn away.

Even had the whole of the letter been left, the writer's style was so wild
and incoherent that it would have been no easy task to understand his
meaning. In its torn and fragmentary state, this scrap of writing left by
George Vane was only a scribble of confused and broken sentences. The
sheet of paper had been torn from the top to the bottom, so that the end
of each line was missing. The following broken lines were therefore all that
Eleanor could decipher, and in these the words were blotted and indistinct.

> My poor Eleanor, – My poor injured
> worst your cruel sister, Hortensia Bannis
> could not be bad enough. I am a thief
> robbed and cheated my own
> been decoyed to this hell upon eart
> wretches who are base enough to
> a helpless old man who had trust
> to be gentlemen. I cannot return
> look in my child's face after
> money which was to have
> education. Better to die and rid
> But my blood be upon the head of
> who has cheated me this night out of
> May he suffer as he has
> forget, Eleanor, never forget Robert Lan
> murderer of your helpless old
> a cheat and a villain who
> some day live to revenge the fate
> poor old father, who prays that God will
> helpless old man whose folly
> madness have

There was no more. These lines were spread over the first leaf of a sheet
of letter-paper; the second leaf, as well as a long strip of the first, had
been torn away.

This was the only clue to the secret of his death which George Vane
had left behind him.

Eleanor Vane folded the crumpled scrap of paper, and put it tenderly in her bosom. Then, falling on her knees, she clasped her hands, and lifted them towards the low ceiling of the little chamber.

'Oh, my God!' she cried; 'hear the vow of a desolate creature, who has only one purpose left in life.'

Signora Picirillo knelt down beside her, and tried to clasp her in her arms.

'My dear, my dear!' she pleaded; 'remember how this letter was written – remember the state of your father's mind——'

'I remember nothing,' answered Eleanor Vane, 'except that my father tells me to revenge his murder. For he was murdered,' she cried, passionately, 'if this money – this wretched money, which he would have died sooner than lose – was taken from him unfairly. He was murdered. What did the wretch who robbed him care what became of the poor, broken-hearted, helpless old man whom he had wronged and cheated? What did he care? He left my father; left him in his desolation and misery; left him after having stripped and beggared him; left him to die in his despair. Listen to me, both of you, and remember what I say. I am very young, I know, but I have learnt to think and act for myself before to-day. I don't know this man's name; I never even saw his face; I don't know who he is, or where he comes from; but sooner or later I swear to be revenged upon him for my father's cruel death.'

'Eleanor, Eleanor!' cried the Signora: 'is this womanly? Is this Christian-like?'

The girl turned upon her. There was almost a supernatural light, now, in the dilated grey eyes. Eleanor Vane had risen from her knees, and stood with her slender figure drawn to its fullest height, her long auburn hair streaming over her shoulders, with the low light of the setting sun shining upon the waving tresses until they glittered like molten gold. She looked, in her desperate resolution and virginal beauty, like some young martyr of the middle ages awaiting to be led to the rack.

'I don't know whether it is womanly or Christian-like,' she said, 'but I know that it is henceforward the purpose of my life, and that it is stronger than myself.'

CHAPTER IX

LOOKING TO THE FUTURE

The story which Richard Thornton had told Eleanor Vane was the simple record of an unhappy truth. The gay and thoughtless spendthrift, the man about town, who had outlived his age and spent three fortunes, had ended his life, by his own desperate hand, in an obscure café near the Barrière Saint Antoine.

Amongst other habits of the age in which George Vane had lived, gambling was pretty prevalent. Mr Vane's sanguine nature was the very nature which leads a man to the gaming-table, and holds him there under the demoniac fascination of the fatal green cloth, hoping against hope, until his pockets are empty, and he must needs crawl dispirited away, having no more money to lose.

This was the one vice of George Vane's life. He had tried to redeem his every-day extravagances by the gamester's frenzied speculations, the gamester's subtle combinations; which are so infallible in theory, so ruinous in practice. Eleanor had never known this. If her father stayed out late at night, and she had to wait and watch for him through long weary hours of suspense and anxiety, she never knew why he stayed, or why he was often so broken down and wretched when he came home. Other people could guess the reason of the old man's midnight absences from his shabby lodging, but they were too merciful to tell his little girl the truth. In Paris, in a strange city, where his acquaintance were few, the old vice grew stronger, and George Vane spent his nights in gambling for pitiful stakes in any low haunts to which his disreputable associates deluded him. He picked up strange acquaintance in these days of his decadence, as poor people very often do: young men who were wandering about the world, penniless adventurers, professionless young reprobates, getting a very doubtful living by the exercise of their wits; men who were content to flatter and pay court to the old beau so long as they could win a few francs from him to pay for the evening's diversion.

With such men George Vane had associated for a long time. They won pitiful sums of him, and cheated him without scruple; but his life was a very dull one, remember; he had lived for the world, and society of some kind or other was absolutely necessary to him. He clung, therefore, to these men, and was fain to accept their homage in the hour of his decline; and it was with such men as these he had spent the night before his death. It was such men as these who had robbed him of the money which, but for an unhappy accident, would have been safely handed over to the schoolmistress in the Bois de Boulogne.

The old man's death caused very little excitement in Paris. Public gambling-houses had been abolished by the order of the Government long before; and it was no longer a common thing for desperate men to scatter their brains upon the table on which they had just squandered their money; but still people knew very well that there was plenty of card-playing, and dice throwing, and billiard-playing, always going on here and there in the brilliant city, and the suicide of a gambler more or less was not a thing to make any disturbance.

Mrs Bannister wrote a stiffly-worded letter in reply to that in which Richard Thornton told her of her father's death, enclosing an order on Messrs Blount for the sum she considered sufficient to pay for the old man's funeral, and to support Eleanor for a few weeks.

'I should advise her early return to England,' the stockbroker's widow wrote, 'and I will endeavour to find her some decent situation – as nursery governess or milliner's apprentice, perhaps – but she must remember that I expect her to support herself, and that she must not look to me for any further assistance. I have performed my duty to my father at a considerable loss to myself, but with his death all claim upon me ceases.'

George Vane had been buried during the early days of his youngest daughter's illness. They placed him amongst a cluster of neglected graves, in a patch of ground upon the outskirts of Père la Chaise, a burial place for heretics and suicides, and Richard Thornton ordered a roughly-hewn cross from one of the stonemasons near the cemetery. So, far away from the lofty monuments of the Russian princes and the marshals of the First Empire; far away from Abelard and Heloise, and all the marble chapels in which devoted survivors pray for the souls of the beloved dead; in a desolate and unhallowed patch of weedy turf, where the bones of the departed were only suffered to rest peaceably for a given number of years, and were stirred up out of their coffins periodically to make room for new-comers, George Vane slept the last sleep. He might have been buried as a nameless suicide, but for the chance which had taken Richard Thornton to the Morgue, where he recognized Eleanor's father in the unknown man who had been last brought to that gloomy shelter; for he had had no papers which could give any clue to his identity about him at the time of his death.

Upon the morning after that quiet September afternoon on which Eleanor Vane had learned the true story of her father's death, Signora Picirillo for the first time spoke seriously of the future. In the intensity of her first great grief, Eleanor Vane had never once thought of the desolation of her position, nor yet of the sacrifices which the Signora and Richard were making for her sake. She never remembered that they were both lingering in Paris solely on her account: she only knew that they were there, and that she saw them daily, and that the sight of them, good and kind as they were, was pain and weariness to her, like the sight of everything else in the world. She had been singularly quiet since the revelation made to her. After the first burst of passionate vehemence which had succeeded her perusal of her dead father's letter, her manner had grown almost unnaturally calm. She had sat all the evening apart near the window, and Richard had tried in vain to beguile her attention even for a moment. She kept silence, brooding upon the scrap of paper which lay in her bosom.

This morning she sat in a listless attitude, with her head resting on her hand. She took no heed of the Signora's busy movements from room to room. She made no effort to give her old friend any assistance in all the little household arrangements which took so long to complete, and when at last the music-mistress brought her needlework to the window, and sat down opposite the invalid, Eleanor looked up at her with a dull gaze that struck despair to the good creature's heart.

'Nelly, my dear,' the Signora said briskly, 'I want to have a little serious conversation with you.'

'About what, dear Signora?'

'About the future, my love.'

'The future!' Eleanor Vane uttered the word almost as if it had been meaningless to her.

'Yes, my dear. You see even I can talk hopefully of the future, though I am an old woman; but you, who are only fifteen, have a long life before you, and it is time you began to look forward to it.'

'I do look forward,' Eleanor said, with a gloomy expression upon her face. 'I do look forward to the future; and to meeting that man, the man who caused my father's death. How am I to find him, Signora? Help me in that. You have been kind to me in everything else. Only help me to do that, and I will love you better than ever I have loved you yet.'

The Signora shook her head. She was a light-hearted, energetic creature, who had borne very heavy burdens through a long life; but the burdens had not been able to crush her. Perhaps her unselfishness had upheld her throughout all her trials. She had thought and cared so much for other people, that she had had little time left for thinking of herself.

'My dear Eleanor,' she said, gravely; 'this will never do. You must not be influenced by that fatal letter. Your poor father had no right to lay the responsibility of his own act upon another man. If he chose to stake this unfortunate money upon the hazard of a pack of cards, and lost it, he had no right to charge this man with the consequences of his own folly.'

'But the man cheated him!'

'As your father thought. People are very apt to fancy themselves cheated when they lose money.'

'Papa would never have written so positively, if he had not *known* that the man cheated him. Besides, Richard says they were heard at high words; that was no doubt when my poor father accused this wretch of being a cheat. He and his companion were wicked, scheming men, who had good reason to hide their names. They were pitiless wretches, who had no compassion upon the poor old man who trusted them and believed in their honour. Are *you* going to defend them, Signora Picirillo?'

'Defend them, Eleanor? no: they were bad men, I have no doubt. But, my darling child, you must not begin life with hatred and vengeance in your heart.'

'Not hate the man who caused my father's death?' cried Eleanor Vane. 'Do you think I shall ever cease to hate him, Signora? Do you think that I shall ever forget to pray that the day may come when he and I will stand face to face, and that he may be as helpless and as dependent upon my mercy as my father was on his? Heaven help him on that day! But I don't want to talk of this, Signora: what is the use of talking? I may be an old woman, perhaps, before I meet this man; but surely, surely I shall meet him, sooner or later. If I only knew his name – if I only knew his name, I think I could trace him from one end of the earth to the other. Robert Lan—— Lan—— what?'

Her head sank forward on her breast, and her eyes fixed themselves dreamily on the sunlit street below the open window. The French poodle, Fido, lay at her feet, and lifted up his head every now and then to lick her hand. The animal had missed his master, and had wandered about the little rooms, sniffing on the thresholds of closed doors, and moaning dismally for several days after Mr Vane's disappearance.

The Signora sighed as she watched Eleanor. What was she to do with this girl, who had taken a horrible vendetta upon herself at fifteen years of age, and who seemed as gloomily absorbed in her scheme of vengeance as any Corsican chieftain?

'My dear,' the music-mistress said presently, with rather a sharp accent, 'do you know that Richard and I will be compelled to leave Paris to-morrow?'

'Leave Paris to-morrow, Signora!'

'Yes. The Phoenix opens early in October, and our Dick will have all the scenes to paint for the new piece. Besides, there are my pupils; you know, my love, they cannot be kept together for ever unless I go back to them.'

Eleanor Vane looked up with almost a bewildered expression, as if she had been trying to comprehend all that Signora Picirillo had said; then suddenly a light seemed to dawn upon her, and she rose from her chair and flung herself upon a hassock at the feet of her friend.

'Dear Signora,' she said, clasping the music-mistress's hand in both her own, 'how wicked and ungrateful I have been all this time! I forget everything but myself and my own trouble. You came over to Paris on my account. You told me so when I was ill, but I had forgotten, I had forgotten. And Richard has stopped in Paris because of me. Oh! what can I do to repay you both – what can I do?'

Eleanor hid her face upon the Signora's lap, and wept silently. Those tears did her good; they beguiled her for a little while, at least, from the one absorbing thought of her father's melancholy fate.

Signora Picirillo tenderly smoothed the soft ripples of auburn hair lying on her lap.

'My dear Eleanor, shall I tell you what you can do to make us both very happy, and to pay us tenfold for any little sacrifice we may have made on your account?'

'Yes, yes; tell me.'

'You have to choose your pathway in life, Nelly, and to choose it quickly. In all the world you have only your half-sisters and brothers to whom you can appeal for assistance. You have some claim upon them, you know, dear; but I sometimes think you are too proud to avail yourself of that claim.'

Eleanor Vane lifted her head with a gesture of superb defiance.

'I would starve rather than accept a penny from Mrs Bannister, or from her sister or brothers. If they had been different, my father would never have died as he did. He was deserted and abandoned by all the world, except his helpless child, who could do nothing to save him.'

'But if you don't mean to apply to Mrs Bannister, what will you do, Nelly?'

Eleanor Vane shook her head hopelessly. The whole fabric of the future had been shattered by her father's desperate act. The simple dream of a life in which she was to have worked for that beloved father was over, and it seemed to Eleanor as if the future existed no longer; there was only the sad, desolate present, – a dreary spot in the great desert of life, bounded by a yawning grave.

'Why do you ask me what I mean to do, Signora?' she said, piteously. 'How does it matter what I do? Nothing I can do will bring my father back. I will stay in Paris, and get my living how I can, and look for the man who murdered my father.'

'Eleanor,' cried the Signora, 'are you mad? How could you stay in Paris, when you don't know a single creature in the whole city? How, in mercy's name, could you get your living in this strange place?'

'I could be a nursery-governess; or a nursery-maid; anything! What do I care how low I sink, if I can only stay here, where I am likely to meet that man?'

'Eleanor, my dear! For pity's sake do not delude yourself in this manner. The man you want to find is an adventurer, no doubt. In Paris one day, in London another, or away in America perhaps, or at the farthest extremity of the globe. Do you hope to find this man by walking about the streets of Paris?'

'I don't know.'

'How do you expect to meet him?'

'I don't know.'

'But, Eleanor, be reasonable. It is utterly impossible that you can remain in Paris. If Mrs Bannister does not claim the right of exercising some authority over you, I claim it as your oldest friend. My dear, you will not refuse to listen to me, will you?'

'No, no, dear Signora. If you think I mustn't stay in Paris, I'll go back to England, to the Miss Bennetts. They'll give me fifteen pounds a year as junior teacher. I may as well live with them, if I mustn't stay here. I must earn some money, I suppose, before I can even try to find the man who caused my father's death. How long it will be before I can earn anything worth speaking of!'

She sighed wearily, and fell again into a gloomy silence, from which the poodle vainly tried to arouse her by many affectionate devices.

'Then we may consider it settled, Nelly, my dear,' the Signora said, cheerfully. 'You will leave Paris to-morrow morning, with Richard and me. You can stay with us, my dear, till you've made up your mind what to do. We've a little spare room, which is only used now as a receptacle for empty boxes and Richard's painting litter. We'll fit it up for you, my darling, and make you as comfortable as we can.'

'Dear, dear Signora!' said Eleanor, kneeling at her friend's chair. 'How good you are to me! But while I have been ill there must have been a great deal of money spent: for the doctor, and the jelly, and fruit, and lemonade you have given me – who found the money, Signora?'

'Your sister, Mrs Bannister, my dear; she sent some money in answer to a letter from Richard.'

Eleanor's face crimsoned suddenly, and the music-mistress understood the meaning of that angry flush.

'Richard didn't ask for any money, my love. He only wrote to tell your sister what had happened. She sent money for all necessary expenses. It is not all gone yet, Nelly; there will be enough to pay your journey back to England; and even then something left. I have kept an account of all that has been spent, and will give it to you when you like.'

Eleanor looked down at her white morning-gown.

'Is there enough left to buy a black frock?' she asked, in a low voice.

'Yes, my darling. I have thought of that. I have had mourning made for you. The dressmaker took one of your muslin frocks for a pattern, so there was no occasion to trouble you about the business.'

'How good you are to me, how very, very good!'

Eleanor Vane could only say this. As yet she only dimly felt how much she owed to these people, who were bound to her by no tie of relationship, and who yet stepped aside from their own difficult pathway to do her service in her sorrow. She could not learn to cling to them, and depend upon them yet. She had loved them long ago, in her father's lifetime; but now that he was dead, every link that had bound her to life, and love, and happiness, seemed suddenly severed, and she stood alone, groping blindly in the thick darkness of a new and dreary world, with only one light shining far away at the end of a wearisome and obscure pathway; and that a lurid and fatal star, which beckoned her onward to some unknown deed of hate and vengeance.

Heaven knows what vague scheme of retribution she cherished in her childish ignorance of the world. Perhaps she formed her ideas of life from the numerous novels she had read, in which the villain was always confounded in the last chapter, however triumphant he might be through two volumes and three-quarters of successful iniquity.

George Vane's sanguine and romantic visions of wealth and grandeur, of retaliation upon those who had neglected and forgotten him, had not been without effect upon the mind of his youngest daughter. That plastic mind had been entirely in the old man's hands, to mould in what form he pleased. Himself the slave of impulse, it was not to be supposed that he could teach his daughter those sound principles without which man, like a rudderless vessel, floats hither and thither before every current on the sea of life. He suffered Eleanor's impulsive nature to have full sway; he put no curb upon the sanguine temperament which took everything in the extreme. As blindly as the girl loved her father, so blindly she was ready to hate those whom he called his enemies. To investigate the nature of the wrongs they had done him would have been to take their side in the quarrel. Reason and Love could not go hand-in-hand in Eleanor's creed; for the questions which Reason might ask would be so many treacheries against Love.

It is not to be wondered, then, that she held the few broken sentences written by her father on the threshold of a shameful death, as a solemn and sacred trust, not to be violated or lost sight of, though her future life should be sacrificed to the fulfilment of one purpose.

Such thoughts as these – indistinct, ignorant, and childish, perhaps, but not the less absorbing – filled her mind. It may be that this new purpose of revenge enabled her the better to endure her loss. She had something to live for, at least. There was a light far away athwart the long gloomy pathway through an unknown world; and, however lurid that guiding star might be, it was better than total darkness.

CHAPTER X

HORTENSIA BANNISTER HOLDS OUT A HELPING HAND

Signora Picirillo was very well contented with her morning's work. She had obtained Eleanor's consent to a speedy departure from Paris; that was the grand point. Once away from the scene of George Vane's death, the young girl's sunshiny nature would reassert itself, and little by little the great grief would be forgotten.

In all this dreary period of sickness and misery the good music-mistress had grown to love Mr Vane's daughter even more than she had loved her long ago, when Eleanor's childish fingers had first stumbled slowly over the keys of the pianoforte, in a feeble endeavour to master the grand difficulties of Haydn's 'Surprise.'

The widow's life had been a very sorrowful one. Perhaps its most tranquil period had come within the last ten years. It was ten years since, her Italian husband and her children having one by one died, she had found herself alone in the world, with a gaunt, long-legged hobbledehoy of eighteen, her dead sister's orphan son, for her sole protector.

This long-legged hobbledehoy was Richard Thornton, the only child of the Signora's pretty younger sister and a dashing cavalry officer, who had married a penniless and obscure girl for the love of her pretty face, and had died within a couple of years of his marriage, leaving his widow to drag out the remnant of a fretful, helpless life in dependence upon her sister. The Signora had been used to carrying other people's burdens from a very early age. She was the eldest child of a clever violinist, for twenty years leader of the orchestra in one of the principal London theatres; and from babyhood she had been a brave-hearted self-reliant creature. When her sister died, therefore, and, with the last words upon her pale, tremulous lips, prayed the Signora to protect the helpless boy, Richard Thornton, Eliza Picirillo freely accepted the charge, and promised to perform it faithfully. The poor faded beauty died with a smile upon her face, and when Signor Picirillo – who was a teacher of languages at a few suburban schools, and a lazy good-tempered nonentity – came home that evening, he found that there was to be another member of his domestic circle, and another mouth to be fed henceforth.

The Signora's cruse of oil held out bravely, in spite of the demands upon it; and by-and-by, when the honest-hearted music-mistress would otherwise have been terribly desolate, there was Richard, a tall lad, ready to stand by her sturdily in the battle of life, and as devoted to her as the most affectionate of sons. The boy had shown considerable talent at a very early age, but it was a versatile kind of talent, which did not promise ever to burst forth into the grander gift of genius. His aunt taught him music, and he taught himself painting, intending to be something in the way of Maclise or Turner, by-and-by, and scraping together some of the shillings he earned with his violin in order to attend a dingy academy somewhere in Bloomsbury.

But the great historical subjects after Maclise – 'The Death of the Bloody Boar at Bosworth,' a grand battle scene, with a lurid sunset in the background, and Richmond's face and armour all ablaze with crimson,

lake and gamboge, from the flaming reflection of the skies, was the
magnum opus which poor Dick fondly hoped to see in the Royal
Academy – were not very saleable; and the Turneresque landscapes,
nymphs and ruins, dryads and satyrs, dimly visible through yellow mist
and rose-coloured fog, cost a great deal of time and money to produce,
and were not easily convertible into ready cash. So when Richard had
gone the usual weary round amongst the picture-dealers, and had
endured the usual heart-burnings and agonies which wait upon ambitious
youth, he was glad to accept the brush flung aside by a scene-painter at
the Phoenix, where Dick received a scanty salary as second violinist; a
salary which was doubled when the young man practised the double duty
of second violin and assistant scene-painter.

These simple people were the only friends of Eleanor Vane's
childhood. They were ready to accept the responsibility of her future
welfare now, when her rich sister would have sent her into the world,
lonely and helpless, to sink to the abject drudgery which well-to-do
people speak so complacently of, when they recommend their poor
relations to get an honest living and trouble them no longer.

Richard Thornton was enraptured at the idea of taking this beautiful
younger sister home with him, although that idea involved the necessity
of working for her till she was able to do something for herself.

'Nothing could be better for us than all this sad business, aunty,' the
scene-painter said, when he called in the Rue de l'Archevêque, and
found his aunt alone in the little sitting-room. Eleanor was lying down
after the morning's excitement, while her friend packed her slender
wardrobe and made all preparations for departure. 'Nothing could be
better for us,' the young man said. 'Why, Nell's golden hair will light up
the Pilasters with perpetual sunshine, and I shall always have a model for
my subject-pictures. Then what a companion she'll be for you in the
long dreary nights, when I am away at the Phoenix, and how capitally
she'll be able to help you with your pupils; for, of course, she plays and
sings like anything by this time.'

'But she wants to go back to the people at the Brixton school, Dick.'

'But, Lord bless you, aunty, we won't let her go,' cried Mr Thornton;
'we'll make a prima donna or a leading tragedy-actress, or something of
that kind, of her. We'll teach her to make a hundred pounds a week out
of her white arms, and her flashing grey eyes. How beautiful she looked
last night when she was on her knees, vowing vengeance against that
scoundrel who won her father's money. How splendid she looked, with
her yellow hair all streaming over her shoulders, and her eyes flashing
sparks of fire! Wouldn't she bring the house down, if she did that at the
Phoenix? She's a wonderful girl, aunty; the sort of girl to set all London
in a blaze some day, somehow or other. Miss Bennett's and Brixton,

indeed!' cried Richard, snapping his fingers contemptuously; 'you could no more chain that girl down to a governess's drudgery, than you could make a flash of forked lightning do duty for a farthing candle.'

So Eleanor Vane went back to England with her friends. They chose the Dieppe and Newhaven route for its economy; and over the same sunlit landscape upon which she had gazed so rapturously less than a month ago, Eleanor's eyes wandered now wearily and sadly, seeing nothing but desolation wherever they looked. She recognized swelling hills and broad patches of low verdure, winding glimpses of the river, far-away villages glimmering whitely in the distance, and she wondered at the change in herself which made all these things so different to her. What a child she had been a month ago; what a reckless, happy child, looking forward in foolish certainty to a long life with her father; ignorant of all sorrows except the petty troubles she had shared with him; ready to hope for anything in the boundless future; with a whole fairy-land of pleasure and delight spreading out before her eager feet!

Now she was a woman, alone in a horrible desert, over whose dreary sands she must toil slowly to the end she hoped to reach.

She sat back in a corner of the second-class carriage, with her face hidden in a veil, and with the dog Fido curled up in her lap. Her father had been fond of the faithful creature, she remembered.

It was early in the grey bleakness of a September morning when the cab, carrying Eleanor and her friends, rattled under an archway leading out of Dudley Street, Bloomsbury, into the queer little retreat called the Pilasters. The grooms were already at work in the mews, and the neighbourhood was enlivened by that hissing noise with which horses are generally beguiled during the trials of the equine toilet. The chimney-sweep had left his abode and was whooping dismally in Northumberland Square. Life began early in the Pilasters, and already the inmates of many houses were astir, and the sharp voices of mothers clamoured denunciations on the elder daughters who acted as unsalaried nursemaids to the younger branches of the family.

The place popularly known as the Pilasters is one of the queerest nooks in London. It consists of a row of tumble-down houses, fronted by a dilapidated colonnade, and filled with busy life from cellar to attic. But I do not believe that the inhabitants of the Pilasters are guilty of nefarious practices, or that vice and crime find a hiding-place in the cellars below the colonnade. The retreat stands by itself, hidden between two highly respectable middle-class streets, whose inhabitants would scarcely tolerate Alsatian habits or Field Lane proclivities in their near neighbours. Small tradesmen find a home in the Pilasters, and emerge thence to work for the best families in Dudley Street and 'the Squares.'

Here, amongst small tailors and mantua-makers, cheap eating-houses, shabby beer-shops, chimney-sweeps and mangles, Signora Picirillo had taken up her abode, bringing her faded goods and chattels, the remnants of brighter times, to furnish the first-floor over a shoemaker's shop. I am afraid the shoemaker was oftener employed in mending old shoes than in making new ones, but the Signora was fain to ignore that fact, and to be contented with her good fortune in having found a very cheap lodging in a central neighbourhood.

This was a shabbier place than any that Eleanor Vane had ever lived in, but she showed no distaste for its simple arrangements. The Signora's hopes were realized by-and-by. At first the girl sat all day in a despondent attitude, with the French poodle in her lap, her head drooping on her breast, her eyes fixed on vacancy, her whole manner giving evidence of an all-absorbing grief which was nearly akin to despair. She went to Brixton very soon after her return to England; but here a cruel disappointment awaited her. The Misses Bennett heard her sorrowful story with pitiful murmurs of regret and compassion; but they had engaged a young person as junior teacher, and could do nothing to help her. She returned to the Pilasters, looking the image of pale despair; but the Signora and Richard both declared to her that nothing could be happier for them than her consenting to remain with them.

So it seemed very much as if the Pilasters was to be Eleanor Vane's permanent abode. The neighbours had stared at her a great deal at first, admiring her pale face and flowing hair, and pitying her because of her black frock; but they were familiar with her now, and gave her a good day in a friendly manner as she passed under the shadow of the colonnade on her way out or in.

Little by little the air of dull despondency gave way before this young woman's earnest desire to be of use to the people who were so kind to her. She played remarkably well, for she had had plenty of the drudgery of pianoforte-playing at the Brixton school, and she was able to take some of the Signora's pupils off her hands. She sang, too, in a rich contralto, which promised to be powerful and beautiful by-and-by; and she practised the ballads in the old operas which the Signora kept, neatly bound, but yellow with age, in her feeble music-stand.

As her friends had hoped, her sunshiny nature reasserted itself. The outer evidence of her great sorrow gradually passed away, though the memory of her loss still filled her mind; the image of her father, and the thought of that father's unhappy death, were still for ever present with her. It was not in her nature to be long reserved or unsocial; and by-and-by, when she had been nearly six months in her new home, and the London sparrows were chirping in the bright spring sunshine about the mews and under the colonnade, Miss Vane began to sing at her work as she flitted to and fro in the low rooms, dusting the grand pianoforte and the old china – touching up the frame of Richard's unsaleable picture, the flaring battle of Bosworth, which illuminated one side of the room. Wherever she went the faithful French poodle ran frisking by her side; whatever sunshine could find its way into the dusky London chamber seemed to concentrate itself about her golden head. Gaiety, life, and brightness went with her up and down the dark staircase – in and out of the dingy rooms. Her youth and beauty turned the shabby lodgings into a fairy palace, as it seemed to Richard and his aunt. When she sat down and ran her agile fingers over the piano, dashing into fantasias and scenas, sparkling and rippling with joyous treble meanderings among the upper notes, the old Clementi grew young again beneath her touch, the worn-out strings were revivified by the wondrous magnetism of her youth and vitality. The flute-like treble trills and triplets seemed like the joyous chirpings of a hundred birds. The music-mistress and the scene-painter used to sit and watch her as she played; their admiring eyes followed her as she flitted to and fro, and they wondered at her grace and beauty.

She had her father's aristocratic elegance, her father's power of fascination. All the dangerous gifts which had been so fatal to George Vane, were inherited by his youngest daughter. Like him, a creature of impulse, spontaneous, sanguine, volatile, she influenced other people by the force of her own superabundant vitality. In her bright hopefulness she made an atmosphere of hope in which other people grew hopeful. The dullest rejoiced in her joyous vivacity, her unconscious loveliness. Yes, perhaps Eleanor Vane's greatest charm lay in her utter ignorance of the fact that she was charming. In the three years' drudgery of a boarding-school she had never learned the power of her own fascination. She knew that people loved her, and she was grateful to them for their affection; but she had never discovered that it was by some wondrous magnetic attraction inherent in herself that she obtained so much love and devotion.

Nobody had ever taken the trouble to tell her that she was beautiful. She had generally worn shabby frocks, and the rippling golden hair had not very often been smooth; so perhaps the school-girls at Brixton scarcely knew how lovely their companion was. The delicate aquiline profile, the flashing grey eyes, pale face, red lips, and amber hair, were counterbalanced by the silk dresses and lace furbelows of young ladies, whose wealthy fathers paid full price for their eduction. Poverty learns its place in the little world of a young ladies' boarding-school quite as surely as in the larger world beyond the garden wall which bounds that establishment. But Eleanor had held her own at the Misses Bennett's seminary, by some mysterious power against which her richer companions had in vain rebelled. Her frank acknowledgement of her poverty, coupled with the fact of her father's former wealth and grandeur, perhaps enabled her to do this. If she wore shabby frocks, she looked more aristocratic in her shabbiness than the other young ladies in their stiff silks and prim finery. They recognized this fact, they acknowledged something in their playfellow which lifted her above themselves, and the half-boarder dealt out patronage and regal condescensions to the most remunerative pupils in the school. She reigned by reason of her unacknowledged beauty, and that divine something, dimly recognized by all about her, but as yet wholly undeveloped. The school-girl was clever, brilliant, fascinating, but it was yet to be discovered what the woman would be. It was yet to be discovered whether these budding qualities would develop into the many flowers of a bright and versatile mind, or burst forth suddenly and mysteriously into that rare tropical blossom, that mental once-in-a-century-flourishing aloe, which men call Genius. The good music-mistress watched her young protégée with love and wonder, not unalloyed by fear. What was she to do with this strange and beautiful bird which she had brought home to her nest? Would it be right to fetter this bright spirit for ever? Was it fair to immure all this joyous loveliness in that shabby lodging; to stifle such superabundant vitality in the close atmosphere of a dull and monotonous existence?

The faithful creature had been accustomed to consider others, and she thought of this seriously and constantly. Eleanor was contented and happy. She was earning money now by giving lessons here and there, and she contributed to the family purse. The days slipped by very rapidly, as it seemed, in that peaceful monotony. Miss Vane's frocks appeared to grow shorter and shorter as the young lady sprang up into bright womanhood. She was nearly seventeen now, and had been more than a year and a half living under the shadow of the Bloomsbury Pilasters. Richard and his aunt consulted together as to what her future life ought to be; but they never came nearer to any conclusion.

'It's all very well to talk of her going away from us, you know, aunty,' the scene-painter said; 'but what are we to do without her? All the sunshine and poetry of our lives will go away with her when she leaves us! Besides! what is she to be? A governess? Bah! who would doom her to that lady-like drudgery? An actress? No, aunty carissima, I should never like to see that bright young beauty behind the glare of the foot-lights. I think I'd rather she should live here for ever and ever, than that her nature should ever be vulgarized by contact with the world. Let us keep her, aunty; she doesn't want to leave us. Those who have any actual claim upon her have abandoned her. She came across my pathway like some wandering homeless angel. I shall never forget her face when I first saw it on the lamplit boulevard, and recognized the little girl I had known three years before in the fair-haired young beauty of fifteen. She doesn't want to go away. Why should you talk of her leaving us, aunty dear?'

Signora Picirillo shrugged her shoulders with a sigh.

'Heaven knows I have no wish to part with her, Dick,' she said; 'but we ought to do what's right for her sake. This is no place for George Vane's daughter.'

But while the music-mistress and her nephew were speculating and theorizing upon the future of their protégée, practical Mrs Bannister was contemplating the infliction of a death-blow which was to shatter the happiness of the humble Bloomsbury circle with one merciless stroke. Early in the bleak March of 1855, Eleanor received a coldly-worded epistle from her half-sister, to the effect that an opportunity had now arisen for her advancement in life; and that if she wished ever to attain a *respectable* position – the adjective was mercilessly underlined – she would do well to avail herself of it. For further information and advice she was to call early the next morning in Hyde Park Gardens. Miss Vane would fain have left this letter unanswered, and at first stoutly refused to obey Mrs Bannister's summons.

'What do I want with her condescension and patronage?' she said, indignantly. 'Does she think that I forget the cruel letter she wrote to my father; or that I forgive her for its heartless insolence? Let her keep her favours for those who solicit them. I want nothing from her. I only want to be left in peace with the friends I love. Do you wish to get rid of me, Signora, that you persuade me to dance attendance upon Mrs Bannister?'

It was very hard for poor Signora Picirillo to be compelled to urge the child's acceptance of the hand so coldly extended to her, but the good creature felt that it was her duty to do so, and Miss Vane loved her protectress far too dearly to persist in opposing her. She went, therefore, early the next morning to her half-sister's house at Bayswater, where the spacious rooms seemed doubly spacious when compared with the little sitting-room over the colonnade, the sitting-room which was more than half filled by Clementi's old-fashioned piano. Here the gorgeous Erard's grand, in a case of carved walnut wood and ebony, and with all manner of newfangled improvements, was only an oasis upon the great desert of velvet piles.

Hortensia Bannister was pleased to be very gracious to her half-sister. Perhaps she was all the more so because Eleanor made no pretence of affection for her. This cold, hard-natured woman would have been suspicious of mercenary motives lurking beneath any demonstration of sisterly love.

'I am glad to hear you have been learning to get your own living, Eleanor,' she said, 'and above all, that you have been cultivating your talent for the piano. I have not forgotten you, you will find. The people

with whom you have been living sent me their address when they
brought you from Paris, and I knew where to find you when any
opportunity should present itself for your advancement. This opportunity
has now presented itself. My old acquaintance, Mrs Darrell, the niece of
your father's friend, Maurice de Crespigny, who is still living, though
very old and infirm, has written to me saying that she requires a young
person who would act as companion and musical governess to a lady
who lives with her. This young lady is no relation of Mrs Darrell's, but is
a kind of ward or pupil, I believe. Your youth, in this instance, Eleanor,
happens to be an advantage, as the young lady requires a companion of
her own age. You will receive a moderate salary, and will be treated as a
member of the family. Let me hear you play, by the bye, in order that I
may be able to speak positively as to your qualifications.'

Eleanor Vane sat down to the piano. The strings of the Erard vibrated
under her touch. She was almost frightened at the grand tones that came
out of the instrument as she dashed over the keys. She played very
brilliantly, however, and her sister condescended to say so.

'I think I may conscientiously give a good account of your playing,' she
said. 'You sing, I suppose?'

'Oh, yes.'

'Very well, then; I think you may consider the engagement a settled
thing. There is only one question to arrange. Of course you must be
aware that the position which your father occupied was once a very
elevated one. Mrs Darrell and her sisters knew your father in his most
prosperous days, and lost sight of him before he became poor. They
know nothing of his second marriage, or of your birth. His most intimate
friend was Mr de Crespigny, the uncle of the lady whose house I wish
you to enter. Under these circumstances you cannot wonder when I tell
you that I should strongly object to Mrs Darrell's knowing who you
really are.'

'How do you mean, Hortensia?'

'I mean that I shall recommend you as a young person in whose career
I feel interested. If you go to Hazlewood at all, you must go under an
assumed name.'

'Hortensia!'

'Well!' cried Mrs Bannister, lifting her handsome black eyebrows.

'I don't want this situation, and I should hate to take a false name. I
would rather stay with my friends, please. I love them very dearly, and am
very happy with them.'

'Good Heavens!' exclaimed Mrs Bannister, 'what is the use of trying to
do some people a service? Here have I been scheming as to how I could
manage to avail myself of this chance, and now this ungrateful girl turns
round and tells me she doesn't want the situation. Do you know what

you are refusing, Eleanor Vane? Have you learnt your father's habit of pauperism, that you prefer to be a burden upon this penniless music-teacher and her son, or nephew, or whatever he is, rather than make an honest effort to get your own living?'

Eleanor started up from the piano: she had been sitting before it until now, softly fingering the keys, and admiring the beauty of the tones. She started up, looking at her sister, and blushing indignantly to the very roots of her auburn hair.

Could this be true? Could she be indeed a burden to the friends she loved so dearly?

'If you think that, Hortensia,' she said, 'if you think I am any burden to the dear Signora, or Richard, I will take any situation you like, however hard. I'll toil night and day, and work my fingers to the bone, rather than be a trouble or a burden to them any longer.'

She remembered how little she earned by her few pupils. Yes, Hortensia was no doubt right. She was a burden to those good people who had taken her to their home in her hour of desolation and misery.

'I'll take the situation, Hortensia,' she cried. 'I'll take a false name. I'll do anything in the world rather than impose upon the goodness of my friends.'

'Very well,' answered Mrs Bannister, coldly. 'Pray do not let us have any heroics about it. The situation is a very good one, I can assure you; and there are many girls who would be glad to snap at such a chance. I will write to my friend, Mrs Darrell, and recommend you to her notice. I can do no more. I cannot, of course, ensure your success; but Ellen Darrell and I were great friends some years since, and I know that I have considerable influence with her. I'll write and tell you the result of my recommendation.'

Eleanor left Hyde Park Gardens after taking two or three sips of some pale sherry which her half-sister gave her. The wine seemed of a sorry vintage, and tasted very much as if the grapes of which it was made had never seen the sun. Miss Vane was glad to set down her wine–glass and escape from the cold splendour of her half-sister's drawing-room.

She walked slowly and sorrowfully back to Bloomsbury. She was to leave her dear friends there – leave the shabby rooms in which she had been so happy, and to go out into the bleak world a dependant upon grand people, so low and humiliated that even her own name must be abandoned by her before she could enter upon the state of dependence. The Bohemian sociality of the Pilasters was to be exchanged for the dreary splendour of a household in which she was to be something a little above the servants.

But it would be cowardly and selfish to refuse this situation, for no doubt cruel Mrs Bannister had spoken the truth. Eleanor began to think that she had been a burden upon her poor friends.

She was very gloomy and despondent, brooding upon these things; but through every gloomy thought of the present a darker image loomed, far away in the black future. This was the image of her vengeance, the vague and uncertain shadow that had filled her girlish dreams ever since the great sorrow of her father's death had fallen upon her.

'If I go to Hazlewood,' she thought, 'if I spend my life at Mrs Darrell's, how can I ever hope to find the murderer of my father?'

CHAPTER XI

RICHARD THORNTON'S PROMISE

Eleanor Vane looked very sadly at all the common everyday sights connected with the domestic economy of the Pilasters, when she went back to Bloomsbury after her interview with Mrs Bannister. She had only lived a year and a half in that humble locality, but it was in her nature to become quickly attached to places as well as persons, and she had grown very fond of the Pilasters. Everybody about the place knew her and loved her. The horses looked out of their open stable-doors as she passed; the dogs came tumbling from their kennels, dragging half-a-dozen yards of rusty iron chain and a heap of straw at their heels, to greet her as she went by; the chimney-sweeps' children courted her notice; and at all the little shops where she had been wont to give orders and pay bills for the Signora, the simple tradespeople tendered her their admiration and homage. Her beauty was a pride to the worthy citizens of the Pilasters. Could all Bloomsbury, from Dudley Street to the Squares, produce sunnier golden hair, or brighter grey eyes than were to be seen under the shadow of the dilapidated colonnade when Eleanor Vane went by?

In this atmosphere of love and admiration, the girl had been very happy. She had one of those natures in which there lies a wondrous power of assimilation with the manners and habits of others. She was never out of place; she was never in the way. She was not ambitious. Her sunny temperament was the centre of perpetual peace and happiness, only to be disturbed by very terrible thunderclaps of sorrow. She had been very happy with the Signora; and to-day she looked sadly round the little sitting-room, her eyes resting now on the old piano, now on a shelf of tattered books – romances dear to Richard and herself, and not too well treated by either – now on the young man's flaming *magnum opus*, the picture she had loved to criticise and abuse in mischievous enjoyment of the painter's anguish. As she looked at these things, and remembered how soon she must go away from them, the

slow tears trickled down her cheeks, and she stood despondent on the
gloomy threshold of her new life.

She had found the familiar rooms empty upon her return from
Bayswater, for the Signora was away teaching beyond the regions of the
New Road, and Richard was hard at work at the Phoenix, where there
were always new pieces to be produced and new scenes to be painted.
Eleanor had the little sitting-room all to herself; she took off her bonnet
and sat down upon the old-fashioned chintz-covered sofa. She buried her
head in the cushions and tried to think.

The prospect of a new existence, which would have been delightful to
most girls of her age, was utterly distasteful to her. Her nature was
adhesive; she would have gone to the farthest end of the world with her
father, if he had lived, or with Richard and the Signora, whom she loved
only less than she had loved him. But to sever every tie, and go out alone
into the world, with nothing between her and desolation, was
unspeakably terrible to this affectionate, impulsive girl.

If it had been simply a question of her own advantage, if by the
sacrifice of her own advancement, her every prospect in life, she might
have stayed with the friends she loved, she would not have hesitated for a
moment. But it was not so. Mrs Bannister had clearly told her that she
was a burden upon these generous people, who had sheltered and
succoured her in her hour of misery. The cruel word pauperism had been
flung in her teeth, and with a racking brain this poor girl set herself to
calculate how much her maintenance cost her friends, and how much she
was able to contribute out of her own pitiful earnings.

Alas! the balance told against her when the sum was done. Her
earnings were very, very small as yet, not because her talent was
unappreciated, but because her pupils were poor; and a music-mistress
whose address was Bloomsbury Pilasters could scarcely demand high
payment for her services, or hope to obtain a very aristocratic
connection.

No; Mrs Bannister – stern, uncompromising, and disagreeable as the
truth itself – had no doubt been right. Her duty lay before her, plainly
indicated by that unpleasant monitor. She was bound to leave these dear
friends, and to go out into the world to fight a lonely battle for herself.

'I may be able to do something for them,' she thought; and this
thought was the only gleam of light which illumined the darkness of her
sorrow. 'I may be able to save money enough to buy the Signora a black
silk dress, and Richard a meerschaum. I should so like to buy Dick a
meerschaum; I know the one he'd like – a bull-dog's head, with a silver
collar around the neck. We looked at it one night at a shop in Holborn.'

She rose from the sofa at last with an aching heart and troubled brain,
when the early shadows of the spring twilight were gathering in the

room. She made up the fire and swept the hearth, and arranged the tea-things on the comfortable round table, and then sat down on a low stool by the fender to toast great rounds of bread, which would be as nothing in comparison to Richard's all-devouring capacity after a hard day's work in the scene-room at the Phoenix. How pleasant it was to perform all these little familiar offices of love and duty! How sorrowfully she looked back to her simple, free-and-easy life, now that she was to go amongst strangers who would exact all manner of ceremonious observances from her! The Bohemianism of her existence had been its greatest charm; and this poor benighted girl trembled at the prospect of a life in which she would have to go through all those terrible performances which she had read of, fearfully and wonderingly, in certain erudite essays upon Etiquette, but which had never yet come within the range of her experiences.

'It is my duty to go away from them,' she kept saying to herself; 'it is my duty to go away.'

She had schooled herself in this difficult duty by the time her friends came home, and she told them very quietly that she had seen Mrs Bannister, and had agreed to accept her patronage and services.

'I am going to be a sort of companion or musical governess – I scarcely know which – to a young lady at a country house called Hazlewood,' she said. 'Don't think I am not sorry to leave you, dear Signora, but Hortensia says it is better that I should do so.'

'And don't think that I am not sorry to lose you, Nelly, when I tell you that I think your sister is right,' the Signora answered gently, as she kissed her protégée.

Perhaps Eleanor was a little disappointed at this reply. She little dreamed how often Eliza Picirillo had struggled against the selfishness of her affection before she had grown thus resigned to this parting.

Mr Richard Thornton groaned aloud.

'I shall go out and pull down a couple of the Pilasters, and bury myself under them, à la Samson,' he said, piteously. 'What is to become of us without you, Eleanor? Who will come over to the Phoenix, and applaud my great scenes with the ferule of an umbrella? Who'll cut up half-quartern loaves into toast when I am hungry, or have Welsh rarebits in readiness on the hob when I come home late at night? Who'll play Mendelssohn's 'Songs without Words' to me, and darn my stockings, and sew buttons – absurd institutions, invented by ignorant people, who have never known the blessing of pins – upon my shirts? Who'll abuse me when I go unshaven, or recommend blacking as an embellishment for my boots? Who'll career in and out of the room with a dirty white French poodle at her heels, looking like a fair-haired Esmeralda with a curly-coated goat? What are we to do without you, Eleanor?'

There was a sharp pain at poor Dick's heart as he apostrophized his adopted sister. Were his feelings quite brotherly? Was there no twinge of the fatal torture so common to mankind mingled with this young man's feelings as he looked at the beautiful face opposite to him, and remembered how soon it would have vanished from that shabby chamber, leaving only dismal emptiness behind?

The Signora looked at her nephew and sighed. Yes, it was far better that Eleanor should go away. She could never have grown to love this honest-hearted, candid, slovenly scene-painter, whose coat was a perfect landscape in distemper by reason of the many-coloured splashes which adorned it.

'My poor Dick would have fallen in love with her, and would have broken his good honest heart,' Eliza Picirillo said. 'I'm very glad she's going away.'

So from the road which Destiny had appointed for her to tread, there was not one voice to call Eleanor Vane aside. The affectionate and the indifferent alike conspired to urge her onward. It was only her own inclination that would have held her back.

'If I could have stayed in London,' she thought, 'there might have been some chance of my meeting that man. All scamps and villains come to hide themselves in London. But in a quiet country village I shall be buried alive. When I pass the threshold of Mrs Darrell's house, I bid good-bye to the hope of crossing that man's pathway.'

The letter came very quickly from Mrs Bannister. Mrs Darrell had accepted her dear friend's recommendation, and was ready to receive Miss Vincent. It was under this name the stockbroker's widow had introduced her half-sister to the notice of her friend.

'You will receive a salary of thirty pounds a year,' Hortensia Bannister wrote, 'and your duties will be very light. Do not forget that your name at Hazlewood is to be Vincent, and that you are carefully to avoid all reference to your father. You will be amongst people who knew him well, and must therefore be on your guard. I have described you as the orphan daughter of a gentleman who died in reduced circumstances, and have thus strictly adhered to the truth. No questions will be asked of you, as Mrs Darrell is satisfied with my recommendation, and is too well bred to feel any vulgar curiosity as to your past history. I send you, per parcel delivery, a box of dresses and other wearing apparel, which will be of use to you. I also send you five pounds for such little extra expenditure as may be necessary. Hazlewood is thirty miles from London, and about seven from Windsor. You will go down by the Great Western, and stop at Slough, where a conveyance will meet you; but I will write further upon this matter before you go. Mrs Darrell has kindly accorded you a fortnight's delay for such preparations as you may require to make. You will be expected at Hazlewood on the 6th of April.

'I have only one other remark to make. I know that your father cherished a foolish notion upon the subject of the Woodlands property. Pray bear in mind that no such idea has ever been entertained by me. I know the Darrell family quite well enough to feel assured that they will take care of their own rights, which I am content to acknowledge. Remember, therefore, that I have no wish or expectation with regard to Maurice de Crespigny's will; but it is, on the other hand, perfectly true, that in his youth he did make a solemn promise that, in the event of his dying a bachelor, he would leave that money to my father or his heirs.'

Eleanor Vane took very little notice of this final paragraph in her sister's letter. Who cared for Maurice de Crespigny's fortune? What was the good of it *now*? It could not bring her father back to life; it could not blot out that quiet, unwitnessed death-scene in the Parisian café; it could not rehabilitate the broken name, or restore the shattered life. What could it matter who inherited the useless dross?

The fortnight passed in a feverish unsatisfactory manner. Richard and the Signora took care to conceal the poignancy of their regret at parting with the girl who had brought such new brightness into their narrow lives. Eleanor wept by stealth; dropping many bitter tears over her work, as she remodelled Mrs Bannister's silk dresses, reducing those garments to the dimensions of her own girlish figure. The last night came by-and-by, the night of the 5th of April, the eve of a sorrowful parting, and the beginning of a new existence.

It happened to be a Sunday evening, and Eleanor and Richard walked out together in the quiet Bloomsbury streets while the bells were ringing for evening service, and the lamps glimmering dimly from the church windows. They chose the loneliest streets in the old-fashioned middle-class quarter. Eleanor was very pale, very silent. This evening walk had been her express desire, and Richard watched her wonderingly. Her face had an expression which he remembered in the Rue de l'Archevêque, when he had told her the story of her father's death – an unnaturally rigid look, strangely opposed to the changeful brightness common to that youthful countenance.

They had strolled slowly hither and thither in the deserted streets for some time. The bells had ceased ringing, and the church-goers had all disappeared. The grey twilight was stealing into the streets and squares, and the lights began to shine out from the lower windows.

'How quiet you are, Nelly,' Richard said at last; 'why were you so anxious that we should come out together alone, my dear? I fancied you had something particular to say to me.'

'I have something particular to say.'

'What about?' asked Mr Thornton.

He looked thoughtfully at his companion. He could only see her profile — that clearly-defined, almost classical outline — for she had not turned towards him when she spoke. Her grey eyes looked straight before her into empty space, and her lips were tightly compressed.

'You love me, don't you, Richard?' she asked presently, with a suddenness that startled the scene-painter.

Poor Dick blushed crimson at that alarming inquiry. How could she be so cruel as to ask him such a question? For the last fortnight he had been fighting with himself — sturdily and honestly — in the heroic desire to put away this one fatal thought from his mind; and now the girl for whose sake he had been doing battle with his own selfishness, struck the tenderest of all chords with her ignorant hand, and wounded her victim to the very quick.

But Miss Vane had no consciousness of the mischief she had done. Coquetry was an unknown science to this girl of seventeen. In all matters connected with that womanly accomplishment she was as much a child, now that her seventeenth birthday was past, as she had been in the old days at Chelsea when she had upset Richard's colour-boxes and made grotesque copies of his paintings.

'I know you love me, Dick,' she continued, 'quite as much as if I were your real sister, instead of a poor desolate girl who flung herself upon you and yours in the day of her affliction. I know you love me, Dick, and would do almost anything for my sake, and I wanted to speak to you to-night alone, because I am going to say something that would distress the dear Signora, if she were to hear it.'

'What is it, my dear?'

'You remember the story of my father's death?'

'Only too well, Eleanor.'

'And you remember the vow I made when you told me that story, Richard?'

The young man hesitated.

'Yes, I do remember, Nelly,' he said, after a pause; 'but I had hoped that you had forgotten that foolish vow. For it was foolish, you know, my dear, as well as unwomanly,' the young man added, gravely.

Eleanor's eyes flashed defiance upon her friend, as she turned to him for the first time that evening.

'Yes,' she cried, 'you thought that I had forgotten, because I was not always talking of that man who caused my father's death! You thought my sorrow for my father was only childish grief, that was to be forgotten when I turned my back upon the country where he lies in his abandoned grave — his unconsecrated grave! You thought that nobody would ever try to avenge the poor, lonely old man's murder — for it was a murder, Richard Thornton! What did the wretch who robbed him care for the anguish of the heart he broke? What did he care what became of his victim? It was as base and cruel a murder as was ever done upon this earth, Richard, though the world would not call it by that name.'

'Eleanor, my dear Eleanor! why do you talk of these things!'

The girl's voice had risen with the vehemence of her passion, and Richard Thornton dreaded the effect which this kind of conversation might have upon her excitable nature.

'Nelly, my dear,' he said, 'it would be better to forget all this. What good can you do by cherishing these painful recollections? You are never likely to meet this man; you do not even know his name. He was a scamp and an adventurer, no doubt; he may be dead by this time. He may have done something to bring himself within the power of the law, and he may be in prison, or transported?'

'He may have done something to bring himself within the power of the law,' repeated Eleanor. 'What do you mean?'

'I mean that he may have committed some crime for which he could be punished.'

'Could he be punished by the law for having cheated my father at cards?'

'That sort of charge is always difficult to be proved, Nell; impossible to be proved after the fact. No, I'm afraid the law could never touch him for that.'

'But if he were to commit some other crime, he might be punished?'

'Of course.'

'If I met him, Richard,' cried Eleanor Vane, with a dangerous light kindling in her eyes, 'I would try and lure him on to commit some crime, and then turn round upon him and say, "The law of the land could not avenge my father's death, but it can punish you for a lesser crime. I have twisted the law to my own purpose, and made it redress my father's wrongs."'

Richard Thornton started aghast at his companion.

'Why, Eleanor,' he exclaimed, 'you talk like a Red Indian! This is quite shocking! You frighten me, really; you do, indeed.'

'I am sorry for that, Richard,' Miss Vane answered, meekly. She was a child in all things which concerned her affections alone. 'I wouldn't grieve you or the dear Signora for the world. But there are some things that are stronger than ourselves, Richard; and the oath that I took a year and a half ago, in the Rue de l'Archevêque, is one of those things. I have never forgotten, Dick. Night after night – though I've been happy and light-hearted enough in the day, for I could not be otherwise than happy with you and the Signora – night after night I have lain awake thinking of my father's death. If that death had been a common one; if he had died in my arms at the will of God, instead of by the cruelty of a wretch, my grief might have worn itself out by this time. But as it is, I cannot forget – I cannot forgive. If all the Christian people in the world were to talk to me, I could never have one merciful feeling towards this man. If he were going to be hung to-morrow, I should be glad, and could walk barefoot to the place of his execution to see him suffer. There is no treachery that I should think base if employed against him. There is no slow torture I could inflict upon him that would seem cruel enough to satisfy my hatred of him. Think what a helpless old man my father was; a broken-down gentleman; the sort of man whom everybody pities, whom everybody respects. Remember this; and then remember the cold-blooded deliberation of the wretch who cheated him out of the money which was more than money to him – which represented honour – honesty – his child's future – all he valued. Remember the remorseless cruelty of the wretch who looked on while this helpless old man suffered a slow agony of six or seven hours' duration, and then left him alone in his despair. Think of this, Richard Thornton, and don't wonder any longer if my feelings towards this man are not *Christian-like*.'

'My dear Eleanor, if I regret the vehemence of your feeling upon this subject, I do not defend the man whose treachery hurried your father to his unhappy death; I only wish to convince you of the folly you commit in cherishing these ideas of vengeance and retribution. Life is not a three-volume novel or a five-act play, you know, Nelly. The sudden meetings and strange coincidences common in novels are not very general in our everyday existence. It is not at all likely that in the whole course of your life you will ever again encounter this man. From the moment of your father's death all clue to him was lost; for it was only your father who could have told us who and what he was, or, at least, who and what he represented himself to be. He is lost in the vast chaos of humanity now, my dear, and you have not the frailest clue by which you might hope to find him. For Heaven's sake, then, abandon all thought of an impossible revenge! Have you forgotten the words we heard in the Epistle a few weeks ago – "Vengeance is mine, I will repay, saith the Lord"? If the melodramatic revenge of the stage is not practicable in real life, we know at least, my dear – for you see we have it from very high authority – that wicked deeds do not go unpunished. Far away at the remotest limits of the earth, this man, whom your puny efforts would be powerless to injure, may suffer for his crime. Try and think of this, Eleanor.'

'*I cannot*,' answered the girl. 'The letter which my father wrote before he died was a direct charge which I will never disobey. The only inheritance I received from him was that letter – that letter in which he told me to avenge his death. I dare say you think me mad as well as wicked, Richard; but, in spite of all you have said, *I believe that I shall meet that man!*'

The scene-painter sighed and relapsed into despondent silence. How could he argue with this girl? What could he do but love and admire her, and entrust himself to her direction if she had need of a slave? While he was thinking this, Eleanor clasped both her hands upon his arm and looked up earnestly in his face.

'Richard,' she said, in a low voice, 'I think you would serve me if you had the power.'

'I would go through fire and water to do so, Nelly.'

'I want you to help me in this matter. You know as little of this man as I do, but you are much cleverer than me. You mix with other people and see something of the world; not much, I know, but still a great deal more than I do. I am going away into a quiet country place, where there is no possible chance of meeting this man; you will stay in London———'

'Where I may brush against him in the streets any day, Nell, without being a shade the wiser as to his identity. My dear child, for any practical purpose you will be as near the man in Berkshire as I shall be in Bloomsbury. Don't let's talk of him any longer, Nelly. I can't tell you how this subject distresses me.'

'I won't leave off talking of him,' said the young lady, resolutely, 'until you have made me a promise.'

'What promise?'

'That if ever you do come across any clue which may lead to the identification of the man I want to find, you will follow it up, patiently and faithfully, sparing neither trouble nor cost. For my sake, Richard, for my sake, will you promise?'

'I will, my dear,' Mr Thornton answered. 'I do promise, and I will keep my promise honestly if ever the chance of doing so should come to me. But I must tell you frankly, Nell, I don't believe it ever will.'

'Bless you for the promise, notwithstanding, Richard,' Eleanor said, warmly. 'It has made me much happier. There will be two people henceforth, instead of one, set against this man.'

A dark frown overshadowed her face. It seemed as if she had uttered those last few words in the form of a threat and a defiance, which the man, whoever he was, and wherever he was, might hear.

'You know all the strange things they say now about second-sight, clairvoyance, odic force, magnetic attraction – all sorts of long words whose meaning I don't understand, Richard. I wonder sometimes if this man *knows* that I hate him, and that I am watching for him, thinking of him, praying to meet him day and night. Perhaps he does know this, and will hold himself on his guard against me, and try and avoid me.'

Richard shrank from entering upon this subject; the conversation had been altogether disagreeable to him. There was a horrible discrepancy between this girl's innocent youthful beauty and all this determined talk of fierce and eager vengeance, which would have been more natural to a Highland or Corsican chieftain than to a young lady of seventeen.

It was dark now, and they went back to the Pilasters, where Eliza Picirillo was spending that last night very mournfully. The shabby room was only illuminated by the glimmer of a low fire, for the Signora had not cared to light the candles until her two children came home. She had been sitting by the dingy window watching for their return, and had fallen asleep in the darkness.

There is no need to dwell upon that last night. It was like the eves of all partings, very sad, very uncomfortable. Everything was disorganized by that approaching sorrow. Conversation was desultory and forced, and Richard was glad to be employed in cording Eleanor's boxes. She had two trunks now, and had a wardrobe that seemed to her magnificent, so liberally had Mrs Bannister bestowed her cast-off dresses upon her half-sister.

So the last night passed away, the April morning came, and Eleanor's new life began.

CHAPTER XII

GILBERT MONCKTON

Eleanor Vane was not to go down to Berkshire alone. The beginning of her new life, that terrible beginning which she so much dreaded, was to make her acquainted with new people.

She had received the following communication from Mrs Darrell: —

'Hazlewood, April 3rd, 1855.
'Madame,
As it would of course be very improper for a young lady of your age to travel alone, I have provided against that contingency.

'My friend Mr Monckton has kindly promised to meet you in the first-class waiting-room at the Great Western Station, at three o'clock on Monday afternoon. He will drive you here on his way home.

'I am, Madam,
'Yours faithfully,
'ELLEN DARRELL.'

Eliza Picirillo worked harder upon a Monday than on any other day in the week. She left the Pilasters immediately after an early breakfast, to go upon a wearisome round amongst her pupils. Richard was in the thick of the preparations for a new piece, so poor Eleanor was obliged to go alone to the station, to meet the stranger who had been appointed as her escort to Hazlewood.

She quite broke down when the time came for bidding farewell to her old friend. She clung about the Signora, weeping unrestrainedly for the first time.

'I can't bear to go away from you,' she sobbed piteously; 'I can't bear to say good-bye.'

'But, my love,' the music-mistress answered, tenderly, 'if you don't really wish to go——'

'No, no, it isn't that. I feel that I must go – that——'

'And I, too, my dear girl. I believe you would do very wrong in refusing this situation. But, Nelly, my darling, remember that this is only an experiment. You may not be happy at Hazlewood. In that case you will not fail to remember that your home is always here; that, come to it when you may, you will never fail to find a loving welcome; and that the friends you leave behind you here are friends whom nothing upon earth can ever estrange from you. Remember this, Eleanor.'

'Yes, yes, dear, dear Signora.'

'If I could have gone with her to the station, I shouldn't have cared so much,' Richard murmured, despondingly; 'but the laws of Spavin and Cromshaw are as the laws of Draco. If I don't get on with the Swiss châlet and moonlit Alpine peaks, the new piece can't come out on Monday.'

So poor Eleanor went to the station alone, and was overcharged by the cabman who carried the two trunks which Richard had neatly addressed to Miss Vincent, Hazlewood, Berks.

She was received by a civil porter, who took charge of her luggage while she went to the waiting-room to look for the stranger who was to be her escort.

She was no more a coquette than she had been nearly two years before when she travelled alone between London and Paris, and she was prepared to accept the care and protection of the elderly gentleman who had taken charge of her upon that occasion.

But how was she to recognize the stranger? She could not walk up to every gentleman in the waiting-room, to ask him if he were Mr Monckton.

She had in almost all her wanderings travelled in second-class carriages, and waited in second-class waiting-rooms. She shrank back, therefore, rather timidly upon the threshold of the capacious carpeted saloon, and looked a little nervously at the occupants of that gorgeous chamber. There was a group of ladies near the fireplace, and there were three gentlemen in different parts of the room. One of these gentlemen was a little man with grey hair and a red face; the other was very young and very sandy; the third was a tall man of about forty, with close-cut black hair, and a square massive face and head – not exactly a handsome face, perhaps, but a countenance not easily to be overlooked.

This tall man was standing near one of the windows, reading a newspaper. He looked up as Eleanor pushed open the swinging door.

'I wonder which of them is Mr Monckton,' she thought. 'Not that fidgety young man with the red hair, I hope.'

While she still stood doubtfully upon the threshold, hesitating what to do – she little knew what a pretty picture she made in that timid, fluttering attitude – the tall man threw down his newspaper upon the sofa beside him, and walked across the room to where she stood.

'Miss Vincent, I believe?' he said.

Eleanor blushed at the sound of that false name, and then bent her head in reply to the question. She could not say yes. She could not fall into this disagreeable falsehood all at once.

'I am Mrs Darrell's friend and legal adviser, Mr Monckton,' the gentleman said, 'and I shall be very happy to perform the duty she has entrusted to me. We are in very good time, Miss Vincent. I know that young ladies are generally *ultra*-punctual upon these occasions; and I came very early in order to anticipate you, if possible.'

Eleanor did not speak. She was looking furtively at the face of Mrs Darrell's friend and legal adviser. A good and wise adviser, Miss Vane thought: for the face, not strictly handsome, seemed to bear in its every feature the stamp of three qualities – goodness, wisdom, and strength.

'I am sure he is very good,' she thought; 'but I would not like to offend him for the world, for though he looks so kind now, I know he must be terrible when he's angry.'

She looked almost fearfully at the strongly-marked black eyebrows, thinking what a stormy darkness must overshadow the massive face when they contracted over the grave, brown eyes – serious and earnest eyes, but with a latent fire lurking somewhere in their calm depths, Eleanor thought.

The girl's mind rambled on thus while she stood by the stranger's side in the sunlit window. Already the blackness of her new life was broken by this prominent figure standing boldly out upon its very threshold. Already she was learning to be interested in new people.

'He isn't a bit like a lawyer,' she thought; 'I fancied lawyers were always shabby old men, with blue bags. The men who used to come to Chelsea after papa were always nasty disagreeable men, with papers about the Queen and Richard Roe.'

Mr Monckton looked thoughtfully down at the girl by his side. There was a vein of silent poetry, and there were dim glimpses of artistic feeling hidden somewhere in the nature of this man, very far below the hard, business-like exterior which he presented to the world. He felt a quiet pleasure in looking at Eleanor's young beauty. It was her youthfulness, perhaps, her almost childlike innocence, which made her greatest charm. Her face was not that of a common beauty: her aquiline nose, grey eyes, and firmly-moulded mouth had a certain air of queenliness very rarely to be seen; but the youth of the soul shining out of the clear eyes was visible in every glance, in every change of expression.

'Do you know much of Berkshire, Miss Vincent?' the lawyer asked, presently.

'Oh, no, I have never been there.'

'You are very young, and I dare say have never left home before?' Mr Monckton said. He was wondering that no relative or friend had accompanied the girl to the station.

'I have been at school,' Eleanor answered; 'but I have never been away from home before – to – to get my own living.'

'I thought not. Your papa and mamma must be very sorry to lose you.'

'I have neither father nor mother.'

'Indeed!' said Mr Monckton; 'that's strange.'

Then after a pause he said, in a low voice:

'I think the young lady you are going to will like you all the better for that.'

'Why?' Eleanor asked involuntarily.

'Because she has never known either father or mother.'

'Poor girl!' murmured Eleanor; 'they are both dead, then?'

The lawyer did not answer this question. He was so far professional, even in his conversation with Miss Vane, that he asked a great many more questions than he answered.

'Do you like going to Hazlewood, Miss Vincent?' he said, by-and-by, rather abruptly.

'Not very much.'

'Why not?'

'Because I am leaving very dear friends to go to——'

'Strangers, who may ill-treat you, eh?' muttered Mr Monckton. 'You need have no apprehension of that sort of thing, I assure you, Miss Vincent. Mrs Darrell is rather rigid in her ideas of life; she has had her disappointments, poor soul, and you must be patient with her; but Laura Mason, the young lady who is to be your companion, is the gentlest and most affectionate girl in Christendom, I should think. She is a sort of ward of mine, and her future life is in my hands; a very heavy responsibility, Miss Vincent; she will have plenty of money by-and-by – houses, and horses, and carriages, and servants, and all the outer paraphernalia of happiness: but Heaven knows if she will be happy, poor girl! She has never known either mother or father. She has lived with all manner of respectable matrons, who have promised to do a mother's duty to her, and have tried to do it, I dare say; but she has never had a mother, Miss Vincent. I am always sorry for her when I think of that.'

The lawyer sighed heavily, and his thoughts seemed to wander away from the young lady in his charge. He still stood at the window, looking out at the bustle on the platform, but not seeing it, I think, and took no further notice of Eleanor until the bell rang for the starting of the train.

'Come, Miss Vincent,' he said, rousing himself suddenly from his reverie; 'I have forgotten all about your ticket. I'll put you into a carriage, and then send a porter for it.'

Mr Monckton scarcely spoke to his companion half-a-dozen times during the brief journey to Slough. He sat with a newspaper before him, but Eleanor noticed that he never turned its leaves, and once, when she caught a glimpse of the lawyer's face, she saw that it wore the same gloomy and abstracted expression that she had observed upon it as Mr Monckton stood in the window of the waiting-room.

'He must be very fond of his ward,' she thought, 'or he could never be so sorry because she has no mother. I thought lawyers were hard, cruel men, who cared for nothing in the world. I always used to fancy my sister Hortensia ought to have been a lawyer.'

By-and-by, as they drew very near to the station, Mr Monckton dropped his newspaper with another sigh, and turning to Eleanor, said, in a low, confidential voice:

'I hope you will be very good to Laura Mason, Miss Vincent. Remember that she stands quite alone in the world: and that, however friendless, however desolate you may be − I say this because you tell me you are an orphan − you can never be so friendless or so desolate as she is.'

CHAPTER XIII

HAZLEWOOD

A phaeton and pair was in waiting for Mr Monckton outside the Slough station. The vehicle was very plain, but had a certain quiet elegance of its own, and the horses had been sold at Tattersall's for something over five hundred pounds.

Eleanor Vane's spirits rose in spite of herself as she sat by the lawyer's side, driving at a rapid rate through the pretty pastoral country. They crossed the river almost immediately after leaving Slough, and dashed into Berkshire. They skirted Windsor Park and Forest, leaving the black outline of the castle keep behind them; and then turned into a quiet

country road, where the green banks were dotted by clumps of early
primroses, and the white-thorns were bursting into flower.

Eleanor looked rapturously at all this rural beauty. She was a Cockney,
poor child, and her experience of the country was confined to rambles in
Greenwich Park, or on Richmond Terrace; happy rambles with her
father, prior to expensive dinners at the Crown and Sceptre, or the Star
and Garter, as the case might be.

But the country, the genuine country, the long roads and patches of
common, the glimpses of wood and water, the great deserts of arable land,
the scattered farm-houses, and noisy farm-yards; all these were strange and
new to her, and her soul expanded in the unfamiliar atmosphere.

If that drive could have lasted for ever, it would have been very
delightful; but she knew that those splendid chestnut horses were
carrying her at a terrible rate to her new home. Her new home! What
right had she to call Hazlewood by that name? She was not going home.
She was going to her first situation.

All the pride of birth, the foolish and mistaken pride in shipwrecked
fortune and squandered wealth which this girl's weak-minded father had
instilled into her, arose and rebelled against this bitter thought. What
humiliation Mrs Bannister's cruelty had inflicted upon her!

She was thinking this when Mr Monckton suddenly turned his horses'
heads away from the main road, and the phaeton entered a lane above
which the branches of the still leafless trees made an overarching roof of
delicate tracery.

At the end of this lane, in which the primroses seemed to grow thicker
than in any other part of the country, there were some low wooden gates,
and an old-fashioned iron lamp-post. On the other side of the gates there
was a wide lawn shut in by a shrubbery and a grove of trees, and beyond
the lawn glimmered the sunlit windows of a low white house; a rambling
cottage, whose walls were half hidden by trellis-work and ivy, and not one
of whose windows or chimneys owned a fellowship with the others.

Pigeons were cooing and hens clucking somewhere behind the house,
a horse began to neigh as the carriage stopped, and three dogs, one very
big, and two very little ones, ran out upon the lawn, and barked furiously
at the phaeton.

Eleanor Vane could not help thinking the low-roofed, white-walled,
ivy-covered irregular cottage very pretty, even though it *was* Hazlewood.

While the dogs were barking their loudest, a delicate little figure, in
fluttering draperies of white and blue, came floating out of a window
under the shadow of a verandah, and ran towards the gates.

It was the figure of a young lady, very fragile-looking and graceful. A
young lady whose complexion was fairer than a snow-drop, and whose
loose floating hair was of the palest shade of flaxen.

'Be quiet, Julius Caesar; be quiet, Mark Anthony,' she cried to the dogs, who ran up to her and leaped and whirled about her, jumping almost higher than her head in an excess of canine spirits. 'Be quiet, you big, wicked Julius Caesar, or you shall go back to the stables, sir. Is this the way you behave yourself when I've had ever so much trouble to get you a half-holiday? Please, don't mind them, Miss Vincent,' the young lady added, opening the gate, and looking up pleadingly at Eleanor; 'they're only noisy. They wouldn't hurt you for the world; and they'll love you very much by-and-by, when they come to know you. I've been watching for you such a time, Mr Monckton. The train must have been slow this afternoon!'

'The train travelled at its usual speed, neither slower nor faster,' the lawyer said, with a quiet smile, as he handed Eleanor out of the phaeton. He left the horses in the care of the groom, and walked on to the lawn with the two girls. The dogs left off barking at a word from him, though they had made very light of Miss Mason's entreaties. They seemed to know him, and to be accustomed to obey him.

'I know the afternoon *seemed* dreadfully long,' the young lady said. 'I thought the train *must* be behind its time.'

'And, of course, you never thought of looking at your watch, Miss Mason,' the lawyer said, pointing to a quantity of jewelled toys which hung at the young lady's blue sash.

'What's the good of looking at one's watch, if one's watch won't go?' said Miss Mason; 'the sun has been going down ever so long, but the sun's so changeable, there's no relying on it. Mrs Darrell has gone out in the pony-carriage to call upon some people near Woodlands.'

Eleanor Vane started at the sudden mention of a name which had been so familiar to her from her dead father's lips.

'So I am all alone,' continued Miss Mason, 'and I'm very glad of that; because we shall get to know each other so much better by ourselves, shan't we, Miss Vincent?'

George Monckton had been walking between the two girls, but Laura Mason came round to Eleanor, and put her hand in that of Miss Vane. It was a fat little childish hand, but there were rings glittering upon it, small as it was.

'I think I shall like you very much,' Miss Mason whispered. 'Do you think you shall like me?'

She looked up into Eleanor's face, with an entreating expression in her blue eyes; they were really blue eyes, a bright forget-me-not, or turquoise blue, as different as possible from Eleanor's clear grey ones, which were for ever changing, sometimes purple, sometimes brown, sometimes black.

How could Miss Vane reply to this childish question, except in the affirmative? She had every inclination to love the babyish young lady,

who was so ready to cling to her and confide in her. She had expected to
find a haughty heiress who would have flaunted her wealth before her
penniless companion. But she had another reason for inclining tenderly
towards this girl. She remembered what Mr Monckton had said to her in
the railway carriage.

'However friendless or desolate you may be, you can never be so
friendless and desolate as she is.'

Eleanor pressed the hand that clung to hers, and said, gravely, 'I'm sure
I shall love you, Miss Mason, if you'll let me.'

'And you'll not be dreadful about triplets, and arpeggios, and
cinquepated passages?' the young lady said, piteously. 'I don't mind music
a bit, in a general way, you know; but I never could play triplets in time.'

She led the way into a sitting-room under the verandah, as she talked.
Eleanor went with her, hand-in-hand, and Mr Monckton followed,
keeping an attentive watch upon the two girls.

The sitting-room was, like the exterior of the cottage, very irregular
and very pretty. It stood at one end of the house, and there were
windows upon three sides of the room, – an oriel at the end opposite the
door, a bay opening on to the verandah, and three latticed windows with
deep oaken seats upon the other side.

The furniture was pretty, but very simple and inexpensive. The chintz
curtains and chair-covers were sprinkled with rose-buds and butterflies;
the chairs and tables were of shining maple-wood; and there was a good
supply of old china arranged here and there upon brackets and cabinets of
obsolete form. The pale cream-coloured walls were hung with a few
prints and water-coloured sketches; but beyond this the chamber had no
adornments.

Laura Mason led Eleanor to one of the window-seats, where a litter of
fancy-work, and two or three open books tumbled carelessly here and
there amongst floss-silks and Berlin wools and scraps of embroidery, gave
token to the young lady's habits.

'Will you take off your things here,' she said, 'or shall I show you to
your own room at once? It's the blue room, next to mine. There's a door
between the two rooms, so we shall be able to talk to each other
whenever we like. How dreadfully you must want something to eat after
your journey! Shall I ring for cake and wine, or shall we wait for tea? We
always drink tea at seven, and we dine very early; not like Mr Monckton,
who has a grand late dinner every evening.'

The lawyer sighed.

'Rather a desolate dinner, sometimes, Miss Mason,' he said, gravely;
'but you remind me that I shall be hardly in time for it, and my poor
housekeeper makes herself wretched when the fish is spoiled.'

He looked at his watch.

'Six o'clock, I declare; good-bye, Laura; good-bye, Miss Vincent. I hope you will be happy at Hazlewood.'

'I am *sure* I shall be happy with Miss Mason,' Eleanor answered.

'Indeed!' exclaimed Mr Monckton, elevating his straight black eyebrows, 'is she so very fascinating, then? I'm sorry for it,' he muttered under his breath, as he walked off after shaking hands with the two girls.

They heard the phaeton driving away three minutes afterwards.

Laura Mason shrugged her shoulders with an air of relief.

'I'm glad he's gone,' she said.

'But you like him very much. He's very good, isn't he?'

'Oh, yes, very, very good, and I do like him. But I'm afraid of him, I think, because he's so good. He always seems to be watching one and finding out one's faults. And he seems so sorry because I'm frivolous, and I can't help being frivolous when I'm happy.'

'And are you always happy?' Eleanor asked. She thought it very possible that this young heiress, who had never known any of those bitter troubles which Miss Vane had found associated with 'money matters' might indeed be *always* happy. But Laura Mason shook her head.

'Always, except when I think,' she said; 'but when I think about papa and mamma, and wonder who they were, and why I never knew them, I can't help feeling very unhappy.'

'They died when you were very young, then?' Eleanor said.

Laura Mason shook her head with a sorrowful gesture.

'I scarcely know when they died,' she answered; 'I know that I can remember nothing about them; the first thing I recollect is being with a lady, far down in Devonshire — a lady who took the charge of several little girls. I stayed with her till I was ten years old, and then I was sent to a fashionable school at Bayswater, and I stayed there till I was fifteen, and then I came here, and I've been here two years and a half. Mr Monckton is my guardian, you know, and he says I am a very lucky girl, and will have plenty of money by-and-by; but what's the use of money if one has no relations in all the wide world? and he tells me to attend to my education, and not to be frivolous, or care for dress and jewellery, but to try and become a good woman. He talks to me very seriously, and almost frightens me sometimes with his grave manner; but for all that, he's very kind, and lets me have almost everything I ask him for. He's tremendously rich himself, you know, though he's only a professional man, and he lives at a beautiful place four miles from here, called Tolldale Priory. I used to ask him questions about papa and mamma, but he would never tell me anything. So now I never speak to him about them.'

She sighed as she finished speaking, and was silent for some few minutes; but she very quickly recovered her spirits, and conducted

Eleanor to a pretty rustic chamber with a lattice window looking on to the lawn.

'Mrs Darrell's man is gone to fetch your luggage,' Miss Mason said, 'so you must have my brushes and combs, please, for your hair, and then we'll go down to tea.'

She led Eleanor into the adjoining apartment, where the dressing-table was littered with all manner of womanly frivolities, and here Miss Vane re-arranged her luxuriant golden-brown hair, which no longer was allowed to fall about her shoulders in rippling curls, but was drawn simply away from her forehead, and rolled in a knot at the back of her head. She was a woman now, and had begun the battle of life.

A pony-carriage drove up to the gate while Eleanor was standing at the glass by the open window, and Mrs Darrell got out and walked across the lawn towards the house.

She was a tall woman, unusually tall for a woman, and she was dressed in black silk, which hung about her angular limbs in heavy, lustreless folds. Eleanor could see that her face was pale and her eyes black and flashing.

The two girls went down stairs hand-in-hand. Tea was prepared in the dining-room, a long wainscoted apartment, older than the rest of the house, and rather gloomy-looking. Three narrow windows upon one side of this room looked towards the shrubbery and grove at the back of the house, and the trunks of the trees looked gaunt and black in the spring twilight. A fire was burning upon the low hearth, and a maid-servant was lighting a lamp in the centre of the table as the two girls went in.

Mrs Darrell welcomed her dependant very politely; but there was a harshness and a stiffness in her politeness which reminded Eleanor of her half-sister, Mrs Bannister. The two women seemed to belong to the same school, Miss Vane thought.

The lamplight shone full upon Mrs Darrell's face, and Eleanor could see now that the face was a handsome one, though faded and careworn. The widow's hair was grey, but her eyes retained the flashing brightness of youth. They were very dark and lustrous, but their expression was scarcely pleasant. There was too much of the hawk or eagle in their penetrating glance.

But Laura Mason did not seem at all afraid of her protectress.

'Miss Vincent and I are good friends already, Mrs Darrell,' she said, gaily, 'and we shall be as happy together as the day is long, I hope.'

'And I hope Miss Vincent will teach you industrious habits, Laura,' Miss Darrell answered, gravely.

Miss Mason made a grimace with her pretty red under-lip.

Eleanor took the seat indicated to her, a seat at the end of the dining-table, and exactly opposite to Mrs Darrell, who sat with her back to the fireplace.

Sitting here, Eleanor could scarcely fail to observe an oil painting – the only picture in the room – which hung over the mantel-piece. It was the portrait of a young man, with dark hair clustering about a handsome forehead, regular features, a pale complexion, and black eyes. The face was very handsome, very aristocratic, but there was a want of youthfulness, an absence of the fresh, eager spirit of boyhood in its expression. A look of listless hauteur hung like a cloud over the almost faultless features.

Mrs Darrell watched Eleanor's eyes as the girl looked at this picture.

'You are looking at my son, Miss Vincent,' she said; 'but perhaps it is scarcely necessary to tell you so. People say there is a strong likeness between us.'

There was indeed a very striking resemblance between the faded face below and the pictured face above. But it seemed to Eleanor Vane as if the mother's face, faded and careworn though it was, was almost the younger of the two. The listless indifference, the utter lack of energy in the lad's countenance, was so much the more striking when contrasted with the youthfulness of the features.

'Yes,' exclaimed Laura Mason, 'that is Mrs Darrell's only son, Launcelot Darrell. Isn't that a romantic name, Miss Vincent?'

Eleanor started. This Launcelot Darrell was the young man she had heard her father speak of; the man who expected to inherit the De Crespigny estate. How often she had heard his name! It was he, then, who would have stood between her father and fortune, had that dear father lived; or whose claim of kindred would, perhaps, have had to make way for the more sacred right of friendship.

And this young man's portrait was hanging in the room where she sat. He lived in the house, perhaps. Where should he live except in his mother's house?

But Eleanor's mind was soon relieved upon this point, for Laura Mason, in the pauses of the business of the tea-table, talked a good deal about the original of the portrait.

'Don't you think him handsome, Miss Vincent?' she asked, without waiting for an answer. 'But of course you do; everybody thinks him handsome; and then Mrs Darrell says he's so elegant, so tall, so aristocratic. He is almost sure to have Woodlands by-and-by, and all Mr de Crespigny's money. But of course you don't know Woodlands or Mr de Crespigny. How should you, when you've never been in Berkshire before? And he – not Mr de Crespigny, he's a nasty, fidgety, hypochon – what's its name? – old man – but Launcelot Darrell is *so* accomplished. He's an artist, you know, and all the water-coloured sketches in the drawing-room and the breakfast-parlour are his; and he plays and sings, and he dances exquisitely, and he rides and plays cricket, and he's a –

what you may call it – a crack shot; and, in short, he's an Admirable Crichton. You mustn't fancy I'm in love with him, you know, Miss Vincent,' the young lady added, blushing and laughing, 'because I never saw him in my life, and I only know all this by hearsay.'

'You never saw him!' repeated Eleanor.

Launcelot Darrell did not live at Hazlewood, then.

'No,' the widow interposed; 'my son has enemies, I am sorry to say, amongst his own kindred. Instead of occupying the position his talents, to say nothing of his birth, entitle him to, he has been compelled to go out to India in a mercantile capacity. I do not wonder that his spirit rebels against such an injustice. I do not wonder that he cannot forgive.'

Mrs Darrell's face darkened as she spoke, and she sighed heavily. By-and-by, when the two girls were alone together in the breakfast room, Laura Mason alluded to the conversation at the tea-table.

'I don't think I ought to have talked about Launcelot Darrell,' she said; 'I know his mother is unhappy about him, though I don't exactly know why. You see his two aunts, who live at Woodlands, are nasty, scheming old maids, and they contrived to keep him away from his great uncle, Mr de Crespigny, who is expected to leave him all his money. Indeed, I don't see who else he can leave it to now. There was an old man – a college friend of Mr de Crespigny's – who expected to get the Woodlands estate; but of course that was an absurd idea; and the old man – the father of that very Mrs Bannister who recommended you to Mrs Darrell, by the bye – is dead. So all chance of that sort of thing is over.'

'And Mr Launcelot Darrell is sure to have the fortune?' Eleanor said, interrogatively, after a very long pause.

'Well, I don't know about that; but I've heard Mrs Darrell say that Launcelot was a great favourite of Mr de Crespigny's when he was a boy. But those two cantankerous old maids, Mrs Darrell's sisters, are nagging at the old man night and day, and they may persuade him at last, or they may have succeeded in persuading him, perhaps, ever so long ago, to make a will in their favour. Of course all this makes Mrs Darrell very unhappy. She idolizes her son, who is an only child, and was terribly spoiled when he was a boy, they say; and she does not know whether he will be a rich man or a pauper.'

'And in the meantime, Mr Darrell is in India?'

'Yes. He went to India three years ago. He's overseer to an indigo-planter up the country, at some place with an unpronounceable name, hundreds and hundreds of miles from Calcutta. He's not at all happy, I believe, and he very seldom writes – not above once in a twelvemonth.'

'He is not a good son, then,' Eleanor said.

'Oh, I don't know about that! Mrs Darrell never complains, and she's very proud of him. She always speaks of him as "my son". But, of course, what with one thing and another, she is often very unhappy. So, if she is a little severe, now and then, we'll try and bear with her, won't we, Eleanor? I may call you Eleanor, mayn't I?'

The pretty flaxen head dropped upon Miss Vane's shoulder, as the heiress asked this question, and the blue eyes were lifted pleadingly.

'Yes, yes; I would much rather be called Eleanor than Miss Vincent.'

'And you'll call me Laura. Nobody ever calls me Miss Mason except Mr Monckton when he lectures me. We shall be very, very happy together, I hope, Eleanor.'

'I hope so, dear.'

There was a sudden pang of mingled fear and remorse at Eleanor Vane's heart as she said this. Was she to be happy, and to forget the purpose of her life? Was she to be happy, and false to the memory of her murdered father? In this quiet country life; in this pleasant girlish companionship which was so new to her; was she to abandon that one dark dream, that one deeply-rooted desire which had been in her mind ever since her father's untimely death?

She recoiled with a shudder of dread from the simple happiness which threatened to lull her to a Sybarite rest; in which that deadly design might lose its force, and, little by little, fade out of her mind.

She disengaged herself from the slight arms which had encircled her in a half-childish caress, and rose suddenly to her feet.

'Laura,' she cried, 'Laura, you mustn't talk to me like this. My life is not like yours. I have something to do, – I have a purpose to achieve; a purpose before which every thought of my mind, every impulse of my heart, must give way.'

'What purpose, Eleanor?' asked Laura Mason, almost alarmed by the energy of her companion's manner.

'I cannot tell you. It is a secret,' Miss Vane replied.

Then sitting down once more in the deep window-seat by Laura's side, Eleanor Vane drew her arm tenderly round the frightened girl's waist.

'I'll try and do my duty to you, Laura, dear,' she said, 'and I know I shall be happy with you. But if ever you see me dull and silent, you'll understand, dear, that there is a secret in my life, and that there is a hidden purpose in my mind that sooner or later must be achieved. Sooner or later,' she repeated, with a sigh, 'but Heaven only knows when.'

She was silent and absent-minded during the rest of the evening, though she played one of her most elaborate fantasias at Mrs Darrell's request, and perfectly satisfied that lady's expectations by the brilliancy of her touch. She was very glad when, at ten o'clock, the two women servants of the simple household and a hobbledehoyish young man, who looked after the pony and pigs and poultry-yard, and smelt very strongly of the stable, came in to hear prayers read by Mrs Darrell.

'I know you're tired, dear,' Laura Mason said, as she bade Eleanor good night at the door of her bedroom, 'so I won't ask you to talk to me to-night. Get to bed, and go to sleep at once, dear.'

But Eleanor did not go to bed immediately; nor did she fall asleep until very late that night.

She unfastened one of her trunks, and took from it a little locked morocco casket, which held a few valueless and old-fashioned trinkets that had been her mother's, and the crumpled fragment of her father's last letter.

She sat at the little dressing-table, reading the disjointed sentences in that melancholy letter, before she undressed, and then replaced the scrap of paper in the casket.

She looked at the lawn and shrubbery. The shining leaves of the evergreens trembled in the soft April breeze, and shimmered in the moonlight. All was silent in that simple rustic retreat. The bare branches of the tall trees near the low white gates were sharply defined against the sky. High up in the tranquil heavens the full moon shone out from a pale background of fleecy cloud.

The beauty of the scene made a very powerful impression upon Eleanor Vane. The window from which she had been accustomed to look in Bloomsbury abutted on a yard, a narrow gorge of dirt and disorder, between the dismal back walls of high London houses.

'I ought never to have come here,' Eleanor thought, bitterly, as she let fall her dimity window curtain and shut out the splendour of the night. 'I ought to have stayed in London; there was some hope of my meeting that man in London, where strange things are always happening. But here——'

She fell into a gloomy reverie. Secluded in that quiet rustic retreat, what hope could she have of advancing, by so much as one footstep, upon the dark road she had appointed for herself to tread?

It was very long before she fell asleep. She lay for hours, tumbling and tossing feverishly upon her comfortable bed.

The memories of her old life mingled themselves with thoughts of her new existence. She was haunted now by the recollection of her father and her father's death; now by her fresh experiences of Hazlewood, by the widow's grey hair and penetrating gaze, and by the pictured face of Launcelot Darrell.

CHAPTER XIV

THE PRODIGAL'S RETURN

The course of Eleanor's life at Hazlewood was peaceful and monotonous. She had been engaged simply as a 'companion' for Laura Mason. That common epithet, which is so often twisted into the signification of a household drudge – an upper-servant, who works harder than any of her fellows – in this case meant purely and simply what it was originally intended to mean. Eleanor's only duties were to teach Laura Mason music, and to be the companion and associate of all her girlish pleasures and industries.

Not that Miss Mason was very industrious. She had a habit of beginning great undertakings in the way of fancy work, and the more gigantic the design the more ardent was her desire to attempt it – but she rarely got beyond the initiative part of her labour. There was always some 'Dweller on the Threshold' in the shape of a stitch, that couldn't be learnt, or a skein of silk that couldn't be matched, or a pattern that *wouldn't* come right; and one after another of the gigantic undertakings was flung aside to decay in dusty oblivion, or to be finished by Eleanor or Mrs Darrell.

Laura Mason was not made for the active service of life. She was one of the holiday soldiers in the great army, fit for nothing but to wear gilded epaulettes and gorgeous uniforms, and to turn out upon gala days to the sound of trumpet and drum.

She was a loving, generous-hearted, confiding creature; but, like some rudderless boat drifting hither and thither before a stormy ocean, this frivolous, purposeless girl flung herself, helpless and dependent, upon the mercy of other people.

The rich City solicitor, Mr Monckton, the head of a celebrated legal firm familiar in the Bankruptcy Court, took the trouble to say very little about his pretty, flaxen-haired, and blue-eyed ward.

He spoke of her, indeed, with an almost pointed indifference. She was the daughter of some people he had known in his early youth, he said, and her fortune had been entrusted to his care. She would be rich, but he was none less anxious about her future. A woman was not generally any the safer in this world for being an heiress. This was all Gilbert Monckton had ever said to Mrs Darrell upon the subject of his ward's past history. Laura herself had talked freely enough of her first two homes. There was little to tell, but, upon the other hand, there seemed nothing to conceal.

Upon one subject Mr Monckton was very strict, and that was the seclusion of the home he had chosen for his ward.

'When Miss Mason is of age she will of course choose for herself,' he said; 'but until that time comes, I must beg, Mrs Darrell, that you will keep her out of all society.'

Under these circumstances it was especially necessary that Laura Mason should have a companion of her own age. Hazlewood was a hermitage, never approached by any visitors except some half-dozen elderly ladies, who were intimate with Mrs Darrell, and Mr Monckton, who came about once a fortnight to dine and spend the evening.

He used to devote himself very much to Laura and her companion during these visits. Eleanor could see how earnestly he watched the flaxen-haired girl, whose childish simplicity no doubt made her very bewitching to the grave man of business. He watched her and listened to her; sometimes with a pleased smile, sometimes with an anxious expression on his face; but his attention very rarely wandered from her.

'He must love her very dearly,' Eleanor thought, remembering how earnestly he had spoken in the railway carriage.

She wondered what was the nature of the affection which the solicitor felt for his ward. He was old enough to be her father, it was true, but he was still in the prime of life; he had not that beauty of feature and complexion which a school-girl calls handsome, but he had a face which leaves its impress upon the minds of those who look at it.

He was very clever, or at least he seemed so to Eleanor; for there was no subject ever mentioned, no topic ever discussed, with which he did not appear thoroughly familiar, and upon which his opinions were not original and forcible. Eleanor's intellect expanded under the influence of this superior masculine intelligence. Her plastic mind, so ready to take any impression, was newly moulded by its contact with this stronger brain. Her education, very imperfect before, seemed to complete itself now by this occasional association with a clever man.

Of course all this came about by slow degrees. She did not very rapidly become familiar with Gilbert Monckton, for his grave manner was rather calculated to inspire diffidence in a very young woman; but little by little, as she grew accustomed to his society, accustomed to sit quietly in the shade, only speaking now and then, while Laura Mason talked familiarly to her guardian, she began to discover how much she had gained from her association with the lawyer. It was not without some bitterness of spirit that Eleanor Vane thought of this. She felt as if she had been an interloper in that quiet Hazlewood household. What right had she to come between Laura and her guardian, and steal the advantages Mr Monckton intended for his ward? It was for Laura's sake he had been earnest or eloquent; it was for Laura's sake he had described this, or explained that. What right, then, had she, Eleanor, to remember what Laura had forgotten, or to avail herself of the advantages Laura was too frivolous to value?

There was a gulf between the two girls that could not be passed, even by affection. Eleanor Vane's mental superiority placed her so high above Laura Mason that perfect confidence could not exist between them. Eleanor's love for the light-hearted, heedless girl, had something almost motherly in its nature.

'I know we shall never quite understand each other, Laura,' she said; 'but I think I could give up my life for your sake, my dear.'

'Or I for you, Nelly.'

'No, no, Laura. I know you are unselfish as an angel, and you'd wish to do so; but yours is not the giving-up nature, my darling. You'd die under a great sorrow.'

'I think I should, Nelly,' the girl answered, drawing closer to her friend, and trembling at the very thought of calamity; 'but how you speak, dear. Had you ever a great sorrow?'

'Yes, a very great one.'

'And yet you are happy with us, and can sing and play, and ramble about in the woods with me, Nell, as if you had nothing on your mind.'

'Yes, Laura, but I can remember my sorrow all the time. It is hidden so deep in my heart that the sunshine never reaches it, however happy I may seem.'

Laura Mason sighed. The spoiled child of fortune could not help wondering how she would act under the influence of a great misery. She would sit down upon the ground in some darkened room, she thought, and cry until her heart broke and she died.

The summer faded into autumn, and autumn into winter, and the early spring flowers bloomed again in the shrubberies and on the lawn at Hazlewood. The primroses were pale upon the tender grass of the sloping banks in the broad lane near the gates, and still no event had happened to break the tranquil monotony of that secluded household. Eleanor had grown familiar with every nook in the rambling old cottage; even with Launcelot Darrell's apartments, a suite of rooms on the bedroom floor, looking out into the grove at the back of the house. These rooms had been shut up for years, ever since Launcelot had sailed for India, and they had a desolate look, though fires had been lighted in them periodically, and every scrap of furniture was kept carefully dusted.

'The rooms must always be ready,' Mrs Darrell said. 'Mr de Crespigny may die, and my son may be called home suddenly.'

So the three rooms, a bedroom, dressingroom, and sitting-room, were kept in perfect order, and Laura and Eleanor wandered into them sometimes, in the idleness of a wet afternoon, and looked at the pictures upon the walls, the unfinished sketches piled one upon the top of another on the easel, or tried the little cottage piano, upon which Mr Darrell had been wont to accompany himself when he sang. His mother

always insisted upon this piano being tuned when the tuner came from
Windsor to attend to Laura Mason's modern grand. The two girls used to
talk a good deal of the widow's handsome son. They had heard him
spoken of by his mother, by the servants, and by the few humble
neighbours in scattered cottages near Hazlewood. They talked of his
uncertain fortunes, his accomplishments, his handsome, haughty face,
which Laura declared was faultless.

Miss Vane had by this time been a twelvemonth at Hazlewood. Her
eighteenth birthday was past, and the girlishness of her appearance had
matured into the serene beauty of early womanhood. The golden tints of
her hair had deepened into rich auburn, her grey eyes looked darker
under the shadow of her dark brows. When she went to spend a brief
Christmas holiday with her old friends, the Signora and Richard
Thornton declared that she had altered very much since she had left
them, and were surprised at her matured beauty. She bought the silk
gown for Eliza Picirillo, and the meerschaum pipe for poor Dick, who
needed no memorial of his adopted sister; for her image haunted him
only too perpetually, to the destruction of all other images which might
else have found a place in the scene-painter's heart.

Eleanor Vane felt a pang of remorse as she remembered how very easily
she had borne her separation from these faithful friends. It was not that
she loved them less, or forgot their goodness to her. She had no such
ingratitude as that wherewith to reproach herself; but she felt as if she had
committed a sin against them in being happy in the calm serenity of
Hazlewood.

She said this to Richard Thornton during the brief Christmas visit.
They had walked out once more in the quiet streets and squares in the
early winter twilight.

'I feel as if I had grown selfish and indifferent,' she said. 'The months
pass one after another. It is two years and a half since my father died, and I
am not one step nearer to the discovery of the man who caused his death.
Not one step. I am buried alive at Hazlewood. I am bound hand and foot.
What can I do, Richard; what can I do? I could go mad, almost, when I
remember that I am a poor helpless girl, and that I may never be able to
keep the oath I swore when I first read my dead father's letter. And you,
Richard, in all this time you have done nothing to help me.'

The scene-painter shook his head sadly enough.

'What can I do, my dear Eleanor? What I told you nearly a year ago, I
tell you again now. This man will never be found. What hope have we?
what chance of finding him? We might hear his name to-morrow, and
we should not know it. If either of us met him in the street, we should
pass him by. We might live in the same house with him, and be ignorant
of his presence.'

'No, Richard,' cried Eleanor Vane. 'I think if I met that man some instinct of hate and horror would reveal his identity to me.'

'My poor romantic Nelly, you talk as if life was a melodrama. No, my dear, I say again, this man will never be found; the story of your father's death is unhappily a common one. Let that sad story rest, Nell, with all the other mournful records of the past. Believe me that you cannot do better than be happy at Hazlewood; happy in your innocent life, and utterly forgetful of the foolish vow you made when you were little better than a child. If all the improbabilities that you have ever dreamt of were to come to pass, and vengeance were in your grasp, I hope and believe, Nell, that a better spirit would arise within you, and prompt you to let it go.'

Richard Thornton spoke very seriously. He had never been able to speak of Eleanor's scheme of retribution without grief and regret. He recognized the taint of her father's influence in this vision of vengeance and destruction. All George Vane's notions of justice and honour had been rather the meretricious and flimsy ideas of a stage play, than the common-sense views of real life. He had talked incessantly to his daughter about days of retribution; gigantic vengeances which were looming somewhere in the far-away distance, for the ultimate annihilation of the old man's enemies. This foolish ruined spendthrift, who cried out against the world because his money was spent, and his place in that world usurped by wiser men, had been Eleanor's teacher during her most impressionable years. It was scarcely to be wondered at, then, that there were some flaws in the character of this motherless girl, and that she was ready to mistake a pagan scheme of retribution for the Christian duty of filial love.

Midsummer had come and gone, when an event occurred to break the tranquillity of that simple household.

The two girls had lingered late in the garden one evening early in July. Mrs Darrell sat writing in the breakfast-parlour. The lamplight glimmered under the shadow of the verandah, and the widow's tall figure seated at her desk was visible through the open bay window.

Laura and her companion had been talking for a long time, but Eleanor had lapsed into silence at last, and stood against the low white gate with her elbow resting upon the upper bar, looking thoughtfully out into the lane. Miss Mason was never the first to be tired of talking. A silvery torrent of innocent babble was for ever gushing from her red babyish lips; so, when at last Eleanor grew silent and absent-minded, the heiress was fain to talk to her dogs; her darling silky Skye, whose great brown eyes looked out from a ball of floss silk that represented the animal's head; and her Italian greyhound, a slim shivering brute, who wore a coloured flannel paletot, and exhibited a fretful and whimpering disposition, far from agreeable to any one but his mistress.

There was no moon upon this balmy July night, and the hulking hobbledehoy-of-all-work came out to light the lamp while the two girls were standing at the gate. This lamp gave a pleasant aspect to the cottage upon dark nights, and threw a bright line of light into the obscurity of the lane.

The boy had scarcely retired with his short ladder and flaming lantern, when the two pet dogs began to bark violently, and a man came out of the darkness into the line of lamplight.

Laura Mason gave a startled scream; but Eleanor caught her by the arm, to check her foolish outcry.

There was nothing very alarming in the aspect of the man. He was only a tramp: not a common beggar, but a shabby-genteel-looking tramp, whose threadbare coat was of a fashionable make, and who, in spite of his ragged slovenliness, had something the look of a gentleman.

'Mrs Darrell still lives here, does she not?' he asked, rather eagerly.

'Yes.'

It was Eleanor who answered. The dogs were still barking, and Laura was still looking very suspiciously at the stranger.

'Will you tell her, please, that she is wanted out here by some one who has something important to communicate to her,' the man said.

Eleanor was going towards the house to deliver this message, when she saw Mrs Darrell coming across the lawn. She had been disturbed at her writing by the barking of the dogs.

'What is the matter, Miss Vincent?' she asked, sharply. 'Who are you and Laura talking to, out here?'

She walked from the two girls to the man, who stood back a little way outside the gate, with the lamplight shining full upon his face.

The widow looked sternly at this man who had dared to come to the gate at nightfall, and to address the two girls under her charge.

But her face changed as she looked at him, and a wild cry broke from her lips.

'Launcelot, Launcelot, my son!'

CHAPTER XV

LAUNCELOT

Mrs Darrell stood for some time clasped in her son's embrace, and sobbing violently. The two girls withdrew a few paces, too bewildered to know what to do, in the first shock of the surprise that had come so suddenly upon them.

This was Launcelot Darrell, then, the long absent son, whose portrait hung above the mantel-piece in the dining-room, whose memory was so tenderly cherished, every token of whose former presence was so carefully preserved.

'My boy, my boy,' murmured the widow, in a voice which seemed strange to the two girls, from its new accent of tenderness; 'my own and only son, how is it that you come back to me thus? I thought you were in India. I thought——'

'I was in India, mother, when my last letter to you was written,' the young man answered; 'but you know how sick and tired I was of the odious climate, and the odious life I was compelled to lead. It grew unbearable at last, and I determined to throw everything up, and come home; so I sailed in the first vessel that left Calcutta after I had formed this determination. You're not sorry to see me back, are you, mother?'

'Sorry to see you, Launcelot!'

Mrs Darrell led her son across the lawn and into the house, through an open window. She seemed utterly unconscious of the presence of her two charges. She seemed to have forgotten their very existence in the wonderful surprise of her son's return. So Laura and Eleanor went up to Miss Mason's room and shut themselves in to talk over the strange adventures of the evening, while the mother and son were closeted together in the breakfast-room below.

'Isn't it all romantic, Nelly, dear?' Miss Mason said with enthusiasm. 'I wonder whether he came all the way from India in that dreadful coat and that horrid shabby hat? He looks just like the hero of a novel, doesn't he, Nell? dark and pale, and tall and slender. Has he come back for good, do you think? I'm sure he ought to have Mr de Crespigny's fortune.'

Miss Vane shrugged her shoulders. She was not particularly interested in the handsome prodigal son who had made his appearance so unexpectedly: and she had enough to do to listen to all Laura's exclamations, and sympathize with her curiosity.

'I shan't sleep a bit to-night, Nelly,' Miss Mason said as she parted from her friend. 'I shall be dreaming of Launcelot Darrell, with his dark eyes and pale face. What a fierce, half-angry look he has, Nell, as if he were savage with the world for having treated him badly. For he must have been badly treated, you know. We know how clever he is. He ought to have been made a governor-general, or an ambassador, or something of that kind, in India. He has no right to be shabby.'

'I should think his shabbiness was his own fault, Laura,' Miss Vane answered, quietly. 'If he is clever, you know, he ought to be able to earn money.'

She thought of Richard Thornton as she spoke, working at the Phoenix Theatre for the poor salary that helped to support the Bohemian comforts of that primitive shelter in the Pilasters; and Dick's paint and whitewash bespattered coat seemed glorified by contrast with that of the young prodigal in the room below.

The two girls went down to the breakfast-room early the next morning, Laura Mason arrayed in her prettiest and brightest muslin morning dress, which was scarcely so bright as her beaming face. The young lady's gossamer white robes fluttered with the floating ribbons and delicate laces that adorned them. She was a coquette by nature, and was eager to take her revenge for all the monotonous days of enforced seclusion which she had endured.

Mrs Darrell was sitting at the breakfast-table when the two girls entered the room. Her Bible lay open amongst the cups and saucers near her. Her face was pale. She looked even more careworn than usual; and her eyes were dimmed by the tears that she had shed. The heroism of the woman who had borne her son's absence silently and uncomplainingly, had given way under the unlooked-for joy of his return.

She gave her hand to each of the girls as they wished her good morning. Eleanor almost shuddered as she felt the deadly coldness of that wasted hand.

'We will begin breakfast at once, my dears,' Mrs Darrell said, quietly; 'my son is fatigued by a long journey, and exhausted by the excitement of his return. He will not get up, therefore, until late in the day.'

The widow poured out the tea, and for some little time there was silence at the breakfast-table. Neither Eleanor nor Laura liked to speak. They both waited – one patiently, the other very impatiently, until Mrs Darrell should please to tell them something about her son's extraordinary return.

It seemed as if the mistress of Hazlewood, usually so coldly dignified and self-possessed, felt some little embarrassment in speaking of the strange scene of the previous night.

'I need scarcely tell you, Laura,' she said, rather abruptly, after a very long pause, 'that if anything could lessen my happiness in my son's return, it would be the manner of his coming back to his old home. He comes back to me poorer than when he went away. He came on foot from Southampton here; he came looking like a tramp and a beggar to his mother's house. But it would be hard if I blamed my poor boy for this. The sin lies at his uncle's door. Maurice de Crespigny should have known that Colonel Darrell's only son would never stoop to a life of commercial drudgery. Launcelot's letters might have prepared me for what has happened. Their brevity, their bitter, despondent tone, might have told the utter hopelessness of a commercial career for my son. He tells me that he left India because his position there – a position which held out no promise of improvement – had become unbearable. He comes back to me penniless, with the battle of life before him. You can scarcely wonder, then, that my happiness in his return is not unalloyed.'

'No, indeed, dear Mrs Darrell,' Laura answered, eagerly; 'but still you must be very glad to have him back: and if he didn't make a fortune in India, he can make one in England, I dare say. He is so handsome, and so clever, and——'

The young lady stopped suddenly, blushing under the cold scrutiny of Ellen Darrell's eyes. Perhaps in that moment a thought flashed across the mind of the widow – the thought of a wealthy marriage for her handsome son. She knew that Laura Mason was rich, for Mr Monckton had told her that his ward would have all the advantages in after life which wealth can bestow; but she had no idea of the amount of the girl's fortune.

Launcelot Darrell slept late after his pedestrian journey. Miss Mason's piano was kept shut, out of consideration for the traveller; and Laura and Eleanor found the bright summer's morning unusually long. They had so few pursuits, or amusements, that to be deprived of one seemed very cruel. They were in a shady nook in the shrubbery, after their early dinner, Laura lying on the ground, reading a novel, and Eleanor engaged in some needlework achievement, which was by-and-by to be presented to the Signora; when the rustling leaves of the laurel screen that enclosed and sheltered their retreat were parted, and the handsome face, the face which had looked worn and haggard last night, but which now had only an aristocratic air of languor, presented itself before them in a frame of dark foliage.

'Good morning, or good afternoon, young ladies,' said Mr Darrell, 'for I hear that your habits at Hazlewood are very primitive, and that you dine at three o'clock. I have been looking for you during the last half-hour, in my anxiety to apologise for any alarm I may have given you last night. When the landless heir returns to his home, he scarcely expects to find two angels waiting for him on the threshold. I might have been a little more careful of my toilet, had I been able to foresee my reception. What luggage I had I left at Southampton.'

'Oh! never mind your dress, Mr Darrell,' Laura answered, gaily, 'we are both so glad you have come home. Ain't we, Eleanor? for our lives are so dreadfully dull here, though your mamma is very kind to us. But do tell us all about your voyage home, and your journey here on foot, and all the troubles you have gone through? Do tell us your adventures, Mr Darrell?'

The young lady lifted her bright blue eyes with a languishing glance of pity; but suddenly dropped them under the young man's gaze. He looked from one to the other of the two girls, and then, strolling into the grassy little amphitheatre where they were sitting, flung himself into a rustic arm-chair, near the table at which Eleanor Vane sat at work.

Launcelot Darrell was a handsome likeness of his mother. The features, which in her face were stern and hard, had in his an almost feminine softness. The dark eyes had a lazy light in them, and were half hidden by the listless droop of the black lashes that fringed their full white lids. The straight nose, low forehead, and delicately moulded mouth, were almost classical in their physical perfection; but there was a something wanting in the lower part of the face; the chin receded a little where it should have projected, the handsome mouth was weak and undecided in expression.

Mr Darrell might have sat as a painter's model for all the lovers in prose or poetry; but he would never have been mistaken for a hero or a statesman. He had all the attributes of grace and beauty, but not one of the outward signs of greatness. Eleanor Vane felt this want of power in the young man as she looked at him. Her rapid perception seized upon the one defect which marred so much perfection.

'If I had need of help against the murderer of my father,' the girl thought, 'I would not ask this man to aid me.'

'And now, Mr Darrell,' said Laura, throwing down her book, and settling herself for a flirtation with the prodigal son, 'tell us all your adventures. We are dying to hear them.'

Launcelot Darrell shrugged his shoulders.

'What adventures, my dear Miss Mason?'

'Why, your Indian experiences, of course, and your journey home. All your romantic escapes, and thrilling perils, tiger-hunting, pig-sticking – that doesn't sound romantic, but I suppose it is – lonely nights in which you lost yourself in the jungle, horrible encounters with rattlesnakes, brilliant balls at the Government House – you see I know all about Indian life – rides on the race-course, flirtations with Calcutta belles.'

The young man laughed at Miss Mason's enthusiasm.

'You know more about the delights of an Indian existence than I do,' he said, rather bitterly; 'a poor devil who goes out to Calcutta with only one letter of introduction, and an empty purse, and is sent up the country, within a few days of his arrival, to a lonely station, where his own face is about the only white one in the neighbourhood, hasn't very much chance of becoming familiar with Government House festivities or Calcutta belles, who reserve their smiles for the favoured children of fortune, I can assure you. As to tiger-hunts and pig-sticking, my dear Miss Mason, I can give you very little information upon those points, for an indigo planter's overseer, whose nose is kept pretty close to the grindstone, has enough to do for his pitiful stipend, and very little chance of becoming a Gordon Cumming or a Jules Gerard.'

Laura Mason looked very much disappointed.

'You didn't like India, then, Mr Darrell?' she said.

'I hated it,' the young man answered, between his set teeth.

There was so much suppressed force in Launcelot Darrell's utterance of these three words, that Eleanor looked up from her work, startled by the young man's sudden vehemence.

He was looking straight before him, his dark eyes fixed, his strongly marked eyebrows contracted, and a red spot burning in the centre of each pale and rather hollow cheek.

'But why did you hate India?' Laura asked, with unflinching pertinacity.

'Why does a man hate poverty and humiliation, Miss Mason? You might as well ask me that. Suppose we drop the subject. It isn't a very agreeable one to me, I assure you.'

'But your voyage home,' pursued Laura, quite unabashed by this rebuff; 'you can tell us your adventures during the voyage home?'

'I had no adventures. Men who travel by the overland route may have something to tell, perhaps: I came the cheapest and the slowest way.'

'By a sailing vessel?'

'Yes.'

'And what was the name of the vessel?'

'*The Indus.*'

'*The Indus,* that's an easy name to remember. But of course you had all sorts of amusements on board: you played whist in the cuddy — what is the cuddy, by the bye? — and you got up private theatricals, and you started an amateur newspaper, or a magazine, and you crossed the line, and——'

'Oh, yes, we went through the usual routine. It was dreary enough. Pray tell me something about Hazlewood, Miss Mason; I am a great deal more interested in Berkshire than you can possibly be in my Indian experiences.'

The young lady was fain to submit. She told Mr Darrell such scraps and shreds of gossip as form the 'news' in a place like Hazlewood. He listened very attentively to anything Miss Mason had to tell about his uncle, Maurice de Crespigny.

'So those tiger cats, my maiden aunts, are as watchful as ever,' he said, when Laura had finished. 'Heaven grant the harpies may be disappointed! Do any of the Vane family ever try to get at the old man?'

Eleanor looked up from her work, but very quietly; she had grown accustomed to hear her name spoken by those who had no suspicion of her identity.

'Oh, no, I believe not,' Miss Mason answered: 'old Mr Vane died two or three years ago, you know.'

'Yes, my mother wrote me word of his death.'

'You were in India when it happened, then?'

'Yes.'

Eleanor's face blanched, and her heart beat with a fierce heavy throbbing against her breast. How dared they talk of her dead father in that tone of almost insolent indifference! The one passion of her young life had as strong a power over her now as when she had knelt in the little chamber in the Rue de l'Archevêque, with her clasped hands uplifted to the low ceiling, and a terrible oath upon her girlish lips.

She dropped her work suddenly, and rising from her rustic seat, walked away from the shade of the laurels.

'Eleanor,' cried Laura Mason, 'where are you going?'

Launcelot Darrell sat in a lounging attitude, trifling with the reels of silk, and balls of wool, and all the paraphernalia of fancy work scattered upon the table before him, but he lifted his head as Laura uttered her friend's name, and perhaps for the first time looked steadily at Miss Vane.

He sat looking at her for some minutes while she and Laura stood talking together a few paces from him. It was perhaps only a painter's habit of looking earnestly at a pretty face that gave intensity to his gaze. He dropped his eyelids presently, and drew a long breath, that sounded almost like a sigh of relief.

'An accidental likeness,' he muttered; 'there are a hundred such likenesses in the world.'

He got up and walked back to the house, leaving the two girls together. Laura had a great deal to say about his handsome face, and the easy grace of his manner; but Eleanor Vane was absent and thoughtful. The mention of her father's name had brought back the past. Her peaceful life, and all its quiet contentment, melted away like a curtain of morning mist that rises to disclose the ghastly horror of a battle-field; and the dreadful picture of the past arose before her; painfully vivid, horribly real. The parting on the boulevard; the long night of agony and suspense; the meeting with Richard on the bridge by the Morgue; her father's torn, disjointed letter; and her own vengeful wrath; all returned to her. Every voice of her heart seemed to call her away from the commonplace tranquillity of her life to some desperate act of justice and retribution.

'What have I to do with this frivolous girl?' she thought; 'what is it to me whether Launcelot Darrell's nose is Grecian or aquiline, whether his eyes are black or brown? What a wretched, useless life I am leading in this place, when I should be hunting through the world for the murderer of my father.'

She sighed wearily as she remembered how powerless she was. What could she do to get one step nearer to the accomplishment of that single purpose, which she called the purpose of her life. Nothing! She remembered with a chill feeling of despair that however, in her moments of exaltation, she might look forward to some shadowy day of triumph and revenge, her better sense always told her that Richard Thornton had spoken the truth. The man whose treachery had destroyed George Vane had dropped into the chaos of an over-crowded universe, leaving no clue behind him by which he might be traced.

CHAPTER XVI

THE LAWYER'S SUSPICION

Mr Monckton came to Hazlewood upon the day after Launcelot Darrell's arrival. The grave solicitor had known the young man before his departure for India, but there seemed no very great intimacy between them, and Mr Darrell appeared rather to avoid any familiarity with his mother's rich friend.

He answered Gilbert Monckton's questions about India and indigo-planting with an air of unwillingness that was almost insolent.

'The last few years of my life have not been so very pleasant as to make me care to look back at them,' he said, bitterly. 'Some men keep a diary of the experiences of each day – I found the experiences tiresome enough in themselves, and had no wish to incur the extra fatigue of writing about them. I told my uncle, when he forced a commercial career upon me, that he was making a mistake; and the result has proved that I was right.'

Mr Darrell spoke with as much gentlemanly indifference as if he had been discussing the affairs of a stranger. He evidently thought that the mistakes of his life rested upon other people's shoulders; and that it was no shame to him, but rather to his credit as a fine gentleman, that he had come home penniless and shabby to sponge upon his mother's slender income.

'And now you have come back, what do you mean to do?' Mr Monckton asked, rather abruptly.

'I shall go in for painting. I'll work hard, down in this quiet place, and get a picture ready for the Royal Academy next year. Will you sit for me, Miss Mason? and you, Miss Vincent? you would make a splendid Rosalind and Celia. Yes, Mr Monckton, I shall try the sublime art whose professors have been the friends of princes.'

'And if you fail——'

'If I fail, I'll change my name, and turn itinerant portrait-painter. But I don't suppose my uncle Maurice means to live for ever. He must leave his money to somebody. If Providence favours me my respected aunts may happen to offend him a few hours before his death, and he may make a will in my favour, in order to revenge himself upon them. I think that's

generally the way of it, eh, Mr Monckton? The testator doesn't consider
the delight of the person who *is* to get the money, but gloats over the
aggravation of the poor wretch who *isn't*.'

The young man spoke as carelessly as if the Woodlands fortune were
scarcely worth a discussion. It was his habit to speak indifferently of all
things, and it was rather difficult to penetrate his real sentiments, so
skilfully were they hidden by this surface manner.

'You had a formidable rival once in your uncle's affections,' Mr
Monckton said, presently.

'Which rival?'

'The Damon of Maurice de Crespigny's youth, George Vandeleur Vane.'

Launcelot Darrell's face darkened at the mention of the dead man's
name. It had always been the habit of the De Crespigny family to look
upon Eleanor's father as a subtle and designing foe, against whom no
warfare could be too desperate.

'My uncle could never have been such a fool as to leave his money to
that spendthrift,' Mr Darrell said.

Eleanor had been sitting at an open window busy with her work
during this conversation; but she rose hastily as Launcelot spoke of her
father. She was ready to do battle for him then and there, if need were.
She was ready to fling off the disguise of her false name, and to avow
herself as George Vane's daughter, if they dared to slander him. Whatever
shame or humiliation was cast upon him should be shared by her.

But before she could give way to this sudden impulse, Gilbert
Monckton spoke, and the angry girl waited to hear what he might say.

'I have every reason to believe that Maurice de Crespigny would have
left his money to his old friend had Mr Vane lived,' the lawyer said. 'I
never shall forget your uncle's grief when he read the account of the old
man's death in a "Galignani" which was put purposely in his way by one
of your aunts.'

'Ah,' said Mr Darrell, bitterly, 'George Vane's death cleared the way for
those harpies.'

'Or for you, perhaps.'

'Perhaps. I have not come home to wait for a dead man's shoes, Mr
Monckton.'

Mrs Darrell had been listening to this conversation, with her watchful
eyes fixed upon Gilbert Monckton's face. She spoke now for the first
time.

'My son is the proper person to inherit my uncle's fortune,' she said;
'he is young, and has a bright future before him. Money would be of
some use to *him*; but it would be almost useless to my sisters.'

She glanced at the young man as she spoke; and in that one kindling
glance of maternal pride the widow revealed how much she loved her son.

The young man was leaning in a lounging attitude over the piano, turning the leaves of Laura's open music-book, and now and then striking his fingers on the notes.

Mr Monckton took up his hat, shook hands with his ward and with Mrs Darrell, and then went over to the window at which Eleanor sat.

'How silent you have been this morning, Miss Vincent,' he said.

The girl blushed as she looked up at the lawyer's grave face. She always felt ashamed of her false name when Mr Monckton addressed her by it.

'When are you and Laura coming to see my new picture?' he asked.

'Whenever Mrs Darrell likes to bring us,' Eleanor answered, frankly.

'You hear, Mrs Darrell?' said the lawyer; 'these two young ladies are coming over to Tolldale to see a genuine Raphael that I bought at Christie's a month ago. You will be taking your son to see his uncle, I have no doubt – suppose you come to lunch at the Priory on the day you go to Woodlands.'

'That will be to-morrow,' answered Mrs Darrell. 'My uncle cannot deny himself to Launcelot after an absence of nearly five years, and even my sisters can scarcely have the impertinence to shut the door in my son's face.'

'Very well; Woodlands and the Priory lie close together. You can cross the park and get into Mr de Crespigny's grounds by the wicket-gate, and so surprise the enemy. That will be the best plan.'

'If you please, my dear Mr Monckton,' said the widow.

She was gratified at the idea of stealing a march upon her maiden sisters, for she knew how difficult it was to effect an entrance to the citadel so jealously guarded by them.

'Come, young ladies,' exclaimed Mr Monckton, as he crossed the threshold of the bay window, 'will you honour me with your company to the gates?'

The two girls rose and went out on to the lawn with the lawyer. Laura Mason was accustomed to obey her guardian, and Eleanor was very well pleased to pay all possible respect to Gilbert Monckton. She looked up to him as something removed from the commonplace sphere in which she felt so fettered and helpless. She fancied sometimes that if she could have told him the story of her father's death, he might have helped her to find the old man's destroyer. She had that implicit confidence in his power which a young and inexperienced woman almost always feels for a man of superior intellect who is twenty years her senior.

Mr Monckton and the two girls walked slowly across the grass; but Laura Mason was distracted by her dogs before she reached the gate, and ran away into one of the shrubberied pathways after the refractory Italian greyhound.

The lawyer stopped at the gate. He was silent for some moments, looking thoughtfully at Eleanor, as if he had something particular to say to her.

'Well, Miss Vincent, how do you like Mr Launcelot Darrell?' he asked at last.

The question seemed rather insignificant after the pause that had preceded it.

Eleanor hesitated.

'I scarcely know whether I like or dislike him,' she said; 'he only came the night before last, and——'

'And my question is what we call a leading one. Never mind, you shall tell me what you think by-and-by, when you have had some more time to form an opinion. You think the young man handsome, I suppose?'

'Oh, yes! very handsome.'

'But you are not the girl to be fascinated by a handsome face. I can see that you mean that by the contemptuous curl of your lip. Quite true, no doubt, Miss Vincent; but there are some young ladies less strong-minded than yourself, who may be easily bewitched by the outline of a classical profile, or the light of a pair of handsome dark eyes. Eleanor Vincent, do you remember what I said to you when I brought you down to Hazlewood?'

Mr Monckton was in the habit of addressing both the girls by their Christian names when he spoke seriously.

'Yes, I remember perfectly.'

'What I said to you then implied an amount of trust which I don't often put in an acquaintance of a couple of hours. That little girl yonder,' added the lawyer, glancing towards the pathway in which Laura Mason flitted about, alternately coaxing and remonstrating with her dogs, 'is tender-hearted and weak-headed. I think you would willingly do anything to serve her and me. You can do her no better service than by shielding her from the influence of Launcelot Darrell. Don't let my ward fall in love with the young man's handsome face, Miss Vincent!'

Eleanor was silent, scarcely knowing how to reply to this strange appeal.

'You think I am taking alarm too soon, I dare say,' the lawyer said, 'but in our profession we learn to look a long way ahead. I don't like the young man, Miss Vincent. He is selfish, and shallow, and frivolous, – false, I think, as well. And, more than this, there is a secret in his life.'

'A secret?'

'Yes; and that secret is connected with his Indian experiences.'

CHAPTER XVII

THE SHADOW ON GILBERT MONCKTON'S LIFE

Tolldale Priory was a red brick mansion, lying deep in a valley, almost hidden amidst the thick woodland that surrounded it; a stately dwelling-place, shrouded and well-nigh entombed by the old trees that shut it in on every side, and made a screen through which only a glimpse of crimson brick could be seen from the bye-road or lane that approached the great iron gates.

From the hill-tops, high above the wooded valley, looking down into the sombre depths of verdure, one could see the gabled roof of the mansion, glimmering amid the woodland, like some rich jewel in its casket; and, at a little distance, the massive square tower of an ivy-grown old church, at which a few tenant-farmers about Tolldale, and the lords of the Priory and their retainers, were wont to worship.

The house was large and handsome; there was a long banqueting hall with a roof of black oak, rich in quaint carvings, and a gloomy corridor, which were said to belong to the reign of Henry the Second; but the rest of the mansion had been built in the time of Queen Anne, and was of that prim and square order of architecture which Sir John Vanbrugh and his followers affected.

The garden was prim and square, like the house, and shut in from the road by high red brick walls, over some part of which the stone-moss had crept, and the ivy trailed for centuries; but the garden had grown out of the stiffness of Queen Anne's day, for every tree and shrub, every flower and weed, patch of grass, or cluster of ivy, grew so luxuriantly in this fertile valley, that it would have needed three times the number of gardeners that had been kept at Tolldale for the last twenty years, to preserve the neat order of the flower-beds and pathways, the holly hedges, the huge bushes of boxwood that had once been fashioned into the grim semblances of lions, swans, dragons, and elephants, and all the other stiff beauties of the pleasure-grounds.

Behind the house a couple of peacocks stalked moodily about a stony courtyard, and a great watch-dog showed his sulky head at the mouth of his kennel, and barked incessantly at the advent of any visitor, as if the Priory had been some weird and enchanted dwelling to which no stranger had right of approach. The entrance to the house most commonly used, opened into this stony courtyard; and in the dusky, flagged hall, hung the ponderous and roomy riding-boots and the heavy saddle of some Tolldale who had distinguished himself in the civil wars.

The rainbow colours that glimmered on the stone pavement of this dusky entrance-hall were reflected from the crests and coats of arms, the interlaced ciphers, the coronets and bloody hands, emblazoned on the mullioned windows, whose splendour chastened and subdued the daylight; tempering the garish glory of heaven for the benefit of aristocratic eyes. But of all these crests and ciphers, of all these honourable insignia, not one belonged to the present owner of the house – Mr Gilbert Monckton, the lawyer.

Tolldale Priory had changed hands several times since the monkish days, in which the older part of the house had been built. Gilbert Monckton had bought the estate twenty years before of a Mr Ravenshaw, a reckless and extravagant gentleman, with an only daughter, whose beauty had been very much talked about in the neighbourhood. Indeed, report had gone so far as to declare that Gilbert Monckton had been desperately in love with this Margaret Ravenshaw, and that it was for her sake he had invested a great part of the splendid fortune left him by his father in the purchase of the Tolldale estate; thereby freeing the young lady's father from very terrible embarrassments, and enabling him to retire to the Continent with his only child.

There had been, certainly, considerable grounds for this report, as, immediately after the transfer of the property, Gilbert Monckton quitted England, leaving his business in the hands of the two junior partners of the house – both much older men than himself, by the bye. He remained abroad for nearly two years; during which time everybody believed him to be travelling with Mr Ravenshaw and his daughter, and at the end of that time returned – an altered man.

Yes; every one who had been intimate with Gilbert Monckton declared that a blight had fallen upon his life; and it was only natural that they should go a little farther than this, and conclude that this change had been brought about by an unhappy attachment; or, in plainer words, that Margaret Ravenshaw had jilted him.

However this might be, the lawyer kept his secret. There was no unmanly sentimentalism in his nature. Whatever his sorrow was, he bore it very quietly, keeping it entirely to himself, and asking sympathy from no living creature. But from the hour of his return to England, he devoted himself to his profession with a determination and an assiduity that he had never before displayed.

This was the great change that his disappointment – whatever that disappointment may have been – had made in him. He did not become either a misanthrope or a bore. He became purely and simply a man of business. The frank, generous-hearted young squire, who had shunned his father's office as if every sheet of parchment or scrap of red tape had been infected by the pestilent vapours of a plague-stricken city, was transformed into a patient and plodding lawyer, whose gigantic grasp of thought and unfailing foresight were almost akin to genius.

For ten years Tolldale Priory was uninhabited by its new master, and left in the care of a snuff-taking old housekeeper, and a deaf gardener, who effectually kept all visitors at bay by a systematic habit of failing to hear the great bell at the iron gates; which might clang never so loudly under the shadow of its wooden pent-house without apparently producing the faintest impression upon the aural nerves of these two superannuated retainers. But at last the day came upon which Mr Monckton grew tired of his London dwelling-place in a dingy square in Bloomsbury, and determined to take possession of his Berkshire estate. He sent a couple of upholsterers to Tolldale Priory, with strict instructions to set the old furniture in order, but to do nothing more; not so much as to alter the adjustment of a curtain, or the accustomed position of a chair or table.

Perhaps he wished to see the familiar rooms looking exactly as they had looked when he had sat by Margaret Ravenshaw's side, a bright and hopeful lad of twenty. He kept the snuff-taking old housekeeper and the deaf gardener, and brought his own small staff of well-trained servants from London. The town-bred servants would have willingly rebelled against their new dwelling-place, and the verdant shades that seemed to shut them in from the outer world; but their wages were too liberal to be resigned for any but a very powerful reason, and they submitted as best they could to the solitude of their new abode.

Mr Monckton travelled backwards and forwards between Tolldale and London almost every day, driving to the station in his phaeton in the morning, and being met by his groom on his return in the evening. The lawyer's professional duties had taxed his strength to the utmost, and grave physicians had prescribed country air and occasional repose as absolutely necessary to him. For nearly ten years, therefore, he had lived at the Priory, forming new acquaintances, and positively no friends. His most intimate associates had been the De Crespignys. This had no doubt arisen from the circumstance of the Woodlands estate adjoining Tolldale. Mr Monckton accepted the acquaintances whom accident forced upon him, but he sought none. Those who knew him best said that the shadow which had so early fallen upon his life had never passed away.

Of course Eleanor Vane had heard these things during her residence at Hazlewood. The knowledge of them invested the grave lawyer with a halo of romance in her girlish eyes. He, like herself, had his secret, and kept it faithfully.

CHAPTER XVIII

UNFORGOTTEN

Mrs Darrell drove her son and the two girls to Tolldale Priory in accordance with Mr Monckton's wish. The widow had no particular desire to bring either Laura or Eleanor into contact with her uncle, Maurice de Crespigny; for she nourished that intense jealousy of all visitors who crossed the threshold of the old man's house, which is only known to expectant heirs whose chances of a fortune tremble in the wavering balance of an invalid's caprice. But Mrs Darrell could not afford to offend Mr Monckton. He paid a high price for her protection of his ward, and was by no means the sort of man to be thwarted with impunity.

Launcelot Darrell lolled by his mother's side, smoking a cigar and taking very little notice of the blossoming hedgerows and glimpses of luxuriant pastoral landscape. The two young ladies sat upon a low seat, with their backs to the ponies, and had therefore ample opportunity of observing the prodigal son's face.

For the first time since Mr Darrell's return Eleanor Vane did watch that handsome face, seeking in it for some evidence of those words which Gilbert Monckton had spoken to her the day before.

'He is selfish, and shallow, and frivolous; false, I think, as well; more than this, he has a secret − a secret connected with his Indian experiences.'

This is what Mr Monckton had said. Eleanor asked herself what right he had to say so much?

It was scarcely likely that a girl of Eleanor's age, so unaccustomed to all society, so shut in from the outer world by her narrow and secluded life, could fail to be a little interested in the handsome stranger, whose advent had not been without a tinge of romance. She was interested in him, and all the more so because of that which Gilbert Monckton had said to her. There was a secret in Launcelot Darrell's life. How strange this was! Had every creature a secret, part of themselves, hidden deep in their breasts, like that dark purpose which had grown out of the misery of her father's untimely death − some buried memory, whose influence was to overshadow all their lives?

She looked at the young man's face. It had an expression of half-defiant recklessness which seemed almost habitual to it; but it was not the face of a happy man.

Laura Mason was the only person who talked much during that drive to Tolldale. That young lady's tongue ran on in a pretty, incessant babble, about nothing in particular. The wild flowers in the hedgerows, the distant glimpses of country, the light clouds floating in the summer sky, the flaming poppies among the ripening corn, the noisy fowl upon the margin of a pond, the shaggy horses looking over farm-yard gates, — every object, animate and inanimate, between Hazlewood and Tolldale, was the subject of Miss Mason's remark. Launcelot Darrell looked at her now and then with an expression of half-admiring amusement, and sometimes aroused himself to talk to her; but only to relapse very quickly into a half-contemptuous, half-sulky silence.

Mr Monckton received his guests in a long low library, looking out into the neglected garden; a dusky chamber, darkened by the shadows of trailing parasites that hung over the narrow windows. But this room was an especial favourite with the grave master of the house. It was here he sat during the lonely evenings that he spent at home. The drawing-rooms on the first floor were only used upon those rare occasions when the lawyer opened his house to his friends of long standing, dashing clients, who were very well pleased to get a week's shooting in the woody coverts about the Priory.

Neither Laura nor Eleanor felt very enthusiastic about the Raphael, which seemed to the two girls to represent an angular and rather insipid type of female beauty; but Launcelot Darrell and his host entered into an artistic discussion that lasted until luncheon was announced by the lawyer's grey-haired butler; a ponderous and dignified individual who had lived with Gilbert Monckton's father, and who was said to know more about his master's history than Gilbert's most intimate friends.

It was nearly three o'clock in the afternoon when luncheon was finished, and the party set out to attempt an invasion upon Woodlands. Launcelot Darrell gave his arm to his mother, who in a manner took possession of her son, and the two girls walked behind with the lawyer.

'You have never seen Mr de Crespigny, I suppose, Miss Vincent?' Gilbert Monckton said, as they went out of the iron gates and struck into a narrow pathway leading through the wood.

'Never! But I am very anxious to see him.'

'Why so?'

Eleanor hesitated. She was for ever being reminded of her assumed name, and the falsehood to which she had submitted out of deference to her half-sister's pride.

Fortunately the lawyer did not wait for an answer to his question.

'Maurice de Crespigny is a strange old man,' he said; 'a very strange old man. I sometimes think there is a disappointment in store for Launcelot Darrell; and for his maiden aunts as well.'

'A disappointment!'

'Yes, I doubt very much if either the maiden ladies or their nephews will get Maurice de Crespigny's fortune.'

'But to whom will he leave it, then?'

The lawyer shrugged his shoulders.

'It is not for me to answer that question, Miss Vincent,' he said. 'I merely speculate upon the chances, in perfect ignorance as to facts. Were I Mr de Crespigny's legal adviser, I should have no right to say as much as this; but as I am not, I am free to discuss the business.'

Mr Monckton and Eleanor were alone by this time, for Laura Mason had flitted on to the party in advance, and was talking to Launcelot Darrell. The lawyer's face clouded as he watched his ward and the young man.

'You remember what I said to you yesterday, Miss Vincent?' he said, after a pause.

'Perfectly.'

'I am very much afraid of the influence that young man's handsome face may have upon my poor frivolous ward. I would move her out of the way of that influence if I could, but where could I remove her? Poor child! she has been shifted about enough already. She seems happy at Hazlewood; very happy, with you.'

'Yes,' Eleanor answered, frankly; 'we love each other very dearly.'

'And you would do anything to serve her?'

'Anything in the world.'

Mr Monckton sighed.

'There is one way in which you might serve her,' he said, in a low voice, as if speaking to himself rather than to Eleanor, 'and yet——'

He did not finish the sentence, but walked on in silence, with his eyes bent upon the ground. He only looked up now and then to listen, with an uneasy expression, to the animated conversation of Launcelot and Laura. They walked thus through the shadowy woodland, where the rustling sound of a pheasant's flight amongst the brushwood, and the gay tones of Laura's voice, only broke the silence.

Beyond the wood they came to a grassy slope dotted by groups of trees, and bounded by an invisible wire fence.

Here, on the summit of a gentle elevation, stood a low white villa – a large and important house – but built in the modern style, and very inferior to Tolldale Priory in dignity and grandeur.

This was Woodlands, the house which Maurice de Crespigny had built for himself some thirty years before; the house whose threshold had so long been jealously guarded by the invalid's maiden nieces.

Mr Monckton looked at his watch as he and Eleanor joined Mrs Darrell.

'Half-past three o'clock,' he said; 'Mr de Crespigny generally takes an airing in his Bath-chair at about this time in the afternoon. You see, I know the habits of the Citadel, and know therefore how to effect a surprise. If we strike across the park we are almost sure to meet him.'

He led the way to a little gate in the fence. It was only fastened by a latch, and the party entered the grassy enclosure.

Eleanor Vane's heart beat violently. She was about to see her father's old and early friend; that friend whom George Vane had never been suffered to approach, to whom he had been forbidden to appeal in the hour of his distress.

'If my poor father could have written to Mr de Crespigny for help when he lost that wretched hundred pounds, he might have been saved from a cruel death,' Eleanor thought.

Fortune seemed to favour the invaders. In a shady avenue that skirted one side of the slope, they came upon the old man and the two sisters. The maiden ladies walked on either side of their uncle's Bath-chair, erect and formidable-looking as a couple of grenadiers.

Maurice de Crespigny looked twenty years older than his spendthrift friend had looked up to the hour of his death. His bent head nodded helplessly forward. His faded eyes seemed dim and sightless. The withered hand lying idle upon the leathern apron of the Bath-chair, trembled like a leaf shaken by the autumn wind. The shadow of approaching death seemed to hover about this feeble creature, separating him from his fellow-mortals.

The two maiden ladies greeted their sister with no very demonstrative cordiality.

'Ellen!' exclaimed Miss Lavinia, the elder of the two, 'this is an unexpected pleasure. I am sure that both Sarah and myself are charmed to see you; but as this is one of our poor dear invalid's worst days, your visit is rather unfortunately timed. If you had written, and given us notice of your coming——'

'You would have shut the door in my face,' Mrs Darrell said, resolutely. 'Pray do not put yourself to the trouble of inventing any polite fictions on my account, Lavinia. We understand each other perfectly. I came here by the back way, because I knew I should be refused admittance at the front door. You keep watch well, Lavinia, and I beg to compliment you upon your patience.'

The widow had approached her uncle's chair, leaving the rest of the party in the background. Pale and defiant, she did battle with her two sisters, fighting sturdily in the cause of her idolized son, who seemed a great deal too listless and indifferent to look after his own interests.

The ladies in possession glared at their sister's pale face with spiteful eyes; they were a little daunted by the widow's air of resolution.

'Who are these people, Ellen Darrell?' asked the younger of the two old maids. 'Do you want to kill my uncle, that you bring a crowd of strangers to intrude upon him at a time when his nerves are at their worst?'

'I have not brought a crowd of strangers. One of those people is my son, who has come to pay his respects to his uncle after his return from India.'

'Launcelot Darrell returned!' exclaimed the two ladies, simultaneously.

'Yes, returned to look after his own interests; returned with very grateful feelings towards those who prompted his being sent away from his native country to waste his youth in an unhealthy climate.'

'*Some* people get on in India,' Miss Lavinia de Crespigny said, spitefully; 'but I never thought Launcelot Darrell would do any good there.'

'How kind it was in you to advise his going, then,' Mrs Darrell answered, promptly. Then, passing by the astonished Miss Lavinia, she went up to her uncle, and bent over him.

The old man looked up at his niece, but with no glance of recognition in his blue eyes, which had grown pale with age.

'Uncle Maurice,' said Mrs Darrell, 'don't you know me?'

The invalid nodded his head.

'Yes, yes, yes!' he said; but there was a vacant smile upon his face, and it seemed as if the words were uttered mechanically.

'And are you glad to see me, dear uncle?'

'Yes, yes, yes!' the old man answered in exactly the same tone.

Mrs Darrell looked up hopelessly.

'Is he always like this?' she asked.

'No,' answered Miss Sarah, briskly, 'he is only so when he is intruded upon and annoyed. We told you it was one of your uncle's bad days, Ellen; and yet you are heartless enough to insist on persecuting him.'

Mrs Darrell turned upon her sister with suppressed rage.

'When will the day come in which I shall be welcome to this place, Sarah de Crespigny?' she said. 'I choose my own time, and seize any chance I can of speaking to my uncle.'

She looked back at the group she had left behind her, and beckoned to her son.

Launcelot Darrell came straight to his uncle's chair.

'You remember Launcelot, Uncle Maurice,' Mrs Darrell said, entreatingly; 'I'm sure you remember Launcelot.'

The two maiden sisters watched their uncle's face with eager and jealous glances. It seemed as if the thick clouds were clearing away from the old man's memory, for a faint light kindled in his faded eyes.

'Launcelot!' he said; 'yes, I remember Launcelot. In India, poor lad, in India.'

'He went to India, dear uncle, and he has been away some years. You remember how unfortunate he was: the indigo planter to whom he was to have gone failed before he got to Calcutta, so that my poor boy could not even deliver the one letter of introduction which he took with him to a strange country. He was thrown upon his own resources, therefore, and had to get a living as he could. The climate never agreed with him, Uncle Maurice, and he was altogether very unhappy. He stayed in India as long as he could endure a life that was utterly unsuited to him; and then flung everything up for the sake of returning to England. You must not be angry with my poor boy, dear Uncle Maurice.'

The old man seemed to have brightened up a good deal by this time. He nodded perpetually as his niece talked to him, but there was a look of intelligence in his face now.

'I am not angry with him,' he said; 'he was free to go; or free to return. I did the best I could for him; but of course he was free to choose his own career, and is so still. I don't expect him to defer to me.'

Mrs Darrell turned pale. This speech appeared to express a renunciation of all interest in her son. She would almost rather that her uncle had been angry and indignant at the young man's return.

'But Launcelot wishes to please you in all he does, dear uncle,' pleaded the widow. 'He will be very, very sorry if he has offended you.'

'He is very good,' the old man answered; 'he has not offended me. He is quite free, quite free to act for himself. I did the best I could for him – I did the best; but he is perfectly free.'

The two maiden sisters exchanged a look of triumph. In this hand-to-hand contest for the rich man's fortune, it did not seem as if either Ellen Darrell or her son were gaining any great advantage.

Launcelot bent over his great-uncle's chair.

'I am very happy to find you alive and well, sir, on my return,' he said, respectfully.

The old man lifted his eyes, and looked earnestly at the handsome face bent over him.

'You are very good, nephew,' he said; 'I sometimes think that, because I have a little money to leave behind me, everybody wishes for my death. It's hard to fancy that every breath one draws is grudged by those who live with us. That's very hard!'

'Uncle!' cried the maiden nieces, simultaneously, with a little shriek of lady-like horror. 'When have you ever fancied that?'

The old man shook his head, with a feeble smile upon his tremulous lips.

'You are very good to me, my dears,' he said, 'very good, but sick men have strange fancies. I sometimes think I've lived too long for myself and others. But never mind that; never mind that. Who are those people there?' he asked, in a different tone.

'Friends of mine, uncle,' Mrs Darrell answered; 'and one of them is a friend of yours. You know Mr Monckton?'

'Monckton! Oh, yes – yes! Monckton, the lawyer,' muttered the old man; 'and who is that girl yonder?' he cried suddenly, with quite an altered voice and manner, almost as if the shock of some great surprise had galvanized him into new life. 'Who is that girl yonder, with fair hair and her face turned this way? Tell me who she is, Ellen Darrell.'

He pointed to Eleanor Vane as he spoke. She was standing a little way apart from Gilbert Monckton and Laura; she had taken off her broad straw hat and slung it across her arm, and the warm summer breeze had swept the bright auburn hair from her forehead. Forgetful of every necessity for caution, in the intensity of her desire to see her dead father's dearest friend, she had advanced a few paces from her companions, and stood watching the group about the old man's chair.

'Who is she, Ellen Darrell?' repeated Mr de Crespigny.

Mrs Darrell looked almost frightened by her uncle's eagerness.

'That young lady is only the musical instructress of another young lady I have in my care, Uncle Maurice,' she answered. 'What is there in her that attracts your attention?'

The old man's eyes filled with tears that rolled slowly down his withered cheeks.

'When George Vane and I were students together at Magdalen,' answered Maurice de Crespigny, 'my friend was the living image of that girl.'

Mrs Darrell turned sharply round; and looked at Eleanor as if she would have almost annihilated the girl for daring to resemble George Vane.

'I think your eyes must deceive you, my dear uncle,' said the widow; 'I knew Mr Vane well enough, and I never saw any likeness to him in this Miss Vincent.'

Maurice de Crespigny shook his head.

'My eyes do not deceive me,' he said. 'It's my memory that's weak, sometimes; my eyesight is good enough. When you knew George Vane his hair was grey, and his handsome looks faded; when I first knew him he was as young as that girl yonder, and he was like her. Poor George! poor George!'

The three sisters looked at each other. Whatever enmity might exist between Mrs Darrell and the two maiden ladies, the three were perfectly agreed upon one point – namely, that the recollection of George Vane and his family must, at any price, be kept out of Maurice de Crespigny's mind.

The old man had not spoken of his friend for years, and the maiden sisters had triumphed in the thought that all memories of their uncle's youth had become obscured and obliterated by the gathering shadows of age. But now, at the sight of a fair-haired girl of eighteen, the old memories came back in all their force. The sudden outburst of feeling came upon the sisters like a thunderbolt, and they lost that common instinct of self-preservation, that ordinary presence of mind, which would have prompted them to hustle the old man off, and carry him at once out of the way of this tiresome, intrusive, fair-haired young woman, who had the impertinence to resemble George Vane.

The sisters had never heard of the birth of Mr Vane's youngest daughter. Many years had elapsed since the intercourse between Mrs Darrell and Hortensia Bannister had extended to more than an occasional epistolary communication, and the stockbroker's widow had not thought it necessary to make any formal announcement of her half-sister's birth.

'Tell that girl to come here,' cried Maurice de Crespigny, pointing with a trembling hand to Eleanor. 'Let her come here; I want to look at her.'

Mrs Darrell thought it would be scarcely wise to oppose her uncle.

'Miss Vincent!' she called, sharply, to the girl; 'come here, if you please; my uncle wishes to speak to you.'

Eleanor Vane was startled by the widow's summons, but she came eagerly to the old man's chair. She was very anxious to see the friend of her dead father. She went close up to the Bath-chair, and stood beside the old man.

Maurice de Crespigny laid his hand upon hers.

'Yes,' he said; 'yes, yes. It's almost the same face – almost the same. God bless you, my dear! It makes me fifty years younger to look at you. You are like a friend who was once very dear to me – very dear to me. God bless you!'

The girl's face grew pale with the intensity of her feeling. Oh! that her father had been alive; that she might have pleaded for him with this old man, and have reunited the broken links of the past. But of what avail now were Maurice de Crespigny's compassionate words? They could not recall the dead. They could not blot out the misery of that horrible night upon which the loss of a pitiful sum of money had driven George Vane to the commission of the fatal act which had ended his life. No! His old friend could do nothing for him; his loving daughter could do nothing for him – except to avenge his death.

Carried away by her feelings; forgetful of her assumed character; forgetful of everything except that the hand now clasped in hers was the same that had been linked in that of her father, years and years ago, in the warm grasp of friendship; Eleanor Vane knelt down beside the old man's chair, and pressed his thin fingers to her lips.

CHAPTER XIX

LIKE THE MEMORY OF A DREAM

Mrs Darrell drove away from Tolldale Priory late in the afternoon, and in a very despondent state of mind. She had done no good by her visit to Woodlands, and it seemed painfully probable that she had done a great deal of harm; for the unfortunate accident of a resemblance between Laura Mason's companion and the late George Vane had stirred up the memories of the past in that turbid stream, the old man's mind. The widow scarcely opened her lips during the homeward drive. She would fain have punished Eleanor for that unlucky chance by which she happened to resemble the dead man, and she did not fail to remark unpleasantly upon Miss Vane's conduct at Woodlands.

'One would really think you wished to trade upon your likeness to Mr Vane, and to insinuate yourself into my uncle's good graces, Miss Vincent,' the widow said, rather sharply.

Eleanor blushed crimson, but did not attempt to reply to her employer's bitter speech. The falsehood of an assumed name was perpetually placing her in positions against which her truthful nature revolted.

If Mrs Darrell had been free to dismiss Eleanor Vane, she would doubtless have done so, for the girl's presence had now become a source of alarm to her. There were two reasons for this sentiment of alarm. First, the likeness which Maurice de Crespigny had discovered between Eleanor and his dead friend, and which might prompt him at any moment to some capricious fancy for the girl; and, secondly, the fact that Eleanor's beauty and fascination might not be without their effect upon Launcelot Darrell.

The widow knew by cruel experience that her son was not a man to surrender his lightest caprice at the entreaty of another. At seven-and-twenty years of age he was as much a spoiled child as he had been at seven. Ellen Darrell looked back at the bitter trials of the past; and remembered how hard it had been to keep her son true even to his own interests. Selfish and self-willed, he had taken his own way; always relying upon his handsome face, his shallow versatility, his showy accomplishments, to carry him through every difficulty, and get him out of every dilemma; always eager for the enjoyment of the present hour, and reckless as to any penalties to be paid in the future.

Mrs Darrell had concentrated every feeling of her heart into one passion: her love for this young man. Frigid and reserved to all the rest of the world, with him she was impulsive, vehement, spontaneous; ready to pour out her heart's blood at his feet, if he had needed such an evidence of her devotion. For him she was jealous and exacting; harsh to others; desperate and unforgiving to those whom she thought his enemies.

For Launcelot she was anxious and ambitious. The hope that her Uncle Maurice would leave his fortune to the young man, whose boyish good looks and precocious talents had made some impression upon him, many years before, never entirely deserted her. But, even if that hope should fail, her sisters were elderly women like herself. If they succeeded in cajoling Maurice de Crespigny out of his fortune, they must surely eventually leave it to their only nephew, Launcelot. This was how the widow reasoned. But there was another chance which she fancied she saw for her son's advancement. Laura Mason, the heiress, evidently admired the young man's handsome face and dashing manners. What more likely than that Launcelot might succeed in winning the hand and fortune of that capricious young lady?

Under these circumstances Mrs Darrell would have been very glad to have removed Eleanor Vane out of her son's way; but this was not easily to be done. When the widow sounded Laura Mason upon the subject, and vaguely hinted at the necessity of parting with Eleanor, the heiress bursts into a flood of tears, and declared passionately that she would not live without her darling Nelly. And when Mrs Darrell went even further than this, and touched upon the subject in a conversation with Mr Monckton, the lawyer replied very decidedly that he considered Miss Vincent's companionship of great benefit to his ward, and that he could not hear of any arrangement by which the two girls would be separated.

Mrs Darrell, therefore, could do nothing but submit; in the hope that for once her son might consent to be governed by his interests, rather than by those erratic impulses which had led him in the reckless and riotous days of his early youth.

She pleaded with him; entreating him to be prudent and thoughtful for the future.

'You have suffered so much from poverty, Launcelot,' she urged, 'that surely you will lose no opportunity of improving your position. Look back, my boy; remember that bitter time in which you were lost to me, led away by low and vicious companions, and only appealing to me when you found yourself in debt and difficulty. Think of your Indian life, and the years you have wasted, − you who are so clever and accomplished, and who ought to have been so fortunate. Oh, Launcelot, if you knew what a bitter thing it is to a mother to see her idolized child waste every opportunity of winning the advancement which should be his by right, − yes, by right, Launcelot, by the right of your talents. I never reproached you, my boy, for coming home to me penniless. Were you to return to me twenty times, as you came back that night, you would always find the same welcome, the same affection. My love for you will never change, my darling, till I go to my grave. But I suffer very bitterly when I think of your wasted youth. You must be rich, Launcelot; you cannot afford to be poor. There are some men to whom poverty seems a spur that drives them on to greatness; but it has clogged your footsteps, and held you back from the fame you might have won.'

'Egad, so it has, mother,' the young man answered, bitterly; 'a shabby coat paralyzes a man's arm, to my mind, and it's not very easy for a fellow to hold his head very high when the nap's all worn off his hat. But I don't mean to sit down to a life of idleness, I can tell you, mother. I shall turn painter. You know I've got on with my painting pretty well during the last few years.'

'I'm glad of that, my dear boy. You had plenty of time to devote to your painting, then?'

'Plenty of time; oh, yes, I was pretty well off for that matter.'

'Then you were not so hard worked in India?'

'Not always. That depended upon circumstances,' the young man answered, indifferently. 'Yes, mother, I shall turn painter, and try and make a fortune out of my brush.'

Mrs Darrell sighed. She wished to see her son made rich by a quicker road than the slow and toilsome pathway by which an artist reaches fortune.

'If you could make a wealthy marriage, Launcelot,' she said, 'you might afford to devote yourself to art, without having to endure the torturing anxieties which must be suffered by a man who has only his profession to depend upon. I wouldn't for the world wish you to sell yourself for money, for I know the wretchedness of a really mercenary marriage; but if——'

The young man flung back the dark hair from his forehead, and smiled at his mother as he interrupted her.

'If I should fall in love with this Miss Laura Mason, who, according to your account, is to have a power of money one of these days, I should prove myself a wise man. That's what you mean, isn't it, *madre mia*? Well, I'll do my best. The young lady is pretty, but her childishness is positively *impayable*. What's the amount of the fortune that is to counterbalance so much empty-headed frivolity? Eh, mother?'

'I can't quite answer that question, Launcelot. I only know that Mr Monckton told me Laura will be very rich.'

'And Gilbert Monckton, although a lawyer, is one of those uncompromising personages who never tell a lie. Well, mother, we'll see about it; I can't say anything more than that.'

The young man had been standing before his easel with his palette and brushes in his hand during this conversation, now and then adding a touch here and there to a picture that he had been working at since his return. He had taken up his abode in his old apartments. His mother spent a good deal of her time with him; sitting at needlework by the open window, while he painted; listening while, in his idler moments, he sat at the piano, composing a few bars of a waltz, or trying to recall the words of some song that he had written long ago; always following him with watchful and admiring eyes, shadowed only by the mother's anxiety for her son's future.

Launcelot Darrell did not seem to be altogether a bad young man. He accepted his mother's love with something of that indolent selfishness common to those spoiled children of fortune upon whom an extra share of maternal devotion has been lavished. He absorbed the widow's affection; and gave her in return an easy-going, graceful attention, which satisfied the unselfish woman, and demanded neither trouble nor sacrifice from the young man himself.

'Now, if the wealthy heiress were the poor companion, mother,' Mr Darrell said, presently working away with his brush as he spoke, 'your scheme would be charming. Eleanor Vincent is a glorious girl; a little bit of a spitfire, I should think, quiet and gentle as she is with us; but a splendid girl; just the sort of wife for an indolent man; a wife who would rouse him out of his lethargy and drive him on to distinction.'

Yes, Launcelot Darrell, who had never in his life resisted any temptation, or accepted any guidance except that of his own wishes, was led by them now; and, instead of devoting himself to the young heiress, chose to fall desperately in love with her fair-haired companion. He fell in love with Eleanor Vane; desperately, after his own fashion. I doubt if there was any great intensity in the young man's desperation; for I do not believe that he was capable of any real depth of feeling. There was a kind of hollow, tinselly fervour in his nature which took the place of true passion. It may be that with him all emotions – love and remorse, penitence, pity, regret, hate, anger, and revenge – were true and real so long as they lasted. But all these sentiments were so short-lived, by reason of the fickleness of his mind, that it was almost difficult to believe even in their temporary truth.

But Eleanor Vane, being very young and inexperienced, had no power of analyzing the character of her lover. She only knew that he was handsome, accomplished, and clever; that he loved her, and that it was very agreeable to be loved by him.

I do not believe that she returned the young man's affection. She was like a child upon the threshold of a new world: bewildered and dazzled by the glorious aspect of the unknown region before her; beguiled and delighted by its beauty and novelty. All the darker aspects of the great passion were unknown to her, and undreamed of by her. She only knew that on the cheerless horizon that had so long bounded her life, a new star had arisen – a bright and wonderful planet, which for a while displaced the lurid light that had so long shone steadfastly across the darkness.

Eleanor Vane yielded herself up to the brief holiday-time which generally comes once in almost every woman's life, however desolate and joyless the rest of that life may be. The holiday comes, – a fleeting summer of gladness and rejoicing. The earth lights up under a new sun and moon; the flowers bloom into new colours and scatter new perfumes on the sublimated atmosphere; the waters of the commonest rivers change to melted sapphires, and blaze with the splendour of a million jewels in the sunshine. The dull universe changes to fairyland; but, alas! the holiday-time is very short: the children grow tired of paradise, or are summoned back to school; the sun and moon collapse into commonplace luminaries; the flowers fade into every-day blossoms; the river flows a grey stream under a November sky; and the dream is over.

Launcelot Darrell had been little more than a fortnight in his mother's house when he declared his love for Miss Mason's companion. The young people had been a great deal together in that fortnight; wandering in the grassy lanes about Hazlewood, and in the shadowy woods round Tolldale Priory, or on breezy hills high up above the lawyer's sheltered mansion. In hope of an alliance between Launcelot and Gilbert Monckton's ward, Mrs Darrell was obliged to submit to the necessity which threw her son very much into the society of the companion as well as of the heiress.

'He will surely never be so foolish as to thwart my plan for his future,' thought the anxious mother. 'Surely, surely, he will consent to be guided by his own interests. Gilbert Monckton must know that it is only likely an attachment may arise between Launcelot and Laura. He would not leave the girl with me unless he were resigned to such an event, and ready to give his consent to their marriage. My son is poor, certainly; but the lawyer knows that he has some hope of inheriting a great fortune.'

While the mother pondered thus over her son's chances of advancement, the young man took life very easily; spending his mornings at his easel, but by no means over-exerting himself; and dawdling away his afternoons in rustic rambles with the two girls.

Laura Mason was very happy in the society of this new and brilliant companion. She was bewitched and fascinated by Mr Darrell's careless talk; which sounded very witty, very profound, sarcastic, and eloquent in the ears of an ignorant girl. She admired him and fell in love with him, and wearied poor Eleanor with her very unreserved rhapsodies about the object of her affection.

'I know it's very bold and wicked and horrid to fall in love with anybody before they fall in love with one, you know, Eleanor,' the young lady said, in not very elegant English; 'but he is so handsome and so clever. I don't think any one in the world could help loving him.

>   "'I have no hope in loving thee,
>   I only ask to love;
>   I ber-rood upon my silent heart,
>   As on its nest a dove;'"

added Miss Mason, quoting that favourite poet of all desponding lovers, poor L.E.L.

I think Mr Monckton's ward rather enjoyed the hopelessness of her attachment. The brooding upon her silent heart was scarcely an accurate exposition of her conduct, as she talked reams of sentiment to Eleanor upon the subject of her unrequited affection. Miss Vane was patient and tender with her, listening to her foolish talk, and dreading the coming of that hour in which the childish young beauty must be rudely awakened from her rose-coloured dream.

'I don't want to marry him, you know, Eleanor,' the young lady said; 'I only want to be allowed to love him. You remember the German story in which the knight watches the window of his lost love's convent cell. I could live for ever and ever near him; and be content to see him sometimes; or to hear his voice, even if I did not see him. I should like to wear boy's clothes, and be his page, like Viola, and tell him my own story, you know, some day.'

Eleanor remembered her promise to Gilbert Monckton, and tried sometimes to check the torrent of sentimental talk.

'I know your love is very poetical, and I dare say it's very true, my pet,' she said; 'but do you think Mr Darrell is quite worth all this waste of affection? I sometimes think, Laura dear, that we commit a sin when we waste our best feelings. Suppose by-and-by you should meet some one quite as worthy of your love as Launcelot Darrell; some one who would love you very devotedly; don't you think you would look back and regret having lavished your best and freshest feelings upon a person who——'

'Who doesn't care a straw for me,' cried the heiress, half crying. 'That's what you mean, Eleanor Vincent. You mean to insinuate that Launcelot doesn't care for me. You are a cruel, heartless girl, and you don't love me a bit.'

And the young lady bemoaned her disappointment, and wept over the hardships of her lot; very much as she might have cried for any new plaything a few years before.

It was upon a burning August morning that Launcelot Darrell declared himself to Eleanor Vane. The two girls had been sitting to him for a picture, – Eleanor as Rosalind, and Laura as Celia, – a pretty feminine

group. Rosalind in her womanly robes, and not her forester's dress of
grey and green; for the painter had chosen the scene in which Celia
promises to share her cousin's exile.

This picture was to be exhibited at the Academy, and was to make Mr
Darrell's fortune. Laura had been called from the room to attend to some
important business with a dressmaker from Windsor, and Eleanor and
Launcelot were alone.

The young man went on painting for some time, and then, throwing
down his brush with a gesture of impatience, went over to the window
near which Eleanor sat, on a raised platform covered with a shabby
drapery of red baize.

'Do you think the picture will be a success, Miss Vincent?' he asked.

'Oh yes, I think so, and hope so; but I am no judge, you know.'

'Your judgment must be as good as the public judgment, I should
think,' Launcelot Darrell answered, rather impatiently. 'The critics will
try to write me down, I dare say, but I don't look to the critics to buy my
picture. They'll call me crude and meretricious, and hard and cold, and
thin and grey, I've no doubt; but the best picture, to my mind, is the
picture that sells best, eh, Miss Vincent?'

Eleanor lifted her arched eyebrows with a look of surprise; this very
low view of the question rather jarred upon her sense of the dignity of
art.

'I suppose you think my sentiments very mercenary and contemptible,
Miss Vincent,' said the painter, interpreting the expression of her face;
'but I have lived out the romance of my life; or one part of that romance,
at any rate; and have no very ardent aspiration after greatness in the
abstract. I want to earn money. The need of money drives men into
almost every folly; farther, sometimes: into follies that touch upon the
verge of crime.'

The young man's face darkened suddenly as he spoke. He was silent for
a few moments, not looking at his companion, but away out of the open
window into vacancy, as it seemed.

The memory of Gilbert Monckton's words flashed back upon Eleanor's
mind. 'There is a secret in Launcelot Darrell's life,' the lawyer had said; 'a
secret connected with his Indian experience.' Was he thinking of that
secret now, Eleanor wondered. But the painter's face brightened almost as
suddenly as it had been overshadowed. He flung back his head with an
impetuous gesture. It seemed almost as if he had cast some imaginary
burden from off his shoulders by that sudden movement.

'I want to earn money, Miss Vincent,' he said. 'Art in the abstract is
very grand, no doubt. I quite believe in the man who stabbed his model
in order to get the death-agony for his picture of the Crucifixion; but I
must make art subservient to my own necessities. I must earn money for

myself and my wife, Eleanor. I might marry a rich woman, perhaps, but I want to marry a poor one. Do you think the girl I love will listen to me, Eleanor? Do you think she will accept the doubtful future I can offer her? Do you think she will be brave enough to share the fortunes of a struggling man?'

Nothing could be more heroic than the tone in which Launcelot Darrell spoke. He had the air of a man who means to strive, with the sturdy devotion of a martyr, to win the end of his ambition, rather than that of a sanguine but vacillating young gentleman who would be ready to fling himself down under the influence of the first moment of despondency, and live upon the proceeds of the pawning of his watch, while his unfinished picture rotted upon the canvas.

He had something of George Vane's nature, perhaps; that fatally hopeful temperament common to men who are for ever going to do great things, and for ever failing to achieve even the smallest. He was one of those men who are perpetually deluding other people by the force of their power of self-delusion.

Self-deluded and mistaken now, it was scarcely strange if he deceived Eleanor Vane, who was carried away by the impetuous torrent of words in which he told her that he loved her, and that the future happiness of his life depended upon the fiat which must issue from her lips.

Only very faltering accents came from those tremulous lips. Miss Vane was not in love; she was only bewildered, and perhaps a little bewitched, by the painter's vehemence. He was the first young, elegant, handsome, and accomplished man with whom she had ever been thrown much in contact. It is scarcely wonderful, then, if this inexperienced girl of eighteen was a little influenced by the ardour of his admiration – by the eloquence of his wild talk.

She had risen from her seat in her agitation, and stood with her back to the sunlit window, trembling and blushing before her lover.

Launcelot Darrell was not slow to draw a flattering inference from these signs of womanly confusion.

'You love me, Eleanor,' he said; 'yes, you love me. You think, perhaps, my mother would oppose our marriage. You don't know me, dearest, if you can believe I would suffer any opposition to come between me and my love. I am ready to make any sacrifice for your sake, Eleanor. Only tell me that you love me, and I shall have a new purpose in life; a new motive for exertion.'

Mr Darrell held the girl's two hands clasped in both his own, as he pleaded thus, using hackneyed phrases with a vehement earnestness that gave new life to the old words. His face was close to Eleanor's, with the broad light of the sunny summer sky full upon it. Some sudden fancy – some vague idea, dim and indistinct as the faint memory of a dream whose details we strive vainly to recall – flashed into the mind of George Vane's orphan daughter as she looked into her lover's black eyes. She recoiled from him a little; her eyebrows contracted into a slight frown: her blushes faded out with the effort which she made to seize upon and analyze that sudden fancy. But her effort was vain: transient as a gleam of summer lightning the thought had flashed across her brain, only to melt utterly away.

While she was still trying to recall that lost idea, while Launcelot Darrell was still pleading for an answer to his suit, the door of the painting-room was pushed open – it had been left ajar by volatile Miss Mason, most likely – and the widow entered, pale, stern, and sorrowful-looking.

CHAPTER XX

RECOGNITION

'I thought Laura was with you,' Mrs Darrell said, rather sharply, as she scrutinized Eleanor's face with no very friendly eyes.

'She was with us until a few minutes ago,' Launcelot answered, carelessly; 'but she was called away to see a milliner or a dressmaker, or some such important personage in the feminine decorative art line. I don't believe that young lady's soul ever soars above laces and ribbons, and all those miscellaneous fripperies which women dignify by the generic title of their "things!"'

Mrs Darrell frowned at her son's contemptuous allusion to the heiress.

'Laura Mason is a very amiable and accomplished girl,' she said.

The young man shrugged his shoulders, and took up his palette and brushes.

'Will you settle yourself once more in the Rosalind attitude, Miss Vincent?' he said. 'I suppose our volatile Celia will be back presently.'

'Will you go and look for her, Launcelot?' interposed Mrs Darrell; 'I want to speak to Miss Vincent.'

Launcelot Darrell flung down his brushes, and turned suddenly towards his mother with a look of angry defiance in his face.

'What have you to say to Miss Vincent that you can't say before me?' he asked. 'What do you mean, mother, by breaking in upon us like this, and scowling at us as if we were a couple of conspirators?'

Mrs Darrell drew herself to her fullest height, and looked half sternly, half contemptuously at her son. His nature, in every quality weaker and meaner than her own, prompted him to shrink from any open contest with her. Dearly as she loved this selfish, handsome scapegrace, there were times in which her better sense revolted against the weakness of her affection; and at such times Launcelot Darrell was afraid of his mother.

'I have a great deal to say to Miss Vincent,' the widow answered, gravely. 'If you refuse to leave us together, I have no doubt Miss Vincent will have the good taste to come elsewhere with me.'

Eleanor looked up, startled by the suppressed passion in the widow's tone.

'I will come with you anywhere, Mrs Darrell,' she said, 'if you wish to speak to me.'

'Come this way, then.'

Mrs Darrell swept out of the room, and Eleanor followed her, before the young man had any opportunity for remonstrance. The widow led the way to the pretty chamber in which Miss Vane slept, and the two women went in together, Mrs Darrell shutting the door behind her.

'Miss Vincent,' she said, taking Eleanor's hand in her own, 'I am going to appeal to you more frankly than one woman often appeals to another. I might diplomatize and plot against you, but I am not base enough for that; though, I dare say, I could stoop to a good deal that is despicable for the sake of my son. And, again, I have so good an opinion of you that I think candour will be the wiser policy. My son has asked you to be his wife.'

'Madam,' stammered Eleanor, looking aghast at the pale face, which had an almost tragic aspect in its earnestness.

'Yes, I told you just now that I could do despicable things for my son's sake. I was passing the door while Launcelot was talking to you. The door was ajar, you know. I heard a few words, enough to tell me the subject upon which he was speaking; and I stopped to hear more. I listened, Miss Vincent. It was very contemptible, was it not?'

Eleanor was silent. She stood before the widow, looking down upon the ground. The colour came and went in her face; she was agitated and confused by what had happened; but in all her agitation and confusion the memory of that sudden fancy that had flashed across her brain while Launcelot Darrell talked to her was uppermost in her mind.

'You despise me for my conduct, Miss Vincent,' said Mrs Darrell, reading the meaning of the girl's silence; 'but the day may come in which you may experience a mother's anguish; the brooding care, the unceasing watchfulness, the feverish, all-devouring anxiety which only a mother can feel. If that day ever comes, you will be able to forgive me; to think mercifully of me. I do not complain of my son; I never have complained of him. But I suffer; I suffer. I see him holding no place in the world, despised by prosperous and successful men, with a wasted youth behind him and a blank future before. I love him; but I am not deceived by him.

The day for all deception is past. He will never be rich or prosperous by any act of his own. There are but two chances for him: the chances of inheriting my uncle's fortune, or the chance of marrying a rich woman. I speak very frankly, you see, Miss Vincent, and I expect equal candour from you. Do you love my son?'

'Madam—— Mrs Darrell – I——'

'You would not answer him just now; I ask you to answer me. The prosperity of his future life hangs upon your reply. I know that he *might* marry a girl who does not love him; and who can bring him a fortune which will place him in the position he ought to occupy. Be generous, Miss Vincent. I ask you to tell me the truth. That is the least you can do. Do you love my son, Launcelot Darrell? Do you love him with your whole heart and soul, as I love him?'

Eleanor lifted her head suddenly, and looked full in the widow's face.

'No, madam,' she answered, proudly, 'I do not.'

'Thank God for that! Even if you had loved him, I would not have shrunk from asking you to sacrifice yourself for his happiness. As it is, I appeal to you without hesitation. Will you leave this place; will you leave me my son, with the chance of planning his future after my own fashion?'

'I will, Mrs Darrell,' Eleanor said, earnestly. 'I thought, perhaps, till to-day – I may have fancied that I – I mean that I was flattered by your son's attention, and perhaps believed I loved him a little,' the girl murmured, shyly; 'but I know now that I have been mistaken. Perhaps it is the truth and intensity of your love that shows me the shallowness and falsehood of my own. I remember how I loved my father,' – her eyes filled with tears as she spoke, – 'and, looking back at my feelings for him, I know that I do not love Mr Darrell. It will be much better for me to go away. I shall be sorry to leave Laura – sorry to leave Hazlewood; for I have been very happy here – too happy perhaps. I will write to your son, and tell him that I leave this place of my own free will.'

'Thank you, my dear,' the widow said, warmly; 'my son would be very hard with me if he thought that my influence had been the means of thwarting any whim of his. I know him well enough to know that this sentiment, like every other sentiment of his, will not endure for ever. He will be angry, and offended, and wounded by your departure; but he will not break his heart, Miss Vincent.'

'Let me go away at once, Mrs Darrell,' said Eleanor; 'it will be better for me to go at once. I can return to my friends in London. I have saved some money while I have been with you, and I shall not go back to them penniless.'

'You are a generous and noble-hearted girl! It shall be my care to provide you with at least as good a home as you have had here. I am not selfish enough to forget how much I have asked of you.'

'And you will let me go at once. I would rather not see Laura, or say good-bye to her; we have grown so fond of each other. I never had a sister – at least never an affectionate sister – and Laura has been like one to me. Let me go away quietly without seeing her, Mrs Darrell; I can write to her from London to say good-bye.'

'You shall do just as you like, my dear,' the widow answered. 'I will drive you over to Windsor in time for the four o'clock train, and you will get into town before dark. I must go now and see what my son is doing. If he should suspect——'

'He shall suspect nothing till I am gone,' said Eleanor. 'It is past one o'clock now, Mrs Darrell, and I must pack all my things. Will you keep Laura out of my room, please, for if she came here, she'd guess——?'

'Yes, yes, I'll go and see – I'll make all arrangements.'

Mrs Darrell hurried out of the room, leaving Eleanor to contemplate the sudden change in her position. The girl dragged one of her trunks out of a recess in the simply-furnished bed-chamber, and sitting down upon it in a half-despondent attitude, reflected on the unlooked-for break in her existence. Once more she was called upon to disunite herself from the past, and begin life anew.

'Am I never to know any rest?' she thought. 'I had grown so accustomed to this place. I shall be glad to see the Signora and Richard once more; but Laura, Mr Monckton, – I wonder whether they will be sorry to lose me?'

By three o'clock in the afternoon all Eleanor's preparations were completed – her trunks packed, and handed over to the factotum of the Hazlewood establishment, who was to see them safely despatched by luggage-train after the young lady's departure. At three o'clock precisely Miss Vincent took her seat beside Mrs Darrell in the low basket-carriage.

Circumstances had conspired to favour the girl's unnoticed departure from Hazlewood. Laura Mason had been prostrated by the intense strain upon her faculties caused by an hour's interview with her dressmaker, and had flung herself upon the sofa in the drawing-room, after sopping up half a pint of eau-de-cologne on her flimsy handkerchief. Worn out by her exertions, and lulled by the summer heat, the young lady had fallen into a heavy slumber of two or three hours' duration.

Launcelot Darrell had left the house almost immediately after the scene in the painting-room, striding out of the hall without leaving any intimation as to the direction in which he was going or the probable hour of his return.

Thus it was that the little pony-carriage drove quietly away from the gates of Hazlewood; and Eleanor left the house in which she had lived for upwards of a year without any one caring to question her as to the cause of her departure.

Very few words were said by either Mrs Darrell or her companion during the drive to Windsor. Eleanor was absorbed in gloomy thought. She did not feel any intense grief at leaving Hazlewood; but some sense of desolation, some despondency, at the thought that she was a wanderer on the face of the earth, with no real claim upon any one, no actual right to rest anywhere. They drove into Windsor while she was thinking thus. They had come through the park, and they entered the town by the gateway at the bottom of the hill. They had driven up the hill, and were in the principal street below the castle wall, when Mrs Darrell uttered an exclamation of surprise.

'Launcelot!' she said; 'and we must pass him to get to the station. There's no help for it.'

Eleanor looked up. Yes, before the door of one of the principal hotels stood Mr Launcelot Darrell, with two other young men. One of these men was talking to him, but he was paying very little attention. He stood upon the edge of the kerbstone, with his back half turned to his companion, kicking the pebbles on the road with the toe of his boot, and staring moodily before him.

In that one moment, – in the moment in which the pony-carriage, going at full speed, passed the young man, – the thought which had flashed, so vague and indistinct, so transient and intangible, through the mind of Eleanor Vane that morning, took a new shape, and arose palpable and vivid in her brain.

This man, Launcelot Darrell, was the sulky stranger who had stood on the Parisian boulevard, kicking the straws upon the kerbstone, and waiting to entrap her father to his ruin.

CHAPTER XXI

ON THE TRACK

The little pony-carriage drove on to the station; and Eleanor, like some traveller in a dream, saw the castle walls and turrets, the busy street and hurrying people, spin past her eyes and melt into confusion. She did not know how she entered the railway station, or how she came to be walking quietly up and down the platform with Mrs Darrell. There was a choking sensation in her dry throat, a blinding mist before her eyes, and a confusion that was almost terrible to bear in her brain. She wanted to get away – anywhere, so long as it was away from all the world. In the meantime she walked up and down the platform, with Launcelot Darrell's mother by her side.

'I am mad,' she thought, 'I am mad! It *cannot* be so!'

Again and again, in the course of Eleanor Vane's brief association with the widow's son, something, – some fancy, some shadowy recollection, vague and impalpable as the faintest clouds in the summer sky above Hazlewood – had flitted across her mind, only to be blotted away before she could even try to define or understand it. But now these passing fancies all culminated in one conviction. Launcelot Darrell was the man whom she had seen lounging on the kerbstone of the boulevard on the night of her last parting with her father.

In vain she reasoned with herself that she had no justifiable grounds for this conviction – the conviction remained, nevertheless. The only foundation for her belief that Launcelot Darrell, from amongst all other men, was the one man whom she sought to pursue, was a resemblance in his attitude, as he stood lounging in the Windsor street, to the attitude of the young man on the boulevard. Surely this was the slightest, the weakest foundation on which belief ever rested! Eleanor Vane could acknowledge this; but she could not lessen the force of that belief. At the very moment when the memory of her father and her father's death had been farthest from her thoughts, this sudden conviction, rapid and forcible as inspiration, had flashed upon her.

The matter was beyond reason, beyond argument.

The young man loitering listlessly upon the kerbstone of the Windsor street was the man who had loitered on the boulevard, waiting, sulkily enough, while his companion tempted George Vane to his destruction.

It seemed as if the girl's memory, suddenly endowed with a new and subtle power, took her back to that August night in the year '53, and placed her once more face to face with her father's enemy. Once more the dark restless eyes, the pale cowering face and moustachioed lip, overshadowed by the slouched hat, flashed upon her for a moment, before the sulky stranger turned away to keep moody silence throughout his companion's babble. And with that memory of the past was interlinked the face and figure of Launcelot Darrell – so closely that, do what she would, Eleanor Vane could not dissociate the two images.

And she had suffered this man, of all other men, to tell her that he loved her; she had taken a romantic pleasure in his devotion. Day after day, and hour after hour, she had been his companion, sharing his enjoyments, sympathizing with his pursuits, admiring and believing him. This day – this very day – he had held her hand, he had looked in her face; and the words she had spoken to Richard Thornton had proved only a vain boast after all. No instinct in her own breast had revealed to her the presence of her father's murderer.

Mrs Darrell looked furtively every now and then at the girl's face. The iron rigidity of that white face almost startled the widow. Was it the expression of terrible grief restrained by a superhuman effort of will?

'Does this girl love my son, I wonder?' the widow thought; and then the answer, prompted by a mother's pride, came quickly after the question: 'Yes, how could she do otherwise than love him? How could any woman on earth be indifferent to my boy?'

Something almost akin to pity stirred faintly in the heart which was so cold to every creature upon earth except this spoiled and prodigal son; and Mrs Darrell did her best to comfort the banished girl.

'I am afraid you are ill, my dear Miss Vincent,' the widow said. 'The excitement of this sudden departure has been too much for you. Pray, my dear, do not think that I submit to this necessity without very great regret. You have given me perfect satisfaction in everything you have done ever since you entered my house. No praises I can bestow upon you in recommending you to a new home will go beyond the truth. Forgive me! Forgive me, my poor child; I know I must seem very cruel; but I love my son so dearly – I love him so dearly!'

There was real feeling in the tone in which these words were spoken; but the widow's voice sounded far away to Eleanor Vane, and the words had no meaning. The girl turned her stony face towards the speaker, and made a feeble effort to understand what was said to her; but all power of comprehension seemed lost in the confusion of her brain.

'I want to get back to London,' she said, 'I want to get away from this place. Will it be long before the train starts, Mrs Darrell?'

'Not five minutes. I have put up your money in this envelope, my dear – a quarter's salary; the quarter began in June, you know, and I have paid you up to September. I have paid for your ticket also, in order that your money might not be broken into by that expense. Your luggage will be sent to you to-morrow. You will get a cab at the station, my dear. Your friends will be very much surprised to see you, no doubt.'

'My friends!' repeated Eleanor, in an absent tone.

'Yes, the good music-mistress and her son. I have your address, Miss Vincent, and you may rely on hearing from me in a few days. I shall take care that you suffer no inconvenience from this sudden change in all our plans. Good-bye; and God bless you, my dear!'

Eleanor had taken her seat in the carriage by this time, and the train was about to move. Mrs Darrell held out her hand; but the girl drew away from her with a sudden movement of terror. 'Oh, please do not shake hands with me!' she cried. 'I am very, very unhappy!'

The train moved away before the widow could reply to this strange speech; and the last thing that Eleanor saw was the pale face of Launcelot Darrell's mother turned towards her with a look of surprise.

'Poor child!' thought Mrs Darrell, as she walked slowly back to the station door, before which her pony-carriage waited. 'She feels this very much, but she has acted nobly.'

The widow sighed as she remembered that the worst part of the struggle was yet to come. She would have her son's indignation to encounter and to endure – not the stormy passion of a strong man unfairly separated from the woman he loves, but the fretful irritation of a spoiled child who has been robbed of a favourite toy.

It was nearly dark when Eleanor Vane reached the Pilasters. She paid and dismissed the cab in Dudley Street, and made her way on foot under the familiar archway and into the Colonnade where the same children seemed to be playing the same games in the dusky light, the same horses peering from the stable-doors, the same cabmen drinking at the old-fashioned public-house at the corner.

The Signora was giving a singing-lesson to a stolid young person, with a fat face and freckles, who was being prepared for the lyric drama, and wished to appear at one of the opera-houses as Norma, after a dozen lessons or so. Eliza Picirillo was trying her hardest to simplify a difficult passage for this embryo Grisi's comprehension, when Eleanor Vane opened the door of the little sitting-room and appeared upon the threshold.

It would have been natural to the girl to have rushed to the piano and flung herself into the arms of the Signora at the risk of upsetting the stolid pupil; and there was something so very *un*natural in her manner as she paused in the open doorway, – something so wan and ghostlike in her appearance, that Eliza Picirillo rose from her music-stool in alarm, and stared aghast at this unexpected visitor.

'Eleanor!' she exclaimed. 'Eleanor!'

'Yes, dear Signora, it is I! I – I know I have come back very unexpectedly; I have a great deal to tell you by-and-by. But I am tired to death. May I sit down, please, while you finish your lesson?'

'*May* you sit down! My darling Nelly! is that the way you talk in your old home? My dear, dear child! do you think you can ever come so unexpectedly as to fail to find a welcome from Eliza Picirillo? Here, my dear, sit down and make yourself as comfortable as you can until I'm able to attend to you. Excuse me, Miss Dodson; we'll go on with the duet directly.'

The music-mistress wheeled forward an old easy-chair, her own favourite seat, and Eleanor dropped wearily into it. Signora Picirillo removed the girl's bonnet, and tenderly smoothed her tumbled hair; murmuring expressions of welcome and affection, and whispering a promise that the lesson should be very soon finished.

She went back to Norma after seeing Eleanor comfortably ensconced
in the arm-chair, and hammered away sturdily and conscientiously at the
'*Deh, con te*' duet, in which Miss Dodson gave a very mild interpretation
of the Italian composer's meaning, and sang about Pollio, her children,
and her wrongs, as placidly as if she had been declaiming her wish to be a
butterfly, or a daisy, or any other sentiment common to English ballad-
singers.

But when Miss Dodson had finished singing, and had put on her
bonnet and shawl (which operation occupied a good deal of unnecessary
time), and had rolled up her music, and found her gloves — which had
fallen off the piano and hidden themselves in an obscure and dusty corner
of the room, — and had further entered into a detailed and intricate
explanation of her arrangements and domestic circumstances before
making an appointment for the next lesson, and had been finally hustled
out of the room and lighted down the stairs, and fully instructed as to the
nearest way from the Pilasters to Camden Town, Eliza Picirillo was able
to give her full attention to the pale-faced girl who had returned so
suddenly to her old shelter. The music-mistress was almost frightened at
the expression of Eleanor Vane's face. She remembered only too well
having seen that look before, upon the September night in Paris, when
the girl of fifteen had sworn to be revenged upon her father's enemies.

'Nelly, my darling,' she said, seating herself beside Eleanor's chair, 'how
is it that you come home so suddenly? Nothing could be greater
happiness than to have you back, my dear. But I know that something has
happened; I can see it in your face, Nelly. Tell me, my love, what is it?'

'It is nothing to be sorry about, dear Signora; I have come away
because — because Mrs Darrell wished it. Her son — her only son — has
come home from India, and she wants him to marry a rich woman, and
— and——'

'And he has fallen in love with *you*, eh, Nelly?' asked the Signora.
'Well, I'm not surprised to hear that, my dear; and you are honourable
enough to beat a retreat, and leave the young man free to make a
mercenary marriage at his mother's bidding. Dear, dear, what strange
things people are ready to do for money now-a-days! I'm sure you've
acted very wisely, my darling; so cheer up, and let me see the bright smile
that we've been accustomed to. There's nothing in all this to make you
look so pale, Nelly.'

'Do I look pale?'

'Yes, as pale as a ghost weary with a long night's wandering. Nelly,
dear,' said the Signora, very gently, 'you weren't in love with this young
man; you didn't return his affection, did you?'

'In love with him!' cried Eleanor Vane, with a shudder, 'oh! no, no.'

'And yet you seem sorry at having left Hazlewood?'

'I am sorry; I – I had many reasons for wishing to stay there.'

'You were attached to your companion, Miss Mason?'

'Yes, I was very much attached to her,' answered Eleanor. 'Don't ask me any more questions to-night, dear Signora. I'm tired out with my journey and the excitement of – all – that has happened to-day; I will explain things more fully to-morrow. I am glad to come back to you – very, very glad to see you once more, dearest friend; but I had a strong reason for wishing to stay at Hazlewood, – I have a powerful motive for wanting to go back there, if I could go back, which I fear I never can.' The girl stopped abruptly, as if absorbed in her own thoughts, and almost unconscious of her friend's presence.

'Well, well, Nelly, I won't question you any further,' Eliza Picirillo said, soothingly. 'Goodness knows, my dear, I am glad enough to have you with me, without worrying you about the why and the wherefore. But I must go and try and get your little room ready again for you, or perhaps, as it's late, you'd better sleep with me to-night.'

'If you please, dear Signora.'

The music-mistress hurried away to make some preparations in the bedchamber adjoining the little sitting-room; and Eleanor Vane sat staring at the guttering tallow-candles on the table before her – lost in the tumult and confusion of her thoughts, which as yet took no distinct form in her brain.

At the very moment in which she had set a barrier between herself and Hazlewood that might prevent her ever crossing the threshold of its gates, she had made a discovery which rendered that retired country dwelling-house the one spot upon earth to which she had need to have free access.

'I fancied that I was going away from my revenge when I left London to go into Berkshire,' she thought; 'now I leave my revenge behind me at Hazlewood. And yet, how can it be as I think? How can it be so? Launcelot Darrell went to India a year before my father died. Can it be only a likeness after all – an accidental likeness – between *that man* and Mrs Darrell's son?'

She sat thinking of these things – reasoning with herself upon the utter improbability of the identity of the two men, yet yielding again and again to that conviction which had forced itself upon her, sudden and irresistible, in the Windsor street, – while the Signora bustled about between the two rooms, stopping to cast a stolen glance now and then at Eleanor Vane's thoughtful face.

Mr Richard Thornton came in by-and-by. The Phoenix was closed as to dramatic performances, but the scene-painter's work never stopped. The young man gave utterance to a cry of delight as he saw the figure sitting in his aunt's easy-chair.

'Nell!' he exclaimed, 'has the world come to an end, and have you dropped into your proper position in the general smash! Eleanor, how glad I am to see you!'

He held out both his hands. Miss Vane rose and, mechanically, put her white fingers in the weatherbeaten-looking palms held out to receive them.

In that moment the scene-painter saw that something had happened.

'What's the matter, Nell?' he cried, eagerly.

'Hush, Dick,' said the girl in a whisper; 'I don't want the Signora to know.'

'You don't want the Signora to know what?'

'I have found that man.'

'What man?'

'The man who caused my father's death.'

CHAPTER XXII

IN THE SHIPBROKER'S OFFICE

Eleanor Vane employed the morning after her arrival at the Pilasters in writing to Laura Mason. She would have written a long letter if she could, for she knew what grief her sudden departure must have caused her childish and confiding companion; but she could not write of anything except the one thought that absorbed her whole brain, leaving her for the common business of life a purposeless and powerless creature. The explanation which she gave of her sudden departure was lame and laboured; her expressions of regard were trite and meaningless. It was only when she came to that subject which was the real purpose of her letter; it was only when she came to write of Launcelot Darrell that there was any vigour or reality in her words.

'I have a favour to ask you, dear Laura,' she wrote; 'and I must beg you to use your best discretion in granting it. I want you to find out for me the date of Mr Darrell's departure for Calcutta, and the name of the vessel in which he sailed. Do this, Laura, and you will be serving me — perhaps serving him also.'

'If I find that he really was in India at the date of my father's death,' Eleanor thought, 'I *must* cease to suspect him.'

Later in the day, Miss Vane went out with Richard into the streets and squares in which all their secret conferences had taken place. She told the scene-painter very simply and briefly of what had happened, and poor Dick listened to her story with a tender respect, as he would have listened to anything from her. But he shook his head with a sad smile when she had finished.

'What do you think now, Richard?' she asked.

'I think that you are the dupe of a foolish fancy, Nelly,' the young man answered. 'You are deceived by some chance resemblance between this Mr Darrell and the man you saw upon the boulevard. Any dark pale-faced man lounging moodily on a kerbstone would have reminded you of the figure which is so interwoven with the memories of that mournful time in Paris. Forget it, Nelly, my dear – forget that dark chapter in the history of your girlhood. Your father's rest will be none the sweeter because the brightness of your youth is blighted by these bitter memories. Do your duty, Eleanor, in the state to which you are called. You are *not* called upon to sacrifice the fairest years of your life to a Quixotic scheme of vengeance.'

'Quixotic!' cried Eleanor, reproachfully; 'you would not speak like this, Richard, if *your* father had suffered as my father suffered through the villany of a gambler and cheat. It is no use talking to me, Dick,' she added, resolutely. 'If this conviction, which I cannot get out of my mind, is a false one, its falsehood must be proved. If it is true – why, then, it will seem to me as if Providence had flung this man across my pathway, and that I am appointed to bring punishment upon him for his wickedness.'

'Perhaps, Eleanor, but this Mr Darrell is *not* the man.'

'How do you know he is not?'

'Because, according to your own account, Launcelot was in India in the year '53.'

'Yes, they *say* that he was there.'

'Have you any reason to doubt the fact?' asked Richard.

'Yes,' answered Eleanor. 'When Mr Darrell first returned to Hazlewood, Laura Mason was very anxious to hear all about what she called his "adventures" in India. She asked him a great many questions, and I remember – I cannot tell you, Dick, how carelessly I listened at the time, though every word comes back to me now as vividly as if I had been a prisoner, on trial for my life, listening breathlessly to the evidence of the witnesses against me – I remember now how obstinately Launcelot Darrell avoided all Laura's questions, telling her at last, almost rudely, to change the subject. The next day Mr Monckton came to us, and he talked about India; and Mr Darrell again avoided the question in the same sullen, disagreeable manner. You may think me weak and foolish, Richard, and I dare say I am so; but Mr Monckton is a very clever man. *He* could not be easily deceived.'

'But what of him?'

'He said, "Launcelot Darrell has a secret; and that secret is connected with his Indian experiences." I thought very little of this at the time, Dick: but I think I understand it now.'

'Indeed! And the young man's secret———?'

'Is that he never went to India.'

'Eleanor!'

'Yes, Richard, I think and believe this; and you must help me to find out whether I am right or wrong.'

The scene-painter sighed. He had hoped that his beautiful adopted sister had long since abandoned or forgotten her utopian scheme of vengeance in the congenial society of a gay-hearted girl of her own age. And behold, here she was, vindictive, resolute, as upon that Sunday evening, a year and a half ago, on which they had walked together in those dingy London streets.

Eleanor Vane interpreted her companion's sigh.

'Remember your promise, Richard,' she said. 'You promised to serve me, and you must do so – you *will* do so, won't you, Dick?'

The avenging fury had transformed herself into a siren as she spoke, and looked archly up at her companion's face, with her head on one side, and a soft light in her grey eyes.

'You won't refuse to serve me, will you, Richard?'

'Refuse!' cried the young man. 'Oh! Nelly, Nelly, you know very well there is nothing in the world I could refuse you.'

Miss Vane accepted this assurance with great composure. She had never been able to dissociate Richard Thornton with those early days in which she had accompanied him to Covent Garden to buy mulberry leaves for his silkworms, and had learned to play 'God save the Queen' upon the young musician's violin. Nothing was farther from her thoughts than the idea that poor Dick's feelings could have undergone any change since those childish days in the King's Road, Chelsea.

The letter which Eleanor so feverishly awaited from Laura Mason came by return of post. The young lady's epistle was very long, and rather rambling in its nature. Three sheets of note-paper were covered with Miss Mason's lamentations for her Eleanor's absence, reproachful complainings against her cruelty, and repeated entreaties that she would come back to Hazlewood.

George Vane's daughter did not linger over this feminine missive. A few days ago she would have been touched by Laura's innocent expressions of regard; now her eyes hurried along the lines, taking little note of all those simple words of affection and regret, and looking greedily forward to that one only passage in the letter which was likely to have any interest for her.

This passage did not occur until Eleanor had reached the very last of the twelve pages which Miss Mason had covered with flowing Italian characters, whose symmetry was here and there disfigured by sundry blots and erasures. But as her eyes rested upon the last page, Eleanor Vane's hand tightened upon the paper in her grasp, and the hot blood rushed redly to her earnest face.

'And I have found out all you want to know, dear Nell,' wrote Miss Mason; 'though I am puzzled out of my wits to know why you should want to know it – when I did exercise in composition at Bayswater, they wouldn't let me put two "knows" so near together; but you won't mind it, will you, dear? Well, darling, I'm not very clever at beating about the bush or finding out anything in a diplomatic way; so this afternoon at tea – I am writing to catch the evening post, and Bob is going to take my letters to the village for sixpence – I asked Launcelot Darrell, who was not drinking his tea, like a Christian, but lolling in the window, smoking a cigar: he has been as sulky as a bear ever since you left – oh, Nelly, Nelly, he isn't in love with you, is he? – I should break my heart if I thought he was – I asked him, point-blank, what year and what day he sailed for India. I suppose the question sounded rather impertinent, for he coloured up scarlet all in a minute, and shrugged his shoulders in that dear disdainful way of his that always reminds me of Lara or the Corsair – L. and the C. were the same person, though, weren't they? – and said, "I don't keep a diary, Miss Mason, or I should be happy to afford you any information you may require as to my antecedents." I thought I should have dropped through the floor, Nelly, – the floor won't let one drop through it, or else I am sure I should, – and I couldn't have asked another question, even for your sake, dear; when, strange to say, Mrs Darrell got me quite out of the difficulty. "I am sorry you should answer Laura so very unkindly, Launcelot," she said; "there is nothing strange in her question. *I* remember the date of your departure from your native country only too vividly. You left this house upon the 3rd of October, '52, and you were to sail from Gravesend on the 4th, in the *Princess Alice*. I have reason to remember the date, for it seemed as if my uncle chose the very worst season of the year for sending you upon a long sea-voyage. But he was prompted, no doubt, by my sisters. I ought to feel no anger against *him*, poor old man!"'

Eleanor Vane glanced hurriedly at the concluding words of the letter. Then, with the last sheet crumpled in her hand, she sat motionless and absorbed, thinking over its contents.

'If Launcelot Darrell sailed for India upon the 4th of October, '52, he is not likely to have been in Paris in '53. If I can only prove to myself that he did sail upon that date, I will try and believe that I have been deluded by some foolish fancy of my own. But why did his face flush scarlet when Laura questioned him about his voyage? – why did he pretend to have forgotten the date?'

Eleanor waited impatiently for the arrival of her friend and counsellor, Richard Thornton. He came in at about three o'clock in the afternoon, while his aunt was still absent amongst her out-of-door pupils, and flung himself, jaded and worn out, on the chintz-covered sofa. But, tired as he was, he aroused himself by an effort to listen to that portion of Laura Mason's letter which related to Launcelot Darrell.

'What do you think now, Dick?' Miss Vane asked, when she had finished reading.

'Pretty much what I thought before, Nell,' answered Mr Thornton. 'This young fellow's objection to talk of his Indian voyage is no proof that he never went upon that voyage. He may have half-a-dozen unpleasant recollections connected with that part of his life. I don't particularly care about talking of the Phoenix; but I never committed a murder in the obscurity of the flies, or buried the body of my victim between the stage and the mezzanine floor. People have their secrets, Nell; and we have no right to pry into the small mysteries which may lurk under a change of countenance or an impatient word.'

Eleanor Vane took very little notice of the young man's argument.

'Can you find out if Launcelot Darrell sailed in the *Princess Alice*, Dick?' she added.

The scene-painter rubbed his chin reflectively.

'I can *try* and find out, my dear,' he said, after a pause; 'that's open to anybody. The *Princess Alice*! She's one of Ward's ships, I think. If the shipbrokers are inclined to be civil, they'll perhaps help me; but I have no justification for bothering them upon the subject, and they *may* tell me to go about my business. If I could give them a good reason for my making such an inquiry, I might very likely find them willing to help me. But what can I tell them — except that a very beautiful young person with grey eyes and auburn hair has taken an absurd crotchet into her obstinate head, and that I, her faithful slave, am compelled to do her bidding?'

'Never mind what they say to you, Richard,' Miss Vane replied, authoritatively; 'they *must* answer your question if you only go on asking them long enough.'

Mr Thornton smiled.

'That's the true feminine method of obtaining information; isn't it, Nell?' he said. 'However, I'll do my best: and if the shipbrokers are to be "got at," as sporting gentlemen say, it shall go hard if I don't get a list of the passengers who sailed in the *Princess Alice*.'

'Dear, dear Dick!' cried Eleanor, holding out both her hands to her companion. The young man sighed. Alas! he knew only too well that all this pretty friendliness was as far away from any latent tenderness or hidden emotion as the blusterous frozen North is from the splendid sunny South.

'I wonder whether she knows what love is,' thought the scene-painter; 'I wonder whether her heart has been touched ever so slightly by the fatal emotion. No; she is a bright virginal creature, all confidence and candour, and she has yet to learn the mysteries of life. I wish I could think less of her and fall in love with Miss Montalembert – her name is plain Lambert, and she has added the Monta for the sake of euphony. I wish I could fall in love with Lizzie Lambert, popularly known as Elise Montalembert, the soubrette at the Phoenix. She is a good little girl, and earns a salary of four pounds a week. She's fond of the Signora, too, and we could leave the Pilasters and go into housekeeping upon our joint salaries.'

Mr Thornton's fancies might have rambled on in this wise for some time, but he was abruptly aroused from his reverie by Eleanor Vane, who had been watching him rather impatiently.

'When are you going to the shipbroker's, Dick?' she asked.

'When am I going?'

'Yes; you'll go at once, won't you?'

'Eh! Well, my dear Nell, Cornhill's a good step from here.'

'But you can take a cab,' cried the young lady. 'I've plenty of money, Dick, and do you think I shall grudge it for such a purpose? Go at once, Richard, dear, and take a cab.'

She pulled a purse from her pocket, and tried to force it into the young man's hand; but he shook his head.

'I'm afraid the shipbroker's office would be closed, Nelly,' he said. 'We'd better wait till to-morrow morning.'

But the young lady would not hear of this. She was sure the shipbroker's office wouldn't close so early, she said, with as much authority as if she had been intimately acquainted with the habits of shipbrokers; and she bustled Dick down stairs and out of the house before he well knew where he was.

He returned in about an hour and a half, very tired and dusty; having preferred his independence and an omnibus to the cab offered by Eleanor.

'It's no use, Nelly,' he said despondently, as he threw off his hat, and ran his dirty fingers through the rumpled shock of dusty brown hair that had been blown about his face by the hot August wind, 'the office was just closing, and I couldn't get anything out of the clerks. I was never so cruelly snubbed in my life.'

Miss Vane looked very much disappointed, and was silent for a minute or so. Then her face suddenly brightened, and she patted Richard's shoulder with a gesture expressive of patronage and encouragement.

'Never mind, Dick,' she said, smilingly, 'you shall go again to-morrow morning early; and I'll go with you. We'll see if these shipbroker's clerks will snub *me*!'

'Snub you!' cried Richard Thornton, in a rapture of admiration. 'I think that, of all the members of the human family, paid officials are the most unpleasant and repulsive; but I don't think there's a clerk in Christendom who could snub you, Miss Vane.'

Eleanor smiled. Perhaps for the first time in her life the young lady was guilty of a spice of that feminine sin called coquetry. Her boxes had arrived from Hazlewood upon the previous evening. She was armed, therefore, with all those munitions of war without which a woman can scarcely commence a siege upon the fortress of man's indifference.

She rose early the next morning – for she was too much absorbed in the one great purpose of her life to be able to sleep very long or very soundly – and arrayed herself for a visit to the shipbroker.

She put on a bonnet of pale blue crape, which was to be the chief instrument in the siege – a feminine battering-ram or Armstrong gun before which the stoutest wall must have crumbled – and smoothed her silken locks, her soft amber-dropping tresses, under this framework of diaphanous azure. Then she went into the little sitting-room where Mr Richard Thornton was loitering over his breakfast, to try the effect of this piece of milliner's artillery upon the unhappy young man.

'Will the clerks snub me, Dick?' she asked, archly.

The scene-painter replied with his mouth full of egg and bread-and-butter, and was more enthusiastic than intelligible.

A four-wheel cab jolted Miss Vane and her companion to Cornhill, and the young lady contrived to make her way into the sanctum-sanctorum of the shipbroker himself, in a manner which took Richard Thornton's breath away from him, in the fervour of his admiration. Every barrier gave way before the blue bonnet and glistening auburn hair, the bright grey eyes and friendly smile. Poor Dick had approached the officials with that air of suppressed enmity and lurking hate with which the Englishman generally addresses his brother Englishman; but Eleanor's friendliness and familiarity disarmed the stoniest of the clerks, and she was conducted to the shipbroker's private room by an usher who bowed before her as if she had been a queen.

The young lady told her story very simply. She wished to ascertain if a gentleman called Launcelot Darrell had sailed in the *Princess Alice* on the 4th of October, '52.

This was all she said. Richard Thornton stood by, fingering difficult passages in his last overture on the brim of his hat, out of sheer perturbation of spirit, while he wondered at and admired Miss Vane's placid assurance.

'I shall be extremely obliged if you can give me this information,' she said in conclusion, 'for a great deal depends upon my being able to ascertain the truth in this matter.'

The shipbroker looked through his spectacles at the earnest face turned so trustingly towards his own. He was an old man, with granddaughters as tall as Eleanor, but was nevertheless not utterly dead to the influence of a beautiful face. The auburn hair and diaphanous bonnet made a bright spot of colour in the dinginess of his dusty office.

'I should be very ungallant were I to refuse to serve a young lady,' the old man said, politely. – 'Jarvis,' he added, turning to the clerk who had conducted Eleanor to his apartment, 'do you think you could contrive to look up the list of passengers in the *Princess Alice*, October 4th, '52?'

Mr Jarvis, who had told Richard to go about his business upon the day before, said he had no doubt he could, and went away to perform this errand.

Eleanor's breath grew short and quick, and her colour rose as she waited for the clerk's return. Richard executed impossible passages on the brim of his hat. The shipbroker watched the girl's face, and drew his own deductions from the flutter of agitation visible in that bright countenance.

'Aha!' he thought, 'a love affair, no doubt. This pretty girl in the blue bonnet has come here to look after a runaway sweetheart.'

The clerk returned, carrying a ledger, with his thumb between two of the leaves. He opened the uninteresting-looking volume, and laid it on the table before his employer, pointing with his spare forefinger to one particular entry.'

'A berth was taken for a Mr Launcelot Darrell, who was to share his cabin with a Mr Thomas Halliday,' the shipbroker said, looking at the passage to which the clerk pointed.

Eleanor's face crimsoned. She had wronged the widow's son, then, after all.

'But the name was crossed out afterwards,' continued the old man, 'and there's another entry farther down, dated October 5th. The ship sailed without Mr Darrell.'

The crimson flush faded out of Eleanor's face and left it deadly pale. She tottered a few paces towards the table, with her hand stretched out, as if she would have taken the book from the shipbroker and examined the entry for herself. But midway between the chair she had left and the table, her strength failed her, and she would have fallen if Richard Thornton had not dashed his hat upon the ground, and caught her sinking figure in his outstretched arms.

'Dear me!' exclaimed the shipbroker, 'bless my soul: a glass of water, Jarvis; this is very sad, very sad, indeed. A runaway lover, I suppose, or a brother, perhaps. These sort of things are always happening. I assure you, if I had the gift that some of you young people have, I could write half-a-dozen romances out of the history of this office.'

The clerk came back with the glass of water; it was rather a murky-looking fluid, but a few drops between Eleanor's pale lips served to bring the life back to her.

She lifted her head with the proud resolution of a queen, and looked at the compassionate shipbroker with a strange smile. She had heard the old man's suppositions about lovers and brothers. How far away his simple fancy led him from the bitter truth!

She held out her hand to him as she rose from her chair, erect and dauntless as a fair-haired Joan of Arc, ready to gird on the sword in defence of her king and country.

'I thank you very much, sir,' she said, 'for what you have done for me to-day. My father was an old man — as old or older perhaps than yourself; and he died a very cruel death. I believe that your kindness of this day will help me to avenge him.'

CHAPTER XXIII

RESOLVED

Launcelot Darrell had not sailed for Calcutta in the *Princess Alice*. This point once established, it was utterly vain for Richard Thornton to argue against that indomitable belief which had taken possession of Eleanor Vane's mind, respecting the identity between the man who had won her father's money at écarté, and Mrs Darrell's only son.

'I tell you, Richard,' she said, when the scene-painter argued with her, 'that nothing but proof positive of Launcelot Darrell's absence in India at the date of my father's death would have dispossessed me of the idea that flashed upon me on the day I left Berkshire. He was not in India at that time. He deceived his mother and his friends. He remained in Europe; and led, no doubt, an idle, dissipated life. He must have lived by his wits, for he had no money from his mother — no one to help him — no profession to support him. What is more likely than that he went to Paris, — the paradise of scoundrels, I have heard you say, Richard, — under an assumed name? What more likely? Why, *he was there!* The man I saw on the boulevard, and the man I saw in the Windsor street, are one and the same. You cannot argue me out of that conviction, Richard Thornton, for it is the truth. It is the truth, and it shall be the business of my life to prove that it is so.'

'And what then, Eleanor?' Mr Thornton asked, gravely. 'Supposing you can prove this; by such evidences as will be very difficult to get at — by such an investigation as will waste your life, blight your girlhood, warp your nature, unsex your mind, and transform you from a candid and confiding woman into an amateur detective. Suppose you do all this, — and you little guess, my dear, the humiliating falsehoods, the pitiful

deceptions, the studied basenesses, you must practise if you are to tread
that sinuous pathway, – what then? What good is effected; what end is
gained? Are you any nearer to the accomplishment of the vow you
uttered in the Rue de l'Archevêque?'

'What do you mean, Richard?'

'I mean that to prove this man's guilt is not to avenge your father's
death. Neither you nor the law has any power to punish him. He may or
may not have cheated your poor father. At this distance of time you can
prove nothing; except that he played écarté in the private room of a café,
and that he won all your father's money. He would only laugh in your
face, my poor Nelly, if you were to bring such a charge as this against
him.'

'If I can once prove that, which I now believe as firmly as if every
mortal proof had demonstrated its truth, I know how to punish
Launcelot Darrell,' replied the girl.

'You know how to punish him?'

'Yes. His uncle – that is to say, his great-uncle – Maurice de Crespigny,
was my father's firmest friend. I need not tell you that story, Dick, for
you have heard it often enough from my poor father's own lips.
Launcelot Darrell hopes to inherit the old man's money, and is, I believe,
likely enough to do so. But if I could prove to the old man that my father
died a melancholy and untimely death through his nephew's treachery,
Launcelot Darrell would never receive a sixpence of that money. I know
how eagerly he looks forward to it, though he affects indifference.'

'And you would do this, Eleanor?' asked Richard, staring aghast at his
companion. 'You would betray the secrets of this young man's youth to
his uncle, and compass his ruin by that revelation?'

'I would do what I swore to do in the Rue de l'Archevêque – I would
avenge my father's death. The last words my poor father ever wrote
appealed to me to do that. I have never forgotten those words. There
may have been a deeper treachery in that night's work than you or I
knew of, Richard. Launcelot Darrell knew who my father was; he knew
of the friendship between him and Mr de Crespigny. How do we know
that he did not try to goad the poor old man to that last act of his
despair? – how do we know that he did not plan those losses at cards, in
order to remove his uncle's friend from his pathway? O God! Richard, if
I thought that——!'

The girl rose from her chair in a sudden tumult of passion, with her
hands clenched and her eyes flashing.

'If I could think that his treachery went beyond the baseness of
cheating my father of his money for the money's sake, I would take *his*
life for that dear life as freely and as unhesitatingly as I lift my hand up
now.'

She raised her clenched hand towards the ceiling as she spoke, as if to register some unuttered vow. Then, turning abruptly to the scene-painter, she said, almost imploringly, –

'It can't be, Richard; he cannot have been so base as that! He held my hand in his only a few days ago. I would cut off that hand if I could think that Launcelot Darrell had planned my father's death.'

'But you cannot think it, my dear Eleanor,' Richard answered, earnestly. 'How should the young man know that your father would take his loss so deeply to heart? We none of us calculate the consequences of our sins, my dear. If this man cheated, he cheated because he wanted money. For Heaven's sake, Nelly, leave him and his sin in the hands of Providence! The future is not a blank sheet of paper, for us to write any story we please upon, but a wonderful chart, mapped out by a Divine and unerring Hand. Launcelot Darrell will not go unpunished, my dear. "My faith is strong in Time," as the poet says. Leave the young man to time – and to Providence.'

Eleanor Vane shook her head, smiling bitterly at her friend's philosophy. Poor mad Constance's reply always rose, in some shape or other, to the girl's lips in answer to Richard's arguments. The Cardinal reasons with wonderful discretion, but the bereaved mother utters one sentence that is more powerful than all the worthy man's moralities: 'He talks to me that never had a son!'

'It is no use preaching to me,' Miss Vane said. 'If *your* father had died by this man's treachery, you would not feel so charitably disposed towards him. I *will* keep the promise made three years ago. I *will* prove Launcelot Darrell's guilt; and that guilt shall stand between him and Maurice de Crespigny's fortune.'

'You forget one point in this business, Eleanor.'

'What point?'

'It may take you a very long time to obtain the proof you want. Mr de Crespigny is an old man and an invalid. He may make a will in Mr Darrell's favour and die before you are in a position to tell him of his nephew's treachery to your poor father.'

Eleanor was silent for a few moments. Her arched brows contracted, and her mouth grew compressed and rigid.

'I must go back to Hazlewood, Dick,' she said, slowly. 'Yes, you are right; there is no time to be lost. I *must* go back to Hazlewood.'

'That is not very practicable, is it, Nell?'

'I *must* go back, if I go in some disguise – if I go and hide myself in the village, and watch Launcelot Darrell when he least thinks he is observed. I don't care how I go, Richard, but I must be there. It can only be from the discoveries I make in the present that I shall be able to trace my way back to the history of the past. I must go there!'

'And begin at once upon the business of a detective! Eleanor, you shall not do this, if I can prevent you.'

Richard Thornton's unavowed love gave him a certain degree of authority over the impulsive girl. There is always a dignity and power in every feeling that is really true. Throughout the story of Notre Dame de Paris, the hunchback's love for Esmeralda is never once contemptible. It is only Phoebus, handsome, glittering, and false, who provokes our scorn.

Eleanor Vane did not rebel against the young man's tone of authority.

'Oh, Dick, Dick!' she cried, piteously, 'I know how wicked I am. I have been nothing but a trouble to you and the dear Signora. But I cannot forget my father's death – I cannot forget the letter he wrote to me. I must be true to the vow I made then, Richard, if I sacrifice my life in keeping my word.'

Eliza Picirillo came in before the scene-painter could reply to this speech. It had been agreed between the two young people that the Signora should know nothing of Miss Vane's discoveries; so Eleanor and Richard saluted the music-mistress in that strain of factitious gaiety generally adopted under such circumstances.

Signora Picirillo's perceptions were perhaps a little blunted by the wear-and-tear of half-a-dozen hours' labour amongst her out-door pupils; and as Eleanor bustled about the room preparing the tea-table and making the tea, the good music-mistress fully believed in her protégée's simulated liveliness. When the table had been cleared, and Richard had gone to smoke his short meerschaum amongst the damp straw and invalid cabs in the promenade before the Pilasters, Eleanor seated herself at the piano, in order to escape the necessity of conversation. Her fingers flew over the keys in a thousand complexities of harmony, but her mind, for ever true to one idea, brooded upon the dark scheme of vengeance which she had planned for herself.

'Come what may,' she thought again and again, 'at any price I must go back to Hazlewood.'

CHAPTER XXIV

THE ONE CHANCE

Eleanor Vane lay awake through the greater part of the night which succeeded her interview with the shipbroker. She lay awake, trying to fashion for herself some scheme by which she might go back to Hazlewood. The discovery which she had to make, the proof positive that she wanted to obtain of Launcelot Darrell's guilt, could only be procured by long and patient watching of the young man himself; the evidence that was to condemn him must come from his own lips. Some chance admission, some accidental word, might afford a clue that would guide her back to the secret of the past. But to obtain this clue she must be in intimate association with the man whom she suspected. In the careless confidence of daily life, in the freedom of social intercourse, a hundred chances might occur which could never be brought about while the gates of Hazlewood were closed upon her.

There was one other chance, it was true. Launcelot Darrell had asked her to become his wife. His love, however feeble to withstand the wear and tear of time, must, for the moment at least, be real. A line from her would no doubt bring him to her side. She could lure him on by affecting to return his affection, and in the entire confidence of such an association she might discover the truth.

No! not for the wide world – not even to be true to her dead father – could she be so false to every sentiment of womanly honour!

'Richard was right,' she thought, as she dismissed this idea with a humiliating sense of her own baseness in having even for one brief moment entertained it. 'He was right. What shame and degradation I must wade through before I can keep my promise!'

And to keep her promise she must go back to Hazlewood. This was the point to which she always returned. But was it possible for her to regain her old position in Mrs Darrell's house? Would not Mrs Darrell take care to keep her away, having once succeeded in banishing her from Launcelot's society?

Miss Vane was not a good schemer. Transparent, ingenuous, and impulsive, she had the will and the courage which would have prompted her to denounce Launcelot Darrell as a traitor and a cheat; but she did not possess one of the attributes which are necessary for the watcher who hopes to trace a shameful secret through all the dark intricacies of the hidden pathway that leads to it.

It was long after daylight when the young lady fell asleep, worn out, harassed, and baffled. The night had brought no counsel. Eleanor Vane dropped off into a fitful slumber, with a passionate prayer upon her lips, – a prayer that Providence would set her in the way of bringing vengeance upon her father's destroyer.

She flung herself upon Providence – after the manner of a great many persons – when she found her own intellect powerless to conduct her to the end she wanted to gain.

Throughout the next day Miss Vane sat alone on the chintz-covered sofa by the window, looking down at the children playing hop-scotch, and gambling for marbles upon the rugged flags below; 'weary of the rolling hours,' and unable to bring herself to the frame of mind necessary

for the ordinary purposes of life. Upon any other occasion she would
have tried to do something whereby she might lighten the Signora's
burden, being quite competent to take the pupils off her friend's hands;
but to-day she had suffered Eliza Picirillo to trudge out under the
broiling August sky, through the stifling London streets, and had made no
attempt to lesson her labours. She seemed even incapable of performing
the little domestic offices which she had been in the habit of doing. She
let the London dust accumulate upon the piano; she left the breakfast-
table scattered with the débris of the morning's meal; she made no effort
to collect the stray sheets of music, the open books, the scraps of
needlework that littered the room; but with her elbow on the smoky sill
of the window, and her head resting on her hand, she sat, looking wearily
out, with eyes that saw nothing but vacancy.

Richard had gone out early, and neither he nor his aunt was expected
to return till dusk.

'I can have everything ready for them when they come back,' she
thought, looking listlessly at the unwashed tea-things, which seemed to
stare at her in mute reproachfulness; and then her eyes wandered back to
the sunny window, and her mind returned with a cruel constancy to the
one idea that occupied it.

Had she been really looking at the objects on which her eyes seemed
to be fixed, she must have been surprised by the advent of a tall and
rather distinguished-looking stranger, who made his way along the
straw-littered promenade, between the Colonnade and the stables,
erasing the chalk diagrams of the hop-scotch players with the soles of
his boots, and rendering himself otherwise objectionable to the juvenile
population.

This stranger came straight to the shop of the shoemaker with whom
Signora Picirillo lodged, and inquired for Miss Vincent.

The shoemaker had only heard Eleanor's assumed name a day or two
before, when Laura's letter had arrived at the Pilasters. He had a vague
idea that the beautiful golden-haired young woman, who had first
entered his dwelling in the early freshness of budding girlhood, was going
to distinguish herself as a great musical genius, and intended to astonish
the professional world under a false name.

'It's Miss Eleanor you want, I suppose, sir?' the man said, in answer to
the stranger's question.

'Miss Eleanor? – yes.'

'Then, if you'll please to step up-stairs, sir. The young lady's all alone
to-day, for Mr Richard he's over the water a scene-paintin' away for dear
life, and the S'nora she's out givin' lessons; so poor young miss is alone,
and dismal enough she must be, cooped in-doors this fine weather. It's
bad enough when one's obliged to it, you know, sir,' the man added,

rather obscurely. 'Will you please to walk up, sir? It's the door facing you at the top of the stairs.'

The shoemaker opened a half-glass door communicating with a dingy back parlour and a steep staircase that twisted corkscrew-wise up to the first floor. The visitor waited for no further invitation, but ascended the stairs in a few strides, and paused for a moment before the door of Signora Picirillo's sitting-room.

'He's one of these here London managers, I dessay,' thought the simple cordwainer, as he went back to his work. 'Mr Cromshaw come here one day after Mr Richard in a pheeaton and pair, and no end of diamond rings and breastpins.'

Eleanor Vane had not noticed the stranger's footsteps on the uncarpeted stair, but she started when the door opened, and looked round. Her unexpected visitor was Mr Monckton.

She rose in confusion, and stood with her back to the window, looking at the lawyer. She was too much absorbed by her one idea to be troubled by the untidiness of the shabby chamber, by the disorder of her own hair or dress, or by any of those external circumstances which are generally so embarrassing to a woman. She only thought of Gilbert Monckton as a link between herself and Hazlewood. She did not even wonder why he had come to see her.

'I may find out something; I may learn something from him,' she thought.

Against the great purpose of her life, even this man, who of all others she most respected and esteemed, sank into utter insignificance. She never cared to consider what he might think. She only regarded him as an instrument which might happen to be of use to her.

'You are very much surprised to see me, Miss Vincent,' the lawyer said, holding out his hand.

The girl put her hand loosely in his, and Gilbert Monckton started as he felt the feverish heat of the slim fingers that touched his so lightly. He looked into Eleanor's face. The excitement of the last three days had left its traces on her countenance.

Mrs Darrell had made a confidant of the lawyer. It had been absolutely necessary to explain Eleanor's absence. Mrs Darrell had given her own version of the business, telling the truth, with sundry reservations. Miss Vincent was a handsome and agreeable girl, she said; it was of vital consequence to Launcelot that he should not form any attachment or entertain any passing fancy, that might militate against his future prospects. An imprudent marriage had alienated her, Mrs Darrell, from her uncle, Maurice de Crespigny. An imprudent marriage might ruin the young man's chance of inheriting the Woodlands estate. Under these circumstances it was advisable that Miss Vincent should leave Hazlewood;

and the young lady had very generously resigned her situation upon the matter being put before her in a proper light.

Mrs Darrell took very good care not to make any allusion to that declaration of love which she had overheard through the half-open door of her son's painting-room.

Mr Monckton had expressed no little vexation at the sudden departure of his ward's companion; but his annoyance was of course felt solely on account of Miss Mason, who told him, with her eyes streaming, and her voice half-choked with sobs, that she could never be happy without her darling Eleanor.

The lawyer said very little in reply to these lamentations, but took care to get Miss Vincent's address from his ward, and on the day after his visit to Hazlewood went straight from his office to the Pilasters.

Looking at the change in Eleanor Vane's face, Mr Monckton began to wonder very seriously if the departure from Hazlewood had been a matter of indifference to her; and whether it might not be that Mrs Darrell's alarms about her son's possible admiration for the penniless companion were founded on stronger grounds than the widow had cared to reveal to him.

'I was afraid that Laura's frivolous fancy might be caught by this young fellow,' he thought, 'but I could never have believed that this girl, who has ten times Laura's intellect, would fall in love with Launcelot Darrell.'

He thought this, while Eleanor's feverish hand lay, loose and passive, in his own.

'It was not quite kind of you to leave Hazlewood without seeing me, or consulting me, Miss Vincent,' he said; 'you must remember that I confided to you a trust.'

'A trust!'

'Yes. You promised that you would look after my foolish young ward, and take care that she did not fall in love with Mr Darrell.'

Mr Monckton watched the girl's face very closely while he pronounced Launcelot Darrell's name, but there was revelation in that pale and wearied countenance. The grey eyes returned his gaze frankly and unhesitatingly. Their brightness was faded, but their innocent candour remained, in all its virginal beauty.

'I tried to do what you wished,' Miss Vane answered. 'I am afraid that Laura does admire Mr Darrell. But I can't quite understand whether she is serious or not, and in any case nothing I could say would influence her much, though I know she loves me.'

'No, I suppose not,' said Mr Monckton, rather bitterly; 'women are not easily to be influenced in these matters. A woman's love is the sublimation of selfishness, Miss Vincent. It is delightful to a woman to throw herself away; and she is perfectly indifferent as to how many unoffending victims she drags to destruction in her downfall. An Indian woman sacrifices herself out of respect to her dead husband. An English woman offers up her husband and children on the altar of a living lover. Pardon me if I speak too plainly. We lawyers become acquainted with strange stories. I should not at all wonder if my ward were to insist upon making herself miserable for life because Launcelot Darrell has a Grecian nose.'

Mr Monckton seated himself, uninvited, by the table on which the unwashed tea-things bore testimonies to Eleanor's neglect. He looked round the room, but not rudely; for in one brief observant glance he was able to see everything, and to understand everything.

'Have you ever *lived* here, Miss Vincent?' he asked.

'Yes; I lived here a year and a half before I went to Hazlewood. I was very happy,' Eleanor added, hastily, as if in deprecation of the lawyer's look, which betrayed a half-compassionate interest. 'My friends are very good to me, and I never wish for a better home.'

'But you have been accustomed to a better home, in your childhood?'

'No, not very much better. I always lived in lodgings, with my poor father.'

'Your father was not rich, then?'

'No, not at all rich.'

'He was a professional man, I suppose?'

'No, he had no profession. He had been rich – very rich – once.'

The colour rose to Eleanor's face as she spoke, for she suddenly recollected that she had a secret to keep. The lawyer might recognize George Vane by this description, she thought.

Gilbert Monckton fancied that sudden blush arose from wounded pride.

'Forgive me for asking you so many questions, Miss Vincent,' he said, gently. 'I am very much interested in you. I have been very much interested in you for a long time.'

He was silent for some minutes. Eleanor had resumed her seat near the window, and sat in a thoughtful attitude, with her eyes cast upon the ground. She was wondering how she was to make good use of this interview, and discover as much as possible of Launcelot Darrell's antecedents.

'Will you forgive me if I ask you a few more questions, Miss Vincent?' the lawyer asked, after this brief silence.

Eleanor raised her eyes, and looked him full in the face. That bright, straight, unfaltering gaze was perhaps the greatest charm which Miss Vane possessed. She had no reason to complain that Nature had gifted her with a niggardly hand; she had beauty of feature, of outline, of colour; but this exquisitely candid expression was a rarer beauty, and a higher gift.

'Believe me,' said Mr Monckton, 'that I am actuated by no unworthy motive when I ask you to deal frankly with me. You will understand, by-and-by, why and by what right I presume to question you. In the meantime I ask you to confide in me. You left Hazlewood at Mrs Darrell's wish, did you not?'

'Yes: it was at her wish that I left.'

'Her son had made you an offer of his hand?'

The question would have brought a blush to the face of an ordinary girl. But Eleanor Vane was removed from ordinary women by the exceptional story of her life. From the moment of her discovery of Launcelot Darrell's identity, all thought of him as a lover, or an admirer, had been blotted out of her mind. He was removed from other men by the circumstances of his guilt; as she was set apart from other women by the revengeful purpose in her breast.

'Yes,' she said. 'Mr Darrell asked me to be his wife.'

'And did you – did you refuse him?'

'No; I gave him no answer.'

'You did not love him, then?'

'Love him! Oh, no, no!'

Her eyes dilated with a look of surprise as she spoke, as if it was most astounding to her that Gilbert Monckton should ask such a question.

'Perhaps you do not think Launcelot Darrell worthy of a good woman's love?'

'I do not,' answered Eleanor. 'Don't talk of him, please. At least, I mean, don't talk of him, and of love,' she added, hastily, remembering that the very thing she wished was that the lawyer should talk of Launcelot Darrell. 'You – you must know a great deal of his youth. He was idle and dissipated, was he not; and – and - a card-player?'

'A card-player?'

'Yes – a gambler; a man who plays cards for the sake of winning money?'

'I never heard any one say so. He was idle, no doubt, and loitered away his time in London under the pretence of studying art; but I never remember hearing that gambling was one of his vices. However, I don't come here to speak of him, but of you. What are you going to do, now that you have left Hazlewood?'

Eleanor was cruelly embarrassed by this question. Her most earnest wish was to return to Hazlewood, or at least to the neighbourhood of Launcelot Darrell's home. Absorbed by this wish, she had formed no scheme for the future. She had not even remembered that she stood alone in the world, with only a few pounds saved out of her slender salary, unprovided with that which is the most necessary of all weapons in any warfare. Money!

'I – I scarcely know what I shall do,' she said. 'Mrs Darrell promised to procure me a situation.'

But as she spoke she remembered that to accept a situation of Mrs Darrell's getting would be in some manner to eat bread provided by the kinswoman of her father's foe, and she made a mental vow to starve rather than to receive the widow's patronage.

'I do not put much confidence in Mrs Darrell's friendship when her own end is gained,' Gilbert Monckton said, thoughtfully. 'Ellen Darrell is only capable of loving one person, and that person is, according to the fashion of the world, the one who has used her worst. She loves her son, Launcelot, and would sacrifice a hecatomb of her fellow-creatures for his advantage. If she can get you a new home, I dare say she will do so. If she cannot, she has succeeded in removing you from her son's pathway, and will trouble herself very little about your future.'

Eleanor Vane lifted her head with a sudden gesture of pride.

'I do not want Mrs Darrell's help,' she said.

'But you would not refuse the counsel, or even the help of any one you liked, would you, Eleanor?' returned the lawyer. 'You are very young, very inexperienced, – the life at Hazlewood suited you, and it might have gone on for years without danger of unhappiness or disquiet, but for the coming of Launcelot Darrell. I have known you for a year and a half, Miss Vincent, and I have watched you very closely. I think I know you very well. Yes, if a lawyer's powers of penetration and habit of observation are to go for anything, I *must* know you by this time. I may have been an egregious fool twenty years ago; but I must be wise enough now to understand a girl of eighteen.'

He said this rather as if reasoning with himself than talking to Eleanor. Miss Vane looked at him, wondering what all this talk would lead to, and what motive, under heaven, could have induced a lawyer of high standing to leave his chambers in the middle of the business day, for the purpose of sitting in a shabby lodging-house chamber, with his elbow resting upon a dirty tablecloth amid the confusion of unwashed breakfast cups and saucers.

'Eleanor Vincent,' Mr Monckton said by-and-by, after a very long pause, 'country people are most intolerable gossips. You cannot have lived at Hazlewood for a year and a half without having heard something of my history.'

'Your history?'

'Yes, you heard that there was some secret trouble in the early part of my life – that there were some unpleasant circumstances connected with my purchase of Tolldale.'

Eleanor Vane was unskilled in the art of prevarication. She could not give an evasive answer to a straight question.

'Yes,' she said, 'I have heard people say that.'

'And you have no doubt heard them say that my trouble — like every other trouble upon this earth, as it seems to me — was caused by a woman.'

'Yes, I heard that.'

'I was very young when that sorrow came to me, Eleanor Vincent, and very ready to believe in a beautiful face. I was deceived. My story is all told in those three words, and it is a very old story after all. Great tragedies and epic poems have been written upon the same theme, until it has become so hackneyed that I have no need to enlarge upon it. I was deceived, Miss Vincent, and for twenty years I have profited by that bitter lesson. Heaven help me if I feel inclined to forget it now. I am forty years of age, but I do not think that the brightness of my life has quite gone yet. Twenty years ago I was in love, and in the ardour and freshness of my youth, I dare say I talked a great deal of nonsense. I am in love once more, Eleanor. Will you forgive me if all my faculty for sentimental talk is lost? Will you let me tell you, in very few and simple words, that I love you; that I have loved you for a long time; and that you will make me unspeakably happy if you can think my earnest devotion worthy of some return?'

Every vestige of colour faded slowly from Eleanor's face. There had been a time — before the return of Launcelot Darrell — when a word of praise, an expression of friendliness or regard from Gilbert Monckton, had been very precious to her. She had never taken the trouble to analyze her feelings. That time, before the coming of the young man, had been the sunniest and most careless period of her youth. She had during that interval been false to the memory of her father — she had suffered herself to be happy. But now a gulf yawned between her and that lapse of forgetfulness. She could not look back clearly; she could not remember or recall her former feelings. Gilbert Monckton's offer might then have awakened some answering sentiment in her own breast. Now his hand struck upon the slackened chords of a shattered instrument; and there was no music to respond harmoniously to the player's touch.

'Can you love me, Eleanor? Can you love me?' the lawyer asked, imploringly, taking the girl's two hands in his own.

'Your heart is free: yes, I know that; and that at least is something. Heaven forgive me if I try to bribe you. But my youth is passed, and I can scarcely expect to be loved for myself alone. Think how dreary and undefended your life must be, if you refuse my love and protection. Think of that, Eleanor. Ah! if you knew what a woman is when thrown upon the world *without* the shelter of a husband's love, you would think seriously. I want you to be more than my wife, Eleanor. I want you to be the guardian and protectress of that poor frivolous girl whose future has been trusted to my care. I want you to come and live at Tolldale, my darling, so as to be near that poor child at Hazlewood.'

Near Hazlewood! The hot blood rushed into Eleanor's face at the sound of those two words, then faded suddenly away and left her deadly white, trembling and clinging to the back of her chair for support. To all else that Gilbert Monckton had said she had listened in a dull stupor. But now her intellect arose and grasped the full importance of the lawyer's supplication. In a moment she understood that the one chance which of all other things upon this earth she had most desired, and which of all other things had seemed farthest removed from her, was now within her reach.

She might go back to Hazlewood. She might return as Gilbert Monckton's wife. She did not stop to consider how much was involved in this. It was her nature to be ruled by impulse, and impulse only; and she had yet to learn submission to a better guidance. She could go back to Hazlewood. She would have returned there as a kitchen-maid, had the opportunity of so doing offered itself to her; and she was ready to return as Gilbert Monckton's wife.

'My prayers have been heard,' she thought. 'My prayers have been heard: Providence will give me power to keep my promise. Providence will set me face to face with that man.'

Eleanor Vane stood with her hands clasped upon the back of her chair, thinking of this, and looking straight before her, in utter unconsciousness of the earnest eyes that were fixed upon her face, while the lawyer waited breathlessly to hear her decision.

'Eleanor,' he cried, entreatingly, 'Eleanor, I have been deceived once; do not let me be a woman's dupe, now that there are streaks of grey amongst my hair. I love you, my dear. I can make you independent and secure; but I do not offer you a fortune or a position of sufficient magnitude or grandeur to tempt an ambitious woman. For God's sake do not trifle with me. If you love me now, or can hope to love me in the future, be my wife. But if any other image holds the smallest place in your heart – if there is one memory, or one regret, that can come between us, Eleanor, dismiss me from you unhesitatingly. It will be merciful to me – to you also, perhaps, to do so. I have seen many a union in which there has been love on one side, and indifference – or something worse than indifference – upon the other. Eleanor, think of all this, and then tell me, frankly, if you can be my wife.'

Eleanor Vane dimly comprehended that there was a depth of passionate feeling beneath the quiet earnestness of the lawyer's manner. She tried to listen; she tried to understand; but she could not. The one idea which held possession of her mind, kept that mind locked against every other impression. It was not his love, it was not his name, or his fortune, that

Gilbert Monckton offered her – he offered her the chance of returning to Hazlewood.

'You are very good to me,' she said. 'I will be your wife. I will go back to Hazlewood.'

She held out her hand to him. No trace of womanly confusion, or natural coquetry, betrayed itself in her manner. Pale and absorbed, she held out her hand, and offered up her Future as a small and unconsidered matter, when set against the one idea of her life – the promise to her dead father.

CHAPTER XXV

ACCEPTED

When a man sets his happiness in the balance, he is apt to be contented with a very slight turning of the scale. He is not likely to be critical as to the wording of the verdict which gives him the prize he has asked for.

Mr Gilbert Monckton had no contemptible opinion of his own judgment and deliberation, his perceptive faculties and powers of reasoning; but as blindly as Macbeth accepted the promises of the oracular voices in the witches' cave, so did this grave and eminent lawyer receive those few cold words in which Eleanor Vane consented to be his wife.

It was not that he refrained from reflecting upon the girl's manner of accepting his offer. He did reflect upon it; and proved to himself, by unerring logic, that she could scarcely have spoken in any other way. There were a thousand reasons why she should have employed those very words, and pronounced them in that very tone. Maidenly modesty, innocent surprise, inexperience, girlish timidity: – he ran over a whole catalogue of causes, naming every possible cause, save one, and that one was the thing he had most dreaded – indifference, or even repugnance to himself. He looked into her face. His professional career had given him the faculty of putting together the evidences of smiles and frowns, involuntary contractions of the eyebrows, scarcely perceptible compressions of the lips, every tone and semi-tone in the facial diapason. He looked at Eleanor Vane's face, and said to himself:

'This girl *cannot* be mercenary. She is as pure as an angel; as unselfish as Jephtha's daughter; as brave as Judith, or Joan of Arc. She *cannot* be anything but a good wife. The man who wins her has reason to thank God for his bounty.'

It was with such thoughts as these that the lawyer received the feminine decision which was to influence his future life. He bent over the

girl's fair head – tall as she was, her face was only on a level with Gilbert
Monckton's shoulder – and pressed his lips to her forehead, solemnly,
almost as if setting a seal upon his own.

'My darling,' he said, in a low voice, 'my darling, you have made me
very happy; I dare not tell you how much I love you. I struggled against
my love, Eleanor. I once meant to have kept the secret till I went down
to my grave. I think I could have kept silence so long as you remained
within my reach, protected and sheltered by people whom I could trust,
happy in the bright years of your innocent girlhood. But when you left
Hazlewood, when you went out into the world, my courage failed. I
wanted to give you my love as a shield and a defence. Better that I should
be deceived, I thought; better that I should be miserable, than that she
should be undefended.'

Eleanor Vane listened to the lawyer's happy talk. He could have talked
to her for ever, now that the ice was broken, and the important step – so
long considered, so long avoided – actually taken. It seemed as if his
youth came back to him, bestowed by some miraculous power; invisible,
but most palpably present in that shabby Bloomsbury dwelling. His
youth came back; the intellectual cobwebs of twenty years were swept
away by one stroke of some benevolent witch's broomstick. Cherished
prejudices, fondly nursed doubts and suspicions, were blotted out of his
mind, leaving the tablet fair and bright as it had been before the coming
of that shadow which had darkened so much of this man's life. Sudden
almost as the conversion of Saul, was this transformation of the
misanthropical solicitor under the master influence of a true and pure
affection.

For twenty years he had sneered at women, and at men's belief in
them; and now, at the end of twenty years, he believed; and, escaping out
of the prison which he had made for himself, he spread his recovered
wings and was free.

A sigh escaped from Eleanor's lips as she listened to her lover. The time
in which she could have hoped to pay him back all this great debt which
he was heaping upon her, was past and gone. She felt a sense of
oppression beneath the load of this obligation. She began to perceive – as
yet only dimly, so intense was the egotism engendered out of the single
purpose of her life – that she was binding herself to something that she
might not be able to perform; she was taking upon herself a debt that she
could scarcely hope to pay. For a moment she thought this, and was
ready, under this new impulse, to draw back and say, 'I cannot become
your wife; I am too much tied and bound by the obligations of the past,
to be able to fulfil the duties of the present. I am set apart from other
women, and must stand alone until the task I have set myself is
accomplished, or the hope of its fulfilment abandoned.'

She thought this, and the words trembled on her lips; but in the next moment the image of her father arose angry and reproachful, as if to say to her, 'Have you so little memory of my wrongs and my sorrows that you can shrink from any means of avenging me?'

This idea banished every other consideration.

'I will keep my promise first, and do my duty to Gilbert Monckton afterwards,' thought Eleanor. 'It will be easy to be a good wife to him. I used to like him very much.'

She recalled the old days in which she had sat a little way apart from the lawyer and his ward, envying Laura Mason her apparent influence over Mr Monckton; and for a moment a faint thrill of pleasure and triumph vibrated through her veins as she remembered that henceforth her claim upon him would be higher than that of any other living creature. He would be her own – her lover, her husband – adviser, friend, instructor; everything in the wide world to her.

'Oh, let me avenge my father's cruel death,' she thought, 'and then I may be a good and happy wife.'

Mr Monckton could have stood for ever by the side of his betrothed wife in the sunny window looking out upon the mews. The prospect of the half-open stable-doors; the lounging grooms smoking and drinking in the intervals of their labour; the scantily draperied women hanging out newly-washed linen, and making as it were triumphal arches of wet garments across the narrow thoroughfare; the children playing hop-scotch, or called away from that absorbing diversion to fetch damp steaming quartern loaves and jugs of beer for their elders, – all these things were beautiful in the eyes of the owner of Tolldale Priory. An overplus of that sunshine which filled his own breast glorified these common objects, and Mr Monckton gazed upon the angular proportions of the bony Roman-nosed horses, the classic outlines of decrepit Hansom cabs, and all the other objects peculiar to the neighbourhood of the Pilasters, with such a radiance of contentment and delight upon his countenance as might have induced the observer, looking at the lawyer's face, and *not* at the prospect, to believe that the bay of Naples was spread out in purple splendour under the open window of Miss Vane's sitting-room.

Signora Picirillo returned from her day's labours, and found Eleanor's visitor thus absorbed; but he understood directly who she was, and greeted her with a cordiality that very much astonished the music-mistress. Eleanor Vane slipped out of the room while Mr Monckton was explaining himself to the Signora. She was only too glad to get away from the man to whom she had so rashly bound herself. She went to the glass to brush her hair away from her hot forehead, and then threw herself on the bed, prostrated by all the excitement she had undergone, powerless even to think.

'I almost wish I could lie here for ever,' she thought: 'it seems so like peace to lie still and leave off thinking.' Her youth had held out bravely against the burdens she had put upon her strength and spirits, but the young energies had given way at last, and she fell into a heavy dreamless slumber: a blessed and renovating sleep, from which nature takes compensation for the wrongs that have been done her.

Gilbert Monckton told his story very briefly and simply. He had no occasion to say much himself, for Eleanor had written a great deal about him in her letters to the Signora, and had often talked of him during her one holiday at the Pilasters.

Eliza Picirillo was too entirely unselfish to feel otherwise than pleased at the idea that Eleanor Vane had won the love of a good man, whose position in life would remove her from every danger and from every trial. But, mingled with this unselfish delight, there was a painful recollection. The music-mistress had fathomed her nephew's secret; and she felt that Eleanor's marriage would be a sad blow to Richard Thornton.

'I don't believe poor Dick ever hoped to win her love,' Signora Picirillo thought; 'but if he could have gone on loving her and admiring her, and associating with her, in a frank brotherly way, he might have been happy. Perhaps it's better as it is, though; perhaps that very uncertainty might have blighted his life, and shut him out from some possible happiness.'

'As my dear girl is an orphan,' Gilbert Monckton said, 'I feel that you, Madame Picirillo, are the only person I need consult. I have heard from Eleanor how much she owes you; and believe me that when I ask her to become my wife, I do not wish her to be less your adopted daughter. She has told me that in the greatest miseries of her life, you were as true a friend to her as her own mother could have been. She has never told me what those miseries were, but I trust her so fully that I do not care to torment her with questions about a past which she tells me was sorrowful.'

Eliza Picirillo's eyelids fell under the earnest gaze of the lawyer: she remembered the deception that had been practised upon Mrs Darrell in deference to the pride of Eleanor's half-sister.

'This Mr Monckton must know Nelly's story before he marries her,' thought the straightforward Signora. She explained this to Eleanor the next morning, when the girl rose, invigorated by a long sleep, and inspired by a desperate hopefulness – the hope of speedily avenging her father's wrongs.

For some time Miss Vane passionately combated the Signora's arguments. Why should she tell Gilbert Monckton her real name? she demanded. She wished to keep it a secret from Mr de Crespigny: from the people at Hazlewood. She must keep it a secret, she said.

But little by little Eliza Picirillo overcame this determination. She explained to the passionate girl that if her marriage was to be legally unassailable, she must be married in her true name. She explained this: and she said a great deal about the moral wrong which would be done if Eleanor persisted in deceiving her future husband.

The marriage was pushed on with terrible haste, as it seemed to Richard Thornton and the Signora; but even the brief delay that occurred between Gilbert Monckton's declaration of his love and the day fixed for the wedding was almost intolerable to Eleanor. The all-important step which was to make her the lawyer's wife seemed nothing to her. She ignored this great crisis of her life altogether, in her desire to return to Hazlewood, to discover and denounce Launcelot Darrell's treachery before Maurice de Crespigny's death.

There were preparations to be made, and a trousseau to be provided. It was a very simple trousseau, fitter for the bride of some young curate with seventy pounds a year, than for a lady who was to be mistress of Tolldale Priory. Eleanor took no interest in the pretty girlish dresses, pale and delicate in colour, simple and inexpensive in texture and fashion, which the Signora chose for her protégée. There was a settlement to be drawn up also; for Gilbert Monckton insisted upon treating his betrothed as generously as if she had been a woman of distinction, with an aristocratic father to bargain and diplomatize for her welfare; but Eleanor was as indifferent to the settlement as about the trousseau, and could scarcely be made to understand that, on and after her wedding-day, she would be the exclusive possessor of a small landed estate worth three hundred a year.

Once, and once only, she thanked Gilbert Monckton for his generosity; and this was when, for the first time, the thought flashed into her mind, that this three hundred a year, to which she was so indifferent, would enable her to place Eliza Picirillo in a position of independence.

'Dear Signora,' she cried, 'you shall never work after I am married. How good it is of you to give me this money, Mr Monckton,' she added, her eyes filling with sudden tears; 'I will try to deserve your goodness, I will indeed.'

It was upon the evening on which Eleanor spoke these few grateful and earnest words to her betrothed husband, that the revelation of her secret was made.

'I am going to Doctors' Commons to-morrow morning, Signora,' the lawyer said, as he rose to leave the little sitting-room – he had spent his evenings in the Pilasters during his brief courtship, perfectly at home and unspeakably happy in that shabby and Bohemian colony. 'Eleanor and I have determined that our marriage is to take place at St George's, Bloomsbury. It is to be a very quiet wedding. My two partners, yourself, and Mr Thornton, are to be the only witnesses. The Berkshire people will be surprised when I take my young wife back to Tolldale.'

He was going away, when the Signora laid her hands on Eleanor's shoulder.

'You *must* tell him to-night, Nelly,' she whispered; 'he must not be allowed to take out the license in a false name.'

The girl bent her head.

'I will do as you wish, Signora,' she said.

Five minutes afterwards, when Gilbert Monckton gave Eleanor his hand, she said, quietly:

'Do not say good night yet. I will come down stairs with you; I have something to say to you.'

She went down the narrow staircase, and out into the colonnade with Mr Monckton. It was ten o'clock; the shops were closed, and the public-house was quiet. Under the August moonlight the shabby tenements looked less commonplace, the dilapidated wooden colonnade was almost picturesque. Miss Vane stood with her face turned frankly towards her lover, her figure resting slightly against one of the slender pillars before the shoemaker's emporium.

'What is it that you want to tell me, Eleanor dearest?' Mr Monckton asked, as she paused, looking half-doubtfully in his face, uncertain what she should say to him.

'I want to tell you that I have done very wrong – I have deceived you.'

'Deceived me! Eleanor! Eleanor!'

She saw the lawyer's face turn pale under the moonlight. That word deception had such a terrible meaning to him.

'Yes, I have deceived you. I have kept a secret from you, and I can only tell it to you upon one condition.'

'Upon what condition?'

'That you do not tell it to Mr de Crespigny, or to Mrs Darrell, until you have my permission to do so.'

Gilbert Monckton smiled. His sudden fears fled away before the truthfulness of the girl's voice, the earnestness of her manner.

'Not tell Mr de Crespigny, or Mrs Darrell?' he said; 'of course not, my dear. Why should I tell them anything which concerns you, and that you wish me to keep from them?'

'You promise, then?'

'Most certainly.'

'You give me your solemn promise that you will not tell Mr de Crespigny, or any member of his family, the secret which I am going to confide to you; under no circumstances whatever will you be tempted to break that promise?'

'Why, Nelly,' cried Mr Monckton, 'you are as serious as if you were the chief of a political society, about to administer some terrible oath to a neophyte. I shall not break my promise, my dear, believe me. My profession has accustomed me to keeping secrets. What is it, Eleanor; what is this tremendous mystery?'

Miss Vane lifted her eyes, and looked full in her lover's face, upon the watch for any change of expression that might indicate displeasure or contempt. She was very fearful of losing the lawyer's confidence and esteem.

'When I went to Hazlewood,' she said, 'I went in a false name, not at my own wish, but to please my sister, who did not want Mrs Darrell to know that any member of her family could be in a dependent position. My name is not Vincent. I am Eleanor Vane, the daughter of Mr de Crespigny's old friend.'

Gilbert Monckton's astonishment was unbounded. He had heard George Vane's history from Mrs Darrell, but he had never heard of the birth of the old man's youngest daughter.

'Eleanor Vane?' he said; 'then Mrs Bannister is your sister.'

'She is my half-sister, and it was at her wish that I went to Hazlewood under a false name. You are not angry with me for having done so, are you?'

'Angry with you? No, my dear, the deception was harmless enough; though it was a piece of foolish pride upon your sister's part. My Eleanor was in no way degraded by having to turn her accomplishments to use and profit. My poor, self-reliant girl,' he added, tenderly, 'going out into the world with a secret to keep. But why do you wish this secret to be still preserved, Eleanor; you are not ashamed of your father's name?'

'Ashamed of his name? Oh, no, no!'

'Why keep your real name a secret, then?'

'I can't tell you why. But you'll keep your promise. You are too honourable to break your promise.'

Mr Monckton looked wonderingly at the girl's earnest face.

'No, my dear, I won't break my promise,' he said. 'But I can't understand your anxiety for this concealment. However, we will say nothing more about it, Nelly,' he added, as if in reply to an appealing look from Miss Vane; 'your name will be Monckton when you go back to Berkshire; and nobody will dare to question your right to that name.'

The lawyer put his lips to the girl's forehead, and bade her good night upon the threshold of the shoemaker's door.

'God bless you, my own darling!' he said, in a very low voice, 'and preserve our faith in each other. There must be no secrets between you and me, Nelly.'

CHAPTER XXVI

AN INSIDIOUS DEMON

On a bright September morning a hired carriage took Miss Vane and her friends to the quiet old church in Hart Street, Bloomsbury. There was a little crowd assembled about the door of the shoemaker's dwelling, and sympathetic spectators were scattered here and there in the mews, for a marriage is one of those things which the cleverest people can never contrive to keep a secret.

Miss Eleanor Vane's pale fawn-coloured silk dress, black mantle, and simple white bonnet did not form the established costume of a bride, but the young lady looked so very beautiful in her girlish dress and virginal innocence, that more than one of the lounging grooms who came out of the stables to see her go by to her hired carriage, confidentially remarked to an acquaintance that he only wished he could get such a young woman for *his* missus. Richard Thornton was not in attendance upon the fair young bride. There was a scene to be painted for Spavin and Cromshaw upon that particular day which was more important than any scene Dick had ever painted before. So the young man set out early upon that September bridal morning, after saluting Eleanor Vane in the most tender and brotherly fashion; but I am sorry to say that instead of going straight to the Royal Phoenix Theatre, Mr Thornton walked with a slow and listless gait across Westminster Bridge, then plunged with a sudden and almost ferocious impetus into the remotest intricacies of Lambeth, scowling darkly at the street boys who came in his way, skirting the Archbishop's palace, glowering at the desolation of Vauxhall, and hurrying far away into the solitudes of Battersea Fields, where he spent the better part of the afternoon in the dreary parlour of an obscure public-house, drinking adulterated beer, and smoking bad tobacco.

The Signora wore a rustling black silk dress – Eleanor's present of the previous Christmas – in honour of her protégée's wedding; but Eliza Picirillo's heart was sadly divided upon their quiet bridal day; half rejoicing in Miss Vane's fortune and advancement; half sorrowful for poor desolate Dick wandering away amongst the swamps by the water-side.

Mr Monckton and his two partners were waiting for the bride in the portico of the church. The senior of the two, an old man with white hair, was to give Eleanor away, and paid her many appropriate though rather obsolete compliments upon the occasion. Perhaps it was now for the first time that Miss Vane began to regard the step she was about to take as one of a somewhat serious and indeed awful nature; perhaps it was now for the first time that she began to think she had committed a sin in accepting Gilbert Monckton's love so lightly.

'If he knew that I did not promise to marry him because I loved him, but because I wanted to get back to Hazlewood,' she thought.

But presently the grave shadows passed away from her face and a faint blush rose to her cheek and brow.

'I will love him by-and-by, when I have avenged my father's death,' she said to herself.

Some such thought as this was in her mind when she took her place beside Gilbert Monckton at the altar.

The autumn sunshine streamed in upon them through the great windows of the church, and wrapped them in yellow light, like the figures of Joseph and Mary in an old picture. The bride and bridegroom looked very handsome standing side by side in this yellow sunshine. Gilbert Monckton's twenty years' seniority only dignified and exalted him; investing the holy marriage promise of love and protection with a greater solemnity than it could have had when spoken by a stripling of one or two and twenty.

Everything seemed auspicious upon this wedding morning. The lawyer's partners were in the highest spirits, the beadle and pew-opener were elevated by the idea of prospective donations. The Signora wept quietly while the marriage service was being read, thinking of her nephew Richard smoking and drinking desperately, perhaps, in his desolate painting-room; but when the ceremony was over the good music-mistress dried her tears, banishing all traces of sorrow before she kissed and complimented the bride.

'You are to come and see us at the Priory, dear Signora,' Eleanor said, as she clung about her friend before leaving the vestry; 'Gilbert says so, you know.'

Her voice faltered a little, and she glanced shyly at her husband as she spoke of him by his christian name. It seemed as if she had no right to allude so familiarly to Mr Monckton, of Tolldale Priory. And presently Eliza Picirillo stood alone – or attended only by the beadle, obsequiously attentive in proportion to the liberality of the donation he had just received – under the portico of the Bloomsbury church, watching the lawyer's carriage drive away towards the Great Northern railway station. Mr Monckton, in the absence of any preference upon Eleanor's part, had chosen a quiet Yorkshire watering-place as the scene of his honeymoon.

Signora Picirillo sighed as she went down the steps before the church, and took her seat in the hired vehicle that was to take her back to the Pilasters.

'So Bloomsbury has seen the last of Eleanor,' she thought, sadly; 'we may go down to see her, perhaps, in her grand new house, but she will never come back to us. She will never wash the tea-things and make tea and toast again for a tired-out old music-mistress.'

The dying glory of red and orange in the last sunset of September sank behind the grey line of the German Ocean, after the closing day of Gilbert Monckton's honeymoon. Upon the first of October the lawyer was to take his young wife to Tolldale Priory. Mr and Mrs Monckton walked upon the broad sands as that low orange light faded out of the western sky. The lawyer was grave and silent, and every now and then cast a furtive glance at his companion's face. Sometimes that glance was succeeded by a sigh.

Eleanor was paler and more careworn than she had looked since the day after her visit to the shipbroker's office. The quiet and seclusion of the place to which Gilbert Monckton had brought his bride had given her ample opportunity of brooding on the one idea of her life. Had he plunged her into a vortex of gaiety, it is possible that she might have been true to that deep-rooted purpose which she had so long nursed in her breast; but, on the other hand, there would have been some hope that the delights of change and novelty, delights to which youth cannot be indifferent – might have beguiled the bride from that for-ever-recurring train of thought which separated her from her husband as effectually as if an ocean had rolled between them.

Yes, Gilbert Monckton had discovered the fatal truth that marriage is not always union, and that the holiest words that were ever spoken cannot weave the mystic web which makes two souls indissolubly one, if there be one inharmonious thread in the magical fabric. Gilbert Monckton felt this, and knew that there was some dissonant note in the chord which should have been such a melodious combination.

Again and again, while talking to his wife – carried away, perhaps, by the theme of which he was speaking, and counting on her sympathy as a matter of course – he had looked into Eleanor's face, and seen that her thoughts had wandered far away from him and his conversation, into some unknown region. He had no clue by which he could follow those wanderings; no chance word ever fell from his wife's lips which might serve as the traitor silk that guided ruthless Eleanor to Rosamond's hiding-place. So thus, before the honeymoon was over, Gilbert Monckton began to be jealous of his bride, thereby fostering for himself a nest of scorpions, or a very flock of young vultures, which were henceforth to make their meals off his entrails.

But it was not the ferocious or Othello-like jealousy. The green-eyed monster did not appear under his more rugged and uncivilized form, finding a vent for his passions in pillows, poisons, and poniards. The monster disguised himself as a smooth and philosophical demon. He hid his diabolical attributes under the gravity and wisdom of a friendly sage. In other words, Gilbert Monckton, feeling disappointed at the result of his marriage, set himself to reason upon the fact; and was for ever torturing himself with silent arguments and mute conjectures as to the cause of that indescribable something in his young wife's manner, which told him there was no perfect union between them. The lawyer reproached himself for his weak folly in having built a fairy palace of hope upon the barren fact of Eleanor's acceptance of his hand. Did not girls, situated as George Vane's daughter had been situated, marry for money, again and again, in these mercenary days? Who should know this better than Gilbert Monckton the solicitor, who had drawn up so many marriage settlements, been concerned in so many divorces, and assisted at so many matrimonial bargains, whose sordid motives were as undisguised as in any sale of cattle transacted in the purlieus of Smithfield? Who should know better than he, that beautiful and innocent girls every day bartered their beauty and innocence for certain considerations set down by grave lawyers, and engrossed upon sheets of parchment at so much per sheet?

He did know this, and in his mad arrogance he had said to himself, 'I – amongst all other men – will be an exception to the common rule. The girl I marry is poor; but she will give herself to me for no meaner considerations than my love, and my truth, and my devotion; and those shall be hers until my dying day.'

Gilbert Monckton had said this; and already a mocking demon had made a permanent perch for himself upon this wretched man's shoulders, for ever whispering insidious doubts into his ear, for ever instilling shadowy fears into his mind.

Eleanor had not seemed happy during those few honeymoon weeks. She had grown weary of the broad sands stretching far away, flat and desolate under the September sky, and weary of the everlasting and unbroken line that bounded that wide grey sea. This weariness she had displayed frankly enough; but she had not revealed its hidden source, which lay in her feverish impatience to go back to the neighbourhood of Hazlewood, and to make the discovery she wished to make, before Maurice de Crespigny's death.

She had sounded her husband upon the subject of the old man's health.

'Do you think Mr de Crespigny will live long?' she asked, one day.

'Heaven knows, my dear,' the lawyer answered, carelessly. 'He has been an invalid for twenty years now, and he may go on being an invalid for twenty years more, perhaps. I fancy that his death will be very sudden whenever it does happen.'

'And do you think that he will leave his money to Launcelot Darrell?'

Eleanor's face grew a little paler as she mentioned the young man's name. The invisible familiar perched upon Mr Monckton's shoulder directed the lawyer's attention to that fact.

'I don't know. Why should you be interested in Mr Darrell's welfare?'

'I am not interested in his welfare; I only asked you a question, Gilbert.'

Even the malice of the familiar could take no objection to the tone in which Eleanor said this: and Mr Monckton was ashamed of the passing twinge which Launcelot Darrell's name had caused him.

'I dare say De Crespigny will leave his money to young Darrell, my dear,' he said, in a more cordial voice; 'and though I have no very high opinion of the young man's character, I think he ought to have the fortune. The maiden ladies should have annuities, of course. Heaven knows they have fought hard enough for the prize.'

'How can people act so contemptibly for the sake of money!' cried Eleanor, with sudden indignation.

The lawyer looked admiringly at her glowing face, which had crimsoned with the intensity of her feeling. She was thinking of her father's death, and of that hundred pounds which had been won from him on the night of his suicide.

'No,' thought Mr Monckton, 'she cannot be mercenary. That bright impulsive creature could never be guilty of any deliberate meanness – and what could be a worse meanness than that of the woman who could marry a man out of sordid and mercenary motives, beguiling him by a simulated affection, in order to compass her own advancement?'

'If I have won her heart, in its untainted freshness,' thought Gilbert Monckton, 'I must be content, though that girlish heart may seem cold. She will love me better by-and-by. She will learn to confide in me; she will learn to sympathize with me.'

By such arguments as these Mr Monckton endeavoured to satisfy himself – and sometimes, indeed, succeeded in doing so – that his young wife's absent and thoughtful manner was a matter of course; the thoughtfulness of a girl unused to her new position, and perhaps a little bewildered by its strangeness. But on the morning of the first of October, Gilbert Monckton perceived a change in Eleanor's manner, and on that morning the demon familiar took up a permanent station upon the lawyer's shoulder.

Mrs Monckton was no longer grave and listless. A feverish impatience, a sudden flow of high spirits, seemed to have taken possession of her.

'You observe,' whispered the demon familiar, as Mr Monckton sat opposite his wife in a compartment of the express train that was to take them to London, *en route* for Berkshire, 'you observe the glow in her cheeks, the brightness of her eyes. You saw her turn pale the other day when she mentioned Launcelot Darrell's name. You know what the young man's mother told you. You can do the commonest sum in logical arithmetic, I suppose. You can put two and two together. Your wife has been wearied to death of the north, and the sea, and the sands – and of *you.* She is in high spirits to-day, and it is very easy to account for the change in her manner. She is glad to go back to Berkshire – she is glad to go back there, because *she will see Launcelot Darrell.*'

Mr Monckton, with a cambric handkerchief thrown over his face, kept a covert watch upon his wife from between its artfully-adjusted folds, and enjoyed such converse as this with the spirit he had chosen for his companion.

CHAPTER XXVII

SLOW FIRES

The new life which began for Eleanor Monckton at Tolldale Priory seemed very strange to her. The prim respectability of the old mansion weighed heavily upon her spirits. The best part of her existence had been spent in a very free-and-easy and Bohemian manner: and her improved position was at first more strange than pleasant to her. The well-trained servants who waited upon her in respectful silence, acknowledging her as their mistress, and obsequiously eager to give her pleasure, were very different people to the familiar landladies of those lodgings in which she had lived with her father, or the good-natured shoemaker-landlord at the Pilasters.

At Hazlewood she had been only a dependent; and those who served her had given her their service out of love for her brightness and beauty; rendering her little benefits with frank smiles and familiar greetings. But the mistress of Tolldale had a certain dignity to support; and new duties to learn in her new position.

At first those duties seemed very hard to the impulsive girl, who had a sort of instinctive contempt for all ceremonial usages and stereotyped observances. They seemed more especially hard, perhaps, because Gilbert Monckton expected his young wife to assume her new position as a thing of course, and was inclined to be very jealous of any omission that derogated from her dignity.

He was inclined to be jealous of her girlish inconstancy of thought and action, seeing in all this an evidence that she regretted the freedom of her girlhood. He was inclined to be jealous. That one sentence reveals the secret of a great deal of misery which this gentleman made for himself. He was inclined to be jealous of anything and everything, where his young wife was concerned.

It was thus that Gilbert Monckton began his married life. It was thus that, of his own doing, he set a breach between himself and the woman he idolized. And when the breach was made, and the dreary gulf of distrust and misapprehension stretched black and impassable between this weak man and that which he loved dearest in all the world, he could only cast himself down beside the yawning ravine and bemoan his desolation.

I have called Gilbert Monckton a weak man advisedly. In all the ordinary business of life, and in all the extraordinary businesses that fell in his professional pathway, the lawyer's clearness of perception and power of intellect were unsurpassed by any of his compeers. Strong; stern; decided and unyielding, where his judgment was once formed; he was trusted as an oracle by those who had dealings with him. But in his love for his wife he was weaker and more irresolute than any desponding swain of five-and-twenty.

He had been deceived once by a woman whom he had loved as he now loved Eleanor; and he could not forget that early deception. The shadow that had fallen upon his life was not to be lifted off by any sunshine of trust and love. He had been deceived once, and he might be deceived again.

The wrong which a woman's falsehood does to the man whom she betrays is a lasting and sometimes irrecoverable wrong. The wound festers, deep down below the outer scar; and while sympathetic friends are rejoicing in the slow obliteration of that surface evidence of the past, the hidden canker still endures, gaining force by time.

The secret sorrow of Gilbert Monckton's youth had made him suspicious of all womanly truth and purity. He watched his wife, as it had been his habit to watch his ward, doubtfully and fearfully; even when he most admired her, regarding her in some wise as a capricious and irresponsible being who might at any moment turn upon him and betray him.

He had fought against his love for his ward's beautiful companion. He had tried to shut his mind against all consciousness of her fascinations; he had endeavoured not to believe in her. If she had stayed at Hazlewood, that silent struggle might have gone on in the lawyer's breast for years; but her sudden departure had taken the grave man of forty off his guard. Hurried away by an impulse, he had revealed the secret that had been so skilfully repressed, and, for the second time in his life, perilled his happiness upon the hazard of a woman's truth.

'What do I know of her more than I knew of Margaret Ravenshaw?' he thought sometimes; 'can I trust her because she looks full in my face, with eyes that are as clear as the sky above my head? There is generally some landmark by which a man's character can be understood, however practised he may be in hypocrisy; but a woman—— Bah! a woman's beauty defies a physiognomist. We trust and believe because we admire. "She can't be wicked with such a Grecian nose," we say. "Those red, smiling lips cannot speak anything but the truth!"'

If Gilbert Monckton's young wife had seemed happy in her new home, he would have accepted the fair omen, and would have sunned himself in the brightness of her gaiety. But she was not happy; he could clearly see that; and day and night he tormented himself with vain endeavours to find out the cause of her uncertain spirits, her fits of abstraction, her long pauses of thoughtful silence.

And while Mrs Monckton's husband was nursing all these tortures, and every day widening the gulf of his own making, his wife, absorbed by her own secret purpose, was almost unconscious of all else in the world. If she saw the lawyer's face thoughtful or gloomy, she concluded that his moodiness arose from business anxieties with which she had no concern. If he sighed, she set down his melancholy to the same professional causes. A tiresome will case, a troublesome chancery suit – something in those dusty offices had annoyed him; and that professional something had of course no concern for her.

Eleanor Monckton had taken upon herself an unnatural office; she had assumed an abnormal duty; and her whole life fashioned itself to fit that unwomanly purpose. She abnegated the privileges, and left unperformed the duties, of a wife – true to nothing except to that fatal promise made in the first madness of her grief for George Vane's death.

She had been more than a week at Tolldale Priory, and she had not advanced one step upon the road which she had so desperately determined to pursue. She had not yet seen Launcelot Darrell.

Gilbert Monckton had spent the day after his return to Berkshire in riding about the neighbourhood, calling upon those few people with whom he kept up any acquaintance, and informing them of his marriage with the young lady who, a few weeks before, had been the companion of his ward. Of course he received friendly congratulations and good wishes from every one to whom he imparted this intelligence; and of course when his back was turned, the same people who had tendered those good wishes set to work to wonder at his folly, and to prognosticate all manner of evil from his absurd and imprudent marriage.

His longest visit was paid to Hazlewood, and here his tidings afforded real and unmixed satisfaction. Launcelot Darrell was at work in his painting-room, and was therefore out of the way of hearing the news. The widow was pleased to think that Eleanor's marriage would secure her son against the immediate danger of taking a penniless wife; and Laura was sincerely rejoiced at the idea of seeing her friend again.

'I may come to Tolldale soon, mayn't I, Mr Monckton?' she asked. 'Dear Nelly, I do so long to see her! But to think of her being married to you! I never was so surprised in my life. Why, you must be old enough to be her father. It does seem so funny!'

Gilbert Monckton did not feel particularly grateful to his ward for the extreme candour of these remarks, but he invited the young lady to spend the following day with Eleanor.

'I shall be in town to-morrow,' he said, 'and I dare say Mrs Monckton will find the Priory dull.'

'Mrs Monckton!' cried Laura; 'oh, to be sure; why, that's Nelly, of course! Find the Priory dull? Yes, I should think she would indeed! Poor Eleanor, in those damp, overgrown gardens, with the high walls all round, and the tops of the trees above the walls. How lonely she'll be.'

'Lonely! I shall come home to dinner every day.'

'Yes, at seven o'clock; and from breakfast time till seven poor Nell must amuse herself in the best way she can. But I'm not going to grumble; I'm only too happy to think she will be near me.'

Mr Monckton stood by the garden gate – that gate near which he had so often loitered with Eleanor – listening with no very great satisfaction to his ward's frivolous prattle. His young wife would feel unhappy in the dulness of her new life, perhaps. If that were to be so, it would be proof positive that she did not love him. He could never have felt dull or lonely in her society, though Tolldale had been some grim and isolated habitation in the middle of an African desert.'

'So you think she will be dull, Laura?' he said, rather despondently.

'Why, *of course* she will,' answered the young lady; 'but now don't think me inquisitive, please,' she added, in a very insinuating tone, 'but I do *so* much want you to tell me something.'

'You want me to tell you what?' asked the lawyer, rather sharply.

Laura linked her hand through his arm, and raising herself on tip-toe, so as to bring her rosy lips within easier reach of his ear, whispered archly,

'Does she *really* love you? Was it *really* a love match?'

Gilbert Monckton started as violently as if that infantine whisper had been the envenomed hiss of a snake.

'What do you mean, child?' he said, turning sharply upon his ward; 'of course Eleanor and I married because we loved each other? Why else should we have married?'

'No, to be sure. Girls marry for money sometimes. I heard Mrs Darrell say that one of the Penwoods, of Windsor, married a horrid, old, rich city man for the sake of his money. But I don't think Eleanor would do that sort of thing. Only it seems so funny that she should have been in love with you all the time.'

'All what time?'

'Why, all the time she and I were together. How could she help talking of you, I wonder?'

The lawyer bit his lip.

'She never talked of me, then?' he said, with a feeble attempt to make his tone careless.

'Oh, yes, she spoke of you sometimes, of course; but not in that way.'

'Not in what way? When will you learn to express yourself clearly, Miss Mason? Are you going to be a child all your life?'

Gilbert Monckton's ward looked up at him with a half comic look of terror. He was not accustomed to speak so sharply to her.

'Don't be angry, please,' she said, 'I know I don't always express myself clearly. I dare say it's because I used to get other girls to do my themes — they call exercises in composition themes, you know — when I was at school. I mean that Eleanor didn't talk of you as if she was in love with you — not as I talk — not as I *should* talk of any one if I were in love with them,' added the young lady, blushing very much as she corrected herself.

Miss Mason had only one idea of the outer evidences of the master-passion. A secret or unrequited affection, which did not make itself known by copious quotations of Percy Shelley and Letitia Landon, was in her mind a very commonplace affair.

Mr Monckton shrugged his shoulders.

'Who set you up as a judge of how a woman should speak of the man she loves?' he said, sharply. 'My wife has too much modesty to advertise her affection for any man. By the bye, Miss Mason, would you like to come and live at Tolldale?'

Laura looked at her guardian with unmitigated surprise.

'Come and live at Tolldale!' she said; 'I thought you didn't like me; I thought you despised me because I'm so frivolous and childish.'

'Despise you, Laura,' cried Gilbert Monckton, 'not like you! My poor dear child, what a brute I must have been if I ever have given you such an impression as that. I am very fond of you, my dear,' he added, gravely, laying his hand upon the girl's head as he spoke, and looking down at her with sorrowful tenderness. 'I am very much attached to you, my poor dear child. If I ever seem vexed with your girlish frivolity, it is only because I am anxious about your future. I am very, very anxious about your future.'

'But why are you so anxious?'

'Because your mother was childish and light-hearted like you, Laura, and she was led to do a very cruel thing for want of thought.'

'My poor mother. Ah, how I wish you would tell me about her.'

Laura Mason looked very serious as she said this. Her hands were folded round the lawyer's arm; her bright blue eyes seemed to grow of a more sombre colour as she looked earnestly upward to his grave face.

'Not now, my dear; some day; some day, perhaps, we'll talk about all that. But not now. You haven't answered my question, Laura. Would you like to live at Tolldale?'

The young lady blushed crimson and dropped her eyelids.

'I should dearly like to live with Eleanor,' she said. 'But——'

'But what?'

'I don't think it would be quite right to leave Mrs Darrell, would it? The money you pay her is of great use to her, you know; I have heard her say she could scarcely get on without it, especially now that Launcelot – now that Mr Darrell has come home.'

The blushes deepened as Laura Mason said this.

The lawyer watched those deepening blushes with considerable uneasiness. 'She is in love with this dark-eyed young Apollo,' he thought.

'You are very scrupulous about Mrs Darrell and her convenience, Laura,' he said. 'I should have fancied you would have been delighted to live with your old friend and companion. You'll come to-morrow to spend the day with Eleanor, I suppose?'

'Oh, yes; if you please.'

'I'll send the carriage for you, after it has taken me to Slough. Good-bye.'

Mr Monckton rode slowly homewards. His interview with Laura had not been altogether agreeable to him. The girl's surprise at his marriage with Eleanor had irritated and disturbed him. It seemed like a protest against the twenty years that divided his age from that of his young wife. There was something abnormal and exceptionable in the marriage, it seemed, then; and the people who had congratulated him and wished him well, were so many bland and conventional hypocrites, who no doubt laughed in their sleeves at his folly.

The lawyer rode back to Tolldale Priory with a moody and overclouded brow.

'That girl is in love with Launcelot Darrell,' he thought. 'She betrayed her secret in her childish transparence. The young man must be wonderfully attractive, since people fall in love with him in this manner. I don't like him; I don't believe in him; I should not like Laura to be his wife.'

Yet in the next moment Mr Monckton reflected that, after all, a marriage between his ward and Launcelot might not be altogether unadvisable. The young man was clever and gentlemanly. He came of a good stock, and had at least brilliant expectations. He might marry Laura and go to Italy, where he could devote a few years to the cultivation of his art.

'If the poor child is in love with him, and he returns her affection, it would be cruel to come between them with any prudential tyranny,' thought Mr Monckton. 'The young man seems really anxious to achieve success as an artist, and if he is to do so he ought certainly to study abroad.'

The lawyer's mind dwelt upon this latter point throughout the remainder of his ride, and when he crossed the stone-paved hall where the cavaliers' boots and saddles hung in the glowing light that stole through the emblazoned windows, he had almost come to the determination that Laura Mason and Launcelot Darrell ought to be married forthwith. He found his wife sitting in one of the windows of the library, with her hands lying idle in her lap, and her eyes fixed upon the garden before her. She started as he entered the room, and looked up at him with a bright eagerness in her face.

'You have been to Hazlewood?' she said.

'Yes, I have just come from there.'

'And you have seen——?'

She stopped suddenly. Launcelot Darrell's name had risen to her lips, but she checked herself before uttering it, lest she should betray her eager interest in him. She had no fear of that interest being misconstrued; no idea of such a possibility had ever entered her head. She only feared that some chance look or word might betray her vengeful hatred of the young man.

'You saw Laura – and – and Mrs Darrell, I suppose?' she said.

'Yes, I saw Laura and Mrs Darrell,' answered Gilbert Monckton, watching his wife's face. He had perceived the hesitation with which she had asked this question. He saw now that she was disappointed in his reply.

Eleanor was incapable of dissimulation, and her disappointment betrayed itself in her face. She had expected to hear something of Launcelot Darrell, something which would have at least given her an excuse for questioning her husband about him.

'You did not see Mr Darrell, then?' she said, after a pause, during which Mr Monckton had placed himself opposite to her in the open window. The afternoon sunshine fell full upon Eleanor's face; lighting up every change of expression; revealing every varying shade of thought that betrayed itself unconsciously in a countenance whose mobility was one of its greatest charms.

'No, Mr Darrell was in his painting-room; I did not see him.'

There was a pause. Eleanor was silent, scarcely knowing how to fashion any question that might lead to her gaining some information about the man whose secrets she had set herself to unravel.

'Do you know, Eleanor,' said the lawyer after this pause, during which he had kept close watch upon his wife's face, 'I think I have discovered a secret that concerns Launcelot Darrell.'

'A secret?'

Sudden blushes lit up Eleanor Monckton's cheeks like a flaming fire.

'A secret!' she repeated. 'You have found out a secret!'

'Yes, I believe that my ward, Laura Mason, has fallen in love with the young man.'

Eleanor's face changed. Her feverish eagerness gave place to a look of indifference.

'Is that all?' she said.

She had no very great belief in the intensity of Miss Mason's feelings. The girl's sentimental talk and demonstrative admiration had to her mind something spurious in their nature; Mrs Monckton was ready to love Laura very dearly when the business of her life should be done, and she could have time to love anybody; but in the meantime she gave herself no uneasiness about Miss Mason's romantic passion for the young painter.

'Laura is as inconstant as the wind,' she thought. 'She will hate Launcelot Darrell when I tell her how base he is.'

But what was Eleanor's surprise when Mr Monckton said, very quietly:

'If the girl is really attached to this young man, and he returns her affection – she is so pretty and fascinating, that I should think he could scarcely help being in love with her – I don't see why the match should not take place.'

Eleanor looked up suddenly.

'Oh, no, no, no,' she cried; 'you would never let Laura marry Launcelot Darrell.'

'And why not, Mrs Monckton?'

The insidious imp which the lawyer had made his bosom companion of late, at this moment transformed himself into a raging demon, and gnawed ravenously at the vitals of its master.

'Why shouldn't Laura marry Launcelot Darrell?'

'Because you have a bad opinion of him. What did you say to me by the garden-gate at Hazlewood, when Mr Darrell first came home? You said he was selfish, shallow, frivolous; false, perhaps. You said there was a secret in his life.'

'I thought so then.'

'And have you ceased to think so now?'

'I don't know. I may have been prejudiced against the young man,' answered Mr Monckton, doubtfully.

'I don't think you were,' Eleanor said; 'I don't think he is a good man. Pray, pray don't let Laura marry him.'

She clasped her hands in her eagerness, as she looked up in her husband's face.

Gilbert Monckton's brow darkened.

'What does it matter to you?' he asked.

Eleanor looked surprised at the almost angry abruptness of her husband's manner.

'It matters a great deal to me,' she said. 'I should be very sorry if Laura were to make an unhappy marriage.'

'But must her marriage with Launcelot Darrell be necessarily unhappy?'

'Yes; because he is a bad man.'

'What right have you to say that, unless you have some special reason for thinking it?'

'I have a special reason.'

'What reason?'

'I cannot tell you – now.'

The ravenous demon's tooth grew sharper than usual when Eleanor said this.

'Mrs Monckton,' the lawyer said, sternly, 'I am afraid that there can be very little happiness in store for you and me if you begin your married life by keeping secrets from your husband.'

Gilbert Monckton was too proud to say more than this. A dull despair was creeping into his breast, a sick loathing of himself and of his folly. Every one of those twenty years which made him his young wife's senior rose up against him, and gibed and twitted him.

What right had he to marry a young wife, and believe that she could love him? What justification could he find for his own folly in taking this girl from poverty and obscurity, and then expecting that she should feel any warmer sentiment than some feeble gratitude to him for having given her an advantageous bargain? He had given her a handsome house and attentive servants, carriages and horses, prosperity and independence, in exchange for her bright youth and beauty, and he was angry with her because she did not love him.

Looking back at that interview in the Pilasters – every circumstance of which was very clear to him now, by the aid of a pair of spectacles lent him by the jealous demon, his familiar – Mr Monckton remembered that no confession of love had dropped from Eleanor's lips. She had consented to become his wife, nothing more. She had, no doubt – in those moments of maidenly hesitation, during which he had waited so breathlessly – deliberately weighed and carefully balanced the advantages that were to be won from the sacrifice demanded of her.

Of course the perpetual brooding upon such fancies as these very much tended to make Gilbert Monckton an agreeable and lively companion for an impulsive girl. There is something remarkable in the persistency with which the sufferer from that terrible disease called jealousy strives to aggravate the causes of his torture.

CHAPTER XXVIII

BY THE SUNDIAL

Laura Mason came to live at Tolldale. Gilbert Monckton argued with himself that his most reasonable motive for marrying Eleanor Vane had lain in his desire to provide a secure home and suitable companionship for his ward. The girl was very glad to be with Eleanor; but a little sorry to leave Hazlewood, now that Mr Launcelot Darrell's presence gave a new charm to the place.

'Not that he is very lively, you know, Nelly,' Miss Mason remarked to her guardian's wife in the course of a long discussion of Mr Darrell's merits. 'He never seems happy. He's always roaming about the place, looking as if he had something upon his mind. It makes him look very handsome, though, you know; I don't think he'd look half so handsome if he hadn't anything on his mind. He was awfully dull and gloomy after you went away, Nell; I'm sure he must have been in love with you. Mrs Darrell says he wasn't; and that he admires another person: quite a different person. Do you think I'm the person, Eleanor dear?' asked the young lady, blushing and smiling, as she looked shyly up at her companion's grave face.

'I don't know, Laura; but I almost hope not, for I should be very sorry if you were to marry Launcelot Darrell,' Eleanor said.

'But why should you be sorry, Nelly?'

'Because I don't think he's a good man.'

Miss Mason pouted her under lip and shrugged her shoulders, with the prettiest air of impatience.

'It's very unkind of you to say so, Nell,' she exclaimed. 'I'm sure he's good! Or if he isn't good, I like him all the better for it,' she added, with charming inconsistency. 'I don't want to marry a good man, like my guardian, or Mr Neate, the curate of Hazlewood parish. The Corsair wasn't good; but see how fond Gulnare and Medora were of him. I don't suppose it was good of the Giaour to kill Hassan; but who could have had the heart to refuse to marry the Giaour?'

Mrs Monckton did not attempt to argue with a young lady who expressed such opinions as these. Laura's romantic infatuation only made Eleanor more impatient for the coming of that hour in which she should be able to denounce Launcelot Darrell as a cheat and a traitor.

'He shall be disappointed in his hope of a fortune, and through me,' she thought. 'He shall be cast off by the woman who has loved him, and through me. And when he suffers most I will be as pitiless to his suffering, as he was pitiless to the old man whom he cheated and abandoned to despair.'

A fortnight passed after Eleanor's arrival at the Priory before she had any opportunity of seeing Launcelot Darrell. She had proposed going to Hazlewood several times, but upon each occasion Mr Monckton had contrived to interpose some objection to her visit. She began to despair of entering upon the silent struggle with her father's destroyer. It seemed as if she had come to Tolldale for no purpose. In her impatience she dreaded that Maurice de Crespigny would die, leaving his fortune to his nephew. She knew that the old man's life hung by a slender thread, which at any moment might be severed.

But at last the opportunity she had so anxiously awaited arrived unexpectedly, not brought about by any scheming or foresight upon her part. Laura had been a few days at the Priory, and the two girls were walking in one of the sheltered pathways of the old-fashioned garden, waiting for Gilbert Monckton's arrival, and the clanging summons of the great dinner-bell.

The October sunshine was bright and pleasant; the autumn flowers enlivened the dark luxuriance of the garden with their gaudy splendour. The tall hollyhocks waved in the breeze.

The two girls had walked up and down the smooth gravel path for some time in silence. Eleanor was absorbed in her own thoughts, and even Laura could not talk for ever without encouragement.

But presently this latter young lady stopped with a blush and a start, clasping her hand tightly about her companion's wrist. At the other end of the sheltered walk, amongst the flickering patches of sunshine that trembled on the filbert-trees, she had perceived Launcelot Darrell advancing towards them.

Eleanor looked up.

'What is the matter, Laura?' she asked.

In the next moment she recognized Mr Darrell. The chance had come at last.

The young man advanced to meet Mrs Monckton and her companion. He was pale, and had a certain gravity in his face expressive of some hidden sorrow. He had been in love with Eleanor Vane, after his own fashion, and was very much disposed to resent her desertion of him. His mother had told him the reason of that desertion very frankly, after Eleanor's marriage.

'I come to offer you my congratulations, Mrs Monckton,' he said, in a tone which was intended to wound the young wife to the quick, but which, like everything else about this young man, had a certain spuriousness, an air of melodrama that robbed it of all force. 'I should have accompanied my mother when she called on you the other day – but——'

He paused abruptly, looking at Laura with an air of ill-concealed vexation.

'Can I speak to you alone, Mrs Monckton?' he asked; 'I have something particular to say to you.'

'But you can say it before Laura, I suppose?'

'No, not before Laura, or before any one. I must speak to you alone.'

Miss Mason looked at the object of her admiration with a piteous expression in her childish face.

'How cruel he is to me,' she thought; 'I do believe he is in love with Eleanor. How wicked of him to be in love with my guardian's wife.'

Mrs Monckton did not attempt to refuse the privilege which the young man demanded of her.

'I am quite willing to hear anything you have to say to me,' she said.

'Oh, very well!' cried Laura. 'I'm sure I'll go away if you want to talk about secrets that I mustn't hear. Only I don't see how you can have any secrets. You haven't known Mr Darrell a day longer than I have, Eleanor; and I can't imagine what he can have to say to you.'

After this protest Miss Mason turned her back upon her companions, and ran away towards the house. She shed a few silent tears behind the shelter of a great clump of chrysanthemums.

'He doesn't care for me a bit,' she muttered, as she dried her eyes: 'Mrs Darrell is a wicked old story-teller. I feel just as poor Gulnare must have felt when the Corsair was so rude to her, after she'd committed a murder for his sake.'

Eleanor and Launcelot left the sheltered pathway, and walked slowly across the broad lawn towards an old sundial, quaint in shape, and covered with the moss that had slowly crept over the grey stonework. Here the young man stopped, lounging against the moss-grown pedestal, and resting his elbow upon the broken dial.

'I have come here to-day to tell you that you have treated me very ill, Eleanor Monckton,' he said.

The young wife drew herself up proudly.

'What do you mean?' she asked.

'I mean that you jilted me.'

'Jilted you!'

'Yes. You played fast and loose with me. You listened to my declaration of love. You suffered me to believe that you loved me.'

'Mr Darrell!'

'You did more, Eleanor,' cried the young man, passionately; 'you *did* love me. This marriage with Gilbert Monckton, a man twenty years your senior, is a marriage prompted by base and mercenary motives. You loved me, Eleanor; your silence admitted it that day, if your words did not. You had no right to be cajoled by my mother; you had no right to leave Hazlewood without a word of explanation to me. You are false-hearted and mercenary, Mrs Monckton; and you have married this man here because he is the owner of a fine house, and can give you money to spend upon your womanly caprices – your selfish vanities.'

He pointed scornfully to her silk dress as he spoke, and to the golden trinkets that glittered at her waist.

She looked at him with a strange expression in her face.

'Think of me as you please,' she said; 'think that I was in love with you, if you like.'

It was as if she had said to him, 'Fall into a trap of your own setting, if you please. I am not base enough to lay such a snare for you.'

'Yes, Eleanor, you were false and mercenary. You were foolish, perhaps, as well: for I may be a rich man before very long. I may be master of the Woodlands property.'

'I don't think you ever will inherit that fortune,' Eleanor said, slowly. 'You talk of being base and mercenary; you are at liberty to think so if you please. But have *you* never done base things for the sake of money, Launcelot Darrell?'

The man's face darkened.

'Nobody is immaculate, I dare say,' he answered. 'I have been very poor, and have been obliged to do what the rest of the world does when its purse is empty.'

As Eleanor watched his moody face she suddenly remembered that this was not the way her cards must be played. The task which she had set herself to perform was not to be accomplished by candour and openness. This man had betrayed her father, and she must betray him.

She held out her hand to Launcelot Darrell.

'Let us be friends,' she said; 'I wish to be friends with you.'

There were two witnesses looking on at this gesture. Laura Mason was standing by her guardian, watching the group beside the sundial. Gilbert Monckton had returned from town, and had come into the garden in search of his wife.

'They sent me away from them,' Laura said, as her guardian looked at Launcelot and Eleanor. 'He had something particular to say to her: so I wasn't to hear it, and they sent me away. You'll ask him to dinner, I suppose?'

'No,' answered the lawyer, sharply.

Launcelot Darrell held Eleanor's hand some moments before he released it.

'I wish to be friends with you, Mr Darrell,' she said; 'I'll come to Hazlewood to-morrow to see your pictures, if you please. I want to see how the Rosalind and Celia goes on.'

She hated herself for her hypocrisy. Every generous impulse of her soul revolted against her falsehood. But these things were only a natural part of the unnatural task which she had set herself to perform.

CHAPTER XXIX

KEEPING WATCH

Two pairs of jealous eyes kept constant watch upon Eleanor Monckton for some time after that October afternoon on which the lawyer and Miss Mason stood side by side, looking at the two figures by the sundial.

Gilbert Monckton was too proud to complain. He laid down the fair hopes of his manhood in the grave that already held the broken dreams of his youth. He bowed his head and resigned himself to his fate.

'I was mistaken,' he thought; 'it was too preposterous to suppose that at forty I could win the love of a girl of eighteen. My wife is good and true, but——'

But what? Could this girl be good and true? Had she not deceived her lover most cruelly, most deliberately, in her declaration of utter indifference towards Launcelot Darrell.

Mr Monckton remembered her very words, her sudden look of astonishment, her almost shuddering gesture of surprise, as he asked the important question,

'And you do not love Launcelot Darrell?'

'Love him! oh, no, no, no!'

And in spite of this emphatic denial, Mrs Monckton had, ever since her arrival at Tolldale Priory, betrayed an intense, an almost feverish interest in the young scapegrace artist.

'If she is capable of falsehood,' thought the lawyer, 'there must surely be no truth upon this earth. Shall I trust her and wait patiently for the solution of the mystery? No; between man and wife there should be no mystery! She has no right to keep any secret from me.'

So Mr Monckton hardened his heart against his beautiful young wife, and set himself sternly and indefatigably to watch her every look, to listen to every intonation of her voice, to keep a rigorous guard over his own honour and dignity.

Poor Eleanor was too innocent to read all these signs aright; she only thought that her husband was changed; that this stern and gloomy companion was not the same Gilbert Monckton whom she had known at Hazlewood; not the patient 'guide, philosopher, and friend,' whose subdued bass voice, eloquent in the dusky evenings long ago – a year is very long to a girl of eighteen – in Mrs Darrell's simple drawing-room, had seemed a kind of intellectual music to her.

Had she not been absorbed always by that one thought, whose intensity had reduced the compass of her mind to a monotone, the young wife would very bitterly have felt this change in her husband. As it was she looked upon her disappointment as something very far away from her; something to be considered and regretted by-and-by; by-and-by, when the grand business of her life was done.

But while the gulf between the young wife and her husband every day grew wider, this grand business made no progress. Day after day, week after week passed by, and Eleanor Monckton found herself no nearer the end.

She had paid several visits to Hazlewood; she had acted her part to the best of her abilities, which were very mediocre in all matters where deception is necessary; she had watched and questioned Launcelot Darrell; but she had obtained no vestige of proof to set before Maurice de Crespigny when she denounced his niece's son.

No; whatever secrets were hidden in the young man's breast, he was so guarded as to baffle Eleanor Monckton at every point. He was so thoroughly self-possessed as to avoid betraying himself by so much as a look or a tone.

He was, however, thrown a good deal in Eleanor's society, for Mr Monckton, with a strange persistence, encouraged the penniless artist's attentions to Laura Mason; while Launcelot Darrell, too shallow to hold long to any infatuation, influenced upon one side by his mother, and flattered upon the other by Laura's unconcealed admiration, was content, by-and-by, to lay down his allegiance at this new shrine, and to forgive Mrs Monckton for her desertion.

'Eleanor and my mother were both right, I dare say,' the young man reflected, contemplating his fate with a feeling of despondent languor. 'They were wiser than I was, I dare say. I ought to marry a rich woman. I could never drag out an existence of poverty. Bachelor poverty is bad enough, but, at least, there's something artistic and Bohemian about that. Chambertin one day, and vin ordinaire the next; Veuve Cliquot at the Trois Frères or the Café de Paris to-night, and small beer in a garret to-morrow morning. But married poverty! Squalid desolation instead of reckless gaiety; a sick wife and lean hungry children, and the husband carrying wet canvases to the pawnbroker! Bah! Eleanor was right; she has done a good thing for herself; and I'd better go in and win the heiress, and make myself secure against any caprice of my worthy great-uncle.'

It was thus that Launcelot Darrell became a frequent visitor at Tolldale Priory, and as, about this time, Mr Monckton's business became so unimportant as to be easily flung entirely into the hands of the two junior partners, the lawyer was almost always at home to receive his guest.

Nothing could have been more antagonistic than the characters of the two men. There was no possibility of sympathy or assimilation between them. The weakness of one was rendered more evident by the strength of the other. The decided character of the lawyer seemed harsh and rigid when contrasted with the easy-going languid good-nature of the artist.

Eleanor Monckton, perceiving this wide difference between the two men, admired her husband as much as she despised Launcelot Darrell.

If the lawyer could have known this, – if he could have known that when his wife's earnest eyes followed every change of expression in the young man's face, when she listened most intently to his careless and rambling, yet sometimes almost brilliant talk, she read his shallow nature and its worthlessness better than that nature had ever yet been read by the closest observer, – if Gilbert Monckton could have understood these things, what wasted agonies, what futile tortures, might have been spared him!

'What would have become of me if I had loved this man?' Eleanor thought, as day by day, with an intellect rendered preternaturally clear by the intensity of her one desire, she grew more familiar with Launcelot Darrell's character.

In the meanwhile, Laura Mason walked along a pathway of roses, whose only thorns were those jealous twinges which the young lady experienced on account of Eleanor Monckton.

'He loved her first,' the heiress thought, despondently, 'I know he did, and he made her an offer upon the day the dressmaker brought home my blue silk, and it was so short-waisted I was obliged to make her take it back for alteration. And that was why she – I mean Eleanor, not the dressmaker – left Hazlewood. And it's not pleasant to think that the man one idolizes has idolized somebody else not three months before he proposes to one; and I don't think it was right of Eleanor to lead him on.'

It was by this latter very vague phrase that Miss Mason was in the habit of excusing her lover's delinquency. Eleanor had led him on; and he was thereby in a manner justified for that brief infatuation which had beguiled him from poor Laura. In what this 'leading on' had consisted the young lady did not seek to understand. She wanted to forgive her lover, and she wanted reasons for her forgiveness; as weak women do when they deliver themselves up to the bondage of a sentimental affection for a handsome face. But although Launcelot Darrell had made his peace with Mr Monckton's ward, wooing her with a great many tender words and pretty stereotyped phrases under the gloomy shadow of the yew-trees in the old-fashioned priory garden, and although he had formally demanded her hand, and had been accepted by her guardian and herself, Laura was not yet quite satisfied. Some lingering sentiment of distrust still held its place in her breast, and the jealous twinges, which, as I have said, constituted the thorns upon her rose-bestrewn pathway, were very sharp and numerous.

Nor was Mr Monckton wholly free from anxiety on his ward's account. He had consented to her engagement with Launcelot Darrell. He had done even more; he had encouraged the young man's suit; and now that it was too late to undo his work, he began to argue with himself as to the wisdom of his conduct.

He tried to palter with his conscience; but he could not disguise from himself that the leading motive which had induced him to consent to his ward's engagement was his desire to remove Launcelot Darrell out of the society of his wife. He could not be so blind to his own weakness as to be unaware of the secret pleasure he felt in being able to demonstrate to Eleanor the worthlessness of an affection which could be so easily transferred from one object to another.

Apart from this, Gilbert Monckton tried to believe that he had taken the best course within his power of choice, for the frivolous girl whom it was his duty to protect. To have opposed Laura's attachment would have been to cause her great unhappiness. The young man was clever and agreeable. He was the descendant of a race which was almost noble by right of its origin. His character would grow stronger with time, and it would be the guardian's duty to foster all that was good in the nature of his ward's husband; and to put him in a fair way of occupying an honourable position.

'I will try and develop his talent – his genius, perhaps,' Gilbert Monckton thought; 'he shall go to Italy, and study the old masters.'

So it was settled that the marriage should take place early in the spring, and that Launcelot and his wife should start immediately afterwards upon a tour through the great art cities on the continent. It was arranged that they should remain away for at least a twelvemonth, and that they should spend the winter in Rome.

Eleanor Monckton grew deathly pale when her husband announced to her the probable date of the marriage.

'So soon!' she said, in a low, half-stifled voice. 'So soon, why, December has already begun – the spring will be here directly.'

Gilbert Monckton watched her face with a thoughtful frown.

'What is there to wait for?' he said.

Eleanor was silent for a few moments. What could she say? Could she suffer this engagement to continue? Could she allow Launcelot Darrell to hold his place amongst these people who so ignorantly trusted in him? She would have spoken, perhaps, and confided at least some part of her secret to her husband, but she refrained from doing so: for might not he too laugh at her, as Richard Thornton had done? Might not he, who had grown lately cold and reserved in his manner towards her, sometimes even sarcastic and severe – might not he sternly reprobate her mad desire for vengeance, and in some manner or other frustrate the great purpose of her life?

She had trusted Richard Thornton, and had implored his help. No good had ever come of that confidence: nothing but remonstrances, reproaches, entreaties; even ridicule. Why, then, should she trust any one else? No, she was resolved henceforward to hold her secret in her own keeping, and to look to herself alone for victory.

'Why should the marriage be delayed?' Mr Monckton demanded, rather sharply, for the second time; 'is there any reason for delay?'

'No,' Eleanor faltered, 'not if you think Mr Darrell worthy of Laura's confidence; not if you think him a good man.'

'Have you any reason to think otherwise of him?'

Mrs Monckton evaded a direct answer to this question.

'It was you who first taught me to doubt him,' she said.

'Indeed!' answered her husband; 'I had quite forgotten that. I wonder, Eleanor, that you should appear so much interested in this young man, since you have so bad an opinion of him.'

Mr Monckton left the room after launching this dart at the breast which he believed was guilty of hiding from him a secret regard for another.

'God help her, poor child!' thought the lawyer, 'she married me for my position; and perhaps thought that it would be an easy thing to conquer some slight sentimental predilection for Launcelot Darrell. She tries to do her duty, I believe; and when this young man is safely out of the way she may learn to love me perhaps.'

Such reflections as these were generally followed by a change in the lawyer's manner, and Eleanor's failing spirits revived in the new sunshine of his affection. She had respected and admired Gilbert Monckton from the hour of her meeting with him at the Great Western terminus; and she was ready to love him truly and cordially whenever she could succeed in her great purpose, and disengage her mind from its one absorbing idea.

CHAPTER XXX

AN OLD MAN'S FANCY

Although Eleanor Monckton's utmost watchfulness revealed to her nothing that could be twisted into a proof of Launcelot Darrell's identity with the man who had been the indirect cause of her father's death, she made some progress in another quarter, very much to the annoyance of several people, amongst whom must be included the young painter.

Maurice de Crespigny, who for some years past had not been known to take an interest in anything, exhibited a very great interest in Gilbert Monckton's young wife.

The old man had never forgotten the day upon which he had been suddenly carried back to the past, by the apparition of a fair-haired girl who seemed to him the living image of his lost friend. He had never forgotten this: and when, a few days after Eleanor's arrival at Tolldale, he happened to encounter her in one of his airings, he had insisted on stopping to talk to her, much to the aggravation of his two maiden warders.

Eleanor caught eagerly at any chance of becoming familiar with her father's friend. It was to him she looked for her promised vengeance. The law could give her no redress; but Maurice de Crespigny held in his hand the disposition of that wealth for which his young kinsman hoped, and thus possessed power to punish the cheat and traitor who had robbed a helpless old man.

Even if this motive had not existed, Eleanor's love for her dead father would have been sufficient to inspire her with every tender feeling towards the owner of Woodlands. Her manner, modified by this tenderness, acted almost like a spell upon Maurice de Crespigny. He insisted upon coming, in the course of his daily airing, to that part of the grounds where the two estates were only divided by a slender wire fence, and where he might hope to meet Eleanor. By-and-by he extorted from her the promise to meet him on every fine day at a particular hour, and it was in vain that the maiden sisters endeavoured by every stratagem they could devise, to detain him in-doors at this appointed time. They were fain to pray for perpetual wet weather, for storms and fogs, whirlwinds, and other caprices of nature, which might keep the invalid a prisoner to the house.

But at last even rain and tempest ceased to be of any avail to these distressed and expectant spinsters, for Maurice de Crespigny insisted upon inviting Mr and Mrs Monckton to Woodlands. They were to come whenever they could, every day if they could, the old man wrote, with a tremulous hand that was apt to go a little astray over the paper; but which was yet strong enough and firm enough to inscribe a decent signature at the foot of a will.

The two sisters never saw him write without thinking of this document. Was it made, and made in their favour? Was it yet to make? Or was it made in accordance with the expectations of Ellen Darrell and her son?

Lavinia and Sarah de Crespigny were agonized by the mere thought of this latter possibility. It was not the money alone that they thought of, the lands and tenements alone that they considered. There was the family house in which they had lived so long, the household treasures which their own careful hands had dusted, as things too sacred to be approached by meaner fingers.

There were the old silver salvers, the antique tea and coffee services, the great dragon-china jars on the staircase, the inlaid card-tables in the green parlour, – would the ruthless young man come into possession, and seize even upon those particular household gods which were most sacred to the maiden sisters?

They knew that they had no claim to any great mercy from Launcelot Darrell. Had they not urged his Indian voyage, and for ever offended him by so doing? It would have been better perhaps to have been friendly towards him, and to have suffered him to remain in England, and to be as much at Woodlands as he pleased, thereby affording him ample opportunity for giving offence to his great-uncle.

'Who can count upon an old man's caprices?' thought the maiden sisters; 'perhaps because our uncle has seen very little of Launcelot, he may be all the more kindly disposed towards him.'

On the other hand, there was now the more imminent danger of this sudden fancy with which Eleanor Monckton had inspired the invalid; and the sisters grew paler and more lugubrious every day as they watched the progress of this eccentric friendship.

Gilbert Monckton placed no obstacle in the way of his wife's visits to Woodlands. He knew how sternly the doors of Mr de Crespigny's house were guarded against his widowed niece and her son; and he knew that there at least Eleanor was not likely to meet Launcelot Darrell.

Mrs Monckton was therefore free to visit her dead father's friend when she pleased; and she was not slow to avail herself of this privilege. It was of vital importance to her to be on familiar terms with Maurice de Crespigny, to be able to enter his house when and how she would. She saw enough in the old man's face, in the fearful uncertainty of his health – which one day suffered him to be bright and cheerful, and on the next laid him prostrate and helpless upon a sick bed – to convince her that his state was terribly precarious. He might linger for years. He might die suddenly. He might die, leaving his fortune to Launcelot Darrell.

The sisters watched, with ever-increasing alarm, the progress that Mrs Monckton was making in their uncle's favour. The old man seemed to brighten under the influence of Eleanor's society. He had no glimmering idea of the truth; he fully believed that the likeness which the lawyer's young wife bore to George Vane was one of those accidental resemblances so common to the experience of every one. He believed this; and yet in spite of this he felt as if Eleanor's presence brought back something of his lost youth. Even his memory was revivified by the companionship of his dead friend's daughter; and he would sit for hours together, talking, as his nieces had not heard him talk in many monotonous years, telling familiar stories of that past in which George Vane had figured so prominently.

To Eleanor these old memories were never wearisome; and Maurice de Crespigny felt the delight of talking to a listener who was really interested. He was accustomed to the polite attention of his nieces, whose suppressed yawns sometimes broke in unpleasantly at the very climax of a story, and whose wooden-faced stolidity had at best something unpleasantly suggestive of being listened to and stared at by two Dutch clocks. But he was not accustomed to see a beautiful and earnest face turned towards him as he spoke; a pair of bright grey eyes lighting up with new radiance at every crisis in the narrative; and lovely lips half parted through intensity of interest.

These things the old man was not accustomed to, and he became entirely Eleanor's slave and adorer. Indeed, the elderly damsels congratulated themselves upon Miss Vincent's marriage with Gilbert Monckton; otherwise Maurice de Crespigny, being besotted and infatuated, and the young woman mercenary, there might have been a new mistress brought home to Woodlands instead of to Tolldale Priory.

Happily for Eleanor, the anxious minds of the maiden sisters were ultimately set in some degree at rest by a few words which Maurice de Crespigny let drop in a conversation with Mrs Monckton. Amongst the treasures possessed by the old man – the relics of a past life, whose chief value lay in association – there was one object that was peculiarly precious to Eleanor. This was a miniature portrait of George Vane, in the cap and gown which he had worn sixty years before, at Magdalen College, Oxford.

This picture was very dear to Eleanor Monckton. It was no very wonderful work of art, perhaps, but a laborious and patient performance, whose production had cost more time and money than the photographic representations of half the members of the Lower House would cost to-day. It showed Eleanor a fair-haired stripling, with bright hopeful blue eyes. It was the shadow of her dead father's youth.

Her eyes filled with tears as she looked at the little ivory portrait in its oval case of slippery red morocco.

'Crocodile!' thought one of the maiden sisters.

'Sycophant!' muttered the other.

But this very miniature gave rise to that speech which had so much effect in calming the terrors of the two ladies.

'Yes, my dear,' Maurice de Crespigny said; 'that portrait was painted sixty years ago. George Vane would have been close upon eighty if he had lived. Yes, close upon eighty, my love. You don't see your own likeness to that picture, perhaps; people seldom do see resemblances of that kind. But the lad's face is like yours, my dear, and you bring back the memory of my youth, just as the scent of some old-fashioned flower, that our advanced horticulture has banished to a cottager's garden, brings back the grass-plot upon which I played at my mother's knees. Do you know what I mean to do, Mrs Monckton?'

Eleanor lifted her eyebrows with an arch smile, as who should say, 'Your caprices are quite beyond my power of divination.'

'I mean to leave that miniature to you in my will, my dear.'

The maiden sisters started simultaneously, agitated by the same emotion, and their eyes met.

'Yes, my dear,' Maurice de Crespigny repeated, 'I shall leave that miniature to you when I die. It's not worth anything intrinsically; but I don't want you to be reminded of me when I am dead and gone, except through your own tender feelings. You have been interested in my stories of George Vane – who, with all his faults, and I'm not slow to acknowledge them, was a brighter and better man than I was – and it may please you sometimes to look at that picture. You've brought a ray of sunlight across a very dismal pathway, my love,' added the invalid, quite indifferent to the fact that this remark was by no means complimentary to his devoted nurses and guardians, 'and I am grateful to you. If you were poor, I should leave you money. But you are the wife of a rich man; and, beyond that, my fortune is already disposed of. I am not free to leave it as I might wish; I have a duty to perform, my dear; a duty which I consider sacred and imperative; and I shall fulfil that duty.'

The old man had never before spoken so freely of his intentions with regard to his money. The sisters sat staring blankly at each other, with quickened breaths and pale faces.

What could this speech mean? Why, clearly that the money must be left to them. What other duty could Maurice de Crespigny owe to any one? Had they not kept guard over him for years, shutting him in, and separating him from every living creature? What right had he to be grateful to any one but them, inasmuch as they had taken good care that no one else should ever do him a service?

But to the ears of Eleanor Monckton, the old man's speech had another signification; the blood mounted to her face, and her heart beat violently. 'He is thinking of Launcelot Darrell,' she thought; 'he will leave his fortune to Launcelot Darrell. He will die before he learns the secret of my father's wrongs. His will is already made, no doubt, and he will die before I can dare to say to him, "Your niece's son is a trickster and a villain!"'

This was the only occasion upon which Maurice de Crespigny ever spoke of his intentions with regard to the fortune that he must leave behind him. He said, plainly enough, that Eleanor was to have none of his money; and the sisters, who had until now kept a jealous watch upon the old man and his favourite, were henceforward content to let Mrs Monckton come and go as she pleased. But for all this Eleanor was no nearer the accomplishment of her great purpose.

Launcelot Darrell came to Tolldale, and in a certain easy and somewhat indifferent manner paid his homage to his affianced wife. Laura was happy by fits and starts; and by fits and starts utterly miserable, when the horrible pangs of jealousy – jealousy of Eleanor, and jealous doubts of her lover's truth – tortured her breast. Gilbert Monckton sat day after day in the library or the drawing-room, or Eleanor's morning-room, as the case might be, keeping watch over his wife and the lovers.

But though the days and weeks went by with an unnatural rapidity, as it seemed to Mrs Monckton – with a wearisome slowness in the opinion of her husband – the progress of time brought George Vane's daughter no further onward, by so much as one step, upon the pathway which she had chosen for herself.

Christmas came; and the girl whose youth had been spent in the shabby lodgings in which her father had hidden the poverty of his decline, the patient young housekeeper who had been used to eke out ounces of tea, and to entreat for brief respite and grace from aggrieved chandlers, was called upon to play my Lady Bountiful at Tolldale Priory, and to dole out beef and bread, blankets and brandy, coals and flannels, to a host of hungry and shivering claimants.

Christmas passed, and the new year struggled into life under every disadvantage of bad weather; while the spring, the dreaded early spring, which was to witness Laura's marriage, approached with a stealthy footfall, creeping day by day nearer and nearer.

Eleanor, in very despair, appealed to Richard Thornton.

She appealed to him from the force of habit, perhaps: as a fretful child complains to its mother: rather than from any hope that he could aid her in her great scheme.

'Oh, Richard,' she wrote, despairingly, 'help me, help me, help me! I thought all would be so easy if I could once come to this place. But I am here, and I see Launcelot Darrell every day, and yet I am no nearer the end. What am I to do? January is nearly over; and in March, Laura Mason is to marry that man. Mr de Crespigny is very ill, and may die at any moment, leaving his money to his niece's son. Is this man, who caused my father's death, to have all the brightest and best things this world can give? Is he to have a noble fortune and an amiable wife? and am I to stand by and permit him to be happy; remembering what happened upon that dreadful night in Paris – remembering that my father lies in his unconsecrated grave, and that his blood is upon this man's head? Help me, Richard. Come to me; help me to find proof positive of Launcelot Darrell's guilt. You can help me, if you please. Your brain is clearer, your perception quicker, than mine. I am carried away by my own passion – blinded by my indignation. You were right when you said I should never succeed in this work. I look to you to avenge my father's death.'

CHAPTER XXXI

A POWERFUL ALLY

Richard Thornton was not slow to respond to Eleanor's summons. The same post which carried Mrs Monckton's letter to the young man conveyed another letter, addressed to the Signora, urging her to abandon her pupils, for a time at least, and to come at once to Tolldale.

Eleanor had not forgotten the faithful friends who had succoured her in the day of her desolation, but the Signora's habits of independence were not to be conquered, and Mrs Monckton found there was very little that Eliza Picirillo would consent to accept from her.

She had insisted upon removing the music-mistress from the eccentric regions of the Pilasters to a comfortable first-floor in Dudley Street. She had furnished this new shelter with easy chairs, and Brussels carpets, an Erard's piano, and proof impressions of the Signora's favourite pictures, and in doing this she had very nearly exhausted her first year's income, much to the satisfaction of Gilbert Monckton, who implored her to call upon him freely for any money she might want for her friends.

It pleased him to see her do these things. It was a delight to him to see her thus tenderly grateful to the friends of her adversity.

'A mercenary woman would have cast off these humble associations,' he thought: 'this girl must be the noble creature I believed her to be, when I flung down my happiness for the second time at a woman's feet.'

But although Eleanor would have gladly lavished every shilling she possessed upon Eliza Picirillo and her nephew, she could not persuade either the music-mistress or the scene-painter to work less hard than it had been their wont to do for many wearisome years. The Signora still went from house to house in attendance upon her out-of-door pupils, and still received young ladies bent upon wearing the laurel crown of the lyric drama. Richard still painted snow-clad mountain-tops, and impossible Alpine passes, impracticably prosperous villages, and wide-spreading farm-lands of yellow corn, bounded by fragile white pailings, and occupied by husbandmen in linen gaiters and chintz waistcoats. It was in vain, therefore, that Mrs Monckton had hitherto implored her friends to come to Tolldale, and it was only in consequence of a very serious misunderstanding with Messrs Spavin and Cromshaw, which for a time threw the scene-painter out of employment, that Richard Thornton was able to respond to Eleanor's earnest appeal.

A January that had been bleaker and colder than even January is expected to be was drawing to a close, when Signora Picirillo and her nephew arrived at the Priory. The woods round Tolldale were shrouded with snow, the broad lawns before Woodlands were as white as Richard's

Alpine passes, and Maurice de Crespigny had been for many weeks a prisoner to the house. Laura's wedding-day was appointed for the fifteenth of March, and that young lady, when unoccupied by her lover's society, was entirely absorbed in the millinery and mantua-making necessary for the preparation of her bridal outfit.

Richard Thornton had considerably modified the eccentric fashion of his beard, and had bought a new suit of clothes in honour of his fair young hostess. The scene-painter had not seen Eleanor since the morning on which he had fled away from the Pilasters to hide his sorrows amongst the swamps of Battersea. The meeting, therefore, was a painful one to him; all the more painful, perhaps, because Mrs Monckton received him with the frankly affectionate welcome which she would have bestowed upon a brother.

'You must help me, Dick,' she said, 'for the sake if others, if not for my sake; you cannot now refuse to fathom this mystery. If Launcelot Darrell is the man I believe him to be, he is no fit husband for an affectionate and trusting girl. He has no right to inherit Maurice de Crespigny's fortune! The marriage between Laura and this man is to take place upon the fifteenth of March. Maurice de Crespigny may die to-morrow. We have very little time before us, Richard.'

So Mr Thornton was fain to obey the imperious young lady, who had been in the habit of ordering him about ever since the days in which he had kept rabbits and silkworms for her gratification. He set himself to his task very faithfully; and did his best to become acquainted with Launcelot Darrell's character.

The well-born young artist, who meant to do something very great in the Academy at his earliest convenience, treated the scene-painter with a supercilious good-nature that was by no means agreeable to Mr Thornton.

Dick had resolved *not* to be prejudiced against Eleanor's fancied enemy, lest that young lady's vehement impulses should have led her into rather an awkward mistake; but there was something in the insolent assurance of Launcelot Darrell that aroused Richard's indignation, and it was not without an effort that he contrived to be commonly civil to poor Laura's affianced husband.

Launcelot dined at Tolldale upon the evening of the arrival of Eleanor's guests, and it was at the dinner-table that Richard first had an opportunity of observing the man he had been entreated to watch. Mr Monckton, sitting at the bottom of the table, and looking at his wife athwart a glittering array of glass and silver, became aware of a change in Eleanor's manner, – a change that mystified and bewildered him, but which was not altogether unpleasant to him.

The lawyer's jealousy had been chiefly aroused by the perpetual uneasiness of Eleanor's manner when Launcelot Darrell was present; by the furtive yet unregarded watch which she kept upon the young man's movements. To-night, for the first time, her manner had changed. It was no longer Launcelot Darrell, but Richard Thornton whom she watched.

Following every varying expression of her face, Gilbert Monckton saw that she looked at the scene-painter with an earnest, questioning, appealing glance, that seemed to demand something of him, or urge him on to the performance of something that she wanted done. Looking from his wife to Richard, the lawyer saw that Launcelot Darrell was still watched; but this time the eyes that observed him were those of the Signora's nephew.

Mr Monckton felt very much like a spectator who looks on at a drama which is being acted in a language that is unknown to him. The *dramatis personae* come in and go out; they are earnest or vehement, joyous or sorrowful, as the case may be; but not having any clue to the plot, the wretched looker-on can scarcely feel intense delight in the performance.

Eleanor contrived to question her ally in the course of the evening.

'Well, Richard,' she said, 'is Launcelot Darrell the man who cheated my father?'

'I don't know about that, Mrs Monckton, but——'

'But you think——?'

'I think he is by no means the most delightful, or the best of men. He snubs me because I paint scenery for the Phoenix; and he accepts that silly little girl's homage with the air of a sultan.'

'Then you don't like him, Dick!'

Mr Thornton drew a long breath, as if by some powerful effort of his will he repressed a vehement and unseemly expression of feeling.

'I think he's – you know what a great tragedian used to call people when they rang down the act-drop three minutes before Lear had finished using bad language to his eldest daughter, or came up in the witches' cauldron with their backs to the audience – and nervous people have been known to do that, Eleanor: – it isn't pleasant to stand on a rickety ladder and talk to a quick-tempered tragedian out of a canvas saucepan, with a smell of burning rosin in your nostrils, and another nervous apparition wanting to get you off the ladder before you've finished your speech. I think Launcelot Darrell is – a BEAST, Mrs Monckton; and I have no doubt he would cheat at cards, if he had the chance of doing it with perfect safety and convenience.'

'You think that?' cried Eleanor, seizing upon this latter part of Richard's speech; 'you think that he would cheat a helpless old man? Prove that, Richard; prove it, and I will be as merciless to Launcelot Darrell as he was to my father – his uncle's friend, too; he knew that.'

'Eleanor Monckton,' Richard said, earnestly, 'I have never been serious before upon this matter; I have hoped that you would outlive your girlish resolution; I hoped above all that when you married' – his voice trembled a little here, but he went bravely on – 'new duties would make you forget that old promise; and I did my best, Heaven knows, to wean you from the infatuation. But now that I have seen this man, Launcelot Darrell, it seems to me as if there may have been something of inspiration in your sudden recognition of him. I have already seen enough of him to know at least that he is no fit husband for that poor little romantic girl with the primrose-coloured ringlets; and I will do my best to find out where he was, and what he was doing, during those years in which he is supposed to have been in India.'

'You will do this, Richard?'

'Yes, Mrs Monckton.' The young man addressed his old companion by this name, using the unfamiliar appellation as a species of rod by which he kept in order and subdued certain rebellious emotions that would arise as he remembered how utterly the beautiful girl, whose presence had made sunshine in the shabbiest, if not the shadiest of places, was now lost to him. 'Yes, Mrs Monckton, I will try and fathom the mystery. This Launcelot Darrell must be very clever if he can have contrived to do away with every vestige of the years in which he was or was not in India. However softly Time may tread, he leaves his footmarks behind him; and it will be strange if we can't find some tell-tale impression whereby Mr Darrell's secret may be discovered. By the bye, Mrs Monckton, you have had a good deal of time for observation. What have you done towards investigating the young man's antecedents?'

Eleanor blushed, and hesitated a little before she answered this very direct question.

'I have watched him very closely,' she said, 'and I've listened to every word he has ever said——'

'To be sure. In the expectation, no doubt, that he would betray himself by frowns and scowls, and other facial contortions, after the manner of a stage villain; or that he wold say, "At such a time I was in Paris;" or "At such a time I cheated at écarté." You go cleverly to work, Mrs Monckton, for an amateur detective!'

'What ought I to have done, then?' Eleanor asked, despondently.

'You should have endeavoured to trace up the history of the past by those evidences which the progress of life can scarcely fail to leave behind it. Watch the man's habits and associations, rather than the man himself. Have you had access to the rooms in which he lives?'

'Yes; I have been with Laura to Hazlewood often since I came here. I have been in Launcelot Darrell's rooms.'

'And have you seen nothing there? no book, no letter; no scrap of evidence that might make one link in the story of this man's life?'

'Nothing – nothing particular. He has some French novels on a shelf in one corner of his sitting-room.'

'Yes; but the possession of a few French novels scarcely proves that he was in Paris in the year '53. Did you look at the titles of the books?'

'No; what could I have gained by seeing them?'

'Something, perhaps. The French are a volatile [race]. The fashion of one year is not the fashion of another. If you had found some work that made a *furore* in that particular year, you might have argued that Launcelot Darrell was a *flâneur* in the Galerie d'Orleans, or on the Boulevard, where the book was newly exhibited in the shop-windows. If the novels were new ones, and not Michel Lévy's eternal reprints of Sand and Soulié, Balzac and Bernard, you might have learnt something from them. The science of detection, Mrs Monckton, lies in the observation of insignificant things. It is a species of mental geology. A geologist looks into the gravel pit, and tells you the history of the creation; a clever detective ransacks a man's carpet-bag, and convicts that man of a murder or a forgery.'

'I know I have been very stupid,' Eleanor murmured, almost piteously.

'Heaven forbid that you should ever be very clever in such a line as this. There must be detective officers; they are the polished bloodhounds of our civilized age, and very noble and estimable animals when they do their duty conscientiously: but fair-haired young ladies should be kept out of this *galère*. Think no more of this business, then, Eleanor. If Launcelot Darrell was the man who played *écarté* with your father on the 11th of August '53, I'll find a proof of his guilt. Trust me to do that.'

'I will trust you, Richard.'

Mrs Monckton held out her hand with a certain queenliness of gesture, as if she would thereby have ratified a bond between herself and her old friend; and as the flower of bygone chivalry were wont to vow the accomplishment of great deeds on the jewelled hilt of a cross-handled sword, so Richard Thornton, bending his honest head, swore allegiance upon the hand of Gilbert Monckton's young wife.

'One word more, Mrs Monckton,' said the scene-painter, 'and then we had better leave off talking, or people will begin to wonder why we are so confidential and mysterious. This Mr Darrell is an artist, I understand. Does he paint much?'

'Oh, yes, a great deal; that is to say, he begins a great many things.'

'Precisely; he does a good many rough sketches, scraps of pencil and crayon, eh?'

'Yes.'

'And he fills portfolios with such scraps, and litters his studio with them?'

'Yes.'

'Then I must have a look at his studio, Mrs Monckton. An artist – yes, even the poorest artist, the furthest away from the sublimity of genius – is sure to be fond of his art. He makes a confidant of it; he betrays a hundred secrets, that he keeps locked from every living creature, in the freedom of his studio. His pencil is the outer expression of his mind; and whatever falsehoods he may impose upon his fellow-men, his sketch-book will tell the truth. It will betray him when he is false, and reveal him when he is true. I must have a look at Launcelot Darrell's studio, Mrs Monckton. Let me see the man's pictures; and I may be able to tell you more about the man himself.'

CHAPTER XXXII

THE TESTIMONY OF THE SKETCH-BOOK

It is only natural that one painter should take an interest in the work of another. Mr Darrell testified no surprise, therefore, when Richard Thornton appeared at Hazlewood the morning after his arrival at Tolldale, under convoy of Mrs Monckton and Laura.

'I've come to say how sorry I was at your not coming to dinner last night, dear Mrs Darrell,' Laura said, to the lady who was so soon to be her mother-in-law; 'and I want to ask you whether I ought to have the sprigged muslin morning dresses trimmed with pink or blue, or whether I ought to have three of them pink and three blue, for Launcelot might get tired of seeing me in the same colours, you know, and I might have two of them trimmed with peach, if it came to that; and Eleanor has come with me; and Mr Thornton – Mr Thornton, Mrs Darrell; Mrs Darrell, Mr Thornton – has come too, because he is an artist and wants to see Launcelot's pictures – especially the beautiful picture that's going into the Academy, and that the committee is sure to hang on the line; and I'm sure Launcelot will let Mr Thornton see his studio – won't you, dear Launcelot?'

Miss Mason pursed up her rosy lips, and put her head on one side like an insinuating canary, as she addressed her affianced husband. She looked very pretty in her winter costume, with a good deal of rich brown fur about her, and a dash of scarlet here and there. She looked like a fashionably-dressed Red Ridinghood, simple enough to be deluded by the weakest-minded of wolves. She was so pretty that her lover glanced down at her with a gratified smile, deriving considerable pleasure from the idea that she belonged to him, and that she was, on the whole, something to be rather proud of; something that added to the young sultan's dignity, and bore testimony to his supreme merits.

Eleanor looked at the lovers with a contemptuous curve lifting her firm upper lip. She despised Launcelot Darrell so utterly, that she was almost cruel enough to despise Laura for loving him.

'Yes,' she thought, 'Mr Monckton is right. Shallow, selfish, and frivolous! He is all these, and he is false as well. Heaven help you, Laura, if I cannot save you from a marriage with this man.'

Mr Darrell was very well pleased to do the honours of his studio to Richard Thornton. It would be quite a new sort of thing to this scene-painting fellow, the embryo Academician thought: the poor devil would pick up fresh ideas, and get a glimpse at the higher regions of art, for the first time in his life perhaps.

Launcelot Darrell led the way to that pleasant, prettily-furnished room which he called his studio. The 'Rosalind and Celia' still occupied the post of honour on the easel. Mr Darrell worked very hard; but in that spasmodic fashion which is antagonistic to anything like progress. The enthusiasm which upon one occasion kept him at his picture long after the fading light had given him notice to leave it, entirely deserted him upon another; and was perhaps followed by a fit of disgust with himself and with his art, which kept him idle for weeks together.

He made a merit of this fitfulness, depreciating a power of steady and persistent labour as the faculty of a tradesman, rather than an artist. He took credit to himself for the long pauses of idleness in which he waited for what he called inspiration; and imposed upon his mother by his grand talk about earnestness, conscientiousness, reverence for the sublimity of art, and a great many more fine phrases by which he contrived to excuse the simple fact of his laziness. So Eleanor Vane, as sorrowful *Rosalind*, still smiled sadly upon a simpering *Celia*: – it had been quite impossible to prevent Miss Mason's assuming the conventional simper of the weak-minded sitter who can't forget that his portrait is being taken, and that he is in the very act of handing down his smile to prosperity, or to the furniture brokers – out of an unfinished background, and clad in robes of unfinished satin and velvet. Mr Thornton wondered as he looked at the young man's work, and remembered how many miles of canvas it had been his own fate to cover since first he had handled his brushes and splashed in sky borders and cloud pieces for the chief scene-painter at the Phoenix.

Launcelot Darrell, with his mahlstick in his hand, smiled with sublime patronage upon Eleanor's humble friend.

'This sort of thing is rather different to what you've been used to, I suppose?' he said; 'rather another kind of work than your pantomime scenes, your grots of everlasting bliss, and caves of constant content, where the waterfalls are spangles sewn upon white tape, and the cloudless skies are blue gauze and silver foil?'

'But we're not always painting transformations, you know,' Mr Thornton answered, in nowise offended by the artist's graceful insolence; 'scene-painting isn't *all* done with Dutch metal and the glue-pot: we're obliged to know a little about perspective, and to have a slight knowledge of colour. Some of my brotherhood have turned out tolerable landscape-painters, Mr Darrell. By the bye, you don't do anything in the way of landscape, do you?'

'Yes,' Launcelot Darrell answered, indifferently, 'I used to try my hand at landscape; but human interest, human interest, Mr Thornton, is the strong point of a picture. To my mind a picture should be a story, a drama, a tragedy, a poem – something that explains itself without any help from a catalogue.'

'Precisely. An epic upon a Bishop's half-length,' Richard Thornton answered, rather absently. He saw Eleanor's watchful eyes fixed upon him, and knew that with every moment she was losing faith in him. Looking round the room he saw, too, that there were a couple of bloated portfolios leaning against the wall, and running over with sheets of dirty Bristol board and crumpled drawing paper.

'Yes,' Launcelot Darrell repeated, 'I have tried my hand at landscape. There are a few in one of those portfolios – the upper one, I think – not the purple one; I keep private memoranda and scraps in that. The green portfolio, Mr Thornton; you may find some things there that will interest you – that might be useful to you, perhaps.'

The artist threw down his mahlstick, and strolled across the room to talk to Laura Mason and his mother, who were sitting near the fire. In doing this he left Eleanor and Richard side by side, near the easel and the corner in which the portfolios leaned against the wall.

There was a large old-fashioned window in this corner of the room, the casement against which Eleanor had stood when Launcelot Darrell asked her to be his wife. The window was in a deep recess, shaded by thick crimson curtains, and in the recess there was a table. Any one sitting at this table was almost concealed from the other inmates of the room.

Richard Thornton lifted both the portfolios, and placed them on this table. Eleanor stood beside him, breathless and expectant.

'The purple portfolio contains private memoranda,' whispered the young man; 'it is in that portfolio we must look, Mrs Monckton. There is no such thing as honour on the road we have chosen for ourselves.'

The scene-painter untied the strings of the loaded scrap-book, and flung it open. A chaotic mass of drawings lay before him. Crayon sketches; pencil scraps; unfinished and finished water-coloured drawings; rough caricatures in pen-and-ink, and in water-colours; faint indications of half-obliterated subjects; heads, profiles, chins, and noses; lithographed costumes; prints; etchings; illustrations torn out of books and newspapers; all flung together in bewildering confusion.

Mr Thornton, seated at the table with his head bent over the papers before him, and with Eleanor standing at his shoulder, began steadily and deliberately to examine the contents of this purple portfolio.

He carefully scrutinized each drawing, however slight, however roughly done, however unpretentious. He looked also at the back of each drawing, sometimes finding a blank, sometimes a faint pencil indication of a rubbed-out sketch, or a rough outline in pen-and-ink.

For a long time he found nothing in which the utmost ingenuity could discover any relation to that period of Launcelot Darrell's existence which Eleanor believed to have been spent in Paris.

'Belisarius. Girl with basket of strawberries. Marie Antoinette. Headsman. Flower-girl. Oliver Cromwell refusing the crown. Oliver Cromwell denouncing Sir Harry Vane. Oliver Cromwell and his daughters. Fairfax,' – muttered Richard, as he looked over the sketches. 'Didn't I tell you, Eleanor, that a man's sketch-book contains the record of his life? These Cromwell drawings are all dated in the same year. Nearly ten years ago; that is to say, when Mr Darrell had very little knowledge of anatomy, and a tremendous passion for republicanism. Further on we come to a pastoral strata, you see. The Watermill: Rosa. There is a perpetual recurrence of Rosa and the Watermill; Rosa in a bridal dress; the mill by moonlight; Rosa in a russet cloak; the mill in a thunderstorm: Rosa sad; the mill at sunset; and the series bears date two years later, when the artist was desperately in love with a rustic beauty in this neighbourhood. Now we lose sight of Rosa, and come upon a Roman period; the artist goes in for the grand and classic. The Roman period lasts a very short time. Now we are in London; yes, we are up to our eyes in student life in the metropolis. Here are sketches of artist existence in Clipstone Street and the purlieus of Fitzroy Square. Here is the Haymarket by night. An opera-box. Lady Clara Vere de Vere. Lady Clara at the flower-show – in Hyde Park – at a concert. Aha! the artist is in love again; and this time the beauty is highborn and unapproachable. Here are pen-and-ink hints at contemplated suicide; a young man lying on a pallet bed, an empty bottle on the floor labelled Prussic Acid; the same young man leaning over the parapet of Waterloo Bridge on a moonlit night, with St Paul's in the background. Yes, there have been wasted love and despair, and a wild yearning for death, and that generally morbid and unpleasant state of mind which is the common result of idleness and strong liquors. Stay!' cried Richard Thornton, suddenly, 'we're all wrong here.'

'What do you mean?' asked Eleanor. She had watched the young man's examination of the drawings with eager interest, with ever-increasing impatience, in her desire to come to something that should be evidence against Launcelot Darrell.

'What do you mean?' she said, and then she added, impatiently, 'How slow you are, Dick! What do I want to know of this man except the one proof that will identify him with that man upon the Boulevard?'

'I'm afraid we've been making a mistake all this time,' Richard said, in a rather despondent tone. 'These sketches must have been done by some companion of Mr Darrell's. I'm afraid they're none of them his.'

'Not his? But why – why not?'

'Because the first lot, the Cromwells and the Rosas, are all signed with a flourishing autograph – "Launcelot Darrell, pinxt.," in full, as if the young man was rather proud of his name.'

'Yes, yes; but what then?'

'The London-life sketches, the Lady Claras, and the suicides, which are much better than the first lot, though I should have thought they had been by the same man, are all signed with a monogram.'

'A monogram?'

'Yes, of two initials. I've been trying to make them out for ever so long, and I've only just succeeded. The two letters are R. L.'

Richard Thornton felt Eleanor's hand, which had been resting lightly upon the back of his chair, tighten suddenly upon the rosewood scroll-work; he heard her breath grow quicker; and when he turned his head he saw that she was deadly pale.

'It is coming home to him, Richard,' she said. 'The man who cheated my father called himself "Robert Lan——" Part of the name was torn away in my father's letter, but the initials of that false name are R.L. Go on, Dick; go on quickly, for pity's sake; we shall find something more presently.'

Eleanor Monckton had spoken in a whisper, but at this moment the scene-painter laid his hand upon her wrist and reminded her by a gesture of the need of caution. But Mr Darrell, and the two ladies at the other end of the roomy studio, were in no manner observant of anything that might be going on in the curtained recess of the window. Laura was talking, and her lover was laughing at her; half pleased, half amused, by her childish frivolity.

Richard Thornton turned over a heap of sketches, without speaking.

But presently he came upon a water-colour drawing of a long lamplit street, crowed with figures in grotesque costumes, and with masks upon their faces.

'We have crossed the Channel, Eleanor,' he said. 'Here is Paris in Carnival time, and here is the assumed name, too, in full, – "Robert Lance, March 2nd, '53." Be quiet, Eleanor, be calm, for Heaven's sake. The man is guilty; I believe that, now, as fully as you do; but we have to bring his guilt home to him.'

'Keep that sketch, Richard,' whispered the girl, 'keep it. It is the proof of his false name. It is the proof that he was in Paris when he was believed to be in India. It is the proof that he was in Paris a few months before my father's death.'

The scene-painter folded the tumbled sheet of drawing-paper and thrust it into the breast-pocket of his loose overcoat.

'Go on, Richard; go on,' said Eleanor; 'there may be something more than this.'

The young man obeyed his eager companion; one by one he looked at the pen-and-ink sketches, the crayon drawings, the unfinished scraps in Indian ink or water-colour.

They all bore evidence of a life in Paris and its neighbourhood. Now a *débardeur* hanging on the arm of a student; now a grisette drinking lemonade with an artisan beyond the barrier; a funeral train entering the gates of Père la Chaise; some children, with garlands in their hands, kneeling by a grave; a showman on the Boulevard; a group of Zouaves; a bit of landscape in the forest of Saint Germain, with equestrian figures beneath an arch of foliage; a scene in the Champs Elysées.

And at last, a rough pencil sketch of a group in a small chamber at a *café*; an old man seated at a lamplit table playing *écarté* with a man whose face was hidden; an aristocratic-looking, shabby-genteel old man, whose nervous fingers seemed to clutch restlessly at a little pile of napoleons on the table before him.

There was a third figure; the figure of a smartly-dressed Frenchman standing behind the old man's chair; and in this watcher of the game Eleanor recognized the man who had persuaded her father to leave her on the Boulevard, – the companion of the sulky Englishman.

The sketch was dated August 12, 1853; the very day on which Richard Thornton had recognized the dead man in the ghastly chamber of the Morgue. On the back of the drawing were written these words, 'Sketch for finished picture, to be called "The last of the Napoleons" – Robert Lance.'

The likeness of the principal figure to George Vane was unmistakable. The man who had been heartless enough to cheat his kinsman's friend, had made this record of the scene of his cruelty; but had not been so callous as to carry out his design after the suicide of his victim.

CHAPTER XXXIII

MAURICE DE CRESPIGNY'S WILL

Richard Thornton folded the pencil sketch and put it in his pocket with the water-coloured drawing.

'I told you that Launcelot Darrell would make a confidant of his pencil,' he said, in a low voice. 'We may as well tie up the portfolio, Mrs Monckton; there will be nothing more in it that can help us. The memory of your father would scarcely be pleasant to this young man after the 12th of August. When he made this sketch he had yet to learn the consequences of what he had done.'

Eleanor stood behind the scene-painter's chair, silent and motionless. Her face was pale, and her mouth compressed and rigid with the effort by which she controlled her agitation. But a flame of fire burned in her eyes, and her nostrils quivered with a convulsive movement. Mr Thornton carefully replaced the sketches in the purple portfolio, tied the strings, and laid the book in its old place against the wall. Then, unfastening the green portfolio, he went rapidly through the landscape scraps which it contained.

'The hand is weak here,' Richard said: 'Mr Launcelot Darrell has no sympathy with nature. He might be a clever figure painter if he had as much perseverance as he has talent. His pictures are like himself; shallow, artificial, and meretricious; but they are clever.'

The scene-painter said this with a purpose. He knew that Eleanor stood behind him, erect and statuesque, with her hand grasping the back of his chair, a pale Nemesis bent on revenge and destruction. He wanted, if possible, to let her down to commonplace feeling, by his commonplace talk, before Launcelot Darrell saw her face. But, looking round at that pale young face, Richard saw how terrible was the struggle in the girl's breast, and how likely she was at any moment to betray herself.

'Eleanor,' he whispered, 'if you want to carry this business to the end, you must keep your secret. Launcelot Darrell is coming this way. Remember that an artist is quick to observe. There is the plot of a tragedy in your face at this moment.'

Mrs Monckton tried to smile; but the attempt was very feeble; the smile wan and sickly. Launcelot Darrell came to the curtained recess, but he was not alone; Laura Mason came with him, talking very fast, and asking innumerable questions, now turning to her lover, now appealing to Eleanor or Richard Thornton.

'What a time you've been looking over the sketches,' she said, 'and how do you like them, and which do you like best? Do you like the sea-side bits, or the forest sketches? There's a picture of Tolldale with the

cupola and the dinner-bell, Eleanor; I like the sketches in the other
portfolio best; Launcelot lets *me* look at them, though he won't allow any
one else to see them. But I don't like Rosa. I'm terribly jealous of Rosa –
yes, I *am*, Launcelot; and it's not a bit of use telling me you were never in
love with her, and you only admired her because she was a pretty rustic
model. Nobody in the world could believe that, could they, Mr
Thornton? Could they, Eleanor? When an artist paints the same face
again and again, and again and again, he must be in love with the
original; mustn't he now?'

Nobody answered the young lady's eager questions. Launcelot Darrell
smiled and twisted his dark moustache between his slender womanish
fingers. Laura's unrestrained admiration of him was very agreeable; and he
was beginning to be in love with her, after his own fashion, which was a
very easy one.

Eleanor looked at her husband's ward with a strange expression in her face
– a stern unpitying gaze, that promised little good to the young heiress.

'What is this foolish girl's fancy to me, that it should weigh against my
father's death?' she thought. 'What is it to me that she may have to suffer?
Let me remember the bitterness of his sufferings; let me remember that
long night upon which I watched for him, – that miserable night in
which he despaired and died. Surely the remembrance of this will shut
every thought of pity from my heart.'

Perhaps Eleanor Monckton had need to reason with herself thus. It
might be difficult to be true to her scheme of vengeance, when, in the
path she had to tread, this girl's heart must be trampled upon; this
innocent, childish, confiding little creature who had clung to her, and
trusted in her, and loved her, from the hour of their first meeting.

'Should I be pitiful, or merciful, or just to her, if I suffered her to
marry a bad man?' Mrs Monckton asked herself. 'No; for her sake, as
much as for the memory of my father, it is my duty to denounce
Launcelot Darrell.'

Throughout the drive back to Tolldale, Mrs Monckton silently
brooded upon the morning's work. Richard Thornton had indeed
proved a powerful ally. How often she had been in that studio, and not
once had the idea occurred to her of looking amongst the artist's sketches
for the evidence of his life.

'I told you that you could help me, Richard,' she said, when she found
herself alone with the scene-painter. 'You have given me the proof which
I have waited for so long. I will go to Woodlands to-night.'

'What for?'

'To show those two sketches to Mr de Crespigny.'

'But will that proof be strong enough to convince a man whose powers
of perception must be weakened by age? What if Mr de Crespigny should

fail to understand the evidence of those sketches? What if he should refuse to believe your accusation of his nephew?'

'I will show him my father's letter.'

'You forget that your father's letter accuses Robert Lance, and not Launcelot Darrell.'

'But the sketches are signed "Robert Lance."'

'And Mr Darrell may deny his identity with the man who signed himself by that name. You cannot ask Maurice de Crespigny to believe in his nephew's guilt on the testimony of a pencil drawing which that nephew may boldly repudiate. No, Eleanor, the work of to-day is only one step upon the road we have to tread. We must be patient, and wait for more conclusive proof than that which we hold in these two sketches.'

Eleanor sighed wearily.

'And in the meantime the 15th of March may come, or Mr de Crespigny may die,' she said. 'Oh, let me go to him at once; let me tell him the cruel story of his old friend's death! He knows nothing but that which he learned from a brief notice in a newspaper. He *cannot* refuse to believe me.'

Richard Thornton shook his head.

'You have asked me to help you, Eleanor,' he said, gravely; 'if I am to do so, you must have some faith in my counsel. Wait until we have fuller power to prove our case, before you reveal yourself to Mr de Crespigny.'

Mrs Monckton could not very well refuse to submit herself to the scene-painter's guidance. He had already most decisively demonstrated the superiority of his deliberate policy, as compared with the impulsive and unconsidered course of action recklessly followed by a headstrong girl.

'I must obey you, Dick,' Eleanor said, 'because you are so good to me, and have done so much to prove that you are a great deal wiser than I am. But if Mr de Crespigny should die while you are waiting for further proof, I——'

'You'll blame me for his death, I suppose, Mrs Monckton,' interrupted Richard, with a quiet smile, 'after the manner of your sex?'

Eleanor had no little difficulty in obeying her counsellor, for when Gilbert Monckton met his wife at dinner, he told her that he had been at Woodlands that morning, and that her friend Maurice de Crespigny was daily growing weaker, and was not expected to live through the early spring months.

'The old man is fading slowly away,' the lawyer said. 'His quiet and temperate habits have enabled him to hold out much longer than the doctors expected. It is like the gradual going out of a candle, they say. The flame sinks little by little in the socket. You must go and see the poor old man, Eleanor, before he dies.'

'Before he dies!' repeated Mrs Monckton, 'before he dies! Do you think he will die very soon, then, or suddenly?'

'Yes, I think he may go off suddenly at last. The medical men say as much, I understand.'

Eleanor looked at Richard Thornton.

'I must see him, and must see him before he dies,' she said. 'Is his mind unimpaired, Gilbert? Is his intellect still as clear as it was a week ago?'

'Yes,' answered Mr Monckton, 'I have every reason to believe so; for while I was talking to the two ladies in the breakfast-parlour, the chief clerk to Henry Lawford, the Windsor attorney, came in, and asked me to go up to Mr de Crespigny's room. What do you think I was wanted for, Eleanor?'

'I have no idea.'

'I was wanted to act as witness to the old man's will, in conjunction with Lawford's clerk. It seems the old man had sent to Windsor in a great hurry for Lawford; but Lawford happened to be out, so his clerk went instead, and De Crespigny had dictated the will to him. I need scarcely tell you I was not a little astonished to find that Maurice de Crespigny had only now made up his mind as to the disposal of his money. I suppose he has made half-a-dozen wills, and destroyed one after another according to his humour. I only hope the maiden sisters may get a decent reward for their long years of patience and expectation.'

Eleanor's trembling fingers trifled nervously with the ornaments at her watch-chain. It was with difficulty that she could control her agitation.

'But to whom is the fortune left?' she asked, breathlessly. 'Did you hear that, Gilbert?'

'No, my dear, it isn't usual to make the witness to a will acquainted with the body of the deed. I saw poor Maurice de Crespigny execute his feeble autograph, and I put my own muscular-looking signature in the place indicated to me, and I asked no questions. It was enough for me to know that *I* had no interest in the document.'

'But did Mr de Crespigny say nothing – nothing that could lead you to guess who——'

'Mr de Crespigny said nothing whatever calculated to throw any light upon his intentions. He seemed relieved by the idea that his will was made and the business settled. The clerk wanted to carry off the document, but the old man insisted on keeping it in his possession. He wished to look over it, he said. He wanted to see if his intentions had been fully carried out, in the spirit as well as in the letter. He put the parchment under his pillow, and then laid down with an air of satisfaction. I dare say he has gone through the same little comedy again and again before to-day.'

'Perhaps he will destroy this will?' Eleanor said, thoughtfully.

'Yes,' Mr Monckton answered, indifferently, 'the old man may change his mind again, if he lives long enough to repent of this new will. But I doubt his surviving so long as to do that.'

'And have you no idea, Gilbert, – have you no idea as to whom the fortune is left?'

Mr Monckton smiled.

'This is a question that concerns you, Laura,' he said, 'a great deal more nearly than it does us.'

'What question?' asked Miss Mason, looking up from an elaborate piece of embroidery which she had been showing to Signora Picirillo.

'We are talking of Mr de Crespigny's fortune, my dear; you are interested in the disposal of that, are you not?'

'Oh, yes, of course,' answered the young lady, 'I ought to be interested for Launcelot's sake, I know; and I know that he ought to have the fortune, and that nobody has any right to deprive him of it, especially those nasty old maids who had him sent to India against his will, and I dare say he will have horrid pains in his liver from the climate when he's older. Of course he ought to have the fortune, and yet sometimes I think it would be nicer for him to be poor. He may never be a great artist if he's rich, perhaps; and I'd rather go to Rome with him and sit by his easel while he works, and pay the hotel bills, and the travelling expenses, and all that sort of thing, out of my own money, than have him a country gentleman. I shouldn't like him to be a country gentleman; he'd have to hunt, and wear top-hats and nasty leather gaiters, like a common ploughman, when he went out shooting. I hate country gentlemen. Byron hasn't one country gentleman in all his poems, and that horrid husband in Locksley Hall will show you what an opinion Tennyson has of them.'

Miss Mason went back to the Signora and the embroidery, satisfied with having settled the business in her own manner.

'He couldn't look like the Corsair if he had Woodlands,' she murmured, despondingly; 'he'd have to shave off his moustache if they made him a magistrate. What would be the good of his talking seriously to poachers if he wore turned-down collars and loose handkerchiefs round his neck? People would never respect him unless he was a Guy, with creaky boots, and big seals hanging to his watch-chain.'

Eleanor pushed the question still further.

'You think that Mr de Crespigny has left his fortune to Launcelot Darrell, don't you, Gilbert?' she asked.

Her husband, prompted by the evil spirit that was his occasional companion, looked at her, rather suspiciously; but her eyes met his own with an unfaltering gaze.

'Why are you so interested in this fortune, and in Launcelot Darrell?' he said.

'I will tell you by-and-by. But tell me now, if you think the estate is left to Mr Darrell?'

'I think it scarcely unlikely that it is so. The fact of Maurice de Crespigny making a fresh will within six months of the young man's return looks rather as if he had been led to relent of some previous determination by the presence of his niece's son.'

'But Mr de Crespigny has seen very little of Launcelot Darrell.'

'Perhaps not,' answered Mr Monckton, coldly. 'I may be quite wrong in my conjecture. You ask for my opinion, and I give it you freely. Pray let us change the subject. I hate the idea of all this speculation as to who shall stand in a dead man's shoes. As far as Launcelot Darrell's interests are concerned, I really think there is an undercurrent of common sense in Laura's romantic talk. He may be all the better for being a poor man. He may be all the better for having to go to Italy and work at his art for a few years.'

Mr Monckton looked sharply at his young wife as he said this. I rather think that the demon familiar had prompted this speech, and that the lawyer watched Eleanor's face in the desire to discover whether there was anything unpleasant to her in the idea of Launcelot Darrell's long absence from his native country.

But, clever as Gilbert Monckton was, the mystery of his wife's face was as yet beyond his power to read. He watched her in vain. The pale and thoughtful countenance told nothing to the man who wanted the master key by which alone its expression could be read.

CHAPTER XXXIV

RICHARD'S DISCOVERY

An almost ungovernable impulse prompted Eleanor Monckton to make her way at once into Maurice de Crespigny's sick-chamber, and say to him, 'Launcelot Darrell is the wretch who caused your old friend's cruel death. I call upon you, by the memory of the past, to avenge that dead friend's wrongs!'

The struggle was a terrible one, but discretion in the end triumphed, and Eleanor submitted herself to the guidance of her devoted slave and ally. She knew now that Launcelot Darrell was guilty; but she had known that from the moment in which she had seen him lounging in the Windsor street. The task that lay before her was to procure such proof as must be convincing to the old man. In spite of her impetuous desire for immediate action, Eleanor was compelled to acknowledge that the testimony of the sketch-book was not strong enough in itself to condemn Launcelot Darrell.

The young man's answer to any accusation brought against him on such evidence would be simple enough.

Nothing could be easier than for him to say, 'My name is not Robert Lance. The drawing abstracted by unfair means from my portfolio is not mine. I am not responsible for the actions of the man who made that sketch.'

And against this simple declaration there would be nothing but Eleanor's unsupported assertion of the identity between the two men.

There was nothing to be done, then, except to follow Richard Thornton's advice, and wait.

This waiting was very weary work. Estranged from her husband by the secret of her life; unhappy in the society of Laura Mason, against whose happiness she felt that she was, in a manner, plotting; restrained and ill at ease even in the familiar companionship of Eliza Picirillo, – Eleanor Monckton wandered about the great rambling mansion which had become her home, restless and unhappy, yearning with a terrible impatience for the coming of the end, however dark that end might be. Every day, and often more than once in the course of the day, she locked herself in her room, and opened the desk in which she kept Launcelot Darrell's sketches and her dead father's last letter. She looked at these things almost as if she feared that by some diabolical influence they might be taken from her before they had served as the instruments of her revenge. So the weary days wore themselves out. The first week of Richard's visit; the second week of Richard's visit passed by; the middle of February came, and nothing more had been done.

Eleanor's health began to suffer from the perpetual mental fever of anxiety and impatience. Her husband saw her day by day growing thinner and paler; a hectic flush crimsoned her cheek now at every trifling agitation, with every surprise, however insignificant; but, except for these transient flushes, her face was as colourless as marble.

Her husband saw this, and made himself miserable because of the change in his young wife. He made himself still more wretched by reason of those unworthy doubts and suspicions that were for ever torturing him. 'Why was Eleanor ill? Why was she unhappy?' He asked himself this latter question a thousand times a day, and always answered it more or less after the same fashion.

She was unhappy because of the swiftly approaching marriage between Laura Mason and Launcelot Darrell. She had opposed that marriage with all the power she possessed. She had over-estimated her own fortitude when she sacrificed her love for the young artist to her desire to win a brilliant position.

'Why should she be different from other women?' the lawyer thought. 'She has married me for my money, and she is sorry for what she has done, and perhaps upon the eve of poor Laura's wedding day, there will be a repetition of the scene that took place at Lausanne nearly twenty years ago.' This was the manner of meditation to which Mr Monckton abandoned himself when the black mood was upon him.

All this time Launcelot Darrell came backwards and forwards between Hazlewood and Tolldale, after the free-and-easy manner of an accepted lover, who feels that, whatever advantages he may obtain by the matrimonial treaty which he is about to form, his own transcendant merits are so far above every meaner consideration as to render the lady the gainer by the bargain.

He came, therefore, whenever it pleased him to come. Now dawdling away a morning over the piano with Laura Mason; now playing billiards with Richard Thornton, who associated with him as it were under protest, hating him most cordially all the time.

'The detectives must have a hard time of it,' reflected Mr Thornton, after one of these mornings. 'Imagine having to hob-and-nob with a William Palmer, on the chance of his dropping out a word or two that might help to bring him to the gallows. The profession is extremely honourable, no doubt, but I don't think it can be a very pleasant one. I fancy, upon the whole, a muddy crossing and a good broom must be more agreeable to a man's feelings.'

The 15th of February came, dark, cold, and dreary, and Eleanor reminded the scene-painter that only one month now remained before the day appointed for Laura's marriage. That young lady, absorbed amongst a chaos of ribbons and laces, silks and velvets, had ceased to feel any jealousy of her guardian's wife. Her lover's easy acceptance of her devotion was sufficient for her happiness. What should the Corsair do but twist his black moustaches and permit Medora to worship him?

It was on this very 15th of February that, for the first time since the visit to Launcelot Darrell's studio, Mr Richard Thornton made a discovery.

It was not a very important one, perhaps, nor did it bear directly upon the secret of the artist's life, but it was something.

The scene-painter left Tolldale soon after breakfast upon this bleak February day, in a light dog-cart which Mr Monckton placed at the disposal of any guest who might wish to explore the neighbouring country. Richard did not return until dusk, and he broke in upon Eleanor's solitude as the shadows were gathering outside the window of the room in which she sat. He found his old companion alone in a little morning-room next her husband's study. She was sitting on a low stool by the hearth, her head resting on her hands, and the red firelight on her face; her attitude altogether expressive of care and despondency.

The door of communication between Gilbert Monckton's study and the room in which Eleanor sat was closed.

The girl started and looked up as Richard Thornton opened the door. The day had been wet as well as cold; drops of rain and sleet hung about the young man's rough great-coat, and he brought a damp and chilly atmosphere into the room.

'Is it you, Richard?' Eleanor said, absently.

'Yes, Mrs Monckton, I have been out all day; I have been to Windsor.'

'Indeed!'

'Yes. I met Launcelot Darrell there.'

'You met Launcelot Darrell!' repeated Eleanor. 'Richard,' she cried, suddenly, rising as she spoke, and going to where the young man stood, 'you have found something more.'

'I have not found what we want, Eleanor. I have not found the proof that you must lay before Mr de Crespigny, when you ask him to leave his estate away from his nephew. But I think I have made a discovery.'

'What discovery?' asked Mrs Monckton, with suppressed eagerness. 'Do not speak loudly, Dick,' she added, in a whisper, 'my husband is in the next room. I sit with him sometimes when he is at work there with his law papers, but I can't help fancying that my presence annoys him. He is not the same to me that he used to be. Oh, Richard, Richard, I feel as if I was divided from every creature in the world, except you: I can trust you, for you know my secret. When will this end?'

'Very soon, my dear, I hope,' Mr Thornton answered, gravely. 'There was a time when I urged you to abandon your purpose, Eleanor, but I do so no longer. Launcelot Darrell is a bad man, and the poor little girl with the blue eyes and flaxen ringlets must not be suffered to fall into his power.'

'No, not, not for the world. But you have made some discovery to-day, Richard?'

'I think so. You remember what Mr Monckton told us the other day. You remember his telling us that Mr de Crespigny had only that day made his will?'

'Yes, I remember it perfectly.'

'Laura Mason was present when her guardian told us this. It is only natural she should tell Launcelot Darrell what had happened.'

'She tells him everything; she would be sure to tell him that.'

'Precisely, and Mr Darrell has not been slow to act upon the hint.'

'What do you mean?'

'I mean that Launcelot Darrell has been guilty of the baseness of bribing Mr Lawford's clerk, in order to find out the secret of the contents of that will.'

'How do you know this?'

'I discovered it by the merest chance. You owe me no praises, Eleanor.
I begin to think that the science of detection is, after all, very weak and
imperfect; and that the detective officer owes many of his greatest
triumphs to patience, and a series of happy accidents. Yes, Eleanor, Mr
Launcelot Darrell's eagerness, or avarice, whichever you will, would not
suffer him to wait until his great-uncle's death. He was determined to
know the contents of that will; and, whatever the knowledge may have
cost him, I fancy that he is scarcely satisfied with his bargain.'

'Why?'

'Because I believe that the Woodlands property is not left to him.'

There was a noise as of the movement of a heavy chair in the next
room.

'Hush!' Eleanor whispered; 'my husband is going to dress for dinner.'

A bell rang while she was speaking, and Richard heard the door of the
next room opened and shut.

CHAPTER XXXV

WHAT HAPPENED AT WINDSOR

'Yes,' repeated Richard Thornton, 'I have reason to believe that the will
witnessed by your husband is a very unpleasant piece of literature in the
estimation of Launcelot Darrell, for I fancy that it gives a death-blow to
all his expectations, and leaves him without even the meagre consolation
of that solitary shilling which is usually inherited by unhappy elder sons.'

'But tell me why you think this, Richard.'

'I will, my dear Mrs Monckton. The story is rather a long one, but I
think I can tell it in a quarter of an hour. Can you dress for dinner in the
other quarter?'

'Oh, yes, yes!'

'What a nuisance civilization is, Nelly. We never dressed for dinner in
the Pilasters; indeed, the fashion amongst the leading families in that
locality leans rather the other way. The gentlemen in the cab and
chimney line generally take off their coats when the mid-day meal is
announced, in order to dine coolly and comfortably in their shirt-sleeves.'

'Richard, Richard!' cried Eleanor, impatiently.

'Well, well, Mrs Monckton, seriously, you shall have my Windsor
adventures. I hate this man, Launcelot Darrell, for I believe he is a
shallow, selfish, cold-hearted coxcomb; or else I don't think I could have
brought myself to do what I've done to-day. I've been playing the spy,
Eleanor, for a couple of hours at least. The Duke of Otranto used to find

plenty of people for this kind of work – artists, actors, actresses, priests, women, every creature whom you would least suspect of baseness. But they manage these things better in France. We don't take to the business so readily upon this side of the water.'

'Richard!'

The girl's impatience was almost uncontrollable. She watched the hands of a little clock upon the chimney-piece: the firelight flashed every now and then upon the dial, and then faded out, leaving it dark.

'I'm coming to the story, Nell, if you'll only be patient,' remonstrated Mr Thornton. He was getting over that secret sorrow which he had nursed for such a long time in the lowest depths of a most true and faithful breast. He was growing reconciled to the Inevitable, as we all must, sooner or later; and he had resumed that comfortable brotherly familiarity which had been so long habitual to him in his intercourse with Eleanor. 'Only be patient, my dear, and let me tell my story my own way,' he pleaded. 'I left here early this morning in your husband's dog-cart, intending to drive over to Windsor and amuse myself by exploring the town, and the castle, if possible, to see if there was anything in the way to be picked up – donjon keeps, turret staircases, secret corridors, and so on, you know. You remember what sort of a morning it was, bleak and dismal enough, but until twelve o'clock no rain. It was within a quarter of an hour of twelve when I got into Windsor, and the rain was just beginning, spiteful drops of rain and particles of sleet, that came down obliquely and cut into your face like so many needle-points. I stopped at an inn in a perpendicular street below the castle, which looks as if it means to topple down and annihilate that part of the town some of these days. I put up the dog-cart, and asked a few questions about the possibility of getting admission to the royal dwelling-place. Of course I was informed that such admission was to-day utterly impracticable. I could have seen the state apartments yesterday. I could see them, most likely, by the end of next week; but I couldn't see them when I wanted to see them. I hinted that my chief desire was to see secret passages, donjon keeps, moats, and sliding panels; but neither the landlord nor the waiter seemed to understand me, and I sat down rather despondently by the window of the tavern parlour to wait till the rain was over, and I could go out and prowl upon the castle terrace to study wintry effects in the park.'

'But Launcelot Darrell, Richard – where did you meet Launcelot Darrell?'

'I am coming to him presently. The perpendicular street wasn't particularly lively upon this wretched February day; so, as there weren't any passers-by to look at, I amused myself by looking at the houses facing the inn. Immediately opposite to me there was a house very superior to the others in style – a red brick house of the Georgian era, modernized by plate-glass windows and green blinds – not a large house, but eminently respectable. A dazzling brass plate adorned the door, and upon this brass plate, which winked and twinkled in the very face of the rain, I read the name of Mr Henry Lawford, solicitor.'

'The lawyer whose clerk made Mr de Crespigny's will?'

'Precisely. Upon one side of the door there was a bell-handle inscribed "Visitors," on the other a duplicate handle inscribed "Office." I hadn't been looking at the house above five minutes, when a young man, with a slender silk umbrella, struggling against the wind, rang the office-bell.'

'The young man was Launcelot Darrell?' Eleanor cried, quickly.

'He was. The door was opened by a boy, of whom Mr Darrell asked several questions. Whatever the answers were, he walked away, and the door was shut. But from his manner of strolling slowly along the street, I was convinced that he was not going far, and that he meant to come back. People don't usually stroll in a sharp rain that comes down obliquely and seems to drift in your face from every point of the compass. He'll come back presently, I thought; so I ordered a bottle of pale ale, and I waited.'

'And he came back?'

'Yes, he came back in about half an hour; but, ten minutes or so before he returned, I saw a shabby-genteel, elderly man let himself in with a latch-key at a small green side door with "Clerks' Office" painted in white letters on the panel. I knew by the look of this man that he must be a clerk. There's a look about an attorney's clerk that you can't mistake, even when he doesn't carry a blue bag; and this man did carry one. Ten minutes afterwards Launcelot Darrell returned. This time he knocked with the handle of his umbrella at the green door, which was opened by the boy, who went to fetch the elderly clerk. This elderly clerk and Mr Darrell stood on the door-step talking confidentially for about five minutes, and then our friend the artist went away: but this time again strolled slowly through the rain; as if he had a certain interval to dispose of, and scarcely knew what to do with himself.

'I suppose the amateur detective business fills a man's mind with all manner of suspicious fancies, Eleanor. However that may be, I could not help thinking that there was something queer in these two visits of Launcelot Darrell to the red brick house opposite me. What did he want with a lawyer in the first place? and if he did want a lawyer, why didn't he go straight to Mr Lawford, who was at home – for I could see his head across the top of the wire blind in one of the plate-glass windows as he bent over his desk – instead of tampering with small boys and clerks? There was something mysterious in the manner of his hanging about the place; and as I had been watching him wearily for a long time without being able to find out anything mysterious in his conduct, I determined to make the most of my chances and watch him to some purpose to-day.

"'He'll come back,' I thought, "unless I'm very much mistaken."

'I was very much mistaken, for Launcelot Darrell did not come back; but a few minutes after the clock struck one, the green door opened, and the elderly clerk came out, without the blue bag this time, and walked nimbly up the street in the direction that Launcelot Darrell had taken.

"'He's going to his dinner," I thought, "or he's going to meet Launcelot Darrell."

'I put on my hat, and went out of the house. The clerk was toiling up the perpendicular street a good way a-head of me, but I managed to keep him in sight and to be close upon his heels when he turned the corner into the street below the towers of the castle. He walked a little way along this street, and then went into one of the principal hotels.

"'Ah, my friend!" I said to myself, "you don't ordinarily take your dinner at that house, I imagine. It's a cut above your requirements, I should think."

'I went into the hotel, and made my way to the coffee-room. Mr Launcelot Darrell and the shabby-genteel clerk were sitting at a table, drinking sherry and soda-water. The artist was talking to his companion in a low voice, and very earnestly. It was not difficult to see that he was trying to persuade the seedy clerk to something which the clerk's sense of caution revolted from. Both men looked up as I went into the room, which they had had all to themselves until that moment; and Launcelot Darrell flushed scarlet as he recognized me. It was evident, therefore, that he did not care to be seen in the company of Mr Lawford's clerk.

"'Good morning, Mr Darrell," I said; "I've come over to have a look at the castle, but I find strangers are not admitted to-day, so I'm obliged to content myself with walking about in the wet for an hour or two."

'Launcelot Darrell answered me in that patronizing manner which renders him so delightful to the people he considers inferior to himself. He had quite recovered from the confusion my sudden appearance had caused, and muttered something about Mr Lawford, the attorney, and "business." Then he sat biting his nails in an uncomfortable and restless manner, while I drank another bottle of pale ale. That's another objection to the detective business; it involves such a lot of drinking.

'I left the hotel, and left Mr Darrell and the clerk together; but I didn't go very far. I contrived somehow or other to be especially interested in that part of the exterior of the castle visible from the street in which the hotel is situated, and, in a manner, kept one eye upon the stately towers of the royal residence, and the other upon the doorway out of which Launcelot Darrell and Mr Lawford's clerk must by-and-by emerge. In about half-an-hour I had the satisfaction of seeing them appear, and contrived, most innocently, of course, to throw myself exactly in their way at the corner of the perpendicular street.

'I was amply rewarded for any trouble I had taken; for I never saw a face that so plainly expressed rage, mortification, disappointment, almost despair, as did the face of Launcelot Darrell, when I came against him at the street corner. He was as white as a sheet, and he scowled at me savagely as he passed me by. Not as if he recognized me; the fixed look in his face showed that his mind was too much absorbed by one thought for any consciousness of exterior things; but as if in his suppressed fury he was ready to go blindly against anybody or anything that came in his way.'

'But why, Richard, why was he so angry?' cried Eleanor, with her hands clenched and her nostrils quivering with the passage of her rapid breath. 'What does it all mean?'

'Unless I'm very much mistaken, Mrs Monckton, it means that Launcelot Darrell has been tampering with the clerk of the lawyer who drew up Mr de Crespigny's last will, and that he now knows the worst——'

'And that is——'

'The plain fact, that unless that will is altered the brilliant Mr Darrell will not inherit a penny of his kinsman's fortune.'

The second dinner-bell rang while Richard was speaking, and Eleanor ran away to make some hurried change in her toilette, and to appear in the drawing-room, agitated and ill at ease, ten minutes after Mr Monckton's punctilious butler had made his formal announcement of the principal meal of the day.

CHAPTER XXXVI

ANOTHER RECOGNITION

Launcelot Darrell came to Tolldale Priory upon the day after Richard's visit to Windsor, and it was easy for Eleanor, assisted by her knowledge of what had transpired, to see the change in his manner. She spent an hour in the drawing-room that morning for the purpose of seeing this change, and thereby finding confirmation of that which Richard Thornton had told her. But the alteration in the young man's manner must have been very obvious, for even Laura, who was not particularly observant of any shades of feeling that did not make themselves manifest by the outward expression of word or gesture, perceived that there was something amiss with her lover, and drove Launcelot Darrell well-nigh mad with her childish questionings and lamentations.

Why was he so quiet? Why was he so much paler than usual? Why did he sigh sometimes? Why did he laugh in that strange way? Oh, no, not in his usual way. It was no use saying that it was so. Had he a headache? Had he been sitting up late at night? Had he been drinking horrid wine that had disagreed with him? Had he been a naughty, naughty, cruel, false, treacherous boy, and had he been to some party that he hadn't told his poor Laura about, drinking champagne and flirting with girls, and dancing, and all that? Or had he been working too much at his new picture?

With such questions as these did the young lady harass and torment her lover throughout that uncomfortable February morning; until at last Mr Darrell turned upon her in a rage, declaring that his head was nearly split asunder, and plainly telling her to hold her tongue.

Indeed, Mr Launcelot Darrell made very little effort to disguise his feelings, but sat over the fire in a low easy chair, with his elbows resting on his knees, and his handsome dark eyes bent moodily upon the blaze. He roused himself now and then from a fit of gloomy thought to snatch up the polished-steel poker, and plunge it savagely amongst the coals, as if it was some relief to him to punish even them. Another man might have feared the inferences which spectators might draw from his conduct, but the principle upon which Launcelot Darrell's life had been based involved an utter contempt for almost every living creature except himself, and he apprehended no danger from the watchfulness of the inferior beings about him.

Laura Mason, sitting on a low ottoman at his feet, and employed in working a pair of embroidered slippers – the third pair she had begun for the use of her future lord and master – thought him more like the Corsair to-day than ever; but thought at the same time that some periods of Medora's existence must have been rather dreary. No doubt it was Conrad's habit to sit and stare at the coals, and to poke the fire savagely when things went amiss with him; when his favourite barque was scuttled by a mutinous crew, or his cargo confiscated by the minions of the law.

Launcelot Darrell was engaged to dine at the Priory upon this 16th of February. Mr Monckton had invited him, in order that some matters connected with Laura's fortune might be discussed.

'It is fully time we should understand each other, Darrell,' the lawyer said; 'so I shall expect you to give me a couple of hours in my study this evening after dinner, if you've no objection.'

Of course Mr Darrell had no objection, but he had an almost spiteful manner that day in his intercourse with poor Laura, who was bewildered by the change in him.

'You think it's strange that I should dislike all this ceremony about settlements and allowance. Yes, Laura, *that's* a pleasant word, isn't it? Your guardian honoured me by telling me he should make us a handsome allowance for the first few years of our married life. You think I ought to take kindly to this sort of thing, I dare say, and drop quietly into my position of genteel pauperism, dependent upon my pencil, or my wife, for the dinner I eat, and the coat I wear. No, Laura,' cried the young man, passionately, 'I don't take kindly to it; I can't stand it. The thought of my position enrages me against myself, against you, against everybody and everything in the world.'

Launcelot Darrell talked thus to his betrothed while Richard and Eleanor were both in the room; the scene-painter sitting in a window making furtive sketches with a fat little stump of lead pencil upon the backs of divers letters; Mrs Monckton standing at another window looking out at the leafless trees, the black flowerless garden beds, the rain-drops hanging on the dingy firs and evergreens.

Mr Darrell knew that he was overheard; but he had no wish that it should be otherwise. He did not care to keep his grievances a secret. The egotism of his nature exhibited itself in this. He gave himself the airs of a victim, and made a show of despising the benefits he was about to accept from his confiding betrothed. He in a manner proclaimed himself injured by the existence of his future wife's fortune; and he forced her to apologize to him for the prosperity which she was about to bestow upon him.

'As if it was being a pauper to take my money,' cried Miss Mason, with great tenderness, albeit in rather obscure English; 'as if I grudged you the horrid money, Launcelot. Why, I don't even know how much I'm to have. It may be fifty pounds a-year – that's what I've had to buy my dresses and things since I was fifteen – or it may be fifty thousand. I don't want to know how much it is. If it *is* fifty thousand a-year, you're welcome to it, Launcelot, darling.'

'Launcelot darling' shrugged his shoulders with a peevish gesture, which exhibited him rather as a discontented darling.

'You talk like a baby, Laura,' he said, contemptuously; 'I suppose the "handsome allowance" Mr Monckton promises will be about two or three thousand a year, or so; something that I'm to eke out by my industry. Heaven knows he has preached to me enough about the necessity of being industrious. One would think that an artist was a bricklayer or a stonemason, to hear him talk.'

Eleanor turned away from the window as Launcelot Darrell said this; she could not suffer her husband to be undefended while she was by.

'I have no doubt whatever Mr Monckton said was right, Mr Darrell,' she exclaimed, lifting her head proudly, as if in defiance of any voice that should gainsay her husband's merits.

'No doubt, Mrs Monckton; but there's a certain sledgehammer-like way of propounding that which is right that isn't always pleasant. I don't want to be reminded that an artist's calling is a trade, and that when the Graces bless me with a happy thought I must work like a slave until I've hammered it out upon canvas and sent it into the market for sale.'

'Some people think the Graces are propitiated by hard labour,' Richard Thornton said, quietly, without raising his eyes from his rapid pencil, 'and that the happiest thoughts are apt to come when a man has his brush in his hand, rather than when he is lying on a sofa reading French novels; though I have known artists who preferred that method of waiting for inspiration. For my own part, I believe in the inspiration that grows out of patient labour.'

'Yes,' Mr Darrell answered, with an air of lazy indifference, – an air which plainly expressed that he disdained to discuss art-topics with a scene-painter, 'I dare say you find it answers – in your line. You must splash over a good deal of canvas before you can produce a transformation-scene, I suppose?'

'Peter Paul Rubens got over a good deal of canvas,' said Richard, 'and Raffaelle Sanzio d'Urbino did something in that way, if we may judge by the cartoons and a few other trifles.'

'Oh, of course, there were giants in those days. I don't aspire to rival any such Patagonians. I don't see why people should be compelled to walk through a picture-gallery a mile long before they can pronounce an opinion upon a painter's merits. I should be very well contented if my chance with posterity rested upon half-a-dozen pictures no bigger than Millais's "Huguenots;" and as good.'

'And I'm sure you could do dozens and dozens as good as that,' cried Laura. 'Why, it's only a lady tying a scarf round her lover's arm, and a lot of green leaves. Of course it's very pretty, you know, and one feels very much for her, poor thing, and one's afraid that he'll let those cruel Catholics kill him, and that she'll die broken-hearted. But you could paint lots of pictures like that, Launcelot, if you chose.'

The young man did not condescend to notice his affianced wife's art-criticism. He relapsed into gloomy silence, and once more betook himself to that savage kind of consolation afforded by a sturdy exercise of the poker.

'But, Launcelot,' pleaded Miss Mason, presently, 'I'm sure you needn't be unhappy about my having money, and your being poor. There's Mr de Crespigny's fortune, you know; he can't be shameful and wicked enough to leave it to any one but you. My guardian said, only the other day, that he thought it would be left to you.'

'Oh, ah, to be sure,' muttered Mr Darrell, moodily; 'there's *that* chance, of course.'

'He couldn't leave Woodlands to those two old maids, you know, Launcelot, could he?'

To the surprise of the two listeners, Richard Thornton and Eleanor, the young man burst into a harsh disdainful laugh.

'My respected maiden aunts!' he exclaimed; 'poor devils, they've had a nice time of it.'

Until this moment Richard and Eleanor had most firmly believed that the will which disinherited Launcelot Darrell bequeathed the Woodlands fortune to the two maiden sisters, Lavinia and Sarah de Crespigny; but the young man's disdainful laugh, and the contemptuous, yet half-pitying tone in which he spoke of the two sisters, plainly revealed that if he knew the secret of the disposal of Maurice de Crespigny's fortune, and knew that it was not left to himself, he knew also that equal disappointment and mortification awaited his aunts.

He had been in the habit of speaking of them with a savage though suppressed animosity. To-day his tone was utterly changed. He had a malicious pleasure, no doubt, in thinking of the disappointment in store for them; and he could afford now to feel a kind of disdainful compassion for all their wasted labours, their useless patience.

But to whom, then, could the fortune be left?

Eleanor and Richard looked at each other in amazement. It might have been supposed that the old man had left his wealth to Eleanor herself, influenced by the caprice that had induced him to attach himself to her, because of her likeness to his dead friend. But this could not be, for the invalid had distinctly declared that he should leave nothing but George Vane's miniature to his new favourite; and Maurice de Crespigny was not a man to say one thing and mean another. He had spoken of a duty to be fulfilled, a duty which he was determined to perform.

Yet, to whom could he possibly owe any duty, except to his kindred? Had he any other relations except his three nieces and Launcelot Darrell? He might have other claims upon him. He might have some poor and modest kindred who had kept aloof from him, and refrained from paying court to him, and whose forbearance he might choose to reward in an unlooked-for, unthought-of manner.

And again, he might have bequeathed his money to some charitable institution, or in trust for some new scheme of philanthropy. Such a course would scarcely be strange in a lonely old man, who in his nearest relations might only recognize eager, expectant harpies keeping anxious watch for the welcome hour of his death.

Eleanor Monckton did not trouble herself much about this question. She believed, from Launcelot Darrell's manner, that Richard Thornton had drawn the right inference from the meeting of the young man and the lawyer's clerk.

She believed implicitly that Launcelot Darrell's name was omitted from his great-uncle's last will, and that he knew it.

This belief inspired her with a new feeling. She could afford to be patient now. If Maurice de Crespigny should die suddenly, he would not die leaving his wealth to enrich the traitor who had cheated a helpless old man. Her only thought now must be to prevent Laura's marriage; and for this she must look to her husband, Gilbert Monckton.

'He will never let the girl whose destiny has been confided to him marry a bad man,' she thought; 'I have only to tell him the story of my father's death, and to prove to him Launcelot Darrell's guilt.'

The dinner went off very quietly. Mr Monckton was reserved and silent, as it had lately become his habit to be. Launcelot Darrell had still the gloomy, discontented air that had made him a very unpleasant companion throughout the day. The young man was not a hypocrite, and had no power of concealing his feelings. He could tell any number of lies that might be necessary for his own convenience or safety; but he was not a hypocrite. Hypocrisy involves a great deal of trouble on the part of those who practise it: and is, moreover, the vice of a man who sets no little value upon the opinion of his fellow-creatures. Mr Darrell was of a listless and lazy temperament, and nourished an utter abhorrence of all work, either physical or mental. On the other hand, he had so good an opinion of himself as to be tolerably indifferent to the opinions of others.

If he had been accused of a crime he would have denied having committed it, for his own sake. But he never troubled himself to consider what other people might think of him, so long as their opinion had no power to affect his personal comfort or safety.

The cloth had been removed; for old fashions held their ground at Tolldale Priory, where a dinner à la Russe would have been looked upon as an absurd institution, more like a child's feast of fruit and flowers, cakes and sugar-plums, than a substantial meal intended for sensible people. The cloth had been removed, and that dreary ceremonial, a good old English dessert, was in progress, when a servant brought Launcelot Darrell a card upon a salver, and presented it to him solemnly, amid the silence of the company.

The young man was sitting next Eleanor Monckton, and she saw that the card was of a highly glazed and slippery nature and of an abnormal size, between the ordinary sizes of a gentleman's and a lady's card.

The blood rushed to Launcelot Darrell's forehead as he read the name upon the card, and Eleanor saw his under lip contract with a sudden movement, expressive of intense vexation.

'How did this – this gentleman come here?' he asked, turning to the servant.

'The gentleman has driven over from Hazlewood, sir. Hearing you were dining here, he came on to see you, he says; is he to be shown into the drawing-room?'

'Yes – no: I'll come out and see him. Will you excuse me, Mr Monckton: this is an old acquaintance of mine? Rather a pertinacious acquaintance, as you may perceive by his manner of following me up to-night.'

Mr Darrell rose, pushed aside his chair, and went out of the dining-room, followed by the servant.

The hall was brilliantly lighted, and in the few moments during which the servant slowly followed Launcelot Darrell, Eleanor had an opportunity of seeing the stranger who had come to the Priory.

He was standing under the light of the large gas-lamp, shaking the rain-drops from his hat, and with his face turned towards the dining-room door.

He was short and stout, smartly-dressed, and foppish-looking even in his travelling costume; and he was no other than the talkative Frenchman who had persuaded George Vane to leave his daughter alone upon the Boulevard on the night of August 11th, 1853.

CHAPTER XXXVII

LAUNCELOT'S TROUBLES

Eleanor Monckton sat looking at the door which had closed upon the scene in the lamplit hall, almost as if the intensity of her gaze could have pierced the solid oaken panel and revealed to her that which was taking place outside the dining-room.

Richard Thornton and her husband, both watching her face, marvelled at the sudden change in its expression, – the look of rapt wonder and amazement that had come over it from the moment in which Launcelot Darrell had gone out into the hall. Richard guessed that something strange and unexpected had occurred, but Gilbert Monckton, who was quite in the dark as to his wife's feelings, could only stare blankly at her face, and mutely wonder at the mystery which tortured him. Laura Mason, who had been throughout the day alarmed by her lover's manner, was too anxious about Launcelot Darrell to observe the face of her friend.

'I'm sure there's something wrong,' she said; 'I'm sure there is, Mr Monckton. You don't know how Launcelot's been going on all day, frightening me out of my wits. Hasn't he, now, Eleanor? Hasn't he, Mr Thornton? Saying he won't be a pauper, dependent upon his wife, and that you've wounded his feelings by talking about art as if you were a bricklayer; or as if he was a bricklayer, I forget which. I had a presentiment all day that something was going to happen; and Launcelot did go on so, staring at the fire, and hammering the coals, and sighing as if he had something awful on his mind – as if he'd committed a crime, you know, and was brooding over it,' added the young lady, with an evident relish of the last idea.

Mr Monckton looked contemptuously at his ward. The girl's frivolous babble was in horrible discord with his own anxiety – a kind of parody of his own alarm.

'What do you mean by committing crimes, Laura?' he said. 'I'm afraid you'll never learn to talk like a reasonable being. Is there anything so very miraculous in the fact that some old acquaintance of Mr Darrell's has come down to Berkshire to see him?'

Laura Mason breathed a sigh of relief.

'You don't think, then, that Launcelot has done something dreadful, and that this man has come to arrest him?' she asked. 'It seems so odd his coming here on a dark winter's night; and Launcelot looked angry when he saw the card the servant gave him. I'm sure it's something dreadful. Let's go into the drawing-room, Eleanor. We shall have to pass through the hall, and if there's anything wrong we can find out all about it.'

Eleanor started as Laura addressed her, and rose suddenly, aroused by the necessity of having to attend to something that had been said to her, but scarcely knowing what that something was.

'Eleanor!' exclaimed her husband, 'how pale you are, and how strangely you look at that door. One would think that you were influenced by Laura's absurd fears.'

'Oh, no! I am not frightened of anything; only I——'

She paused, hesitating, and looking down in painful embarrassment.

'Only what?'

'I happened to see the person who has come to speak to Mr Darrell, and – and – his face reminded me of a man I saw a long time ago.'

Richard looked up quickly.

'But was there anything so very startling in the mere coincidence of a likeness?'

'Oh, no, nothing startling.'

'Upon my word, Eleanor,' exclaimed Gilbert Monckton, impatiently, 'we seem to live in an atmosphere of mystery, which, to say the least of it, is far from agreeable to those who only occupy the position of lookers-on. There, there, go to the drawing-room with Laura. Mr Thornton and I will follow you almost immediately. We shall have very little pleasure in sitting over our wine with a consciousness that a kind of Gunpowder Plot is going on in the hall outside.'

The lawyer filled his glass with claret, and pushed the crystal jug towards Richard; but he left the wine untasted before him, and he sat silently brooding over his suspicions, with a bent brow and rigidly-compressed lips.

It was no use to struggle against his destiny, he thought. Life was to be always a dreary French novel, in which he was to play the victim husband. He had loved and trusted this girl. He had seen innocence and candour beaming in her face, and he had dared to believe her; and from the very hour of her marriage a horrible transformation had taken place in this frank and fearless creature. A hundred changes of expression, all equally mysterious to him, had converted the face he loved into a wearisome and incomprehensible enigma, which it was the torment of his life to endeavour vainly and hopelessly to guess. Richard Thornton opened the door, and Eleanor gladly made her escape from the dining-room, holding Laura's hand in hers, and with the Signora following close behind her. The three women entered the hall in a group, and paused for a moment looking at Launcelot Darrell and the stranger.

Mr Darrell stood near the open hall-door with his hands in his pockets, and his head bent in that sulky attitude which Eleanor had good reason to remember. The stranger, smoothing the wet nap of his hat with a careful hand, seemed to be talking in a tone of remonstrance, and, as it were, urging something upon his companion. This was only to be guessed by the expression of his face, as the voice in which he spoke was scarcely above a whisper.

The three ladies crossed the hall and went into the drawing-room. Eleanor had no need to confirm her sudden recognition of the Frenchman by any second scrutiny of his face. She sat down near the broad hearth, and began to think how this man's unlooked-for coming might affect the fulfilment of her purpose. Would he be likely to thwart her? or could he not, perhaps, be induced to help her?

'I must talk to Richard,' she thought. 'He knows the world better than I do. I am almost as much a child as Laura.'

While Mrs Monckton sat looking absently at the fire, and trying to imagine how the advent of the Frenchman might be made subservient to the scheme of her life, Miss Mason burst into a torrent of panegyric upon the stranger's appearance.

'He's such a good-natured-looking dear,' she exclaimed, 'with curly hair and a moustache just like the Emperor's; and the idea of my frightening myself so about him, and thinking he was a dreadful creature in a slouched hat, and with his coat-collar turned up to hide his face, come to arrest Launcelot for some awful crime. I'm not a bit frightened now, and I hope Launcelot will bring him in to tea. The idea of his being a foreigner, too! I think foreigners are *so* interesting. Don't you, Nelly?'

Eleanor Monckton looked up at the sound of her name. She had not heard a word that Laura had said.

'What, dear?' she asked, listlessly.

'Don't you think foreigners interesting, Nelly?' repeated the young lady.

'Interesting? No.'

'What! not Frenchmen?'

Mrs Monckton gave a faint shiver.

'Frenchmen!' she said. 'No, I don't like them, I——. How do I know, Laura? Baseness and treachery belong to no peculiar people, I suppose?'

Mr Monckton and the scene-painter came into the drawing-room at this moment, followed pretty closely by Launcelot Darrell.

'What have you done with your friend, Darrell?' Gilbert Monckton asked, with a look of surprise.

'Oh, he's gone,' the young man answered, indifferently.

'You've let him go without asking him to rest, or take some refreshment?'

'Yes, I contrived to get rid of him.'

'We don't usually "contrive to get rid" of people when they come here on a wet winter night,' said Mr Monckton. 'You'll give Tolldale Priory a reputation for inhospitality, I fear. Why did you not ask your friend to stop?'

'Because I didn't care to introduce him to you,' Launcelot Darrell answered, coolly. 'I never said he was a friend of mine. He's only an acquaintance, and a very intrusive acquaintance. He had no right to ferret out my whereabouts, and to come down here after me. A man doesn't want past associations forced upon him, however agreeable they may have been.'

'And still less when those associations are disagreeable. I understand. But who is this man?'

'He's a Frenchman, a *commis voyageur*, or something of that kind; by no means a distinguished acquaintance. He's a good fellow, in his own particular fashion, and would go out of his way to do me a service, I dare say; but he's rather too fond of absinthe, or brandy, or any other spirit he can get hold of.'

'You mean that he is a drunkard,' said Mr Monckton.

'I don't say that. But I know that the poor devil has had more than one attack of delirium tremens in the course of his life. He's over here in the interests of a patent mustard, I believe, lately invented by some great Parisian gastronomer.'

'Indeed; and where did you make his acquaintance?'

The same crimson hue that had mounted to Mr Darrell's forehead when the Frenchman's card was handed to him dyed his face now, and he hesitated for a few moments before replying to Gilbert Monckton's straight question. But he recovered himself pretty quickly, and answered with his accustomed carelessness of manner:

'Where did I know him? Oh, in London, of course. He was an inhabitant of that refuge for the destitute of all nations, some years ago, while I was sowing my wild oats there.'

'Before you went to India?'

'Yes, of course, before I went to India.'

Mr Monckton looked sharply at the young man's face. There were moments when the lawyer's prudence, when the conscientious scruples of an honest man got the better of the husband's selfish fears; and in those moments Gilbert Monckton doubted whether he was doing his duty towards his ward in suffering her to marry Launcelot Darrell.

Was the young man worthy of the trust that was to be confided to him? Was he a fitting husband for an inexperienced and frivolous girl?

Mr Monckton could only answer this question in one way. He could not satisfy his conscience by taking a cynical view of the matter.

'Launcelot Darrell is as good as other young men, I dare say,' he argued. 'He's good-looking, and conceited, and shallow, and idle; but the poor little girl has chosen to fall in love with him, and if I come between them, and forbid this marriage, and make the silly child unhappy by forcing my choice upon her, I may be quite as much mistaken as she, and after all marry her to a bad man. I may just as well let her draw her own number in the great lottery, and trust to Providence for its being a lucky one.'

But to-night there was something in Launcelot Darrell's manner which aroused a vague suspicion in the breast of the lawyer.

'Then your friend the *commis voyageur* has gone back to Windsor, I suppose?' he said.

'No; I couldn't very well avoid giving him shelter, as he chose to come, though he came uninvited. I sent him back to Hazlewood with a few lines addressed to my mother, who will do her best to make him comfortable, I dare say. Poor soul, she would scarcely refuse to shelter a stray dog, if the wandering cur were in any way attached to me.'

'Yes, Mr Darrell, you have reason to value your mother's affection,' answered the lawyer, gravely. 'But we must not forget that we've a good deal of business to transact to-night. Will you come with me into my study, as soon as you've finished that cup of tea?'

Launcelot Darrell bowed, and set down his teacup on the nearest table. Eleanor and Richard had both watched him closely since his coming into the drawing-room. It was easy to see that he had by no means recovered from the unpleasant surprise caused him by the Frenchman's visit. His careless manner was only assumed, and it was with evident difficulty that he responded to each new demand made upon his attention.

He followed Gilbert Monckton slowly and silently from the room, without having lingered to speak so much as a word to Laura, without having even made her happy by so much as a look.

'He might have spoken to me,' the young lady murmured, disconsolately, as she watched her lover's retreating figure.

Two hours elapsed before the gentlemen returned to the drawing-room; two dreary hours for Laura, who sat yawning over a book, or playing with her two dogs, which, by virtue of their high breeding and good conduct, were constant occupants of the drawing-room at Tolldale. Richard Thornton and Mrs Monckton played a game of chess, the strangest game, perhaps, that ever was played, for the moving backwards and forwards of the ivory pieces was a mere pretence, by means of which Eleanor contrived to take counsel with her faithful ally.

'Do you think this man's coming will help us, Dick?' she asked, when she had told the story of her recognition of the Frenchman.

Richard shook his head, not negatively, but reflectively.

'How can I tell?' he said; 'the man may or may not be inclined to betray his friend. In any case it will be very difficult for us to get at him.'

'Not for *you*, Richard,' murmured Eleanor, persuasively.

'Not for *me*,' echoed the young man. 'Syren, mermaiden, witch of the sea, avaunt! It was you and the blue bonnet that settled for the shipbroker and his clerks. Have you the blue bonnet still, Nell; or have you any other influence in the millinery line that you can bring to bear upon this traveller in mustard?'

'But if he should remember me?'

'That's scarcely likely. His face was impressed upon your mind by the awful circumstance that followed your meeting with him. You have changed very much since you were fifteen years of age, Mrs Monckton. You were a feminine hobbledehoy then. Now you are – never mind what. A superb Nemesis in crinoline, bent on deeds of darkness and horror. No, I do not see any reason to fear this man's recognition of you.'

The expression of Launcelot Darrell's face had subsided into a settled gloom when he reappeared in the drawing-room with Mr Monckton.

The lawyer seated himself at a reading-table, and began to open the evening papers, which were sent from Windsor to Tolldale. Launcelot strolled over to Laura Mason, and, sitting down beside her, amused himself by pulling the silky ears of the Skye terrier.

'Do tell me everything, Launcelot,' said Miss Mason. 'You don't know how much I've suffered all this evening. I hope the interview was a pleasant one?'

'Oh, yes, remarkably pleasant,' answered the young man, with a sneer. 'I shall not be exposed to the reproach of having made a mercenary marriage, Laura, at any rate.'

'What do you mean, Launcelot?' cried the young lady, staring aghast at her lover. 'You don't mean that my guardian's been deceiving me all this time, and that I'm a poor penniless creature after all, and that I ought to have been a companion, or a nursery governess, or something of that kind, as Eleanor was before her marriage. You don't mean that, Launcelot!'

'Not precisely,' answered Mr Darrell; 'but I mean that the noble allowance of which your guardian has talked so much is to be two hundred a year: which, as we are so unfortunate as to possess the habits of a gentleman and a lady, will not go very far.'

'But ain't I rich, – ain't I an heiress?' cried Miss Mason. 'Haven't I what-you-may-call-'ems – expectations?'

'Oh, yes. I believe there is some vague promise of future wealth held out as a compensation for all present deprivations. But really, although your guardian took great pains to explain the dry business details to me, I was almost too tired to listen to him; and certainly too stupid to understand very clearly what he meant. I believe there is some money which you are to have by-and-by, upon the death of somebody. But as it seems that the somebody is a person in the prime of life, who has the power of altering his will at any moment that he may take it into his head to do so, I look upon that expectation as rather a remote contingency. No, Laura, we must look our position straight in the face. A life of hard work lies before me; a life of poverty before you.'

Miss Mason made a wry face. Her mind had little power to realize anything but extremes. Her idea of poverty was something very horrible. An existence of beggary, with the chance of being called upon to do plain needlework for her daily bread, and with a workhouse at the end of the prospect.

'But I shall love you all the same, Launcelot,' she whispered, 'however poor we may be, and I'll wear dresses without any trimming, and imitation lace. I suppose *you* wouldn't know imitation lace from real Valenciennes, Launcelot, and it's so cheap. And I'll try and make pies and puddings, and I'll learn to be economical, and I've lots of jewellery that my guardian has given me, and we can sell that, if you like. I'll work as hard as that poor woman in the poem, Launcelot, for your sake. "Stitch, stitch, stitch, band and gusset and seam." I don't mind the seams, dear; *they'd* be easy if one didn't prick one's fingers and make knots in one's thread; but I'm afraid I shall never be able to manage the gussets. Only promise me that you'll love me still, Launcelot. Tell me that you don't hate me because I'm poor.'

The young man took the soft little hand that was laid with an imploring gesture on his wrist, and pressed it tenderly.

'I should be a brute if I wasn't grateful for your love, Laura,' he said. 'I didn't wish *you* to be rich. I'm not the sort of fellow who could contentedly accept a degraded position, and sponge upon a wife's fortune. I only wanted – I only wanted what I had been taught to expect,' he muttered, with a savage accent; 'I'm set upon and hemmed in on every side, and I've a hundred mortifications and miseries to bear for want of money. But I'll try and make you a good husband, my dear.'

'You will, Launcelot,' cried the girl, melted by some touch of real earnestness in her lover's tone that was new and welcome to her. 'How good it is of you to say that. But how should you be otherwise than good; and you will be a great painter, and all the world will admire you and talk about you, and we shall be so happy, – shan't we, Launcelot? – wandering through Italy together.'

The young man answered her with a bitter laugh.

'Yes, Laura,' he said, 'the sooner we get to Italy the better. Heaven knows, I've no particular interest that need keep me in England, now.'

CHAPTER XXXVIII

MR MONCKTON BRINGS GLOOMY TIDINGS FROM WOODLANDS

For some few days after the Frenchman's arrival, Launcelot Darrell stopped away from the Priory, much to the regret of his betrothed, whose delight in her *trousseau* was not sufficient to fill the blank made by her lover's absence. Miss Mason roamed disconsolately about the house, looking out at the bare trees, and the desolate garden walks, and quoted Tennyson until she became obnoxious to her fellow-creatures by reason of her regret that *he* did not come, and her anxiety that the day should be done, and other lamentations to the same effect.

She ran out of doors sometimes under the bleak February sky, with a cambric handkerchief over her head as a sensible protection from the bitter atmosphere, and her light ringlets flying in the wind, to stand at a little doorway in the high garden wall, and watch for her lover's coming by a narrow pathway through the wood, by which it was his wont to make a short cut for himself in dry weather.

She was standing in this narrow doorway upon the afternoon of the 22nd of February – only twenty-one days before that eventful morning which was to make her Launcelot Darrell's wife – with Eleanor Monckton by her side. The short winter's day was closing in, and the shadows were thickening in the low woodland, whatever light might linger on the hill-tops above Tolldale. The two women were silent: Eleanor was in very low spirits, for on this day she had lost her friend and counsellor, Richard Thornton, who had had no alternative but to leave Tolldale, or to forfeit a very remunerative and advantageous engagement

at one of the Edinburgh Theatres, whither he had been summoned to
paint the scenery for a grand Easter burlesque, about to be produced with
unusual splendour, by a speculative Scottish manager; and who had,
therefore, departed, taking his aunt with him. George Vane's daughter felt
terribly helpless in the absence of this faithful ally. Richard had promised
to attend to her summons, and to return to Tolldale at any hour, if she
should have need of his services; but he was separated from her by a long
distance, and how could she tell when the moment of that need might
come? She was alone, amongst people who had no sympathy with the
purpose of her life, and she bitterly felt the desolation of her position.

It was no very great wonder, then, if she was thoughtful and silent, and
by no means the joyous, light-hearted companion whom Laura Mason
had loved and clung to at Hazlewood, before the coming of Launcelot
Darrell. This young lady watched her now, furtively, almost fearfully,
wondering at the change in her, and speculating as to the cause of it.

'She *must* have been in love with Launcelot,' Laura thought; 'how
could she help being in love with him? And she married my guardian
because he's rich, and now she's sorry for having done so. And she's
unhappy because I'm going to be married to Launcelot. And, oh!
suppose Launcelot should still be in love with her; like the hero of a
dreadful French novel!'

The dusk was deepening in the wood, when two figures emerged from
the narrow pathway. A tall, slenderly-built young man, who switched the
low brushwood and the fern with his light cane as he walked along, and a
puffy little individual with a curly-brimmed hat, who trotted briskly by
his side.

Laura was not slow to recognize her lover even in that doubtful light,
and Eleanor knew that the young man's companion was the French
commercial traveller.

Mr Darrell introduced his friend to the two ladies.

'Monsieur Victor Bourdon, Mrs Monckton, Miss Mason,' he muttered,
hastily. 'I dare say you have thought me very neglectful, Laura,' he added;
'but I have been driving Monsieur Bourdon about the neighbourhood
for the last day or two. He's a stranger in this part of the country, though
he's almost as much an Englishman as I am.'

Monsieur Bourdon laughed as he acknowledged the compliment, with
an air that was evidently intended to be fascinating.

'Y-a-a-se,' he said, 'we have been to Windsor. It is very naice.'

Launcelot Darrell frowned, and looked angrily at his companion.

'Yes, Bourdon wanted to have a look at the state apartments,' he said;
'he wanted to compare them with those interminable galleries at
Versailles, I suppose, to the disparagement of our national glory.'

'But the apartments are closed,' said Eleanor.

'Oh! of course,' answered Mr Darrell, looking at her rather suspiciously, 'they always are closed when you happen to want to see them. Just like everything else in this world of anomalies and paradoxes.'

'He has taken his friend to Windsor,' Eleanor thought; 'had this visit any relation to his last visit? Did he go there to see Mr Lawford's clerk?'

She was helpless without Richard, and could not answer this question.

'I'll write to him to-night,' she thought, 'and ask him to come back to me directly.'

But in the next moment she was ashamed of herself for her selfishness. She might sacrifice her own life to her scheme of vengeance. The voice of her father crying to her from his unsanctified grave, seemed for ever urging her to do that; but she had no right to call upon others to make the same sacrifice.

'No,' she thought, 'wherever the road I have chosen may lead me, however difficult the path may be to follow, I will henceforward tread it alone. Poor Dick! I have tormented him long enough with my sorrows and my helplessness.'

'You've come to dine, of course, Launcelot,' Miss Mason said, while Eleanor stood motionless and silent in the doorway, absorbed in these thoughts, and looking like some pale statue in the dusk; 'and you've brought your friend, Monsieur – Monsieur Bourdon, to dine——'

'Ah, but no, mademoiselle,' exclaimed the Frenchman, in a transport of humility. 'I am not one of yours. Monsieur Darrell is so good as to call me his friend, but——'

The Frenchman murmured something of a deprecatory nature, to the effect that he was only a humble commercial traveller in the interests of a patent article that was very much appreciated by all the crowned heads of Europe, and which would doubtless, by the aid of his exertions and those of his compatriots, become, before long, a cosmopolitan necessity, and the source of a colossal fortune.

Eleanor shuddered and shrank away from the man with a gesture almost expressive of disgust, as he turned to her in his voluble depreciation of himself and glorification of the merchandise which it was his duty to praise.

She remembered that it was this man, this loquacious vulgarian, who had been Launcelot Darrell's tool on the night of her father's death. This was the wretch who had stood behind George Vane's chair, and watched the old man's play, and telegraphed to his accomplice.

If she could have forgotten Darrell's treachery, this presence would have been enough to remind her of that pitiless baseness, to inspire her with a tenfold disgust for that hideous cruelty. It seemed as if the Frenchman's coming had been designed by Providence to urge her to new energy, new determination.

'The man who could make this creature his accomplice in a plot against my father shall never inherit Maurice de Crespigny's fortune,' she thought; 'he shall never marry my husband's ward.'

She linked her arm in Laura's as she thought this; as if by that simple and involuntary action she would have shielded her from Launcelot Darrell.

In the next moment a footstep – the firm tread of a man – sounded on the crisp gravel of the garden walk behind the two girls, and presently Gilbert Monckton laid his hand lightly upon his wife's shoulder.

She was startled by his unexpected coming, and turning suddenly round, looked at him with a scared face; which was a new evidence against her in his troubled mind, a new testimony that she was keeping some secret from him.

He had left Tolldale Priory early that morning to give a day's attention to that business of which he had been lately so neglectful, and had returned a couple of hours before his usual time for coming home.

'What brings you out into the garden this bitter afternoon, Eleanor?' he said, sternly; 'you'll catch cold in that thin shawl; and you, too, Laura; I should have thought a seat by the drawing-room fire far more comfortable than this dreary garden. Good evening, gentlemen; you had better bring your friend into the house, Mr Darrell.'

The young man muttered something of an apologetic nature, and Monsieur Bourdon acknowledged the lawyer's cold salutation with an infinite number of bows and smirks.

'You have come home by an earlier train than usual, Gilbert,' Mrs Monckton said, by way of saying something that might break the silence which had followed her husband's coming; 'we did not expect you until seven.'

'I came to Windsor by the three o'clock express,' answered Mr Monckton. 'I have not come straight home. I stopped at Woodlands to inquire after the invalid.'

Eleanor looked up with a new and eager expression in her face.

'And Mr de Crespigny – he is better, I hope.'

'No, Eleanor, I fear that you will never see him again. The doctors scarcely hope that he will last out the week.'

The girl set her lips firmly, and raised her head with a resolute gesture – a mute expression of determination and defiance.

'I *will* see him again,' she thought; 'I will not trust my hope of vengeance to a chance. He may have altered his will, perhaps. Come what may, I will stand beside his sick bed. I will tell him who I am, and call upon him, in my dead father's name, to do an act of justice.'

Launcelot Darrell stood with his head bent and his eyes fixed upon the ground.

As it was the habit of Eleanor to lift her forehead with something of the air of a young war-horse who scents the breath of the battle-field afar, so it was this young man's manner to look moodily earthward under the influence of any violent agitation.

'So,' he said, slowly, 'the old man is dying?'

'Yes,' answered Mr Monckton; 'your great-uncle is dying. You may be master of Woodlands, Launcelot, before many days are past.'

The young man drew a long breath.

'Yes,' he muttered; 'I may: *I may*.'

CHAPTER XXXIX

LAUNCELOT'S COUNSELLOR

Mr Darrell, and his friend the commercial traveller, did not linger long at the garden gate. There was nothing very cordial or conciliatory in Gilbert Monckton's manner, and he had evidently no wish to cultivate any intimate relations with Monsieur Victor Bourdon.

Nor was Launcelot Darrell by any means anxious that his companion should be invited to stop at Tolldale. He had brought the Frenchman to the Priory, but he had only done so because Monsieur Bourdon was one of those pertinacious gentlemen not easily to be shaken off by the victims who are so unfortunate as to have fallen into their power.

'Well,' said the artist, as the two men walked away from the Priory in the murky dusk, 'what do you think of her?'

'Of which *her*? *La belle future*, or the otha-i-r?'

'What do you think of Mrs Monckton? I don't want your opinion of my future wife, thank you.'

Monsieur Bourdon looked at his companion with a smile that was half a sneer.

'He is so proud, this dear Monsieur Lan—— Darrell,' he said. 'You ask of me what I think of Mrs Monck-a-tonne,' he continued, in English; 'shall I tell you what I think without reserve?'

'Yes, of course.'

'I think, then, that she is a woman of a thousand – in all that there is of resolute – in all that there is of impulsive – in all that there is of daring – a woman unapproachable, unsurpassable; beautiful to damn the angels! If in the little business that we came to talk about lately this woman is to be in the way, I say to you, my friend, beware! If there is to be any contest between you and her, beware!'

'Pray don't go into heroics, Bourdon,' answered Launcelot Darrell, with evident displeasure. Vanity was one of the artist's strongest vices; and he writhed at the notion of being considered inferior to any one, above all to a woman. 'I knew Mrs Monckton, and I knew that she was a clever, high-spirited girl before to-day. I don't want you to tell me that. As to any contest between her and me, there's no chance of that arising. *She* doesn't stand in my way.'

'And you refuse to tell to your devoted friend the name of the person who does stand in your way?' murmured Monsieur Bourdon, in his most insinuating tones.

'Because that information cannot be of the least consequence to my devoted friend,' answered Launcelot Darrell, coolly. 'If my devoted friend has helped me, he will expect to be paid for his help, I dare say.'

'But, certainly!' cried the Frenchman, with an air of candour; 'you will recompense me for my services if we are successful; and above all for the suggestion which first put into your head the idea——'

'The suggestion which prompted me to the commission of a——'

'Hush, my friend, even the trees in this wood may have ears.'

'Yes, Bourdon,' continued Launcelot, bitterly, 'I have good reason to thank you, and to reward you. From the hour in which we first met until now, you have contrived to do me some noble services.'

Monsieur Bourdon laughed a dry, mocking laugh, which had something of the diabolically grotesque in its sound.

'Ah, what a noble creation of the poet's mind is Faust!' he exclaimed; 'that excellent, that amiable hero; who would never, of his own will, do any harm; but who is always led into the commission of all manner of wickedness by Mephistopheles. And then, when this noble but unhappy man is steeped to the very lips in sin, he can turn upon that wicked counsellor and say, "Demon, it is for your pleasure these crimes have been committed!" Of course he forgets, this impulsive Faust, that it was he, and not Mephistopheles, who was in love with poor Gretchen!'

'Don't be a fool, Bourdon,' muttered the artist, impatiently. 'You know what I mean. When I started in life I was too proud to commit a dishonourable action. It is you, and such as you, who have made me what I am.'

'Bah!' exclaimed the Frenchman, snapping his fingers with a gesture of unutterable contempt. 'You ask me just now to spare you my heroics; I say the same thing now to you. Do not let us talk to each other like the personages of a drama at the Ambigu. It is your necessities that have made of you what you are, and that will keep you what you are, so long as they exist, and are strong enough to push you to disagreeable courses. Who says it is pleasant to go out of the straight line? Not I, faith of a

gentleman, Monsieur Lance! Believe me, it is more pleasant, as well as
more proper, to be virtuous than to be wicked. Give me an annuity of a
few thousand francs, and I will be the most honourable of men. You are
afraid of the work that lies before you, because it is difficult, because it is
dangerous; but *not* because it is dishonourable. Let us speak frankly, and
call things by their right names. You want to inherit this old man's
fortune?'

'Yes,' answered Launcelot Darrell. 'I have been taught from my
babyhood to expect it. I have a right to expect it.'

'Precisely; and you don't want this other person, whose name you
won't tell me, to get it.'

'No.'

'Very well, then. Do not let us have any further dispute about the
matter. Do not abuse poor Mephistopheles because he has shown the
desire to help you to gain your own ends, and has already, by decision
and promptitude of action, achieved that which you would never have
effected by yourself alone. Tell Mephistopheles to go about his business,
and he will go. But he will not stay to be made a – what you call – an
animal which is turn out into the wilderness with other people's sins
upon his shoulders? – a scapegoat; or a paws-cat, which pull hot
chestnuts from the fire, and burn her fingers in the interests of her
friend. The chestnuts, in this case, this, are *very* hot, my friend; but I risk
to burn my fingers with the shells in the hope to partake the inside of
the nut.'

'I never meant to make a scapegoat of you, nor a cat's-paw,' said
Launcelot Darrell, with some alarm in his tone. 'I didn't mean to offend
you, Bourdon. You're a very good fellow in your way, I know; and if
your notions are a little loose upon some subjects, why, as you say, a
man's necessities are apt to get the upper hand of his principles. If
Maurice de Crespigny has chosen to make an iniquitous will, for the
mere gratification of an old madman's whim, the consequences of his
injustice must rest on his head, not on mine.'

'Most assuredly,' cried the Frenchman, 'that argument is not to be
answered. Be happy, my friend; we will bring about a posthumous
adjustment of the old man's errors. The wrong done by this deluded
testator shall be repaired before his ashes are carried to their resting-place.
Have no fear, my friend; all is prepared, as you know, and, let the time
come when it may, we are ready to act.'

Launcelot Darrell gave a long sigh, a fretful, discontented inspiration,
that was expressive of utter weariness. This young man had in the course
of his life committed many questionable and dishonourable actions; but
he had always done such wrong as it were under protest, and with the air
of a victim, who is innocently disposed but too easily persuaded, and

who reluctantly suffers himself to be led away by the counsels of evil-minded wretches.

So now he had the air of yielding to the subtle arrangements of his friend, the agent for patent mustard.

The two men walked on in silence for some little time. They had left the wood long ago, and were in a broad lane that led towards Hazlewood. Launcelot Darrell strolled silently along, with his head bent and his black eyebrows contracted. His companion's manner had its usual dapper airiness; but every now and then the Frenchman's sharp greenish-blue eyes glanced from the pathway before him to the gloomy face of the artist.

'There is one thing that I forgot in speaking of Mrs Monckton,' Monsieur Bourdon said, presently; 'and that is, that I fancy I have seen her somewhere before.'

'Oh, I can account for that,' Launcelot Darrell answered, carelessly. 'I was inclined to think the same thing myself when I first saw her. She is like George Vane's daughter.'

'George Vane's daughter?'

'Yes, the girl we saw on the Boulevard upon the night——'

The young man stopped abruptly, and gave another of those fretful sighs by which he made a kind of sulky atonement for the errors of his life.

'I do not remember the daughter of George Vane,' murmured the Frenchman, reflectively. 'I know that there was a young girl with that wearisome old Englishman – a handsome young person, with bright yellow hair and big eyes; an overgrown child, who was not easily to be shaken off; but I remember no more. Nevertheless, I think I have seen this Mrs Monckton before to-day.'

'Because, I tell you, Eleanor Monckton is like that girl. I saw the likeness when I first came home, though I only caught one glimpse of the face of George Vane's daughter on the Boulevard that night. And, if I had not had reason for thinking otherwise, I should have been almost inclined to believe that the old schemer's daughter had come to Hazlewood to plot against my interests.'

'I do not understand.'

'You remember George Vane's talk about his friend's promise, and the fortune that he was to inherit?'

'Yes, perfectly. We used to laugh at the poor hopeful old man.'

'You used to wonder why I took such an interest in the poor old fellow's talk. Heaven knows I never wished him ill, much less meant him any harm——'

'Except so far as getting hold of his money,' murmured Monsieur Bourdon, in an undertone.

The young man turned impatiently upon his companion.

'Why do you delight in raking up unpleasant memories?' he said, in a half-savage, half-peevish tone. 'George Vane was only one amongst many others.'

'Most certainly! Amongst a great many others.'

'And if I happened to play *écarté* better than most of the men we knew——'

'To say nothing of that pretty little trick with an extra king in the lining of your coat sleeve, which I taught you, my friend. – But about George Vane, about the friend of George Vane, about the promise——'

'George Vane's friend is my great-uncle, Maurice de Crespigny; and the promise was made when the two were young men at Oxford.'

'And the promise was——'

'A romantic, boyish business, worthy of the Minerva Press. If either of the two friends died unmarried, he was to leave all his possessions to the other.'

'Supposing the other to survive him. But Monsieur de Crespigny cannot leave his money to the dead. George Vane is dead. You need no longer fear him.'

'No, I have no reason to fear *him!*'

'But of whom, then, have you fear?'

Launcelot Darrell shook his head.

'Never you mind that, Bourdon,' he said. 'You're a very clever fellow, and a very good-natured fellow, when you please. But it's sometimes safest to keep one's own secrets. You know what we talked about yesterday. Unless I take your advice I'm a ruined man.'

'But you will take it? Having gone so far, and taken so much trouble, and confided so much in strangers, you will surely not recede?' said Monsieur Bourdon, in his most insinuating tones.

'If my great-uncle is dying, the crisis has come, and I must decide one way or the other,' answered Launcelot Darrell, slowly, in a thick voice that was strange to him. 'I – I – can't face ruin, Bourdon. I think I *must* take your advice.'

'I *knew* that you would take it, my friend,' the commercial traveller returned, quietly.

The two men turned out of the lane and climbed a rough stile leading into a meadow that lay between them and Hazlewood. The lights burned brightly in the lower windows of Mrs Darrell's house, and the clock of the village church slowly struck six as Launcelot and his companion crossed the meadow.

A dark figure was dimly visible, standing at a low wicket-gate that opened from the meadow into the Hazlewood shrubbery.

'There's my mother,' muttered Launcelot, 'watching for me at the gate. She's heard the news, perhaps. Poor soul, if I didn't care about the fortune for my own sake, I should for hers. I think a disappointment would almost kill her.'

Again a coward's argument, – a new loophole by means of which Launcelot Darrell tried to creep out of the responsibility of his own act, and to make another, in a manner, accountable for his sin.

CHAPTER XL

RESOLVED

Eleanor Monckton walked slowly back to the house by the side of her husband, whose eyes never left his wife's face during that short walk between the garden-gate and the long French window by which the two girls had left the drawing-room. Even in the dusk, Gilbert Monckton could see that his wife's face was unusually pale.

She spoke to him as they entered the drawing-room, laying her hand upon his arm as she addressed him, and looking earnestly at him in the red firelight.

'Is Mr de Crespigny really dying, Gilbert?' she asked.

'I fear that, from what the medical men say, there is very little doubt about it. The old man is going fast.'

Eleanor paused for a few moments, with her head bent, and her face hidden from her husband.

Then, suddenly looking up, she spoke to him again; this time with intense earnestness.

'Gilbert, I want to see Mr de Crespigny before he dies; I want to see him alone – I must see him!'

The lawyer stared at his wife in utter bewilderment. What in Heaven's name, was the meaning of this sudden energy, this intense eagerness, which blanched the colour in her cheeks, and held her breathless? Her friendly feeling for the invalid, her womanly pity for an old man's infirmities, could never have been powerful enough to cause such emotion.

'You want to see Maurice de Crespigny, Eleanor?' repeated Mr Monckton, in a tone of undisguised wonder. 'But why do you want to see him?'

'I have something to tell him – something that he *must* know before he dies.'

The lawyer started. A sudden light broke in upon his bewildered mind, – a light that showed him the woman he loved in very odious colours.

'You want to tell him who you are?'

'To tell him who I am? yes!' Eleanor answered, absently.

'But for what reason?'

Mrs Monckton was silent for a moment, looking thoughtfully at her husband.

'My reason is a secret, Gilbert,' she said; 'I cannot even tell it to you – yet. But I hope to do so very, very soon. Perhaps to-night.'

The lawyer bit his under lip and walked away from his wife with a frown upon his face. He left Eleanor standing before the fireplace, and took two or three turns up and down the room, pacing backwards and forwards in moody silence.

Then, suddenly returning to her, he said, with an air of angry resolution that chilled her timid confidence in him, and cast her back upon herself, 'Eleanor, there is something in all this that wounds me to the very quick. There is a mystery between us; a mystery that has lasted too long. Why did you stipulate that your maiden name should be kept a secret from Maurice de Crespigny? Why have you paid him court ever since your coming to this place? And why, now that you hear of his approaching death, do you want to force yourself into his presence? Eleanor, Eleanor, there can be but one reason for all this, and that the most sordid, the most miserable and mercenary of reasons.'

George Vane's daughter looked at her husband with a stare of blank dismay, as if she was trying, but trying in vain, to attach some meaning to his words.

'A sordid reason – a mercenary reason,' she repeated slowly, in a half whisper.

'Yes, Eleanor,' answered Gilbert Monckton, passionately. 'Why should you be different from the rest of the world? It has been my error, my mad delusion, to think you so; as I once thought another woman who crushed my hopes of happiness as recklessly as a child shatters a plaything it has got tired of. It has been my folly to trust and believe in you, forgetful of the past, false to the teaching of most bitter experience. I have been mistaken – once more – all the more egregiously, perhaps, because this time I thought I was so deliberate, so cautious. You are *not* different to the rest of the world. If other women are mercenary, you too are mercenary. You are not content with having sacrificed your inclination for the sake of making what the world calls an advantageous marriage. You are not satisfied with having won a wealthy husband, and you seek to inherit Maurice de Crespigny's fortune.'

Eleanor Monckton passed both her hands across her forehead, pushing back the loose masses of her hair, as if she would by that movement have cleared away some of the clouds that overshadowed her brain.

'*I* seek to inherit Mr de Crespigny's fortune!' she murmured.

'Yes! Your father no doubt educated you in that idea. I have heard how obstinately he built upon the inheritance of his friend's wealth. He taught you to share his hopes: he bequeathed them to you as the only legacy he had to give——'

'No!' cried Eleanor, suddenly; 'the inheritance I received at my father's death was no inheritance of hope. Do not say any more to me, Mr Monckton. It seems as if my brain has no power to bear all this to-night. If you can think these base things of me, I must be content to endure your bad opinion. I know that I have been very forgetful of you, very neglectful of you, since I have been your wife, and you have reason to think badly of me. But my mind has been so full of other things: so full, that it has seemed to me as if all else in life – except those thoughts, that one hope – slipped by me like the events of a dream.'

Gilbert Monckton looked half-fearfully at his wife as she spoke. There was something in her manner that he had never seen before. He had seen her only when her feelings had been held in check by her utmost power of repression. That power was beginning to wear out now. The strain upon Eleanor's intellect had been too great, and her nerves were losing their power of tension.

'Do not say anything more to me,' she cried, imploringly; 'do not say anything more. It will soon be over now.'

'What will soon be over, Eleanor?'

But Eleanor did not answer. She clasped her hands before her face; a half-stifled sob broke from her lips, and she hurried from the room before her husband could repeat his question.

Mr Monckton looked after her with an expression of unmingled anguish on his face.

'How can I doubt the truth?' he thought; 'her indignant repudiation of any design on Maurice de Crespigny's fortune exonerates her at least from that charge. But her agitation, her tears, her confusion, all betray the truth. Her heart has never been mine. She married me with the determination to do her duty to me, and to be true to me. I believe that. Yes, in spite of all, I will believe that. But her love is Launcelot Darrell's. Her love, the one blessing I sought to win, – the blessing which in my mad folly I was weak enough to hope for, – is given to Laura's betrothed husband. What could be plainer than the meaning of those last broken words she spoke just now: "It will soon be over; it will soon be over?" What should she mean except that Launcelot Darrell's marriage and departure will put an end to the struggle of her life?'

Mingled with the bitterness of his grief, some feeling akin to pity had a place in Gilbert Monckton's heart.

He pitied her – yes, he pitied this girl, whose life it had been his fate to overshadow. He had come between this bright young creature and the affection of her innocent girlhood, and, presenting himself before her in the hour of her desolation, had betrayed her into one of those mistakes which a lifetime of honest devotion is not always able to repair.

'She consented to marry me on the impulse of the moment, clinging to me in her loneliness and helplessness, and blinded to the future by the sorrow of the present. It was an instinct of confidence, and not love, that drew her towards me; and now, now that there is no retreat – no drawing back – nothing but a long vista of dreary years to be spent with a man she does not love, this poor unhappy girl suffers an agony which can no longer be concealed, even from me.'

Mr Monckton paced up and down his spacious drawing-room, thinking of these things. Once he looked with a sad, bitter smile at the evidence of wealth that were so lavishly scattered about the handsome chamber. On every side those evidences met his eyes. The Guido, upon which the firelight gleamed, kindling the face of a martyr into supernatural glory, was worth a sum that would have been a fortune to a poor man. Every here and there, half hidden amongst the larger modern pictures, lurked some tiny gem of Italian art, a few square inches of painted canvas, worth full a hundred times its weight of unalloyed gold.

'If my wife were as frivolous as Laura,' thought Mr Monckton, 'I could make her happy, perhaps. Fine dresses, and jewels, and pictures, and furniture, would be enough to make happiness for an empty-headed woman. If Eleanor had been influenced by mercenary feelings when she married me, she would have surely made more use of my wealth; she would have paraded the jewellery I have given her, and made herself a lay figure for the display of milliner's work; at least while the novelty of her position lasted. But she has dressed as plainly as a village tradesman's wife, and the only money she has spent is that which she has given to her friend the music-mistress.'

The second dinner-bell rang while Gilbert Monckton was pacing the empty drawing-room, and he went straight to the dining-room in his frock-coat, and with no very great appetite for the dishes that were to be set before him.

Eleanor took her place at the top of the table. She wore a brown silk dress, a few shades darker than her auburn hair, and her white shoulders gleamed like ivory against bronze. She had bathed her head and face with cold water, and her rippling hair was still wet. She was very pale, very grave; but all traces of violent emotion had passed away, and there was a look of quiet determination about her mouth.

Laura Mason came rustling and fluttering into the room, as Mr and Mrs Monckton took their places at the dinner-table.

'It's my PINK,' said the young lady, alluding to a very elaborate toilette of blush-rose coloured silk, bedizened with innumerable yards of lace and ribbon.

'I thought you would like to see my pink, and I want to know how it looks. It's the new colour. Launcelot says the new colour is like strawberry ices, but I like it. It's one of the dinner dresses in my trousseau, you know,' she murmured, apologetically, to Mr Monckton; 'and I wanted to try the effect of it, though of course it's only to be worn at a party. The trimmings on the cross set beautifully; don't they, Eleanor?'

It was fortunate, perhaps, on this occasion at least, that Miss Mason possessed the faculty of keeping up a kind of conversational monologue, for otherwise there must have been a very dreary silence at the dinner-table upon this particular evening.

Gilbert Monckton only spoke when the business of the meal compelled him to do so. But there was a certain tenderness of tone in the very few words he had occasion to address to his wife which was utterly different to his manner before dinner. It was never Mr Monckton's habit to sit long over the dismal expanse of a dessert-table; but to-night, when the cloth had been removed and the two women left the room, he followed them without any delay whatever.

Eleanor seated herself in a low chair by the fireplace. She had looked at her watch twice during dinner, and now her eyes wandered almost involuntarily to the dial of the clock upon the chimney-piece.

Her husband crossed the room and leant for a few moments over her chair.

'I am sorry for what I said this afternoon, Eleanor,' he murmured, in a low voice; 'can you forgive me?'

His wife lifted her eyes to his face. Those luminous grey eyes had a look of mournful sweetness in them.

'Forgive you!' exclaimed Eleanor, 'it is you who have so much to forgive. But I will atone – I will atone – after to-night.'

She said these last words almost in a whisper, rather as if she had been speaking to herself than to her husband; but Gilbert Monckton heard those whispered syllables, and drew his own conclusions from them. Unhappily, every word that Mrs Monckton uttered tended to confirm her husband's doubts and to increase his wretchedness.

He seated himself in a reading-chair upon the opposite side of the hearth, and, drawing a lamp close to his elbow, buried himself, or appeared to bury himself, in his newspapers.

But every now and then the upper margin of the 'Times,' or the 'Post,' or the 'Athenaeum,' or the 'Saturday,' or whatever journal the lawyer happened to be perusing – and he took up one after the other with a fretful restlessness that betokened a mind ill at ease – dropped a little

lower than the level of the reader's eyes, and Mr Monckton looked across
the edge of the paper at his wife.

Almost every time he did so he found that Eleanor's eyes were fixed
upon the clock.

The discovery of this fact speedily became a torture to him. He
followed his wife's eyes to the slowly moving hands upon the enamelled
dial. He watched the minute hand as it glided from one figure to another,
marking intervals of five minutes that seemed like five hours. Even when
he tried to read, the loud ticking of the wretched timepiece came
between him and the sense of the page upon which his eyes were fixed,
and the monotonous sound seemed to deafen him.

Eleanor sat quite still in her low easy chair. Scraps of fancy-work and
open books lay upon the table beside her, but she made no effort to
beguile the evening by any feminine occupation. Laura Mason, restless
for want of employment and companionship, fluttered about the room
like some discontented butterfly, stopping every now and then before a
looking-glass to contemplate some newly-discovered effect in the elegant
costume which she called her 'pink;' but Eleanor took no notice
whatever of her murmured exclamations and appeals for sympathy.

'I don't know what's come to you, Nelly, since your marriage,' the
young lady cried at last; after vainly trying to draw Mrs Monckton's
attention to the manifold beauties of gauze puffings and floating streamers
of ribbon; 'you don't seem to take any interest in life. You're quite a
different girl to what you were at Hazlewood – before Launcelot came
home.'

Mr Monckton threw down the 'Athenaeum,' and took up 'Punch,' at
this juncture. He stared with a stony face at one of Mr Leech's most
genial cartoons, and glanced almost vengefully at the familiar double
columns of jokes. Eleanor looked away from the clock to answer her
companion's peevish complaint.

'I am thinking of Mr de Crespigny,' she said; 'he may be dying while
we are sitting here.'

Mr Monckton dropped 'Punch,' and looked, openly this time, at his
wife's face.

Could it be, after all, that her abstraction of manner really arose from
no deeper cause than her regret for the loss of this old man, who was her
dead father's friend, and who had displayed an especial affection for her?

Could it be so? No! Her words that night had revealed more than a
common sorrow such as this. They had betrayed the secret of a hidden
struggle – a woman's grief – not easily to be repressed or overcome.
There is no knowing how long the lawyer might have sat brooding over
his troubles under cover of the newspapers, but presently he remembered
some papers which he had brought from London that afternoon, and

which it was his imperative duty – in the interests of a very important client – to read that night.

He pushed away the lamp, rose from his low chair, and went to the door of the drawing-room.

'I am going to my study, Eleanor;' he said; 'I shall most likely spend the rest of the evening there, and I may be obliged to be very late. You won't sit up for me?'

'Oh, no; not unless you wish it.'

'On no account. Good night. Good night, Laura.'

Even while his wife wished him good night, her eyes wandered uneasily back to the clock. A quarter to ten.

'And he hasn't once looked at my pink!' murmured Miss Mason, as her guardian left the drawing-room.

Scarcely had the door closed when Eleanor Monckton rose from her chair.

Her flushed cheeks flamed with crimson brightness; her eyes were lighted up as if a fire had burned in her dilated pupils.

'I am going to bed, Laura,' she said, abruptly; 'I am very tired. Good night!'

She took a candle from a table near the door, lit it, and hurried from the room before Laura could question her or remonstrate with her.

'She doesn't *look* tired,' thought Miss Mason; 'she looks as if she were going to a ball; or going to have the scarlatina. I think I looked like that when I was going to have the scarlatina; and when Launcelot proposed to me.'

Five minutes after the stable-clock had struck ten, the great door of Tolldale Priory was opened by a cautious hand, and Mrs Monckton stole out of her house with a woollen cloak wrapped about her, and her head almost buried in the hood belonging to the thick winter garment. She closed the door softly; and then, without stopping to look behind her, hurried down the broad stone steps, across the courtyard, along the gravelled garden pathway, out at the narrow wooden door in the wall, and away into the dreary darkness of the wood that lay between the Priory grounds and the dwelling-place of Maurice de Crespigny.

CHAPTER XLI

A TERRIBLE SURPRISE

With the chill winds of February blowing in her face, Eleanor Monckton entered the wood between Tolldale and Mr de Crespigny's estate.

There were no stars in the blank grey sky above that lonely place; black masses of pine and fir shut in the narrow path upon either side;

mysterious noises, caused by the capricious moaning of the winter wind, sounded far away in the dark recesses of the wood, awfully distinct amid the stillness of the night.

It was very long since Eleanor had been out alone after dark, and she had never before been alone in the darkness of such a place as this. She had the courage of a young lioness, but she had also a highly nervous and sensitive nature, an imaginative temperament; and the solemn loneliness of this wood, resonant every now and then with the dismal cries of the night-wind, was very terrible to her. But above and beyond every natural womanly feeling was this girl's devotion to her dead father; and she walked on with her thick shawl gathered closely round her, and with both her hands pressed against her beating heart.

She walked on through the solitude and the darkness, not indifferently, but devotedly; in sublime self-abnegation; in the heroic grandeur of a soul that is elevated by love; as she would have walked through fire and water, if by the endurance of such an ordeal she could have given fresh proof of her affection for that hapless suicide of the Faubourg Saint Antoine.

'My dear father,' she murmured once, in a low voice, 'I have been slow to act, but I have never forgotten. I have never forgotten you, lying far away from me in that cruel foreign grave. I have waited, but I will wait no longer. I will speak to-night.'

I think she believed that George Vane, divided from her by the awful chasm which yawns, mysterious and unfathomable, betwixt life and death, was yet near enough akin to her, in his changed state of being, to witness her actions and hear her words. She spoke to him as she would have written to him had he been very far away from her, in the belief that her words would reach him, sooner or later.

The walk, which in the daytime seemed only a pleasant ramble, was a weary pilgrimage under the starless winter sky. Eleanor stopped once or twice to look back at the lighted windows of Tolldale, lying low in the hollow behind her; and then hurried on with a quicker step.

'If Gilbert should miss me,' she thought, 'what will he do? what will he think?'

She quickened her pace even more as she thought of her husband. What unlooked-for difficulties might she not have to combat if Mr Monckton should discover her absence, and send or go himself in search of her.

She had reached the outskirts of the wood by this time, and the low gate in the iron fence – the gateway through which she had passed upon the day when, for the first time, she saw her father's old friend, Maurice de Crespigny.

This gate was very rarely locked or bolted, but to-night, to her surprise, she found it wide open.

She did not stop to wonder at this circumstance, but hurried on. She had grown very familiar with every pathway in the grounds during her walks beside Mr de Crespigny's invalid chair, and she knew the nearest way to the house.

This nearest way was across a broad expanse of turf, and through a shrubbery into the garden at the back of the rooms occupied by the old man, who had for many years been unable to go up and down stairs, and who had, for that length of time, inhabited a suite of rooms on the ground-floor, opening with French windows on to a tiny lawn, shut in and sheltered by a thick belt of pine and evergreens. It was in this shrubbery that Eleanor paused for a few moments to recover her breath after hurrying up the hill, and to reassure herself as to the safety of the papers which she carried in the bosom of her dress – Launcelot Darrell's water-colour sketch, and her father's letter. The picture and the letter were safe. She reassured herself of this, and was about to hurry on, when she was arrested by a sound near her. The laurel branches close beside her had rustled, as if parted by a man's strong hand.

Many times in her journey through the wood, Eleanor had been terrified by a rustling amongst the long grass about the trunks of the trees; but each time the sight of a pheasant flying across her pathway, or a frightened hare scudding away into the darkness, had reassured her. But this time there could be no mistake as to what she had heard. There was no game in Mr de Crespigny's garden. She was not alone, therefore. There was a man lurking somewhere under the shadow of the evergreens.

She stopped; clutched the documents that she carried in her breast, and then emerged from the shrubbery on to the lawn, ashamed of her fears.

The man whose presence had alarmed her was, no doubt, one of the servants – the gardener, most likely – and he would admit her to the house and save her any encounter with the maiden sisters.

She looked about the garden, but could see no one. Then, in a low voice, she called to the man by name: but there was no answer.

Lights were burning in Mr de Crespigny's bedroom, but the windows of the room which the old man called his study, and the windows of his dressing-room, a little apartment between the bed-chamber and the study, were dark.

Eleanor waited a few minutes in the garden, expecting to hear or see one of the servants emerge from the shrubbery; but all was quiet, and she had no alternative except to go round to the principal door of the house, and take her chance of being admitted.

'I am certain that there was some one close to me,' she thought. 'It must have been Brooks, the gardener; but how odd that he didn't hear me when I called to him.'

The principal entrance to Mr de Crespigny's house was by a pair of half-glass doors, approached by a double flight of stone steps, either from the right or the left, as might suit the visitor's convenience. It was a handsome entrance; and the plate glass which formed the upper halves of the doors appeared a very slight barrier between the visitor waiting on the broad stone platform without and the interior of the house. But, for all this, no portcullis of the Middle Ages, no sturdy postern-gate of massive oak studded by ponderous iron nails, was ever more impregnable to the besieger than these transparent doors had been under the despotic sway of the rich bachelor's maiden nieces. Despairing poor relations, standing hopeless and desperate without those fatal doors, had been well-nigh tempted to smash the plate-glass, and thus make their way into the citadel. But, as this would have scarcely been a likely method by which to ingratiate themselves into the favour of a testy old man, the glass remained undamaged; and the hapless kinsfolk of Maurice de Crespigny were fain to keep at a distance and hope − almost against hope − that he would get tired of his maiden watchers, and revenge himself upon their officiousness by leaving his money away from them.

It was outside these glass doors that Eleanor Monckton stood to-night, with very different feelings in her breast to those which were wont to animate the visitors who came to Woodlands.

She pulled the brass handle of the bell, which was stiff from little usage, and which, after resisting her efforts for a long time, gave way at last with an angry spring that shook the distant clapper with a noisy peal which seemed as if it would have never ceased ringing sharply through the stillness.

But, loud as this peal had been, it was not answered immediately, and Eleanor had time to contemplate the prim furniture of the dimly-lighted hall, the umbrella-stand and barometer, and some marine views of a warlike nature on the walls; pictures in which a De Crespigny of Nelson's time distinguished himself unpleasantly by the blowing up of some very ugly ships, which exploded in blazes of yellow ochre and vermilion, and the bombardment of some equally ugly fortresses in burnt sienna.

A butler or factotum, − for there was only one male servant in the house, and he was old and unpleasant, and had been cherished by the Misses de Crespigny because of those very qualifications, which were likely to stand in the way of his getting any important legacy, − emerged at last from one of the passages at the back of the hall, and advanced, with indignation and astonishment depicted on his grim features, to the doors before which Eleanor waited, Heaven only knows how impatiently.

'Launcelot Darrell may have come here before me,' she thought; 'he may be with his uncle now, and may induce him to alter his will. He must be desperate enough to do anything, if he really knows that he is disinherited.'

The butler opened one of the hall doors a very little way, and suspiciously. He took care to plant himself in the aperture, in such a manner as would have compelled Eleanor to walk through his body before she could enter the hall; and as the butler was the very reverse of Mr Pepper's ghost in consistency, Mrs Monckton could only parley with him in the faint hope of taking the citadel by capitulation. She did not know that the citadel was already taken, and that an awful guest, to whom neither closely guarded doors nor oaken posterns lined with stoutest iron formed obstacle or hindrance, had entered that quiet mansion before her; she did not know this, nor that the butler only kept her at bay out of the sheer force of habit, and perhaps with a spiteful sense of pleasure in doing battle with would-be legatees.

'I want to see Mr de Crespigny,' Eleanor cried, eagerly; 'I want to see him very particularly, if you please. I know that he will see me if you will be so good as to tell him that I am here.'

The butler opened his mouth to speak, but before he could do so a door opened, and Miss Lavinia de Crespigny appeared. She was very pale, and carried a handkerchief in her hand, which she put to her eyes every now and then; but the eyes were quite dry, and she had not been weeping.

'Who is that?' she exclaimed, sharply. 'What is the matter, Parker? Why can't you tell the person that we can see nobody to-night?'

'I was just a-goin' to tell her so,' the butler answered; 'but it's Mrs Monckton, and she says she wants to see poor master.'

He moved away from the door, as if his responsibility had ceased on the appearance of his mistress, and Eleanor entered the hall.

'Oh, dear Miss Lavinia,' she cried, almost breathless in her eagerness, 'do let me see your uncle. I know he will not refuse to see me. I am a favourite with him, you know. Please let me see him.'

Miss Lavinia de Crespigny applied her handkerchief to her dry eyes before she answered Eleanor's eager entreaty. Then she said very slowly, –

'My beloved uncle departed this life an hour ago. He breathed his last in my arms.'

'And in mine,' murmured Miss Sarah, who had followed her sister into the hall.

'And I was a-standing by the bedside,' observed the butler, with respectful firmness; 'and the last words as my blessed master said before you come into the room, Miss Lavinia, was these: "You've been a good servant, Parker, and you'll find you're not forgotten." Yes, miss, "You'll find you're not forgotten, Parker," were his last words.'

The two ladies looked very sharply and rather suspiciously at Mr Parker, as if they were meditating the possibility of that gentleman having fabricated a will constituting himself sole legatee.

'*I* did not hear my dear uncle mention you, Parker,' Miss Sarah said stiffly; 'but *we* shall not forget any one he wished to have remembered; you may be sure of that.'

Eleanor Monckton stood, silent and aghast, staring straight before her, paralyzed, dumbfounded, by the tidings she had just heard.

'Dead!' she murmured at last. 'Dead! dead! – before I could see him, before I could tell him——'

She paused, looking round her with a bewildered expression in her face.

'I do not know *why* you should be so eager to see my uncle,' said Miss Lavinia, forgetting her assumption of grief, and becoming very genuine in her spiteful feeling towards Eleanor, as a possible rival, 'nor do I know *what* you can have had to say to him. But I do know that you have not exhibited very good taste in intruding upon us at such an hour as this, and, above all, in remaining, now that you hear the sad affliction' – the handkerchief went to the eyes again here – 'which has befallen us. If you come here,' added Miss Lavinia, suddenly becoming spiteful again, 'in the hope of ascertaining how my uncle's money has been left – and it would be only like *some* people to do so – I can give you *no* information upon the subject. The gardener has been sent to Windsor to summon Mr Lawford's clerk. Mr Lawford himself started some days ago for New York on business. It's very unlucky that he should be away at such a time, for we put every confidence in him. However, I suppose the clerk will do as well. He will put seals on my uncle's effects, I believe, and nothing will be known about the will until the day of the funeral. But I do not think *you* need trouble yourself upon the subject, my dear Mrs Monckton, as I perfectly remember my beloved relative telling you very distinctly that he had no idea of leaving you anything except a picture, or something of that kind. We shall be very happy to see that you get the picture,' concluded the lady, with frigid politeness.

Eleanor Monckton stood with one hand pushing the glossy ripples of auburn hair away from her forehead, and with a look upon her face which the Misses de Crespigny – whose minds had run in one very narrow groove for the last twenty years – could only construe into some disappointment upon the subject of the will. Eleanor recovered her self-command with an effort, as Miss Lavinia finished speaking, and said, very quietly:

'Believe me, I do not want to inherit any of Mr de Crespigny's property. I am very, very sorry that he is dead, for there was something that I wanted to tell him before he died; something that I ought to have told him long ago. I have been foolish – cowardly – to wait so long.'

She said the last words not to the two ladies, but to herself; and then, after a pause, she added, slowly:

'I hope your uncle has left his fortune to you and your sister, Miss Lavinia. Heaven grant that he may have left it so!'

Unfortunately the Misses de Crespigny were in the humour to take offence at anything. The terrible torture of suspense which was gnawing at the heart of each of the dead man's nieces disposed them to be snappish to any one who came in their way. To them, to-night, it seemed as if the earth was peopled by expectant legatees, all eager to dispute for the heritage which by right was theirs.

'We are extremely obliged to you for your good wishes, Mrs Monckton,' Miss Sarah said, with vinegary politeness, 'and we can perfectly appreciate their sincerity. *Good* evening.'

On this hint, the butler opened the door with a solemn flourish, and the two ladies bowed Eleanor out of the house. The door closed behind her, and she went slowly down the steps, lingering without purpose, entirely bewildered by the turn that events had taken.

'Dead!' she exclaimed, in a half-whisper, 'dead! I never thought that he would die so soon. I waited, and waited, thinking that, whenever the time came for me to speak, he would be alive to hear me; and now he is dead, and I have lost my chance; I have lost my one chance of avenging my father's death. The law cannot touch Launcelot Darrell; but this old man had the power to punish him, and would have used that power, if he had known the story of his friend's death. I cannot doubt that. I cannot doubt that Maurice de Crespigny dearly loved my father.'

Eleanor Monckton stopped for a few minutes at the bottom of the steps, trying to collect her senses – trying to think if there was anything more for her to do.

No, there was nothing. The one chance which fortune, by a series of events, not one of which had been of her own contriving, had thrown into her way, was lost. She could do nothing but go quietly home, and wait for the reading of the will, which might, or might not, make Launcelot Darrell the owner of a noble estate.

But then she remembered Richard Thornton's visit to Windsor, and the inferences he had drawn from the meeting between Launcelot and the lawyer's clerk. Richard had most firmly believed that the property was left away from the young man; and Launcelot Darrell's conduct since that day had gone far towards confirming the scene-painter's assertion. There was very little doubt, then, that the will which had been drawn up by Mr Lawford and witnessed by Gilbert Monckton, was a will that left Maurice de Crespigny's fortune away from Launcelot Darrell. The old man had spoken of a duty which he meant to perform. Surely he must have alluded to his two nieces' devotion, and the recompense which they had earned by their patient attendance upon him. Such untiring watchers generally succeed in reaping the reward of their labours; and why should it be otherwise in this case?

But then, on the other hand, the old man was fretful and capricious. His nerves had been shattered by a long illness. How often, in the watches of the night, he might have lain awake, pondering upon the disposal of his wealth, and doubtful what to do with it in his desire to act for the best! It was known that he had made other wills, and had burned them when the humour seized him. He had had ample opportunity for changing his mind. He had very likely destroyed the will witnessed by Gilbert Monckton, in order to make a new one in Launcelot's favour.

Eleanor stood at the bottom of the broad flight of steps, with her hand upon the iron railing, thinking of all this. Then, with a regretful sigh, she walked away from the front of the house.

CHAPTER XLII

IN THE PRESENCE OF THE DEAD

The rooms that had been occupied by Maurice de Crespigny were at the back of the house, and Eleanor, returning by the way that she had come, had occasion to pass once more through the garden and shrubbery upon which the windows of these rooms looked.

Mrs. Monckton paused amongst the evergreens that grew near the house, sheltering and darkening the windows with their thick luxuriance. The Venetian shutters outside the windows of the room in which the dead man lay were closed, and the light within shone brightly between the slanting laths.

'Poor old man,' Eleanor murmured, as she looked mournfully towards this death-chamber; 'he was very good to me; I ought to be sorry for his death.'

The evergreens which grew in groups on either side of the windows made a thick screen, behind which half-a-dozen people might have safely hidden themselves upon this moonless and starless February night. Eleanor lingered for a few moments amongst these clustering laurels before she emerged upon the patch of smooth turf, which was scarcely large enough to be dignified with the title of a lawn.

As she lingered, partly because of a regretful tenderness towards the dead man, partly because of that irresolution and uncertainty that had taken possession of her mind from the moment in which she had heard of his death, she was startled once more by the rustling of the branches near her. This time she was not left long in doubt: the rustling of the branches was followed by a hissing whisper, very cautious and subdued, but at the same time very distinct in the stillness; and Eleanor Monckton was not slow to recognize the accent of the French commercial traveller, Monsieur Victor Bourdon.

'The shutters are not fastened,' this man whispered; 'there is a chance yet, *mon ami.*'

The speaker was within two paces of Eleanor, but she was hidden from him by the shrubs. The companion to whom he had spoken was of course Launcelot Darrell; there could be no doubt of that. But why were these men here? Had the artist come in ignorance of his kinsman's death, and in the hope of introducing himself secretly into the old man's apartments, and thus outmanoeuvring the maiden nieces?

As the two men moved nearer one of the windows of the bed-chamber, moving very cautiously, but still disturbing the branches as they went, Eleanor drew back, and stood, motionless, almost breathless, close against the blank wall between the long French windows.

In another moment Launcelot Darrell and his companion were standing so close to her that she could hear their hurried breathing as distinctly as she heard her own. The Frenchman softly drew back one of the Venetian shutters a few inches, and peeped very cautiously through the narrow aperture into the room.

'There is only an old woman there,' he whispered, 'an old woman, very grey, very respectable; she is asleep, I think; look and see who she is.'

Monsieur Bourdon drew back as he spoke, making way for Launcelot Darrell. The young man obeyed his companion, but in a half-sulky, half-unwilling fashion, which was very much like his manner on the Parisian Boulevard.

'Who is it?' whispered the Frenchman, as Launcelot leant forward and peered into the lighted room.

'Mrs Jepcott, my uncle's housekeeper.'

'Is she a friend of yours, or an enemy?'

'A friend, I think. I know that she hates my aunts. She would rather serve me than serve them.'

'Good. We are not going to trust Mrs Jepcott; but it's as well to know that she is friendly towards us. Now listen to me, my friend; we must have the key.'

'I suppose we must,' muttered Launcelot Darrell, very sulkily.

'You suppose we must! Bah!' whispered the Frenchman, with intense scornfulness of manner. 'It is likely we should draw back, after having gone so far as we have gone, and made such promises as we have made. It is like you Englishmen to turn cowards at the very last, in any difficult business like this. You are very brave and very great so long as you can make a great noise about your honour, and your courage, and your loyalty; so long as the drums are beating and the flags flying, and all the world looking on to admire you. But the moment there is anything of difficult – anything of a little hazardous, or anything of criminal, perhaps – you draw back, you have fear. Bah! I have no patience with you. You are a great nation, but you have never produced a great impostor. Your Perkin Warbecks, your Stuart Pretenders, they are all the same. They ride up hills with forty thousand men, and,' – here Monsieur Bourdon hissed out a very big French oath, to give strength to his assertion, – 'when they get to the top they can do nothing better than ride down again.'

It is not to be supposed that, in so critical a situation as that in which the two men had placed themselves, the Frenchman would have said all this without a purpose. He knew Launcelot Darrell, and he knew that ridicule was the best spur with which to urge him on when he was inclined to come to a stand-still. The young man's pride took fire at his companion's scornful banter.

'What do you want me to do?' he asked.

'I want you to go into that room and look for your uncle's keys. I would do it, and perhaps do it better than you, but if that woman woke and found me there, she would rouse the house; if she wakes up and sees you, any sentimental story of your desire to look for the last time upon your kinsman and benefactor will satisfy her and stop her mouth. *You* must search for the keys, Monsieur Robert Lance, pardon! – Monsieur Launcelot Darrell.'

The young man made no immediate answer to this speech. He stood close to the window, with the half-open shutter in his hand, and Eleanor could see, by the motion of this shutter, that he was trembling.

'I can't do it, Bourdon,' he gasped, after a long pause; 'I can't do it. To go up to that dead man's bedside and *steal* his keys. It seems like an act of sacrilege – I – I – *can't* do it.'

The commercial traveller shrugged his shoulders so high that it almost seemed he never meant to bring them down again.

'Good!' he said, '*C'est fini!* Live and die a pauper, Monsieur Darrell, but never again ask me to help you in a great scheme. Good night.'

The Frenchman made a show of walking off, but went slowly, and gave Launcelot plenty of time to stop him.

'Stay, Bourdon,' the young man muttered; 'don't be a fool. If you mean to stand by me in this business, you must have a little patience. I'll do what must be done, of course, however unpleasant it may be. I've no reason to feel any great compunction about the old man. He hasn't shown so much love for me that I need have any very sentimental affection for him. I'll go in and look for the keys.'

He had opened the shutter to its widest extent, and he put his hand upon the window as he spoke, but the Frenchman checked him.

'What are you going to do?' asked Monsieur Bourdon.

'I'm going to look for the keys.'

'Not that way. If you open that window the cold air will blow into the room and awaken the old woman – what you call her – Madame Jepcott. No, you must take off your boots, and go in through one of the windows of the other rooms. We saw just now that those rooms are empty. Come with me.'

The two men moved away towards the windows of the sitting-room. Eleanor crept to the Venetian shutters which Launcelot had closed, and, drawing one of them a little way open, looked into the room in which the dead man lay. The housekeeper, Mrs Jepcott, sat in a roomy easy-chair, close to the fire, which burned brightly, and had evidently been very lately replenished. The old woman's head had fallen back upon the cushion of her chair, and the monotonous regularity of her snores gave sufficient evidence of the soundness of her slumbers. Voluminous curtains of dark green damask were drawn closely round the massive four-post bed; a thick wax candle, in an old-fashioned silver candlestick, burned upon the table by the bedside, and a pair of commoner candles, in brass candlesticks, brought, no doubt, from the housekeeper's room, stood upon a larger table near the fireplace.

Nothing had been disturbed since the old man's death. The maiden ladies had made a merit of this.

'We shall disturb nothing,' Miss Lavinia, who was the more loquacious of the two, had said; 'we shall not pry about or tamper with any of our beloved relative's effects. You will take care of everything in your master's room, Jepcott; we place everything under your charge, and you will see that nothing is touched; you will take care that not so much as a pocket-handkerchief shall be disturbed until Mr Lawford's clerk comes from Windsor.'

In accordance with these directions, everything had remained exactly as it had been left at the moment of Maurice de Crespigny's death. The practised sick-nurse had retired, after doing her dismal duty; the stiffening limbs had been composed in the last calm sleep; the old man's eyelids had been closed upon the sightless eyeballs; the curtains had been drawn; and that was all.

The medicine bottles, the open Bible, the crumbled handkerchiefs, the purse, and paper-knife, and spectacles, and keys, lying in disorder upon the table by the bed, had not been touched. Eager as the dead man's nieces were to know the contents of his will, the thought of obtaining that knowledge by any surreptitious means had never for one moment entered into the head of either. They were conscientious ladies, who attended church three times upon a Sunday, and who would have recoiled aghast from before the mere thought of any infraction of the law.

Eleanor, with the Venetian shutter a very little way open, and with her face close against the window, stood looking into the lighted room, and waiting for Launcelot Darrell to appear.

The great four-post bedstead stood opposite the windows; the door was on Eleanor's right hand. About five minutes elapsed before there was any sign of the intruder's coming. Then the door was opened, very slowly, and Launcelot Darrell crept into the room.

His face was almost livid, and he trembled violently. At first he looked helplessly about him, as if paralyzed by fear. Then he took a handkerchief from his pocket, and wiped the cold perspiration from his forehead, still looking helplessly right and left.

But presently the Frenchman's head appeared round the edge of the door, which Launcelot Darrell had left a little way open, a fat little hand pointed to the table by the bed, and Monsieur Bourdon's hissing whisper vibrated in the room.

'V'là, – the table – the table – straight before you.'

Following this indication, the young man began with trembling hands to search amongst the disorder of the littered table. He had not occasion to seek very long for what he wanted. The dead man's keys lay under one of the handkerchiefs. They jingled a little as Launcelot took them up, and Mrs Jepcott stirred in her sleep, but she did not open her eyes.

'Come away, come!' whispered the Frenchman, as Launcelot stood with the keys in his hand, as if too much bewildered even to know that his purpose was accomplished. He obeyed Monsieur Bourdon, and hurried from the room. He had taken off his boots at his companion's instigation, and his stockinged feet made no sound upon the thick carpet.

'What is he going to do with those keys?' Eleanor thought. 'If he knows the contents of the will, as Richard believed, what good can the keys be to him?'

She still looked into the lighted bed-chamber, wondering what could happen next. Where had Launcelot Darrell gone, and what was he going to do with the keys? She crept along by the side of the house, past the window of the dressing-room, which was still dark, and stopped when she came to the window of the old man's study. All the windows upon this floor were in the same style – long French windows, opening to the ground, and they were all sheltered by Venetian shutters. The shutters of the study were closed, but the window was open, and through the bars of the shutters Eleanor saw a faint glimmer of light.

She drew the shutter nearest her a little way open, and looked into the room. The light that she had seen came from a very small bull's-eye lantern, which the Frenchman held in his hand. He was standing over Launcelot Darrell, who was on his knees before the lower half of an old-fashioned *secrétaire*, at which Mr de Crespigny had been in the habit of writing, and in which he had kept papers.

The lower half of this *secrétaire* contained a great many little drawers, which were closed in by a pair of inlaid ebony doors. The doors were open now, and Launcelot Darrell was busy examining the contents of the drawers one by one. His hands still trembled, and he went to work slowly and awkwardly. The Frenchman, whose nerves appeared in no way shaken, contrived to throw the light of the bull's-eye always upon the papers in the young man's hand.

'Have you found what you want?' he asked.

'No, there's nothing yet; nothing but old leases, receipts, letters, bills.'

'Be quick! Remember we have to put the keys back, and to get away. Have you the other ready?'

'Yes.'

They spoke in whispers, but their whispers were perhaps more distinct than their ordinary tones would have been. Eleanor could hear every word they said.

There was a long pause, during which Launcelot Darrell opened and shut several drawers, taking a hurried survey of their contents. Presently he uttered a half-smothered cry.

'You've got it?' exclaimed the Frenchman.

'Yes.'

'Put in the substitute, then, and lock the cabinet.'

Launcelot Darrell threw the document which he had taken from the drawer upon the chair near him, and took another paper from his pocket. He put this second paper in the place from which he had taken the first, and then shut the drawer, and closed and locked the doors of the cabinet. He did all this in nervous haste, and neither he nor his companion perceived that a third paper, very much like the first in shape and size, had fallen out of one of the drawers and lay upon the carpet before the cabinet.

Now, for the first time, Eleanor Monckton began to comprehend the nature of the conspiracy which she had witnessed. Launcelot Darrell and his accomplice had substituted a fictitious paper for the real will signed by Maurice de Crespigny and witnessed by Gilbert Monckton and the lawyer's clerk. The genuine document was that which Launcelot Darrell had flung upon the chair by the side of the *secrétaire*.

CHAPTER XLIII

A BRIEF TRIUMPH

Eleanor Monckton's first impulse was to rush into the room and denounce Launcelot Darrell in the presence of those who would be sure to come in answer to her call. He would be scarcely likely to find much mercy at the hands of his aunts: he would stand before them a detected wretch, capable of any crime, of any treachery, for the furtherance of his own interest.

But a second impulse, as rapid as the first, restrained the impetuous girl. She wanted to know the end, she wanted to see what these two plotters would do next. Under the influence of her desire to rush into the room, she had moved forward a few paces, rustling the leaves about her as she stirred. The Frenchman's acute hearing had detected that rustling sound.

'Quick, quick,' he whispered; 'take the keys back; there is some one in the garden.'

Launcelot Darrell had risen from his knees. The door between the study and the dressing-room had been left ajar; the young man pushed it open, and hurried away with the keys in his hand. Victor Bourdon closed his lantern, and came to the window. He thrust aside the Venetian shutters, and stepped out into the garden. Eleanor crouched down with her back flat against the wall, completely sheltered by the laurels. The Frenchman commenced his search, amongst the bushes on the right of the window. Eleanor's hiding-place was on the left. This gave her a moment's breathing time.

'The will!' she thought in that one moment; 'they have left the genuine will upon the chair by the cabinet. *If* I could get that!'

The thought had flashed like lightning through her brain. Reckless in her excitement, she rose from her crouching position, and slid rapidly and noiselessly across the threshold of the open window into the study, before Victor Bourdon had finished his examination of the shrubs on the right.

Her excitement seemed to intensify every sense. The only light in the room was a faint ray which came across the small intermediate chamber from the open door of Maurice de Crespigny's bedroom. This light was very little, but the open door was opposite the cabinet, and what light there was fell upon the very spot towards which Eleanor's dilated eyes looked. She could see the outline of the paper on the chair; she could see the other paper on the floor, faint and grey in the dim glimmer from the distant candles.

She snatched the will from the chair, and thrust it into the pocket of her dress; she picked up the other paper from the floor, and placed it on the chair. Then, with her face and figure obscured in the loose cloak that shrouded her, she went back into the garden.

As she drew back into the shelter of the laurels she felt a man's garments brushing against her own, and a man's hot breath upon her cheek. The Frenchman had passed her so closely that it was almost impossible he could have failed to perceive her presence; and yet he had seemed utterly unconscious of it.

Launcelot Darrell came back to the study almost the moment after Eleanor had left it. He was breathing quickly, and stopped to wipe his forehead once more with his handkerchief.

'Bourdon!' he exclaimed, in a loud whisper. 'Bourdon, where are you?'

The Frenchman crossed the threshold of the window as the young man called to him.

'I have been on the look-out for spies,' he said.

'Have you seen any one?'

'No; I fancy it was a false alarm.'

'Come, then,' said Launcelot Darrell, 'we have been luckier than I thought we should be.'

'Hadn't you better unlock that door before we leave?' asked Monsieur Bourdon, pointing to the door which communicated with the other part of the house. Launcelot had locked it on first entering the study, and had thus secured himself from any surprise in that direction. The two men were going away when Monsieur Bourdon stopped suddenly.

'You've forgotten something, my friend,' he whispered, laying his hand on Launcelot's shoulder.

'What?'

'The will, the genuine will,' answered the Frenchman, pointing to the chair. 'It would be a clever thing to leave that behind, eh?'

Launcelot started, and put his hand to his forehead.

'I must be mad,' he muttered; 'this business is too much for my brain. Why did you lead me into it, Bourdon? Are you the Devil, that you must always prompt me to some new mischief?'

'You shall ask me that next week, my friend, when you are the master of this house. Get that paper there, and come away: unless you want to stop till your maiden aunts make their appearance.'

Launcelot Darrell snatched up the paper which Eleanor had put upon the chair by the cabinet. He was going to thrust it into his breast-pocket, when the Frenchman took it away from him.

'You don't particularly want to keep that document; or to drop it anywhere about the garden; do you? We'll burn it, if it's all the same to you, and save them all trouble at − what you call your law court − Common doctors, Proctor's Commons, eh?'

Monsieur Bourdon had put his bull's-eye lantern in his coat-pocket, after looking for spies amongst the evergreens. He now produced a box of fusees, and setting one of them alight, watched it fizz and sparkle for a moment, and then held it beneath the corner of the document in his left hand.

The paper was slow to catch fire, and Monsieur Bourdon had occasion to light another fusee before he succeeded in doing more than scorching it. But it blazed up by-and-by, and by the light of the blaze Eleanor Monckton saw the eager faces of the two men. Launcelot Darrell's livid countenance was almost like that of a man who looks on at an assassination. The commercial traveller watched the slow burning of the document with a smile upon his face – a smile of triumph, as it seemed to Eleanor Monckton.

'V'là!' he exclaimed, as the paper dropped, a frail sheet of tinder, from his hand, and fluttered slowly to the ground. 'V'là!' he cried, stamping upon the feathery grey ashes; 'so much for that; and now our little scheme of to-night is safe, I fancy, my friend.'

Launcelot Darrell drew a long breath.

'Thank God, it's over,' he muttered. 'I wouldn't go through this business again for twenty fortunes.'

Eleanor, still crouching upon the damp grass close against the wall, waited for the two men to go away. She waited, with her hands clasped upon her heart; thinking of her triumph.

The vengeance had come at last. That which she had said to Richard Thornton was about to be fulfilled. The law of the land had no power to punish Launcelot Darrell for the cowardly and treacherous act that had led to an old man's miserable death: but the traitor had by a new crime placed himself at the mercy of the law.

'The will he has placed in the cabinet is a forgery,' she thought; 'and I have the real will in my pocket. He cannot escape me now, – he cannot escape me now! His fate is in my hands.'

The two men had walked past the laurels out on to the grass-plat. Eleanor rose from her crouching position, rustling the branches as she did so. At the same moment she heard voices in the distance, and saw a light gleaming through the leaves.

One of the voices that she had heard was her husband's.

'So much the better,' she thought. 'I will tell him what Launcelot Darrell is. I will tell him to-night.'

The voices and the lights came nearer, and she heard Gilbert Monckton say:

'Impossible, Miss Sarah. Why should my wife stop here? She must have gone back to Tolldale; and I have been unlucky enough to miss her on the way.'

The lawyer had scarcely spoken when, by the light of the lantern which he held, he saw Launcelot Darrell making off into the shrubbery that surrounded the grass-plat. The young man had not succeeded in escaping from the open space into this friendly shelter before Gilbert Monckton perceived him. Monsieur Bourdon, perhaps better accustomed to take to his heels, had been more fortunate, and had plunged in amongst the evergreens at the first sound of the lawyer's voice.

'Darrell!' cried Mr Monckton, 'what in Heaven's name brings you here?'

The young man stood for a few moments, irresolute, and sullen-looking.

'I've as good a right to be here as any one else, I suppose,' he said. 'I heard of my uncle's death – and – and – I came to ascertain if there was any truth in the report.'

'You heard of my beloved uncle's death!' cried Miss Sarah de Crespigny, peering sharply at her nephew from under the shadow of a pent-house-like garden-hood, in which she had invested herself before venturing into the night air. 'How *could* you have heard of the sad event? My sister and I gave special orders that no report should go abroad until to-morrow morning.'

Mr Darrell did not care to say that one of the Woodlands servants was in his pay; and that the same servant, being no other than Brooks, the gardener, had galloped over to Hazlewood, to communicate the tidings of his master's death, before starting for Windsor.

'I *did* hear of it,' Launcelot said, 'and that's enough. I came to ascertain if it was true.'

'But you were going away from the house when I saw you!' said Mr Monckton, rather suspiciously.

'I was not going away from the house, for I had not been to the house,' Launcelot answered, in the same tone as before.

He spoke in a sulky, grudging manner, because he knew that he was telling a deliberate lie. He was a man who always did wrong acts under protest, as being forced to do them by the injustice of the world; and held society responsible for all his errors.

'Have you seen my wife?' Gilbert asked, still suspiciously.

'No. I have only this moment come. I have not seen anybody.'

'I *must* have missed her,' muttered the lawyer, with an anxious air. 'I must have missed her between this and Tolldale. Nobody saw her leave the house. She went out without leaving any message, and I guessed at once that she had come up here. It's very odd.'

'It *is* very odd!' Miss Sarah repeated, with spiteful emphasis. 'I must confess that for my own part I do not see what motive Mrs Monckton could have had for rushing up here in the dead of the night.'

The time which Miss Sarah de Crespigny spoke of as the dead of the night had been something between ten and eleven o'clock. It was now past eleven.

The lawyer and Miss de Crespigny walked slowly along the gravelled pathway that led from the grass-plat and shrubbery to the other side of the house. Launcelot Darrell went with them, lounging by his aunt's side, with his head down, and his hands in his pockets, stopping now and then to kick the pebbles from his pathway.

It was impossible to imagine anything more despicable than this young man's aspect. Hating himself for what he had done; hating the man who had prompted him to do it; angry against the very workings of Providence – since by his reasoning it was Providence, or his Destiny, or some power or other against which he had ample ground for rebellion, that had caused all the mischief and dishonour of his life – he went unwillingly to act out the part which he had taken upon himself, and to do his best to throw Gilbert Monckton off the scent.

His mind was too much disturbed for him to be able clearly to realize the danger of his position. To have been seen there was ruin – perhaps! If by-and-by any doubts should arise as to the validity of the will that would be found in Maurice de Crespigny's *secrétaire*, would it not be remembered that he, Launcelot Darrell, had been seen lurking about the house on the night of the old man's death, and had been only able to give a very lame explanation of his motives for being there. He thought of this as he walked by his aunt's side. He thought of this, and began to wonder if it might not be possible to undo what had been done? No, it was impossible. The crime had been committed. A step had been taken which could never be retraced, for Victor Bourdon had burned the real will.

'Curse his officiousness,' thought the young man. 'I could have undone it all but for that.'

As the lawyer and his two companions reached the angle of the house on their way to the front entrance, whence Mr Monckton and Miss de Crespigny had come into the garden, a dark figure, shrouded in a loose cloak, emerged from amidst the shrubs by the windows of the dead man's apartments, and approached them.

'Who is that?' cried the lawyer, suddenly. His heart began to beat violently as he asked the question. It was quite a supererogatory question; for he knew well enough that it was his wife who stood before him.

'It is I, Gilbert,' Eleanor said, quietly.

'You here, Mrs Monckton!' exclaimed her husband, in a harsh voice, that seemed to ring through the air like the vibration of metal that has been struck – 'you here, hiding in this shrubbery?'

'Yes, I came here – how long ago, Miss Sarah? It seems half a century to me.'

'You came here exactly twenty minutes ago, Mrs Monckton,' Miss de Crespigny answered, icily.

'And by a really remarkable coincidence,' cried Gilbert Monckton, in the same unnatural voice in which he had spoken before, 'Mr Darrell happens to be here too: only I must do you the justice to say, Mrs Monckton, that *you* appear less discomposed than the gentleman. Ladies always have the advantage of us; they can carry off these things so easily; deception seems to come natural to them.'

'Deception!' repeated Eleanor.

What did he mean? Why was he angry with her? She wondered at his manner as she walked with him to the house. No suspicion of the real nature of her husband's feelings entered her mind. The absorbing idea of her life was the desire to punish her father's destroyer; and how could she imagine that her husband was tortured by jealous suspicions of this man: of this man, who of all the living creatures upon the earth was most hateful to her? How could she – knowing her own feelings, and taking it for granted that these feelings were more or less obvious to other people – how could she imagine the state of Gilbert Monckton's mind?

She went into the hall with her husband, followed by Miss Sarah de Crespigny and Launcelot Darrell, and from the hall into the sitting-room usually occupied by the two ladies. A lamp burned brightly upon the centre table, and Miss Lavinia de Crespigny sat near it, with some devotional book in her hand. I think she tried her best to be devout, and to employ herself with serious reflections upon the dread event that had so lately happened; but the fatal power of the old man's wealth was stronger than any holier influence, and I fear that Miss Lavinia's thoughts very often wandered away from the page on which her eyes were fixed, into sundry intricate calculations of the cumulative interest upon Exchequer bills, India five per cents., and Great Western Railway shares.

'I must have an explanation of this business,' Mr Monckton said: 'it is time that we should all understand each other. There has been too much mystification, and I am most heartily tired of it.'

He walked to the fireplace and leaned his elbow upon the marble chimney-piece. From this position he commanded a view of every one in the room. Launcelot Darrell flung himself into a chair by the table, nearly opposite his aunt Lavinia. He did not trouble himself to notice this lady, nor did he bow to Eleanor; he sat with his elbow resting upon the arm of his chair, his chin in the palm of his hand, and he employed himself by biting his nails and beating his heel upon the carpet. He was still thinking, as he had thought in the garden, 'If I could only undo what I have done. If I could only undo the work of the last quarter of an hour, and stand right with the world again.'

But in this intense desire that had taken possession of Launcelot Darrell's mind there was mingled no regretful horror of the wickedness of what he had done; no remorseful sense of the great injustice which he had plotted; no wish to atone or to restore. It was selfishness alone that influenced his every thought. He wanted to put *himself* right. He hated this new position, which for the last few minutes he had occupied for the first time in his life; the position of a deliberate criminal, amenable to the laws by which the commonest felons are tried, likely to suffer as the commonest felons suffer.

It seemed to him as if his brain had been paralyzed until now; it seemed to him as if he had acted in a stupor or a dream; and that he now for the first time comprehended the nature of the deed which he had done, and was able to foresee the possible consequences of his own act.

'I have committed forgery,' he thought. 'If my crime is discovered I shall be sent to Bermuda to work amongst gangs of murderous ruffians till I drop down dead. *If* my crime is discovered! How shall I ever be safe from discovery, when I am at the mercy of the wretches who helped me?'

Eleanor threw off her cloak, but she refused to sit down in the chair which Miss Sarah offered her. She stood divided by the width of half the room from her husband, with her face fronting his, in the full glare of the lamplight. Her large grey eyes were bright with excitement, her cheeks were flushed, her hair fell loosely about her face, brown in the shadow, and glittering like ruddy gold in the light.

In all the beauty of her girlhood, from the hour in which Gilbert Monckton had first seen her until to-night, she had never looked so beautiful as she looked now. The sense that she had triumphed, the thought that she held the power to avenge her father's death, lent an unnatural brilliancy to her loveliness. She was no longer an ordinary woman, only gifted with the earthly charms of lovely womanhood: she was a splendid Nemesis, radiant with a supernatural beauty.

CHAPTER XLIV

LOST

'You asked me why I came here to-night,' she said, looking at her husband. 'I will tell you, Gilbert: but I must tell you a long story first, almost all the story of my life.'

Her voice, resonant and musical, roused Launcelot Darrell from his gloomy abstraction. He looked up at Eleanor, and for the first time began to wonder how and why she had come there. They had met her in the garden. Why had she been there? What had she been doing there? Could it be possible that she had played the spy upon him? No! Surely there could be no fear of that? What reason should *she* have for suspecting or watching him? *That* terror was too cowardly, too absurd, he thought; but such foolish and unnecessary fears would be the perpetual torment of his life henceforward.

'You remember, Gilbert,' Eleanor continued, 'that when I promised to be your wife, I told you my real name, and asked you to keep that name a secret from the people in this house; and from Launcelot Darrell.'

'Yes,' answered Mr Monckton, 'I remember.'

Even in the midst of the tortures which arose out of his jealousy and suspicion, and which to-night had reached their climax, and had taken entire possession of the lawyer's mind, there was some half-doubtful feeling of wonder at Eleanor's calm and self-assured manner.

And yet she was deceiving him. He knew that. He had long ago determined that this second hazard of his life was to result in ignominious failure like the first. He had been deceived before; gulled, hoodwinked, fooled, jilted: and the traitress had smiled in his face, with the innocent smile of a guileless child. Eleanor was perhaps even more skilled in treachery than the first traitress; but that was all.

'I will not be deluded by her again,' he thought, as he looked gloomily at the beautiful face opposite to him: '*nothing* she can say shall make me her dupe again.'

'Shall I tell you why I asked you to keep that secret for me, Gilbert?' continued Eleanor. 'I did so because I had a motive for coming back to the neighbourhood of this place. A motive that was stronger than my love for you – though I did love you, Gilbert, better than I thought; if I thought at all of anything except that other motive which was the one purpose of my life.'

Mr Monckton's upper lip curled scornfully. Love him! That was too poor a fancy. What had he ever been but a dupe and a cat's-paw for a false woman; fooled and cheated many years ago in his early manhood; fooled and cheated to-day in his prime of life. He smiled contemptuously at the thought of his own folly.

'Launcelot Darrell,' cried Eleanor, suddenly, in an altered voice, 'shall I tell *you* why I was so eager to come back to this neighbourhood? Shall I tell you why I wanted the secret of my name kept from you and from your kindred?'

The young man lifted his head and looked at Eleanor. Wonder and terror were both expressed in his countenance. He wondered why Gilbert Monckton's wife addressed him with such earnestness. He was afraid, without knowing what he feared.

'I don't know what you mean, Mrs Monckton,' he faltered. 'What could I have to do with your false name, or your coming back to this place?'

'EVERYTHING!' cried Eleanor: 'it was to be near you that I came back here.'

'I thought as much,' muttered the lawyer, under his breath.

'It was to be near you that I came back,' Eleanor repeated; 'it was to be near you, Launcelot Darrell, that I was so eager to come back: so eager, that I would have stooped to any stratagem, encountered any risk, if by so doing I could have hastened my return. It was for this that I took the most solemn step a woman can take, without stopping to think of its solemnity. It was to deceive you that I kept my name a secret. It was to denounce you as the wretch who cheated a helpless old man out of the money that was not his own, and thus drove him to a shameful and a sinful death, that I came here. I have watched and waited long for this moment. It has come at last. Thank Heaven, it has come at last!'

Launcelot Darrell rose suddenly from his chair. His white face was still turned towards Eleanor; his eyes were fixed in a stare of horror. At first, perhaps, he contemplated rushing out of the room, and getting away from this woman, who had recalled the sin of the past, at a moment when his brain was maddened by the crime of the present. But he stopped, fascinated by some irresistible power in the beautiful face before him. Eleanor stood between the coward and the door. He could not pass her.

'You know who I am now, Launcelot Darrell, and you know how much mercy you can expect from me,' this girl continued, in the clear, ringing voice in which she had first addressed her enemy. 'You remember the eleventh of August. You remember the night upon which you met my father upon the Boulevard. I stood by his side upon that night. I was hanging upon his arm, when you and your vile associate tempted him away from me. Heaven knows how dearly I loved him; Heaven knows how happily I looked forward to a life in which I might be with him and work for him. Heaven only knows how happily that bright dream might have been realized – but for you – but for you. May an old man's sin rest upon your head. May a daughter's blighted hope rest upon your head. You can guess now why I am here to-night, and what I have been doing; and you can guess, perhaps, what mercy you have to expect from George Vane's daughter.'

'George Vane's daughter!'

Sarah and Lavinia de Crespigny lifted up their hands and eyes in mute dismay. Was this woman, this viper, who had gained access to the very heart of the citadel which they had guarded so jealously, the very creature who of all others they would have kept remote from the dead man?

No! it was impossible. Neither of Maurice de Crespigny's nieces had ever heard of the birth of George Vane's youngest child. The old man had received tidings of the little girl's advent in a letter sent by stealth, and had kept the intelligence a secret.

'It is too absurd!' Miss Lavinia exclaimed; 'George Vane's youngest daughter is Hortensia Bannister, and she must be at least five-and-thirty years of age.'

Launcelot Darrell knew better than this. *He* could recall a dismal scene that had occurred in the pale grey light of an August morning. He could remember a white-haired old man, sitting amidst the sordid splendour of a second-rate coffee-house, crying about his youngest daughter, and bewailing the loss of the money that was to have paid for his darling's education; a wretched, broken-hearted old man, who had held his trembling hands aloft, and cursed the wretch who had cheated him.

He could see the figure now, with the shaking hands lifted high. He could see the wrinkled face, very old and worn, in that grey morning light, and tears streaming from the faded blue eyes. He had lived under the shadow of that curse ever since, and it seemed as if it was coming home to him to-night.

'I am Eleanor Vane,' Gilbert Monckton's wife said, in answer to Miss Lavinia. 'I am Hortensia Bannister's half-sister. It was because of her foolish pride that I came to Hazlewood under a false name. It was in order to be revenged upon Launcelot Darrell that I have since kept my real name a secret.'

Eleanor Vane! Eleanor Vane! Could it be true? Of all whom Launcelot Darrell had reason to fear, this Eleanor Vane was the most to be dreaded. If he had never wronged her father, even if he had not been indirectly the cause of the old man's death, he would still have had reason to fear Eleanor Vane. He knew what that reason was, and he dropped back into his chair, livid and trembling, as he had trembled when he stole the keys from his dead uncle's bedside.

'Maurice de Crespigny and my father were bosom friends,' continued Eleanor. Her voice changed as she spoke of her father, and the light in her face faded as a tender shadow stole over her countenance. She could not mention her father's name without tenderness, speak of him when or where she might. 'They were bosom friends; everybody here knows that; and my poor dear father had a foolish fancy that if Mr de Crespigny died before him, he would inherit this house and estate, and that he would be rich once more, and that we should be very happy together. *I* never thought that.'

Launcelot Darrell looked up with a strange, eager glance, but said nothing. The sisters, however, could not suffer Eleanor's words to pass without remarks.

'You never thought that; oh dear no, I dare say not,' Miss Lavinia observed.

'Of course you never entered this house with any mercenary ideas upon the subject of my dear uncle's will,' Miss Sarah exclaimed, with biting irony.

'I never built any hope upon my dear father's fancy,' resumed Eleanor, so indifferent to the remarks of the two ladies that it seemed as if they had been unheard by her; 'but I humoured it as I would have humoured any fancy of his, however foolish. But after his death I remembered that Mr de Crespigny had been his friend, and I only waited to convince myself of that man's guilt' – she pointed to Launcelot Darrell as she spoke – 'before I denounced him to his great-uncle. I thought that my father's old friend would listen to me, and knowing what had been done, would never let a traitor inherit his wealth. I thought that by this means I should be revenged upon the man who caused my father's death. I heard to-day that Mr de Crespigny had not long to live; and when I came here to-night I came with the intention of telling him the real character of the man who was perhaps to inherit his fortune.'

The maiden ladies looked at each other. It would not have been a bad thing, perhaps, after all, if Eleanor had arrived in time to see the dying man. It was a pity that Maurice de Crespigny should have died in ignorance of his nephew's character, when there was just a chance that he might have left a will in that nephew's favour. But on the other hand, George Vane's daughter was even a more formidable person than Launcelot. Who could tell how she might have contrived to tamper with the old man?

'I have no doubt you wished to denounce Mr Darrell; and to denounce us, too, for the matter of that, I dare say,' observed Miss Sarah, 'in order that you yourself might profit by my uncle's will.'

'*I* profit!' cried Eleanor; 'what should I want with the poor old man's money?'

'My wife is rich enough to be above any suspicion of that kind, Miss de Crespigny,' Gilbert Monckton said, proudly.

'I came too late,' Eleanor said; 'I came too late to see my father's friend, but not too late for what I have so long prayed for – revenge upon my father's destroyer. Look at your sister's son, Miss de Crespigny. Look at him, Miss Lavinia; you have good reason to be proud of him. He has been a liar and a traitor from first to last; and to-night he has advanced from treachery to crime. The law could not punish him for the cruelty that killed a helpless old man; the law can punish him for that which he has done to-night, for he has committed a crime.'

'A crime!'

'Yes. He has crept like a thief into the house in which his uncle lies, dead, and has introduced some document – a will of his own fabrication, no doubt – in the place of the genuine will left in Mr de Crespigny's private *secrétaire.*'

'How do *you* know this, Eleanor?' cried Gilbert Monckton.

'I know it because I was outside the window of the study when he changed the papers in the cabinet, and because I have the real will in my possession.'

'It is a lie!' shouted Launcelot Darrell, starting to his feet, 'a damnable lie, the real will——'

'Was burnt, as you think, Mr Darrell; but you are mistaken. The document which your friend, Monsieur Victor Bourdon, burnt was a paper which you dropped out of the *secrétaire* while you were searching for the will.'

'And where is the genuine document, Eleanor?' Gilbert asked.

'Here,' answered his wife, triumphantly.

She put her hand into her pocket. It was empty. The will was gone.

CHAPTER XLV

AT SEA

The will was gone. Eleanor tried to think how or where she could have lost it. It might have dropped from her pocket, perhaps. That was the only solution of the mystery that presented itself to her mind. The open pocket of her dress might have been caught by one of the laurel boughs as she crouched upon the ground, and when she rose the paper had dropped out. There was no other way in which she *could* have lost it. She had been so absorbed in the watch she had kept on Launcelot Darrell, as to forget the value of the document which she had thrust carelessly into her pocket. Her father's letter and Launcelot Darrell's sketch were still safe in the bosom of her dress; but the will, the genuine will, in place of which the young man had introduced some fabrication of his own, was gone.

'Let me see this will, Eleanor,' Gilbert Monckton said, advancing to his wife. Although she had been the most skilful actress, the most accomplished deceiver amongst all womankind, her conduct to-night could not be all acting, it could not be all deception. She did not love him: she had confessed that, very plainly. She did not love him; and she had only married him in order to serve a purpose of her own. But then, on the other hand, if her passionate words were to be believed in, she did not love Launcelot Darrell. There was some comfort in that. 'Let me see the will, Eleanor,' he repeated, as his wife stared at him blankly, in the first shock of her discovery.

'I can't find it,' she said, hopelessly. 'It's gone; it's lost. Oh, for pity's sake, go out into the garden and look for it. I must have dropped it amongst the evergreens outside Mr de Crespigny's room. Pray go and look for it.'

'I will,' the lawyer said, taking up his hat and walking towards the door of the room.

But Miss Lavinia de Crespigny stopped him.

'No, Mr Monckton,' she said; 'pray don't go out into the night air. Parker is the proper person to look for this document.'

She rang the bell, which was answered by the old butler.

'Has Brooks come back from Windsor?' she asked.

'No, miss, not yet.'

'A paper has been dropped in the garden, Parker, somewhere amongst the evergreens, outside my uncle's rooms. Will you take a lantern, and go and look for it?'

'Dear, dear!' exclaimed Miss Sarah, 'Brooks has been a very long time going from here to Windsor and back again. I wish Mr Lawford's clerk were come. The place would be taken care of then, and we should have no further anxiety.'

The lady looked suspiciously from her nephew to Eleanor, and from Eleanor to Gilbert Monckton. She did not know whom to trust, or whom to fear. Launcelot Darrell sat before her, biting savagely at his nails, and with his head bent upon his breast. Eleanor had sunk into the chair nearest here, utterly dumbfounded by the loss of the will.

'You need not fear that we shall long intrude upon you, Miss de Crespigny,' Gilbert Monckton said. 'My wife has made an accusation against a person in this room. It is only right, in your interest, and for the justification of her truth and honour, that this business should be investigated – and immediately.'

'The will *must* be found,' Eleanor cried; 'it *must* have fallen from my pocket in the shrubbery.'

Launcelot Darrell said nothing. He waited the issue of the search that was being made. If the will was found he was prepared to repudiate it; for there was no other course left to him. He hated this woman, who had suddenly arisen before him as an enemy and denouncer, who had recalled to him the bitter memory of his first great dishonour, and who had detected him in the commission of his first crime. He hated Eleanor, and was ready to sacrifice her for his own safety.

He lifted his head presently, and looked about him with a scornful laugh.

'Is this a farce, or a conspiracy, Mrs Monckton?' he asked. 'Do you expect to invalidate my great-uncle's genuine will – wherever that will may happen to be found – by the production of some document dropped

by you in the garden, and which has, very likely, never been inside this
house, much less in my uncle's possession? You surely don't expect any
one to believe your pretty, romantic story, of a suicide in Paris, and a
midnight scene at Woodlands? It would be an excellent paragraph for a
hard-up penny-a-liner, but, really, for any other purpose——'

'Take care, Mr Darrell,' Gilbert Monckton said, quietly, 'you will gain
nothing by insolence. If I do not resent your impertinence to my wife, it
is because I begin to believe that you are so despicable a scoundrel as to
be unworthy of an honest man's anger. You had much better hold your
tongue.'

There was no particular eloquence in these last few words, but there
was something in the lawyer's tone that effectually silenced Launcelot
Darrell. Mr Monckton's cane lay upon a chair by the fireplace, and while
speaking he had set down his hat, and taken up the cane; unconsciously,
perhaps; but the movement had not escaped the guilty man's furtive
glance. He kept silence; and with his face darkened by a gloomy scowl,
still sat biting his nails. The will would be found. The genuine document
would be compared with the fabrication he had placed amongst his
great-uncle's papers, and perpetual shame, punishment, and misery would
be his lot. What he suffered to-night, sitting amongst these people, not
one of whom he could count as a friend, was only a foretaste of what he
would have to suffer by-and-by in a criminal dock.

For some time there was silence in the room. The two sisters, anxious
and perplexed, looked almost despairingly at each other, fearful that at
the end of all this business they would be the sufferers; cheated, in their
helplessness, either by George Vane's daughter or by Launcelot Darrell.
Eleanor, exhausted by her own excitement, sat with her eyes fixed upon
the door, waiting for the coming of the old butler.

'You have found it!' cried Eleanor, starting to her feet.

'No, ma'am. No, Miss Lavinia,' added the butler. 'I have searched every
inch of the garding, and there is nothink in the shape of a paper to be
found. The 'ousemaid was with me, and she searched likewise.'

'It *must* be in the garden,' exclaimed Eleanor, 'it must be there – unless
it has been blown away.'

'There's not wind enough for that, ma'am. The s'rubberies are 'igh,
and it would take a deal of wind to blow a paper across the tops of the
trees.'

'And you've searched the ground under the trees?' asked Mr
Monckton.

'Yes, sir. We've searched everywhere; me and the 'ousemaid.'

Launcelot Darrell burst into a loud laugh, an insolent, strident laugh.

'Why, I thought as much,' he cried; 'the whole story is a farce. I beg
your pardon, Mr Monckton, for calling it a conspiracy. It is merely a

slight hallucination of your wife's; and I dare say she is as much George Vane's daughter as I am the fabricator of a forged will.'

Mr Darrell's triumph had made him foolhardy. In the next moment Gilbert Monckton's hand was on the collar of his coat, and the cane uplifted above his shoulders.

'Oh my goodness me!' shrieked Sarah de Crespigny, with a dismal wail, 'there'll be murder done presently. Oh, this is too dreadful; in the dead of the night, too.'

But before any harm could happen to Launcelot Darrell, Eleanor clung about her husband's upraised arm.

'What you said just now was the truth, Gilbert,' she cried; 'he is not worthy of it; he is not indeed. He is beneath an honest man's anger. Let him alone; for my sake let him alone. Retribution must come upon him, sooner or later. I thought it had come to-night, but there has been witchcraft in all this business. I *can't* understand it.'

'Stay, Eleanor,' said Gilbert Monckton, putting down his cane, and turning away from Launcelot Darrell as he might have turned from a mongrel cur that he had been dissuaded from punishing. 'This last will – what was the wording of it – to whom did it leave the fortune?'

Launcelot Darrell looked up eagerly, breathlessly waiting for Eleanor's answer.

'I don't know,' she said.

'What, have you forgotten?'

'No, I never knew anything about the contents of the will. I had no opportunity of looking at it. I took it from the chair on which Launcelot Darrell threw it, and put it in my pocket. From that moment to this I have never seen it.'

'How do you know, then, that it was a will?' asked Gilbert Monckton.

'Because I heard Launcelot Darrell and his companion speak of it as the genuine will.'

The young man seemed infinitely relieved by the knowledge of Eleanor's ignorance.

'Come, Mr Monckton,' he said, with an air of injured innocence, 'you have been very anxious to investigate the grounds of your wife's accusation, and have been very ready to believe in a most absurd story. You have even gone so far as to wish to execute summary vengeance upon me with a walking-stick. I think it's my turn now to ask a few questions.'

'You can ask as many as you please,' answered the lawyer.

His mind was bewildered by what had happened. Eleanor's earnestness, which had seemed so real, had all ended in nothing. How if it was all acting; how if some darker mystery lurked beneath all this tumult of accusation and denial? The canker of suspicion, engendered by one woman's treachery, had taken deep root in Gilbert Monckton's breast. He had lost one of the purest and highest gifts of a noble nature – the power to trust.

'Very well, then,' said Launcelot Darrell, turning to Eleanor: 'perhaps you will tell me how I contrived to open this cabinet, out of which you say I stole one document, and into which you declare I introduced another?'

'You took the keys from Mr de Crespigny's room.'

'Indeed! But is there no one keeping watch in that room?'

'Yes,' cried Miss Sarah, 'Jepcott is there. Jepcott has been there ever since my beloved uncle expired. Nothing has been disturbed, and Jepcott has had the care of the room. We could trust Jepcott with untold gold.'

'Yes,' said Miss Lavinia, 'with untold gold.'

'But she was asleep!' cried Eleanor, 'the woman was asleep when that man went into the room.'

'Asleep!' exclaimed Miss Sarah; 'oh, surely not. Surely Jepcott would not deceive us; I can't think that of her. The last words I said to her were, "Jepcott, do you feel at all sleepy? If you feel in the least degree sleepy, have the housemaid to sit with you – make assurance doubly sure, and have the housemaid!" "No, Miss," Jepcott said, "I never felt more wakeful in my life, and as to the girl, she's a poor, frightened silly, and I don't think you could induce her to go into master's room, though you were to offer her a five-pound note for doing it." And if Jepcott went to sleep after this, knowing that everything was left about just as it was when my uncle died, it was really too bad of her.'

'Send for Mrs Jepcott,' said Launcelot Darrell; 'let us hear what she has to say about this very probable story of my stealing my great-uncle's keys.'

Miss Lavinia de Crespigny rang the bell, which was answered by Mr Parker, who, though usually slow to respond to any summons, was wonderfully prompt in his attendance this evening.

'Tell Mrs Jepcott to come here,' said Miss Lavinia; 'I want to speak to her.'

The butler departed upon this errand, and again there was a silent pause, which seemed a very long one, but which only extended over five minutes. At the end of that time Mrs Jepcott appeared. She was a respectable-looking woman, prim, and rather grim in appearance. She had been in the dead man's service for five-and-thirty years, and was about fifteen years older than the Misses de Crespigny, whom she always spoke of as 'the young ladies.'

'Jepcott,' said Miss Sarah, 'I want to know whether anybody whatever, except yourself, has entered Mr de Crespigny's room since you have been placed in charge of it?'

'Oh, dear no, miss,' answered the housekeeper, promptly, 'certainly not.'

'Are you sure of that, Jepcott?'

'Quite sure, miss; as sure as I am that I am standing here this moment.'

'You speak very confidently, Jepcott, but this is really a most serious business. I am told that you have been asleep.'

'Asleep, Miss de Crespigny! Oh, dear, who *could* say anything of the kind? Who could be so wicked as to tell such a story?'

'You are certain that you have not been asleep?'

'Yes, miss, quite certain. I closed my eyes sometimes, for my sight is weak, as you know, miss, and the light dazzled me, and made my eyes ache. I close my eyes generally when I sit down of an evening, for my sight doesn't allow me to do needlework by candlelight, neither to read a newspaper; and I may have closed my eyes to-night, but I didn't go to *sleep*, miss, oh dear no; I was too nervous and anxious for that, a great deal; besides, I am not a good sleeper at any time, and so I should have heard if a mouse had stirred in the room.'

'You didn't hear me come into the room, did you, Mrs Jepcott?' asked Launcelot Darrell.

'*You*, Mr Darrell? Oh, dear, no; neither you nor anybody else, sir.'

'And you don't think that I could have come into the room without your knowing it? You don't think I could have come in while you were asleep?'

'But I *wasn't* asleep, Mr Darrell; and as for you or anybody comin' in without my hearin' 'em -- why I heard every leaf that stirred outside the windows.'

'I fear that at least this part of your charge must drop to the ground, Mrs Monckton,' Launcelot Darrell said, scornfully.

'Jepcott,' said Miss Lavinia de Crespigny, 'go back and see if my uncle's keys are safe.'

'Yes, do, Mrs Jepcott,' exclaimed Launcelot Darrell; 'and be sure you take notice whether they have been disturbed since your master died.'

The housekeeper left the room, and returned after about three minutes' absence.

'The keys are quite safe, Miss Lavinia,' she said.

'And they have not been disturbed?' asked Launcelot.

'No, Mr Darrell, they haven't been moved a quarter of an inch. They're lyin' just where they lay when my poor master died, half hid under a pocket-handkerchief.'

Launcelot Darrell drew a long breath. How wonderfully these foolish women had played into his hands, and helped him to escape.

'That will do, Jepcott,' said Miss Sarah; 'you may go now. Remember that you are responsible for everything in my uncle's room until the arrival of Mr Lawford's clerk. It would have been a very bad business for you if Mr de Crespigny's keys had been tampered with.'

Mrs Jepcott looked rather alarmed at this remark, and retired without delay. Suppose she had been asleep, after all, for five minutes or so, and some mischief had arisen out of it, what might not her punishment be. She had a very vague idea of the power of the law, and did not know what penalties she might have incurred by five minutes' unconscious doze. This honest woman had been in the habit of spending the evening in a series of intermittent naps for the last ten years, and had no idea that while closing her eyes to shade them from the glare of the light, she often slumbered soundly for an hour at a stretch.

'Well, Mrs Monckton,' Launcelot Darrell said, when the housekeeper had left the room, 'I suppose now you are convinced that all this midwinter night's dream is a mere hallucination of your own?'

Eleanor looked at him with a contemptuous smile, whose open scorn was not the least painful torture he had been obliged to bear that night.

'Do not speak to me,' she said; 'remember who I am; and let that memory keep you silent.'

The door-bell rang loudly as Eleanor finished speaking.

'Thank Heaven!' exclaimed Miss de Crespigny, 'Mr Lawford's clerk has come at last. He will take charge of everything, and *if* anybody has tampered with my uncle's papers,' she added, looking first at Launcelot and then at Eleanor, 'I have no doubt that he will find out all about it. We are poor unprotected women, but I dare say we shall find those who will be able to defend our rights.'

'I don't think we have any occasion to stop here,' said Mr Monckton; 'are you ready to come home, Eleanor?'

'Quite ready,' his wife answered.

'You have nothing more to say?'

'Nothing.'

'Put on your cloak, then, and come. Good night, Miss de Crespigny. Good night, Miss Lavinia.'

Mr Lawford's clerk came in while Gilbert Monckton and his wife were leaving the room. He was the same old man whom Richard Thornton had seen at Windsor. Eleanor perceived that this man was surprised to see Launcelot Darrell. He started, and looked at the artist with a half-frightened, half-inquiring glance; but the young man did not return the look.

CHAPTER XLVI

LAURA'S TROUBLES

Gilbert Monckton offered Eleanor his arm as they went out of the hall and down the steps before the front entrance.

'I would have got a conveyance for you if it had been possible, Eleanor,' he said; 'but of course at this time of night that is utterly out of the question. Do you think that you can manage the walk home?'

'Oh, yes; very well indeed.'

She sighed as she spoke. She felt completely baffled by what had occurred; terribly prostrated by the defeat which had befallen her. There was no hope, then. This base and treacherous man was always to triumph, however wicked, however criminal.

'Is it very late?' she asked, presently.

'Yes, very late – past one o'clock.'

The husband and wife walked homewards in silence. The road seemed even drearier than before to Eleanor, though this time she had a companion in her dismal journey. But this time despair was gnawing at her breast; she had been supported before by excitement, buoyed up by hope.

They reached Tolldale at last. The butler admitted them. He had sent all the other servants to bed, and had sat up alone to receive his master. Even upon this night of bewilderment Gilbert Monckton endeavoured to keep up appearances.

'We have been to Woodlands,' he said to the old servant. 'Mr de Crespigny is dead.'

He had no doubt that his own and his wife's absence had given rise to wonderment in the quiet household; and he thought by this means to set all curiosity at rest. But the drawing-room door opened while he was speaking, and Laura rushed into the hall.

'Oh, my goodness gracious,' she exclaimed, 'here you are at last. What I have suffered this evening! Oh! what agonies I have suffered this evening, wondering what had happened, and thinking of all sorts of horrid things.'

'But, my dear Laura, why didn't you go to bed?' asked Mr Monckton.

'*Go to bed!*' screamed the young lady. 'Go to bed, with my poor brain bursting with suspense. I'm sure if people's brains *do* burst, it's a wonder mine hasn't to-night, and I thought ever so many times it was going to do it. First Eleanor goes out without leaving word where *she's* gone; and then you go out without leaving word where *you're* gone; and then you both stay away for hours, and hours, and hours. And there I sit all the time watching the clock, with nobody but the Skye to keep me company: until I get so nervous that I daren't look behind me, and I almost begin to feel as if the Skye was a demon dog! And, oh, do tell me what in goodness' name has happened.'

'Come into the drawing-room, Laura; and pray don't talk so fast. I'll tell you presently.'

Mr Monckton walked into the drawing-room, followed by Laura and his wife. He closed the door, and then sat down by the fire.

'I've had coals put on five times,' exclaimed Miss Mason; 'but all the coals in the world wouldn't keep me from shivering and feeling as if somebody was coming in through the door and looking over my shoulder. If it hadn't been for the Skye I should have gone mad. What *has* happened?'

'Something has happened at Woodlands——' Mr Monckton began, gravely; but Laura interrupted him with a little shriek.

'Oh, don't,' she cried, 'don't, please; I'd rather you didn't. I know what you're going to say. You must come and sleep with me to-night, Eleanor, if you don't want to find me raving mad in the morning. No wonder I felt as if the room was peopled with ghosts.'

'Don't be foolish, Laura,' Mr Monckton said, impatiently. 'You asked me what has happened, and I tell you. To speak plain, Mr de Crespigny is dead.'

'Yes, I guessed that, of course, directly you began to speak in that solemn way. It's very dreadful – not that he should be dead, you know; because I scarcely ever saw him, and when I did see him he always seemed to be deaf, or grumpy – but it seems dreadful that people should die at all; and I always fancy they'll come walking into the room at night when I'm taking my hair down before the glass, and look over my shoulder, as they do in German stories.'

'Laura!'

'Oh, please don't look contemptuously at me,' cried Miss Mason, piteously; 'of course, if you haven't got nerves it's very easy to despise these things; and I wish *I'd* been born a man or a lawyer, or something of that sort, so that I might never be nervous. Not that I believe in ghosts, you know; I'm not so childish as that. I don't believe in them, and I'm not afraid of them; *but I don't like them!*'

Gilbert Monckton's contemptuous expression changed to a look of pity. This was the foolish girl whom he had been about to entrust to the man he now knew to be a villain. He *now* knew; – bah, he had paltered with his own conscience. He had known it from the first. And this poor child loved Launcelot Darrell. Her hopes, like his own, were shipwrecked; even in the egotism of his misery the strong man felt some compassion for this helpless girl.

'So, Mr de Crespigny is dead,' Laura said, after a pause; 'does Launcelot know it yet?'

'He does.'

'Was he there to-night – up at Woodlands, in spite of his nasty old aunts?'

'Yes, he was there.'

Eleanor looked anxiously, almost piteously, at Laura. The great disappointment, the death-blow of every hope, was coming down upon her; and Eleanor, who could see the hand uplifted to strike, and the cruel knife bared ready to inflict the fatal stab, shivered as she thought of the misery the thoughtless girl must have to suffer.

'But what can her misery be against my father's,' she thought, 'and how am *I* accountable for her sorrow? It is all Launcelot Darrell's work; it is his wicked work from first to last.'

'And do you think he will have the fortune?' Laura asked.

'I don't know, my dear,' her guardian answered, gravely, 'but I think it matters very little either to you or me whether he may get the fortune or not.'

'What do you mean?' cried the girl, 'how strangely you speak; how cruelly and coldly you speak of Launcelot, just as if you didn't care whether he was rich or poor. Oh, good heavens,' she shrieked, suddenly growing wild with terror, 'why do you both look at me like that? Why do you both look so anxious? I know that something dreadful has happened. Something has happened to Launcelot! It's not Mr de Crespigny, it's Launcelot that's dead!'

'No, no, Laura, he is not dead. It would be better perhaps if he were. He is not a good man, Laura, and he can never be your husband.'

'Oh, I don't care a bit about his not being good, as long as he isn't dead,' exclaimed Laura. 'I never said he was good, and never wanted him to be good. *I'm* not good; for I don't like going to church three times every Sunday. The idea of your saying my poor dear Launcelot mustn't marry me because he isn't good! I like him to be a little wicked; like the Giaour, or Manfred – though goodness gracious only knows what *he'd* done that he should go on as he did – I never asked him to be good. Goodness wouldn't go well with his style of looks. It's fair people, with wishy-washy blue eyes and straight hair, and no eyebrows or eyelashes in particular, that are generally good. I hate *good* people, and if you don't let me marry Launcelot Darrell now, I shall marry him when I'm of age, and that'll be in three years' time.'

Miss Mason said all this with great vehemence and indignation, and then walked towards the door of the room; but Eleanor stopped her, and caught the slender little figure in her arms.

'Ah! Laura, Laura,' she cried, 'you must listen to us, you must hear us, poor darling. I know it seems very cruel to speak against the man you love, but it would be fifty times more cruel to let you marry him, and leave you to discover afterwards, when your life was linked to his, and never, never could be a happy life again if parted from him, that he was unworthy of your love. If it is terrible to be told this now, Laura, it would be a thousand times more terrible to hear it then. Come with me to your room, dear; I will stay with you all to-night. I will tell you all I know about Launcelot Darrell. I ought to have told you before, perhaps; but I waited; I waited for what I begin to think will never come.'

'I won't believe anything against him,' cried Laura, passionately, disengaging herself from Eleanor's embrace; 'I won't listen to you. I won't hear a word. *I* know why you don't want me to marry him. You were in love with him yourself, you know you were, and you're jealous of me, and you want to prevent my being happy with him.'

Of all the unlucky speeches that could have been made in the presence of Gilbert Monckton, this was perhaps the most unlucky. He started as if he had been stung, and rising from his seat near the fire, took a lighted candle from a side table, and walked to the door.

'I really can't endure all this,' he said. 'Eleanor, I'll leave you with Laura. Say what you have to say about Launcelot Darrell, and for pity's sake let me never hear his name again. Good night.'

The two girls were left alone together. Laura had thrown herself upon a sofa, and was sobbing violently. Eleanor stood a few paces from her, looking at her with the same tender and compassionate expression with which she had regarded her from the first.

'When I see your troubles, Laura,' she said, 'I almost forget my own. My poor dear child, God knows how truly I pity you.'

'But I don't want your pity,' cried Laura. 'I shall hate you if you say anything against Launcelot. Why should anybody pity me? I am engaged to the man I love, the only man I ever loved – you know that, Eleanor; you know how I fell in love with him directly he came to Hazlewood, – and I will marry him in spite of all the world. I shall be of age in three years and then no horrid guardian can prevent my doing what I like!'

'But you would not marry him, Laura, if you knew him to be a bad man?'

'I would never believe that he is a bad man!'

'But, my darling, you will listen to me. I must tell you the truth. I have kept it from you too long. I have been very guilty in keeping it from you. I ought to have told you when I first came back to Tolldale.'

'*What* ought you to have told me?'

'The story of my life, Laura. But I thought you would come between me and the victory I wanted to achieve.'

'What victory?'

'A victory over the man who caused my father's death.'

Then, little by little, interrupted by a hundred exclamations and protestations from the sobbing girl whose head lay on her shoulder, and whose waist was encircled by her arm, Eleanor Monckton told the story of her return to Paris, the meeting on the Boulevard, and George Vane's suicide. Little by little she contrived to explain to the wretched girl who clung about her, and who declared again and again that she *would* not believe anything against Launcelot, that she could not think him cruel or treacherous, – how the artist and his vile associate, Victor Bourdon, had cheated the old man out of the money which represented his own honour and the future welfare of his child.

'You think me hard and merciless, Laura,' she cried, 'and I sometimes wonder at my own feelings; but remember, only remember what my father suffered. He was cheated out of the money that had been entrusted to him. He was afraid to face his own child. Oh, my poor dear, how could you wrong me so cruelly,' she murmured, in a low voice, as if addressing her dead father, 'how could you think that I should have spoken one word of reproach, or loved you any the less, if you had lost a dozen fortunes of mine? No, Laura, I *cannot* forget what my father suffered; I *cannot* be merciful to this man.'

Eleanor's task was a very hard one. Laura would not believe; that is to say, she would not acknowledge that she believed; but she had none of the calm assurance which a perfect and entire faith in her lover should have given her. It was useless to reason with her. All Eleanor's logic was powerless against the passionate force of this girl's perpetual cry, the gist of which was, 'I will believe no harm of him! I love him, and I will not cease to love him!'

She would not argue, or listen to Eleanor's calm reasoning; for Mrs Monckton was very calm in the knowledge of her own defeat, almost despairingly resigned, in the idea that all struggle against Launcelot Darrell was hopeless. Laura would not listen, would not be convinced. The man whom Eleanor had seen in Paris was not Launcelot. He was in India at that very time. He had written letters from India, and posted them thence, with foreign postage stamps. The shipbroker's books were all wrong; what was more likely that that stupid shipbroker's clerks should make wrong entries in their horrid books? In short, according to poor Laura's reasoning, Launcelot Darrell was the victim of a series of coincidences. There had happened to be a person who resembled him in Paris at the time of George Vane's death. There happened to be a mistake in the shipbroker's books. The figure in the water-coloured sketch that Eleanor had stolen happened to be like the old man. Miss Mason rejected circumstantial evidence in toto. As for the story of the forgery, she declared that it was all a fabrication of Eleanor's, invented in order that the marriage should be postponed.

'You're very cruel, Eleanor,' she cried, 'and you've acted very treacherously, and I shouldn't have thought it of you. First you fall in love with Launcelot Darrell; and then you go and marry my guardian; and then, when you find that you don't like my guardian, you begrudge me my happiness; and you now want to set me against Launcelot; but I will not be set against him. THERE!'

This last decisive monosyllable was uttered amidst a torrent of sobs, and then, for a long time, the two girls sat in silence upon the sofa before the expiring fire. By-and-by, Laura nestled her head a little closer upon Eleanor's shoulder: then a little hand, very cold, by reason of its owner's agitation, stole into the open palm lying idle upon Mrs Monckton's lap; and at last, in a low voice, almost stifled by tears, she murmured:

'*Do* you think that he is wicked? Oh! Eleanor, do you *really* think that it was he who cheated your poor old father?'

'I know that it was he, Laura.'

'And do you believe that he has made a false will, for the sake of that dreadful money? Oh, how could he care for the money, when we might have been so happy together poor! Do you *really* believe that he has committed – forgery?'

She dropped her voice to a whisper as she spoke the word that was so awful to her when uttered in relation to Launcelot Darrell.

'I believe it, and I know it, Laura,' Eleanor answered, gravely.

'But what will they do to him? What will become of him? They won't hang him – will they, Eleanor? They don't hang people for forgery now. Oh, Eleanor, what will become of him? I love him so dearly, I don't care what he is, or what he has done. I love him still, and would die to save him.'

'You need not be afraid, Laura,' Mrs Monckton answered, bitterly. 'Launcelot Darrell will escape all evil consequences of what he has done. You may be sure of that. He will hold his head higher than he ever held it yet, Laura. He will be master of Woodlands before next week is over.'

'But his conscience, Eleanor, his conscience! He will be so unhappy – he will be so miserable.'

Laura disengaged herself from the loving arm that had supported her, and started to her feet.

'Eleanor!' she cried, 'where is he? Let me go to him! It is not too late to undo all this, perhaps. He can put back the real will, can't he?'

'No, the real will is lost.'

'He can destroy the false one, then.'

'I don't think he will have the chance of doing that, Laura. If his heart is not hardened against remorse, he will have plenty of time for repentance between this and the time when the will is read. If he wishes to undo what he has done, he may make a confession to his aunts, and throw himself upon their mercy. They are the only persons likely to be injured by what he has done. The money was left to them in the original will, no doubt.'

'He *shall* confess, Eleanor!' cried Laura. 'I will throw myself upon my knees at his feet, and I won't leave him till he promises me to undo what he has done. His aunts will keep the secret, for their own sakes. They wouldn't like the world to know that their nephew could do such a wicked thing. He shall confess to them, and let them have the fortune, and then we can be married, and then we shall be as happy together as if he had never done wrong. Let me go to him.'

'Not to-night, Laura. Look at the clock.'

Eleanor pointed to the dial of the timepiece opposite them. It was half-past two o'clock.

'I will see him to-morrow morning, then, Eleanor. I *will* see him.'

'You shall, my dear; if you think it wise or right to do so.'

But Laura Mason did not see her lover the next morning; for when the morning came she was in a burning fever, brought on by the agitation and excitement of the previous night. A medical man was summoned from Windsor to attend upon her; and Eleanor sat by her bed-side, watching her as tenderly as a mother watches her sick child.

Gilbert Monckton, too, was very anxious about his ward, and came to the door of Laura's room to make inquiries many times in the course of that day.

CHAPTER XLVII

GETTING OVER IT

Laura Mason was not dangerously ill. Her malady was by no means of a serious nature. The pink-blossom tint of her cheeks was intensified into vivid carnation; the turquoise-blue eyes shone with a feverish light; the little hands were very hot and dry. It was in vain that the physician from Windsor prescribed composing draughts. His patient would not be quiet or composed. In vain Eleanor tried to soothe the wounded spirit. It would not be at rest.

'It's no use, Nelly,' the invalid cried, impatiently. 'I *must* talk to him; I must talk of my sorrows, unless you want me to go mad. Oh, my poor Launcelot! my own dear Launcelot! how cruel it is to keep me from you!'

This was the worst part of the business. Poor Laura was perpetually entreating to be allowed to see Launcelot. Would they let her go to him; or would they send and ask him to come to her? They were the most cruel and heartless creatures, if they could refuse to let her see him.

But Eleanor did refuse.

'It is impossible, my darling,' she said; 'I cannot send for him. It is quite impossible that he and I should ever meet again, except as enemies. The will must be read in a few days. Let us wait till then. If Launcelot Darrell is sorry for what he has done, he will try to undo it. If he is not sorry, and takes possession of the estate upon the strength of a forged will, he must be a villain, unworthy even of your pity, Laura.'

'But I *do* pity him; and I love him.'

It was strange to see what a hold this unhappy affection had taken upon Laura's shallow nature. This frivolous girl was as impressionable as she was volatile. The blow was more terrible to her than it would have been to a woman of higher and grander nature; but to such a woman the consequences of the blow would be, perhaps, life-long, while it was scarcely likely that Laura would suffer for ever. She did not try to endure the grief that had fallen upon her. She was entirely without pride; and had no more shame in bemoaning her loss of Launcelot Darrell than she would have had fifteen years before in crying over a broken doll. She did not care who knew her sorrows, and would have made a confidante of the servant who waited upon her if Eleanor had not interfered to prevent her.

'I'm very miserable and wretched, Jane,' she said, while the girl was smoothing her pillows and arranging the tumbled bed-clothes, which had been twisted into mere wisps of linen by the perpetual tossings to and fro of the invalid. 'I'm the most miserable creature that ever was born, Jane, and I wish that I was dead. I know it's wicked, but I do. What's the good of Dr Featherstone prescribing for me, when I don't want to be prescribed for? What's the good of my taking lime-draughts, when I'd much rather die? What's the use of those horrid opiates, that taste like stale London porter? Opiates won't give me back Launce——'

She stopped abruptly at this point, checked by a warning look from Eleanor.

'You must not speak of Launcelot Darrell to these people, Laura,' Mrs Monckton said, when the servant had left the room, 'unless you want them to suspect that something strange has happened.'

'But they'll know it, if my wedding is put off.'

'Your guardian will explain all that, Laura.'

Miss Mason bemoaned her fate even more piteously than before.

'It's hard enough to be miserable,' she cried, 'but it's still worse to be miserable, and not to be allowed to say so.'

'Many people have sorrows to endure that cannot be spoken of,' Eleanor answered, quietly. 'I had to bear the sorrow of my father's death when I dared not speak of it.'

Mrs Monckton saw very little of her husband during the few days of Laura's illness. She only saw him, indeed, when he came to the door to make inquiries about his ward; but even in the few brief sentences exchanged by them, she could perceive that his manner was altered towards her. He had been cold and distant for a long time since their marriage; but now his manner had the icy reserve of a man who feels that he has been wronged. Eleanor comprehended this, and was sorry for it; but she had a dull, hopeless feeling that nothing she could do would alter it. The great purpose of her life had failed; and she began to think that nothing but failure could come to any hope of hers.

This feeling separated her completely from her husband. In her ignorance of the suspicions which tortured him, she could of course make no effort to set him right. The girl's innocence and the man's pride made a gulf that no power of affection could pass. If Eleanor could have guessed, ever so vaguely, at the cause of her husband's reserve, a few words from her might have melted the ice; but she had not the faintest notion of the hidden source from which came those bitter waters that had swept away all outward tokens of her husband's love; and those words remained unspoken. Gilbert Monckton thought that if his wife was not false, she was at least indifferent; and he bowed his head before the gloomy face of his Destiny.

'I am not to be loved,' he said. 'Good-bye once more to that dream. And let me try to do my duty, and be in some way useful to my fellow-creatures. Half my life has been swallowed up by egotistical regrets. May God give me grace to use the remnant of it more wisely.'

He had told Eleanor that as soon as Laura was a little better he should take her to the seaside.

'The poor child cannot remain here,' he said; 'every gossip in the neighbourhood will be eager to know why the wedding is postponed; and unless we assign some simple reason for the change in our arrangements, there will be no limit to people's speculations and conjectures. Laura's illness will be the best possible excuse; and I will take her to the south of France. She may forget Launcelot Darrell by-and-by, when she finds herself in a strange place, surrounded by new associations.'

Eleanor eagerly assented to this.

'Nothing could be wiser than such an arrangement,' she answered. 'I almost think the poor girl would die if she remained here. Everything reminds her of her disappointment.'

'Very well, then, I shall take her to Nice as soon as she is well enough to go. Will you tell her that I mean to do so, and try and make her feel some interest in the idea of the change?'

Eleanor Monckton had a very hard time of it in the sick-room. Those frivolous people who feel their misfortunes very acutely for the time being, are apt to throw a heavy share of their burden upon the shoulders of their friends. Laura's lamentations were very painful and not a little monotonous to hear; and there was a great deal of hard work to be done in the way of going over the same ground again and again, for that young lady's consolation. She had no idea of turning her face to the wall and suffering in silence. Her manner had none of that artificial calm which often causes uneasiness to those who watch a beloved sufferer through some terrible crisis. Everything reminded her of her grief; and she would not be courageous enough to put away the things that recalled her sorrows. She could not draw a curtain over the bright picture of the past, and turn her face resolutely to the blank future. She was for ever looking back, and bewailing the beauty of that vanished hope, and insisting that the dream palace was not utterly ruined; that it might be patched up again somehow or another; not to be what it was before; that was impossible, of course; but to be *something*. The broken vase could surely be pieced together, and the scent of the faded roses would hang round it still.

'If he repents, I will marry him, Eleanor,' she said, at the end of almost every argument, 'and we will go to Italy and be happy together, and he will be a great painter. Nobody would dare to say he had committed a forgery if he was a great painter like Holman Hunt, or Mr Millais. We'll go to Rome together, Nelly, and he shall study the old masters, and sketch peasants from the life; and I won't mind even if they're pretty; though it isn't pleasant to have one's husband always sketching pretty peasants; and that will divert his mind, you know.'

For four days Laura was ordered to keep to her bed, and during that time Eleanor rarely quitted the invalid's apartments, only taking brief snatches of rest in an easy-chair by the fire in Laura's dressing-room. On the fifth day Miss Mason was allowed to get up, and then there were terrible scenes to be gone through; for the young lady insisted upon having her trousseau spread out upon the bed, and the chair, and the sofas, and hung upon every available peg in the two rooms; until both those apartments became a very forest of finery, about which the invalid prowled perpetually, indulging in a separate fit of weeping over each garment.

'Look at this darling parasol, Nelly,' she cried, gazing at the tiny canopy of silk and whalebone with streaming eyes; 'isn't the real point lace over the pale pink silk lovely? And then it's so becoming to the complexion, too! Oh, how happy I thought I should be when I had this parasol. I thought I should drive on the Corso with Launcelot, and *now* – ! And the violet satin boots with high heels, Nelly, made on purpose to wear with my violet silk dress; I thought nobody *could* be unhappy with such things as those, and *now!*'

Every speech ended in fresh tears, which sometimes trickled over a shining silken garment, and flecked the lustrous fabric with spots of water that took the brightness out of the splendid hues.

'To think that I should be so miserable as to cry over silk at nine and sixpence a yard, and not to care!' exclaimed Laura Mason; as if, in these words, she described the highest anguish-point that human misery can reach.

She had a few presents given her by Launcelot; they were *very* few, and by no means valuable; for Mr Darrell, as we know was essentially selfish, and did not care to spend his small stock of money upon other people; and she sat with these trifles in her lap for hours together, lamenting over them, and talking about them.

'There's my silver thimble – my dear, darling little silver thimble,' she said, perching the scrap of glistening metal upon her little finger, and kissing it with that degree of rapture which the French vaudevilleists call 'explosion!' – 'that nasty, spiteful Amelia Shalders said a silver thimble was a vulgar present, just what a carpenter, or any other common man, would have given to his sweetheart, and that Launcelot ought to have given me a ring or a bracelet; as if he could go buying rings and bracelets without any money. And I don't care whether my thimble's vulgar or not, and I love it dearly, because he gave it me. And I'd do lots of needlework for the sake of using it, only I never could learn to use a thimble – quite. It always seems so much easier to work without one, though it does make a hole in the top of one's finger. Then there's my tablets! Nobody can say that ivory tablets are vulgar. My darling little tablets, with the tiny, *tiny* gold pencil-case,' – the gold pencil-case was *very* tiny – 'and the wee mite of a turquoise for a seal. I've tried to write "Launcelot" upon every leaf, but I don't think ivory tablets are the very nicest things to write upon. One's writing seems to slide about somehow, as if the pencil was tipsy, and the lines won't come straight. It's like trying to walk up and down the deck of a steamer; one goes where one doesn't want to go.'

The bewailings over the trousseau and the presents had a beneficial effect upon the heart-broken invalid. On the evening of the fifth day her spirits began to revive a little; she drank tea with Eleanor at a table by the fire in the dressing-room, and after tea tried on her wedding bonnet and mantle before the cheval glass.

This performance seemed to have a peculiarly consoling effect; and after surveying herself for a long time in the glass, and lamenting the redness of her eyelids, which prevented full justice being done to the beauty of the bonnet, Miss Mason declared that she felt a great deal better, and that she had a presentiment that something would happen, and that everything would come right somehow or other.

As it would have been very cruel to deprive her of this rather vague species of comfort, Eleanor said nothing, and the evening ended almost cheerfully. But the next day was that appointed for Mr de Crespigny's funeral and the reading of the will; and Laura's anxiety was now really greater than it had ever been. She could not help believing Eleanor's story of the forgery, though she had struggled long against the conviction that had been forced upon her; and her only hope was that her lover would repent, and suffer his aunts to inherit the wealth which had been no doubt bequeathed to them. Frivolous and shallow as this girl was, she could not for a moment contemplate marrying Launcelot under any other circumstances. She could not think of sharing with him a fortune that had been gained by fraud.

'I know he will confess the truth,' she said to Eleanor, upon the morning of the funeral; 'he was led into doing wrong by his friend that wicked Frenchman. It was only the impulse of the moment. He has been sorry ever since, I dare say. He will undo what he has done.'

'But if the real will has been destroyed?'

'Then his two aunts and his mother would share the estate between them. My guardian told me so the other day when I asked him some question about the fortune. And he told Launcelot the same thing that night in the library, when they had the conversation about my fortune.'

If Laura was anxious upon this eventful day, Eleanor was anxious too. It was a new crisis in her life. Would Launcelot Darrell attempt to restore himself to the position he had occupied before the night of his uncle's death, or would he hold to that which he might acquire by his deliberate fraud, and remain a hardened and impenitent criminal, defiant of the law he had outraged?

CHAPTER XLVIII

THE READING OF THE WILL

Gilbert Monckton went up to Woodlands immediately after the funeral, in order to be present at the reading of the will. He felt that he had a right to see the end of this business, in which his wife had played so extraordinary a part. The will was to be read by Henry Lawford's clerk, in the sitting-room, or study, which Maurice de Crespigny had occupied for many years before his death.

There were a great many people who, like Gilbert Monckton, thought they had a right to be present upon this occasion; people who had been kept out of the old man's house by the rigid watchfulness and the inflexible will of the two maiden ladies for the last twenty years or so, but who were freely admitted now, as no longer capable of doing mischief. All manner of distant relationships, so remote as to be almost untraceable, came to light upon this occasion: cousins by marriage; sisters-in-law of dead first cousins, once removed; widowers who attached themselves to the house of Crespigny by right of departed wives; widows who declared themselves near relations on the strength of claims held by defunct husbands; poor connections who came on foot, and who were so poor that it was really an impertinence in them to expect the smallest legacy; rich connections who came in splendid carriages, and who seemed even more eager for any stray twenty pounds for a mourning ring that might be set against their names, than the poorest of the brotherhood. And indeed these owners of splendid carriages might have been needier than the dusty and weather-beaten pedestrians; for when people try to make fifteen hundred a-year do the work of three thousand, every accidental twenty pounds is a God-send to them.

However it might be, everybody in the Woodlands drawing-room upon that particular morning was influenced by the same feeling, a compound sensation of hope and distrust, expectancy and despair. Surely there could never before have been so many eager faces assembled together in the same small space. Every face, young or old, handsome or ugly, aristocratic or plebeian, wore the same expression; and had thus a common likeness, which bore out the idea of some tie of relationship binding the whole assembly.

Every one regarded his or her neighbour as the possible inheritor of something worth having, and therefore a personal enemy. Smiling relations were suspected of being acquainted with the contents of the will, and secretly rejoicing in the certainty of their own names being pleasantly mentioned therein. Frowning relations were looked at darkly as probable arch-plotters who had worked upon the mind of the dead man. Diffident relations were feared as toadies and sycophants, who had no doubt plied Mr de Crespigny with artful flatteries. Confident relations were dreaded as people who perhaps had some secret claim upon the estate, and were silently gloating over the excellence of their chances. Every one of these outsiders hated each other with vengeful and murderous hate; but they all sympathized in a far deeper hatred of the four favourites for these great legacy stakes, the two maiden ladies, Mrs Darrell, and her son. It was almost certain that one or other of these four people would inherit the Woodlands property, and the bulk of the dead man's fortune; unless, indeed, by one of those caprices common to eccentric valetudinarians, he should have left his wealth to some distant connexion, who had been too proud to toady him – and had, moreover, never had the chance of doing so. Yes, the three nieces and Launcelot were the first favourites in this eager race; and the outsiders speculated freely amongst themselves as to the chances and the 'condition' of these four fortunate creatures. And if the outsiders hated each other desperately for the sake of very small chances, how much more desperate must have been the feelings of these four who were to enter for the great stake.

Launcelot Darrell met Mr Monckton this morning for the first time since that strange scene upon the night of Maurice de Crespigny's death. The young man had called at Tolldale Priory during the interval, but both the lawyer and his ward had been denied to him.

Perhaps amongst all those assembled in the chamber which had so lately been tenanted by the dead man, there was not one more painfully anxious than Gilbert Monckton, into whose mind no mercenary thought had ever entered.

It was in the hope of seeing his wife justified that Mr Monckton had come to Woodlands upon this day. He had brooded over Eleanor's denunciation of Launcelot Darrell perpetually during the week that had elapsed since the old man's death; but the more he pondered upon that passionate accusation the more bewildered and perplexed he became.

Let it be remembered that he was a man whose nature had been rendered jealous and suspicious by one cruel deception which had embittered his youth and soured a generous disposition. His mind was penetrated with the idea that Eleanor had never loved him, and that she *had* loved Launcelot Darrell. This believe was the tormenting spirit, the insidious demon which had held possession of his breast ever since his brief honeymoon on the northern coast. He could not dismiss it all in a moment. The fiend was in possession, and was not very easily to be exorcised. That vehement denunciation, that passionate accusation which had rushed, impetuous and angry, from Eleanor Monckton's lips, might be the outburst of a jealous woman's fury, and might have its roots in love. Eleanor had loved this young man, and was indignant against him for his intended marriage with Laura. If the desire to avenge her father's death had alone actuated her, surely this passionate girl would have spoken before now. It was thus Gilbert Monckton argued. He did not know how eager Eleanor had been to speak, and how she had only been held back by the worldly wisdom of Richard Thornton. How should he know the long trial of patience, the bitter struggle between the promptings of passion and the cold arguments of policy which his wife had endured? He knew nothing except that something – some secret – some master passion – had absorbed her soul, and separated her from him.

He stood aloof in the dead man's study while Mr Lamb, the clerk, a grey-haired old man, with a nervous manner and downcast eyes, arranged his papers upon a little table near the fire, and cleared his throat preparatory to commencing the reading of the will.

There was an awful silence in the room, as if everybody's natural respiration had been suspended all in a moment, and then the clerk's low voice began very slowly and hesitatingly with the usual formula.

'I, Maurice de Crespigny, being at this time,' &c., &c. The will was of some length, and as it began with a great many insignificant legacies – mourning rings, snuff-boxes, books, antique plate, scraps of valuable china, and small donations of all kinds to distant relations and friends who had been lost sight of on the lonely pathway along which the old man had crawled to his tomb under the grim guardianship of his two warders – the patience of the chief expectants was very sorely tried. But at last, after modest little annuities to the servants had been mentioned, the important clauses were arrived at.

To every one of the three sisters, Sarah and Lavinia de Crespigny and Ellen Darrell, the testator bequeathed money in the funds to the amount of two hundred a year. All the 'rest and residue' of the estate, real and personal, was left to Launcelot Darrell absolutely, without condition or reserve.

The blood rushed up to the widow's face, and then as suddenly receded, leaving it ghastly white. She held out her hand to her son, who stood beside her chair, and clasped his clammy fingers in her own.

'Thank God,' she said, in a low voice, 'you have got your chance at last, Launcelot. I should be content to die to-morrow.'

The two sisters, pale and venomous, glared at their nephew. But they could only look at him. They could do nothing against him. He had won and they had lost; that was all. They felt strange buzzing noises in their ears, and the carpeted floor of the room seemed reeling up and down like the deck of a storm-tossed vessel. This was all that they felt just at present. The shock was so great that its first effect was only to produce a kind of physical numbness which extended even to the brain.

I don't suppose that either of these elderly ladies, each of whom wore stuff shoes and crisp little curls of unnaturally brown hair upon her forehead, could, by any possibility, have spent upon her own wants more than a hundred pounds a year, nor had either of them been accustomed to indulge in the sweet luxury of charity; they were neither generous nor ambitious. They were entirely without the capacity of spending money either upon themselves or on other people, and yet they had striven as eagerly for the possession of this fortune as ever any proud, ambitious spirit strove for the golden means by which he hoped to work his way upon the road that leads to glory.

They were fond of money; they were fond of money *per se*; without reference to its uses, either noble or ignoble. They would have been very happy in the possession of their dead kinsman's fortune, though they might have gone down to their graves without having spent so much as the two hundred a year which they received by this cruel will. They would have hoarded the government securities in an iron safe; they would have added interest to principal; they would have nursed the lands, and raised the rents, and been hard and griping with the tenants, and would have counted their gains and calculated together the increase of their wealth; but they would have employed the same cobbler who had worked for them before their uncle's death; they would still have given out their stuff shoes to be mended; and they would have been as sharp as ever as to an odd sixpence in their dealings with the barber who dressed their crisp brown curls.

Launcelot Darrell kept his place beside his mother's chair, though the reading of the will was finished, and the clerk was folding the sheets upon which it was written. Never had any living creature shown less elation than this young man did upon his accession to such a very large fortune.

Mr Monckton went up to the little table at which the lawyer's clerk sat, folding up the papers.

'Will you let me look at that will for a moment, Mr Lamb?' he asked.

The clerk looked up at him with an expression of surprise.

'You wish to look at it?——' he said, hesitating a little.

'Yes. There is no objection to my doing so, is there? It will be sent to Doctors' Commons, I suppose, where anybody will be able to look at it for a shilling.'

The clerk handed Gilbert Monckton the document with a feeble little laugh.

'There it is, Mr Monckton,' he said. 'You remember your own signature, I dare say; you'll find it there along with mine.'

Yes, there was the signature. It is not a very easy thing for the cleverest man, who is not a professional expert, to decide upon the authenticity of his own autograph. There it was. Gilbert Monckton looked at the familiar signature, and tried in vain to find some flaw in it. If it was a forgery, it was a very skilful one. The lawyer remembered the date of the will which he had witnessed, and the kind of paper upon which it had been written. The date and the paper of this corresponded with that recollection.

The body of the will was in the handwriting of the clerk himself. It was written upon three sheets of foolscap paper, and the signatures of the testator and the two witnesses were repeated at the bottom of every page. Every one of the three autographs differed from the others in some trifling point, and this circumstance, small in itself, had considerable influence upon Gilbert Monckton.

'If this will had been a forgery, prepared by Launcelot Darrell, the signatures would have been fac-similes of each other,' thought the lawyer; 'that is a mistake which forgers almost always fall into. They forget that a man very rarely signs his name twice alike. They get hold of one autograph and stereotype it.'

What was he to think, then? If this will was genuine, Eleanor's accusation must be a falsehood. Could he believe this? Could he believe that his wife was a jealous and vindictive woman, capable of inventing a lie in order to avenge herself upon the infidelity of the man she had loved? To believe this would be most everlasting misery. Yet how could Gilbert Monckton think otherwise, *if* the will was genuine? Everything hinged upon that, and every proof was wanting against Launcelot Darrell. The housekeeper, Mrs Jepcott, declared most distinctly that nobody had entered the dead man's room or touched the keys upon the table by the bed. This alone, if the woman's word was to be depended upon, gave the lie to Eleanor's story.

But this was not all. The will was in every particular the very opposite of such a will as would be likely to be the work of a forger.

It contained legacies to old friends of the dead man whom he had not himself seen for twenty years, and whose very names must have been unknown to Launcelot Darrell. It was the will of a man whose mind lived almost entirely in the past. There was a gold snuff-box bequeathed 'to my friend Peter Sedgewick, who was stroke in the Magdalen boat at Henley-on-the-Thames, fifty-seven years ago, when I was six in the same boat;' there was an onyx shirt-pin left 'to my old boon companion Henry Laurence, who dined with me at the Beefsteak Club with George Vane and Richard Brinsley Sheridan on my birthday.' The will was full of personal recollections dated fifty years back; and how was it possible that Launcelot Darrell could have fabricated such a will; when by Eleanor's own admission he had no access to the genuine document until he came to substitute the forgery after his uncle's death? The forgery must therefore, Gilbert Monckton argued, have been prepared while the young man was in utter ignorance as to the tenor of the actual will, according to Eleanor's story; and this, the lawyer reasoned, was proof conclusive against his wife.

Launcelot could not have fabricated such a will as this. This will, therefore, was genuine, and Eleanor's accusation had been only prompted by a sudden burst of jealous rage, which had made her almost indifferent to consequences. Mr Monckton examined the signatures again and again, and then, looking very sharply at the clerk, said, in a low voice –

'The body of this will is in your handwriting, I believe, Mr Lamb?'

'It is, sir.'

'Can you swear that this is the genuine document; the same will which you wrote and witnessed?'

'Most decidedly,' the clerk answered, with a look of astonishment.

'You have no suspicion whatever as to its authenticity?'

'No, sir, none! Have *you* any suspicion, Mr Monckton?' he added, after a moment's pause.

The lawyer sighed heavily.

'No,' he said, giving the paper back to the clerk; 'I believe the will is genuine.'

Just at this moment there was a stir in the assembly, and Gilbert Monckton turned round to see what was taking place.

It was Mrs Jepcott, the housekeeper, who was saying something to which everybody listened intently.

The reason of this attention which the housekeeper's smallest word received from every member of that assembly, was the fact that she held a paper in her hand. Every eye was fixed upon this paper. It might be a codicil revoking the will, and making an entirely new disposition of the property.

Faint streaks of red began to light up the wan cheeks of the two old maids, and Launcelot Darrell grew more livid than death. But it was not a codicil; it was only a letter written by Maurice de Crespigny, and addressed to his three nieces.

'The night before my poor dear master died,' the housekeeper said, 'I was sitting up with him all alone, and he called me to him, and he told me to fetch him his dressing-gown, which he'd been wearing all through his illness, whenever he sat up; and I fetched it; and he took a sealed letter out of the breast-pocket, and he said to me, "Jepcott, when my will is read, I expect my three nieces will be very much disappointed and will think I have not treated them fairly; so I've written them a letter, begging them not to be angry with me after I'm dead and gone: and I want you to keep it, and take care of it, until the will has been read, and then give it to my eldest niece, Sarah, to read aloud to her two sisters in the presence of everybody." And this is the letter, miss,' added Mrs Jepcott, handing the sealed letter to Sarah de Crespigny.

'Thank God!' thought Gilbert Monckton, 'I shall know now whether the will is genuine. If it is a fabrication, this letter must bring detection upon the forger.'

CHAPTER XLIX

DESERTED

The letter written by the old man to his three nieces was read aloud by Miss Sarah in the presence of the eager assembly. Amongst all those anxious listeners there was no one who listened more intently than Gilbert Monckton.

Maurice de Crespigny's letter was not a long one.

'My dear Nieces – Sarah, Lavinia, and Ellen,

'You will all three be perhaps much surprised at the manner in which I have disposed of my estate, both real and personal; but believe me that in acting as I have done I have been prompted by no unkind feeling against you; nor am I otherwise than duly grateful for the attention which I have received from you during my declining years.

'I think that I have done my duty; but be that as it may, I have done that which it has been my fixed intention to do for the last ten years. I have made several wills, and destroyed one after another, but they have all been in the main point to the same effect; and it has only been an old man's whimsical fancy that has prompted me to make sundry alterations in minor details. The income of two hundred a year which I have left to each of you will, I know, be more than enough for your simple wants. The three incomes, by the wording of my will, will descend to my nephew, Launcelot Darrell, after your deaths.

'I have tried to remember many old friends who have perhaps long ere this forgotten me, or who may laugh at an old man's foolish bequests.

'I do not believe that I have wronged any one; and I trust that you will think kindly of me when I am in my grave, and never speak bitterly of

'Your affectionate uncle,
'MAURICE DE CRESPIGNY.
'Woodlands, February 20th.'

This was the old man's letter. There was not one syllable of its contents which in any way disagreed with the wording of the will.

Launcelot Darrell drew a long breath; and his mother, sitting close to him, with her hand in his, could feel the clammy coldness of his fingers, and hear the loud thumping of his heart against his breast.

Gilbert Monckton took up his hat and walked out of the room. He did not want to have any explanation with the man whom he fully believed – in spite of all Eleanor had said – to be the fortunate rival who had robbed him of every chance of ever winning his wife's heart.

He had only one feeling now; and that was the same feeling which had taken possession of him twenty years before – an eager desire to run away, to escape from his troubles and perplexities, to get free of this horrible atmosphere of deceit and bewilderment; to cast every hope, every dream behind; and to go out into the world once more, joyless, unloved, hopeless; but, at any rate, not the dupe of a false woman's specious pretences.

He went straight back to Tolldale while the crowd at Woodlands slowly dispersed, more or less discontented with the day's proceedings. He went back to the grand old mansion in which he had never known happiness. He asked whether his wife was with Miss Mason. No, the man told him; Mrs Monckton was in her own room, lying down.

This was the very thing he wished. He didn't want to see Eleanor's beautiful face, framed in shining bands of hazel-brown hair; that irresistible face whose influence he dared not trust. He wanted to see his ward alone.

Laura ran out of her dressing-room at the sound of her guardian's footsteps.

'Well!' she cried, 'is it a forgery?'

'Hush, Laura; go back into your room.'

Miss Mason obeyed, and Mr Monckton followed her into the pretty little apartment, which was a modern bower of shining maplewood and flowery chintz, and flimsy lace and muslin, frivolous and airy as the young lady herself.

'Sit down in a comfortable seat, guardian[, she said, fetch]ing the lawyer a slippery chintz-covered lounging-chair, so low as to bring Mr Monckton's knees inconveniently near his chin as he sat in it. 'Sit down and tell me all about it, for goodness gracious sake. *Is* it forged?'

'I don't know, my dear, whether the will is genuine or not. It would be a very difficult question to decide.'

'But oh! good gracious me,' exclaimed Miss Mason, 'how can you be so unkind as to talk about it like that, as if it didn't matter a bit whether the will is forged or not. If it isn't forged, Launcelot isn't bad; and if he isn't bad, of course I may marry him, and the wedding things won't be all wasted. I knew that something would happen to make everything come right.'

'Laura,' cried Mr Monckton, 'you must not talk like this. Do you know that you are no longer a child, and that you are dealing with the most solemn business in a woman's life? I do not know whether the will by which Launcelot Darrell inherits the Woodlands property is genuine or not; I certainly have reason to *think* that it *is* genuine, but I will not take upon myself to speak positively. But however that may be, I know that he is not a good man, and you shall never marry him with my consent.'

The young lady began to cry, and murmured something to the effect that it was cruel to use her so when she was ill, and had been taking oceans of lime-draughts; but Mr Monckton was inflexible.

'If you were to have a dozen illnesses such as this,' he said, 'they would not turn me from my purpose or alter my determination. When I voluntarily took upon myself the custody of your life, Laura, I undertook that charge with the intention of accomplishing it as a sacred duty. I have faltered in that duty; for I suffered you to betroth yourself to a man

whom I have never been able to trust. But it is not yet too late to repair
that error. You shall never marry Launcelot Darrell.'

'Why not? If he didn't commit a forgery, as Eleanor says he did, why
shouldn't I marry him?'

'Because he has never truly loved you, Laura. You admit that he was
Eleanor's suitor before he was yours? You admit that, don't you?'

Miss Mason pouted, and sobbed, and choked once or twice before she
answered. Gilbert Monckton waited impatiently for her reply. He was
about as fit to play the Mentor as the young lady whom he had taken
upon himself to lecture. He was blinded and maddened by passionate
regret, cruel disappointment, wounded pride, every feeling which is most
calculated to paralyze a man's reasoning power, and transform a Solomon
into a fool.

'Yes,' Laura gasped at last; 'he did propose to Eleanor first, certainly.
But then she led him on.'

'She led him on!' cried Mr Monckton. 'How?'

Laura looked at him with a perplexed expression of countenance,
before she replied to this eager question.

'Oh, *you* know!' she said, after a pause; 'I can't exactly describe *how* she
led him on, but she *did* lead him on. She walked with him, and she
talked to him; they were always talking together and leaving me out of
the conversation, which was very rude of them, to say the least, for if I
wasn't intellectual enough for them, and couldn't quite understand what
they were talking about – for Launcelot would talk meta – what's its
name? you know; and who *could* understand such conversation as that? –
they might have talked about things I *do* understand, such as Byron and
Tennyson. And then she took an interest in his pictures, and talked about
chiaro – thingembob, and foreshortening, and middle distances, and
things just like an artist. And then she used to let him smoke in the
breakfast-parlour when she was giving me my music lessons; and I should
like to know who *could* play cinquapated passages in time, with the smell
of tobacco in their nose, and a fidgety young man reading a crackling
newspaper, and killing flies with his pocket-handkerchief against the
window. And then she asked for Rosalind in his picture. But, good
gracious me, it's no good going all over it; she led him on.'

Mr Monckton sighed. There wasn't much in what his ward had said,
but there was quite enough. Eleanor and Launcelot had been happy and
confidential together. They had talked of metaphysics, and literature, and
poetry, and painting. The young artist had lounged away the summer
mornings, smoking and idling in Miss Vane's society.

There was very little in all this, certainly, but quite as much as there
generally is in the history of a modern love affair. The age of romance
is gone, with tournaments, and troubadours, and knight errantry; and

if a young gentleman now-a-days spends money in the purchase of a private box at Covent Garden, and an extra guinea for a bouquet, or procures tickets for a fashionable flower-show, and is content to pass the better part of his mornings amidst the expensive litter of a drawing-room, watching the white fingers of his beloved in the messy mysteries of *Decalcomanie*, he may be supposed to be quite as sincerely devoted as if he were to plant his lady's point-lace parasol cover in his helmet, and gallop away with a view to having his head split open in her service.

Mr Monckton hid his face in his hands and pondered over what he had heard. Yes, his ward's foolish talk revealed to him all the secrets of his wife's heart. He could see the pretty, sunny morning-room, the young man lounging in the open window, with fluttering rose-leaves all about his handsome head. He could see Eleanor seated at the piano, making believe to listen to her pupil, and glancing back at her lover. He made the prettiest cabinet picture out of these materials for his own torment.

'Do you think Eleanor ever loved Launcelot Darrell?' he asked, by-and-by.

'*Do* I think so?' cried Miss Mason. 'Why, of course I do; and that's why she tries to persuade me not to marry him. I love her, and she's very good to me,' Laura added, hastily, half ashamed of having spoken unkindly of the friend who had been so patient with her during the last few days. 'I love her very dearly; but if she hadn't cared for Launcelot Darrell, why did she go against my marrying him?'

Gilbert Monckton groaned aloud. Yes, it must be so. Eleanor had loved Launcelot, and her sudden anger, her violent emotion, had arisen out of her jealousy. She was not a devoted daughter, nursing a dream of vengeance against her dead father's foe; but a jealous and vindictive woman, bent upon avenging an infidelity against herself.

'Laura,' said Mr Monckton, 'call your maid, and tell her to pack your things without a moment's delay.'

'But why?'

'I am going to take you abroad – immediately.'

'Oh, good gracious! And Eleanor——'

'Eleanor will stay here. You and I will go to Nice, Laura, and cure ourselves of our follies – if we can. Don't bring any unnecessary load of luggage. Have your most useful dresses and your linen packed in a couple of portmanteaus, and let all be ready in an hour's time. We must leave Windsor by the four o'clock train.'

'And my wedding things – what am I to do with them?'

'Pack them up. Burn them, if you like,' answered Gilbert Monckton, leaving his ward to get over her astonishment as she best might.

He encountered her maid in the passage.

'Miss Mason's portmanteau must be packed in an hour, Jane,' he said. I am going to take her away at once for change of air.'

Mr Monckton went down stairs to his study, and shutting himself in, wrote a very long letter, the composition of which seemed to give him a great deal of trouble.

He looked at his watch when this letter was finished, folded, and addressed. It was a quarter past two. He went up stairs once more to Laura's dressing-room, and found that young lady in the wildest state of confusion, doing all in her power to hinder her maid, under the pretence of assisting her.

'Put on your bonnet and shawl and go down stairs, Laura,' Mr Monckton said, decisively. 'Jane will never succeed in packing those portmanteaus while you are fidgeting her. Go down into the drawing-room, and wait there till the boxes are packed and we're ready to start.'

'But mustn't I go and say good-bye to Eleanor?'

'Is she still in her own room?'

'Yes, sir,' the maid answered, looking up from the portmanteau before which she was kneeling. 'I peeped into Mrs Monckton's room just now, and she was fast asleep. She has had a great deal of fatigue in nursing Miss Mason.'

'Very well, then, she had better not be disturbed.'

'But if I'm going to Nice,' remonstrated Laura, 'I can't go so far away without saying good-bye to Eleanor. She has been very kind to me, you know.'

'I have changed my mind,' Mr Monckton said; 'I've been thinking over the matter, and I've decided on not taking you to Nice. Torquay will do just as well.'

Miss Mason made a wry face.

'I thought I was to have change of scene,' she said; 'Torquay isn't change of scene, for I went there once when I was a child. I might have forgotten Launcelot in quite a strange place, where people talk bad French and wear wooden shoes, and everything is different, but I shall never forget him at Torquay.'

Gilbert Monckton did not notice his ward's lamentation.

'Miss Mason will want you with her, Jane,' he said to the girl. 'You will get yourself ready, please, as soon as you've packed those portmanteaus.'

He went down stairs again, gave his orders about a carriage to take him to the station, and then walked up and down the drawing-room waiting for his ward.

In half-an-hour both she and her maid were ready. The portmanteaus were put into the carriage – the mail phaeton which had brought Eleanor to Hazlewood two years before – and Mr Monckton drove away from Tolldale Priory without having uttered a word of adieu to his wife.

CHAPTER L

GILBERT'S LETTER

It was late in the afternoon when Eleanor awoke, aroused by the clanging of the dinner-bell in the cupola above her head. She had been worn out by her patient attendance upon Laura during the last week, and had slept very heavily, in spite of her anxiety to hear what had happened at the reading of the will. She had seen very little of her husband since the night of Mr de Crespigny's death, and, though the coldness and restraint of his manner had much distressed her, she had no idea that he was actually alienated from her, or that he had suffered his mind to become filled with suspicions against her.

She opened the door of her room, went out into the corridor, and listened. But all was very still. She could only hear the faint jingling of glass and silver in the hall below, as the old butler went to and fro putting the finishing touches to the dinner-table.

'Mr Monckton might have come to me to tell me about the will,' she thought: 'he must surely know how anxious I am to hear what has been done.'

She bathed her flushed face, and dressed for dinner as usual. She put on a black silk dress out of respect for her father's friend, whose funeral had been solemnized during her sleep, and with a black lace shawl upon her shoulders she went down stairs for look for her husband.

She found all very quiet – unnaturally quiet. It is strange how soon the absence of an accustomed inhabitant makes itself felt in a house, however quiet the habits of that missing person. Eleanor looked into the drawing-room and the study, and found them both empty.

'Where is Mr Monckton?' she asked of the old butler.

'Gone, ma'am.'

'Gone!'

'Yes, ma'am; two hours ago, a'most. You knew he was going, didn't you, ma'am?'

The old man's curiosity was excited by Eleanor's look of surprise.

'Didn't you know as master was a-going to take Miss Mason away to the seaside for change of air, ma'am?' he asked.

'Yes, yes, I knew that he was going to do so, but not immediately. Did Mr Monckton leave no message for me?'

'He left a letter, ma'am. It's on the mantelpiece in the study.'

Eleanor went to her husband's room with her heart beating high, and her cheeks flushed with indignation against him for the slight he had put upon her. Yes; there was the letter, sealed with his signet-ring. He was not generally in the habit of sealing his letters, so he must have looked

upon this as one of some importance. Mrs Monckton tore open the
envelope. She turned pale as she read the first few lines of the letter. It
was written over two sheets of note paper, and began thus:–

'Eleanor,

'When I asked you to be my wife I told you that in my early youth I
had been deceived by a woman whom I loved very dearly, though not as
dearly as I have since loved you. I told you this, and I implored you to
remember my blighted youth, and to have pity upon me. I entreated you
to spare me the anguish of a second betrayal, a second awakening from
my dream of happiness.

'Surely, if you had not been the most cruel of women, you would have
been touched by the knowledge that I had already suffered so bitterly
from a woman's treachery, and you would have had mercy upon me. But
you had no mercy. It suited you to come back to this neighbourhood, to
be near your former lover, Launcelot Darrell.'

The letter dropped from Eleanor's hands as she read these words.

'My former lover!' she cried; 'my lover, Launcelot Darrell! Can my
husband think that? *Can* he think that I ever loved Launcelot Darrell?'

She picked up the letter and seated herself at her husband's writing-
table. Then she deliberately reperused the first page of the lawyer's epistle.

'How could he write such a letter?' she exclaimed, indignantly. 'How
could he think such cruel things of me after I had told him the truth –
after I had revealed the secret of my life?'

She went on with the latter: –

'From the hour of our return to Tolldale, Eleanor,' wrote Gilbert
Monckton, 'I knew the truth – the hard and cruel truth – very difficult
for a man to believe, when he has built up his life and mapped out a
happy future under the influence of a delusion which leaves him desolate
when it melts away. I knew the worst. I watched you as a man only
watches the woman upon whose truth his every hope depends, and I saw
that you still loved Launcelot Darrell. By a hundred evidences, small in
themselves, but damning when massed together, you betrayed your
secret. You had made a mercenary marriage, looking to worldly
advantages to counterbalance your sacrifice of feeling; and you found too
late that the sacrifice was too hard for you to bear.

'I watched you day by day, and hour by hour; and I saw that as the time
for Laura's marriage approached, you grew hourly more unhappy, more
restless, more impatient and capricious in your manner towards Launcelot.

'On the night of Maurice de Crespigny's death the storm burst. You
met Launcelot Darrell in the Woodlands garden – perhaps by chance,

perhaps by appointment. You tried to dissuade him against the marriage with Laura, as you had tried to dissuade Laura from marrying him; and, failing in this, you gave way to a frenzy of jealousy, and accused your false lover of an impossible crime.

'Remember, Eleanor, I accuse you of no deadly sin, no *deliberate* treachery to me. The wrong you have done me lies in the fact that you married me while your heart was still given to another. I give you credit for having tried to conquer that fatal attachment, and I attribute your false accusations against Launcelot Darrell to a mad impulse of jealousy, rather than the studied design of a base woman. I try to think well of you, Eleanor, for I have loved you most dearly; and the new life that I had made for myself owed all its brightness to my hope of winning your regard. But it is not to be so. I bow my head to the decree, and I release you from a bond that has no doubt grown odious to you.

'I beg you, therefore, to write me a final letter, demanding such terms of separation as you may think fit. Let the ground of our parting be incompatibility of temper. Everything shall be done to render your position honourable; and I trust to you to preserve the name of Gilbert Monckton's wife without taint or blemish. Signora Picirillo will no doubt act for you in this business, and consent to assume the position of your guardian and friend. I leave you in full possession of Tolldale Priory, and I go to Torquay with my ward, whence I shall depart for the Continent as soon as our separation has been adjusted, and my business arrangements made.

'My address for the next fortnight will be the Post-office, Torquay.

'GILBERT MONCKTON.'

This was the letter which the lawyer had written to his young wife. Its contents were like a thunderbolt in the shock which they caused to Eleanor's senses. She sat for a long time, reading it over and over again. For the first time since her marriage she put aside the thought of her revenge, and began to think seriously of something else.

It was too cruel. Unmixed indignation was the feeling which took possession of her mind. She had no comprehension of the despair which had filled Gilbert Monckton's breast as he wrote that farewell letter. She did not know how the strong man had done battle with his suspicions, struggling with every new doubt, and conquering it as it arose, only to be conquered himself at last, by the irresistible force of circumstances, every one of which seemed a new evidence against his wife. Eleanor could not know this. She only knew that her husband had most bitterly wronged her, and she could feel nothing but indignation – yet.

She tore the letter into a hundred fragments. She wanted to annihilate its insulting accusations. How dared he think so vilely of her? Then a feeling of despair sank into her breast, like some actual burden, chill and heavy, that bowed her down to the earth, and for the time paralyzed her energies.

Nothing but failure had met her upon every side. She had been too late in her attempt to see Maurice de Crespigny before his death. She had failed to prove Launcelot Darrell's guilt; though the evidence of his crime had been in her hands, though she had been herself the witness of his wrong-doing. Everything had been against her. The chance which had thrown her across the pathway of the very man she wished to meet had only given rise to delusive hopes, and had resulted in utter defeat.

And now she found herself suspected and deserted by her husband — the man whom she had loved and respected with every better feeling of a generous nature that had become warped and stunted by the all-absorbing motive of her life. In her indignation against Gilbert Monckton her hatred of Launcelot Darrell became even more bitter than before, for it was he who had caused all this — it was he whose treachery had been the blight of her existence, from the hour of her father's death until now.

While Eleanor sat thinking over her husband's letter, the old butler came to announce dinner, which had been waiting some time for her coming. I fancy the worthy retainer had been prowling about the hall meanwhile with the hope of surprising the clue to some domestic mystery in his mistress's face as she emerged from the study.

Mrs Monckton went into the dining-room and made a show of eating her dinner. She had a motive for doing this, beyond the desire to keep up appearances which seemed natural even to the most impulsive people. She wanted to hear all about Mr de Crespigny's will, and she knew that Jeffreys, the butler, was sure to be pretty well informed upon the subject.

She took her accustomed seat at the dinner-table, and Mr Jeffreys placed himself behind her. She took a spoonful of clear soup, and then began to trifle with her spoon.

'Have you heard about Mr de Crespigny's will, Jeffreys?' she asked.

'Well, ma'am, to tell the truth, we had Mr Banks, the baker, from Hazlewood village, in the servants' hall not a quarter of an hour ago, and he *do* say that Mr Darrell has got all his great-uncle's estate, real and personil — leastways, with the exception of hannuities to the two old mai—— the Miss de Crespignys, ma'am, and bein' uncommon stingy in their dealin's, no one will regret as *they* don't come into the fortune. Sherry, ma'am, or 'ock?'

Eleanor touched one of the glasses before her almost mechanically, and waited while the old man — who was not so skilful and rapid as he had been in the time of Gilbert Monckton's father — poured out some wine and removed her soup-plate.

'Yes, ma'am,' he continued, 'Banks of Hazlewood do say that Mr Darrell have got the fortune. He heard it from Mrs Darrell's 'ousemaid, which Mrs Darrell told all the servants directly as she come back from Woodlands, and were all of a tremble like with joy, the 'ousemaid said; but Mr Launcelot, he were as white as a sheet, and hadn't a word to say to any one, except the foreign gentleman that he is so friendly with.'

Eleanor paid very little attention to all these details. She only thought of the main fact. The desperate game which Launcelot had played had been successful. The victory was his.

Mrs Monckton went from the dinner-table to her own room, and with her own hands dragged a portmanteau out of a roomy old-fashioned lumber-closet, and began to pack her plainest dresses and the necessaries of her simple toilet.

'I will leave Tolldale to-morrow morning,' she said. 'I will at least prove to Mr Monckton that I do not wish to enjoy the benefits of a *mercenary* marriage. I will leave this place and begin the world again. Richard was right; my dream of vengeance was a foolish dream. I suppose it is right, after all, that wicked people should succeed in this world, and we must be content to stand by and see them triumph.'

Eleanor could not think without some bitterness of Laura's abrupt departure. *She* could not have been actuated by the same motives that had influenced Gilbert Monckton. Why, then, had she left without a word of farewell? Why, Launcelot Darrell was the cause of this sorrow as well as of every other, for it was jealousy about him that had prejudiced Laura against her friend.

Early the next morning Eleanor Monckton left Tolldale Priory. She went to the station at Windsor in a pony carriage which had been reserved for the use of herself and Laura Mason. She took with her only one portmanteau, her desk, and dressing-case.

'I am going alone, Martin,' she said to the maid whom Mr Monckton had engaged to attend upon her. 'You know that I am accustomed to wait upon myself, and I do not think you could be accommodated where I am going.'

'But you will not be away long, ma'am, shall you?' the young woman asked.

'I don't know. I cannot tell you. I have written to Mr Monckton,' Eleanor answered, hurriedly.

In the bleak early spring morning she left the home in which she had known very little happiness. She looked back at the stately old-fashioned mansion with a regretful sigh.

How happy she *might* have been within those ivied walls! How happy she might have been with her husband and Laura; but for the one hindering cause, the one fatal obstacle – Launcelot Darrell. She thought of what her life might have been, but for the remembrance of that solemn vow which was perpetually urging her on to its fulfilment. The love of a good man, the caressing affection of a gentle girl, the respect of every living creature round about her, might have been hers; but for Launcelot Darrell.

She looked back at the old house, gleaming redly behind the leafless branches of the bare oaks that sheltered it. She could see the oriel window of the morning-room that Gilbert Monckton had furnished on purpose for her, the dark crimson of the voluminous curtains, and a Parian statuette, of his own choosing, glittering whitely against the red light of the fire within. She saw all this, and regretted it; but her pride was soothed by the thought that she was running away from this luxurious home, and all its elegance, to go out alone into a bleak, uncomfortable world.

'He shall know, at least, that I did not marry him for the sake of a fine house and horses and carriages,' she thought, as she watched the terrace chimneys disappear behind the trees. 'However meanly he thinks of me, he shall have no cause to think that.'

It was still very early in the day when Eleanor arrived in London. She was determined not to go to the Signora, since she must relate all that had happened, and would no doubt have considerable difficulty in convincing her old friend that she had chosen the right course.

'The Signora would want me to go back to Tolldale, and to try and justify myself in the opinion of Gilbert Monckton,' Eleanor thought. 'But I will never humiliate myself to him. He has wronged me; and the consequences of that wrong must rest upon his own head.'

You see, this young lady's nature was as undisciplined as it had been in her girlhood, when she flung herself on her knees in the little Parisian chamber to take an oath of vengeance against her father's destroyer. She had not yet learnt to submit. She had not yet learnt the most sublime lesson that the Gospel teaches, to suffer unmerited wrong, and 'take it patiently.'

The letter she had written to Gilbert Monckton was very brief.

'Gilbert,' she wrote, 'you have most cruelly wronged me, and I cannot doubt that the day will come in which you will know how baseless your suspicions have been. Every word that I uttered in Mr de Crespigny's house upon the night of the death was true. I am quite powerless to prove my truth, and I cannot be content to see Launcelot Darrell triumph. The mystery of the lost will is more than I can comprehend, but I declare that it was in my possession five minutes before I met you in the garden. If ever that will should be found, my justification will be found with it. I look to you to watch my interests in this matter, but I am quite incapable of remaining an inmate of your house while you think me the base creature I should be if my accusations against Launcelot Darrell were in the slightest degree false. I will never return to Tolldale until my truth has been proved. You need not fear that I will do anything to bring discredit upon your name. I go out into the world to get my own living, as I have done before.

'ELEANOR MONCKTON.'

This letter expressed very little of the indignation which filled Eleanor's breast. Her pride revolted against the outrage which her husband had inflicted upon her; and she suffered all the more acutely because beneath her apparent indifference there lurked, in the innermost recesses of her heart, a true and pure affection for this cruel Gilbert Monckton, whose causeless suspicions had so deeply wounded her.

In proportion to the strength of her love was the force of her indignation, and she went away from Tolldale with angry thoughts raging in her breast, and buoying her up with a factitious courage.

This influence was still at work when she reached London. She had only a few pounds in her purse, and it was necessary therefore that she should begin to get her own living immediately. She had thought of this during her journey between Windsor and London, and had determined what to do. She took a cab, and drove to a quiet little hotel in the neighbourhood of the Strand, left her portmanteau and other packages there, and then walked to a certain institution for governesses in the neighbourhood of Cavendish Square. She had been there before, during her residence with the Signora, to make an inquiry about pupils for the pianoforte, but had never given her name to the principal.

'I must call myself by a new name,' she thought, 'if I want to hide myself from Gilbert Monckton and from the Signora. I must write to her directly, by the bye, poor dear, and tell her that I am safe and well; or else she will be making herself unhappy about me, directly she hears I have left Tolldale.'

The principal of the Governesses' Institution was a stately maiden lady, with a rustling silk dress and glossy braids of grey hair under a cap of point lace. She received Eleanor with solemn graciousness, demanded her requirements and her qualifications, and then, with a gold pencil-case poised lightly between the tips of her taper fingers, deliberated for a few minutes.

Eleanor sat opposite to her, watching her face very anxiously. She wanted some home, some asylum, some hiding-place from a world that seemed altogether against her. She scarcely cared where or what the place of refuge might be. She wanted to get away from Gilbert Monckton, who had wronged and insulted her, and from Launcelot Darrell, whose treachery was always strong enough to triumph over the truth.

But of course she didn't say this. She only said that she wanted a situation as musical governess, nursery governess, or companion, and that the amount of salary was of very little importance to her.

'I understand,' the lady principal replied, slowly, 'I perfectly understand your feeling, Miss—— Miss——'

'My name is Villars,' Eleanor answered, quickly, looking down at her muff as she spoke,

The lady principal's eyes followed her, and looked at the muff too. It was a very handsome sable muff, which had cost five-and-twenty pounds, and had been given by Mr Monckton to his wife at the beginning of the winter. It was not at all in accord with Eleanor's plain merino dress and woollen shawl, or with her desire to go out as a governess without consideration of salary. Miss Barkham, the lady principal, began to look rather suspiciously at her visitor's handsome face, and forgot to finish the sentence she had commenced.

'You can command excellent references, Miss Villars, I suppose?' she said, coldly.

Eleanor flushed crimson. Here was an insurmountable difficulty at the very outset.

'References,' she stammered, 'will references be necessary?'

'Most decidedly. We could not think of sending out any young lady from this establishment who could not command first-class references or testimonials. Some people are satisfied with written testimonials; for myself, I consider a personal reference indispensable, and I would not upon my own authority engage any lady without one.'

Eleanor looked very much distressed. She had no idea of diplomatizing or prevaricating. She blurted out the truth all at once, unappalled by the stern glances of Miss Barkham.

'I can't possibly give you a reference,' she said; 'my friends do not know that I am in search of a situation, and they must not know it. I assure you that I belong to a very respectable family, and am quite competent to do what I profess to do.'

CHAPTER LI

MRS MAJOR LENNARD

Miss Barkham stared at her visitor with a look of mingled horror and astonishment.

'You do not surely imagine, Miss Villars,' she said, 'that anybody will engage you in the responsible position of governess to their children upon no better recommendation than your own, I must confess, rather *confident* assertion of your merits?'

'I never told a falsehood in my life, Miss Barkham,' Eleanor answered, indignantly. 'If I am without a friend whom I can ask to testify to my respectability, it is on account of circumstances which——'

'To be sure,' exclaimed Miss Barkham; 'that is the very thing we have to contend against. This establishment is completely overrun by young ladies who think there is nothing easier than to turn their backs upon their friends and their homes, and go out into the world to become the instructresses of the rising generation. You think me very punctilious and strait-laced, I dare say, Miss Villars; but I don't know what would become of the rising generation if *somebody* didn't keep watch and ward over the doors of the schoolroom. Young ladies who choose to feel unhappy in the society of their parents; young ladies who are disappointed in some sentimental affection; young ladies who fancy themselves ill-used by their elder sisters; young ladies who, from the very shallowness of their own minds, cannot be contented anywhere, all come to us, and want to go out as governesses, – just for a change, they say, in the hope of finding a little employment that will divert their minds; as if they had any minds to be diverted! These are the amateur hangers-on of a very grave and respectable profession, to which hundreds of estimable and accomplished women have devoted the best and brightest years of their lives. These are the ignorant and superficial pretenders who bring their cheap and worthless wares into the market, in order to undersell the painstaking and patient teachers who have themselves learned the lessons they profess to teach. And these amateurs will continue to flourish, Miss Villars, so long as ladies, who would shudder at the idea of entrusting an expensive silk dress to an incompetent dressmaker, are willing to confide the care of their children to an instructress whose highest merit lies in the fact that she is – cheap. I do not wish to wound your feelings, Miss Villars; but I assure you I often feel sick at heart, when I see a lady who offers thirty years' experience, and all the treasures of a mind carefully and sedulously cultivated, rejected in favour of some chit of nineteen who can play one showy fantasia, and disfigure glass vases with scraps of painted paper, and who will accept twenty pounds a year in payment of services that are not worth five.'

Eleanor smiled at Miss Barkham's energetic protest.

'I dare say you are often very much worried by incompetent people,' she said; 'but I assure you *I* have made no attempt to deceive you. I don't profess to do much, you know. I believe I can play pretty well. May I play you something?' she asked, pointing to an open pianoforte at one end of the room, a handsome grand, with all Erard's patient improvements, on which governesses upon their promotion were in the habit of showing off.

'I have no objection to hear you play,' Miss Barkham answered; 'but remember, I cannot possibly procure you a situation without either references or testimonials.'

Eleanor went to the piano, took off her gloves, and ran her fingers over the keys. She had played very little during the last few months, for in the feverish preoccupation of her mind she had been unequal to any feminine employment; too restless and unsettled to do anything but roam about the house, or sit brooding silently with her hands lying idle in her lap.

The familiar touch of the keys filled her with a strange pleasure: she was surprised at the brilliancy of her execution, as good players often are after an interval of idleness. She played one of Beethoven's most sparkling sonatas; and even Miss Barkham, who was perpetually listening to such performances, murmured a few words of praise.

But before Eleanor had been seated at the piano more than five minutes, a servant came into the room and presented a card to Miss Barkham, who rose from her seat with some appearance of vexation.

'Really, I scarcely know what to do about it,' she muttered to herself. 'It's almost impossible to arrange anything at such very short notice. Excuse me, Miss Villars,' she added, aloud, to Eleanor; 'I am obliged to see a lady in the next room. Don't go until I return.'

Eleanor bowed, and went on playing. She finished the sonata; and then, suddenly catching sight of her wedding-ring and the thick band of gold studded with diamonds that her husband had given her on her wedding-day, she stopped to draw the two rings off her finger, and put them into her purse amongst the few sovereigns that formed her whole stock of worldly wealth.

She sighed as she did this, for it seemed like putting off her old life altogether.

'It's better so,' she said to herself; 'I know now that Gilbert must have thought me false to him from the very first. I can understand his cold reserve *now*, though it used to puzzle me so much. He changed almost immediately after our marriage.'

Eleanor Monckton grew very pensive as she remembered that she had been perhaps herself to blame for the altered manner and no doubt equally altered feelings of her husband. She had neglected her duty as a wife, absorbed in her affection as a daughter; she had sacrificed the living to the dead; and she began to think that Richard Thornton's advice had been wiser than she had believed when she refused to listen to it. She had been wrong altogether. Classic vows of vengeance were all very well in the days when a Medea rode upon flying dragons and slaughtered her children upon principle; but a certain inspired teacher, writing a very long time after that much-to-be-regretted classic age, has declared that vengeance is the right of divinity alone, and far too terrible an attribute to be tampered with by fallible mortals, blindly hurling the bolts of heaven against each other's earthly heads.

She thought this, and grew very melancholy and uncomfortable, and began to fancy that her impulses had been about the worst guides that she could have chosen. She began to think that she had not acted so very wisely in running away from Tolldale Priory in the first heat of her indignation, and that she might have done better perhaps by writing a temperate letter of justification to Gilbert Monckton, and quietly abiding the issue. But she had chosen her path now, and must stand by her choice, on pain of appearing the weakest and most cowardly of women.

'My letter is posted,' she said to herself. 'Gilbert will receive it to-morrow morning. I *should* be a coward to go back; for, however much I may have been to blame in the matter, he has treated me very badly.'

She wiped away some tears that had come into her eyes as she took the rings from her wedding finger, and then began to play again.

This time she dashed into one of the liveliest and most brilliant fantasias she could remember, a very *pot pourri* of airs; a scientific hodge-podge of Scotch melodies; now joyous, now warlike and savage, now plaintive and tender, always capricious in the extreme, and running away every now and then into the strangest variations, the most eccentric cadences. The piece was one of Thalberg's *chef-d'oeuvres*, and Eleanor played it magnificently. As she struck the final chord, sharp and rapid as a rattling peal of musketry, Miss Barkham re-entered the room.

She had the air of being rather annoyed, and she hesitated a little before speaking to Eleanor, who rose from the piano and began to put on her gloves.

'Really, Miss Villars,' she said, 'it is most incomprehensible to me, but since Mrs Lennard herself wishes it, I——'

She stopped and fidgeted a little with the gold pencil-case hanging to her watch-chain.

'I can't at all understand this sort of thing,' she resumed; 'however, of course I wash my hands of all responsibility. Have you any objection to travel, Miss Villars?' she asked, suddenly.

Eleanor opened her eyes with a look of astonishment at this abrupt question.

'Objection to travel?' she repeated; I——'

'Have you any objection to go abroad – to Paris, for instance, – if I could obtain you a situation?'

'Oh, no,' Eleanor answered, with a sigh, 'not at all; I would just as soon go to Paris as anywhere else.'

'Very well, then, if that is the case, I think I can get you a situation immediately. There is a lady in the next room who was here yesterday, and who really gave me a most severe headache with her fidgety, childish ways.

However, she wants to meet with a young lady as a companion *immediately* – that is the grand difficulty. She leaves London for Paris by this evening's mail, and she put off engaging the person she required until yesterday afternoon, when she came to me in a fever of anxiety, and wanted me to introduce her to a lady instanter. She stopped all the afternoon in the next room, and I took ever so many young ladies in to her, all of whom seemed well qualified for the situation, which really demands very little. But not one of them would suit Mrs Lennard. She was very polite to them, and made all kinds of affable speeches to them, and dismissed them in the most ladylike manner; and then she told me afterwards that she didn't take a fancy to them, and she was determined not to engage any one she didn't take a fancy to, as she wanted to be very fond of her companion, and make quite a sister of her. That was what she said, and good gracious me,' cried Miss Barkham, 'how am I to find her somebody she can take a fancy to, and make a sister of, at a quarter-of-an-hour's notice? I assure you, Miss Villars, my head felt quite in a whirl after she went away yesterday afternoon; and it's beginning to be in a whirl again now.'

Eleanor waited very patiently while Miss Barkham endeavoured to collect her scattered senses.

'I can scarcely hope this very capricious lady will take a fancy to me,' she said, smiling.

'Why, my dear,' exclaimed Miss Barkham, 'that's the very thing I came to tell you. She *has* taken a fancy to you.'

'Taken a fancy to me!' repeated Eleanor; 'but she has not seen me.'

'Of course not, my dear. But she really is the most confusing, I may almost say bewildering, person, I ever remember meeting with. I was in the next room talking to Mrs Lennard, who is very pretty and fashionable-looking, only a little untidy in her dress, when you began to play that Scotch fantasia. Mrs Lennard stopped to listen, and after she had listened a few moments she cried out suddenly, "Now I dare say that's an old frump!" I said, "What, ma'am?" for upon my word, my dear, I didn't know whether she meant the piece, or the piano, or what. "I dare say the lady who is playing is an old frump," she said. "Old frumps almost always play well; in point of fact old frumps are generally very clever. But I'm determined not to have any one I can't make a sister of, and I *must* have one by three o'clock this afternoon, or Major Lennard will be cross, and I shall go mad." Well, Miss Villars, I told Mrs Lennard your age, and described your appearance and manners, that is to say, as well as I was able to do so after our very brief acquaintance, and I had no sooner finished than she exclaimed, "That will do; if she can play Scotch melodies like that, and is nice, I'll engage her." I then explained to Mrs Lennard that you could give no references; "and that, of course," I added, "would be an insuperable objection;" but she interrupted me in a manner that would have appeared very impertinent in any one but her, and cried out, "Insuperable fiddlesticks! If she's nice I'll engage her. She can play to me all the morning, while I paint upon velvet;" and you're to come with me, please, Miss Villars, and be introduced to her.'

Eleanor took up her muff and followed Miss Barkham on to the landing, but at this moment three ladies appeared upon the top stair, and the principal of the establishment was called upon to receive them.

'If you'll go in by yourself, my dear,' she whispered to Eleanor, pointing to the door of the back drawing-room, 'I shall be much obliged. You'll find Mrs Lennard a most affable person.'

Eleanor readily assented. She opened the door and went into the primly-furnished back drawing-room. Mrs Major Lennard was a little woman, and she was standing on tiptoe upon the hearth-rug, in order to survey herself in the chimney-glass while she re-arranged the pale blue strings of her black velvet bonnet. Eleanor paused near the door, waiting for her to turn round, and wondering what she was like, as the face in the glass was not visible from where Mrs Monckton stood.

The lady employed a considerable time in the important operation of tying her bonnet-strings, then suddenly hearing the rustlings of Eleanor's dress as she advanced a few paces, Mrs Lennard uttered an exclamation, and turned round.

'You naughty girl, you quite startled me,' she cried.

Not so much as she had startled Eleanor, who could not repress a cry of surprise at the sight of her face. It was a very pretty face, very young-looking, though Mrs Major Lennard was nearly forty years of age. A fair childish face, with pink cheeks, turquoise-blue eyes, and the palest, softest bands of flaxen hair; rather an insipid, German kind of beauty, perhaps, but very perfect of its kind.

But that which had startled Eleanor was not the babyish, delicate prettiness of the face, but the strong resemblance which it bore to Laura Mason. It was the same face after twenty years, not of wear and tear, but of very careful preservation. This lady, in appearance and manner, was exactly what Laura must most surely become if she lived to be seven-and-thirty years of age.

CHAPTER LII

GOING BACK TO PARIS

Eleanor was so completely bewildered by this extraordinary likeness that she remained for some moments staring at Mrs Major Lennard in silent surprise.

'Goodness me, my dear!' exclaimed the lady, 'how astonished you look! I hope I'm not a GUY. Frederick – that's Major Lennard, you know – never liked this bonnet, and really I'm beginning quite to dislike it myself. I do think it's *pokey*. But never mind that, my dear Miss – Villars, I think Miss Barkham said, – a very nice person, Miss Barkham, isn't she? but rather prim. I've got all sorts of business to settle between this and eight o'clock, for Fred *will* travel by the night mail, because he sleeps all the way, and of course that makes the journey shorter – in consequence of which I've never seen Dover, except in the dark, and I always think of it with the lamps lighted and the pier slippery, and everybody hurrying and pushing, like a place in a dream. But the first question, my dear, that we've got to settle, is whether you like me, and think you could make a sister of me?'

This question, asked very eagerly, was really too much for poor Eleanor.

'Oh, please don't look so surprised,' Mrs Lennard exclaimed, entreatingly; 'you make me fancy I'm a guy, and you see there's really no time to be lost, and we must decide immediately if you please. I was here all yesterday afternoon, and I saw legions of ladies, but there wasn't one that I could take a fancy to, and my only motive for engaging a companion is to have somebody that I shall like very much, and always feel at home with; and I want some one who can play the piano and be agreeable and lively, and I'm sure you're the very person, dear, and if you only think you can like me as well as I'm sure I shall like you, we can settle the business at once.'

'But you know that I can give you no references,' Eleanor said, hesitatingly.

'Of course I do,' answered Mrs Lennard. 'Miss Barkham told me all about it. As *if* I thought you'd committed a murder, or done something horrid, just because you can't pounce upon half-a-dozen people ready to declare you're an uncanonized saint all in a moment. I like your looks, my dear, and when I like people's looks at first sight, I generally like *them* afterwards. And you play magnificently; I only wish I could; and I used to play the overture to "Semiramide" before I was married, but as Frederick doesn't like overtures, and as we've been scampering about the world ever since, in the cabins of ships, and in tents, and all sorts of places where you couldn't have pianos unless you had them made on purpose, without legs, I've gone backwards in my music till I can't play so much as a polka, without skipping the difficult parts.'

Mrs Lennard went on to say that the matter of salary was a question to be settled between Miss Villars and the Major.

'I always leave money matters to Frederick,' she said, 'for though he can't add up the bills, he looks as if he could, and that's *some* check upon

people. But you'll have to wait for your quarter's money now and then, I
dare say, dear, because we're often a little behind-hand, you know, and if
you don't mind that, it'll be all the better for you, as Fred's almost sure to
give you a silk dress when your quarter comes due and he can't pay you;
that's what he calls a sop to Cerberus, and I'm sure the money he spends
in keeping people "sweet," as he calls it, would keep us altogether if we
paid ready money. Now, is it a settled thing, Miss Villars? Will you accept
the situation?'

Eleanor assented without hesitation. She heard very little of Mrs
Lennard's good-natured babble. Her whole mind was absorbed by the
sense of her defeat, and by the feeling that she had no further chance of
victory over Launcelot Darrell. She despaired, but she did not submit.
She was only desperate and reckless, ready to go anywhere, and finish the
useless remainder of her existence anyhow. She was not prepared to begin
a new life upon a new plan, casting the old scheme of her life behind her,
as a mistake and a delusion. She was not able to do this yet.

While Mrs Lennard was gathering together a lot of frivolous looking
little whity-brown paper parcels that seemed to bear a strong family
resemblance to herself, Miss Barkham came into the room to ascertain
the result of the interview between the two ladies. Mrs Lennard
expressed herself in the most rapturous manner about Eleanor, paid some
small fee for the benefit of the institution, and departed, carrying her
parcels and taking Eleanor with her.

She allowed her companion to assist her with the parcels, after a little
good-natured contention, and at the nearest corner summoned a cab
which was dawdling lazily along.

'Of course the man will overcharge us,' Mrs Lennard said, 'but we must
be prepared for that, and really I'd rather be overcharged than have a row,
as we generally have when I'm with the major, and summonses and
counter-summonses, and all sorts of disagreeables; not that I mind that
half so much as foreign cabmen, who get excited, and dance upon the
pavement and make wild noises if you don't satisfy them; and I'm sure I
don't know what *would* satisfy foreign cabmen.'

Mrs Lennard took out her watch, which was a pretty little Geneva toy
with an enamelled back, ornamented with the holes that had once held
diamonds. An anxious and intensely studious expression came over Mrs
Lennard's face as she looked at this watch, which was overweighted by a
heap of incomprehensible charms, amongst which chaotic mass of golden
frivolity, a skeleton, a watering-pot, a coffin, and a Dutch oven were
distinguishable.

'It's half-past five by *me*,' Mrs Lennard said, after a profound
contemplation of the Geneva, 'so I should think it must be *about* a
quarter to three.'

Eleanor took out her own watch and settled the question. It was only half-past two.

'Then I've gained another quarter of an hour,' exclaimed Mrs Lennard: 'that's the worst of pretty watches; they always will go too much, or else stop altogether. Freddy bought me my watch, and he gave me my choice as to whether he should spend the money in purple enamel and diamonds, or works, and I chose the purple enamel. But then, of course, I didn't know the diamonds would drop out directly,' Mrs Lennard added, thoughtfully.

She drove about to half-a-dozen shops, and collected more whity-brown paper parcels, a band-box, a bird-cage, a new carpet-bag, a dog's collar, a packet of tea, and other incongruous merchandise, and then ordered the man to drive to the Great Northern Hotel.

'We're staying at the Great Northern, my dear,' she said, after giving this order. 'We very often stay at hotels, for Frederick thinks it's cheaper to pay fifteen shillings a day for your rooms than to have a house, and servants' wages, and coals and candles, and lard, and blacklead, and hearthstone, and all those little things that run away with so much money. And I should like the Great Northern very much if the corridors weren't so long and the waiters so stern. I always think waiters at grand hotels *are* stern. They seem to look at one as if they knew one was thinking of the bill, and trying to calculate whether it would be under ten pounds. But, oh, good gracious!' exclaimed Mrs Lennard, suddenly, 'what a selfish creature I am; I've quite forgotten all this time that of course you'll want to go home to your mamma and papa, and tell them where you're going, and get your boxes packed, and all that.'

Eleanor shook her head with a sad smile.

'I have no mother or father to consult,' she said; 'I am an orphan.'

'Are you?' cried Mrs Lennard; 'then it must have been our destiny to meet, for I am an orphan, too. Ma died while I was a baby, and poor pa died soon after my marriage. He was disappointed in my marriage, poor dear old thing, though I'm glad to think it wasn't that, but gout in the stomach, that killed him. But you'll want to see your friends, Miss Villars, won't you, before you leave London?'

'No,' Eleanor answered: 'I shall write to the only friends I have. I don't want to see any one; I don't want any one to know where I am going. I left my portmanteau at an hotel in Norfolk Street, and I shall be glad if you will let me call for it.'

Mrs Lennard gave the necessary order; the cabman drove to the hotel where Eleanor had left her portmanteau, and thence to the Great Northern, where Mrs Lennard conducted her new companion to a very handsome apartment on the ground-floor, opening into a palatial bed-chamber, whose splendour was a good deal impaired by the circumstances that the stately Arabian bed, the massive easy-chairs, the sofa, the dressing-table, and even the washhand-stand were loaded with divers articles of male and female attire, which seemed to have been flung here and there by some harmless maniac disporting himself about the room.

In the very centre of all this disorder, upon a great black leather military travelling-case, sat a big broad-chested man of about forty, with a good-natured, sunburnt face, a very fierce auburn moustache, and a thick stubble of crisp, wavy, auburn hair, cut close to his head, in the development of which a disciple of Mr George Coombe would have scarcely discovered the organs that make a man either a general or a philosopher. This sunburnt, good-humoured looking gentleman had taken off his coat for the better accomplishment of his herculean labours; and, with his arms folded and his legs crossed, with an embroidered slipper balanced upon the extremity of his toes, and a meerschaum pipe in his mouth, he sat resting himself, after taking the initiatory step of dragging everything out of the drawers and wardrobe.

'Oh, you *lazy* Freddy!' cried Mrs Lennard, looking in at her lord and master with a reproachful countenance, 'is that all you've done?'

'Where's the blue barège with the flounces to go?' roared the major, in the voice of an amiable Stentor. 'I couldn't do anything till I knew that, and I've been waiting for you to come home. Have you got a companion?'

'Hush! yes! she's in the next room; such a dear, and awfully pretty. If you stare at her much I shall be jealous, Freddy, for you know you *are* a starer, though you never will confess it. *I've* seen you, in Regent Street, when you've thought I've been looking at the bonnets,' added the lady, reproachfully.

Upon this the major got up, and, lifting his wife in his arms, gave her such a hug as a well-disposed bear might have bestowed upon the partner of his den. Major Lennard was about six feet one and a half in the embroidered slippers, and was as strong as a gladiator in good training.

'Come and be introduced to her,' exclaimed Mrs Lennard; and she led her husband, in his shirt-sleeves, nothing abashed, into the adjoining sitting-room.

The major's conversational powers were not very startling. He made a few remarks about the weather, which were more courteous than original. He asked Eleanor if she was hungry, if she would have luncheon, or wait for a six o'clock dinner, and if she was a good sailor. Then, suddenly coming to a standstill, he demanded soda water and brandy.

It was the habit of this amiable man to require this beverage on every possible occasion. He was by no means a drunkard, though he was one of those good-natured noisy creatures who can never be convivial without getting tipsy; but his existence was one perpetual absorption of soda water and brandy. Why he drank this mixture, which the uninitiated are apt to consider insipid, was a mystery only to be explained by himself. He could not have been perpetually thirsty; and I am inclined to think that this soda water and brandy was the desperate resource of a feeble intellect craving some employment, rather than a physical want.

The major and his wife retired to the bedroom and began their packing. When matters grew very desperate Eleanor was summoned as a forlorn hope, and did her best to reduce the chaos into something like order. This process occupied the time until six o'clock, when the major put on his coat and sat down to dinner.

But even during dinner the packing business was not altogether suspended, for every now and then, when there was a little pause in the banquet, Mrs Lennard jumped up from the table, and ran into the next room with her workbox, or her desk, or something from the mantelpiece or one of the sofa-tables – sometimes a book, sometimes a paper-knife, a thimble, a pair of scissors, a pen-wiper, or a packet of envelopes, – and then scampered back to her place before the waiter re-entered the room, and tried to look as if she hadn't left her seat. The major meanwhile worked steadily on with his knife and fork, only looking up from his plate to attend to the wants of Eleanor and his wife.

At last everything was ready. The addresses were fastened to the boxes and portmanteaus. A bewildering canary-bird – which rejoiced in every kind of noise and confusion, and had been excruciatingly loud and shrill all the afternoon – was inducted into the new brass cage which Mrs Lennard had bought for it. A sharp little black-and-tan terrier, the property of the major, was invested in the new collar, and securely padlocked; Eleanor and Mrs Lennard put on their shawls and bonnets; the major made himself gigantic by the addition of a rough great-coat, a Scotch plaid, and half-a-dozen yards of woollen comforter to his normal bulk; the bill was paid at the very last moment, while the luggage was being piled up on the top of an extra cab; and Major Lennard and his companions departed at a rattling pace for the London Bridge terminus. There was just time enough for the major to get the tickets and choose a comfortable carriage, before the train started. Away they flew through the darkness of the bleak March night, and Eleanor felt that every throb of the shrieking engine made the step that she had taken more irrevocable.

'There was not a word in Gilbert's letter that expressed sorrow at parting from me,' she thought. 'I had worn out his love, I suppose.'

It was eleven o'clock when they got to Dover. Major Lennard slept all the way, with the lappets of his travelling cap which was a sort of woollen caricature of a Knight Templar's helmet, drawn closely over his ears. Mrs

Lennard, who was very wide awake all the time, sat opposite to her husband, with the canary bird on her lap. He had grown quiet at last, and had retired from the world under a tent of green baize. The bird's mistress made up for his silence by talking incessantly throughout the journey; but it only seemed to Eleanor as if she had a second Laura for her companion, and the succession of her own sad thoughts was scarcely broken by Mrs Lennard's conversation.

They arrived in Paris the next morning in time for breakfast at the great Hôtel du Palais, a monstrous building, newly erected, and rich in the glitter of gilding and the glow of colour. Here the major took up his abode, after deliberately expounding to his wife and Eleanor the theory that the best and most expensive hotels are always the cheapest – in the end. This moral had been the rule of the major's life, and had very often brought him alarmingly near the awful abysses of insolvency.

The gorgeous apartments in which Eleanor found herself were very unlike the low-ceilinged little sitting-room in the Rue de l'Archevêque; but her mind went back to that sad time, nevertheless. She spent the morning in the agreeable employment of unpacking Mrs Lennard's wardrobe, while the major and his wife sailed out of the great hotel to sun themselves in the Rue Rivoli and on the Boulevards, and to wind up with a drive in the Bois, and a little dinner at Vèfour's. When she had completed this most wearisome task, and had arranged all the scraps of lace and ribbons, the gloves and collars, and feminine furbelows, in a buhl chest of drawers and a gorgeous ebony and gold wardrobe, Mrs Monckton put on her bonnet and shawl, and went out into the busy street.

The tears rushed up to her eyes as she looked at the bright vista before her, and heard the roll of the drum, and the tramp of soldiers' feet in the courts of the Louvre. Yes, there was the street along which she had walked by her father's side on the last day of his blighted life. Her hands clenched themselves involuntarily as she remembered that day; and that other bitter day of anguish in which she had knelt upon the ground and sworn to be revenged upon George Vane's enemy.

How had she kept her oath? She smiled bitterly as she thought of the four years that had passed since then, and the strange chance that had flung Launcelot Darrell in her way.

'I went away from this place while he was here,' she thought. 'I come back to it now that he is in England. Is it my destiny, I wonder, always to fail in everything I attempt?'

She went to the Rue de l'Archevêque. Nothing was changed. The same butcher was busy in the shop; the same faded curtains of flowered damask hung behind the windows.

CHAPTER LIII

MARGARET LENNARD'S DELINQUENCIES

Mrs Major Lennard was very kind to Eleanor, and if kindness and friendliness on the part of her employers could have made Mrs Monckton comfortable, she might have been entirely so in her new position.

But comfort was a noun substantive whose very meaning must, I think, have been utterly incomprehensible to Major and Mrs Lennard. They had married very young, had started in life all wrong, and had remained in a perpetual state of muddle, both mental and physical, ever since. They were like two children who had played at being grown-up people for twenty years or so; and who were as entirely childish in their play now as they had been at the very beginning. To live with them was to exist in an atmosphere of bewilderment and confusion; to have any dealings whatever with them was to plunge at once into a chaos of disorder, out of which the clearest intellect could scarcely emerge without having suffered complete disorganization. The greatest misfortune of these two people was the likeness they bore to each other. Had Major Lennard been a man of vigorous intellect and strong will, or had he been merely possessed of the average allowance of common sense, he might have ruled his wife, and introduced some element of order into his existence. On the other hand, if Mrs Lennard had been a sensible woman, she would no doubt have henpecked her husband, and would have rescued the good-natured soldier from a hundred follies, by a well-timed frown, or a sharp matronly nudge, as the occasion might demand.

But they were both alike. They were two overgrown children of forty years of age; and they looked upon the world as a great play-room, whose inhabitants had no better occupation than to find amusement, and shirk the schoolmaster. They were generous and kind-hearted to a degree that, in the opinion of their wiser acquaintance, bordered upon foolishness. They were imposed upon on every side, and had been imposed upon during twenty years, without acquiring any moral wealth in the way of wisdom, from their very costly experience. The major had within the last twelve months left the army on half-pay, on the death of a maiden aunt, who had left him eight hundred a year. Up to the date of receiving this welcome legacy, the soldier and his wife had been compelled to exist upon Major Lennard's pay, eked out by the help of stray benefactions which he received from time to time from his rich relatives. The family to which the ponderous officer belonged was very numerous and aristocratic, owning as its chief a marquis, who was uncle to the major.

So the two big children had decided upon enjoying themselves very much for the rest of their days, and as a commencement of this new life of idleness and enjoyment, Major Lennard had brought his wife to Paris, whence they were to go to Baden-Baden, to meet some of the major's aristocratic cousins.

'He might come in for the title himself, my dear,' Mrs Lennard told Eleanor, 'if seventeen of his first cousins, and first cousins once removed, would die. But, as I told poor papa, when he grumbled at my marrying so badly, you can't expect seventeen cousins to go off all in a minute, just to oblige us by making Freddy a marquis.'

Perhaps nothing could have been happier for Eleanor than this life of confusion, this scrambling and unsettled existence, in which the mind was kept in a tumult by trifling cares and agitations; for in this perpetual disorganization of her intellect, the lonely girl had no time to think of her own troubles, or of the isolated position which she had chosen for herself. It was only at night, when she went to bed, in a small apartment very high up in the Hôtel du Palais, and about a quarter of an hour's walk from the chamber of the major and his wife, that she had time to think of Launcelot Darrell's triumph and her husband's unjust suspicions; and even then she could rarely brood very long upon her troubles, for she was generally exhausted alike in mind and body by the confusion and excitement of the day, and more likely to fall asleep and dream of her sorrows than to lie awake and think of them.

Those dreams were more troublesome to her than all the bewilderment of the day, for in them she was perpetually renewing the old struggle with Launcelot Darrell, perpetually upon the eve of victory, but never quite victorious.

The major lingered in Paris much longer than he had intended, for the big children found the city of boulevards a most delightful playground, and frittered away a great deal of money upon expensive dinners at renowned restaurants, ices, opera tickets, new bonnets, Piver's gloves, Lubin's perfumes, and coach hire.

They stopped at the Hôtel du Palais, still acting on the major's theory, that the most expensive hotels are the cheapest – in the end. They dined occasionally at the table-d'hôte, with two or three hundred companions, and wasted a good deal of time in the great saloons, playing at bagatelle, peering into stereoscopes, turning over the daily papers, reading stray paragraphs here and there, or pouring over a chapter of a romance in the *feuilleton*, until brought to a standstill by a disheartening abundance of difficult words.

After breakfast, the major left his wife and her companion, either to loll in the reading-room, to stroll about the great stone quadrangle, smoking cigars, and drinking occasional brandy and soda, or to read the English papers at Galignani's, or to wait for the post, or to meet a British acquaintance at Hill's café, or to stare at the raw young soldiers exercising in the courtyards of the Louvre, or the copper-faced Zouaves who had done such wonderful work in the Crimea; or perhaps to stumble across some hoary-headed veteran who had fought under Napoleon the First, to make friendly speeches to him in bad French, with every verb in a bewilderingly impossible tense, and to treat him to little glasses of pale cognac.

Then Mrs Lennard brought out her frame and her colour-box, and her velvets and brushes, and all the rest of her implements, and plunged at once into the delightful pursuit of painting upon velvet – an accomplishment which this lady had only newly acquired in six lessons for a guinea, during her last brief sojourn in London.

'The young person who taught me called herself Madame Ascanio de Brindisi – but, oh! Miss Villars, if ever there was a Cockney in this world, I think she was one – and she said in her advertisement, that anybody could earn five pounds a week easily at this elegant and delightful occupation; but I am sure I don't know how *I* should ever earn five pounds a week, Miss Villars, for I've been nearly a month at this one sofa cushion, and it has cost five-and-thirty shillings already, and isn't finished yet, and the major doesn't like to see me work, and I'm obliged to do it while he's out; just as if it was a crime to paint upon velvet. If you *would* mend those gloves, dear, that are split across the thumb – and really Piver's gloves at four francs, five-and-twenty what's its names? oughtn't to do so, though the major says it's my own fault, because I will buy six-and-a-quarters – I should be *so* much obliged,' Mrs Lennard added, entreatingly, as she seated herself at her work in one of the long windows. 'I shall get on splendidly,' she exclaimed, 'if the Emperor doesn't go for a drive; but if he does, I must leave off my work and look at him – he's such a dear!'

Eleanor was very willing to make herself what the advertisements call 'generally useful,' to the lady who had engaged her. She was a very high-spirited girl, we know, quick to resent any insult, sensitive and proud; but she had no false pride. She felt no shame in doing what she had undertaken to do; and if, for her own convenience, she had taken the situation of a kitchen-maid, she would have performed the duties of that situation to the best of her ability. So she mended Mrs Lennard's gloves, and darned that lady's delicate lace collars, and tried to infuse something like order into her toilette, and removed the damp ends of cigars, which it was the major's habit to leave about upon every available piece of furniture, and made herself altogether so useful that Mrs Lennard declared that she would henceforward be unable to live without her.

'But I know how it will be, you nasty provoking thing!' the major's wife exclaimed; 'you'll go on in this way, and you'll make us fond of you, and just as we begin to doat upon you, you'll go and get married and leave us, and then I shall have to get another old frump like Miss Pallister, who lived with me before you, and who never would do anything for me scarcely, but was always talking about belonging to a good family, and not being used to a life of dependence. I'm sure I used to wish she had belonged to a bad family. But I know it'll be so; just as we're most comfortable with you, you'll go and marry some horrid creature.'

Eleanor blushed crimson as she shook her head.

'I don't think that's very likely,' she said.

'Ah! you say that,' Mrs Lennard answered, doubtfully, 'but you can't convince me quite so easily. I know you'll go and marry; but you don't know the troubles you may bring upon yourself if you marry young – as I did,' added the lady, dropping her brush upon her work, and breathing a profound sigh.

'Troubles, my dear Mrs Lennard!' cried Eleanor. 'Why, it seems to me as if you never could have had any sorrow in your life.'

'"Seems, Hamlet!"' exclaimed Mrs Lennard, casting up her eyes tragically; '"nay, it is; *I* know not seems," as the Queen says to Hamlet – or perhaps it's Hamlet says so to the Queen, but that doesn't matter. Oh, Miss Villars! my life might have been very happy, perhaps, but for the blighting influence of my own crime; a crime that I can never atone for – *nev-arr!*'

Eleanor would have been quite alarmed by this speech, but for the tone of enjoyment with which Mrs Lennard gave utterance to it. She had pushed aside her frame and huddled her brushes together upon the buhl table – there was nothing but buhl and ormolu, and velvet-pile and ebony, at the Hôtel du Palais, and an honest mahogany chair, a scrap of Kidderminster carpet, or a dimity curtain, would have been a relief to the overstrained intellect – and she sat with her hands clasped upon the edge of the table, and her light blue eyes fixed in a tragic rapture.

'Crime, Mrs Lennard!' Eleanor repeated, in that tone of horrified surprise which was less prompted by actual terror, than by the feeling that some exclamation of the kind was demanded of her.

'Yes, my dear, ker-rime! ker-rime! is not too harsh a word for the conduct of a woman who jilts the man that loves her on the very eve of the day appointed for the wedding, after a most elaborate trousseau has been prepared at *his* expense, to say nothing of heaps of gorgeous presents, and diamonds as plentiful as dirt – and elopes with another man. Nothing could be more dreadful than that, could it, Miss Villars?'

Eleanor felt that she was called upon to say that nothing *could* be more dreadful, and said so accordingly.

'Oh, don't despise me, then, or hate me, please, Miss Villars,' cried Mrs Lennard; 'I know you'll feel inclined to do so; but don't. I did it! – I did it, Miss Villars. But I'm not altogether such a wretch as I may seem to you. It was chiefly for my poor pa's sake; it was, indeed.'

Eleanor was quite at a loss to know how Mrs Lennard's bad conduct to her affianced husband could have benefited that lady's father, and she said something to that effect.

'Why, you see, my dear, in order to explain that, I must go back to the very beginning, which was when I was at school.'

As Mrs Lennard evidently derived very great enjoyment from this kind of conversation, Eleanor was much too good-natured to discourage it; so the painting upon velvet was abandoned, for that morning at least, and the major's wife gave a brief synopsis of her history for the benefit of Mrs Monckton.

'You must know, my dear,' Mrs Lennard began, 'my poor pa was a country gentleman; and he had once been very rich; or at least his family – and he belonged to a very old family, though not as aristocratic as the major's – had on[ce been very rich] but somehow or other, through the extravagance of one and another, poor pa was dreadfully poor, and his estate, which was in Berkshire, was heavily – what's its name? – mortgaged.'

Eleanor gave a slight start at the word 'Berkshire,' which did not escape Mrs Lennard.

'You know Berkshire?' she said.

'Yes, some part of it.'

'Well, my dear, as I said before, poor papa's estate was very heavily mortgaged, and he'd scarcely anything that he could call his own, except the rambling old country-house in which I was born; and beyond that he was awfully in debt, and in constant dread of his creditors sending him to prison, where he might have finished his days, for there wasn't the least possibility of his ever paying his debts by anything short of a miracle. Now, of course, all this was very sad. However, I was too young to know much about it, and papa sent me to a fashionable school at Bath, where his sisters had gone when they were young, and where he knew he could get credit for my education to be finished.'

Eleanor, hard at work at the split gloves, listened rather indifferently to this story at first; but little by little she began to be interested in it, until at last she let her hands drop into her lap, and left off working, in order the better to attend to Mrs Lennard's discourse.

'Well, Miss Villars, it was at that school that I met the ruling star of my fate – that is to say, the major, who was then dreadfully young, without even the least pretence of whiskers, and always sitting in a pastrycook's shop in the fashionable street, eating strawberry ices. He had only just got his commission, and he was quartered at Bath with his regiment, and his sister Louisa was my schoolfellow at Miss Florathorne's, and he called one morning to see her, and I happened that very morning to be practising in the drawing-room, the consequence of which was that we met, and from that hour our destinies were sealed.

'I won't dwell upon our meetings, which Louisa managed for us, and which were generally dreadfully inconvenient, for Fred used to clamber up the garden wall by the toes of his boots – and he has told me since that the brickwork used to scratch off all the varnish, which of course made it dreadfully expensive – but what will not love endure? – and hook himself on as it were; and it was in that position, with nothing of him visible below his chin, that he made me a most solemn offer of his hand and heart. I was young and foolish, Miss Villars, and I accepted him, without one thought of my poor papa, who was the most indulgent of parents, and who had always let me do everything I liked, and indeed owed upwards of fifty pounds, at a toyshop in Windsor, for dolls and things that he bought me before I was grown up.

'Well, from that hour Frederick and I were engaged, and he dropped a turquoise ring in among the bushes at the bottom of the garden the next morning, and Louisa and I had upwards of an hour's work to find it. We were engaged! But we were not long allowed to bask in the sunshine of requited affection, for a fortnight after this Frederick's regiment was ordered out to Malta, and I was wretched. I will pass over my wretchedness, which might not be interesting to you, Miss Villars, and I will only say that, night after night, my pillow was wet with tears, and that, but for Louisa's sympathy, I should have broken my heart. Frederick and I corresponded regularly under cover of Louisa, and that was my only comfort.

'By-and-by, however, the time for my leaving school came – partly because I was seventeen years of age, and partly because papa couldn't settle Miss Florathorne's bills – and I went home to the old rambling house in Berkshire. Here I found everything at sixes and sevens, and poor papa in dreadfully low spirits. His creditors were all getting horribly impatient, he had all sorts of writs, and attachments, and judgments, and contempt of courts, and horrors of that kind, out against him; and if they could have put him into two prisons at once, I think they would have done it, for some of them wanted him in Whitecross Street, and others wanted him in the Queen's Bench, and it was altogether dreadful.

'Well, papa's only friend of late years had been a very learned gentleman, belonging to a grand legal firm in the city, who had managed all his business matters for him. Now this gentleman had lately died, and his only son, who had succeeded to a very large fortune upon his father's death, was staying with my poor papa when I came home from school.

'I hope you won't think me conceited, Miss Villars, but in order to make my story intelligible, I'm *obliged* to say that at that time I was considered a very pretty girl. I had been the belle of the school at Miss

Florathorne's, and when I went back to Berkshire and mixed in society, people made a tremendous fuss about me. Of course, you know, my dear, troubles about money matters, and a wandering life, and French dinners, which are too much for a weak digestion, have made a very great difference in me, and I'm not a bit like what I was then. Well, the young lawyer who was staying with papa – I shall not tell you his name, because I consider it very dishonourable to tell the name of a person you've jilted, even to a stranger – was very attentive. However, I took no notice of that – though he was very handsome and elegant-looking, and awfully clever – for my heart was true to Frederick, from whom I received the most heart-rending letters under cover to Louisa, declaring that, what with the mosquitoes and what with the separation from me, and owing debts of honour to his brother officers, and not clearly seeing his way to pay them, he was often on the verge of committing suicide.

'I had not told papa of my engagement, you must know, my dear, because I felt sure he'd grumble about my engaging myself to a penniless ensign; though Fred might have been a marquis, for at that time there were only eleven cousins between him and the title. So one day papa took me out for a drive with him, while Mr—— while the young lawyer was out shooting; and he told me that he was sure, from several things the young lawyer had let drop, that he was desperately in love with me, and that it would be his salvation – pa's – if I would marry him, for he was sure that in that case the young man, who was very generous and noble-minded, would pay his debts – pa's – and then he could go on the continent and end his days in peace.

'Well, my dear Miss Villars, the scene between us was actually heart-rending. I told papa that I loved another – I dared not say that I was actually engaged to poor dear Frederick – and pa entreated me to sacrifice what he called a foolish schoolgirl's fancy, and to give some encouragement to a noble-hearted young man, who would no doubt get him out of the most abominable trouble, and would make me an excellent husband.'

'And you consented?'

'Yes, my dear, after a great deal of persuasion, and after shedding actual oceans of tears, and in compliance with papa's entreaties, I began to give the young lawyer – I'm obliged to call him the *young* lawyer, because one is so apt to associate lawyers with grey hair, and grumpiness, and blue bags – a little encouragement, and in about a week's time he made me an offer, and I accepted it, though my heart was still true to Frederick, and I was still corresponding with him under cover of Louisa.'

Eleanor looked very grave at this part of the story, and Mrs Lennard interpreted her companion's serious face as a mute reproach.

'Yes, I know it was very wrong,' she exclaimed; 'but then, what in goodness' name was I to do, driven to distraction upon one side by pa, driven to distraction upon the other side by Fred, who vowed that he would blow out his brains if I didn't write to him by every mail?'

'Well, my dear, the young lawyer, whom I shall call in future my affianced husband, for short, behaved most nobly. In the first place he bought pa's estate – not that he wanted it, but because pa wanted the money – and then he lent pa enough money, over and above the price of the estate, to settle with all his creditors, and to buy an annuity, upon which he could live very comfortably abroad. Of course, this was very generous of him, and he made quite light of it, declaring that my love would have repaid him for much greater sacrifices. You know he thought I loved him, and I really did try to love him, and to throw over poor Frederick, for papa's sake: but the more I tried to throw Frederick over, and the more distant and cold I made my letters, the more heart-rending he became, reminding me of the vows I had uttered in the garden at Bath, and declaring that if I jilted him, his blood should be upon my head. So, what with one thing and another, my life was a burden.

'It took papa some time to settle all his debts, even with the assistance of my affianced husband, but at last everything was arranged, and we started for a continental tour. My affianced husband accompanied us, and the marriage was arranged to take place at Lausanne. I need not say that I was very unhappy all this time; and I felt that I was a very wicked creature, for I was deceiving one of the best of men. Perhaps the worst of all was, that my affianced husband had such perfect confidence in me, that I scarcely think anything I could have said or done – short of what I did at the very last – could have shaken his faith. He talked sometimes of my youth, and my childishness, and my simplicity, until I used to feel a perfect LUCRETIA BORGIA. Ah! Miss Villars, it was dreadful, and I often felt inclined to throw myself at his feet and tell him all about poor Frederick; but the thought of my poor papa, and the recollection of the money for the estate, which could not be paid back again, sealed my lips, and I went on day after day deceiving the best of men. You see, I'd gone too far to recede, and oh, my dear, that is the awful penalty one always pays for one's wickedness – if you begin by deceiving any one, you're obliged to go on, and on, and on, from one deception to another, until you feel the basest creature in the world.

'At least that's how I felt when all the lovely dresses, and jewels, and things that my affianced husband had ordered arrived from Paris. If I could have walked upon gold, Miss Villars, I do think that foolish man – for he was quite foolish about me, though in a general way he was so very clever – would have thought the purest bullion only fit for paving stones under my feet. The silks and satins – satin wasn't *outré* then, you know – would have stood alone if one had wanted them to do so; the lace – well, I won't dwell upon that, because I dare say you think already that I shall never have done talking, and are getting dreadfully tired of this long story.'

'No, Mrs Lennard,' Eleanor answered, gravely, 'I am very much interested in your story. You cannot tell how deeply it interests me.'

The major's wife was only too glad to receive permission to run on. She was one of those people who are never happier than when reciting their own memoirs, or relating remarkable passages in the history of their lives.

'The very eve of the wedding-day had arrived,' resumed Mrs Lennard, in a very solemn, and, indeed, almost awful voice, 'when the unlooked-for crisis of my destiny came upon me like a thunderbolt. Pa and my affianced husband had gone out together, and I was alone in one of the apartments which we occupied at Lausanne. It was about an hour before dinner, and I was dressed in one of the silks that had come from Paris, and I was tolerably resigned to my fate, and determined to do my best to make my affianced husband happy, and to prove my gratitude for his goodness to my father. Imagine my horror, then, when I was told that a lady wished to see me – an English lady – and before I could decide whether I was at home or not, in rushed Louisa Lennard, very dusty and tumbled, for she had only just arrived, and of course there was no railway to Lausanne from anywhere, at that time.

'Well, my dear Miss Villars, it seems that Frederick's silence, which I had taken for resignation, was quite the reverse. Louisa had heard of my intended marriage, and had written about it to her brother, and her brother had gone nearly mad, and, being on the eve of obtaining leave of absence on account of his bad health – the climate had knocked him up – contrived to get away from Malta immediately. He and his sister had managed to persuade their rich maiden aunt, who was very fond of Frederick, and who left him all her money the other day, to take them both to Switzerland, and there they were, with the rich maiden aunt, who was very much knocked up by the journey, and who had not the least shadow of a suspicion that she had been made a catspaw.

'Well, Miss Villars, anybody – even the hardest-hearted of creatures – would have been touched by such devotion as this, and for the moment I forgot all about my affianced husband's generosity, and I gave that enthusiastic Louisa, who really was the moving spirit of everything, a solemn promise that I would see Frederick that night, if only for ten minutes. Of course I didn't tell her that the next day was appointed for my wedding, because I was too much afraid of her anger, as she was devotedly attached to her brother, and had heard my solemn vows in the garden at Bath; but the people at the hotel told her all about it, in their

nasty gossiping way; the consequence of which was, that when I met
Fred in the porch of the cathedral, while papa and my affianced husband
were taking their wine after dinner, his goings-on were really awful.

'I can never describe that scene. When I look back at it, it seems like a
dream – all hurry, and noise, and confusion. Frederick declared that he
had come all the way from Malta to claim me as his bride, and called my
affianced husband a baron all covered with jewels and gold, from the
ballad of "Alonzo the Brave," which he had been in the habit of reciting
at school. And, poor dear fellow, now that I saw him again, my heart,
which had always been true to him, seemed more true to him than ever;
and what with Louisa, who was very strong-minded, going on at me, and
calling me mercenary and faithless and deceitful, and what with
Frederick going down upon his knees in that chilly porch, and getting up
suddenly every time the person who showed the cathedral to strangers
happened to look our way, I scarcely knew what I said or did, and
Frederick extorted from me the promise that I would run away with him
and Louisa that very night, and be married to him as soon as ever we
could find anybody that would marry us.

'I can never describe that dreadful night, Miss Villars; suffice it to say,
that I ran away without a bit of luggage, and that Frederick, Louisa, and
I, performed the most awful journey – almost all by diligence – and
were nearly jolted to death between Lausanne and Paris, where Fred, by
the help of some English friends, contrived to get the ceremony
performed by a Protestant clergyman, at the house of the British
Consul, but not without a great deal of difficulty and delay, during
which I expected every day that my affianced husband would come
tearing after me.

'He did nothing of the kind, however. I heard afterwards from papa
that he didn't show the least disposition to pursue me, and he particularly
requested that no attempt should be made to prevent my doing exactly as
I pleased with regard to Fred. If he had pursued me, Miss Villars, I have
no doubt I should have gone back and married him; for I am very weak,
and it is my nature to do whatever people wish me to do. But all he did
was to walk about very quietly, looking as pale as a ghost for a day or
two, and braving out all the ridicule that attached to him because of his
bride's running away from him upon the eve of the wedding-day, and
then he parted company with papa, and went away to Egypt, and went
up the Nile, and did all sorts of outlandish things.'

'And have you never seen him since?' Eleanor asked, anxiously.

'Yes, once,' answered Mrs Lennard, 'and that's the most singular part of
the story. About three years after my marriage I was in London, and Fred
and I were very, very poor, for his aunt hadn't then forgiven him for
making a catspaw of her at Lausanne, and he had no remittance from her,

and nothing but his pay and an occasional present from Louisa, who married a rich city man soon after our elopement. I had had one baby, a little girl, who was then a year and a half old, and who was christened after Fred's rich aunt; and Fred's regiment was ordered out to India, and I was getting ready to join him at Southampton, and I was very unhappy at having to take my darling out there, for people said the climate would kill her. I was in lodgings in the neighbourhood of Euston Square, and I was altogether very wretched, when one evening, at dusk, as I was sitting by the fire, with my little girl in my lap, who should walk into the room but the very man I had jilted.

'I gave a scream when I saw him, but he begged me not to be frightened of him; and then I asked him if he had forgiven me. He said he had tried to forgive me. He was very grave and quiet; but though I think he tried to be gentle, there was a sort of suppressed sternness in his manner which made me feel afraid of him. He had not very long returned from the East, he said, and he was very lonely and wretched. He had heard from my father that I was going to India, and that I had a little girl, whom I was obliged to take abroad with me for want of the means of providing her with a comfortable home in England. He proposed to me to adopt this little girl, and to bring her up as his own daughter, with my husband's consent.

'He promised to leave her very well off at his death, and to give her a fortune if he lived to see her married. He would be most likely, he said, to leave her all his money; but he made it a condition that neither I nor her father should have any further claim upon her. We were to give her up altogether, and were to be satisfied with hearing of her from time to time, through him.

'"I am a lonely man, Mrs Lennard," he said; "even my wealth is a burden to me. My life is purposeless and empty. I have no incentive to labour – nothing to love or to protect. Let me have your little girl; I shall be a better father to her than your husband can be."

'At first I thought that I could never, never consent to such a thing; but little by little he won me over, in a grave, persuasive way, that convinced me in spite of myself, and I couldn't afford to engage a nurse to go out to Calcutta with me, and I'd advertised for an ayah who wanted to return, and who would go with me for the consideration of her passage-money, but there had been no answers to my advertisements: so at last I consented to write to Fred to ask him if he would agree to our parting with the pet. Fred wrote me the shortest of letters by return of post; "Yes," he said, "the child would be an awful nuisance on shipboard, and it will be much better for her to stop in England." I sent his letter to the lawyer, and the next day he brought a nurse, a respectable elderly person, and fetched away my precious darling.

'You see, Miss Villars, neither Fred nor I had *realized* the idea that we were parting with her for ever; we only thought of the convenience of getting her a happy home in England for nothing, while we went abroad to be broiled to death's door out in India. But! ah! when years and years passed by, and the two babies who were born in India died, I began to grieve dreadfully about my lost pet; and if I hadn't been what some people call frivolous, and if Fred and I hadn't suited each other so exactly, and been somehow or other always happy together in all our troubles, I think I should have broken my heart. But I tried to be resigned,' concluded Mrs Lennard, with a profound sigh, 'and I hear *of* my pet once in six months or so, though I never hear from her, and indeed I doubt if she knows she's got such a thing as a mamma in the universe – and I have her portrait, poor darling, and she's very like what I was twenty years ago.'

'I know she is,' Eleanor answered, gravely.

'You know she is! You know her, then?'

'Yes, dear Mrs Lennard. Very strange things happen in this world, and not the least strange is the circumstance which has brought you and me together. I know your daughter intimately. Her name is Laura, is it not?'

'Yes, Laura Mason Lennard, after Fred's rich aunt, Laura Mason.'

'And your maiden name was Margaret Ravenshaw.'

'Good gracious me, yes!' cried Mrs Lennard. 'Why, you seem to know everything about me.'

'I know this much, – the man you jilted was Gilbert Monckton, of Tolldale Priory.'

'Of course! Tolldale was poor papa's place till he sold it to Mr Monckton. Oh, Miss Villars, if you know him, how you must despise me!'

'I only wonder that you could——'

Eleanor stopped abruptly; the termination of her speech would not have been very complimentary to the good-tempered major. Mrs Lennard understood that sudden pause.

'I know what you were going to say, Miss Villars. You were going to say you wondered how I could prefer Fred to Gilbert Monckton; and I'm not a bit offended. I know as well as you do that Mr Monckton is very, VERY, VERY superior to Frederick in intellect, and dignity, and elegance, and all manner of things. But then, you see,' added Mrs Lennard, with a pleading smile, 'Fred *suited me*.'

CHAPTER LIV

VERY LONELY

Eleanor had considerable difficulty in parrying Mrs Lennard's questions as to how she had come to know Gilbert Monckton and his ward; and she was obliged to confess that she had been musical governess to Laura at Hazlewood.

'But I must beg you not to tell Mr Monckton that I am with you, if you should happen to write to him,' Eleanor said. 'I have a very particular reason for wishing him to remain in perfect ignorance of my present home.'

'To be sure, my dear,' answered Mrs Lennard, 'of course I won't tell him if you don't wish me to do so. And as to writing to him, I should no more think of doing so than of flying in the air, except just a civil note of a few lines, to thank him for sending me news of Laura. He only writes to me once in six months or so, to tell me how my lost darling is, and though I've implored him again and again, he won't let me see her. "She is still little more than a child," he wrote in his last letter, "and I dread the effect of your influence upon her. It is out of no revengeful feeling that I keep your daughter apart from you. When her character is formed and her principles fixed, you shall know her." As if I was a wretch!' cried Mrs Lennard, in conclusion, 'and should contaminate my own daughter.'

Eleanor smiled as she shook her head.

'Dear Mrs Lennard,' she said, 'your daughter is perhaps better off in the care of such a man as Gilbert Monckton. She is as kind-hearted and good-tempered as yourself, but she is rather weak, and——'

'And I'm weak, too. Yes, I quite understand you, Miss Villars. It is my misfortune to be weak-minded. I can't say "no" to people. The arguments of the person who talks to me last always seem so much stronger than those of the person who talked to me first. I take impressions quickly, and don't take them deeply. I was touched to the heart by Gilbert Monckton's kindness to my father, and I meant to marry him as I promised, and to be his true and obedient wife; and then when that poor silly Fred came all the way to Lausanne, and went on so about being ill-used and deserted, and wanted to commit suicide, I thought it was my duty to run away with Fred. I haven't any opinions of my own, you see, and I'm always ready to be influenced by the opinions of other people.'

Eleanor thought long and deeply over the story she had heard from Mrs Lennard. This was the root of all Gilbert Monckton's suspicions. He had been deceived, most cruelly, most unexpectedly, by a beautiful, childish creature, in whose innocence he had implicitly believed. He had been fooled and hoodwinked by a fair-haired angel whose candid azure eyes had seemed to beam upon him with all the brightness of truth. He had been deceived most egregiously, but he had not been deliberately betrayed: for up to the time of her treacherous desertion of her affianced lover, Margaret Ravenshaw had meant to be true to him. Unhappily Gilbert Monckton did not know this. It is difficult for the man who finds himself as cruelly jilted as he had been, not to believe that the false one has intended all along to turn traitor at the last. There had been no explanation between Margaret and the lawyer; and he was entirely ignorant of the manner of her flight. He only knew that she had left him without a word to prepare him for the death-blow, without a line of regretful farewell to make his sorrow lighter to him. The frivolous shallow woman had been unable to fathom the depth of the strong man's love. Margaret Ravenshaw knew there was a very little of the divine in her own nature, and she had never expected to inspire the mighty affection of a grand and noble soul. She was able to understand the love of Frederick Lennard: which was demonstrated by noisy protestations, and disclosed itself in long schoolboy letters in which the young man's doubtful orthography was blistered by his tears. But she could not understand the intensity of feelings that did not make themselves visible in any stereotyped fashion.

Unluckily for the harmony of creation, wise men do not always fall in love wisely. The wisest and the best are apt to be bound captive by some external charm, which they think must be the outward evidence of an inward grace; and Gilbert Monckton had loved this frivolous, capricious girl as truly as if she had been the noblest and greatest of womankind. So the blow that had fallen upon him was a very heavy one; and its most fatal effect was to transform a confiding nature into a suspicious one.

He argued as many men argue under the same circumstances. He had been deceived by one woman, *ergo*, all women were capable of deception. I don't suppose the 'Stranger' placed very much confidence in the Countess, or had by any means too high an opinion of Charlotte; and the best of men are apt to feel very much after the manner of Mrs Haller's husband.

It seemed very strange to Eleanor to be living with Gilbert Monckton's first love. It was almost as if some one had risen out of the grave; for she had looked upon that old story which she had heard hinted at by the Hazlewood gossips, as something so entirely belonging to the past, that the heroine of the romance must of necessity be dead.

And here she was, alive and merry, knowing no greater uneasiness than a vague dread of increasing plumpness, induced by French dinners. Here she was the very reverse of the image that Eleanor had conjured up in her mind in association with Gilbert's false love; a good-tempered, commonplace, pretty, middle-aged woman. Mrs Monckton felt a little pang of jealousy at the thought that her husband had once loved this woman so dearly. Her husband! Had she still the right to call him by that name? Had he not severed the link between them of his own free will? Had he not outraged her honour, insulted her truth by his base and unfounded suspicions? Yes! he had done all this, and yet Eleanor loved him! She knew the strength of her love now that she was away from him, and might perhaps never see his face looking at her in kindness again. She knew it now that her scheme of vengeance against Launcelot Darrell had failed, and left a great blank in her mind. She thought of her husband seriously now for the first time, and she knew that she loved him.

'Richard was right,' she thought again and again; 'the purpose of my life was cruel and unwomanly. I had no right to marry Gilbert Monckton while my mind was full of angry thoughts. Richard was right. My poor father's rest would be no more peaceful if I had made Launcelot Darrell pay the penalty of his wickedness.'

She did not abandon her idea of vengeance all at once; but little by little, by very slow degrees, her mind became reconciled to the idea that she had failed in her scheme of retribution, and that there was nothing left her but to try and justify herself in the sight of the husband she loved.

She loved him; and the angry feelings which had prompted her to run away from Tolldale Priory, willingly abandoning all claim to his name and his protection, were beginning to give way now. Mrs Lennard's story had thrown new light upon the past, and Eleanor made all kinds of excuses for her husband's conduct. It was his habit to bear all sorrows quietly. Who could tell what anguish he might have felt in the thought of his young wife's falsehood?

'He would not pursue Margaret Ravenshaw,' Eleanor thought, 'and he makes no attempt to find me. And yet he may love me as truly as he loved her. Surely if God refused to hear my prayers for revenge, he will grant me the power to justify myself.'

She could only blindly hope for some unknown chance that might bring about her justification; and that chance would perhaps never come. She was very unhappy when she thought of this; and it was only the perpetual confusion in which Major Lennard and his wife contrived to keep everybody belonging to them, that saved her from suffering very cruelly.

All this time she was quite ignorant of the appearance of an advertisement which had been repeated at the top of the second column of the *Times* supplement every day for nearly a month, and about which idle people hazarded all many of conjectures –

Eleanor, come back. I was rash and cruel. I will trust you.

G.M.

Major Lennard was in the habit of seeing the *Times* every day at Galignani's; but, as he was not a very acute observer or original thinker, he took no notice of the repetition of this advertisement beyond an occasional, 'By Jove! Haw! that poor dayv'l's still advertising for El'ner!' nor did he ever make any allusion to the circumstances in his domestic circle.

So Eleanor hugged her sorrows secretly in the gayest city of the world, while Gilbert Monckton was hurrying hither and thither, and breaking his heart about his lost wife.

I think that pitying angels must sometimes weep over the useless torments, the unnecessary anguish, which foolish mortals inflict upon themselves.

CHAPTER LV

VICTOR BOURDON GOES OVER TO THE ENEMY

Major and Mrs Lennard and Eleanor Monckton had stayed for nearly two months at the Hôtel du Palais. April was fast melting into May, and the atmosphere in the city of Boulevards was very different to the air of an English spring. Miniature strawberries were exposed in the windows of the cheap restaurants in the Palais Royal, side by side with monstrous asparagus, and green peas from Algeria; until the mind of the insular-bred stranger grew confused as to the succession of the months, and was beguiled into thinking that May must be omitted in the French almanack, and that capricious April skipped away in a farewell shower to give place at once to glowing June.

It was difficult for a thorough-bred Briton to believe that the Fête of the First Napoleon had not yet come to set the fountains playing at Versailles: for the asphalte on the Boulevards was unpleasantly warm under one's boots; airily-attired ladies were lounging upon the chairs in the gardens of the Tuileries; only the most fragile and vaporous bonnets were to be seen in the Bois de Boulogne; vanille and strawberry ices were in constant demand at Tortoni's; idle Parisians spent the dusky spring evenings seated outside the lighted cafés, drinking iced lemonade; and a hundred other signs and tokens bore witness that the summer had come.

Upon one of these very warm April days, Major Lennard insisted upon taking his wife and her companion to dine at a restaurant not very far from the Bourse; where the pastorally-inclined epicure could take his dinner in a garden, a pleasant quadrangle, festooned with gay blossoms, and musical with the ripple of a fountain. Eleanor did not often accompany the major and his wife in their pleasure excursions, the culminating attraction of which was generally a dinner; but this time Major Lennard insisted upon her joining them.

'It's the last dinner I shall give, Meg, in Paris,' he said; 'for we must start for Brussels on Saturday, and I mean it to be a good one.'

Eleanor submitted, for her new friends had been very kind to her, and she had no motive for opposing their wishes. It was much better for her to be with them in any scene of gaiety, however hollow and false that gaiety might be, than alone in the splendid saloon at the Hôtel du Palais, brooding over her troubles in the dusky twilight, and thinking of the horrible night on which she had watched for her father's coming in the Rue de l'Archevêque.

The restaurant near the Place de la Bourse was very much crowded upon this sunny April afternoon, and there was only one table vacant when the major and his party entered the flowery little quadrangle, where the rippling of the fountain was unheard amidst the clattering of plates and the chinking of silver forks. It was seven o'clock, and the dinners were in high progress; the diners eating very fast, and talking a great deal faster.

The little arbour-like box to which Major Lennard conducted the two ladies was next to a similar arbour, in which there was a group of Frenchmen. Eleanor sat with her back to these men, who had very nearly finished dining, and who, from the style of their conversation, appeared to have taken plenty of wine. The man who was evidently the entertainer sat with his legs amongst a forest of empty bottles; and the jingling of glasses and the 'cloop' of newly-drawn corks drowned a good deal of the conversation.

It was not very likely that Eleanor would listen to these men's talk; or, indeed, distinguish one voice from another, or one word from another, amid the noise of the crowded garden. She had quite enough to do to attend to Mrs Lennard, who chattered all dinner time, keeping up an uninterrupted babble, in which remarks upon the business of the dinner-table were blended with criticisms upon the dress of ladies sitting in the other boxes.

'You should eat those little red things — baby lobsters — écrivisses, I think they call them, dear; I always do. How do you like that bonnet; no, not that one — a little more St Jaques, major — the black one, with the peach-coloured strings? I wonder why they call all the Clarets saints, and not the Burgundies: Do you think she's pretty in the box opposite? No, you don't think much of her, do you? — I don't — I like the one in the blue silk, pretty well, if her eyebrows weren't so heavy.'

The dinner was drawing to a close, the major was up to his eyes in roast fowl and water-cress, and Mrs Lennard was scraping the preserved fruit out of a shellwork of heavy pastry with the point of her spoon, trifling idly now that the grand business was done, when Eleanor rose suddenly from her seat, breathless and eager, as much startled by the sound of a voice in the next arbour as if a shell had just exploded amidst the débris of the dinner.

'After?' some one had said, interrogatively.

'After,' answered a man whose voice had grown hoarser and thicker, as the empty bottles about the legs of the president had become more numerous, 'my stripling has refused me a little bank-note of a thousand francs. Thou art too dear, my friend, he has said to me; *that* has been paid already, and enough largely. Besides, *that* was not great things. Ah! ha! I said, thou art there, my drôle; you begin to fatigue yourself of your confederate. He is too much. Very well; he has his pride, he also. Thou art the last of men, and I say to you, adieu Monsieur Launcelot Darrell.'

This was the name that struck upon Eleanor's ear, and aroused the old feeling in all its strength. The snake had only been scotched after all. It reared its head at the sound of that name, like a war-horse at the blast of a trumpet. Eleanor, starting to her feet, turned round and faced the party in the next box. The man who had spoken had risen also, and was leaning across the table to reach a bottle on the other side. Thus it was that the faces of the two were opposite to each other; and Victor Bourdon, the commercial traveller, recognized Gilbert Monckton's missing wife.

He dropped the glass that he was filling, and poured some wine into the cuff of his coat, while he stared at Eleanor in drunken surprise.

'You are here, madame?' he cried, with a look in which astonishment was blended with intense delight, a sort of tipsy radiance that illuminated the Frenchman's fat face. Even in the midst of her surprise at seeing him, Eleanor perceived that blending of expression and wondered at it.

Before she could speak, Monsieur Bourdon had left his party and had deliberately seated himself in the empty chair next her. He seized her hand in both his own, and bent over her as she shrank away from him.

'Do not recoil from me, madame,' he said, always speaking in French that was considerably disguised by wine. 'Ah, you do not know. I can be of the last service to you; and you can be of the last service to me also. I have embroiled myself with this Monsieur Long – cell – lotte, for always; after that which I have done for him, he is an ingrate, he is less than that,' Monsieur Bourdon struck the nail of his thumb upon his front tooth with a gesture of ineffable contempt. 'But why do I tell you this, madame? You were in the garden when this poor old, – this Monsieur de Crespigny, was lying dead. You remember; you know. Never mind, I lose myself the head; I have dined a little generously. Will you find yourself to-morrow, madame, in the gardens of the Palais Royal, at five hours?

There is music all the Tuesdays. I have something of the last importance
to tell you. Remember you that I know everything, I know that you hate
this Long-cellotte. I will give you your revenge. You will come; is it not?'

'Yes,' Eleanor answered, quickly.

'Upon the five hours? I shall wait for you near to the fountain.'

'Yes.'

Monsieur Bourdon rose, put on his hat with a drunken flourish, and
went back to his friends. The major and Mrs Lennard had been all this
time staring aghast at the drunken Frenchman. He had spoken in a loud
whisper to Eleanor, but neither Frederick Lennard nor his wife retained
very much of that French which had been sedulously drilled into them
during their school-days, and beyond ordering a dinner, or disputing
with a landlord as to the unconscionable number of wax-candles in a
month's hotel bill, their knowledge of the language was very limited; so
Eleanor had only to explain to her friends that Monsieur Bourdon was a
person whom she had known in England, and that he had brought her
some news of importance which she was to hear the following day in the
gardens of the Palais Royal.

Mrs Lennard, who was the soul of good-nature, readily assented to
accompany Eleanor to this rendezvous.

'Of course I'll go, my dear, with pleasure; and really I think it's quite
funny, and indeed actually romantic, to go and meet a tipsy Frenchman –
at least, of course, he won't be tipsy to-day – near a fountain; and it
reminds me of a French novel I read once in English, which shows how
true it must have been to foreign manners; but as the major knows we're
going, there's no harm, you know,' Mrs Lennard remarked, as they
walked from the Hôtel du Palais to the gardens. The diners were hard at
work already at the cheap restaurants, and the brass band was braying
lively melodies amidst the dusty trees and flowers, the lukewarm fountain,
the children, the nursemaids, and the rather seedy-looking Parisian
loungers. It was a quarter past five, for Mrs Lennard had mislaid her
parasol at the last moment, and there had been ten minutes employed in
skirmish and search. Monsieur Victor Bourdon was sitting upon a bench
near the fountain, but he rose and darted forward with his hat in his hand
as the two ladies approached.

'I'll go and look in the jewellers' shops, Miss Villars,' Mrs Lennard said,
'while you're talking to your friend; and please come and look for me
when you want me. The major is to join us here, you know, at half-past
six, and we're to dine at Véfours'. *Good* morning.'

Mrs Lennard bestowed these final words upon the Frenchman,
accompanied by a graceful curtsey, and departed. Victor Bourdon
pointed to the bench which he had just left, and Eleanor sat down. The
Frenchman seated himself next her, but at a respectful distance. Every

trace of the tipsy excitement of the previous night had vanished. He was quite cool to-day; and there was a certain look of determination about his mouth, and a cold glitter in his light, greenish-grey eyes that did not promise well for any one against whom he might bear a grudge.

He spoke English to-day. He spoke it remarkably well, with only an occasional French locution.

'Madame,' he began, 'I shall not waste time, but come at once to the point. You hate Launcelot Darrell?'

Eleanor hesitated. There is something terrible in that word 'hate.' People entertain the deadly sentiment; but they shrink from its plain expression. The naked word is too appalling. It is the half-sister of murder.

'I have good reason to dislike him——' she began.

The Frenchman shrugged his shoulders as he interrupted her.

'Yes, you hate him!' he said; 'you do not like to say so, because the word is not nice. You are — what is it you call it? — you are *shocked* by the word. But it is so, nevertheless; you hate him, and you have cause to hate him. Yes, I know now who you are. I did not know when I first saw you in Berkshire, but I know now. Launcelot Darrell is one who cannot keep a secret, and he has told me. You are the daughter of that poor old man who killed himself in the Faubourg Saint Antoine — that is enough! You are a great heart; you would like to avenge the death of your father. You saw us that night — the night the wills were change?'

'I did,' Eleanor answered, looking at the man with sovereign contempt. He had spoken of the transaction as coolly as if it had been the most honourable and commonplace business.

'You are there in the darkness, and you see us,' exclaimed Monsieur Bourdon, bending over Eleanor and speaking in a confidential whisper, 'you watch, you look, you listen, and after, when you go into the house, you denounce Launcelot. You declare the will is forge. The will is change. You were witness, you say; you tell all that you saw! But they do not believe you. But why? Because when you say you have the true will in your pocket, you cannot find it; it is gone.'

The Frenchman said this in a tone of triumph, and then paused suddenly, looking earnestly at Eleanor.

As she returned that look a new light flashed upon her mind. She began to understand the mystery of the lost will.

'It is gone,' cried Monsieur Bourdon, 'no trace, no vestige of it remains. You say, search the garden; the garden is search; but no result. Then the despair seizes itself of you. Launcelot mocks himself of you; he laughs at your nose. You find yourself unhappy; they do not believe you; they look coldly at you; they are harsh to you, and you fly from them. It is like that; is it not?'

'Yes,' Eleanor answered.

Her breath came and went quickly; she never removed her eyes from the man's face. She began to think that her justification was perhaps only to be obtained by the agency of this disreputable Frenchman.

'What, then, of the lost will? It was not swallowed up by the earth. It could not fly itself away into the space! What became of it?'

'YOU TOOK IT FROM ME!' cried Eleanor. 'Yes, I remember how closely you brushed against me. The paper was too big to go altogether into the pocket of my dress. The ends were sticking out, and you——'

'I did all my possible to teach you a lesson! Ah, when young and beautiful ladies mix themselves with such matters, it is no wonder they make mistakes. I was watching you all the time, dear madame. I saw you change the papers, and I drew the will out of your pocket, as easily as I could rob you of that handkerchief.'

The corner of a lace-bordered handkerchief was visible amid the folds of Eleanor's dress. The Frenchman took the scrap of lace between his fingers, and snatched the handkerchief away with an airy lightness of touch that might have done credit to a professional adept in the art of picking pockets. He laughed as he returned the handkerchief to Eleanor. She scarcely noticed the action, so deeply was she absorbed in the thought of the missing will.

'You have the will, then?'

'Si, madame.'

'Why did you take it from me?'

'But why, madame? For many reasons. First, because it is always good to seize upon anything that other people do not know how to keep. Again, because it is always well to have a strong hand, and a card that one's adversary does not know of. An extra king in one's coat-cuff is a good thing to have when one plays écarté, madame. That will is my extra king.'

The Frenchman was silent for some little time after having made what he evidently considered rather a startling *coup*. He watched Eleanor with a sidelong glance, and with a cunning twinkle in his small eyes.

'Is it that we are to be friends and allies, madame?' he asked, presently.

'Friends!' cried Eleanor. 'Do you forget who I am? Do you forget whose daughter I am? If Launcelot Darrell's was the only name written in my father's last letter, you were not the less an accomplice in the villany that led to his death. The pupil was no doubt worthy of the master.'

'You reject my friendship, then, madame? You wish to know nothing of the document that is in my possession? You treat me from high to low? You refuse to ally yourself with me? Hein?'

'I will use you as an instrument against Launcelot Darrell, if you please,' Eleanor answered, 'since it seems that you have quarrelled with your fast friend.'

'But yes, madame. When pussy has pulled the chestnuts out of the fire, she is thenceforward the most unuseful of animals and they chase her. Do you understand, madame?' cried the Frenchman, with a sudden transformation from the monkey to the tiger phase of his character, that was scarcely agreeable. 'Do you understand?' he hissed. 'Monsieur Launcelot has ennuied himself of me. I am chased! ME!'

He struck his gloved fingers upon his breast to give emphasis to this last word.

'It is of the last *canaille*, this young man,' he continued, with a shrug of disgust. 'Ingrate, poltroon, scoundrel! When the forge will, forge at my suggestion by the clerk of the avoué de Vindsor, has been read, and all is finish, and no one dispute his possession, and he enter his new domain as master, the real nature of the man reveal itself. The *genuine* will is burn, he think. He defies himself of his dear friend, this poor Bourdon, and he will not even tell him who would have benefit by that genuine will. It is burn! Did he not see it scorch and blaze with his own eyes? There is nothing to fear; and for this poor comrade, who has helped my gentleman to a great fortune he is less than that!'

Monsieur Bourdon snapped his fingers derisively, and stared fiercely at Eleanor. Then he relapsed into a sardonic smile, and went on.

'At first things go on charmingly. Monsieur Launcelot is more sweet than the honey. It is new to him to be rich, and for the first month he scatters his money with full hands. Then suddenly he stops. He cries out that he is on the road to ruin; that his friend's claims are monstrous. Faith of a gentleman, I was, perhaps, extravagant; for I am a little gamester, and I like to see life *en grand seigneur. A bas la moutarde*, I said. My friend is *millionaire*. I am no more commercial traveller. Imagine, then, when mon garçon shuts up his – what is it you call it, then – cheque-book, and refuse me a paltry sum of a thousand francs. I smile in his face,' said Monsieur Bourdon, nodding his head slowly, with half-closed eyes, 'and I say, "Bon jour, Monsieur Darrell; I shall make you hear some news of me before I am much older."'

'You did not tell him that the will was in your possession?'

'A thousand thunders! No!' exclaimed the Frenchman. 'I was not so much foolish as to show him the beneath the cards. I come over here to consult a friend, an avoué.'

'And he tells you——?'

'No matter. You are better than the avoué, madame. You hate Launcelot Darrell; this will is all you want to prove him a cheat and a blacksmith – pardon, a forger.'

'But to whom does Mr de Crespigny leave his estate in this genuine will?' asked Mrs Monckton.

The Frenchman smiled, and looked at Eleanor thoughtfully for a few moments before he answered her.

'Wait a little, madame,' he said; 'that is my little secret. Nothing for nothing is the rule here below. I have told you too much already. If you want to know more you must pay me.'

'Prove that I spoke the truth upon that night,' exclaimed Eleanor, 'and I promise you that my husband, Gilbert Monckton, shall reward you handsomely.'

'But if monsieur should repudiate your promise, madame, since he has not authorized you to give it? I am not very wise in your English law, and I would rather not mix myself in this affair. I do not want to be produced as witness or accomplice. I want, all simply, to get a price for this document. I have something to sell. You wish to buy it. Name your price.'

'I cannot,' answered Eleanor; 'I have no money. But I might get some, perhaps. Tell me, how much do you want?'

'A thousand pounds.'

Eleanor shook her head despondently.

'Impossible!' she said; 'there is no one, except my husband, from whom I could get such an amount, and I could not ask him for money until after I had proved Launcelot Darrell's infamy.'

The Frenchman watched her closely. He saw that she had spoken the truth.

'You do not know how much this will is worth to you, madame,' he said. 'Remember, I could make terms with Launcelot Darrell, and sell it to him for perhaps ten times the sum I ask of you. But Monsieur Darrell was insolent to me; he struck me once with the butt end of his hunting-whip; I do not forget. I could get more money from him; but I can get my revenge through you.'

He hissed out these words between his teeth and glared vindictively at the fountain, as if the phantom of Launcelot Darrell had been looking at him out of the sparkling water-drops. Revenge was not a beautiful thing, as represented by Victor Bourdon. Perhaps Eleanor may have thought of this as she looked at him.

'I want my revenge,' he repeated; 'after all, gold is a villain thing. Revenge is more dear – to gentlemen. Besides, I do not think you would pay me ungenerously if I helped you to crush this scoundrel, and helped you to something else by the market, Hein?'

'I tell you again that you shall be well rewarded,' Mrs Monckton said, gravely.

'Very well, then, listen to me. It is to-day Tuesday. In a week I shall have time to think. In a week you will have leisure to gather together a little money – all you can get. At the end of that time come to me at my

apartment – bring with you any friend you like. I do not think that you
are traitor – or ingrate – and you see I trust you. I will have my friend,
the – what you call him – attorney, with me – and we may come to an
arrangement. You shall sign a contract – well ruled – for to pay me in the
future, and then the will is to you. You return to England; you say, "Aha,
Monsieur Launcelot, walk out of that. It is your turn to be chased."'

Victor Bourdon grinned ferociously, then took a memorandum-book
from his pocket, wrote a few words in pencil, tore out the leaf upon
which they were written, and handed it to Mrs Monckton.

'That is my address,' he said. 'On Tuesday, at seven o'clock in the
evening, I shall expect to see you there, and your friend. But if you think
to betray me, remember I am not the man to forgive an injury. I have the
honour to salute you, madame. Bon jour.'

He took off his hat with a flourish, and walked away. Eleanor sat for
some minutes where he had left her, thinking over what had happened,
before she went into the arcades to look for Mrs Lennard.

That night she told the Lennards who she was, and all her story. She
felt that it was better to do so. She must have freedom now to act, and to
act promptly. She could not do this, and yet preserve her secret. Her old
ally, Richard Thornton, would be indispensable to her in this crisis, and
she wrote to him early on the morning after her interview with
Monsieur Bourdon, imploring him to come to her immediately.

CHAPTER LVI

THE HORRORS OF DELIRIUM TREMENS

No letter came from Richard Thornton. Eleanor was seized with a kind
of panic as the days went by, and there was no answer from the young
man, the faithful friend, without whose help she felt herself so powerless.

Eleanor had addressed her letter to the Pilasters, enclosed in an
envelope directed to Signora Picirillo, with a few hurried lines requesting
that it might be immediately forwarded to the scene-painter. He was in
Scotland still, very likely, and some days must elapse before he could
respond to Eleanor's summons. She felt assured that he would come to
her. There are some friends whose goodness we no more doubt than we
doubt the power of God; and Richard Thornton was one of these.

But the week passed, and no reply came to Eleanor's appeal for help; so
she began to feel that she stood alone, and must act for herself. She must
act for herself, since to think of getting any assistance from either the
major or his wife in this business, which demanded foresight, coolness,

and diplomacy, would have been about as reasonable as to apply to one of the children playing under the trees in the gardens of the Tuileries.

As far as sympathy went, Major and Mrs Lennard were all that the most exacting individual could require. The major offered to do anything in a muscular way on behalf of his wife's friend. Should he punch the head of that scoundrelly Frenchman? Should he go over to England and horsewhip Launcelot Darrell, and bring Gilbert Monckton to reason, and play up old gooseberry altogether? This good-natured Hercules was ready to hit out right and left in the defence of poor Eleanor.

But the one friend whom Mrs Monckton wanted in this crisis was Richard Thornton. Richard, the clear-sighted, even-tempered, unprejudiced young man, who was ready to go through fire and water for the sake of his beautiful adopted sister, without noise or bluster; and when the Tuesday, the day appointed by the Frenchman for Eleanor's visit to his apartments, came, and Richard Thornton did not come with it, the lonely girl almost gave way to despair.

She felt that she had to encounter a wretch who was utterly without honour or honesty, and who, seeing the value which she set upon the possession of Maurice de Crespigny's will, would be all the more exacting in his demands. And she had nothing to bribe him with; nothing.

She had been too proud to appeal to her husband. For ever impulsive, for ever inconsiderate, she had not stopped to think that he of all others was the most fitting person to stand by her in this crisis. At first the thought of writing to Gilbert Monckton had indeed flashed across her mind, but in the next moment she had remembered the bitter humiliation of her last failure.

She could not endure another such degradation; and she had seen treachery and dishonour so long triumph over the simple force of truth, that she had begun to think that wrong was stronger than right, and always must be victorious.

'If I were to write and ask Gilbert to come to me, this Frenchman would perhaps disappear before my husband could arrive; or he would be afraid of Gilbert, very likely, and would deny any knowledge of the will, and I should appear a convicted trickster, who had heaped up one falsehood upon another, in the weak attempt to justify herself. No, Gilbert Monckton shall hear nothing of me until I can go to him with Maurice de Crespigny's will in my hands.'

But in the meantime this helpless girl's anxiety grew every hour more intense. What reliance could she place upon the words of the Frenchman? She had encountered him while he was still smarting under the sense of his wrongs, and in that stage of his feelings, revenge had seemed even sweeter to him than gain. But this state of things might not endure very long. The commercial traveller might listen to the dictates of

reason rather than to the fiery promptings of passion, and might begin to
think that a substantial recompense in the shape of money was better than
any sugar-plum in the way of revenge. He had said that Launcelot Darrell
would be willing to give him ten times a thousand pounds for the
genuine will. What more likely than that Monsieur Victor Bourdon
should have thought better of his original design, and opened
negotiations with the new master of Woodlands?

Monsieur Bourdon would in all probability have done precisely this,
had he not been hindered by one of those unlooked-for and purely
providential circumstances which so often help single and simple-minded
Truth in her encounters with versatile and shifty Falsehood.

At half-past six o'clock upon the appointed evening, Eleanor
Monckton left the Hôtel du Palais, escorted by Major Lennard, on her
way to the Frenchman's lodging. She had waited until the last moment in
the hope of Richard Thornton's arrival, but he had not come; and she
had been fain to accept the aid of this good-natured over-grown
schoolboy, who still persisted that the immediate punching of Victor
Bourdon's head would be the best and surest means of getting possession
of the will.

'Let me punch the feller's head, Miss Vil – beg pardon, Mrs
Monckton. The idea of your being married to old Monckton! He ain't
any older than me, you know; but I always call him old Monckton. Let
me punch this dam Frenchman's head; that'll bring the feller to book in
next to no time, and then we can do what we like with him.'

But Eleanor impressed upon her stalwart protector that there must be
no muscular demonstration, and that the conduct of the interview was to
be left entirely to her.

'I don't in the least hope that he'll give up the will without a bribe,'
Eleanor said; 'he is the last man upon earth to do that.'

'I'll tell you what, then, Mrs Monckton,' exclaimed the major; 'I
haven't any *ready* money; I never had, since I borrowed sixpences of a
sucking bill-discounter at the first school I ever went to; but I'll give you
my acceptance. Let this fellow draw upon me for a thousand at three
months, and give up the document for that consideration. Monckton will
enable me to meet the bill, no doubt, when he finds I was of service to
you in this business.'

Eleanor looked at the major with a gleam of hope in her face. But that
transient gleam very quickly faded. She had only a vague idea of the
nature and properties of accommodation bills; but she had a very positive
notion of Victor Bourdon's character, and, though this plan *sounded*
feasible enough, she did not think it would succeed.

'You are very good to me, Major Lennard,' she said, 'and believe me, I
appreciate your kindness; but I do not think that this Frenchman will

consent to take anything but ready money. He could get that from Launcelot Darrell, remember, at any time.'

Eleanor's only hope was the one chance that she might induce Victor Bourdon to accept her promise of a reward from Gilbert Monckton *after* the production of the will.

The neighbourhood in which the commercial traveller lived, whenever he made Paris his head-quarters, was one of the dingiest localities in the city. Major Lennard and Eleanor, after making numerous inquiries, and twice losing their way, found themselves at last in a long narrow street, one side of which was chiefly dead-wall, broken here and there by a dilapidated gateway or a dingy window. At one corner there was a shop for the sale of unredeemed pledges; a queer old shop, in whose one murky window obsolete scraps of jewellery, old watch-keys, impossible watches with cracked enamel dials and crippled hands that pointed to hours whose last moments had passed away for half a century; mysterious, incomprehensible garments, whose fashion was forgotten, and whose first owners were dead and gone; poor broken-down clocks, in tawdry ormolu cases, that had stood upon lodging-house mantelpieces, indifferently telling the wrong time to generations of lodgers; an old guitar; a stringless violin; poor, frail, cracked cups and saucers, that had been precious once, by reason of the lips that had drunk out of them; a child's embroidered frock; a battered christening cup; a tattered missal; an odd volume of 'The Wandering Jew;' amid a hundred other pitiful relics which poverty barters for a crust of bread, faded in the evening sunlight, and waited for some eccentric purchaser to take a fancy to them. Next door to this sarcophagus of the past, there was an eating-house, neat and almost cheerful, where one could have a soup, three courses, and half a bottle of wine for fivepence. The whole neighbourhood seemed to be, somehow or other, overshadowed by churches, and pervaded by the perpetual tramp of funerals; and, lying low and out of the way of all cheerful traffic, was apt to have a depressing effect upon the spirits of frivolous people.

Eleanor, leading the major — who was of about as much use to her as a blind man is to his dog — succeeded at last in finding the house which boasted Monsieur Victor Bourdon amongst its inhabitants. I say 'amongst' advisedly; for as there was the office of a popular bi-weekly periodical upon the first floor, a greengrocer in the *rez-de-chaussée*, a hairdresser, who professed to cut and friz the hair, on the second storey, and a mysterious lady, whose calling was represented by a faded pictorial board, resident somewhere under the roof, the commercial traveller was a very unimportant inhabitant, an insignificant nomad, replaced to-day by a student *en droit*, to-morrow by a second-rate actor at a fifth-rate theatre.

Eleanor found this when she came to make inquiries of the portress as to the possibility of seeing Monsieur Bourdon. This lady, who was knitting, and whose very matronly contour made it impossible for her to see her knitting-needles, told Eleanor that Monsieur Bourdon was very unlikely to be at home at that time. He was apt to return late at night, upon the two hours, in effect, between two wines, and at those times he was enough abrupt, and was evidently by no means a favourite with madame the portress. But on looking into a dusky corner where some keys were hanging upon a row of rusty nails, madame informed Eleanor that Monsieur Bourdon *was* at home, as his key was not amongst the rest, and it was his habit to leave it in her care when he went out. The portress seemed very much struck by this discovery, for she remarked that the last time she had seen Monsieur Bourdon go out had been early in the morning of Sunday, and that she did not remember having seen him re-enter.

But upon this a brisk young person of twelve or thirteen, who was busy getting up fine linen in the recesses of the lodge, cried out in a very shrill voice that Monsieur Bourdon had returned before mid-day on Sunday, looking a little ill, and dragging himself with a fatigued air.

He was at home, then, the portress exclaimed; at least she did not utter any equivalent to our English word home, and in that evinced considerable wisdom, since a French lodging is a place so utterly unhomelike, that the meanest second-floor at Islington or Chelsea, presided over by the most unconscionable of British landladies, becomes better than all the pleasures and palaces we can roam amidst – and it is not everybody who has the chance of roaming amidst pleasures and palaces – by the very force of comparison. Monsieur was *chez lui*, the portress said, and would madame ascend? Monsieur's apartment was on the entresol, with windows giving upon the street. Madame would see a black door facing her upon the first landing.

Eleanor went up a short flight of steps, followed by the major. She knocked upon the panel of the black door – once, twice, three times; but there was no answer.

'I'd lay a five the feller's gone out again,' the major exclaimed; 'that jabbering Frenchwoman didn't seem to know what she was talking about.'

But Eleanor knocked a fourth time, and very much louder than she had knocked before. There was no answer even this time; but a voice was heard within, blaspheming aloud with horrible French execrations that seemed to freeze Eleanor's blood as she listened to them.

She did listen to them involuntarily, as people often listen in a crowded thoroughfare to the obnoxious clamour of a drunken man, paralyzed for the moment by the horror of his hideous oaths.

Eleanor turned very pale, and looked despairingly at the major.

'Hark!' she whispered; 'he is quarrelling with some one.'

The big soldier deliberately turned himself into a convenient position for listening, and flattened his ear against the keyhole.

'No, he ain't quarrellin' with any one,' the major said, presently. 'I can't make much out of his lingo, but there's only one voice. He's all alone, and goin' on like a madman.'

The major opened the door softly as he spoke. Monsieur Bourdon's apartment was divided into two low-roofed chambers, a little larger than comfortable pigeon-holes; and in the inner and smaller chamber Eleanor and her companion saw the commercial traveller wandering backwards and forwards in his obscure den, only dressed in his trousers and shirt, and gesticulating like a madman.

Mrs Monckton clung to the soldier's arm. She had some cause for fear, for in the next moment the Frenchman descried his visitors and, with a howl of rage, rushed at the major's throat.

The most intellectual and diplomatic individual in Christendom would have been of very little service to Eleanor at that moment, if he had been also a coward. Major Lennard lifted the commercial traveller in his arms, as easily as if that gentleman had been a six months' old baby, carried him into the next room, where there was a narrow little bedstead, flung him on to the mattress, and held him there.

'You'll find a silk handkerchief in my pocket, my dear,' he said to Eleanor, 'if you'll be so kind as to pull it out. Voulez-vous gardez-vous trangkeel, dong, vous – scoundrel!' he exclaimed, addressing himself to the struggling Frenchman.

Mrs Monckton obeyed. She fell into her place quite naturally, giving way before the major. He was the hero of the moment. Frederic Soulié has said that the meanest actor who ever trod the boards of a theatre, has some inspired moment in which he is great. I fancy it must be pretty much the same in the drama of life. This was the major's moment; and he arose out of his normal inanity, resplendent with unconscious grandeur.

The silk handkerchief was a large one, and Major Lennard used it very dexterously about Monsieur Bourdon's wrists; then he found another handkerchief in another pocket, and used it as a bandage for the Frenchman's ankles; and having done this he sat down by the bedside and contemplated his handiwork complacently, puffing and blowing a little while he did so.

Victor Bourdon lay very still, glaring at the ponderous soldier with eyes that were like those of a wild beast.

'I know thee,' he exclaimed; 'thou hast been with me all the night, thou hast sat upon my chest; ah, Grêdin! thou art the biggest of all the demons that torment me. Thou breathest the fire and the sulphur, and thy breath burns me, and now thou hast attached my hands with bands of iron, white hot, and thou hast tied my ankles with living scorpions!'

Eleanor stood at a few paces from the bed, listening with horror to the man's delirious ravings.

'What is it?' she asked, in a subdued voice. 'Is it a fever that makes him like this. Or has he gone mad?'

The major shook his head.

'I think I can guess pretty well what's the matter with the poor devil,' he said; 'he's been going it a little too fast. He's got a touch of del. trem.'

'Del. trem!'

'Delirium tremens, my dear,' answered the major. 'Yes, you can hear his teeth chattering now this minute. I had it once when I was up the country, and our fellers took to living upon brandy pawnee. I had rather a sharp time of it, while it lasted; used to fancy the tent was on fire; wanted to go out tiger-hunting in the middle of the night; tried to set the bedclothes alight to cure myself of the hiccough: and ran after Meg with a razor early one morning. This man has got a touch of it, Mrs Monckton, and I don't think we shall get much reason out of him to-night.'

The conduct of Monsieur Victor Bourdon, who was at that moment holding a very animated discourse with a dozen or so of juvenile demons supposed to be located in the bed-curtains, went very far towards confirming the major's assertion.

Eleanor sat down at the little table, upon which the dirty litter of the Frenchman's last meal was huddled into a heap and intermixed with writing materials; an ink-bottle, and a mustard-pot, a quill pen, and a teaspoon lying side by side. The girl's fortitude had given way before this new and most cruel disappointment. She covered her face with her hands and sobbed aloud.

Major Lennard was very much distressed at this unexpected collapse upon the part of his chief. He was very big, and rather stupid; but he had one of those tender childish natures which never learn to be hard and unmerciful. He was for ever patting the shock heads of dirty pauper children, for ever fumbling in his pockets for copper coin, always open to the influence of any story of womanly distress, and quite unable to withstand the dingiest female, if she could only produce the merest phantom of a tear to be wiped away furtively from one eye, while the other looked round the corner to see if the shot went home.

He looked piteously at Eleanor, as she sat sobbing passionately, half unconscious of his presence, forgetful of everything except that this last hope had failed her.

'I thought that he might leave Paris, and go back to Launcelot Darrell,' she said, in a broken voice, 'but I never thought of anything like this.'

'Sh-sh-sh-sh!' cried Monsieur Bourdon from the bed. 'Ftz! Cats, cats! Sh-sh-sh-sh! Chase those cats, somebody! There's the girl Faust saw upon the Bracken with the little rat running out of her mouth! There, sitting at the table! Go then, Voleuse, Gueuse, Infâme!' screamed the Frenchman, glaring at Eleanor.

The girl took no notice of him. Her sobs grew every moment louder and more hysterical. The major looked at her helplessly.

'Don't,' he said, 'my good creature, don't now. This is really dreadful, 'pon my soul, now. Come, come now; cheer up, my dear, cheer up. You won't do anything by giving way, you know. I always tell Margaret that, when she thinks she can catch the train by sitting on the ground and crying because her portmanteaus won't shut. Nobody ever did, you know, and if you don't put your shoulder to the wheel——'

The major might have rambled on in this wise for some time; but the sobbing grew louder; and he felt that it was imperatively necessary that something energetic should be done in this crisis. A bright thought flashed upon him as he looked hopelessly round the room, and in another moment he had seized a small white crockery-ware jug from the Frenchman's toilet table, and launched its contents at Eleanor's head.

This was a second master-stroke. The girl looked up with her head dripping, but with her courage revived by the shock her senses had received.

She took off her wet bonnet, and pushed the drenched hair from her forehead.

'Oh, major,' she said, 'I know I have been very silly. But I was so taken by surprise. It seems so cruel that this should happen. I shall never get the will now.'

'Stuff and nonsense, my dear,' exclaimed Major Lennard. 'What's to prevent your getting it?'

'What do you mean?'

'What's to prevent *your taking it?* We're not going to stand upon ceremony with such a feller as this, are we, Mrs Monckton? He stole the will from you, and if you can get the chance, you'll return the compliment by stealing it from him. Fair play's a jewel, my dear Mrs. M., and nothing could be fairer than that. So we'll set to work at once; and I hope you'll excuse the cold water, which was meant in kindness, I assure you.'

Eleanor smiled, and gave the major her hand.

'I'm sure it was,' she said. 'I scarcely liked the idea of your coming with me, major, for fear you should do some mischief by being a little too impetuous. But I don't know what I should have done without you.'

Major Lennard shrugged his shoulders with a deprecating gesture.

'I *might* have been useful to you, my dear,' he said, 'if the feller had been all right and I could have punched his head; but one can't get any credit out of a chap when he's in that state,' added the major, pointing to the commercial traveller, who was taking journeys on his own account into the horrible regions of an intemperate man's fancy.

'Now, the first thing we shall want, Mrs Monckton,' said the major, 'is a candle and a box of lucifers. We must have a light before we can do anything.'

It was not dark yet; but the twilight was growing greyer and greyer, and the shadows were gathering in the corners of the room.

Victor Bourdon lay glaring at his two visitors through the dusk, while the major groped about the mantelpiece for a box of lucifers. He was not long in finding what he wanted. He struck a little waxen match against the greasy paper of the wall, and then lighted an end of candle in a tawdry cheap china candlestick.

'Ease her, ease her!' cried the Frenchman; 'I see the lights ahead off Normandy, on this side of the wind. She'll strike upon a rock before we know where we are. What are they about, these English sailors? are they blind, that they don't see the light?'

Major Lennard, with the candle in his hand, set to work to look for the missing document. He did not look very systematically, but as he pulled out every drawer and opened every cupboard, and shook out the contents of every receptacle, flinging them remorselessly upon the floor, he certainly looked pretty effectually. Eleanor, kneeling on the ground amongst the chaotic heap of clothes and papers, tattered novels, broken meerschaum pipes and stale cigar ends, examined every pocket, every book, and every paper separately, but with no result. The drawers had been ransacked, the cupboards disembowelled, a couple of portmanteaus completely emptied. Every nook and corner of the two small rooms had been most thoroughly searched, first by the major in a slap-dash and military manner; afterwards by Eleanor, who did her work with calmness and deliberation, though her heart was beating, and the hot blood surging in on her over-excited brain. Every possible hiding-place in the two rooms had been examined, but the will had not been found.

Every possible hiding-place had been examined; except the pockets of Victor Bourdon's trousers, and the bed upon which he lay.

The major stopped to scratch his head in despair, and stood staring hopelessly at the unhappy victim of his own vices, who was still raving, still remonstrating with invisible demons. But Eleanor aroused her friend from this state of stupefaction.

'He may have the will about him, major,' she said.

'Aha!' cried the soldier, 'if he has, I'll have it out of him. Give it me, you unconscionable blackguard,' he exclaimed, pouncing upon the delirious Frenchman. 'I'll have it out of you, you scoundrel. Tell me where it is directly. *Dites-moi où il est, dong!* What have you done with it, sir? What have you done with Maurice de Crespigny's will?'

The familiar name aroused a transitory gleam of consciousness in Victor Bourdon.

'Ha, ha!' he cried, with a malicious chuckle. 'Maurice de Crespigny, the old, the parent of that Long – cellotte; but I will have my revenge; but he shall not enjoy his riches. The will, the will; that is mine; it will give me all.'

He raised himself by a great effort into a sitting posture, and made frantic endeavours to disengage his hands.

'He is thinking of the will,' cried Eleanor; 'loosen his wrists, major! Pray, pray, do, before the thought leaves him.'

Major Lennard obeyed. He loosened the knot of the silk handkerchief, but before he could remove it, Victor Bourdon had pulled his hands through the slackened noose, and clutched at something in his breast. It was a folded paper which he snatched out of the bosom of his shirt, and waved triumphantly above his head.

'Aha, Monsieur Long – cellotte!' he screamed. 'I will pay thee for thy insolence, my friend.'

But before the Frenchman's uplifted arm had described a second circle in the air above his head, the major swooped down upon him, snatched away the paper, handed it to Eleanor, and resecured Monsieur Bourdon's wrists with the silk handkerchief.

So brief had been the interval of semi-consciousness, that the commercial traveller had already forgotten all about Launcelot Darrell and his own wrongs, and had rambled off again into impotent execrations against the imaginary demons amongst the bed-curtains.

Eleanor unfolded the paper, but she only read the first few words, 'I, Maurice de Crespigny, being at this time, &c.,' for before she could read more, the door of the outer room was suddenly opened, and Richard Thornton hurried through into the bed-chamber.

But not Richard only; behind him came Gilbert Monckton, and it was he into whose outstretched arms Eleanor flung herself.

'You will believe me now, Gilbert,' she cried. 'I have found the proof of Launcelot Darrell's guilt at last.'

CHAPTER LVII

MAURICE DE CRESPIGNY'S BEQUEST

Richard Thornton had received Eleanor's letter in Edinburgh, and had been travelling perpetually since his receipt of the girl's eager epistle. He had calculated that by travelling day and night he should be able to accomplish a great achievement in the four days that were to elapse between the hour in which he received Eleanor's letter and the hour appointed for the interview with the Frenchman. This achievement was the reconciliation of Gilbert Monckton and his wife.

For this purpose the devoted young man had travelled from Edinburgh to London, and from London to Torquay, back to London again, with Mr Monckton for his companion, and from London to Paris, still in that gentleman's companionship. Gilbert Monckton would have thought it a small thing to have given half his fortune in payment of the tidings which the scene-painter carried to him.

He should see his wife again; his bright and beautiful young wife, whom he had so cruelly wronged, and so stupidly misunderstood.

Human nature is made up of contradictions. From the hour in which Gilbert Monckton had turned his back upon Tolldale Priory, deserting his young wife in a paroxysm of jealous anger until now, he had done nothing but repent of his own work. Why had he disbelieved in her? How had he been vile enough to doubt her? Had she not stood before him, with the glorious light of truth shining out of her beautiful face? Even had he not already repented, Eleanor's letter would have opened the jealous husband's eyes to his own folly; that brief offended letter in which the brave girl had repudiated her husband's offer of wealth and independence; and had declared her proud determination to go out into the world once more, and to get her own living, and to accept nothing from the man who doubted her truth.

The lawyer had made every effort to lure the lost bird back to its deserted nest. But if you render your wife's existence intolerable, and she runs away from you in despair, it is not always possible to bring her back to your halls; though you may be never so penitent for your offences against her. Gilbert Monckton had employed every possible means to discover his wife's whereabouts; but had failed most completely to do so. His search was futile; his advertisements were unanswered; and, very lonely and miserable, he had dragged out the last six weeks, in constant oscillation between London and Torquay; always making some new effort to obtain tidings of the missing girl; perpetually beguiled a little way onward with false hopes, only to be disappointed. He had gone again and again to Signora Picirillo; but had received no comfort from her, inasmuch as the music mistress knew no more about Eleanor than he did.

It is not to be wondered, then, that when Richard Thornton appeared at Torquay, carrying with him Eleanor's letter, he was received with open arms by the penitent husband. Not an hour was wasted by the eager travellers, but use what haste they might, they could not hasten the Dover express, or the Calais packets, or the comfortable jog-trot pace of the train between Calais and Paris; so they had only been able to arrive at eight o'clock in the dusky April evening, just in time to behold Major Lennard in his moment of triumph.

Gilbert Monckton extended his hand to the stalwart soldier, after the events of the evening had been hurriedly related by Eleanor and her companion.

'You robbed me of a wife twenty years ago, Major Lennard,' he said, 'but you have restored another wife to me to-night.'

'Then I suppose we're quits,' the major exclaimed, cheerfully, 'and we can go back to the Palais and have a devilled lobster, Hay? I suppose we must do something for this poor devil, though, first, Hay?'

Mr Monckton heartily concurred in this suggestion; and Richard Thornton, who was better acquainted with Paris than any of his companions, ran down stairs, told the portress of the malady which had stricken down the lodger in the entresol, despatched the sharp young damsel with the shrill voice in search of a sick nurse, and went himself to look for a doctor. In a little more than half an hour both these officials had arrived, and Mr Monckton and his wife, Major Lennard, and Richard departed, leaving the Frenchman in the care of his two compatriots. But before Gilbert Monckton left the apartment, he gave the nurse special orders respecting the sick man. She was not to let him leave his rooms upon any pretence whatever; not even if he should appear to become reasonable.

Mr Monckton went to the Hôtel du Palais, with his young wife, and for the first time since he had been wronged forgave the frivolous woman who had jilted him. She had been very kind to Eleanor, and he was in a humour to be pleased with any one who had been good to his wife. So the lawyer shook hands very heartily with Mrs Lennard, and promised that she should see her daughter before long.

'The poor little girl has had a hard trial lately, Mrs Lennard, through my folly, and I owe her some atonement. I separated her from her natural protectors, because I was presumptuous enough to imagine that I was better fitted to plan her destiny; and after all I have wrecked her girlish hopes, poor child! But I don't think the damage is irreparable; I think she'll scarcely break her heart about Launcelot Darrell.'

In all this time nobody had cared to ask any questions about the will. Eleanor had handed it to her husband; and Gilbert Monckton had put it, still folded, into his pocket. But when the devilled lobster and the sparkling Moselle, which the major insisted upon ordering, had been discussed, and the table cleared, Mr Monckton took the important document from his pocket.

'We may as well look at poor De Crespigny's last testament,' he said, 'and see who has been most injured by the success of Launcelot Darrell's fabrication.'

He read the first two sheets of the will to himself, slowly and thoughtfully. He remembered every word of those two first sheets. So far the real will was verbatim the same as the forged document. Gilbert Monckton could therefore now understand why that fabricated will had seemed so genuine. The fabrication had been copied from the original paper. It was thus that the forgery had borne the stamp of the testator's mind. The only difference between the two documents lay in the last and most important clause.

The lawyer read aloud this last sheet of Maurice de Crespigny's will.

'I devise and bequeath all the residue and remainder of my real and personal property unto Hortensia Bannister, the daughter of my old and deceased college friend, George Vane, and my valued friend Peter Sedgewick, of Cheltenham, their heirs, executors, administrators and assigns, upon trust, for the sole and separate use of Eleanor, the daughter of my said dear deceased friend, George Vane, by his last wife, Eleanor Thompson, during her life, free from the control, debts, or engagements of any husband she may at any time have, and so that she shall not have power to anticipate the rents, interest, and annual proceeds thereof, and upon and after her decease, for such persons, estates, and in such manner as she shall, whether covert or uncovert, by will appoint; and in default of and subject to any such appointment, for the said Eleanor, the daughter of the said George Vane, her heirs, executors, administrators, and assigns, according to the nature of the said property. And in case the said Eleanor shall have departed this life during my lifetime, or in case the said last-named trustees cannot discover the said Eleanor Vane within four years after my decease, then they shall consider the said Eleanor Vane dead, and therefrom I give and devise the said residuary estates to be equally divided between my said three nieces, Sarah, Lavinia, and Ellen, absolutely.

'It is fortunate that the money is left to trustees for your separate use, Eleanor,' Mr Monckton said. 'If it had been otherwise, the gift would have been invalid, since I, your husband, was one of the witnesses to the will.'

A torrent of congratulations from Major and Mrs Lennard, and Richard Thornton, almost overwhelmed Eleanor; but she was still more overwhelmed by her astonishment at the wording of the will.

'The money left to me!' she exclaimed. 'I didn't want it. I am sorry it should be so. It will seem now as if I had been plotting to get this fortune. I don't want it; I only want my revenge.'

Gilbert Monckton narrowly watched his wife's astonished face. He saw no look of triumph, no smile of gratification. At least she was free from any mercenary baseness. He took her a little way from the rest of the party, and looked earnestly into her fearless eyes.

'My own dear love,' he said, 'I have learned a hard lesson, and I believe that I shall profit by it. I will never doubt you again. But tell me, Eleanor, tell me once and for ever! have you ever loved Launcelot Darrell? Have any of your actions been prompted by jealousy?'

'Not one,' cried Mrs Monckton. 'I have never loved him, and I have never been jealous of him. From first to last I have been actuated by one motive, and one alone – the duty I owe to my dead father.'

She had not abandoned her purpose, then. No; the lurid star that had beckoned her forward still shone before her. It was so near now, that its red splendour filled the universe. The young wife was pleased to be reconciled to her husband; but with the sense that he was restored to her once more, the memory of the dreary interval in which she had lost him melted away from her mind, and Launcelot Darrell – Launcelot Darrell, the destroyer of her dead father, became once more paramount in her thoughts.

'Oh, Gilbert!' she said, clasping her hands about her husband's arm and looking up in his face, 'you'll take me back to England at once, won't you?'

'Yes, my dear,' Mr Monckton answered, with a sigh. 'I'll do whatever you wish.'

There was a jealous pain at his heart as he spoke. His wife was pure, and true, and beautiful; but this strange purpose of her life divided her from him, and left his own existence very blank.

CHAPTER LVIII

THE DAY OF RECKONING

Launcelot Darrell and his mother had inhabited Woodlands for a little more than a fortnight. The painters, and paper-hangers, and upholsterers had done a great deal to alter the handsome country-house; for Mr Darrell had no wish to be reminded of his dead uncle; and familiar chairs and tables have an unpleasant faculty of suggesting tiresome thoughts, and recalling faded faces that had better be forgotten. Almost all the old furniture had been swept away, therefore, and the young man had behaved very generously to his maiden aunts, who had furnished a small house in Windsor with the things that Launcelot had banished from Woodlands. These poor disappointed ladies had located themselves in a quiet little *cul-de-sac*, squeezed in between the hilly street and the castle, with the idea that the wild dissipations of a town life would enable them to forget their wrongs.

So Launcelot Darrell and his mother reigned at Woodlands instead of the maiden sisters; and Parker, the butler, and Mrs Jepcott, the housekeeper, waited upon a new master and mistress.

The young man had chafed bitterly at his poverty, and had hated himself and all the world, because of those humiliations to which a man who is too idle to work, and too poor to live without work, is always more or less subject. But, alas! now that by the commission of a crime he had attained the great end of his ambition, he found that the game was not worth the candle; and that in his most fretful moments before Maurice de Crespigny's death, he had never suffered as much as he now suffered, daily and hourly.

The murderers of the unfortunate Mr Ware ate a hearty supper of pork chops while their victim lay, scarcely cold, in a pond beside the high road; but it is not everybody who is blessed with the strength of mind possessed by those gentlemen. Launcelot Darrell could not shake off the recollection of what he had done. From morning till night, from night till morning, the same thoughts, the same fears, were perpetually pressing upon him. In the eyes of every servant who looked at him; in the voice of every creature who spoke to him; in the sound of every bell that rang in the roomy country-house, there lurked a something that inspired the miserable terror of detection. It haunted him in every place; it met him at every turn. The knowledge that he was in the power of two bad, unscrupulous men, the lawyer's clerk and Victor Bourdon, made him the most helpless of slaves. Already he had found what it was to be in the power of a vicious and greedy wretch. The clerk had been easily satisfied by the gift of a round sum of money, and had levanted before his employer returned from America. But Victor Bourdon became insatiable. He was a gamester, and a drunkard; and he expected to find in Launcelot Darrell's purse a gold mine that was never to be exhausted.

He had abandoned himself to the wildest dissipation in the worst haunts of London after Maurice de Crespigny's death; and had appeared at Woodlands at all times and seasons, demanding enormous sums of his miserable victim. At first terror sealed Launcelot Darrell's lips, and he acceded to the most extravagant demands of his accomplice; but at last his temper gave way, and he refused that 'paltry note for a thousand francs,' to which the Frenchman alluded in his interview with Eleanor. After this refusal there was a desperate quarrel between the two men, at the end of which the commercial traveller received a thrashing, and was turned out of doors by the master of Woodlands.

The young man had been quite reckless of consequences in his passion; but when he grew a little calmer he began to reflect upon the issue of this quarrel.

'I cannot see what harm the man can do me?' he thought: 'to accuse me is to accuse himself also. And then who would believe his unsupported testimony? I could laugh at him as a madman.'

Launcelot Darrell had no knowledge of the existence of the real will. He implicitly believed that it had been burned before his own eyes, and that Eleanor's assertion to the contrary had been only a woman's falsehood invented to terrify him.

'If the girl had once had the will in her possession she would never have been such a fool as to lose it,' he argued.

But notwithstanding all this he felt a vague fear, all the more terrible because of its indefinite character. He had placed himself in a false position. The poet is born, and not made; and perhaps the same thing may be said of the criminal. The genius of crime, like the genius of song, may be a capricious blossom, indigenous to such and such a soil, but not to be produced by cultivation. However this may be, Launcelot Darrell was not a great criminal. He had none of the reckless daring, the marvellous power of dissimulation, the blind indifference to the future, which make a Palmer, a Cartouche, a Fauntleroy, or a Roupell. He was wretched because of what he had done; and he allowed everybody to perceive his wretchedness.

Mrs Darrell saw that her son was miserable in spite of his newly-acquired wealth; and a horrible terror seized upon her. Her sisters had taken good care to describe to her the scene that had occurred at Woodlands upon the night of the old man's death. She had watched her son, as only mothers can watch the children they love; and she had seen that his dead kinsman's fortune had brought him no happiness. She had questioned him, but had received only sulky, ungracious answers; and she had not the heart to press him too closely.

The mother and son were alone in the dining-room at Woodlands about a week after the scene in Monsieur Victor Bourdon's apartment. They had dined tête-à-tête. The dessert had not been removed, and the young man was sitting at the bottom of the long table, lounging lazily in his comfortable chair, and very often refilling his glass from the claret jug on his right hand. The three long windows were open, and the soft May twilight crept into the room. A tall shaded lamp stood in the centre of the table, making a great spot of yellow light in the dusk. Below the lamp there was a confused shimmer of cut glass, upon which the light trembled like moonbeams upon running water. There were some purple grapes, and a litter of vine leaves in a dessert dish of Sèvres china; the spikey crown of a pine-apple; and scarlet strawberries that made splashes of vivid colour amid the sombre green. The pictured face of the dead man hanging upon the wall behind Launcelot Darrell's chair seemed to look reproachfully out of the shadows. The ruby draperies shading the open windows grew darker with the fading of the light. The faint odour of lilacs and hawthorn blossoms blew in from the garden, and the evening stillness was only broken by the sound of leaves stirred faintly by a slow night wind that crept amongst the trees.

Mrs Darrell was sitting in the recess of one of the open windows, with some needlework in her lap. She had brought her work into the dining-room after dinner, because she wished to be with her son; and she knew that Launcelot would sit for the best part of the evening brooding over his half-filled glass. The young man was most completely miserable. The great wrong he had done had brought upon him a torture which he was scarcely strong enough to endure. If he could have undone that wrong – if——! No! That way lay such shame and degradation as he could never stoop to endure.

'It was all my great-uncle's fault,' he repeated to himself, doggedly. 'What business had he to make the will of a madman? Whom have I robbed, after all? Only a specious adventuress, the intriguing daughter of a selfish spendthrift.'

Such thoughts as these were for ever rising in the young man's mind. He was thinking them to-night, while his mother sat in the window, watching her son's face furtively. He was only roused from his reverie by the sound of wheels upon the gravel drive, the opening of a carriage-door, and a loud ringing of the bell.

The arrival of any unexpected visitor always frightened him; so it was nothing unusual for him to get up from his chair and go to the door of the room to listen for the sound of voices in the hall.

To-night he turned deadly pale, as he recognized a familiar voice; the voice of Gilbert Monckton, whom he had not seen since the reading of the will.

Launcelot Darrell drew back as the servant approached the door, and in another moment the man opened it, and announced Mr Monckton, Mrs Monckton, Mr Thornton, Monsieur Bourdon. He would have announced Mr John Ketch, I dare say, just as coolly.

Launcelot Darrell planted his back against the low marble chimney-piece, and prepared to meet his fate. IT had come; the realization of that horrible nightmare which had tormented him ever since the night of Maurice de Crespigny's death. IT had come: detection, disgrace, humiliation, despair; no matter by what name it was called; the thing was living death. His heart seemed to melt into water, and then freeze in his breast. He had seen the face of Victor Bourdon lurking behind Gilbert and Eleanor, and he knew that he had been betrayed.

The young man knew this, and determined to make a gallant finish. He was not a coward by nature, though his own wrong-doing had made him cowardly; he was only an irresolute, vacillating, selfish Sybarite, who had quarrelled with the great schoolmaster Fate, because his life had not been made one long summer's holiday. Even cowards sometimes grow courageous at the last. Launcelot Darrell was not a coward: he drew himself up to his fullest height, and prepared to confront his accusers.

Eleanor Monckton advanced towards him. Her husband tried to restrain her, but his effort was wasted; she waived him back with her hand, and went on to where the young man stood, with her head lifted and her nostrils quivering.

'At last, Launcelot Darrell,' she cried, 'after watching that has wearied me, and failures that have tempted me to despair, at last, I can keep my promise; at last I can be true to the lost father whose death was your cruel work. When last I was in this house, you laughed at me and defied me. I was robbed of the evidence that would have condemned you: all the world seemed leagued together against me. Now, the proof of your crime is in my hands, and the voice of your accomplice has borne witness against you. Cheat, trickster, and forger; there is no escape for you now.'

'No,' exclaimed Monsieur Bourdon, with an unctuous chuckle, 'it is now your turn to be chased, my stripling; it is now your turn to be kick out of the door.'

'From first to last, from first to last,' said Eleanor, 'you have been false and cruel. You wronged and deceived the friends who sent you to India——'

'Yaase!' interrupted the commercial traveller, who was very pale, and by no means too steady in his nerves, after the attack of delirium tremens. He had dropped into a chair, and sat trembling and grinning at his late patron, with a ghastly jocosity that was far from agreeable to behold. 'Yaase, you cheat your mo-thair, you cheat your friends. You make belief to go to the Indias, but you do not go. You what you call — shally shilly, and upon the last moment, when the machine is on the point of depart, you change the mind, you are well in England; there is a handsome career for you, as artist, you say. Then you will not go. But you have fear of your uncle, who has given the money for your — fit-out — and for your passage, and you make believe to do what they wish from you. You have a friend, a *confrère*, a Mr, who is to partake your cabin. You write to *heem*, you get *heem* to post your letters; you write to your mo-thair, in Clip-a-stone Street, and you say to her, "Dear mo-thair, I cannot bear this broil climate; I am broil, I work the night and the day; I am indigo planter;" and you send your letter to the Indias to be posted; and your poor mo-thair belief you; and you are in Paris to enjoy yourself, to lead the life of a student, a little Bohemian, but very gay. You read Balzac, you make the little sketches for the cheap Parisian journals. You are gamester, and win money from a poor old Englishman, the father of that lady there; and you make a catspaw of your friend, Victor Bourdon. You are a villain man, Monsieur Darrell, but it is finished with you.'

'Listen to me, Launcelot Darrell,' Gilbert Monckton said, quietly. 'Every falsehood and trick of which you have been guilty, from first to last, is known. There is no help for you. The will which my wife holds in her hand is the genuine will signed by Maurice de Crespigny. This man is prepared to testify that the will by which you took possession of this estate is a forgery, fabricated by you and Henry Lawford's clerk, who had in his possession a rough draft of the real will which he had written at Mr de Crespigny's dictation, and who copied the three different signatures from three letters written by the old man to Henry Lawford. You are prepared to bear witness to this,' added the lawyer, turning to Victor Bourdon.

'But certainly,' exclaimed the Frenchman, 'it being well understood that I am not to suffer by this candour. It is understood that I am innocent in this affair.'

'Innocent!' cried Launcelot Darrell, bitterly. 'Why, you were the prime mover in this business. It was your suggestion that first induced——'

'It is possible, my friend,' murmured Monsieur Bourdon, complacently; 'but is it, then, a crime to make a little suggestion – to try to make oneself useful to a friend? I do not believe it! No matter, I have studied your English law: I do not think it can touch me, since I am only prepared to swear to having *found* this real will, and having before that *overheard* a conversation between you and the clerk of the avoué de Vindsor.'

'You use noble tools, Mrs Monckton,' said Launcelot Darrell; 'but I do not know by what right you come into my house, uninvited, and bringing in your train a very respectable transpontine scene-painter with whom I have not the honour to be intimate, and a French commercial traveller, who has chosen to make himself peculiarly obnoxious to me. It is for the Court of Chancery to decide whether I am the rightful owner of this house and all appertaining to it. I shall await the fiat of that court; and in the meantime have the honour to wish you good evening.'

He laid his hand upon the handle of the bell as he spoke, but he did not pull it.

'You defy me, then, Launcelot Darrell?' said Eleanor.

'I do.'

'I am glad that it is so!' exclaimed the girl. 'I am glad that you have not prayed to me for mercy. I am glad that Providence has suffered me to avenge my father's death.'

Eleanor Monckton was moving towards the door.

In all this time Ellen Darrell had not once spoken. She had stood apart in the recess of the window, a dark and melancholy shadow, mourning over the ruin of her life.

I think that she was scarcely surprised at what had happened. We sometimes know the people we love, and know them to be base; but we go on loving them desperately, nevertheless; and love them best when the world is against them, and they have most need of our love. I speak here of maternal love, which is so sublime an affection as to be next in order to the love of God.

The widow came suddenly into the centre of the room, and cast herself on her knees before Eleanor, and wound her arms about the girl's slender waist, pinning her to the spot upon which she stood, and holding her there. The mother's arms were stronger than bands of iron, for they were linked about the enemy of her son. It has been demonstrated by practical zoologists that the king of beasts, his majesty the lion, is after all a cowardly creature. It is only the lioness, *the mother*, whose courage is desperate and indomitable.

'You shall not do this,' Ellen Darrell cried; 'you shall not bring disgrace upon my son. Take your due, whatever it is; take your paltry wealth. You have plotted for it, I dare say. Take it, and let us go out of this place penniless. But no disgrace, no humiliation, no punishment, *for him!*'

'Mother,' cried Launcelot, 'get up off your knees. Let her do her worst. I ask no mercy of her.'

'Don't hear him,' gasped the widow, 'don't listen to him. Oh, Eleanor, save him from shame and disgrace! Save him! save him! I was always good to you, was I not? I meant to be so, believe me. If ever I was unkind, it was because I was distracted by regrets and anxieties about him. Oh, Eleanor, forgive him, and be merciful to me! Forgive him. It is my fault that he is what he is. It was my foolish indulgence that ruined his childhood. It was my false pride that taught him to think he had a right to my uncle's money. From first to last, Eleanor, it is I that am to blame. Remember this, and forgive him, forgive——'

Her throat grew dry, and her voice broke, but her lips still moved, though no sound came from them, and she was still imploring mercy for her son.

'Forgive!' cried Eleanor, bitterly. 'Forgive the man who caused my father's death! Do you think I have waited and watched for nothing? It seems to me as if all my life had been given up for this one hope. Do you know how that man has defied me?' she exclaimed, pointing to Launcelot Darrell. 'Do you know that through him I have been divided from my husband? Bah! why do I speak of my own wrongs? Do you know that my father, a poor, helpless old man, a lonely, friendless old man, a decayed gentleman, killed himself because of your son? Do you expect that I am to forget that? Do you think that I can forgive that man? Do you want me to abandon the settled purpose of my life – the purpose to which I have sacrificed every girlish happiness, every womanly joy – now that the victory is mine, and that I can keep my vow?'

She tried to disengage herself from Ellen Darrell's arms, but the widow still clung about her, with her head flung back, and her white face convulsed with anguish.

'Forgive him for my sake,' she cried; 'give him to me – give him to me! He will suffer enough from the ruin of his hopes. He will suffer enough from the consciousness of having done wrong. He *has* suffered. Yes. I have watched him, and I know. Take everything from him. Leave him a penniless dependant upon the pittance my uncle left to me, but save him from disgrace. Give him to me. God has given him to me. Woman, what right have you to take him from me?'

'He killed my father,' Eleanor answered, in a sombre voice; 'my dead father's letter told me to be revenged upon him.'

'Your father wrote in a moment of desperation. I knew him. I knew George Vane. *He* would have forgiven his worst enemy. He was the last person to be vindictive or revengeful when his first anger was passed. What good end will be gained by my son's disgrace? You shall *not* refuse to hear me. You are a wife, Eleanor Monckton: you may one day be a mother. If you are pitiless to me now, God will be pitiless to you then. You will think of me then. In every throb of pain your child may suffer; in every childish ailment that makes your heart grow sick with unutterable fear, you will recognize God's vengeance upon you for this night's work. Think of this, Eleanor; think of this, and be merciful to me – to *me* – not to him. What *he* would have to endure would be only a tithe of *my* suffering. I am his mother – his mother!'

'Oh, my God!' cried Eleanor, lifting her clasped hands above her head. '*What* am I to do?'

The hour of her triumph had come; and in this supreme moment doubt and fear took possession of her breast. If this was her victory, it was only half a victory. She had never thought that any innocent creature would suffer more cruelly by her vengeance upon Launcelot Darrell than the man himself would suffer. And now, here was this woman, whose only sin had been an idolatrous love of her son, and to whom his disgrace would be worse than the anguish of death.

The widow's agony had been too powerful for the girl's endurance. Eleanor burst into a passion of tears, and turning to her husband, let her head fall upon his breast.

'What am I to do, Gilbert?' she said. 'What am I to do?'

'I will not advise you, my dear,' the lawyer answered, in a low voice. 'To-night's business is of your own accomplishing. Your own heart must be your only guide.'

There was silence in the room for a few moments, only broken by Eleanor's sobbing. Launcelot Darrell had covered his face with his hands. His courage had given way before the power of his mother's grief. The widow still knelt, still clung about the girl, with her white face fixed now, in an awful stillness.

'Oh, my dear, dead father!' Eleanor sobbed, 'you – you did wrong yourself sometimes; and you were always kind and merciful to people. Heaven knows, I have tried to keep my oath; but I cannot – I cannot. It seemed so easy to imagine my revenge when it was far away: but now – it is too hard – it is too hard. Take your son, Mrs Darrell. I am a poor helpless coward. I cannot carry out the purpose of my life.'

The white uplifted face scarcely changed, and the widow fell back in a heap upon the floor. Her son and Gilbert Monckton lifted her up and carried her to a chair in one of the open windows. Richard Thornton dropped on his knees before Eleanor, and began to kiss her hands with *effusion*.

'Don't be frightened, Nelly,' he exclaimed. 'I was very fond of you once, and very unhappy about you, as my poor aunt can bear witness; but I am going to marry Eliza Montalembert, and we've got the carpets down at the snuggest little box in all Brixton, and I've made it up with Spavin and Cromshaw in consideration of my salary being doubled. Don't be frightened if I make a fool of myself, Eleanor; but I think I could worship you to-night. This is your victory, my dear. This is the only revenge Providence ever intended for beautiful young women with hazel-brown hair. God bless you!'

Launcelot Darrell, with a greyish pallor spread over his face, like a napkin upon the face of a corpse, came slowly up to Eleanor.

'You have been very generous to me, Mrs Monckton, though it is a hard thing for me to say as much,' he said; 'I have done wicked things, but I have suffered – I have suffered and repented perpetually. I had no thought of the awful consequences which would follow the wrong I did your father. I have hated myself for that wicked act ever since; I should never have forged the will if that man had not come to me, and fooled me, and played upon my weaknesses. I will thank you for the mercy you have shown me by-and-by, Mrs Monckton, when I am better worthy of your generosity.'

CHAPTER LIX

THE LAST

Gilbert Monckton seconded his wife in all she wished to do. There was no scandal. All legal formalities were gone through very quietly. Those troublesome people who require to be informed as to the business of their neighbours, were told that a codicil had been found, which revoked the chief clause of Mr de Crespigny's will. Mr Peter Sedgewick and Mrs Bannister were ready to perform all acts required of them; though the lady expressed considerable surprise at her half-sister's unexpected accession of wealth. Eleanor Monckton entered into possession of the estates. The impulsive girl, having once forgiven her father's enemy, would fain have surrendered the fortune to him into the bargain – but practical, matter-of-fact people were at hand to prevent her being too generous. Mrs Darrell and her son went to Italy, and Mrs Monckton, with her husband's concurrence, made the young man a very handsome allowance, which enabled him to pursue his career as an artist. He worked very hard and with enthusiasm. The shame of the past gave an impetus to his pencil. His outraged self-esteem stood him his friend, and he toiled valiantly to redeem himself from the disgrace that had fallen upon him.

'If I am a great painter, they will remember nothing against me,' he said to himself; and though it was not in him to become a great painter, he became a popular painter; a great man for the Royal Academy, and the West-End engravers, if only a small man for future generations, who will choose the real gems out of the prodigal wealth of the present. Mr Darrell's first success was a picture which he called 'The Earl's Death,' from a poem of Tennyson's, with the motto, 'Oh, the Earl was fair to see,' – a preternaturally ugly man lying at the feet of a preternaturally hideous woman, in a turret chamber lighted by lucifer matches – the blue and green light of the lucifers on the face of the ugly woman, and a pre-Raphaelite cypress seen through the window; and I am fain to say that although the picture was ugly, there was a strange weird attraction in it, and people went to see it again and again, and liked it, and hankered after it, and talked of it perpetually all that season; one faction declaring that the lucifer-match effect was the most delicious moonlight, and the murderess of the Earl the most lovely of womankind, till the faction who thought the very reverse of this became afraid to declare their opinions, and thus everybody was satisfied.

So Launcelot Darrell received a fabulous price for his picture, and, having lived without reproach during three years of probation, came home to marry Laura Mason Lennard, who had been true to him all this time, and who would have rather liked to unite her fortunes with those of a modern Cartouche or Jack Sheppard for the romance of the thing. And although the artist did not become a good man all in a moment, like the repentant villain of a stage play, he did take to heart the lesson of his youth. He was tenderly affectionate to the mother who had suffered so much by reason of his errors; and he made a very tolerable husband to a most devoted little wife.

Monsieur Victor Bourdon was remunerated, and very liberally – for his *services*, and was told to hold his tongue. He departed for Canada soon afterwards, in the interests of the patent mustard, and never reappeared in the neighbourhood of Tolldale Priory.

Eleanor insisted on giving up Woodlands for the use of Mr Darrell, his wife, and mother. Signora Picirillo lived with her nephew and his merry little wife in the pretty house at Brixton; but she paid very frequent visits to Tolldale Priory, sometimes accompanied by Richard and Mrs Richard, sometimes alone. Matrimony had a very good effect upon the outward seeming of the scene-painter: for his young wife initiated him in the luxury of shirt-buttons as contrasted with pins; to say nothing of the delights of a shower-bath, and a pair of ivory-backed hair-brushes, presented by Eleanor as a birth-day present to her old friend. Richard at first suggested that the ivory-backed brushes should be used as chimney ornaments in the Brixton drawing-room: but afterwards submitted to the popular view of the subject, and brushed his hair. Major and Mrs Lennard were also visitors at Tolldale, and Laura knew the happiness of paternal and maternal love – the paternal affection evincing itself in the presentation of a great deal of frivolous jewellery, purchased upon credit; the maternal devotion displaying itself in a wild admiration of Launcelot Darrell's son and heir, a pink-faced baby, who made his appearance in the year 1861, and who was in much better drawing than the 'Dying Gladiator,' exhibited by Mr Darrell in the same year. Little children's voices sounded by-and-by in the shady pathways of the old-fashioned Priory garden, and in all Berkshire there was not a happier woman than Gilbert Monckton's beautiful young wife.

And, after all, Eleanor's Victory was a proper womanly conquest, and not a stern, classical vengeance. The tender woman's heart triumphed over the girl's rash vow; and poor George Vane's enemy was left to the only Judge whose judgments are always righteous.

COMETH UP AS A FLOWER

RHODA BROUGHTON

Wild, endearing, unconventional Nell Le Strange is a misfit in mid-nineteenth-century society. But the individuality which makes her so different delights both the reader and the man with whom she discovers a powerful, enduring first love.

Must Nell bow to the constraints of poverty and marry to please others, or should she defy sense to follow her heart? Ironically it is not she but her sister Dolly who decides.

In a disturbing chain of events told with disarming honesty, Nell finds herself helpless in the face of Dolly's selfish ambition. Dolly is the epitome of ideal womanhood who turns out to be little better than a fiend: a fiend prepared to sacrifice the life of even her own sister.

VIXEN

MARY E. BRADDON

Violet Tempest is Vixen by virtue of her auburn hair and spirited temper. But as the novel unfolds her name assumes a greater significance.

Confronted by treachery and deceit, she is forced to use all her ingenuity and courage to preserve her integrity. Thwarted by the villainous Captain Winstanley, arson, banishment, and immorality are the among the trials she has to overcome to find happiness with the man she loves. Yet family honour has betrothed him to another. . . .

This is a Sensation Novel with a serious message: the need for money induces vicious, unscrupulous behaviour, threatens lives, divides families and undermines marriages. Mary E. Braddon terrifyingly depicts the need for Vixen's strength of character to survive in a society where men and wealth dominate a woman's fate.

JEZEBEL'S DAUGHTER

WILKIE COLLINS

Following the death of her husband, a famous chemist, Madame Fontaine is left penniless. Rumoured to have been the source of his downfall through her extravagant and scandalous behaviour, when a medicine chest that held his most potent potions is found to have disappeared, she is suspected of stealing it. So she becomes known as Jezebel, and her sweet-tempered daughter, Minna, is Jezebel's Daughter.

In another city, Ephraim Wagner, a successful merchant, dies. His widow determines to carry out his last wishes: to extend his policy of employing women equally with men, and to rescue Jack Straw, a simple man held in chains at Bedlam, from his plight and bring him to live with her. Both seem to presage disaster.

As this late and intricate story of Wilkie Collins's unfolds, the paths of the two women cross. For Minna is in love with Wagner's partner's son and although the affair is forbidden by his father, her mother determines to secure her daughter's happiness at any cost, even raising the dead to life again. . . .